Romance Treasury

THE ROMANCE TREASURY ASSOCIATION

TORONTO · NEW YORK · LONDON
AMSTERDAM · PARIS · SYDNEY · HAMBURG
STOCKHOLM · ATHENS · TOKYO · MILAN

These stories were originally published as follows:

GREEK ISLAND MAGIC
Copyright © 1983 by Gloria Bevan
First published by Mills & Boon Limited in 1983

YOURS...FAITHFULLY
Copyright © 1983 by Claudia Jameson
First published by Mills & Boon Limited in 1983

SWEET VIXEN
Copyright © 1983 by Susan Napier
First published by Mills & Boon Limited in 1983

ROMANCE TREASURY is published by
The Romance Treasury Association

Story Illustrations by Muriel Hughes
Book Design by Charles Kadin
Printed and bound by Arcata Graphics
Kingsport, Tennessee U.S.A.

ISBN 0-373-04198-5

Printed in U.S.A.   A198

CONTENTS

Page 9

GREEK ISLAND MAGIC
Gloria Bevan

Page 203

YOURS...FAITHFULLY
Claudia Jameson

Page 391

SWEET VIXEN
Susan Napier

Greek
Island Magic

Gloria Bevan

Adam seemed to mean it when he said, "You could try believing in me for a change."

But Liz *had* believed in him. Out of greed, he'd tried to charm her into selling the Greek villa she'd inherited. Luckily his dazzling campaign hadn't succeeded.

Only now Liz was more in love with Adam than the villa . . . and somehow she had to break free without forfeiting her dreams

CHAPTER ONE

'SO YOU'RE Elizabeth Kay, the girl from New Zealand?' the Greek lawyer said in his excellent English, and motioned her to a seat opposite him at the wide office desk.

'That's me!' She smiled cheerfully and dropped down to a low chair. 'Only no one ever calls me anything but Liz. I couldn't *wait* to get here!' she ran on in her eager husky voice. 'I booked a seat on the first plane leaving for Athens after I got your letter telling me about—' the excitement in her eyes clouded over, 'about my uncle having died and leaving me his property in Crete.'

'Quite, quite. Naturally you will wish to see the place...' His voice trailed into silence as he took in his client, a slim girl with a cloud of dark curly hair springing away from a golden-tanned forehead, a sweetly curved mouth and those huge grey-blue eyes. All at once his expression changed to warm intimacy, and Liz was acutely aware of his interest in her as a woman. How could she help it? There was no mistaking the unspoken significance of his look. She could feel his eyes raking her, mentally stripping her, but she willed herself to an attitude of cool detachment and said with what she hoped was an air of nonchalance, 'You knew my uncle? I guess you must have done, seeing that you attended to his legal affairs.'

The warm expression in his dark eyes lingered, but at least, Liz thought with relief, his tone was perfectly controlled.

'For many years. Although I didn't see him often. He visited me only when he had affairs that must be attended to, like drawing up a new will. A fairly straightforward one in this case, there seem to be no complications.' Wrenching his glance away from Liz's face, he rose to take a file from a shelf above his head and seating himself once again, ran his gaze over the typed paper in his hand. 'Under the terms of the will, the Villa Athene and the beach taverna are to be shared equally between you and your uncle's stepdaughter, Katina, who I understand is continuing to live at the villa. She is a Greek girl of about your own age,' another warmly intimate glance which Liz countered with a blank expression, 'not a blood relative, of course. It seems that your uncle married a Greek woman, a widow with one child. Unfortunately the wife died soon after the marriage and the girl was brought up by relatives in the country. When she was old enough to earn her living she came to help her step-father in the taverna on the beach. In the circumstances I would have thought—' He broke off. 'However, that was your uncle's decision. There was a small legacy also, suf-ficient, your uncle told me at the time he made the will, for you to make a trip out to Greece. You have already re-ceived the cheque for the amount?'

'Oh yes,' Liz assured him in her breathless way. 'That was wonderful of him, to make it possible for me to come here! There was enough money for the return fare,' she con-fided, 'but I'm not worrying about that.' A throaty laugh had the effect of evoking an even warmer glance from the swarthy-looking man seated opposite her. 'I just wanted to get out here and stay.'

He didn't seem to share her enthusiasm. 'You do re-alise—' He was back to his legal approach, Liz thought with relief, 'that sale of the property would require the consent of both you and your—'

'Cousin?' Liz put in helpfully. 'She's near enough to be-ing my cousin, and I've always thought of her that way.' But he seemed anxious only to get his point across to her, and after all, the thought flashed through Liz's mind, anything was preferable to the amorous expression on the dark face.

Such a foreign-looking face, she mused, that big beaky nose
and thick, thick black hair. He looked far too plump for a
young man, but maybe that was the effect of the olive oil
that featured so highly in Greek cooking. She brought her
wandering thoughts back to the smooth tones. 'I have
Katina's assurance that she is most anxious to dispose of the
property. With her no doubt it is a matter of obtaining
money for her dowry.'

'A dowry?' Liz stared at him in disbelief. 'Really? These
days?'

He smiled at her expression of astonishment. 'It is the
custom in our country, when marriage is being discussed by
the parents of the two young people, that the girl brings a
dowry to the union. The man provides the land, the home,
the furnishings.'

Liz was thinking that the subject was bringing back the
smouldering warmth to his eyes, and in an effort to change
the conversation she said briskly, 'Well, I don't see how that
affects me one way or the other.'

'Oh, but there you are mistaken! I assure you that it does!
Without your agreement to sell your share of the property
the whole estate is tied up and nothing can be done.' All at
once his tone was dominating and definite. 'I must point out
that it would be to your advantage to meet your—er—
cousin, as you term her, in this matter. Especially in view of
the fact,' he leaned back in his swivel chair regarding her
with appreciative melting dark eyes, 'that I have already received an offer to sell on your and Katina's behalf, a most
generous offer when one considers the general state of disrepair of the villa and the isolation of the area.' Liz felt there
was something mesmeric in his fixed brown stare. 'My client
is at the moment most eager to purchase and I would
strongly advise you to take advantage of the offer.'

'But—'

He raised a hand to brush aside her objections and swept
on. 'Actually the property is situated in a remote area along
the coast and wouldn't attract buyers as a general rule, but

my client happens to be the owner of one of the luxury hotels built not far away—one moment, I will tell you his
name—'

'Don't trouble,' she cut in, 'I'm not interested one little
bit!' She flashed him a brilliant smile. 'So what does it
matter who he is?'

The lawyer took not the slightest notice of her words.
Clearly he was a man who didn't submit to defeat easily. His
smile was tolerant and confident. 'You will change your
mind when you see the property. So much repair is needed,
so much money would have to be spent on the villa—' He
spread out plump hands in an expressive gesture. 'After all,
when you live on the other side of the world—'

'Sell my property in Crete? Goodness, no!' Liz stared
back at him with wide, incredulous eyes. 'I wouldn't dream
of parting with it. I've only just got it!'

He pursed thick red lips. 'We shall see.' At last, Liz
thought with relief, she had managed to get her own ideas
through to him. She brought her mind back to the lawyer's
tones. 'I see you have already made up your mind, but if in
future you should change your mind in the matter, you must
let me know. Meantime, I shall tell my client—'

'Tell him anything you like! I don't care, so long as you
make it clear to him that there's nothing doing in that direction and if he's counting on me selling out he's wasting
his time. Do you know, I've been looking forward to coming to Crete for ages and ages—'

Her companion however was not to be diverted. 'My
client is most insistent on purchase, and the price he has offered is far in excess of market value, an opportunity you
would be wise to consider before it is too late.'

Liz laughed. 'Too late for what? Not for me!' At his disapproving expression she ran on, 'Don't you see? It's not
just a matter of money. It means an awful lot to me, this
property of my uncle's. I wouldn't give it up for anything.
Now now—or ever!'

'I see.' Liz felt a surge of relief that he appeared convinced that he really meant what she had said. He made no further protest, nor did he advance any more arguments. So why did she get the impression that whatever his appreciation of her physical charms, he put her down as a silly little fool with no business acumen whatever? That when it came to a question of self-interest she registered zero, not even bothering to ascertain the identity of the prospective buyer. As if she cared! Probably he was some Greek businessman, so what did it matter? Confidingly she leaned towards him. 'Shall I tell you something? It doesn't seem at all strange to me being here in Crete, even though I come from a country that's so far away.'

'Indeed?' He was eyeing her attentively, as though he had all the time in the world, Liz thought, and banished a niggling suspicion that he was interested in the curves of her mouth rather than in what she was telling him. Dropping her gaze for fear he might read the thoughts that were passing through her mind, she ran on.

'I guess I was attached to Uncle Jim because he was the only relative I had. My parents were drowned in a boating accident when I was a small child, and you can't really count foster-parents, even if they're kind and look after you. But Uncle Jim was different.'

'He corresponded with you?'

'All the time! Even when I was a little girl at school—' Her tone softened. 'He used to send me the funniest letters, the sort with sketches on them and big print that even a seven-year-old could read. He was fifteen years older than my dad. Uncle Jim put his age up a year or two when World War Two broke out. He went away with an N.Z. Army contingent and was sent to Crete. He liked the island so much that after years spent in a prison camp he decided not to return to New Zealand, but to make his home in Crete. He bought property there and married a Greek woman he'd got to know in wartime. It was such a pity that she died soon afterwards.' A tender smile played around Liz's soft lips.

'So then he just stayed on at his villa, working at the taverna. He wrote me long letters about his life and I knew I could recognise the Villa Athene right away just from his descriptions of it. He told me all about the taverna on the beach too. He used to work there himself with the help of a Greek couple, a middle-aged man and his wife, and much later, when she was old enough to leave home, Katina came to help too. He served meals at the taverna, Greek food, of course. And the beach—he sent me pictures of it and it looked fabulous. He wrote me that he swam every day in the bay,' her bright expression clouded over, 'until he got ill and had to rest a lot. But he still went on writing to me! I'd been saving up for ages for a trip to Greece. It was something that I'd set my heart on, a surprise visit to my uncle here. You wouldn't believe how hard it was.' Her soft lips twitched at the corners. 'I really had to work at it.' Silently she added, especially when it came to not letting myself get too deeply involved in love affairs. That way I knew I would never get here. She ran on, 'I'd got about half of my air fare money saved when I got your letter. I couldn't believe it at first,' her voice thickened, 'that he wouldn't be here to meet me...not ever.' Her eyes misted over. 'Now everything's different. It's such a pity,' she choked on the last word.

'I understand your feelings.' The Greek lawyer leaned forward to place his plump hand over hers and Liz felt the pressure of his moist palm. She swallowed the lump in her throat and recovered her hand. 'So now you know,' she said briskly, 'why I don't want to sell my share of the place that Uncle left me.'

He threw her a thoughtful glance. 'You say you have no capital, only your return fare to New Zealand. It would not be possible for you to find employment at the village. Had it been at Heraklion, now, or Chania—What did you do for a living at home? Nursing? Schoolteaching?'

Liz shook her head. 'I just did office work—typing, keeping accounts, all that stuff.'

He raised his eyes heavenwards. 'If you want my opinion—'

Liz didn't, but she could see he was determined to hand her out advice, so she sighed impatiently and forced herself to listen. 'You have no choice in the matter—none at all. How can you stay here without capital or employment of any sort?'

'Don't worry about me,' Liz said cheerfully. 'I'll find something. So long as I can stay...'

To her surprise he was growing red in the face, a dark unbecoming brick colour. With hands gesticulating wildly in the air he shouted, 'Me, I am trying to tell you for your own good and you will not listen!'

There was no doubt, the thoughts ran through her mind, that he was a man who couldn't endure to have his counsel ignored. After all, she conceded, folk came here to ask, and pay, for his advice. But to become so wildly excited over her refusal to take his words seriously...it must be the Greek way.

'I just want to live here for a while,' she said in an effort to calm his ruffled feelings. Her throaty laugh rang out. 'Wouldn't it be funny if history repeated itself and I got so wrapped up in the island that I couldn't leave it either, and just stayed on forever?'

In a lightning change of mood he was smiling, his warm intimate glance lingering on her face before travelling over her slim body. If only he wasn't becoming amorous again!

He smirked. 'Marry a Greek man, maybe?'

Liz laughed, mainly in an effort to dispel his fatuous expression. 'Who's talking about husbands?' In spite of herself she felt a tinge of pink creeping up her cheeks and before he could make something of the innocent remark, she said hurriedly the first words that rushed into her head. 'What's wrong with my living at the villa? It can't be all that dilapidated if Katina is still living there. Maybe we could run the taverna together and live at the villa. From what you've told me there's only my Greek cousin living there, and I'm sure there'd be room for both of us.'

All at once he was back to her legal adviser. He regarded her reprovingly. 'You do not understand—so much you do not understand about our country. You should listen to me.'

A shaft of remorse struck her. After all, the man was trying to help her in his own way. If only his way wasn't an amorous one! 'All right, then,' she threw him a smile, 'I'm listening.'

'It will not be suitable for you to live at the Villa Athene.'

His words surprised her and she stared back at him in disbelief.

'Why ever not? There's room for me, isn't there?'

'That is not the problem. Has it not occurred to you that your cousin, as you term her, may not be pleased at sharing her inheritance from her stepfather with a stranger, someone she has never set eyes on? She may well feel resentment towards you, and even more so when she hears that you are not agreeable to parting with the property.' Was he having another dig at her? Liz wondered. 'She could be angry with you, and Greek girls,' he said significantly, 'show their feelings. If I were you—'

'But you're not, are you?' Liz cut in. 'If that's all you're warning me about, my cousin...' She couldn't imagine anything going wrong for her on this sundrenched summer day, when things were happening and she was on her way to claim her inheritance. She said with a smile, 'Don't worry about it. I'll soon talk her out of it.'

He looked unconvinced. The next moment his gaze dwelt on Liz's alive face, the sort of face, he noted, that mirrored every emotion, and right at this moment, happiness was there plain to see. 'You have a saying in your country,' he observed smilingly, 'something about not meeting trouble halfway? So that was your only connection with the Greek islands?'

She laughed. 'Not quite. Would you believe? I had a neighbour at home who came from Crete, a nice girl with

two little children. Her brother had come out to New
Zealand to work in a restaurant in Auckland and he sent for
his sister to come over to New Zealand for a holiday. When
she decided to make her home there her parents in Crete sent
her photographs of three different young men who were interested in a wife. So she didn't have much choice in the
matter of picking a husband. Isn't it amazing!'

He looked unimpressed. 'It is the custom in Greece—'

'Yes, I know. The funny thing about it all is,' Liz admitted reluctantly, 'that they're awfully happy and really in love
with each other.' She put her head on one side, considering. 'Odd, isn't it?'

'Not at all.' His voice dropped to a low intimate tone. 'A
man can want a girl to be his woman. The manner of meeting, it is of no importance.' His eyes said, 'I could feel that
way about you.'

To avoid a dangerous moment Liz hurriedly changed the
subject, scarcely thinking of what she was saying. 'So of
course when Yanni and Angeliké knew I was coming here
they were ever so excited. They gave me gifts to pass on to
their families and loads of photographs of the children. I've
been looking at my Crete map, and it doesn't seem too far
away from where I'll be at my uncle's villa to take a bus ride
up there to see them one day.'

His swarthy plump face was set and resentful, no doubt
because of her rejection of his intimate words. If only Greek
men weren't subject to swift changes from light-heartedness
to rage, even rage that they were trying to conceal. She had
to make it clear to him that she wasn't interested in him, as
a man, that was.

She brought her mind back to the words of the man facing her. Sulkily he murmured, 'You should ring for a taxi
from the hotel. Meantime,' all at once he was brisk and
businesslike once more, 'here are the keys to the villa and
taverna.' He handed her a sealed envelope. 'If your stepsis-
ter happens to be away from the villa when you arrive, you
may need them. I will arrange transport for you on a bus

leaving at two this afternoon from the depot outside the old
Venetian wall. You must look for the Kolos destination
sign.'

'Thanks! That's super!' Liz got to her feet and reached
down to pick up her travel pack, then slipped the straps over
her shoulders.

'Ask the driver to put you down at the Hotel Hermes,' he
was saying. He rose from the desk and stood facing her, a
dark-eyed man of medium height with black curly hair and
a prominent nose. 'You must promise me that if you have
any problems at all you will call on me for help.'

'Problems?' she echoed bewilderedly. 'Oh, you mean
language difficulties and all that?'

'Anything! Anything at all!' His warm glance lent the
words significance, or was she merely imagining it? Maybe
he really did want to help her and she had misjudged him.

Taking her small hand in a soft clammy clasp, he pressed
her fingers to his moist lips. 'If there's any way I can be of
service to you, you won't hesitate to let me know? Remember, I will be only as far away from you as the nearest telephone!'

'I'll remember,' said Liz, and recovered her hand. Privately she was of the opinion that she would need to be in
desperate straits indeed to throw herself on the mercy of this
amorous Greek. Her bright smile, however, gave nothing
away.

He ushered her to the door, his gaze lingering on her slim
figure as she went along the passage. Well, he congratulated himself, he had done what he could for this attrac-
tive-looking girl with the dancing light of excitement in her
eyes. With luck he would be seeing her again before long,
because once she realised the state of disrepair of her newly
acquired property she would change her mind soon enough
about getting rid of the old place. He'd take a bet with anyone that she would be back with him in his office within a
week.

Liz emerged from the dimness of the office building into the strangely brilliant white light of the Greek islands. The town, she saw, was ringed with hills, blue in the distance. Ahead of her stretched the winding cobbled street with its shops and taverns, and below were the thick Venetian walls and stone archways that had once guarded the old port. Along the waterfront quaint dark little stores had muslin dresses and blouses hung in doorways, and in the harbour the cruise liners were bright with coloured flags and canvas awnings. All at once she was swept by a sense of heightened perception, born of the dazzling clear air and her exotic surroundings. It was all just as her uncle had described it to her in his letters, and now she was really, really here! If only he were here to welcome her. She brushed the regretful thoughts away. He would want her to enjoy her stay in Crete, to fall a victim to its lure just as he had done. It's true, she told herself in amazement, all they say in novels and travel brochures about the Aegean Sea. It really is that un-believable blue.

She went on up the narrow street past a medieval church where sanctuary bells were tolling over town and harbour. Bells are ringing for me too, she mused, and once again felt that surge of elation. Presently she found herself merging into the flow of people who were milling around a stone fountain where water rose high in the air in the tree-shaded square. Liz made her way through the crowd—well-dressed tourists with guide books and cameras, Greek Orthodox priests, bearded men in black robes and tall black hats, Greek women, their sun-dried brown faces shaded by dark coifs. She made her way towards a taverna with its checked red tablecloths, wooden chairs, small tables and blue can-opies. The outdoor eating place was crowded and as she made her way towards a secluded corner, Liz tried to ig-nore the obvious interest of swarthy men seated at the main cluster of tables.

As she waited for a waiter to take her order, her gaze drifted over the chattering crowd around her. So many

Greek men, and all so volatile. Did they not take their wives or girl-friends for coffee? she wondered. Suddenly her gaze was arrested by a party of Greeks at a nearby table where the men were wildly gesticulating and shouting, obviously engaged in an argument of such passionate intensity that she expected a fist fight to flare up at any moment. The next moment, she saw to her surprise that the men were now smiling and chatting with one another, apparently the best of friends. Unfortunately they were eyeing her with bright interested glances. Liz promptly averted her eyes from the exuberant group, telling herself that it was her own interest in the party that had evoked the spate of Greek comments, clearly concerning herself, that were echoing around the table. She was beginning to realise that as a stranger in a foreign country, travelling alone, she must learn to cope with the Greek male's uninhibited interest. If only she knew the language of the country—but the trip had come about without warning and there had been no time for her to do more than buy a small language travel guide of basic phrases, and what use was that, she asked herself, when what was needed for a girl travelling solo was some instruction on how to say 'Get lost!' or 'I'm waiting for my husband!'

She lingered over the thick Greek coffee, enjoying the brilliant sunshine, fascinated by the variety of accents echoing around her—Canadian, English, American, even the Australian 'twang'.

Time fled by, and almost before she realised it, a glance at her wristwatch told her it was time to adjust the shoulder straps of her nylon pack and make her way to the depot to board the bus for the small village along the coast that was her destination.

The Greek driver recognised the name of the village at once when she enquired of him, but she had no idea whether her efforts to make him understand that she wished to be put off at the hotel stop when they arrived there registered with him. She would just have to hope that he did, she told herself, and took her seat next to an elderly Greek woman, whose nut-brown face was wrinkled from the hot summer suns of the island.

Except for herself, she noticed, the passengers were all Greek who were talking and laughing amongst themselves. Liz stared out of the window as the vehicle moved away, taking in the jumble of little streets with their small dimly lighted stores, where shopkeepers stood in doorways amongst the beads and bells and muslin embroidered dresses fluttering in the breeze. Presently they left the town behind, taking a quiet highway where wild flowers, blood-red poppies and white daisies lined the roadsides, and mountains were clear cut against a translucent blue sky. They were out of sight of the sea now, climbing high hills sparsely covered with silvery green olive trees and fragrant with the scent of herbs, rosemary and thyme. After a time they swung into a road running along the sea coast and Liz eagerly took in the passing scenes—blue bays where tavernas were built at the water's edge, stark white stone houses clinging to steep dry hillsides. She craned her neck backwards to watch a young Greek boy riding a donkey ambling down a rocky slope.

It was a long drive, longer than she had expected, and the white heat of the day was fading when at last the bus turned a bend and ran down towards a rocky coast where waves dashed against dark cliffs and the only building in sight was an opulent hotel, a luxuriously appointed modern building with an imposing facade and great glass windows facing the sea. Liz wondered why the driver was drawing up here as no one seemed to be moving, then all at once she realised he was eyeing her enquiringly. The next moment he burst into a flood of Greek. At last she managed to pick up a word, Kolos. But that was her destination. There must be some mistake. The thoughts rushed confusedly through her mind—there was no village anywhere in sight, no houses, nothing but this immense impressive hotel.

Helplessly she appealed to the driver, gesticulating, appealing to him in her own language, but his answering spate of Greek did nothing to reassure her. At last, to her relief, a passenger rose from his seat at the back of the vehicle and came to join them. He was a Greek, by his accent, she realised, middle-aged and friendly, and thank heaven, he spoke English. Rapidly he translated the excitable Greek words into her own language. 'I know it's Kolos,' she replied distractedly, 'but I want to go to the Villa Athene! It's near a beach and there's a taverna there too. I can't understand it—the name is the same, unless there are two places named Kolos—please will you tell him?'

Swiftly he translated the message and a rapid interchange of words ensued, then the stranger turned to her with a reassuring smile. 'He says you are to get out here. It is not far to the next bay. You must follow the goat track through the olive trees over the hill,' he gestured to a dry slope, 'and there you will find the Villa Athene.'

'Oh, *thank* you!' Her wide smile included her benefactor as well as the Greek driver. Suddenly everyone was happy, the sun-wrinkled face of the Greek woman at her side broke into a beaming smile and the passengers talked, waved and gesticulated with what Liz took to be friendly good wishes towards her. Then she found herself out on the white dust of the road. She hesitated, her gaze taking in the opulent hotel that appeared so bright and welcoming. Could it be the masses of green growing plants cascading over stark white walls, or maybe the pink geraniums spilling from great urns at the entrance, that made it seem so attractive to her travel-weary senses?

'Come to think of it,' she told herself, 'I'm not sure whether or not there'll be anyone at the villa, not really. There could be no food there, nothing to drink. I've only got vague directions as to how to find the place,' she reasoned. 'I'm not sure if I'll be able to recognise it, especially as it will soon be dark.'

Liar. A tiny voice of truth piped deep in her mind. You're feeling awfully weary all of a sudden and not in a mood for a confrontation with that Greek sort-of-cousin of yours.

The uneasy thoughts flickered through her mind. Who said anything about a confrontation?

That Greek lawyer with the unpronounceable name, that's who! Well, he hinted as much.

But I thought, jeered the voice, that you were going to talk Katina out of any mistaken ideas she might have about you?

I will! I will! Tomorrow. In the morning I'll be feeling fresher, more able to cope with whatever turns up. After all, came the sneaky thought, what difference could a few hours make? It would be sheer joy to stay just for the night in this luxurious hotel, to revel in a warm shower, eat a meal already prepared and be certain of somewhere to spend the night. Why not? The battle was won.

Liz went through the iron gates and into a spacious foyer. At the reception desk a smiling Greek girl with friendly dark eyes arranged a night's stay for Liz, handed her a room key and then a porter escorted her into a lift that shot them up to a carpeted corridor. The room into which Liz was shown was a delight, she thought. She threw her nylon pack on to the linen bedcover and explored the balcony, the spacious bedroom, the luxuriously fitted bathroom with its blue and white tiled flooring. How could she help but enjoy herself during her brief stay in these unfamiliar, if expensive, surroundings?

The shower, she found, was all she had hoped for, with thick and thirsty towels and delicately perfumed soap. Afterwards she brushed her damp hair until it sprang back in natural waves and curled around her face. Leaving her complexion clear, she made up her eyes with shadow and slipped into a dress she had hesitated about buying, back home in New Zealand. At least she had hesitated about paying the price, but now, glancing in the mirror, she decided that the garment had been well worth it. The soft cot-

ton in a misty shade of lilac set off her dark hair to
advantage and did something for her glowing skin. As she
met her mirrored reflection she couldn't help the thought
that it was too bad there was no one to notice—no one special, that was—someone masculine, of course. To be here
alone in Greece...it seemed a pity. And yet, she mused, the
Greek Islands were the home of pagan gods, of myth and
legend, and maybe, who knows, the ancient magic still
worked! She flashed a wink in the direction of the mirror
girl. *He,* that special someone, could be waiting for her in
Crete. Maybe he was right here in the hotel at this moment.
And maybe, she pulled a face at her reflection, he wasn't!
She turned away and soon she was stepping down the great
marble stairway and entered the vast dining room that
seemed, at first glance, to stretch away for ever.

A Greek waiter showed Liz to a corner table where long
windows reflected a dark sea. Picking up the menu he
handed her, she ran her eyes down the items without com-
prehending their meaning. She smiled up at the waiter at her
side. '*Karpousi?* Now what—'

'Iced melon, madam.'

'That'll do me for starters.' Once again she consulted the
menu. 'Oh, here's something I'd like to try, squid with
salad.'

As the waiter took her order any doubts she had entertained about difficulty in ordering food at the hotel faded
away. Why, it was easy! Especially as one dessert, crème
caramel, was a familiar name. The meal proved to be delicious. So much so that she boldly ordered a bottle of the
native wine, retsina—but one sip of the strong liquid was
sufficient to make her push her glass aside, for the wine had
to her a strong flavour of—could it be turpentine?

Afterwards she moved into the spacious lounge room,
dropping down to a low couch at the side of an attractive-
looking woman of middle age. 'I'm Mary Denton,' the
stranger had a pleasant easy manner of speaking, 'all the

way from Winnipeg. Are you travelling alone through the Greek Islands too?'

'Not any further.' Liz smiled. 'I'm Liz, all the way from New Zealand. Shall we have coffee together?'

'Love to.' Presently they were sipping strong dark Greek coffee from pottery mugs. 'I'm on a world trip,' the Canadian woman told Liz. 'And I'm looking up my family on the way. I've a son in Mexico and a married daughter living in Australia. But Greece is the country I love most of all,' she confided. 'I've been teaching my college students Greek history for years and I never tire of it. It's the one country I never want to leave, although,' she smiled wryly, 'there's just one thing I'd like to see here, and that is tavernas especially for tourists and overseas travellers where one could drop in for coffee and a toasted roll with fillings like we have back home. You know? If there are any such eating places around the Greek Islands, I haven't come across them. I know if I had money to invest in this country I'd put it into building a taverna for tourists, and I'm sure it would be worthwhile. Listen—' On the other side of the wide room Greek musicians were playing bouzoukis, and as the plaintive melody drifted through the room, a group of swarthy-looking men wearing mulberry-coloured cummerbunds of their native Cretan style joined together with arms thrown around their partners' shoulders, as their feet performed the intricate steps.

When the dance was over the two women crossed the room to wander down some steps towards small shops with their attractive window displays of fashion garments with a Greek influence, miniature urns and gold necklaces. 'This place must be going to my head,' Liz told her companion ruefully, holding against her slim waist an exquisitely cut black skirt, its full folds bordered with a traditional design in heavy gold.

'Go on, take it!' Mary Denton encouraged her. 'If you don't you'll be sorry! I'll tell you something—if I were your age and a garment did that much for me I'd skip dinner for a week to pay for it!'

Laughing, Liz shrugged her shoulders. 'You have a bad influence on me! All the same—' She threw caution to the winds and made the purchase. 'Though heaven only knows,' she confided to her new-made acquaintance, 'where I'll ever go to wear a garment like this!'

'Don't be too sure,' the older woman told her with a smile. 'Don't forget you're in Greece now, where anything can happen! The thing is to be prepared for it, and then one of these days or nights you'll be glad you bought that Grecian skirt, you'll see!'

'I only hope you're right.' Already Liz was having second thoughts about the amount of money she had spent, and this was only the start of her stay.

Back in the immense lounge room, however, she soon forgot her qualms, for dance music was pulsing from a stereo and partners appeared at her side as if from nowhere, attracted by the girl with the expression of excitement lighting her blue-grey eyes. Liz danced with a Swiss tour guide staying the night with his party on their way to a beach resort further up the coast, then with a middle-aged businessman with a quiet smile and a charming manner.

'Who was that?' Mary Denton enquired smilingly as the music drew to a close and Liz was escorted back to her seat by a dark man with a heavy moustache.

'Don't ask me!' Liz was breathless and flushed from exertion and the heat of the night. 'He didn't say one word, maybe he didn't know the language!'

It was much later in the evening when she resisted the attempts of the English businessman to persuade her to stay on. 'There'll be dancing here for hours yet,' he told her. But Liz held firmly to her decision, and soon she stepped into a lift and was wafted up to her room.

Somehow, in spite of the comfortable mattress, she found difficulty in getting to sleep. Hour after hour, restlessly she turned over her pillow and flung herself from side to side.

She had been asleep for only a few minutes, it seemed to her, when she was awakened by sounds of masculine singing, shouting and roars of laughter from the floor below. She eyed her little illuminated travel clock. Three o'clock in the morning! It was too bad, she thought crossly, for that noisy party below to keep others awake with their revelry! Just let them go on with their noisy exuberance for another half hour and she would do something about it! In the end she couldn't wait that long. Suddenly incensed at the uproar echoing from the floor below, she sprang from bed and without bothering with a wrap, flung wide the french windows and went out on the balcony, determined to put an end to the disturbance.

Moonlight silvered the grounds below, making the scene almost as bright as day, and as she peered over the railings she saw it was just as she had thought. A noisy party of Greeks were wandering in and out of a room on the floor below and out to a balcony directly beneath her. Clearly they had been imbibing freely, for some of the group were unsteady in their movements and one of the party, a swarthy man with a black moustache, caught sight of Liz and waved a bottle of retsina in the air.

'The noise!' she called down to him. 'Stop the noise! It's terrible! I can't sleep with that racket going on down there!'

The next moment she realised to her chagrin that her angry outburst had had the effect of bringing others out on to the balcony below. They clustered around the railing, laughing loudly and brandishing bottles of wine in her direction. Clearly they were happily unaware of what she was trying to get through to them and were inviting her to join their party. Oh, she could kill them! She would soon disillusion them about that being the reason for her being out here on the balcony at this hour in the morning. 'No! No!' She glared down at them angrily. At that moment she caught behind her an ominous sound. The next moment she realised that the wide plate glass doors opening on to the balcony had been caught in a gust of the night breeze and

slammed shut. Forgetting the Greek party below, in sudden
panic she ran to the door, wrenching at the heavy handles—but it was no use, the doors could only now be opened
from the inside.

Scarcely knowing what she was doing, she ran to the balcony rail. 'Help, somebody! Help!' The cry seemed to leave
her lips without her volition. Her call for help had the effect of bringing her once more to the unwelcome attention
of the party of men below. They crowded out to their balcony, calling up to her in a spate of Greek. Panic shot
through her. Suppose the revellers below had got the mistaken impression that she was inviting them up to her
apartment? Although somewhat the worse for drink, they
appeared a young and athletic lot—and definitely amorous. Were all Greek men unashamedly womanisers? she
wondered. What if they tried to scramble up to her balcony? The thought was so appalling that she turned and
hurried back into the shadows, her heart beating fast as if
she had been running. Only there was nowhere to run to!
Wildly she glanced around her. There must be someone besides herself in this great building who had heard the uproar in the night, someone to whom she could appeal for
help.

There was, she realised the next minute, as a man's tall
muscular figure appeared on the adjoining balcony. 'You
little fool!' To think he was actually blaming her for the
noise that had disturbed his slumber! 'What do you think
you're doing?'

Liz ran to the corner of the railing and leaned towards
him. 'Me?' Her voice emerged as an indignant squeak. 'It's
not *my* fault! It's those Greeks down there on the next floor!
They've been driving me crazy with all the racket they've
been making, and now,' she finished breathlessly, 'they've
been making a nuisance of themselves. They're...annoying
me!'

At that moment the moon, emerging from behind a
cloud, flooded the scene with silver radiance. She had an

impression of a strong masculine face, all planes and angles in the fitful gleam of light, of wide shoulders and a tall
lean frame. He was tying the cord of his dark robe around
his waist. 'What can you expect,' the deep vibrant tones
were tinged with contempt, 'when you go flaunting yourself at Greek men looking like that? They're in a party mood
and out you come in night gear that doesn't leave much to
the imagination. What the hell did you think their reaction
would be?'

A wave of anger surged through her. Of all the horrible,
beastly men! Judging by his accent he was English, but he
was just as bad as the Greeks. 'Flaunting myself?' she cried
in horrified protest. 'I don't know what you mean! If you're
trying to tell me that I've been inviting trouble from them,
that I . . .' Her voice died away. Up till this moment she had
been too distraught to give a thought to her attire. Now as
the soft night breeze stirred the diaphanous folds of the
single garment she wore, she realised the revealing trans-
parency of the sea-green nightgown she had bought especially for her trip to Crete. Hurriedly she stepped back into
the shadows.

'What else would you call it?' The contemptuous tones
stung her. He made to turn away, and panic gripped her.
'Wait! Don't go!' she cried in desperate entreaty. Hateful
though he was, he was her only chance of escape. A sudden
onslaught of tears threatened and the words came in a rush.
'You don't understand! You've *got* to help me! I'm in a
spot! I came out here to tell those noisy Greek guys to qui-
eten down their party so that I could get some sleep and the
door slammed shut behind me and now I can't get back to
my room!'

'Really?' She could tell by his tone that he didn't believe
her. Callous, unfeeling brute!

'Oh, you're just no help at all!' she threw at him. 'Pretending you don't understand, not believing a word of what
I'm telling you. I tried to get those Greeks down there to
help me. They don't know any English, but *you* do! And all

you can do is to stand there and sneer and say things,' her voice dropped to a sibilant whisper, 'that aren't true at all.'

'How was I to know what your problem was?' he enquired with deceptive gentleness. Oh, he was an unfeeling brute, keeping her out here talking when he had no intention of being the slightest help to her. All at once she decided to throw dignity and resentment to the Cretan moon that had caused her so much trouble tonight. 'Look,' she had no choice but to crush down her anger and appeal to him, 'you've just *got* to help me.' Her tones were low and tense with emotion. 'If you don't, I don't know what I'm going to do!' In spite of herself her voice cracked. *'Please!'*

'Now if only you'd asked me nicely before.' The maddening injustice of his remark almost sparked her to forget her resolution to hold on to her temper at all costs if she knew what was good for her. If she didn't—the worrying thoughts chased through her mind—she would be forced to spend what was left of the night a prisoner on the balcony, the butt of coarse jokes (even if she didn't understand them she knew they'd be coarse) from the inebriated group below.

The bland tones cut across her thoughts. 'Now if you'd explained it to me before—'

Exasperated, she cried angrily, 'I've told and told you!' In the heat of her feelings she forgot all about using a soft approach for her own advantage. 'And all you do,' she threw at him, 'is go on and on about my looking provocative, and I'm not.' She stumbled. 'I don't... Anyway,' she caught herself up and rushed on, almost incoherent with frustration and rage, 'you're insufferable—you just don't care!' Suddenly all hope of obtaining any assistance from him fled. 'You've no intention of helping me!' she cried. 'It's all just a game to you! It amuses you no end to keep me on tenterhooks!'

'Is that the way you think of me?' His soft innocent tone was infuriating to her taut nerves. 'I must have given you the wrong impression. Something to do with that dark hair of yours falling around your shoulders put me off, made me forget what I was saying. You really shouldn't wear those narrow straps if you don't want your shoulders to be seen.'

'Never mind about my shoulders,' Liz said fiercely. She had abandoned her plan of enlisting the assistance of the dark-haired Englishman. He was nothing but a sadistic brute! 'If I could only open my door,' she breathed, 'I wouldn't stay out here arguing with you one more minute—'

'But you can't, can you? Not when it's locked on the inside,' he reminded her with maddening truth. 'Not to worry. No one should ever get all that het up about things here. Greece is a happy place, didn't anyone ever tell you?'

'Are you going to help me get back to my room or aren't you?' she cut in tersely. To her horror the words ended on a sob, and she couldn't go on. Now he would think, blast him, that she was making a play for his pity. Not that it would affect him in the least, he was so cold and uncaring and generally hateful. She blinked away the moisture from her eyes and said thickly, 'Oh, what's the use!'

'You can relax!' All at once the satirical note was gone from his deep tones. 'Your troubles are over. I'm on my way!'

Liz held her breath. She wouldn't put it past him to climb right back to bed and put her out of his mind. A few minutes later, however, her gloomy thoughts were dispelled as a dark tousled head appeared over the adjoining balcony. 'I've just got through to the night porter on the phone and he's on his way up with your key.'

'Oh, that's wonderful!' breathed Liz on a long sigh of relief. 'You managed to make him understand then? You speak Greek?'

Once again the deep resonant tones were tinged with amusement, but now somehow she didn't mind. 'Well enough. Don't worry, you'll be quite safe in Greece—so long as you keep out of the bright moonlight!'

'Oh, you—' The angry words died on her lips, because he had vanished back into his room. For a moment she knew an odd regret. She supposed, she reflected reluctantly, that she owed him some thanks for his help, but really he didn't deserve it, not after the way he had kept her waiting all that time. Anyway, she defended herself, it had *seemed* a long time. The sound of a key turning in the lock was the most welcome sound she had heard in all her life.

Strangely, in the deep silence of a pre-dawn world, she found that sleep eluded her. With senses alert, she lay back on the pillows, arms crossed behind her head as she went over and over the events of the last half hour. Odd how the image of the man in the shadows of the next balcony stayed with her—the dark planes of the strong face, the broad shoulders, the slightly sardonic tone of his voice. She would be leaving in the morning, so there was little chance of their ever meeting again. She couldn't understand why the thought was depressing. She'd give a lot to see him just once more. Mere curiosity on her part, of course, for no man could really be so devastatingly good-looking, not in the clear Greek sunlight.

CHAPTER TWO

LIZ AWAKENED in the morning to dazzling sunshine streaming over her face, and for a moment she blinked in disbelief. What was she doing here in this unfamiliar room that faced the glittering blue sea? Then, as recollection came back in a rush, she dropped her feet to the tiled floor and, crossing the room, opened the glass doors the merest trifle. She wasn't going to be caught that way again, not without being fully dressed! Silence lay all around her and with luck, she mused, the Greek party on the floor below were still sleeping off the effects of their night of revelry. She couldn't bear it if any of them should recognise her in the light of day. Probably they would sleep for hours yet, she comforted herself, and by the time they began to function once again, she would have left the hotel.

If only she could meet her helper once again—the thought came unbidden. She hadn't yet decided whether he was friend or foe, but could she meet him again, just once, she could settle the matter in her own mind. It was odd, she mused as she pulled her nightdress over tousled dark hair and slipped into panties and bra and a dress of cool cotton, how easy it was for her to forget his mockery, the hateful way in which he had taken his time before coming to her rescue. Now all that seemed important was that he had finally solved her problem.

When she entered the dining room only a few tables were occupied—no doubt the tour party had already left to continue their sightseeing, and she could see no tall masculine figure. She knew she would recognise him again at sight de-

spite the shadows of the balcony. What was the matter with
her, she scolded herself, that she couldn't seem to get his
lean dark face or the ironic tones of his voice out of her
mind?

Back in her room she packed away her dress and nightdress in her nylon travel gear, stuffed in her toilet bag, then
adjusting the straps over her shoulders, she made her way
down the winding staircase. As she settled her account at the
reception desk she realised that the girl seated there spoke in
English, and Liz decided to check on her destination.

'It is only a short way to the Villa Athene.' The friendly
Greek girl rose from her chair to escort Liz out of the wide
foyer and into the dazzling sunshine outside. 'If you take the
goat track over the hill,' she indicated a narrow path winding over the rise, 'you will see that it is the only dwelling in
the bay. You will come back here?'

'Goodness, no!' Liz's tone was laced with excitement and
anticipation. 'I'm going to live there!' She flashed an impish smile. 'Don't you think I'm lucky?'

The girl made no answer and Liz imagined there was a
puzzled expression in the dark eyes. She thrust the thought
aside. As if anything could possibly go wrong with her
wonderful new life! Up till now the only thing at all worrying had been last night's episode on the hotel balcony, and
that had been entirely due to her own foolishness in allowing herself to be trapped there. An episode that had ended
without harm, thanks to the reluctant assistance of the man
in the next room. There she went again, thinking of him! He
was a stranger, a shadow-man. Why, she didn't even know
his name.

She hurried up the dusty white track winding through the
silvery green of sparsely growing olive trees, breathing in air
that was redolent with a spicy perfume that was new to her.
When she reached the top of the rise she paused, gazing
down at the small sheltered bay below. In sharp contrast
with the rugged rocky coastline from which she had come,
here was an expanse of golden sand washed by a translu-

cent blue sea. Her gaze moved to the foot of the hill where on a grassy strip, half obscured by trees and bushes, she glimpsed the whitewashed walls of a stone villa with faded blue shutters and a tiled roof. From the front, entrance steps led down to the sand and a short distance further down the beach was a small dwelling where under the shade of shabby canvas awnings, wooden tables and chairs spilled out on to the sand. Could it be the emptiness of the scene, she wondered, that lent the taverna such a desolate air? But of course, she reminded herself, her uncle would have had to close the taverna at the onset of his illness.

All at once she couldn't wait to take a closer look at her inheritance. Her pack bumping on her shoulders, she ran down the curving track, to emerge hot and flushed amid a screen of tall oleander bushes with their clouds of pink blossoms. Liz, however, had eyes only for the villa. She was intrigued by an old grapevine with a giant trunk that climbed from ground level to twine itself up white walls and around a railing of a small balcony above. Opening a gate, she found herself in a courtyard that was flanked by cypress trees, and oh, so neglected. Overgrown rose bushes rose from between broken paving stones and a broken statue of a small boy, stained and discoloured with age, was visible behind high bushes. In the centre of the courtyard a marble dolphin balanced on his tail, but no water spouted from his mouth into a bowl discoloured with mould. Only the great stone urns cascading with pink geraniums appeared to have survived the ravages of time and neglect. Liz crushed down a feeling of dismay and disappointment.

Hadn't the Greek lawyer with the unpronounceable name—Kostas someone—warned her of the villa's state of disrepair? Or he had tried to. But it's mine, she rallied herself—well, half mine anyway, and wondered why she so often forgot about her cousin's share in the inheritance. Making her way over broken paving stones, she reached the weathered unpainted door and raised the ornamentally carved knocker.

It was very still, nothing seemed to move in the shimmering clear air. Or had she heard a movement somewhere inside the villa? She couldn't be certain. Her gaze moved to a window and a girl's face stared back at her, an anger-torn face with smouldering dark eyes. The next moment the image had vanished and presumably, Liz thought, the girl had moved to answer the door. Another lift of the knocker, however, elicited no response, and feeling piqued by the silence when she knew quite well there was someone inside, Liz kept right on knocking. Even if Katina—it must be Katina—for some reason of her own refused to welcome her here, surely someone would answer the summons. The next moment the heavy door swung open and a girl stood facing her in the opening, a remarkably lovely young Greek girl, Liz thought, even with an expression of fury darkening her aquiline features. 'Well,' hands planted aggressively on slim hips and dark head held high, 'what do *you* want?' Katina demanded fiercely. The great dark eyes in a swarthy face blazed angrily and she burst into a spate of Greek of which Liz could understand only two words, 'Katina' and 'New Zealand'. All at once the flood of words changed to English. 'You're *her,* aren't you? The one my stepfather used to tell me about.' She spat contemptuously, and her glance as she eyed Liz was pure malice. 'Go away, you are not wanted here!'

She made to close the heavy door, but Liz, sensing the movement was too quick for her, slipped inside. Crushing down the hot words that trembled on her lips, she forced her voice to an even tone. 'You don't understand. I'm your cousin and I—'

'Cousin!' Katina's tone of voice rose hysterically. 'You are not my cousin! I will never welcome you here, never!' she spat the words out.

'But—' Liz tried vainly to stem the torrent of words. Only her heightened colour betrayed her inner turmoil and her thoughts were rioting.

All at once the Greek girl broke into a storm of weeping, the tears running unrestrained down her cheeks. 'Why did it have to be you?' she sobbed. 'Why did my stepfather give you half of his property? He never told me about that. I thought it would be mine, all mine—' She broke off to glare at Liz through a mist of tears. 'It would have been all for me but for you. Now you have ruined my life. I cannot sell my share and get the money for my dowry.' Her voice thickened, pulsing with emotion. 'It was me he should have left it to. What did you ever do for him?' she demanded fiercely.

'I used to write him letters—'

'Words, just words!' once again Katina spat expressively. 'What use are they? I was the one who helped him every day in the taverna. I looked after him when he was ill, cooked his meals, washed his clothes. And you,' her tone was infinitely contemptuous, 'you didn't even know him. You were nothing to him—nothing!' The thought seemed to rouse her to a fresh surge of anger. 'Why couldn't he have left it all to me?' she cried again. 'You didn't need it! But me, I could have sold it for my dowry. My aunt and uncle, they thought I would have the dowry from my stepfather. It would have made everything right for me. I could have had many suitors asking me in marriage. Now you have spoiled it all! It's all your fault!' Her expression was so menacing that involuntarily Liz stepped backward. 'What do you know about a Greek girl and her dowry?' she flung at Liz. 'In your country you do not need a dowry, my stepfather told me. It's easy for you—' she stopped short and Liz saw with surprise that the dark anger in the swarthy face had given way to an expression of eager hope. 'You have come today about selling your share also? Together we will have the money for the sale and then—'

'No!' Now it was Liz's turn to feel indignation. 'Never! I won't do that! You'll have to find some other way of getting your dowry money.'

'Easy for you to say that,' Katina muttered resentfully. 'What do you care?' she cried bitterly. 'You come here for

a holiday, swim in the sea and lie on the beach all day, bring
your friends here too maybe. *Why* won't you sell?' she cried,
almost beside herself with rage and frustration. 'The lawyer in Heraklion told me he has an offer. It is a chance, he
said, not to be missed. But you, you will not help me, you
do not care! If it was you who needed the money—'

'Listen to me! You've got it all wrong!' The hot colour
flooded Liz's cheeks, but somehow she managed to speak
calmly. 'I haven't any money. I just don't want to sell my
share of the place, that's all.' All at once she realised how
much her decision affected the Greek girl, and she added,
'But I'm sorry about your dowry.'

'Sorry! Sorry!' Katina's red lips curved in a sneer. 'If you
were sorry you would sell today, this minute. Soon, let me
tell you, it will be too late. But you, you do not care! Not
about me, not about my stepfather either. He was nothing
to you, nothing!'

Stung to anger, Liz cried, 'That's not true—' The next
minute, however, she realised that nothing she could say
would make the slightest difference to the Greek girl's
opinion of her. Clearly Katina was beside herself with frustration and resentment—and guess who she held responsible for the twist of fate that had deprived her of her dowry
at a moment when she most needed it! The thoughts
churned through her mind. If only she had sufficient funds
to buy out Katina's share in the estate—but that was out of
the question. Clearly she wanted to get rid of Liz, and just
as determinedly, Liz knew she would never give up her
dream of just being here. Flinging up her small rounded
chin, she looked directly into the blazing black eyes.
'Whether you like it or not,' she announced calmly, 'I'm
staying right here! And if you imagine this is just a holiday
trip,' she ran on, 'you're way off beam. I haven't any
money, as you seem to think, only enough to pay my return
fare back to New Zealand.'

'Why don't you go, then?' screamed Katina. 'You have
nothing to stay for. No husband, no job to go to! Soon you

will have to give up your share and sell, and then it will be my turn to say yes or no! Then you will see—'

'No!' Liz's resolute tones cut across the angry words. 'I'll find something to do to keep myself!'

'*You!*' cried Katina contemptuously. 'What could *you* do?'

'I—' Liz sought wildly in her mind for an answer. Stung to resentment by the other girl's jeering tone, she gave utterance to the first words that entered her mind. 'I'll work in the taverna, that's what!'

The swarthy hands gesticulated wildly in the air. 'You do not know what you are saying!'

'Why not?' Liz told herself that she would make a last effort at reconciliation and that would be it! 'Maybe you could help me?' She waited for a fiery reaction.

It came. 'Help you!' screamed Katina, her voice high, out of control. 'Never will I do such a thing! *You!* How could you do the work in the taverna? I cooked and cleaned and made coffee and meals and served at the tables. My stepfather, he helped me, and later on Xenia and Nikos came—'

'Okay,' Liz refused to be daunted, 'I'll try to get them to come back and work for me.'

'They have gone away,' Katina's black eyes sparkled with anger, 'and the taverna is closed. Closed! Closed! Do you understand?'

'I can see that.' Liz's gaze strayed to the deserted café with its empty seats and faded blue canvas awnings flapping in the sea breeze. 'But you made a living, you and my uncle,' she persisted. 'Lots of Greek folk must have come to the taverna—'

The moment the words left her lips she realised she had played right into her opponent's hands.

'Yes! Yes!' Katina cried triumphantly. 'With our Greek food we made a living! Our people like their own food. You—' her tone was infinitely contemptuous, 'what would you know about our food?'

'Nothing, really,' Liz admitted cheerfully, 'but I could learn.' Refusing to be daunted by the other girl's contemptuous stare, she ran on, 'I've often heard about the wonderful dishes of Greece, like rolls of minced lamb and rice and herbs all wrapped in young vine leaves ... sounds delicious. And at the hotel last night—'

'Hotel meals!' Katina cut in scornfully. 'It is Greek food altered and mixed up to please the foreigners—like you! You had better try the food of our country before you talk about cooking and serving it at the taverna!' She still looked sulky and resentful, but she spoke in a quieter tone and Liz had a wild hope that maybe the Greek girl's rage had spent itself. Hadn't she heard that Greek folk were volatile and changeable in mood?

'Shall I cook you a Greek dish, one that comes from our village high in the mountains, and that way you will know if you wish to cook such food for the taverna? You will try it?'

Liz hesitated, taken aback by the unexpected offer. Her thoughts churning in confusion, she wondered if this were Katina's way of holding out the traditional olive branch. Maybe the Greek girl was just a little sorry for her outburst. She decided to give her the benefit of the doubt. She wasn't at all hungry, but coffee would be appreciated. Aloud she agreed, 'All right, then,' and catching the sudden triumphant gleam in the black eyes she added hastily, 'So long as it's something plain, I never could take black olives.' She tried for something not too highly spiced. 'How about an omelette?'

'You like omelette? I will make one with my special filling.'

'Oh yes, I always like omelettes.'

Katina muttered some words under her breath and Liz found herself hoping that they hadn't been what she imagined they had, 'You won't like this one!' The thought sparked her to say, 'So long as they aren't too spicy.'

She might just as well have been talking to the marble boy in the courtyard, because Katina took not the slightest notice of the remark. 'Go out to the courtyard,' she was saying, 'there is a table there and I will bring the meal out to you.'

Her tone was so friendly that Liz sent her a quick glance, but the other girl's face was turned away and Liz could not glimpse her expression. 'Thank you,' she said. 'I'll just wash my hands.' As she went along the hall she could hear the rattle of pots and pans in the kitchen.

The bathroom she found to be a big cool room with taps, basin and bath and thin towels hanging from a rail. She washed her hands in the basin, then turned to the mirror as she ran a comb through her hair. How pale her face was, she thought in surprise—and she had imagined she had handled the unexpected attack of the Greek girl with complete composure! Oh well, she mused hopefully, maybe everything would turn out all right after all. If only, she reflected on a sigh, her cousin weren't such a let-down. Or had she misjudged her?

She moved through the living room with its icons on white walls and the pottery-crowded mantel and made her way out to the sun-drenched courtyard. As she stepped over the broken paving stones and dropped down on the sun-warmed marble bench at the side of a small iron table, she was struck once again by the air of neglect that pervaded the area. Yet once, long ago, this had been a gracious Cretan dwelling, the entrance gates guarded by tall cypress trees and the sunny courtyard studded with marble statues. The years had taken their toll, but all the same, she cheered herself, there was still the sunshine filtering down through a screen of grapevines overhead, the little marble bench that had survived the ravages of the years, and everywhere the strangely luminous white light. Could it be because she had newly arrived from a New Zealand winter with its soft rains and cloud-enshrouded hills that the sky seemed such a tremulous, incredible blue?

All at once she spied an old stone vessel lying half hidden in weeds and, filling it from a nearby tap, she splashed water around the dust-dry roots of the struggling overgrown rose bush that somehow, despite heat and neglect, had contrived to produce clusters of fragrant white blooms. Then, stepping carefully to avoid crushing the blood-red poppies growing wild amongst the tall grass underfoot, she pulled away spent roses.

'It is ready for you.' She turned to see Katina, who was approaching her, carrying a wicker tray. Soon she had banged it down on the table and Liz saw there was a folded-over golden omelette, light and fluffy, on a plate, and a tiny cup of dark coffee served with the traditional glass of water. Katina, she thought, must have prepared the food in a remarkably short time. As she seated herself at the table, Liz realised that the omelette lay in a pool of olive oil, but what matter, she could always ignore the oil, which to her palate was anything but appetising.

'Coffee? Lovely!' She took a sip of the liquid, sickly sweet and half full of sediment. Discomfitingly aware of the close scrutiny of the Greek girl, she put down the cup.

'You don't like our Greek coffee?'

Liz shrugged slim shoulders. 'Not very much. It's so strong and thick. I guess I'm just not used to it.'

Katina said nothing, but remained standing. If only, Liz thought, the other girl wouldn't watch her in that disconcerting way. Katina's narrowed gaze was a little unnerving, but maybe the Greek girl had taken trouble to prepare the dish as a peace-offering, as it were, and was anxious to have her efforts appreciated. Liz decided to ignore Katina's scrutiny and put a forkful of the omelette to her mouth. The next moment she was choking and gasping, her mouth burning and her eyes smarting—never had she tasted food so revolting! There was a strong flavour of herbs, garlic and fennel, together with spices she couldn't identify. Wildly she snatched up the glass and took great gulps of water, gasping as the cooling liquid slid down a throat that seemed to be afire.

Still breathing with difficulty, she sprang to her feet and faced Katina's triumphant glance. 'How could you!' She put her hand to her mouth as nausea threatened, 'You made that revolting mess just to try to scare me away. It's horrible, and so are you! And if you think you can get rid of me by scaring me away with your nauseating cooking, you're way off beam. It won't work!' A flush had mounted to her delicate cheekbones and with a shock of surprise she realised her arms were trembling. As she met the malicious gleam in the black eyes she cried tersely, 'And don't think you can get me to change my mind about working in the taverna either!'

Katina let out a peal of derisive laughter. 'Stay, then! Work in the taverna, make the food my people want to eat! See if you can! I don't need to stay here. I have a friend who manages the big hotel over the hill. I have often worked there before when my stepfather didn't need me and I have a room there too. I can work there until you come to me and beg me to sell my share. My friend he has begged me to go back and work at his hotel. He knows I will take charge of the kitchen, direct the girls who do the housework, even welcome the tourists at the reception desk when the other girl is away. He is glad for me to do these things and he pays me well. So,' she screamed in sudden fury, 'stay here by yourself! See if I care! You won't help me!' she shouted accusingly 'so why should I help you!' All at once she burst into a spate of Greek of which Liz understood not one word, and throwing out a hand in a swift angry gesture, she sent the tray and its contents spinning to the ground, shattering the china to fragments and sending black olives and strong-smelling sauce spilling over the paving stones below. Then with a toss of her dark head, she swung around and hurried away.

Liz stared after her in horrified silence, one hand pressed to her burning throat. She must have been out of her skull, she scolded herself, ever to have trusted Katina. Well, she

vowed, let the Greek girl try all the sneaky tricks she knew,
it would make no difference. She was determined to stay
here and enjoy her inheritance, no matter what! All at once
her own land seemed far away and she felt very much alone
in a foreign environment where she didn't even know the
language, and the one person to whom she could appeal for
help, the man at the hotel, was probably already on his way
to another part of the island after a brief stop-over here.
Anyway, she reminded herself bleakly, he despised her. He
had made that plain enough last night. As for herself, she
couldn't decide whether he was friend or enemy, but she
couldn't help wishing she could meet him again, if only to
settle the question in her own mind. It was only that charisma of his that made her think about him so often, she
reasoned with herself, that and his heart-knocking appearance.

Still feeling slightly dazed by the Greek girl's unexpected
attack, Liz wandered back into the house. As she entered the
main room she almost collided with Katina, who came hurrying out of a bedroom, a soft embroidered bag bulging in
all directions held in one hand and in the other a hairbrush
and espadrilles. Clearly she was taking with her all the possessions she could carry.

'Now see how you will get on by yourself!' she hissed, and
hurrying past Liz, she slammed the heavy door behind her
with such force that the pottery vessels arranged along the
mantel rattled alarmingly. The next moment Liz ran to the
door and flung it open, watching as Katina's crimson skirt
glimmered through a screen of pink oleander blossom, to
vanish a few minutes later amongst the olive trees at the top
of the rise.

A little later, as she took herself on a tour of the villa, she
told herself that there seemed one big advantage in Greek
homes. For the whitewashed walls, tiled floors and absence
of clutter presented little difficulties in the way of housework. She glanced around the small room with icons on the
whitewashed walls and a woven homespun cover on the bed.

Evidently this had been Katina's room, she reflected, for there was a smudge of lipstick on the mirror and a drift of perfume lingered on the air. A tiny blue stone lay on the bureau. Hadn't she heard Greek girls used them as charms? The kitchen she found to be a sunny room with a colourful tiled floor and an old black stove above which hung bunches of dried herbs, rosemary, thyme and sage. She shuddered at the unpleasant aroma clinging to a blackened frying pan to which some sauce still adhered. But thank heaven, she thought, her uncle had evidently recently been connected with electricity, for a shining new range and kettle appeared scarcely to have been used. A swift glance along the open shelves revealed a stock of essential foodstuffs, flour, sugar, tinned milk—instant coffee. Goody, goody! And wouldn't you know—massive containers of olive oil! Liz wrinkled her small nose at the sight of jars of black olives—a luxury food where she came from in the south Pacific but one she had never developed a taste for, and after today's episode, she knew she never would!

She opened a door from the passage and found herself in a sparsely furnished bedroom. Could this have been her uncle's room? It was difficult to know, as someone had removed all traces of personal belongings. There was just a narrow bed, a shabby chest of drawers, a faded woven rug on the tiled floor. There was nothing to tell her if he had used the room. A pity, for she would have liked to have had something of his, just as a keepsake. Absently she opened a drawer of the wooden chest, but it was empty. The next moment she realised she had been mistaken, for tucked away at the back of the drawer and evidently overlooked by whoever it was who had tidied away his possessions she found a bundle of letters. Her eyes misted over as she recognised the childish writing. To think he had kept the letters she had written him all through the years! Suddenly a photograph fell from the open bundle, herself as a smiling thirteen-year-old. Heavens, she mused, how plump she had been in those days! For a long time she pored over the handwritten pages, then at last she replaced them in the drawer and went to get her travel pack. As she threw it on the bed she reflected that for the first time she was beginning to feel a little at home here. The small balcony-room upstairs with its vine-encrusted terrace was inviting, but she knew that this was the room she would use for herself.

Happily she began draping dresses and tops on hangers and hanging them on a rail. Her brief blue bikini she tossed on the bed, promising herself that as soon as she had a look through the taverna below she would christen the garment in the sapphire sea she could see from the window. She lost no time in hurrying over the long grass and down to the sand, already warm to the touch of her bare feet. Soon she was crossing the concrete strip and unlocking the weathered door of the timber building, to find herself in a long room with a counter built along one wall. Woven baskets held stocks of glasses and pottery mugs and a drawer below the counter took care of the cash takings. Liz pushed open a long shutter, to find herself looking out on a sun-drenched scene where waves creamed in soft curves on the stretch of sand. She turned away and crossed the room to open a swing door leading into the kitchen. Her glance roved over a blackened stove, heavy pots and pans and long benches. Open shelves were stocked with cooking materials and on the wall hung bunches of dried onions and tomatoes. As she had heard was the custom in Greek dwellings, everything was immaculate. All at once she spied a doorway that opened into a small room where whitewashed walls were hung with icons with their oil dips. There was a wooden table, a couple of rush chairs, rough bunks covered with woven spreads. Up till this moment she hadn't realised that the taverna held living quarters—but then, she mused on a sigh, there were so many aspects of her uncle's life that were unknown to her. Had this room, she wondered, been the home of the Greek couple who had helped Katina in the taverna during the owner's illness? But she didn't wish to dwell on the Greek girl. She'd think instead of a swim in the inviting blue water below.

Although it was early in the day the heat was increasing, and back in the villa she went to her room and slipped out of her garments, pulled on a pale blue bikini, then threw over her head a loose dress of soft Indian cotton printed in muted tonings of crimsons and blues. Soon she was making her way to the courtyard. Already it was her favourite spot, and once she had cleared away the long grass... She had stooped to pull aside the encroaching weeds from around the marble statue when a masculine voice from behind arrested her. 'Hope I'm not too early for you. I just called in to—'

Liz froze. Her heart was behaving strangely, and all at once bells were ringing all over the place. That voice! That deep, vibrant, *unforgettable* voice. She straightened and spun around to face brilliant dark blue eyes in a deeply tanned face. Realisation came to both at the same moment, and in an instinctive reaction their voices merged in a cry of delight and astonishment, 'It's you! It's really you!'

CHAPTER THREE

'SO—' SHE found herself enmeshed in his brilliant gaze, 'we meet again. Adam's the name, Adam Farmsworth. And you're Jim Kay's niece, Elizabeth?'

Liz smiled up into the strong dark face. Somehow she was finding it easy to smile right now. 'That's right. But I usually answer to Liz. How did you know about me?'

He laughed. 'The local grapevine functions pretty well around here.'

'Oh!' All the time her mind was registering how attractive he was, in a casual, sun-bronzed sort of way—the athletic figure, the strength of the masculine face with its black-lashed eyes and sensitive mouth. Oh, she had just known that he would be like this, seen in the hot white light of day. Aloud she heard herself say stupidly, 'I didn't think I'd ever see you again!'

'That goes for me too!' His deep tones were still tinged with pleasure. She caught the veiled amusement in his glance. 'Moonlight becomes you. Did anyone ever tell you?'

She could feel the tell-tale colour creeping up her cheeks and hastily she changed the subject. 'I wanted to see you—just to thank you.' Suddenly it seemed very important that she should put matters straight between them. 'You do understand about last night?' Her grey-blue eyes, clear as a child's, swept up to meet his gaze, 'It's true what I told you... it was just an accident. You do believe me?'

He grinned and she caught the flash of teeth, extraordinarily white against the dark tan of his skin. 'Why do you think I called the night porter?'

'You took your time about it.' She couldn't resist the jibe.

'Can you blame me?' His dark blue eyes held a lively expression. 'The Cretan moonlight is very revealing.' At the glint of amusement in his gaze, the colour in her cheeks deepened, but now she knew it was only amusement. The note of contempt in his tones that had so distressed her last night had gone, replaced by warm appreciation. 'I looked for you at the breakfast table this morning.' Heavens, she thought, aghast, why am I letting my tongue run away with me like this? Swiftly she added, 'Just to thank you.'

'I never eat breakfast,' he sent her a grin, 'but if anyone offers me coffee around about this time of the day—'

She smiled back at him. 'I'll see what I can do!' All at once the scene around her seemed to shimmer in the crystalline air. Or could that be her imagination? 'I've only just moved in here today, all the way from a New Zealand winter.'

Again she glimpsed the glimmer of laughter in his eyes. 'So that's why your shoulders are so pale.'

She refused, however, to allow herself to be drawn into that particular trap by his mocking voice. 'Not for long. I haven't had a swim in the bay yet, but that's my first priority—after coffee, of course!' She took in his sun-bronzed limbs, the cotton shirt open to the waist revealing his tanned torso and the dark line of his swimming trunks. 'Do you often come over here to swim?'

'All the time.' His tone was careless. 'I happen to live around here, just over the hill. It's no distance over the goat track.'

Liz turned away. 'Come into the house and I'll fix coffee.' Together they strolled into the coolness of the villa and Adam Farmsworth followed her down the whitewashed hall and into the kitchen. A fresh breeze, spiced with an aroma strange to her, drifted in at the open window. 'Nice,' Liz sniffed appreciatively. 'What is it? Do you know?'

'An aromatic herb called dittany that grows only on the island—I'll give you a hand.' He was taking coffee mugs from hooks on the wall and putting them on the table. Then he found instant coffee on a shelf. 'Goodness,' said Liz in amazement, 'you've been here before!' A sudden thought occurred to her and she looked at him excitedly. 'If you live around here you would have known my uncle.'

'That's right.' He was watching her fill the electric kettle from the tap. 'Nice old boy. I used to drop in to see him now and again. Only one thing wrong with him,' was she imagining a sharper tone in his voice, the lazy laughter in it quenched? 'he was pigheaded as they come. Once he'd made up his mind to anything,' he threw up well-shaped bronzed hands, 'you couldn't shift him. That was it. Finish!' His tone changed to a teasing inflection. 'Don't tell me that you take after him?'

She rushed to his defence. 'I never found him to be that way at all! Anyway,' she said with spirit, 'lots of folk call that strength of character.'

Adam shrugged broad shoulders. 'Whatever it was, there was no arguing him out of anything once he'd made up his mind—Hey!' he looked at her in surprise, 'I didn't know you two had ever met! He used to talk about you a lot, but he never put me in the picture about that.'

Liz shook her head. 'Only in letters. We corresponded for years and years. You'd be surprised how much I know of his life in Crete.'

She caught a sudden flicker of interest in his dark blue eyes. 'Like what?'

'Oh, local customs. Friends he'd made on the island, all those things.'

'I get it.' He appeared to have lost interest in the matter. 'So long as you don't take after him,' he grinned, 'in "strength of character", as you call it.'

She threw him a teasing look. Somehow it was easy to talk to him on this sundrenched day in exciting, unfamiliar surroundings. 'Would it matter so much?'

All at once in a swift change of mood, he was withdrawn, serious.

'It could to me.'

Her eyes widened and she stared up at him in amazement. 'What do you mean?'

'Forget it!' He took the mug of coffee she was handing to him, then went to perch on the scrubbed table, swinging a long tanned leg. 'Katina told me all about you months ago. She didn't ever expect you to make the trip out here.' He shot her a grin. 'Staying long?'

Such a matter-of-fact enquiry, yet to Liz the words seemed to hang in the air with an odd significance. It *must* be her imagination. 'As long as I can! I'm fascinated by this island,' she said confidingly. 'I have been for years. It was just so terrible Uncle Jim dying before I could get here. I'd been saving up for the trip to Greece for years, and then when I did finally get here, my uncle wasn't here any longer and Katina, my cousin—' she pulled a face, 'I call her my cousin, but she's only a "step" really—'

'Didn't put out the welcome mat for you, I gather?' Adam said, grinning.

Liz shrugged slim shoulders. 'Anything but! She made it fairly plain that she doesn't want to have me around, refuses to have anything to do with me. It's awkward,' she stirred her coffee thoughtfully, 'when we both have shares in the place. Oh well,' she said with more confidence than she felt, deep down, 'maybe she'll change her mind in time.'

'Actually she called in to see me this morning. She's often worked for me—'

At last the penny dropped. 'Now I know where you live! At the hotel!'

He nodded. 'I run the show and staff difficulties can be a problem. Luckily Katina lives fairly close and I can always call on her in an emergency. She's worked for me on and off since last summer when I was looking for someone to superintend the kitchen staff and keep the household side of things ticking along. I've found her to be first class, and she happens to speak English, so when she turned up today wanting employment at the hotel it suited me fine. Now that the summer season's starting I'm in luck having someone on the staff like Katina, whom I can depend on.'

Liz's mouth fell open and she said incredulously, 'Depend—on Katina!'

He laughed at her expression of amazement. 'Sure, why not? Oh, I grant you she can fly into a fury half a dozen times in a day, Greeks are like that. They can carry on like nobody's business one minute and be the best of buddies the next! It's a national characteristic, you'll get used to it!'

'Maybe,' Liz said doubtfully. She was finding difficulty in imagining the Greek girl being really friendly with her—ever. She brought her mind back to his deep tones.

'So here you are all on your own on a Greek island on the most fabulous holiday that anyone could wish for—' He broke off and shot her an enquiring glance. 'Or is it just a holiday?'

Liz got a strange impression that her answer was in some way important to him, but she told herself that was ridiculous. 'I'm going to play it by ear,' she told him, 'coast along for a while and see how I get along.' No use confiding to him at this early stage the exciting solution to her financial problems that had just this moment flashed into her mind. It was an idea, she thought jubilantly, with infinite possibilities, but one she would need to think over carefully before making her plans public. Her glance went to the window with its vista of hazy blue hills. 'It's so beautiful here—'

'With the best swimming beach for miles.' Adam grinned. 'Why don't we try it out? It's a waste of time being in the bay without taking a dip.'

She laughed. 'I'm all ready—well, almost. Just give me time to put on some sun-lotion. Won't be a minute!' She found her Greek bag and tossed into it a bottle of lotion, tinted sunglasses and a towel, worn and freshly laundered, that she found in a drawer.

Adam was waiting for her in the bright sunlight of the courtyard, holding out towards her a bunch of white grapes he had plucked from the vine clinging to the sagging supports. 'Try some! They're recommended! You uncle was no end proud of his *rosaki* grapes.' He was watching her as she sampled a sun-warmed delicious grape. 'He always said—' He broke off, his gaze resting on the low scooped neckline of her sun-frock. 'You are sun-tanned, after all!'

Acutely conscious of his gaze, Liz rushed into speech. 'This is just a winter tan, left over from summer. In Auckland, where I come from, the city's bang between two huge harbours and there are so many lovely swimming beaches you wouldn't believe! It's not like here, though, where the tides don't seem to vary much. Pretty soon I guess I'll have my Cretan variety of suntan. A swim every day, that's what I've promised myself. Maybe two.'

'Great! I'll join you!' The words were carelessly said, yet they sent her spirits soaring.

Still plucking at the grapes in her hand, she went with him over the strip of grass and down on the sand, warm to her bare feet.

'Looks dreary, doesn't it?' She glanced towards the taverna they were passing. 'Empty tables, folded sun-umbrellas, closed doors! I had ideas that Katina and I might run it between us,' she confided, 'but she didn't go for that one little bit! Anyway,' all at once she was conscious of a surge of pure happiness, 'I'm not worrying about that right now.' Her glance went to the sandy shore, washed by a translucent sea.

When they neared the shoreline Adam paused to take off his light cotton shirt, tossing it down on the sand, and she took in the supple strength of his chest and wide shoulders, sun-darkened to an even tan. The next moment she pulled her sun-frock over her head and threw it down. 'Beat you in!'

She sped away, bare feet flying over the sand and her hair streaming behind her shoulders. He caught up with her at the water's edge and together they plunged into the foaming sea. 'It's gorgeous!' Liz cried, delighting in the warmth

and buoyancy of seawater that caressed her skin like the
touch of silk. Soon they waited their chance to drop down
on an incoming breaker to be carried into the shallows, then
wade through a frothing sea back into deeper water. At last
they swam out into the deep. A moderately good swimmer
herself, Liz had to admit that Adam's powerful crawl as he
sliced through the water was a delight to see. Just for fun she
waited until they paused to tread water, then swam a short
distance away, calling back over her shoulder, 'Race you to
the rocks at the end of the point!'

'Right! You're on!'

She was hopelessly outpaced, of course, she knew that
from the start. Indeed, the distance was further than she had
imagined and before long her strength was flagging, though
she would never admit it. All at once he was at her side, but
instead of moving ahead, he grasped her arm. 'Take it easy.
Had enough? Those rocks are a hell of a lot further away
than you'd think! Come on, I'll practise my life-saving act
and we'll head for the shore!'

Liz hadn't any breath left to answer him, but she turned
to float on her back. The next moment she felt his strong
arms around her, then he was propelling them through the
water.

'Wow!' She dropped her feet down to firm sand. 'I don't
know what happened to me. I really thought I could make
it.' She pushed back the wet curtain of hair from her face.
'Just as well you were there!'

He laughed. 'Your own fault for throwing challenges
around!'

'I know, I know.'

They dropped down on the towels they spread on the sand
and lay back, letting the dazzling sunshine stream down on
their faces. It was a world of their own where the only sound
was the gentle murmuring of the waves and the cry of seagulls wheeling overhead. Time ceased to matter and she was
conscious only of a delicious lassitude and an odd sense of
belonging. No doubt she felt that way, she thought dream-

ily, because of having no folk of her own and becoming so attached to this uncle in Crete. The singleminded determination to get here had given her the necessary strength of mind to forgo new clothes, entertainments, expensive make-up, anything that might cut into her hard-won savings. All the time, deep down, she had been aware of a hazard that could well put an end to her dream. She knew that whatever happened she mustn't allow herself to get too deeply involved in a romantic relationship. Fortunately, she congratulated herself, the decision to end a promising love affair that she had made on two occasions in the past hadn't really worried her unduly. How could it, when her own private dream beckoned ahead?

She stole a sideways glance at Adam, whose eyes were closed and she could take her fill of looking at him, something she was finding she enjoyed a lot. Could she have dealt so resolutely and lightheartedly with a blossoming romance had the man who loved her devotedly been Adam Farmsworth? Now where, she asked herself the next moment, could that absurd thought have sprung from?

Lulled to a companionable silence by the dazzling sunshine that was drying the salt on their bodies, she was conscious all over again of a feeling of dreamy content. She raised herself a little, leaning on her elbow and once again letting her gaze rest on Adam. He was lying on his back, his arms crossed behind his neck. There was a special magic about him, she mused—the thickly-growing dark hair, the erect lean body, the eyes that seemed so full of light. He was a man, the thought came unbidden, that a girl would find it all too easy to lose her heart to, if she weren't on her guard!

All at once she realised his eyes were open, just a slit but sufficient to reveal the glint of amusement in his sideways gaze. Thank heaven, she thought, her face was already flushed with the touch of the sun and disguised the hot tide of colour running up her cheeks. Forgetting all about her resolution not to divulge her plans, she rushed into speech. 'Guess what? I'm going into business!'

'What?' All at once he was alert, interested, his tone questioning. 'I got the idea you were over here on an extended holiday. You mean you're leaving the villa, going to stay at Chania or Heraklion?'

His sharp tone sent a tingle of excitement flicking along her nerves. Could it matter to him, so much, so soon? Would he really miss her if she left the villa? The thought was intoxicating and she raised herself to lean on an elbow, looking down at the sand she was sifting through her fingers so he wouldn't catch the expression of happiness in her face. 'No, no, you'd never catch me leaving here.'

The urgency in his gaze died away. 'That's all right, then.' At his sudden relaxation she felt again that flicker of joy. 'You don't seem much interested in my project,' she complained.

'You haven't let me in on it yet, but if you're planning on selling crocheted lampshades or handmade cushions—'

'Don't worry,' said Liz, 'All I'm doing is to carry on the family tradition. I'm going to open up the taverna.'

'You're having me on!' His incredulous expression was anything but flattering to her ambitions.

'What's wrong with my having a go at running it?' Her eyes were dreamy. 'There was this nice Canadian woman, she was staying at your hotel when I was there, and she gave me the idea.'

'You can't be serious!' He was eyeing her with amusement. 'You don't mean you're taking that on, Greek cooking and all?'

Her eyes fell before his mocking glance. It must be because of his dark blue gaze, so penetrating and full of light, that she couldn't sustain his look. 'No Greek cooking!'

'What, then?'

'Would you believe? Good old English tea and American coffee and chilled fruit drinks. It will be something different for the tourists—'

The lurking amusement in his eyes deepened. 'It won't, you know! Tourists can soon find that sort of thing if they know where to look for it!'

'Aha,' she cried triumphantly, 'but not right here, with homemade rolls toasted and served with the filling of their choice!' As always when she was feeling enthusiastic about anything, her huge grey-blue eyes glowed with excitement. 'The Canadian lady I met had been to Greece lots of times, and she really did seem to know what she was talking about! From what she said I gathered that Greek food is fine for people who appreciate it (she gave an involuntary shudder at the remembrance of the supposedly native dish prepared especially for her by Katina), but lots of tourists especially the older variety, miss the foods they're accustomed to having at home. Oh, I know it sounds awfully stupid and plain and downright boring to you,' she hastened to say, 'but in a way I can understand how they feel.'

Warned by the discouraging expression in his eyes, she ran on before he could argue the matter. 'Oh, I know that the equipment I'll need for a start-off will cost me plenty. I'll have to have a freezer, a cabinet with lots and lots of glass-topped compartments and a toasting machine. I'm so lucky having electricity already installed at the taverna and the villa—' A sudden thought flashed through her mind. 'I guess I've got you and your hotel to thank for that! So,' she pretended not to see the disapproval in his eyes, 'if you feel like a cup of good old English tea—sorry I can't promise to provide anything stronger—you'll know where to find it! You look a bit off-putting,' she chided him smilingly. 'What's wrong with it, for heaven's sake?'

'If you want it straight,' his face had sobered, 'you could find yourself up against a few financial problems. Away down here, miles from the towns, it isn't easy to arrange deliveries. There'd be hefty cartage as well as installing costs.'

'Oh, that's all right!' She refused to be discouraged by his unhelpful attitude. 'I'm so lucky! Uncle Jim gave me my return fare to Greece. Being here suits me just fine, and I can easily use the money for the return fare and pay myself back later.'

He pinned her with his unrelenting blue gaze. 'No going back?' There was a glint of amusement in his eyes. 'What are you planning on doing? Going to marry a Greek?'

'No!' she protested hotly, and realised the next moment it was the very reaction he had hoped to provoke from her.

'Not a Greek?' he enquired blandly. 'You'd prefer—'

Liz dropped her eyes before his gaze. 'Not any man! At least—'

'You don't seem very sure about it.'

'You know what I mean! What I mean to do,' she rushed on breathlessly, 'is to pay myself back from the profits I'll make this summer!'

Adam squinted into the clear blue bowl of the sky. 'And if you don't make a profit, what then?'

'Stop!' She threw her hands up and cupped her ears. 'You're just trying to ruin my plans!'

He took not the slightest notice of her protest. 'For a kick-off you'd better realise right here and now that you could be billed for a lot more drachmas than you're counting on for the stuff you need. Then you'll need help in the kitchen—'

'Who says so?' She flashed him an impish grin. 'I've made up my mind to go it alone!'

He threw her a sceptical look. 'Your uncle used to employ a Greek couple who worked in the kitchen at the taverna. Katina used to give him a hand too—'

'And now she works for you!'

'That's right.' His tone was noncommittal. 'One of the few Greeks on my payroll who can speak English fluently. That means I can rely on her to fill in at the reception desk when the regular girl is away.'

Liz was scarcely listening. She was sick and tired of being forced to listen to his praises of Katina. All at once she found herself wondering if the Greek girl had told Adam of her arrival at the villa. Katina had flounced off in such a rage that she had probably given him a colourful account of the confrontation between herself and Liz in the courtyard. Or had she? In view of the rapid changes of mood that seemed to be characteristic of Greeks, Liz had a faint hope that the other girl may have calmed down by the time she arrived at the hotel. One thing was for sure—Adam wasn't giving anything away in that direction. Still, the question continued to nag at her. 'Did Katina tell you that I was here?' The words seemed to come without her volition.

'She mentioned it.' He appeared scarcely interested in the matter. Maybe, she thought, he was accustomed to Katina's emotional outbursts and took little notice of her excitability. She wrenched her mind back to his deep tones. 'That's why I came over to see you today, just to say hi!'

'Hi!' She smiled across at him. 'So you don't think much of my project?'

'Not much. You could end up by running up debts you couldn't meet, get in too deep.'

'I won't—'

'It's on the cards,' he pursued inexorably. 'What would you do then?'

She refused to be deterred by his negative attitude. 'I don't know!' Then, on an inspiration, 'Get a loan from that lawyer in Heraklion, I suppose. Kostas someone—I never can pronounce his name. He said to ask him if I needed any help with anything at all. I'm sure he would arrange something for me through the bank.'

You could tell by his expression, Liz thought, that Adam didn't think much of the idea. He said briefly, 'You'd be so lucky!'

'He promised to help me. And he seemed awfully kind...' The words faltered into an uneasy silence. She had a disquieting suspicion that a girl who was going it alone in a strange land would be more than a fool to put herself under an obligation to the Greek lawyer. There was something about the intimacy of his hot, dark eyes... She thrust the uneasy thoughts aside. It wasn't as if she would ever need to ask him for monetary help to tide her over. She'd manage somehow, of course she would!

She brought her mind back to Adam's admonishing tones. 'So long as you don't let yourself in for more than you bargain for!'

It was precisely the thought that had been going through her own mind, but she had no intention of giving him the satisfaction of letting him know. 'I thought maybe you'd help me,' she wrinkled her nose at him, 'tell me the name and address of the shop where I can send in my order for the equipment I need.'

'Right, I'll give it to you later. You can get it all in Heraklion.' He sent her a sharp glance. 'Except the kitchen help you'll be needing. You'd have to go to the village for that.'

'You keep going on about it,' she complained, 'and I keep telling you I don't need anyone else. Anyway, I'll worry about that one when I come to it!' The sundrenched day, the dreamy sense of relaxation laced with the heady excitement of the man at her side with his lean tanned body and sardonic expression, all conspired to go to her head a little, and she heard herself saying happily, confidently, 'It'll all work out, you'll see! 'Anyway,' she threw back the long damp hair from around her face, 'you shouldn't be doing your best to discourage me from opening up the taverna. Just think of your middle-aged clientele,' she threw him a teasing smile, 'who'll come hiking over the hill just for some good old plain filled restaurant rolls, as a change from your horrible Greek dishes at the Hermes dining room—'

Adam rose to his feet and stood looking down at her. 'I take that as a challenge! Take it back or I'll have to make you—'

'You'll have to catch me first!' Quick as a flash Liz had leaped to her feet and dodged between his sinewy arms. 'Race you to the water!'

She was barely a step ahead of him as she splashed into the foaming tide. The next minute he caught up with her and catching her up in purposeful arms he carried her out to deeper water, then—'No!' She was kicking and struggling in his grasp, but he took no notice and dumped her unceremoniously in the water. She emerged with streaming hair, breathless, dashing moisture from her eyes with the backs of her hands. 'Just wait until I catch up with you!' She took after him, then stopped to tread water, breaking into laughter. It was that sort of heat-hazy day, and soon they were making for the shore together.

Much later, when at last they splashed through the shallows after another dip in the sea, Liz paused to wring out the long dark rope of her hair. 'Heaven only knows what the time is! I—' Her voice died away as her gaze rested on Adam, his thick black hair in curly disorder, drops of seawater glistening on his muscular tanned chest. With an effort she wrenched her mind back to his voice. What was he saying? she wondered wildly. Something about having to meet someone, a builder who was coming to see him about making alterations to the structure of the hotel. 'He'll be waiting for me now, I guess.' Reluctantly they made their way over the sand, warm to the touch of their bare feet, past the empty taverna and up to the villa. Somehow she hated to see him go, and on an impulse she said, 'Oh, you were going to let me have the name and address of the electrical firm in town, maybe they'll supply the cabinet with the containers as well.'

For a moment he was silent. Then, 'Over to you. You'd better get a quote from them before you do anything drastic.' Moving into the living room of the dwelling, he went to a cabinet and took out pen and paper. He knows where everything's kept here, Liz thought once again, and wondered just how well Adam had known her uncle.

He handed her a slip of paper. 'You can drop your letter in at the hotel for posting any time,' she caught the hard note of disapproval in his voice, 'that is if you insist on going through with your scheme!'

She pulled a face at him. 'You're trying to knock me—spoil everything!'

'Would I do that to you, Liz?'

'Well, you do your best to pour cold water on my ideas all the time.'

His tone softened. 'Someone's got to look after you. You're in Greece now and the Greeks believe in protecting their womenfolk, especially the unmarried girls—'

She wrinkled her nose at him. 'But you're not a Greek!'

'As good as.' The warmth in his brilliant eyes seemed to deepen. 'You know the old saying, "When in Rome…" Tell you what, I'll pick you up on Sunday and we'll take a look at Aghios Nikolaos, it's a picturesque little village down the coast—that is if you've nothing else on?'

'No, no! I'd love that!' Did she sound as excited as she felt about the invitation? To try and tone down the eager happiness in her voice she added, 'I've got to make the most of my free time here. Once I get going with the taverna—'

'Oh yes, your taverna—'

Swiftly she picked up the satirical note in his dry tone. 'Why do you say it like that? Don't you think I can make a go of it?'

'Frankly, no.'

'Why not?' she demanded.

Adam shrugged broad shoulders. 'Just a matter of good old drachmas. If it was a matter of carrying on like your uncle did you might pull it off, but even then you'd need a lot of help.'

'My uncle managed well enough,' she said stiffly. She added reluctantly, 'Of course he had Katina to help him— well, some of the time.'

He grinned. 'And the Greeks who used the rooms at the back of the taverna…nice old couple. They knew the place inside out and he'd have managed fine with them, even without Katina's help.'

'I see. When did they go away from here?'

'They stayed on until just before you came, the taverna was closed for the winter anyway, and went to live in the village. You'll have to meet them some time, you'd like Xenia and Nikos. Honest as they come, and loyal as hell to your uncle.'

All at once her eyes were alight with enthusiasm. 'Maybe they'd come back and work for me?'

'Sure they would, they'd come like a shot.'

'Of course, I couldn't afford it right away, but maybe later on when I get the money—Oh, I know what you're thinking—more drachmas, and I've barely enough to get started—but don't worry, I'll get the money to put myself in business.' And she spoiled the brave statement by adding a trifle uncertainly, 'Somehow ... you'll see.

'Don't worry about it!' His grin was infectious. 'You're in a country that's new to you, all set to explore one of the loveliest villages in the Greek islands—'

With a man who I'd rather be with than anyone else ... anywhere! The thought came unbidden.

CHAPTER FOUR

LIZ WAS feeling so excited about the trip to Aghios Niko-laos with Adam that she awoke very early in the morning. 'It's really me,' she exulted, 'I'm here in Crete at last, about to go with Adam to Aghios Nikolaos!' The name rang a bell in her mind then she recalled viewing with breathless inter-est a TV series entitled *Who Pays the Ferryman,* filmed in that particular village in Crete.

A glance through the window showed her a luminous blue sky giving promise of a hot day to come, and she chose a dress of cool white cotton printed with green palm trees and the word 'Paradise'. The dress she had brought with her from New Zealand seemed to fit the occasion, for what could be more exciting than to be taken by Adam to the lo-cale of *The Lotus Eaters?* She wandered into the kitchen, where she mixed a mug of instant coffee, made a tomato sandwich for herself and nibbled some of the goat's milk cheese she liked.

Today she decided she wouldn't use much make-up, just sun-lotion and waterproof eye make-up. The excitement glowing in her eyes was there for all to see, but what mat-ter? Soon she was slipping into her capacious Greek bag her blue bikini, camera, towel, comb and sunglasses. Then, fit-ting her feet into woven string sandals, she made her way out to the courtyard to wait for Adam.

It was very still, the only sound the waves washing up on the beach below. A small lizard clung motionless to the whitewashed wall. Idly Liz plucked the spent blossoms from a rose-bush growing wild, the thorny branches spreading high overhead, then she decided to take a snapshot of the courtyard to send home. But *this* was her home now, the thought flickered through her mind. At least, that was the way she already felt about it. It was amazing.

She was snapping the picture when a car pulled up outside, and the first she knew of Adam's arrival was the sight of his tall figure approaching her.

She greeted him with her wide smile. 'Hi! This picture is for the girls in the office, back home.'

'Now I'll take one of you!'

'Oh, would you?' She glanced up, eyes alight. 'They'd never believe how lovely it is here unless I send them some evidence to prove it, broken fountain and all!' She offered him her tiny Instamatic, but he waved it away.

'I've got my own, that way I can be sure of getting one for myself!'

Delight vibrated along her nerves, but she made her voice casual. 'If you really want one?'

Liz found the answer to her question in the warmth that had leaped into his eyes. 'All right, then.' She stood motionless, trying not to blink against the bright sunlight. She had no need to force a smile. Trouble was, she thought, she couldn't seem to stop smiling today!

The next moment she caught the click of the shutter. 'Got it!' said Adam with satisfaction. 'All ready to go?'

'I've been ready for ages!' Why must she say things like that, she scolded herself inwardly, betraying all too clearly the heady excitement she was feeling?

A little later. seated beside Adam in his long red car, she was conscious once again of a surge of pure happiness. 'It's the day,' she assured herself, 'and the air, this crystal-clear air.'

'And being with Adam,' her heart supplied.

She wound down the car window and the light breeze blew softly over her face, stirring the dark hair at her temples and bringing with it an elusive aroma, something she couldn't put a name to.

He seemed to tune in on her thoughts. 'Bet you don't know what that tang is in the air?'

'I haven't a clue. It's something new to me.' She laughed with a sheer joy of living. 'It's all new to me here.'

'A lot of different herbs grow over the hillsides.'

She laughed again. 'I'm learning all the time!'

They took a road winding up a slope that was sparsely covered with the silvery green of olive trees and bright with blood-red poppies, white daisies and small blue wildflowers growing along the roadside. Far ahead Liz could see the hazy blue of distant hills. The next moment she realised they were swiftly overtaking another traveller on the road, a swarthy Greek man seated on the wooden slatted saddle of a donkey while a woman wearing long dark shirts, her face shaded by a black coif, walked alongside. 'Well,' breathed Liz indignantly, 'just look at that! I suppose the woman hurrying alongside the donkey is the Greek's wife?'

Adam threw her a grin. 'No Women's Lib in the villages around here!'

'I think it's awful, his poor wife having to trot alongside the donkey! I thought you told me—' She turned towards him, her words dying into silence as she took in his tanned profile, clear-cut as if cast in bronze. It was amazing the pleasure she took in just...looking at him. With an effort she pulled her thoughts together and said hurriedly, '—that womenfolk in Greece are protected and looked after by their men?'

'True. But after marriage they're expected to work out in the fields, tending the grapevines, working in the olive groves, gathering the herbs. The hours are long and hard and the hot sun of the Greek islands doesn't do much for their complexions.'

'I can see what you mean.' Liz recalled the sun-dried, nut-brown faces of the women working in the fields. Maybe, she thought, they weren't as old as she had thought but prematurely aged by a burning Cretan sun and endless physical toil.

Adam's eyes glinted with amusement. 'Don't look so het-up about it! I hear that the women do have one day off a year and on that day they kick the men out of the tavernas, and instead of the men sitting around there all day, drinking endless cups of Turkish coffee and playing with their worry beads, the women take over!'

'Good for them!'

'It's not a bad idea, the Greek way—' She surprised a teasing light in his eyes.

'Oh, you would say that!' she disclaimed. 'You're a man!'

He said dryly, 'You've noticed?'

Oh, she'd noticed all right. She couldn't seem to keep her gaze from straying endlessly towards him, taking her fill of looking at the lean dark face and eyes that didn't miss a thing! What if he should suspect the way she was feeling about him right at this minute? The possibility was so un-nerving that she broke into speech, saying the first words that came into her mind. 'All those black clothes the Cretan women wear—they look as if they're in perpetual mourning!'

His eyes were fixed on the winding highway ahead.

'Blame the sun for that too!'

'And with all that,' she marvelled aloud, 'Greek girls still need to produce a dowry to find themselves a husband! They do, don't they? It seems so far back in the past, that sort of thing!' She was thinking that she wouldn't put it past Katina to tell her any old lie that would serve to get her what she wanted.

'Do they ever! It's the custom of the country,' he explained. 'Seems to work well enough in this part of the world. You've got to remember that a Greek man doesn't get very high wages, either before or after marriage.' He grinned across at her. 'But you still don't go along with it?'

'No, I don't!' she said with spirit.

He only laughed and sped on. Soon they were taking a smooth highway cutting between hills covered in low-growing olive trees, to drop down to a plain planted with

olives and almonds. Presently they passed a tour bus
crowded with sightseers, then merged into the line of cars
moving ahead of them. Then all at once they rounded a
curve, and looking down on the scene spread below, Liz
drew a sharp breath of delight.

'It's so beautiful,' she breathed, leaning forward to take
in the vista of the seaside town that appeared to be built
around a deep circular lake. Pleasure craft met their reflec-
tions in the still depths and blue and white sun-umbrellas,
shaded tables and seats of tavernas set at the water's edge.
The narrow winding streets were lined with small stores. Liz
caught sight of proprietors standing in doorways while embroidered muslin dresses swung on hangers around them.

Adam guided the car down to the lake's edge, manoeuvring the vehicle amongst cars and tour buses to find a parking space in the crowded area. Soon he and Liz were
strolling down a narrow winding street where each store
displayed attractive ornaments and locally made souvenirs.
The scene sparkled in the clear white light and presently, a
hand on her elbow, Adam guided her down a street where
store displays breathed wealth and opulence. The treasures
seemed endless—porcelain and pottery, small urns made in
the style of the originals. It was, however, the golden glitter
of a small jewellery store that held Liz's fascinated gaze. She
had never owned anything but a few pieces of costume jewellery, had never even been tempted, but there was something about this bright Greek gold...She looked at the
glittering jewelled amulets and earrings and hair ornaments, all fashioned with exquisite craftsmanship and made
with a simplicity of design that could have belonged to the
stylised form of today.

'Come along inside and take a closer look.' A hand laid
on her warm tanned arm, he piloted her into a room that
breathed wealth and luxury and the patronage of an international clientele.

Liz paused before a glass display case, attracted by
gleaming necklaces fashioned in triple curves of Greek gold.

Somehow, she mused, the gold seemed to gleam with a special lustre. Just the air here, the sunshine—all at once she was very much aware of Adam's nearness—her own golden day! Aloud she commented, 'Isn't that the style worn by Greek maidens thousands of years ago?'

'Sure is. Lots of these ornaments are copies of treasures unearthed by archaeologists—tell me, which is it to be?' He was teasing her, of course, he must be, Liz thought as he ran on, 'A silver slave bangle, emerald earrings, a pearl-studded comb for your hair?'

Smilingly, she shook her head. 'All far too expensive.'

Leaning an elbow on the counter, he studied her with lazy detachment. 'But if you had a choice?' he persisted.

'Well,' she smiled up into his tanned face, 'if I had all the money in the world I wouldn't go for any of those, where on earth would I wear them? But this . . .' Her voice died away as her gaze went to a thin gold chain from which hung a tiny golden bee, its jewelled wing and sting tips attached by the finest of gold wires. 'I've seen pictures of the original,' she told him, looking up at him excitedly. As she met his deep brilliant gaze she wrenched her glance aside and heard herself floundering in a tumble of words. 'The pendant of the bees, it was called. And it's at the Museum at Heraklion.'

'That's right. The famous Minoan Golden Bee pendant. The archaeological boys found it not so long ago, amongst the ruins of a king's palace. Luckily it was surprisingly preserved. I'll take you to see it, if you're interested.'

'Oh, I am, I am! I'm interested in anything, everything in Crete.'—*So long as I can see it with you.* The thought came unbidden. She brought her mind back to his deep vibrant tones.

'We haven't started our sightseeing tours yet. I know the island so well.'

He was speaking, she thought, on a wave of excitement, as though the future held many more meetings, as if he had in mind taking her to the many places of interest that abounded in this most fascinating of Greek islands. There was a warmth, a special something in his eyes when he looked at her that made her think he felt the same way about her as she did about him.

'Right,' he was saying, 'that's it, then! I'll get it for you.'

'Me?' She was taken by surprise. 'Goodness, no! It must cost the earth!'

'Not really. It's not the original, you know!'

'I couldn't let you,' she protested. She had a dreadful suspicion that he might have imagined she was hinting for the pendant.

'Why not?' He sent her the heart-knocking grin she found so difficult to resist. 'Give me one good reason.'

'I told you, it's too pricey!'

'Well, that's out for a start!'

'I mean—' something in his bright steady gaze was sending happiness pulsing through her, making it awfully difficult to concentrate. She said the first words that came into her mind. 'It's not as if it were just a little souvenir.'

'What else?'

She could feel the hot colour running up the apricot tan of her cheeks. Heavens, she thought with dismay, what if he imagines—? The next moment, however, she realised that he was pressing home the advantage she had handed him. 'You must have a souvenir. Something to take back with you from Crete.'

She twinkled up at him. 'What makes you think I'm ever going back?' All at once she realised that a man and girl standing nearby were taking an interest in the conversation and hurriedly she said, 'All right, then, if you insist.' At that moment an assistant stepped towards them, as if on cue, or had he too been an interested listener of her and Adam's words? she wondered. The money changed hands, then Adam slipped the small jeweller's box into the pocket of his jacket.

As they went out into the hot sunshine of the pavement Liz said, 'You shouldn't have done this. I didn't want—'

'Yes, you did! I could tell by your face! It's nothing, just a small souvenir.'

She eyed him suspiciously, uncertain whether or not to believe him.

'Well,' she said at last, 'if you're quite sure—' In spite of herself she couldn't keep the note of excitement from her voice. 'Let me see—'

'Sorry, but you'll have to wait!' Liz felt she could drown in the brilliant light that was flooding his eyes. 'Until you can thank me properly.'

'I can thank you now!'

'In the street? I know a much better place. You'll just have to be patient.'

She wrinkled her nose at him. 'It's unfair! I haven't even seen the original and you have! Lucky you!'

'Lucky!' Adam took her arm and they strolled on down the sunshiny street. 'I've been to that museum so many times I just about know every exhibit that's there off by heart.'

Swinging her bag, she paused to look at him in surprise. 'I had no idea you were a student of Greek mythology.'

'I'm not, but my father was. He earned his living teaching languages at university and he was absorbed in Greek mythology. For years my parents spent their holidays in the Greek Islands, studying temples and buried treasures and amphitheatres. As a kid I didn't go for it much, but later on I used to manage to get a holiday job in the holidays in Greece, so I guess something of my dad's interest in the country must have rubbed off on me after all.' All at once his face sobered. 'He died suddenly, a year after my mother, leaving me enough capital to start some sort of business. I'd spent a few years managing tourist hotels around the holiday spots in England, and I decided to take a chance and put all the money I had into building a big luxury place somewhere by the sea in Greece. Crete had always been my dad's favourite Greek island, and somehow I felt that investing the money this way would be something that would have ap-

pealed to him. Not as much as helping to finance a new
museum of Greek artifacts, of course, but I couldn't handle that. The way I figured it, I wanted a spot away from the
usual tourist circuit, a place where guests could relax and do
their own thing, sit around the bar, try out Greek food in the
villages, hire a car if they wanted to and explore the coast. I
got together with an architect friend in London and we drew
up the plans together. We both agreed on the main points—
lots of space and air, a marble staircase to the first floor,
lounge and bedroom windows to look right over the sea.
The Greek builders took their time putting up the place, but
it's finished at last.'

'And things are working out all right for you?'

'Financially, you mean?' He shrugged broad shoulders.
'This is my first season and the summer travel trade hasn't
got into full swing yet, but if a special plan of mine turns up
trumps—'

Liz looked at him enquiringly. 'Special plan?'

He brushed the matter aside. 'It's a long-term thing, so
I'm just keeping my fingers crossed!'

They sauntered on down a twisting narrow street, pausing to look in at windows of tiny stores with their displays
of woven floor mats in brilliant shades of reds and yellows,
Turkish slippers with turned-up toes, miniature bouzoukis,
richly decorated coffee cups, vessels that were replicas of
pottery unearthed from the ruins of buried cities. There were
florist shops, fragrant with growing greenery, art shops ex-
hibiting paintings so expensive that Liz gasped at the price
tags. She recognised a glamorous-looking woman strolling
by as a famous American movie star.

'One could meet people here you only read about at
home,' she told Adam.

He said with a grin, 'According to Greek mythology,
Athene used to bathe in the little lake here.'

'I don't wonder. This must be one of the loveliest villages
in the whole world,' Liz breathed.

He smiled down at her. 'Depends on who you happen to be with!'

Her heart shouted assent, and as they moved over the sun-dried plaza she felt her spirits rise on a tide of elation. For a moment the scene before her, the blue enclosed lake, the passing crowd, shimmered with a feeling of heightened perception. 'Make it last,' she prayed, 'my wonderful, wonderful day!'

'Where would you like a meal?' Adam's deep purposeful tones wrenched her back to mundane matters. 'At a taverna down by the lake or bread and cheese on the beach?'

'I'll settle for the beach every time!' The prospect, she thought, was entrancing.

'Me too.'

They wandered up a winding, narrow street, to pause, attracted by an appetising aroma of newly-baked bread that drifted out through an open doorway. Inside the shop were loaves of all shapes and sizes, still hot from the oven. Further along the street, Adam purchased a bottle of the local wine, and soon Liz's bag was bulging with bunches of white grapes, feta cheese and great yellow Cretan oranges.

Suddenly, at the top of the rise, they came in sight of white cottages tumbling down to the sea. Below, bikini-clad girls and men in swimming shorts were lying sunbathing on the golden sands washed by the Aegean Sea.

A little later they changed into swimming gear and left their garments together with Liz's bag beneath a shady tree on the grassy bank. Soon they were running together over smooth sand to plunge into water so warm and buoyant that meeting the surge of the waves was no shock at all. Not half such a shock to Liz as when Adam swam up behind her to duck her in the water. She came to the surface with streaming hair, dashing seawater from her eyes, and immediately gave chase, but of course it was hopeless trying to catch up with him.

Later they spread towels on the warm sand and let the hot sunlight play on their bodies, lulling them into a state of

dreamy content. After a while Adam appeared to have fallen
asleep and she turned towards him, acutely aware of his lithe
tanned body lying so close. All at once impelled by a longing to touch him, she stretched her hand, to find her fingers imprisoned in his warm grip. For a moment the
sundrenched scene shimmered around her and a wild happiness pulsed through her. How could his touch electrify her
like this? Swiftly he flung himself around and kissed her full
on the lips. In his eyes she glimpsed a glint. 'That's for
starters!'

Suddenly nervous of the effect his caress had had on her,
she got to her feet. 'What's the matter, Liz?' He was regarding her lazily through half-closed eyes.

'Nothing, nothing!' Murmuring something about lunch,
she moved away, making her way between the sun-umbrellas
that dotted the sand. The thoughts whirled through her
mind. How could he affect her in this way, a stranger about
whom she knew nothing? It's the day, she told herself, and
as he caught up with her she managed to get her runaway
emotions under sufficient control to school her voice to a
light note. 'I thought you wanted to sunbathe a bit longer?'

'Not without you beside me, Liz.'

She sent him a swift sideways glance from under her eyelashes, surprised to find that he was perfectly matter-of-fact.
He really meant what he'd said! Once again the warm happiness surged through her.

It was a meal to remember, Liz decided a short time later,
as she munched happily on freshly baked bread. If this were
a sample of Greek food she was all for it. Not like—Determinedly she switched her mind away from Katina and the
nauseating dish she had prepared especially for her. She refused to allow thoughts of Katina to dim the radiance of her
day with Adam. The Cretan oranges, she thought, were like
no others she had ever tasted and the wine, with its delicate
flavour of almonds, was delicious.

Afterwards they sunbathed once again on the warm sand
and time ceased to matter. It was a day to plunge into the

azure sea, then relax on the beach. To run down to the water once more, to laugh and splash each other and float with faces upturned to the sky on the buoyant sun-sparkled sea. The hours drifted by and it was a long time later when the lavender light of a Crete twilight crept over the darkening sea and they watched the night fishermen climb aboard their boats and guide their caiques into the sunset.

As they made their way back to the main square of the village the soft purple twilight deepened into darkness and lights sprang up in the clusters of white cottages running down to the sea. The narrow twisting lanes were alive with music, and as they came into the square they found the streets lined with onlookers as they watched Cretan dancers in their colourful costumes, the women wearing white muslin blouses and dark red skirts with necklaces of gold coins swinging around their necks.

Liz was enchanted as she watched the Cretans sweep into their wildly energetic dances to the lively beat of their native lyre. She held her breath as male dancers linked hands with their girl partners, swinging them off their feet and whirling them through the air, embroidered skirts flying around them in a wild crescendo.

Much later, Adam escorted Liz through the crowd. 'Would you care to try out a little café I know along the coast, or would you prefer that I took you to a restaurant for a meal?'

'Oh no, the café will be fun!' *Everything is fun when I'm with you, Adam!* she thought happily.

The haunting music of the lyre drifted out to them as they moved away from the main square. Dimly lighted tavernas threw a glow on the dark street and soon they had reached the parking area. Adam saw Liz into the car and they turned into the main road. Presently he drew the vehicle to a stop at the side of a dimly-lit café. As he escorted Liz to the open doorway she hesitated, laughter glimmering in her eyes. 'Are you sure women are permitted in here?' She caught echoes of bursts of masculine laughter and loud talk and, peering inside she dimly discerned, in the faint blue glow, the crowd of swarthy male faces. 'It's not one of those all-men tavernas I've heard about?'

'With all those international tourists cluttering up the place?' Adam urged her forward, a hand on her arm. 'Come in and meet my friend Nikolaos.' As they made their way through the crowded room, he said, 'He owns the show, and he'd be no end offended if he couldn't show us himself what he's offering on the menu tonight.'

An aromatic, appetising smell of cooking greeted them as they went into a kitchen where Greek men were busy cooking food at a blackened stove.

'Adam!' At their approach an older man swung around, his swarthy face beaming. He broke into an excited spate of Greek, nodding every now and again towards Liz, who did the best she could with an answering smile. She had no need to know the Greek language to understand that Nikolaos, with much gesticulating and loud talk, was inviting them to make their choice from the foods steaming in smoke-blackened pots. All at once, as the group moved towards the stove, Nikolaos's face darkened. His dark eyes flashed angrily and he waved both hands wildly in the air. 'What's he saying?' Liz whispered to Adam. 'Don't say we've offended him in some way?'

'Good lord, no! He's apologising for the lack of fresh fish today.'

'But he sounds so angry—'

'He is. He says the fishermen of the village sold their entire catch today in the market in Athens. But he can recommend the pilaf, soups, dolmades—'

'Dolmades!' Liz clapped her hands. 'Isn't that a gorgeous dish wrapped in vine leaves that I'm always reading about? I'd love to try it!'

'Right! You won't be sorry you ordered it, Nikolaos will see to that!' He gave the order to the Greek owner of the café for egg and lemon soup followed by dolmades.

Nikolaos escorted them to a table and Liz, casting a swift glance around her, took in the raftered ceiling and smoke-darkened walls that were lined with huge wooden wine barrels. Now that her eyes were becoming accustomed to the smoke-filled room she realised that, as Adam had told her, there were other women seated around her, well-dressed Greek women accompanied by their escorts and parties of overseas tourists who were no doubt staying in the colourful village.

Around them groups of Greeks talked, argued and roared with laughter. With their dark aquiline faces and black moustaches, wearing black beaded kerchiefs on their foreheads and jackboots on their feet, they looked, Liz thought, like brigands. All at once she became conscious of a noisy group of Greek men at the next table who were laughing and talking loudly as they gesticulated excitely in her direction. 'Those men at the next table,' she whispered to Adam, 'I know they're talking about you and me.' His eyes glinted with amusement and she ran on indignantly, 'And it's no use your trying to tell me they're not, because I distinctly heard them mention your name and then they all turned around to look at me. You heard what they've been saying,' she accused him indignantly, 'I can tell by your face! Come on, tell me, what did they say—about us?'

He sent her an enigmatic look. 'You really want me to tell you?'

She smiled back at him. 'Can't wait!'

'"Prettiest girl in the room", they said.' His eyes held a glint of amusement. 'They wanted to ask the waiter to give you wine with their compliments, but they weren't quite sure about that, thought they might have a fight on their hands, because anyone could see that you weren't just a dinner companion but something much more. That you were my *gheńeke*—'

'*Gheńeke?*'

'My woman.'

'Oh!' Liz was taken aback in spite of herself and tried for lightness. 'I'd like to know,' she said in the most nonchalant tone she could summon up, 'just what gave them that idea.'

'They said,' he announced calmly, 'it was the way we look at each other.'

Now she didn't dare look into his eyes. She managed a brief laugh that even to her own ears didn't sound genuine. 'Is that all?'

Adam said quietly, 'Isn't that enough?'

Liz didn't know whether she was relieved or sorry when at that moment a young Greek boy brought soup, steaming hot, in bowls made from local pottery.

'Like it?' Adam was eyeing her attentively.

'It's delicious.' He was beckoning to a waiter, saying something in the boy's native tongue, and she guessed he was ordering wine. 'Cretan Minos,' he told her. 'You'll like it, I promise.' When it came to the table she sipped the sweet wine with enjoyment.

The stuffed vine leaves too, with their filling of minced lamb and delicate flavour of herbs, she found delicious. 'I'll have to get the recipe,' she told Adam with her quick smile. 'If I'm going to stay on here there's lots of things I'll have to learn about.'

'You're still counting on staying, then?' She sensed an odd note in his voice.

'As long as I can! I was telling you, all I have to do to make a living is get myself going with toasted rolls in the taverna my uncle left me and I'm away.'

All at once his voice hardened. 'And if you can't make a go of it—'

In the moment of silence the thoughts raced through her mind. There was a sort of listening look on his dark good-looking face, as if it mattered to him a lot whether she stayed in Crete or not. The wild sweet happiness tingled along her nerves, for that meant that he was interested in her, that he cared about her. Maybe even he had plans that included

both her and himself. The thought was so intoxicating that
she had difficulty in bringing her mind back to his deep resonant tones. 'What if you can't get your project off the
ground?'

She wrinkled her nose at him. 'Oh, don't be so dampen-
ing! If it's finance you're thinking of—'

'It is, actually.'

'I told you,' she said airily, 'that my lawyer will see to
that. He told me he'd give me some help if I got into any
difficulties.'

Still Adam appeared unconvinced, regarding her
thoughtfully. 'But if he doesn't?'

She laughed with sheer exhilaration. 'I'll tell you one
thing, I'm not leaving my villa!'

'Yours?' Once again she caught the strange, enigmatic
note in his voice.

'Well, half mine,' she admitted reluctantly. Why must she
keep forgetting about Katina's share of the property? she
asked herself. Some trick of the mind, because she wanted
to forget? But she refused to allow herself to be discouraged on this exciting night out with Adam. 'I'll find something to keep me going,' she said lightly. At the wry twist of
his lips, his disbelieving glance, she added, 'I don't think
even the Oracle at Delphi could answer that one offhand!
Don't look like that, all disapproving,' she begged him. 'I'll
think of something! Maybe,' she teased, 'if all else fails, I'll
join in the evening parade down the village street that I've
heard about, where the girls dress up in their prettiest frocks
and the boys may look but not touch. The *volta,* isn't that
what they call it? The bride market?'

Her laughing gaze rose to his and as their glances met and
held, tiny flames seemed to glow in his eyes. Hurriedly she
dropped her gaze, unable to sustain his brilliant look.

'You won't need to do that, Liz.'

She would need to watch her words, the thought came
through the confusion of her senses. There was something
about this man that affected her as no other man had ever

done. He made life so different that a Crete village became
a place of enchantment, a dimly-lit café was shot with
magic.

They lingered over the Greek coffee, rich and strong, that
had been served with a glass of water, watching as a Greek
man at a nearby table got to his feet. The next moment his
rich notes rang out to the accompaniment of the plaintive
notes of a lyre.

'What's the song about?' Liz whispered.

'Poetry the Cretans have set to music,' Adam explained,
'all about the ups and downs of love.'

'Love?'

'That's right.' His glance rested on her downcast face and
he asked softly, 'Know anything about it, Liz?'

She flashed him a laughing glance. 'Do you?' The
thought ran through her mind that he was a man apparently in his early thirties, very presentable, rich, attractive.
He must have had affairs, even perhaps a wife.

Adam seemed to pick up her thoughts. He was twirling
his wine glass, his eyes veiled. 'I was married once. Eleni was
Greek. We were both young and we thought we had it made.
Just goes to show how mistaken you can be.' His tone was
thoughtful and he seemed to have forgotten her, Liz
thought. 'I took Eleni back to England with me and we'd
only been married a year when she was killed in a car
smash—one of those freak accidents. She was driving with
a friend to the local shops,' his eyes darkened, 'when a
drunken driver met them head-on on a bend and both the
women were killed instantly. That happened a long time ago,
and I've never found anyone to take Eleni's place—' his
sombre glance lifted to Liz's face, 'yet.' All at once he was
back to his impersonal manner. 'Well, that's me—How
about you?'

She sneaked a look at him from under her lashes and took
a sip of coffee. 'Nothing!'

'Nothing? Looking like you do?' His warm appreciative
glance swept over her wide blue-grey eyes, alight with ex-

citement, the sweetly curved mouth and short nose. 'I don't believe it.'

'It's true,' she answered smilingly. 'I guess I'm just not the falling-madly-in-love type,' she added, and made the mistake of looking up, directly into those brilliant eyes that seemed to possess the disconcerting knack of being able to read her mind. She looked away, fearful he might read in her glance the feelings he aroused in her. 'I have to admit,' she ran on, saying the first words that entered her mind in order to cover her confusion, 'there could be a reason.'

'And that is—?' His attentive gaze was fixed on her face.

Thoughtfully Liz stirred what was left of the coffee in her tiny cup. 'Believe it or not, it was Crete!'

He sent her a sceptical glance. 'Don't give me that! You'd never even set foot on the island.'

'But that's just it—don't you see? I was so wrapped up in the place. It was Uncle's letters from here that started it and kept my obsession, I suppose you could call it, alive for me all those years. I read every book about the island that I could get my hands on, found out all I could and saved every cent I could for the trip.' She raised clear eyes to his attentive gaze. 'I guess I must be a pretty determined type after all,' her lips twitched at the corners, 'because I wouldn't let anything or anyone—especially any man—' she spread her hands expressively, 'stop me. Know what I mean? I just wouldn't let myself get too involved with anyone, that way I knew would be the end of my dream.'

'Funny girl!'

'I know it sounds silly, but that's me! It was just as well that my uncle arranged the trip for me,' she ran on with a rueful smile. 'I'd been out of work for ages and my savings had just melted away. I was just starting on another "get myself to Greece fund, no matter what" when the letter arrived from the solicitor in Heraklion. I suppose,' she finished on a breath, 'you think I'm crazy to get so obsessed by a place I'd never seen.'

To her surprise Adam grinned. 'Why should I think that? We happen to be two of a kind. I haven't any ideas of leaving this island. It's got something, and whatever it is, it draws you back.'

But you can afford to live anywhere in the world you wish. Liz said the words silently.

She sipped her wine. 'You know something? Sometimes I can't believe I'm really here.'

He grinned. 'You've got that excited look in your eyes again!'

'Can't help it! It's all so—so far away from anything I've ever known. Everything's new and exciting—' Especially you. The words came to her mind of their own volition and she lowered her lashes, fearful of what her expression might betray. But apparently she need not have concerned herself on that score.

'I can take you to lots of other places well worth a trip,' Adam was saying. 'A sail to one of the smaller islands around here, a look at the Palace of Knossos.' His smile drew her into a warm intimacy. 'Stick around for a while and I'll show you one of the mountain villages.'

'Oh, I'll be here! Anyway, you'd never believe it, but I have to look up a family in a mountain village on this side of the island. My neighbour at home comes from there, and you should see all the goodies she's given me to take to her family. Lots of photographs of her Kiwi husband and their two children too. Angeliké will have written to her people letting them know I'm coming to see them, so I'll have to make it soon. I guess it's a big event in their lives, getting first-hand news of their daughter and son too, from someone who knows them both so well. It's a village called Kaminaki and it's way up in the mountains. Does the bus go there from our part of the world?'

Amusement glinted in Adam's eyes. 'There is a bus, but it's pretty erratic—quite an experience, that bus trip to the mountains, actually. Why bother when I'll be picking you up and we'll take in a drive to the village? It's quite a sight-seeing place up there.'

'Oh, I didn't mean that!' she protested in some confusion.

'I did! A pleasure, Liz, especially when you open wide those big eyes of yours and get such a kick out of everything. Better watch it,' he grinned, and threw an arm around her shoulders, 'the way you're going you'll never get back to New Zealand!'

She pulled a face at him. 'Who said I wanted to?'

'You've made your point—want to dance?'

'Dance?' She was bemused by the wine and the music, the noise, the dark aquiline faces all around her. Now she realised that Greeks and tourist visitors were forming a circle, hands laid on one another's shoulders. The beat of the lyre was slow and measured.

'Come on.' Taking her hand in his, Adam drew her to her feet, but Liz pulled back. 'I can't do the Greek dances, I don't know the steps—'

'There's nothing to it,' he assured it. 'It's the *stae tria,* the Greek dance that everyone knows and can pick up. Just remember there's a lot of one, two, three, kick, kick—there's the leader who puts everyone in the picture!' With arm thrown around her slim waist, he guided her to the laughing group who were still forming a circle. Diffidently Liz took her place between Adam and a burly Greek with an impressive drooping black moustache and a ferocious expression. Adam's arm tightened around her with an encouraging squeeze. 'Put your hand on my shoulder and follow my steps, then it's easy.' At that moment the beat of lyre music quickened in the smoke-filled room and Liz found herself giggling helplessly as she attempted to follow Adam's lead. She quickly picked up the pattern of the simple dance steps and, along with the rest of the incomplete circle, kept in time with the rhythm, although she couldn't even attempt to emulate the young Cretan leader whose wild leaps and skips were apparently accomplishments of his own.

'You're doing fine,' Adam encouraged.

'Think so?' Never would she admit that being with him was doing things to her that made the simple steps of the Greek dance of little importance.

All at once the music of the stringed instruments picked up, changing to a quicker and quicker tempo until the dance came to an end and Liz, still breathless, returned with Adam to their table.

As she sipped her wine she was aware of his warm glance. 'Enjoying it?'

'Oh *yes!*' She leaned an elbow on the table, looking across at him, her eyes dreamy. 'I guess you could say that I'm in love with this island.' *I'm in love with you!* It was almost as if she had said the words aloud, and swiftly she lowered her lashes to hide the expression in her eyes. Could this be love? she wondered. This wild sweetness that was coursing through her veins, the longing she felt to trace the outline of Adam's firm, sensitive mouth with her fingers? It's the wine, she told herself, the music, that's making me so I can't think straight.

As the hours slipped by the Greek dancing became more unrestrained, the music of the stringed instruments louder, and Liz suspected the songs that accompanied the lyre were bawdier. Greeks were noisily talking, laughing, arguing, and a Greek woman was climbing up on a table to dance. The next moment Liz caught the sound of a plate crashing to the floor, then another.

'Time to go, by the sound of it!' Adam's voice was matter-of-fact. Together they pushed their way through the shouting throng in the smoke-filled room, eventually moving with tourists towards the door and out into the clear night air. In the dim light Liz glanced at her wristwatch. Four o'clock! And the night wasn't yet ended, because ahead—the thought was intoxicating—was the long drive back to the villa, a perfect end to an unforgettable evening.

When they reached the village, lights gleamed on craft anchored on the tranquil waterfront and only a few cars were standing in the car park. Adam saw her seated in the vehicle, then folded his long length into the driver's seat, then they were leaving the village and turning into the darkening road that curved over the hills. They were alone on the dark highway, and when he threw an arm around her shoulders, she nestled closer to his chest. They didn't talk much on the journey. Liz was in a blissful state of deep content, and the moon riding high in a star-ridden sky was only a part of the enchantment.

She enjoyed being with Adam, she mused happily. She enjoyed looking at him too—she stole a glance at the strong masculine profile, shadowy in the dim light of the dashboard. When at last they came in sight of the soaring white building against the backdrop of a dark sea, Adam guided the car towards the main entrance and leaping to the ground, went around the vehicle to open the passenger door for Liz. 'I'll see you back to the villa.' He clasped her hand in his warm grasp and they made their way along the dusty white path winding amongst the olive trees.

CHAPTER FIVE

ALL TOO soon, Liz thought, they had reached the secluded courtyard, and as they paused in the shadows Adam drew her close—so close that she could feel the warmth of his sinewy chest through the thin fabric of his shirt. He bent his head to drop light butterfly kisses that brushed her forehead, the tip of her nose, then his seeking lips found her mouth. Fire was singing along her veins and she was scarcely aware of her own ardent response to his caress.

At last she stirred in his arms. 'I've got to go—'

'Maybe you'd better,' his voice was deep with emotion. 'You won't forget our date next week?'

As if she could!

'Pick you up on Tuesday,' his tone softened, roughened, 'that is, if I can wait that long! How about a trip to Knossos? Buried palaces that have been unearthed after four thousand years are a part of your education on a trip to Greece.'

Over the rioting of her senses Liz was scarcely aware of what she was saying. 'I'm not one for visiting old ruins, but when you put it that way—'

'So long as I've got you with me,' gently he raised her fingers to his lips, 'what matter where we go?'

Liz could scarcely believe her ears. Zeus, coming down from the heights of Mount Olympus, preferring the company of an ordinary mortal like herself to the wealthy international visitors with whom his work brought him in constant contact!

'I'll see you soon,' she murmured, and slipped from his grasp.

His low tone halted her. 'Haven't you forgotten something?'

She hadn't really, but she made a pretence of having done so. 'Oh, you mean—'

'I mean your Minoan honey bee. Come back here, young Liz,' he said softly, 'and try it on for size!'

He looked very tall and impressive, the thought ran through her mind as she turned back towards him. The next minute he was putting a hand to the pocket of his jacket, then he slipped the fine chain of the pendant over her dark hair. Once again his nearness was doing things to her composure and she heard her own voice saying breathlessly, 'You'll never see to do it up,' but already his deft fingers had secured the fastening and in the pale gleam of fading stars she caught the golden gleam of gauzy wings.

'It's lovely, lovely,' she whispered, fingering the tiny stylized bee. 'I didn't need it, though,' she added very low, 'to remember today.'

'Liz—' All at once Adam's tone was husky with emotion. She felt his breath on her face as he gathered her close, then her arms linked themselves around his neck. The next moment his mouth was on hers, sending her senses spinning wildly. He took his time about his kiss on her soft lips, and Liz felt as though she were drowning in waves of deep sweet happiness. She clung to him, her lips responding in a torrent of feeling. Then abruptly the moment was shattered, for in another part of her mind she had realised that a light had flashed on in a room in the villa and a girl's face was visible at the uncurtained window.

'What's wrong?' asked Adam.

'It's Katina!' she gasped. 'I've just seen her at a window. What on earth is she doing here?'

'Probably wondering what's happened to you.'

'Me? She doesn't care one little bit about me!'

'Maybe,' his voice was careless, 'she came back here for something she left here and decided to stay the night.' Liz's mind went to the small blue stone on the bureau 'It's her home too,' he reminded her gently. 'Guess she's got a right to come back here now and again if she gets bored with hotel living. Don't worry about her. She'll be back at work at the hotel in an hour or so. She won't hang around the place, not a chance.'

'I guess not.' Somehow the spell was broken, and a chill sense of foreboding touched her. Trust Katina to spoil the happiest day she had ever known! 'I'll see you soon,' she whispered, and gently Adam released her.

'Night, Liz.' He turned and strode away into the shadows.

The sense of deep happiness enveloped Liz like a cloud as she neared the door of the villa. The warmth and passion of Adam's kiss was still with her, and she had forgotten Katina—until the Greek girl came out of the bedroom and stood in the lighted room. She had evidently been asleep, for she wore a light wrap over her slim body. The dark eyes that regarded Liz were sulky and resentful.

All at once Liz became aware of tousled hair and flushed cheeks. She just knew she had the soft dreamy look of a girl who had just been kissed by a man with whom she was falling in love, why not admit it? The thought made her say the first words that entered her mind. 'What are *you* doing here?'

'What are you?' Katina's lips curved contemptuously. 'It is my house too!'

'You could have told me you were coming—'

'Why should I?' demanded Katina. 'You couldn't stop me!'

It was true, Liz admitted to herself. Why, oh, why had the other girl chosen to come here tonight, ruining everything, making a nuisance of herself?

'I come and go as I please! I'll go out with Adam too, when he asks me. And when he does,' venom dripped in her tone, 'it will be because he wants me to go out with him,' infinite scorn tinged the mocking words, 'not like you!'

Liz was conscious of a niggling sense of unease, but she thrust the feeling aside. Katina was just being vindictive, of course, making up some wild story for her own ends. Aloud she said coldly, 'What do you mean, not like you?'

'Can't you see for yourself?' screamed Katina. 'You must be as blind as the bats in the mountain caves!'

But Liz was becoming impatient with the Greek girl and her histrionics. 'See what? I've no idea what you're getting at!'

'He didn't tell you, then,' a vindictive note of triumph coloured the words, 'what he told me? We used to talk about it a lot before you came to Crete.'

'Talk over—me?' Liz was so taken aback she forgot to be angry. 'How could Adam have done that? He didn't know anything about me.'

Katina tossed her head so that the black hair swirled around her shoulders. 'Stupid, stupid, New Zealand girl! He knew all about you!'

All at once Liz let out her breath on a sigh of relief. She must have been out of her mind to fear anything the Greek girl could tell her, or to take any notice of the veiled insinuations. 'Of course Adam knew my uncle. He told me he used to talk to him. Uncle would have told him about having a niece in New Zealand.'

'Do you think Adam cared about that?' The words came on a scornful breath. 'All he cares about is getting the villa and the taverna for himself. He made an offer through his lawyer to buy it from you, he knew I would be agreeable. Long before you came here, he wrote to the lawyer in Heraklion offering lots and lots of money.'

Liz felt stunned by the other girl's words, her mind feverishly trying to escape the import of the conversation. 'Are you telling me,' the words came slowly, dragged from a pain-filled well deep inside her, 'that Adam is the hotel owner who made that offer?'

Katina's glittering angry eyes said it all. 'Who else would want to buy this place so far from any town?'

Liz clutched at a shred of hope that entered her mind. 'But it couldn't possibly be Adam. He already has a brand new luxury hotel he's built around the point. Why would he want another one so close?'

'Not another hotel, stupid! It is the bay he wants for his tourists, so that they can swim and take walks and enjoy themselves on the beach. So quiet, so peaceful, he said, away from the big cities of Crete.'

'You're crazy!' Liz's tone was low and distraught. 'I don't know why I listen to you!'

Katina's dark face was thrust so close that instinctively Liz recoiled from the other girl's nearness. 'Because you know that I speak the truth, that's why! What do you care,' she ran wildly on, 'that I don't have my dowry in money now when I need it? When men want to marry me and my aunt and uncle, they have to decide. All you care about is yourself!' The spate of words flowed around Liz without her being aware of them. Only one fact registered in her mind. There must be some mistake, she told herself doggedly. Aloud she said, 'He would have told me!'

'Told you! Told you!' jeered Katina. 'Why would he do that when all the time he knew you would say no, no, no, like you always do! The day you arrived here, I told Adam that you were crazy about keeping the property and staying on here. Do you know what he said to me?' Without waiting for an answer she swept on, swarthy hands gesticulating. '"Do not concern yourself, Katina. Be patient and soon, I promise you, all will be changed, and you will have your dowry. I haven't met this girl yet, but when I do I'll soon talk her into my way of thinking. I've got my methods and I'll be able to persuade her to change her ideas."'

Persuade her, persuade her! The words beat a dull tattoo in Liz's mind. The other girl's vindictive tones seemed to be coming from a distance, 'Soften you up? Isn't that what you call it? And you think,' came the sneering tones, 'that he likes taking you out, being nice to you! I tell you it is all a trick to get his own way. He is making you get fond of him in the ways of a man. So easy for him,' the contemptuous gaze flickered over Liz's rumpled hair and hot cheeks, 'when already you think he is some sort of god! You will see, when the time is right, he will get from you what he wants,' the cruel words were arrows aimed straight for the heart, 'and then he will think it was worth all the trouble he had to take to make you love him!'

'Stop!' Liz covered her ears with her hands. 'You've never wanted me to come here, so you're telling me all these lies!'

'Lies, you say?' Fury exploded in the dark eyes. 'Did he tell you that he had a wife once, a Greek girl who he took to England with him to live? He likes Greek girls.' Without waiting for an answer she swept on. 'No, it is only to me he speaks of such things. She died in England and since then he is alone, he can please himself. Why should he waste his time with you,' she hissed, 'when he can have any woman he wants,' she snapped her fingers in the air, 'just like that! It is only that you are so stubborn, so stupid about money matters, that he has to pretend to like you!'

The flush had died away from Liz's cheeks, leaving her very pale. A cold resolve took the place of shock and anger. 'I don't believe you!'

'Why don't you sell your share, then,' a cunning gleam had flashed into Katina's dark eyes, 'and see how much he wants you then?'

'I'll never sell, don't you understand, never, never, never!'

'You say that so that you can keep him hanging around you, pretending to like you. That is all it is with Adam, just pretending!'

A black tide of anger mushroomed up inside Liz and spilled over. 'You're making all this up!' Lifting her chin, she pushed past the Greek girl and made her way to her own room. Katina's voice, high, out of control, echoed in her ears. 'Ask him then if you don't believe me! Ask him! Ask him!'

Liz threw herself down on the bed, not bothering to un-
dress, shock and disbelief struggling in her distraught mind.
She watched the trembling of her hands as if they belonged
to another girl. It wasn't true, it couldn't be true that Adam
was cultivating her friendship for purposes of his own! A
gleam of hope struggled through the dark confusion of her
mind. She suspected Katina of being capable of inventing
any wild story that might serve to frighten Liz away from the
villa. Of course it wasn't the truth, she assured herself.
Adam really did like her for herself, of course he did!

Close on the thought came a sickening reminder. Hadn't
she brushed aside the lawyer's attempt to acquaint her with
the name of the would-be buyer for the property here? She
had taken it for granted that the hotel owner in question
would be a Greek. If only she had listened to the lawyer and
become familiar with the man's name she would know the
truth for sure. *You know already.* The thought welled up
from the deep recesses of her mind. For who else but Adam
with his recently constructed palatial building, so close to
beach and villa, would have an interest in the place? Small
things, insignificant in themselves and unnoticed at the time,
returned to mind to pierce her with painful clarity. Adam's
deep vibrant tones as he said to her, 'If my plans work
out—''Plans?' she had echoed. She hadn't really been listening because at the time she had been more interested in
him than in his evasive answer to her query. What had he
said? Something about a 'long-term' plan. Another thing,
the daunting manner in which he had reacted to her confi-
dences about her staying on in Crete, starting up the taverna again in her own way.

It isn't true, it can't be true what Katina told me about
him, she thought. She would say anything just to get rid of
me. But deep down where it counted she knew there could
be no mistake. It was all too clear now. There was but one
luxury hotel in the vicinity and only one owner who would
have an interest in acquiring the beach property. So much

interest, in fact, that he had offered an extremely high figure in an effort to acquire it for himself.

It all added up to a sickeningly inescapable conclusion. Liz lay very still, sick with shock and pain and a searing sense of let-down. Adam, his traitor's smile, his lively challenging eyes that looked at you so straight that you believed without question every word that he said. And all the time...Unconsciously her fingers went to the tiny golden bee hanging from its fine chain. *The bee with a sting,* she reminded herself and, suddenly angry, she tugged the pendant roughly over her hair and tossed it into a corner of the room. So much for dreams. If only she had used her brains and hadn't been so naïve. Fool, she chided herself, you've played right into his hands! I suppose I'm lucky, she told herself with tight lips, that I've found him out in time. Otherwise I might even have fallen in love with him.

What do you mean, 'might'? jeered a small voice deep in her mind.

Nonsense! How could I love a man who's been only pretending to like me for myself?

What else do you call it? She thrust the insistent voice aside and, scarcely aware of her movements, flung off her garments and reached for her nightdress. No! Not that one! All at once her glazed expression had flickered into life, for she held in her hands the pale green wisp of nylon that she had worn on the night she had first met Adam. Hurling it angrily to the floor, she fumbled in a drawer for a white cotton nightdress and crawled between the sheets.

It was then that the tears came, great choking sobs that racked her body mercilessly. She buried her face in the pillow, fearful that Katina might catch the sound of muffled sobbing.

As she lay there, her eyelids swollen with weeping, it came to her that Adam's plans of 'softening her up' had misfired only because Katina had let out his intentions. Why had Katina done it? Could it be that the Greek girl's volatile temperament had made her temper fly out of control? That, beside herself with jealousy and resentment, Katina had taken her own method of revenge? It was unlikely that she would confide in Adam, so no doubt he would imagine that his plan of campaign was succeeding, as it had done. Up to a point, Liz assured herself hastily. It was left to her to let him know that she knew all about his underhand methods of doing business, tell him that he had failed miserably in his intentions, because she had no ideas of leaving Crete. Funny, she thought bleakly, how the decision gave her little pleasure. Somehow nothing seemed to matter any longer. If only his face wasn't always in her mind, strong and masculine and smiling, the special smile he seemed to keep just for her. The traitorous thought pierced her of his lips, his well-shaped lips seeking hers, and a cold hand seemed to close around her heart.

The thoughts crowded in. Adam was a man of substance and authority, attractive, at home in the world, a man to whom women would be instantly attracted. That was, Liz amended, if they didn't know the sneaky things he was capable of to gain his own ends. Even now she was finding it difficult to believe that everything was changed between them. But she must believe it. Somehow she had to break free from his masculine charisma.

In the end she must have fallen asleep, for she awoke to the sun's rays touching her eyelids and a dull feeling that something was wrong. Then recollection came flooding back, bringing with it the heartache there was no assuaging. She tried to gather comfort from the thought that had she gone on seeing him, revelling in the happiness of being with him, she would end up by falling in love with the man, and then where would she be? It was too late, the thought came unbidden, else why does it hurt so much to give him up? Love...how could she have known that it could sneak up on you and before you knew it, you were caught fast, even when the man you loved was unworthy of your affection! But it was all a fantasy, for Adam was merely acting a part for purposes of his own and she, fool that she was, had let herself be taken in by his tanned good looks and heart-knocking smile.

Listlessly she wrenched her thoughts aside to glance at the small gold travelling clock on the bureau. It was later than she had imagined and by now, she told herself, Katina would have left the villa to take up her duties at the hotel. She avoided glancing in the mirror, conscious of red-rimmed eyes, and pushing the hair back from her forehead, she slipped a cotton robe over her shoulders and went bare-footed into the kitchen. An empty coffee cup was a mute reminder that Katina had long left the house. Liz wandered restlessly across the room to fill the kettle at the sink. Why, she wondered, had she never before been conscious of the emptiness of the villa, with only the pounding of the waves on the beach below to break the silence? She reached out a hand to switch on her small transistor, but today she wasn't in a mood for haunting Greek love songs. Irritatedly she silenced the radio and mixed instant coffee in a pottery mug. Anything to help her throw off the heavy sense of heartache that enveloped her like a storm cloud, on this blue and gold day.

Later in the morning she slipped a cotton shift over her bikini and picking up her woven Greek bag with its suncream, beach towel and tinted glasses, she made her way out of the room. Thoughts of Adam's perfidy had driven everything else from her mind, and it was with a vague sense of surprise that she picked up from beneath the front door a letter that was lying there. The next moment she ripped open the envelope, her lacklustre gaze scarcely taking in the import of the words. Kostas—it was from Kostas Baltsa the lawyer in Heraklion, who had written in reply to her enquiries. The information penetrated her disturbed senses. Regret to have to inform you...costs prohibitive...your finance not sufficient to meet cost of goods...As to a loan, he was sorry to inform her she was not eligible at short notice...a foreigner in the country...but he himself would be happy to oblige in order that she could start up her busi-

ness...a short-term loan, say two years at usual interest
rates...Will be happy to visit you in order to discuss matter...obtain signature on documents...Tuesday next unless I hear to the contrary...Liz thrust the letter into her bag
and made her way over the sand, warm to the touch of her
bare feet, past the empty taverna and down towards the
beach, shimmering in the hot sunshine. Waves were whipped
into a myriad sparkling points in the sea breeze, and except
for a group of children playing in the shallows, the shore was
empty. Soon Liz was floating on her back in the water,
moving with the waves and letting the sensuous touch of the
sea soothe away a little of her crashing disappointment and
sense of let-down. Afterwards she splashed through a
shower of white foam tumbling on the sand and spreading
out her towel a little further up the shore, she dropped
down. The next moment she slipped on the dark glasses that
successfully concealed the evidence of reddened eyelids and
traces of tears. As the time went by, small groups of tourists, probably staying at Adam's hotel, made their way
through the screen of pink oleanders to wander down to the
shore. More than one masculine gaze rested appreciatively
on the slim curves of Liz's lightly tanned young body, but,
aware of the strangers' interest, she feigned sleep and before long she was once again alone.

She stayed there for a long time, watching the lazy curl of
the breakers, the liquid green fire rippling along the wave to
break lazily and splinter into a shower of white foam running along the wet sand.

'Hi, beach girl, remember me?' She was jerked into sudden awareness. That deep familiar voice that could make her
perfectly ordinary name sound like a caress! She stiffened,
summoning up all her defences as Adam, relaxed and smiling, dropped down at her side.

'Hey, take those off—I can't see you!' Before she could
protest he had whipped away her sunglasses, revealing all
too clearly a face blotched and swollen with weeping.

'Tears, Liz?' His smiling expression gave way to one of concern. Indeed, the thought ran through her mind, if she hadn't known better she would have taken it for a look of downright caring! He threw an arm around her smooth shoulders. 'What's the problem, honey? Tell me, I might be able to help.'

Idiot that she was, the tenderness in his voice all but unnerved her. Swiftly she jerked herself away. 'You should know!' She expected to see guilt in his face, but instead he appeared to be genuinely puzzled.

'What are you getting at?'

'As if you didn't know!' She raised accusing eyes to his bewildered gaze. 'All this time and you didn't let on to me that you were the hotel owner who'd made a high offer for the villa and the taverna! Katina,' she choked on the word, 'told me all about it! At least she was open and above-board about wanting me to sell my share, but you—' she raised heavy eyes, then found she was unable to sustain his brilliant, *honest*-looking gaze. 'Why didn't you tell me,' she said very low, 'that you were the one who wanted to buy the place?' A wild hope stirred in her. 'It is true, isn't it?'

His tone was ice-cold. 'If you mean I knew who you were all along, that's right.'

'Then why didn't you come right out with your offer to me?'

He shrugged his broad shoulders. 'What would have been the point? You didn't make any secret about hanging on to the place. I decided to let things ride for a while, especially as by then—' He broke off.

'By then—what?' And you'd better think up a good excuse, she thought.

There was an enigmatic look in his eyes. 'I guess,' despite all she now knew of him, his twisted smile all but broke through her defences, 'the way I figured it, by rushing my fences I stood a good chance of losing you as well as the beach place.'

Liz threw him a disbelieving glance from under her lashes. She said very low, 'Would it matter?'

Adam rose to his feet and stood looking down at her. All at once he was remote, cold and unyielding, his lips no longer curved in a rueful smile but hard and set. *What have I done?* The thought ripped through her senses. But I had to do it!

She forced herself to say the words that must be said. 'You were determined to get around me and persuade me to sell to you, to change my mind about things,' in spite of herself she winced, 'one way or another!'

'Look,' grated Adam, 'if you want me to give it to you straight, sure, I did hope to have a shot at getting you to change your mind about selling the place—who wouldn't in my position? A friendly discussion, what's wrong with that?'

'Nothing,' she shot back, 'only you didn't say a word to me about it.' She said very low, 'Were you waiting until we—got to know each other better? Was that it?'

His eyes were ice-cold. 'Something like that.'

She threw him an accusing look. 'If only you'd told me—'

'I planned to, at the right time!'

It was just as Katina had told her, she thought on a wave of anger. All the frustration and heartache and disappointment gathered in a hard knot in her stomach and the words seemed to fall from her lips without her volition. 'It would have been easy then for you to talk me around to your way of thinking—' She broke off. The thought cut deep, because she knew it was the truth. The next moment, horrified, she realised she had betrayed her growing feeling for him. Swiftly she attempted to cover the slip. 'That's what you thought, isn't it?'

'The hell it's not!' She saw a muscle twitch in Adam's tanned cheek. There was no doubt but that she had got through to him, for plainly he was furious with her.

'If you want it straight,' he grated, 'after I met you—and "after" is the operative word—I rather valued your...' a momentary pause, 'friendship. I thought, hell, if I make an offer for her place she'll refuse me right off and I'll have lost out for good—'

'You'll lose out anyway,' she said with bitter irony.

His tone was steel. 'I wasn't meaning just a matter of property—forget it.' He added curtly, 'You've evidently made up your mind that the whole thing is a put-up job for the purpose of buttering you up—'

'A long-term project, wasn't that the way you put it?'

His face darkened with anger and she suspected he was holding on to his temper with an effort. 'If that's what you want to believe—'

'What else can I think?'

He was silent for a moment, the brilliant eyes raking her pale face. 'You could have a go at believing what I tell you.'

'But I did,' she flashed back at him, 'though it was more what you didn't tell me. And look,' she added bitterly, 'where that got me!'

'A bit of trust in me might help.' The words seemed to cost him an effort. 'What do you say?'

She looked across at him, unaware of the wistfulness in her gaze as she took in the lean tanned face and muscular body, the soft dark hair she'd always longed to touch. How was it that Adam could affect her so—so physically, when all the time she knew his motives were devious and calculating? She must make herself remember what he was really like, or else she was lost. It was easier to answer him, the thoughts ran through her mind, if she avoided looking at him, because that made her think him incapable of ulterior motives or deception. How could she ever trust him again? The truth is, deep in her mind a small voice spoke, that you don't trust *yourself* where Adam is concerned! She thrust the thought away and steeling herself to harden her resolve, shook her head.

'I get it,' he gritted in a low harsh tone. 'You've made up your mind that I was softening you up to put the big question?'

Liz said very low, 'What else can I think?'

'Okay!' His face was dark with anger. 'If that's the way you want it! If you're so ready to take the word of a Greek girl who has an axe to grind—'

'Haven't you?' she flared. 'You're the one who wants the whole set-up, the one whose business depends on getting it. You managed to get around Katina, that was easy—'

He said savagely. 'I had no need to "get around her", as you put it! She's been breaking her neck to sell out from the word go—and you know it!'

It was the humiliating thought of the other two scheming together to outwit the naïve New Zealand girl that made the hot anger rise in her. Oh, she hated them both! 'I guess,' the pain-filled words came from the heart, 'that it was easy for you to fool me. At first I just couldn't believe that you would do such a thing!'

'Don't believe it now! If only you'd listen to me! Look—' he took her hands in his and for a moment the trembling in her put everything else from her mind. Swiftly he pursued his advantage. 'All right then, I did want to get you to change your mind and sell me your uncle's place. I got the idea that when we got to know each other a bit better, we could talk it over between us, come to an arrangement—'

'Get to know each other!' His touch was setting her nerves on fire, raising in her a flame of longing that threatened to take control. Wildly she gathered her thoughts together. 'Is that what you call it?'

His voice was gentle. 'Believe me, Liz, I wouldn't trick you for the world.'

She wrenched her hands from his warm clasp.

'So you say.'

If only she could believe him. If only she didn't know that the kisses that had stirred her so, sent her winging into that wild unaccustomed happiness, to him were of no importance. Oh, he might not term his caresses 'a trick', but that was what it all amounted to. To Adam, his light lovemaking hadn't meant a thing, how could it? And thank heaven he would never know the way that just being with him affected her. The thought made her say stonily, 'I just wish you'd told me—'

He cut in swiftly. 'What good would that have done? You'd have brushed me off with a quick "nothing doing". Even if you'd been any girl—' quickly he caught himself up. 'What I mean is, I figured that given time to weigh up the pros and cons you'd come to realise that it was no good your hanging on to the place here, there'd be no future in it, and that's when I planned to put it to you to settle up with me over the deal!'

'Any girl?' Her mind was still puzzling over the words. 'What could he mean? Surely not that in his mind she meant something to him, even at the start? Ridiculous, in the light of what she now knew of his real nature. He must have been referring to her relationship with Jim Kay, her uncle. Aloud she said coldly, 'Too bad that I happened to have other ideas!' A betraying wobble in her voice spoiled the bravado of her words.

'That's it, then!' Adam's voice was taut with anger. And another part of her mind registered that his deep tan couldn't hide the whiteness around his lips. Strange. But of course he was upset, bitterly disappointed at losing the property he had set his heart on obtaining. Look at the way in which he had schemed to make her part with it, *one way or another.* The words tolled like a bell in her heart. How could she have allowed herself to be so easily fooled? she asked herself. The answer came unbidden. It was because she had believed in him, regarded him as a man of integrity, someone who was honest and straight—*and damned good-looking,* a tiny voice spoke in her mind. Liz thrust the thought away. It was over, over. What did the past matter now? All at once she felt drained of all emotion. Could that be her own voice, thick with unshed tears? 'It's—goodbye, then?'

He made no move to go. 'I'll make you see reason,' he muttered, 'one of these days!'

Now she had her emotions firmly in hand. 'I'll be right here,' she taunted him, 'all the time!'

'What makes you so sure?' He bent on her his deep disturbing stare.

All at once she remembered the crumpled letter in her bag. Humiliation and a fierce desire to get even with him sparked her to say triumphantly, 'I've got news for you! I've got the finance I needed to ahead with my taverna, American-style, so you won't be getting rid of me after all!'

'Good for you!' His voice was deadpan. 'You've managed to raise the cash you needed?'

'No problem at all!' Deliberately she made her tone light and carefree. 'My lawyer's lending it to me—a personal loan, so he told me in his letter. He's coming to see me about it and once it's fixed up I'll be away. I—' She stopped short, aware of his thunderous expression. 'What's wrong with it, for heaven's sake?'

'Everything!'

'I don't know what you're getting at,' she flung at him.

'Don't you?' His lips had a satirical twist.

'No, I don't!' But her heart was thudding. 'It's only a matter of business!'

'You're dead wrong if that's what you think!' She barely caught his low muttered words. 'Put him off, Liz! Tell him you've changed your mind about the loan!'

'I will not!' she flared. 'Why should I?'

His eyes were blazing. 'Can't you see what you're letting yourself in for? A man with his unenviable reputation where women are concerned? Don't you realise that asking him to lend you money puts you right in his power? He calls the tune, and it doesn't need to be a matter of hard cash, when it comes to the repayment. Alone as you are here—'

Her eyes flashed angrily. 'And stupidly naïve? Isn't that what you were going to say?'

'No, it's not!' All at once the barely controlled anger she sensed in him boiled over and his hands were on her shoulders, digging into the flesh with painful pressure. 'You little fool, Liz! Can't you see what you're doing when you make a deal with a man of Kostas Baltsa's reputation?'

'You've no need to worry yourself about me!' she cried, breathing hard, 'and take your hands from my shoulders! You're hurting me!'

Immediately his hands fell away. 'Sorry—sorry about that.' She had to strain to catch the low tones, 'I wouldn't want to hurt you—not you, Liz.'

All at once she felt a wild urge towards hysteria. For clearly Adam was more concerned regarding the danger of her losing her virginity to the Greek lawyer than the matter of his setting out on the chance of acquiring the property from her. Aloud she demanded, 'Don't you think I can look after myself?' And before he could make an answer, 'Not that I need to. Honestly, the things you're suggesting about a perfectly respectable lawyer! The way you're going on about him anyone would think he was a brigand from way back in the mountains of Crete and primitive as they come!'

'He is,' Adam said harshly. 'Where women are concerned, he's earned himself a reputation all over the island as a fairly unsavoury character—cruel type.'

'Oh, you just don't like him!' she countered swiftly. 'He's been very good to me. He told me when I first arrived in Crete that I must let him know if I needed any help, and I could tell by the way he spoke that he really meant what he said!'

'I'll bet he did!' Adam's mouth was a hard line. 'When's he coming to see you?' He shot the words towards her.

'Tuesday of next week.'

'Liz,' all at once his face was dark with anger, 'will you listen to me?'

She wrinkled her nose at him. 'Not when you insist on playing the heavy father—'

He said exasperatedly, 'At least arrange to have someone else in the house with you.'

She threw him a mocking glance. 'Like you?'

Adam ignored the taunting note in her voice. 'I'd be there like a shot! Just say the word—' His voice hardened. 'Good grief, do something to protect yourself, girl!' His mouth tightened. 'Do I have to spell it out?' He looked as incensed, Liz thought in some surprise, as if the matter were of importance to him—which of course was absurd. His voice, threaded with urgency, cut across her thoughts. 'Look, Liz, do what you like. Stay on at the villa and forget about starting up the taverna again. Something might turn up. But do me a favour and don't let that guy come to the villa!' Suddenly his voice was low and persuasive. 'Come on, Liz, I happen to know what I'm talking about. Can't you take my word for it?'

His word! That did it, she thought on a spurt of anger. Weakly she had been tempted to put her trust in him all over again, even after what had happened to her owing to that very mistake in judgement. Summoning up her determination, she said stiffly, 'No, I can't! Not after the way you've let me down!'

His lips were a tight line and anger blazed in his eyes. 'Right!' He had turned away and was striding away from her. Liz stared after him as he moved swiftly over the sand. He hadn't even said, 'So long, be seeing you!' He'd just . . . gone. She blinked the stupid tears from her eyes. It was what she'd wanted, wasn't it, to show him that she refused to be dictated to by him and that his advice was wasted on her? Already she had been taken in by his force and strength and sheer male magnetism one time too many. She'd had to show him, hadn't she, that he couldn't talk away her objections, not this time.

She had certainly achieved what she had set out to do, because plainly he was furious with her. It was almost as if she had somehow hurt as well as angered him. As if he'd cared about what happened to her—but of course, she told herself a moment later, he had good reason to be angry with her. For Kostas's loan to get her started on her project would mean the end of any hopes Adam might still have of her having to sell out and leave the country. Why must she keep forgetting the real reason for his annoyance?

She had had the satisfaction of evening the score with Adam, hadn't she? She should be feeling triumphant and happy and smug. Somehow, though, there was only this dull ache in her heart and an odd sense of regret.

CHAPTER SIX

LIZ STAYED on the sand, hands linked around her knees, staring over the sparkling sea with eyes that saw only Adam, walking away from her, moving out of her life. Don't think of him! Determinedly she sprang to her feet and ran down the sand to plunge into the sea, but the cool invigorating contact with the waves eased her mind only temporarily, and at last she splashed back through foaming breakers to spread her towel once more on the sand. Conscious of heartache and a vague sense of regret, today she found little pleasure in sunbathing. Fool! Forget Adam! In an effort to follow her own advice she took the Greek lawyer's letter from her bag and smoothed it out as she tried to concentrate on the typewritten words that formerly she had merely skimmed over. 'Regret not able to oblige you with loan owing to certain rules pertaining to foreigners...' Funny, she thought dully, she had never thought of herself as a foreigner here. 'However, as a favour I will be glad to help you by arranging a personal loan at a special low rate of interest on a two-year term. By good fortune I happen to have business to attend to in your area on Tuesday and will call and discuss arrangements with you, let us hope to our mutual advantage. Kindest regards, Kostas.'

Somehow she couldn't believe that Greek lawyers were in the habit of signing only their first names on business letters to new clients. And he was coming to see her at the villa! The niggle of unease refused to go away. Why must she recall at this moment the hot dark eyes that had raked her body mercilessly at their meeting in his office? A cold finger of apprehension touched her. Suppose Adam were right and Kostas demanded from her a higher return for his loan than she was prepared to pay? There was something about him. Beneath the suave businesslike exterior she sensed a certain ruthlessness—primitive, male, demanding. The next moment she took herself in hand. She would take Kostas' letter at its face value and curb her over-active imagination. Immediately she spoiled the resolution by a thought: Even if her worst fears were realised she could cope, of course she could! It was Adam who had put these groundless fears into her mind, she told herself. No doubt, she mused on a sigh, he was discrediting the lawyer as a part of his "Get rid of Liz" campaign. There she went, thinking of him again!

All at once a restlessness consumed her. She couldn't lie in the sun any longer. Now that Adam had left her she felt a conspicuous figure on the beach, and ignoring the appreciative glances and shouted comments of a group of Greek Romeos who happened to be passing by, she wandered up the stretch of sand. Today the taverna seemed to her to appear more than ever abandoned with its empty tables and faded canvas awnings flapping in the breeze. But not for long, she vowed silently. The Greek lawyer had offered to help her (she thrust aside the memory of his intimate glance). He would see her through her financial problems, so she had best stop feeling sorry for herself and get on with living. She told herself she had had a lucky escape from falling even more deeply in love with a man whose devious and cunning ways had almost succeeded in deluding her.

If Katina's boasts were to be believed, the taverna had once been a happy, noisy place, crowded with customers. Would it be that way again, she wondered, when she had only the plainest of fare to offer? But her clientele would be different, she encouraged herself—guests from the big hotel over the hill, relaxing after a swim in the sea in the shade of the taverna or beneath sun-umbrellas set out on the sand. It would be a huge success. Why not? And what a triumph that would be! Then she could prove to Adam—resolutely she wrenched her thoughts aside, forcing herself to concentrate on plans for the future. Tomorrow, she promised herself, she would have a trial run, have a go at baking rolls—she had noticed a bottle of dried yeast and a bag of flour in the kitchen of the villa. How fortunate that at the last moment she had slipped into her travel pack the well-used notebook she had brought with her with its recipes she had used while flatting in Auckland. Maybe, she thought bleakly, she had been lucky too that her flatmate had loathed cooking and it was left to Liz, who enjoyed trying out new dishes, to provide the meals. And while she was counting her blessings, there was something she had to thank Adam for, she thought bleakly, one thing he had done for her, even if unwittingly. For the erection of the luxury hotel nearby, she mused, had no doubt been the means of her uncle having electricity at the villa, even though the old blackened stove remained in the kitchen.

Next morning she awoke feeling unrefreshed, with a dull ache at her temples. With a heavy heart, she told herself that it was time she was up and about, she had work to do. She should count herself lucky, she told herself, being able to practise her cooking here in the villa, with nothing else to do and all the time in the world to do it. Yet somehow all her shining enthusiasm in her planned project had left her, and all she could think of was Adam. Who would have believed his smiling strong face could be so cold and forbidding?

To her relief, a mug of hot coffee lifted the little hammer blows of pain in her forehead, and after she had cleared away the few dishes from her frugal breakfast, she changed her nightdress for a green and white spotted cotton frock, short and sleeveless, and coiled her hair in a careless knot on the top of her head for coolness.

Back in the kitchen she tied around her slim waist an apron she found in a drawer. It was such a small size that she suspected it had been worn by the Greek girl, and in an angry gesture she tugged it away. She wanted nothing to do with anything belonging to Katina. Not clothing, or pity or contempt. Or Adam? Now where had that absurd thought come from? she wondered. Just because the two appeared to be on friendly terms, to know each other so well . . . And yet wasn't it strange that Adam hadn't blamed Katina for having betrayed his secret? Could it be that he was making certain of one part of the inheritance by cultivating the Greek girl's friendship? Even, perhaps, marriage? True, Katina had spoken of a dowry, but that was a matter arranged by parents or guardians. How neatly marriage with Katina would solve his problem—well, half of it! Liz couldn't understand why she was feeling so deeply about the matter. But it would do him no good, she told herself, for he would never succeed in persuading her to alter her mind regarding the sale.

As the day wore on the heat in the kitchen became all but unbearable, but despite the discomfort, Liz worked doggedly on. Her face was flushed and tendrils of dark hair clung damply to her forehead. The first batch of baking emerged from the oven passably successful but far short of the standard she was aiming for. She wiped a floury hand over her forehead, glistening with perspiration. She'd have to do better than this if she were to make a success of her venture. Time slipped by and now a profusion of crusty rolls was spread over bench and table top, and the kitchen was filled with the aroma of freshly baked yeasty cooking.

Engrossed in her task, she was unaware of anything else until she noticed with surprise a plump dark hand encrusted with heavy gold rings, that appeared around the edge of the door. The next moment a swarthy, thickly set man wearing an immaculate business suit, stood in the opening. Kostas! He'd come a day early, she thought in confusion.

'I could not make anyone hear with the door knocker,' he was saying, 'so I let myself in. So, you are already starting to make the bread!'

Liz straightened, aware of his intimate glance that lingered on the plunging neckline of her dress. His gaze lifted to her flushed, surprised face. 'You got my letter saying I was coming to see you?'

'Yes, of course.' She was recovering her wits. 'Tomorrow. I thought you were coming tomorrow.'

He was regarding her with a fatuous smile. 'I knew you would like me to come sooner to tell you that I can help you—so here I am.'

She asked quickly, 'Have you been to the villa before?'

He shook his head. 'Your uncle, always he came to see me in my office as do all my clients—except you, Elizabeth. With you I make an exception. It is a long drive, but I do not mind. I asked at the hotel for directions.' Taking a spotless white handkerchief from his pocket, he mopped the beads of moisture on his forehead. 'It is not a day for walking over hills, but,' his warm significant glance made her feel vaguely apprehensive, 'it will be worth it all to you—and me.'

Liz said briskly, 'If I'd known you were coming today I'd have been more presentable.' All at once she was aware of long red burn marks on her hands, a scorched dress, and she suspected that she had smeared flour over her face.

'Do not worry yourself. Me, I like you this way.'

Something in his tone sent a tremor of apprehension running along her nerves. Could she handle a situation that could possibly be fraught with danger? The next moment she told herself she was being stupidly imaginative, overreacting to Kostas's intimate manner. She wrenched her mind back to his deep tones.

'In our country our women stay in the home looking after their men and the children they bear them. They work in the fields—'

'Yes, I know,' Liz tried for lightness. 'I've seen them gathering herbs and olives, working all day in the hot sun.' Nervousness made her run on breathlessly, 'And the older women, I'm not so sure they're as old as they look either, they're so burned and brown, dressed in that blacker-than-black clothing. It must be so depressing for them.'

He eyed her in astonishment and she saw with relief that she had succeeded in diverting his conversation from personal channels. 'Many of them are widows. It is only right that they should give up all attempts to please Greek men. It is the custom. They do not wish for anything else.'

'How do you know?' Liz demanded indignantly. 'How would any man know how a woman would feel about that sort of thing?'

'Ah,' with a sudden misgiving she realised too late she had fallen into a trap, 'between a man and a woman, who knows the feelings?' His ingratiating smile, Liz thought, was more in the nature of a leer. 'Me, I have a feeling for you. That was why I came to see you here, to tell you you have no need to worry any more about the money. I will see that you have it. You understand, Elizabeth? You can rely on me.'

I only hope I can, Liz told herself silently. She was beginning to have mixed feelings regarding her visitor. It would be a wonderful relief to have the loan she had requested of him, but if the offer carried conditions she couldn't and wouldn't agree to in any circumstances...the disturbing thoughts ran through her mind.

'I'll make coffee,' she said abruptly. 'That long drive in the heat,' she heard herself babbling on, 'you must be feeling like some refreshment. I'll let you try out one of my rolls. Why don't you go into the other room,' she suggested, 'and I'll bring in a tray. It's cooler in there.' He made no move to leave the room, but remained standing motionless watching her, just watching. 'I like it here.' Once again she was disconcertingly aware of his warm glance.

To her chagrin she could feel the colour rising in her cheeks and felt a wave of thankfulness that her face was already flushed from the heat of the room. With hands that were unsteady in spite of herself she switched on the electric kettle and reached above the bench for pottery mugs hanging from their hooks.

'It's only instant,' she waffled on, spooning coffee powder from a glass jar. 'I expect you would prefer Greek?'

'It is of no importance.' His significant glance said, 'Only you are of importance to me today.' Liz, however, made a pretence of not noticing the unspoken message beamed from his dark orbs. Soon she was carrying a tray into the cool and uncluttered living room where Kostas dropped down on to a wooden chair. Liz thought wryly that even Kostas couldn't do much mischief when handling a freshly baked roll!

As she sipped her coffee she kept up a light conversation, anything to avoid his significant words and glances. At last, however, coffee mugs were emptied and he leaned confidentially towards her. 'So now we come to business, the little matter you wrote me about.'

'It might be little to you,' said Liz with spirit, 'but it happens to be very important to me! You see, I've got this idea for serving refreshments at the taverna,' she ran on, 'tea, coffee, fruit drinks, baked rolls with fillings inside and then toasted. Plain food, but I think the Canadians and Americans and English tourists would appreciate it—anyway, it's worth a try!' She warmed to her subject. 'I'm sure I could make a go of it!' Rising to her feet, she moved to the window, looking out at the taverna on the sandy beach below. She forgot her apprehensions concerning the man seated opposite her and her eyes were dreamy. 'It looks so deserted somehow, but I could change all that, once I get a start! Actually, it doesn't need a lot doing to it, but I need a reliable toaster, a deep-freeze to store food in the heat and some glass-topped containers to display the various types of fillings.' Her eyes were alight with enthusiasm. 'I know I could make a success of it, once I get myself organised. I really thought,' she ran on, 'that I'd have enough money to get myself started. It sounded such a lot in drachmas—but it seems it's not enough, not by a long way.'

'That is true.'

Liz sighed. 'So that's why I wrote to ask you about costs and if you could let me have a loan. I couldn't think of any other way. Now, though, with your help I'll be able to—' She stopped short, aware that he wasn't really listening to what she was telling him, even though his attention was centred on her lips, and in his smouldering gaze she glimpsed a lambent flame, deep and dangerous.

Wildly she rushed into speech, saying the first words that came into her head. 'Talking of tavernas, tell me, why is it that in the villages, it's always men who sit there playing with their blue worry beads?'

Kostas looked taken aback by the question. 'But of course men sit all day in the taverna. The *kafenenion,* the true Greek café, serves only Greek coffee and there men can play cards or backgammon. Such a place is by custom out of bounds for women, but in a *kafenenion* that is not entirely full, she may sit outside for coffee.'

'Sit outside!' echoed Liz indignantly, 'They allow her to do that? How very bighearted of the menfolk!'

It seemed, however, that sarcasm was wasted on Kostas. 'It is our way, and the women here are lucky, for when they get too old to work they get a pension from the Government earlier than the older men.'

'Well, I think that's awful!' His amused glance took in Liz's indignant expression. 'Do not concern yourselves with such matters, *thespinis,* these are old customs, a part of the life of a village.' A knowing grin. 'You are thinking you would not like to marry a Greek man, but I tell you that in Chania and Heraklion a man of business would not send his wife off to work in the fields.'

Liz remembered the dark-suited men she had seen in the city, well-dressed masculine figures with hands behind their backs as they endlessly clicked their worry beads between their fingers. The next moment she realised that Kostas's thoughts were running along a slightly different channel. 'A man like me.' A plump swarthy hand covered hers.

'I should think not!' exclaimed Liz, and pulled her hand from his moist grasp. 'But you would expect your wife to provide a dowry? Now that to me is an awfully old-fashioned idea.'

'You do not understand our customs. It is an arrangement made by the parents of a girl who comes of marriage-
able age. More than one man may approach the parents of
the girl. There are meetings, there are discussions, and it is
arranged what she will bring to the union. In the villages her
father will provide goats, cattle, a pig—'

'It's like selling the poor girl!' Liz burst out.

Kostas regarded her with the long-suffering patience of an
adult dealing with a fractious child. 'He provides her with
a place to live, sometimes it is a room built on to the parents' house, children—'

'Children!' She regarded him incredulously. 'You call that
providing?'

He said complacently, 'It is what she wants above all else
in life. A good man to look after her, a home of her own, a
family—'

'And work,' she reminded him.

'In the villages, she must work,' he agreed. 'In the cities
the marriage settlements are arranged in the same way, but
the girl will bring drachmas or maybe property, a house,
land—it is all part of the dowry.'

'Or a beach and a taverna?' Liz spoke unthinkingly, she
couldn't resist the jibe.

All at once a light flared in his eyes and she knew she had
made a dreadful mistake. He was a womanizer, she'd known
it instinctively from the moment she had met him. She had
tried to brush the feeling away, but now she wondered if she
had acted rashly in appealing to him for help. He was a
heavily built man with physical strength against which she
would be powerless—she thrust the disquieting thoughts
aside. Ridiculous to think this way. He was only her lawyer, a trifle amorous in his manner maybe, but she would
just have to get used to that and stop dreaming up a dangerous situation out of nothing.

The next moment, however, she knew she had not been
mistaken. He was leaning towards her, the swarthy face
thrust close to hers. 'I knew when you asked me to come to

you,' his tone was hoarse with passion, 'that you wanted me.'

Liz quelled the suddenly rising panic. 'I didn't ask you! You just came—'

'You asked me to come here!' A tide of red had risen beneath the swarthiness of his face and there was a glitter in the dark eyes. 'You agreed to my terms.'

'Interest terms,' she said faintly, knowing he wasn't even listening to her, 'interest on the money.'

He said hoarsely, 'Between a man and a woman there are other ways. Do not tell me that in your country such things are not known—'

'Yes—no—' Liz scarcely knew what she was saying. Then all at once a cold steely anger took possession of her. She would show this easily excited man who imagined because he was physically stronger than she that he could bend her to his will. 'You listen to me! I don't want your loan! I don't want anything to do with you!' Her voice rose high and clear. 'You can keep your money, I don't want it—or you either. Just—get out of my house!'

Kostas made no move to go but remained standing, his arms folded as he gazed down at her. 'You do not tell me to go.' She caught a threatening note in his voice. 'I am the one who, how do you say in your country, "calls the tune".' Liz saw his expression change from anger to a self-satisfied hateful smirk. 'Is it so bad for you to be my woman?'

'Yes, it is!' She flung at him. 'Get out!'

'Come my little one—' The low voice throbbing with passion sent panic quivering along her nerves and all at once she felt very much alone and at his mercy. The next moment he lunged himself towards her and she was caught in arms that were like steel bands. His hot breath was on her face and Liz struggled fiercely in his suffocating embrace. A black tide of anger surged through her and she sank her teeth in the fleshy arm that pinned her so securely. She caught his muttered oath of pain and rage, and something else. Was it a fleeting impression of a shadow passing by the

window or a desperate need that sparked her cry, born of
terror and urgency, that pierced the stillness? 'Adam! Help
me, Adam!'

Her assailant gave a deep triumphant laugh. 'It is no use
shouting, no one will help you!' He was fumbling with unsteady hands with the strap of her sundress.

The next moment the door was flung open and Adam
stood inside, his eyes blazing, his lips a hard accusing line.
Never in her life, Liz thought on a breath of relief, had she
been so glad to see anyone. Dazedly she watched as Adam's
bronzed sinewy arm shot forward to deal a clean blow to
Kostas's chin, felling the heavy man to the floor. He lay
sprawled on the floor tiles, his mouth slack and eyes wide
with fear. But Adam had turned to Liz, 'Tell me,' the words
came on an angry breath, 'has he hurt you? Because if he
has—'

'No, no, he was only trying it on.' She pulled the strap of
her sundress back over her shoulder, hiding a dark bruise.

Kostas had scrambled to his feet, his hand pressed to his
bleeding chin. 'It was nothing, nothing!' warily he eyed
Adam. 'A lovers' quarrel! Elizabeth invited me to come
here. Ask her and she will tell you—' He stopped short in
the face of Adam's threatening expression.

'Get out!' Adam's tone was low and menacing and Liz
suspected it was only by an effort of will he was restraining
himself from dealing out further punishment to Kostas. 'Let
him go!' she said on a breath. 'He's not worth worrying
about!'

'You heard what Liz said,' Adam's tone was threatening, 'so get on your way while you have the chance! Fast!
And take that with you!' He flung the leather briefcase towards Kostas, who snatched it up, then turned and hurried
away. The next minute the slamming of a door echoed
through the room.

Liz realised that Adam was eyeing her with real concern,
his eyes dark and troubled. 'You're quite sure he didn't
harm you?' Reaching out a hand, he traced his palm down

her smooth cheek, and as always his touch started the trembling in her. For a crazy moment she forgot everything else in the world, then somehow she dragged herself back to sanity. Because she could no longer sustain his brilliant gaze she busied herself gathering up long strands of hair that had fallen loose in her struggle and coiling them in a knot at the top of her head.

'He did scare me a bit,' she acknowledged tremulously. An instinctive honesty made her add, 'You did warn me! I guess you know Kostas a whole lot better than I do. His coming here to arrange with me about the loan I wanted was just an excuse. I should have known.' She bit her lip. 'Deep down I did know really, only I wouldn't let myself admit it.'

Adam grinned and the lift of his mobile lips made her feel once again a surge of warm happiness even though she had lost all faith in him. She *must* remember about losing faith in him even though he had chanced to arrive here at the right moment. And that was odd, her thoughts were rioting, because Kostas had planned to come here tomorrow, and anyway, after their stormy parting, she hadn't expected ever to see Adam again. 'How did you know,' she said very low, 'that I needed you?'

He laughed, a chuckle deep in his throat. 'I happen to know Kostas, and someone had to be around to show him a thing or two!'

'But you thought he was coming here tomorrow?'

'He asked for directions to the villa from the receptionist at the hotel. I was a bit late getting the message, but I did get it. Funny thing,' she caught the glimmer of amusement in his eyes, 'I was just lifting my hand to the doorbell when I could have sworn I heard someone yelling out for me.'

Liz's face went pinker... and pinker. Wildly she groped in her mind for a plausible excuse for the cry that had come instinctively from some deep recess in her mind. At last she said, 'I thought I heard someone coming and I was hoping it would be you!'

He raised heavy brows and tiny flames flickered in his eyes.

'Only because,' she rushed on wildly, 'I knew you were so strong and could handle him easily.' She took in his lithe tanned body, his muscular chest revealed by his cotton shirt, open to the waist. 'I mean, you're as fit as can be, and Kostas is anything but.' Adam studied her with amused interest. 'Nice try, Liz.'

'Well, anyway,' she hastened to change the subject, 'I've learned my lesson the hard way with Kostas. To think you told me that Greek men respect and look after their womenfolk, that they've got strict ideas on the subject—'

'They have! But Kostas is no more a typical Greek than a pickpocket is typically English!' He threw her an unreadable look. 'Trouble with you, Liz, is that you're so damned appealing. Didn't anyone ever tell you?'

She laughed, the warm happiness flooding through her. 'I bet you say that to all the maidens you rescue from the wicked villain!'

'Liz—' Excitement quivered along her veins and for a dizzy moment she forgot...forgot. Adam made an effort to take her in his arms, but with an effort she wrenched herself back to sanity. Don't let yourself be caught in that particular trap again! She summoned all her defences and said slowly, 'I'm very grateful to you for turning up here today, but it doesn't really make any difference. Things are just the same between us.'

Instantly his arms fell away. 'I get it.' There was a cutting edge to his voice.

A vague feeling of guilt niggled at her. Or could it be the hurt she saw in his eyes that pricked her conscience? There were words that must be said. She raised clear blue eyes to his ice-cold gaze. 'I just don't know how to thank you for what you did just now.'

His face was unsmiling and she thought how remote he looked all of a sudden. Zeus back on his mountain heights once more, far, far removed from ordinary mortals? She had to strain to catch the muttered words, 'You could try believing in me for a change.'

'Oh, that...' It was the last thing she had expected him to say. Spiritedly she took up his challenge. 'If you mean—'

'You know very well what I mean.'

To change a dangerously emotional subject, Liz said quickly, 'You were right about something else too! Accord ing to what Kostas told me the amount I need to start up the taverna again my way is way beyond what I've got. That's why I'd asked him to loan me the money to get started. I guess,' she finished on a sigh, 'I can kiss all those ideas goodbye right now.'

This is the moment, she told herself, for him to make me an offer for the property, and waited for him to say the words. To her surprise, however, he appeared to have lost interest in the matter. He shrugged powerful shoulders. 'That's the way the cookie crumbles—See you!'

She could almost *feel* the emptiness of the room after he left her.

She stood motionless, the slow tears trickled down her face. She had done the right thing, the only possible thing now she knew of his real feelings towards her, so why did she feel this devastating sense of loss? Could it be because of the way he had helped her out of a desperate situation? He has his good points, she conceded, he knew I was alone here and unprotected. No doubt he would have done the same for any girl on her own. But that didn't give him the right to take up their friendly relationship once again, as though nothing had happened between them. As if she weren't aware of his true purpose to keep right on with his 'buttering up Liz' campaign. Her soft lips firmed. Because it wouldn't work— and anyway, she told herself determinedly, he won't get the chance!

The troubled thoughts chased round and round in her mind. The hurt she had glimpsed in his eyes when she had told him her feelings about him. But of course he was disappointed with her decision because of his own interest in the property. The mistake she had made, she chided herself, was in letting herself forget that despite his male charisma, his devastating smile and dark good looks, Adam was first and foremost a businessman. A man who had invested the main part of his capital in a project on the coast of a Greek island in a venture that had yet to prove its popularity with the tourists arriving at Heraklion from planes and tourist ships at the start of the summer season. One factor only stood in the way of making his luxury hotel a glittering financial success, and that was an unknown girl from the other side of the world. A girl who could be as determined as himself. True, she had at first allowed herself to be taken in by Adam, but, she steeled herself, now that she knew his real reason for cultivating her friendship, she was forearmed. For a time, she admitted, she had been—well, attracted to him, but not now, not any longer.

CHAPTER SEVEN

As THE next few days dragged by, Liz felt restless and unhappy. Who wouldn't, she reasoned with herself, after the crashing disappointment of having all hopes of making a new life for herself come to an end? Only when she was down on the beach, swimming in the clear water, could she dispel a little the sense of letdown, forget her problems—and Adam.

Today, as she slipped a light cotton robe over her yellow bikini and closed the door behind her, she was struck as always by the luminous quality of the light. On the sun-dappled waters a caique sailed by, but otherwise she and the seagulls crying overhead had the bay to themselves. The dolphins rising from the water far out at sea, the piercingly blue sky, it was all so beautiful, she mused as she strolled over the warm sand. A dream island. So why couldn't she just enjoy it instead of letting her mind dwell endlessly on a man who she knew full well wasn't worth a single thought? The ache of longing that spoiled even the attraction of sun and sea warned her that she was allowing Adam to take over her thoughts, her life, and she would be wise to avoid seeing him ever again—if she could.

She roused herself to plunge into the bracing, tumbling froth of the surf, then struck out for deep water. Soon she lay floating on her back, her face upturned to the clear blue bowl of the sky and her dark hair drifting like seaweed around her shoulders. She stayed in the water for a long time, then at last she splashed through the waves at the shoreline and paused to wring seawater from the thick fall of her hair. For an hour she lay sunbathing on her towel spread out on the sand, then she dusted the sand from her knees, slipped on her robe and moved away. 'I've got to organise myself into some sort of activity,' she told herself resolutely.

Anything to make her forget Adam's dark good looks and masculine attraction against which she seemed powerless. Maybe today she would take herself on a tour of Knossos, the site of the long-buried and excavated palace of the Minoans of which she had read in her guide book. She couldn't imagine herself finding much interest in three-thousand-year-old ruins, but it would be something to do. Besides, the thought came unbidden, she wouldn't be here for more than a few months, not in her present low state of finances, so she must make the most of her time and see as much of the island as she could. On the day of her arrival here she had noticed tour buses bearing the destination name of the famous place. The vehicles had made a stop at the hotel in order to pick up passengers, so evidently all she need do would be to wait there until a tour bus came along.

Presently she was back in the villa, showering the salt from her hair, finding fresh underwear and slipping into a dress of cool, creamy-coloured muslin. Copper jewellery had been her usual choice when wearing the dress, but today she would wear the gold honey-bee pendant that Adam had given her. Why not? It would be absurd to leave such an exquisite piece of jewellery here when it complemented so perfectly the low scoop of the neckline of her dress. Besides, she wanted to prove to herself that she had no emotional hang-ups about a gift from a man who, despite all she knew of him, nevertheless held for her a deep and powerful attraction.

She had little appetite of late—blame that infuriating man over at the hotel—but she made herself a tomato sandwich and mixed a mug of instant coffee, then she cleared away the dishes and picked up her Greek embroidered bag. Her cheeks were flushed with the touch of the sun, making her eyes look a deep smoky blue and her damp hair clustered in tendrils around her forehead as she set off along the track. I wish I'd taken the trouble to read up the history of Knossos, she thought regretfully as she made her way up the dusty path winding between the silvery green of olive trees.

When she arrived at the concrete surround of the hotel, there appeared to be no bus in sight and, feeling a little conspicuous in this holiday atmosphere where couples strolled together in the sunshine or sat at tables under blue and white beach umbrellas, Liz moved into the shadows of a white wall.

Through the window she caught a glimpse into the reception lounge. Katina was seated at the desk and Adam was bending over her shoulder, scanning an open guest book lying on the desk. Liz was a little surprised to find Katina at the reception desk, then she remembered Adam having told her that the Greek girl sometimes filled in in the capacity of receptionist. Odd, she mused once again, that he had never blamed Katina in the slightest for letting on his sneaky intention to persuade Liz to sell him her share of the beach properties. It seemed that in his eyes the Greek girl could do no wrong. Now, seeing the two dark heads so close together, Liz was pierced by a pang of jealousy. With it came the reflection that with Katina as his wife, Adam would have no need to worry about a half share of the inheritance, that was for sure, nor would Katina have any problems about finding money for her dowry. The thought was unaccountably depressing, and Liz stared resolutely up the empty road.

She was still there ten minutes later when a voice said, 'Waiting for someone?'

She spun around, her thoughts whirling. Only one man she knew spoke in that deep vibrant tone. 'Adam!'

His eyes were glinting with an emotion she couldn't define. Amusement? Interest? Surprise? And he gave not the slightest indication of remembering his punishing kiss in the darkness of the courtyard. And that, she thought swiftly,

was a game at which two could play. She pulled herself together and tried out her newest, most carefree smile. 'The
bus, actually. There'll be one along for Knossos at any
minute, I expect.'

'You'd be so lucky!' Diamonds of light flickered in his
eyes and his mouth had the upward twist at the corners that
Liz didn't quite trust. 'Knossos, you said?'

'That's right,' she answered with carefully assumed nonchalance. 'The buses were making a stop here on the day I
arrived.'

'Not for you, I'm afraid.' His tone was deceptively regretful.

Liz forgot all about being carelessly unconcerned in the
matter. 'Why ever not?' She stared up at him, wide-eyed.
'There is public transport, isn't there?'

'Sure, but it happens to be excursion buses, all booked up
by travel agents for overseas tourists. To get public ones
you'd have to start from scratch from Heraklion—'

'Oh!' He was looking amused once again and hurriedly
Liz said, 'I'll order a taxi, then. If I could ring for one from
the office?'

'No need, you've got yourself one right now!' There was
a dancing light in his eyes and he appeared to be enjoying
himself hugely, she thought. Could this be a further attempt at friendly persuasion? Aloud she queried, 'With you,
you mean?'

'Why not? The old bus is ready and waiting!' He jerked
a hand towards the gleaming red car standing in the garages nearby.

She hesitated, her thoughts spinning wildly. Just being
with him sent her spirits soaring excitedly. Clearly he had
decided to ignore the circumstances of their last parting. Or
had he already forgotten? She brought her mind back to his
deep vibrant tones. 'Everyone who comes to Crete should
see the old Minoan palace,' he told her with a grin. 'And
now that you—'

'Haven't much time left? Is that what you were going to say?' she flashed. Somehow he sparked her to anger, and she suspected he did it deliberately.

'Not really,' his eyes had a veiled expression. Then all at once he was friendly. 'Come on, Liz,' his voice was low and persuasive, 'let me take you on a personal sightseeing tour. Greek mythology a speciality!' And as she hesitated, 'You'll have to have somewhere to go now that you're all dressed up—honey-bee pendant and all!'

So he had noticed the gold pendant. She threw him a suspicious look, a look, she realised the next minute, that was entirely wasted, for he merely turned away, throwing over his shoulder, 'Right! We're on our way!'

She might as well take up his offer, she reflected as she watched him move towards the car park. What harm could it do to go with him?

Plenty, piped up the small voice deep in her mind, but she thrust it aside. Just an hour or so spent rambling around the ancient courtyards and palace rooms, she reasoned with herself; she'd be foolish to refuse the invitation.

'Hop in, Liz!' Adam was pulling up at her side, leaning from his seat at the wheel of the red car to fling open the side door.

What else could she do? she asked herself as she slid into the passenger seat and he moved around the car to close the door. Clearly it was an opportunity not to be missed. But deep down where it counted she knew she really had no choice in the matter, not when Adam eyed her with his glinting eyes and heart-knocking smile!

He slipped the car into gear and as they took a rise then sped along a road cut between the thyme-scented hills, she forgot everything else in the world but Adam, his bronzed profile and his well-shaped hands on the steering wheel.

His deep tones broke the silence. 'With a bit of luck we'll get to Knossos before the main tour buses for the day show up and I can take you around without tourists getting in the way.'

'Is the palace very big?'

'Is it ever! The palace had a thousand rooms in its hey-day—that's how it got its reputation as a labyrinth, and would you believe, the frescoes are almost as vivid as the day they were created and the plumbing still works!' They had swung into a dusty road winding between sparsely growing olive trees and from somewhere far away Liz caught the faint echoes of a flute.

'Pan pipes,' Adam told her. 'Some lonely shepherd way down in the valley who's keeping an eye on his sheep.'

'I like the sound.' Liz thought she would always remember the haunting thread of music borne on the fresh, herb-scented breeze. The sound was almost as fascinating, she mused, as the warm tones of Adam's voice as he described to her a race who had been far ahead of their time and had lived thousands of years ago on this island. Funny, she had tried to study a book of Crete legends before coming here, but it had failed to hold her interest, yet Adam seemed to be able to communicate to her something of his own enthusiasm for the past. She couldn't seem to wrench her gaze from his face, and for something to say, she commented, 'You seem to know the palace ruins well!'

'I should do!' She took pleasure in his quick, sideways grin. 'As a kid back in England I was brought up on Greek myths and pagan gods—my dad saw to that! Every summer we spent a holiday on one of the Greek islands and I was taken to every museum in the place. Not that I appreciated the outings much at the time, but now...The odd thing about the history of Crete is that it gets you once you start delving into it. They were quite a race, the Minoans, good-looking and lively and graceful, and there was nothing stuffy or pompous about their court. Judging by the pictures and frescoes in the palace rooms they were a happy people. They loved to dance and loved life and built their court with lots of corridors open to the sky. Their paintings are really something, and their stylised gold jewellery could have been fashioned by a leading jeweller of today.'

'Tell me,' said Liz, 'what were the women like, the court ladies?'

'The court ladies?' He flicked her a sideways glance and at something in his expression, her spirits soared. Stupid of her to feel this way. She wrenched her mind back to his words.

'Like you, actually. You see pictures of them on frescoes in the Throne Room of the palace. Slim, dark, sensitive-looking with slender waists and dark curly hair. Only they didn't have your eyes. No one else could have eyes like you!'

She threw him an enquiring look and could have sworn that he really had meant what he had said about her. Maybe he did feel something for her, who could tell? She turned her face aside to hide her burning cheeks and stared out at the piles of rubble beside the road showing the danger of rock falls, as they swung around a hairpin bend. 'You're having me on.'

He said softly, 'Would I do that to you, Liz?'

A loaded question and one to which she knew the answer only too well. 'Well...' she let the word drift into silence and was relieved when they turned another bend in the road and Adam braked to a stop just in time to avoid the sheep that were meandering along the highway in the care of a shepherd.

'Just a matter of being patient,' Adam was leaning back in his seat. 'You don't mind a bit of a wait, do you?'

I don't mind anything when I'm with you, Adam. Now where, she wondered, had that thought come from?

'The shepherd's probably bound for a farm further down the road.' She followed his gaze to a hillside where dark-garbed Cretan women with donkeys were gathering herbs amongst the blood-red poppies and yellow daisies growing amongst the grass. 'They certainly make the most of their herbs growing on the island,' she observed.

He nodded. 'Use them too. A Cretan woman's kitchen always has mint for indigestion and a good supply of origani to give her Greek dishes a lift.'

'Really?' She eyed him wonderingly. 'How about the dittany I can smell on the air right now?'

'Oh, that's the most important of the lot.' He threw his arm lightly around her shoulders. 'It's said to have therapeutic qualities for women in childbirth.'

Liz, however, had forgotten her question. Thank heaven, she thought through rioting senses, Adam couldn't know the effect his touch was having on her. The scattered sheep were still moving around the car, and to break the moment of silence she said, 'That peasant over there working in his field—he surely can't expect to make much of a living, with his primitive wooden plough.'

Adam's arm tightened around her shoulders and she found herself blissfully relaxing against him, only half aware of what he was saying. 'More likely he's hoping for a much more lucrative harvest, real treasure that the plough might turn up in the earth anywhere any time, if he's lucky! And there's always a chance—'

She roused herself to look at him incredulously. 'You don't mean buried treasure! Not these days!'

'You're in Crete now, Liz, and it's happening all the time—one of the big draws of archaeology, I guess. Every day new sites and priceless finds are being unearthed all over the island. Take the original version of the honey-bee pendant you're wearing,' gently he put out a hand and lifted the fine gold wire hanging with shining discs, that was strung around her slender throat. For a long moment she was tinglingly aware of his hand on her skin and fought a wild impulse to hold his hand there, close and warm and exciting. Over the confusion of her senses she made an effort to concentrate on his voice. His matter-of-fact tones calmed her tumultuous thoughts. 'It was discovered in a burial ground, a royal one that had been untouched for centuries.' All at once his tone was warm and intimate. 'So you like your Minoan pendant?'

'Oh, I do! I do! It's the loveliest piece of jewellery I've ever owned!' Too late she realised the excited enthusiasm of her tone. Would he imagine that she cherished the pendant because of the giver? She added on a breath, 'It suits my dress.'

'And your suntanned throat.'

Liz was almost sorry to see the last sheep zigzagging its way past the car to join its woolly companions, and the next moment Adam put a hand to the starter motor.

Presently they were moving up a slope where sunlight made a filtered pattern through the grapevines, and ahead on high land surrounded by hills was the rambling site of the long-buried and excavated Minoan palace. Adam guided the car into a parking area, then escorted Liz through the entrance gates. While he paused to purchase admission tickets at a counter, she stood looking around her, struck by the silence and peacefulness of the place. Could this be what Adam had referred to when he had spoken of being free of the tour buses with their guides and chattering passengers? In the soft bright sunlight she caught glimpses of immense walls of stone, secluded shady courtyards, and everywhere light flooded the ruins of the palace, streaming down through open stairways and light wells.

'You've got yourself a tour guide.' Adam had come to join her. Taking her arm, he led her up a path winding amongst tall grass and wild corn, to emerge amongst grey, time-worn stones. As she gazed over the dark red columns of high walls half buried in weeds Liz said wonderingly, 'Is the palace just as it was thousands of years ago?'

He stood at her side, following her gaze. 'More or less. When it was first discovered and excavated, the thousand-year-old sunbaked bricks couldn't take the daylight, so the palace and courtyard buildings were reconstructed—red pillars, stone walls, the lot. Right here is the central courtyard,' he led the way over silvery-grey stones half covered in encroaching weeds. 'If you stand here beside me,' he drew her to him and she was aware once again of the thrilling awareness his touch evoked, so that she had to force herself to concentrate on his words, 'from here the courtyard frames a view of Mount Jouktas.'

At last she had her runaway emotions in hand. 'Isn't that the sacred mountain, home of the Earth Goddess, the mother of all living creatures?'

'You've been boning up on Cretan mythology!'

'Not enough. I never thought it was interesting until now.' She broke off. Fool! she scolded herself, you can't speak without betraying yourself! Hurriedly she attempted to rectify the blunder. 'Only because I like that bit about the Minoans worshipping the Earth Goddess!' She twinkled up at him. 'It appeals to me much more than the modern Greek idea of the womenfolk getting dried-up skins and old-looking working in the fields in the hot sun while the men sit around in the taverna and play with their worry beads. Yet the Minoans lived so long ago.'

'They were way ahead of any other civilisation of their time—Come on, I'll take you down to the cellars and storehouses.'

They moved beneath the clear dazzling light above, down wide stone steps with black inverted columns, to make their way along low passageways and past great red columns, then down a staircase into the old cellars.

'I don't believe it!' Liz started in amazement at great seven-foot-high pottery jars with their ornate decorations of coloured scenes. 'They could have come right out of a stage production of Ali Baba and the Forty Thieves!'

The air was cool in the dim passageways as they wandered through workshops and storehouses, all arranged around the great Central Court. Liz looked with amazement at the Queen's toilet with its incredibly modern fitments, the luxurious bathroom with its red clay tub. Then they climbed a stone stairway to stroll out on to sun-splashed terraces and through royal suites with their exquisitely decorated rooms in this palace open to the sky.

'Now for the Throne Room.' Adam took her up some steps to the restored room with its gypsum throne and guardian griffons.

'It's not a bit like the throne room I'd pictured.' In the room flooded with light from the opening above, Liz took in the richly glowing colours of frescoes depicting the court ladies in their topless, long-skirted gowns, their dark hair curling in ringlets around their delicate faces. Murals showed the bare-breasted Snake Goddess, and everywhere on doorways and walls was the sacred symbol she had come to know all over Crete, the double axe and the bull's horns. 'It's beautiful!' Her eyes were alight. 'What did you say it was called, this palace? The Palace of the Double Axe? Anyone can see that the folk who lived in the court here were a happy people who loved beauty. You've only got to look at the frescoes and the hairstyles and jewellery of the women.' Once again Liz's gaze was drawn to the frescoes with their pictures of tiny, delicate-featured people who looked full of gaiety and charm. 'Can't you just see them moving about the shady courtyards and enjoying themselves on the dancing floor? And the throne—it's more like an ordinary dining chair of today. So simple, and so little.'

Adam was leaning lazily against a pillar, regarding her with speculative grey eyes. 'Big enough for you.'

She twinkled back at him. 'King Minos must have been a very small person. I don't think I—'

'Want to bet?' Before she could argue the matter he had scooped her up in his arms, then gently he seated her on the tiny throne.

The next moment an echo of voices warned them of the approach of a tour party. Swiftly Liz sprang to her feet, Adam grasped her hand and like conspirators, laughingly they made their escape. Presently they came out into the hot sunshine of a sun-drenched terrace, to wander down a curving path and drop down to stones half hidden in a riot of golden daisies. It was very still, the only sound the droning of bees in air that was heavy with the perfume of trailing honeysuckle. A short distance away groups of tourists were moving towards the ticket booth, milling amongst the stone stairways of the palace rooms and wandering through the souvenir store. Yet here she and Adam were alone in a secluded spot where corn grew high amongst the flagstones and scarlet poppies flamed between great silvery-grey stones half hidden in encroaching weeds.

'I can see why you said those Minoan people were way ahead of other civilisations of their time.' Liz spoke dreamily with one half of her mind. Her gaze was fixed on Adam's dark, lean face. He was gazing out towards the surrounding hills and she took her fill of looking at him...just looking. His sensitively shaped hands and suntanned throat, the thatch of dark hair falling over his bronzed forehead—everything about him drew her to him, and to be alone here with him was a happiness beyond belief. She pulled her thoughts up with a jerk, aghast at the direction in which they were drifting, and attempted to concentrate on his voice. What was he saying, something about the Minoans?

'You have to hand it to a race where just for fun, the girls and boys took on a sport of bull-jumping, a ritual leaping over the horns of a charging bull!'

At last she had herself in control. 'They couldn't!' Her eyes widened. 'Or could they?'

'All the time! The thing was to face the charging bull, then take a firm grip on the lowered horns and be flung up in the air as the bull tossed. The trick was then to let go of the horns, do a somersault up on to the bull's back and take a flying leap down before it could swerve to charge again!'

'Wow-ee! If that wasn't split-second timing—' She added thoughtfully, 'They seemed very concerned with the ritual thing, especially the symbol of the bull's horns and the double axe.'

He nodded. 'One of the Cretan myths. Seems that Queen Pasiphaë had an unnatural passion for the bulls sacred to Knossos, especially the white ones, because the Priest King

Minos was a creature from a dynasty that had a sky bull for its emblem—am I boring you?'

You could never bore me, Adam. Aloud she said, 'Tell me more. It's fascinating.'

'Right, you've asked for it! Anyways, it seems the Queen produced this bull creature, half man, half bull, and he had to be hidden away in the palace and King Minos persuaded the gods to agree to his demand that once a year, seven boys and seven girls should be sent from Athens to Crete, to be thrown to the Minotaur.'

'Gruesome! What happened to him in the end?'

'Theseus—he was the son of the king of Athens—took pity on the victims and offered to go to Crete himself to kill the monster and put an end to the human sacrifices.'

'Good for him! How did he do that?'

'No problem. It seems that Ariadne, the daughter of King Minos, fell in love with the young man and showed him how to overcome the Minotaur by getting at him through his weakest point. She was right on the ball, handed him a big reel of thread which he was to unwind as he made his way through the corridors of the labyrinth. So after he had felled the monster with a single blow he followed the thread Ariadne had given him and found his way back again. Then he took the young people he'd saved, picked up Ariadne, and left for Athens.'

'Golly,' said Liz, 'that's an exciting story, especially the bit about the Minotaur! Poor old thing, I feel quite sorry for him, locked away for years in a gloomy labyrinth because he was so repulsive-looking. Just as well,' she laughed, 'that it wasn't a true story.'

Adam said slowly, 'It could be. My dad was a great one for doing research on the Greek myths and legends, and he came across a theory that the Minotaur story could be based on real facts.'

She stared at him incredulously. 'No! It couldn't be—'

'Oh, not on the face of it, but you'd be surprised how many of these old legends turn out to be real life happenings disguised in story form so as not to be recognised.'

'Like the old English nursery rhymes,' Liz said, 'that were composed by people who didn't dare come right out and say what they knew of the court people, so they made up rhymes for children to disguise the truth. But the Minotaur story— no, I couldn't go along with that being the real thing.'

'It's just a theory, Liz, but it's got something going for it all the same. Can you picture the scene right here in the palace grounds?' His tone was tinged with enthusiasm. 'It's the night of a great religious ceremony. There's chanting to their adored god Zeus and ritual dancing to the Life Goddess under a Cretan moon. Much, much later that night the religious fervour mounts to a climax and men and women put on their bulls head masks for the ceremonial marriage dance. Suppose, just suppose, Liz, that the Priest King danced, and not only danced with the Moon Priestess, what then?'

A bird's song sounded loud in the stillness and Liz had an eerie sensation of being back in a pagan past. She shook away the impression. 'I'll stick with my myth,' she said.

They wandered down an overgrown path, passing broken stone walls, and when they came in sight of the souvenir store Adam said, 'Let me get you some worry beads. And how about some postcards to send home?'

She flashed him a defiant smile. 'But Crete is my home!' At least, she told herself, I've let him know that I'm not giving up without a struggle. As he made no comment she said, 'It's a thought, all the same, especially the postcards. I've got a girlfriend back in Auckland who's interested in pottery. She's got her own kiln in her backyard, and a picture of those monstrous Ali Baba jars would really make her day. I know she'd never believe the size of them otherwise.'

'And what would you like, Liz? Something to take back from Knossos is a must, you know. Let me—'

This time her smile was the real thing, warm and happy. 'Only if it doesn't cost the earth.' She had a suspicion that the honey-bee pendant she was wearing was far from that category.

'Right! You choose!' They strolled around the display shelves with their replicas of Greek urns, charms to keep away the evil spirits and hand-embroidered bags and muslin blouses. Liz picked up a tiny exquisitely fashioned lyre and plucked the miniature strings. 'Listen,' she said delightedly, 'it really plays!' As with all the souvenirs she had seen in Greece, the articles were of tasteful design and high quality workmanship. At last she selected a ceramic tile picture depicting a cluster of white cottages tumbling down to a sapphire sea, a cobbled street, a donkey. Adam paid the trifling cost of the gift and Liz placed it in her embroidered Greek bag. All at once she was filled with a feeling of high elation born of the unfamiliar surroundings, the golden sunshiny day and, why not admit it, being here with Adam. Why not forget, just for today, that there were problems between them, no reason why they couldn't be happy together as friends, even perhaps—lovers?

The thought was intoxicating. Time slipped swiftly by, and it was with a feeling of regret that Liz got into the car for the homeward journey. As they took the winding road over the hills she mused that she wouldn't mind one little bit if a group of straggling sheep once again delayed their progress. All too quickly, however, they sped over slopes with their sparsely growing olive trees, and past the fields where women herb-gatherers still worked beneath the scorching rays of the sun. Then Adam was drawing up at the hotel. He got out of the car and came around the vehicle to open the passenger door. 'I'll see you home—'

'Really,' she protested, 'there's no need!' *Liar! You're longing for him to stay with you until the last possible moment.*

'It's no use arguing with me, Liz. Haven't you discovered that yet?' As they took the dusty white goat track over the slope he clasped her hand in his, and once again Liz felt her heart lift on a great surge of pleasure. When they reached the shady secluded courtyard she hesitated, looking up at him. 'Coffee? It would only take me a minute to make it.'

'Thanks, no. I've got a man turning up for an appointment—a builder I've got to see about some alterations and extensions I'm planning to the place.'

'Oh!' There was a cold feeling inside her and her wild happiness fell away. How could she have forgotten the reason Adam had insisted on taking her to Knossos, had given such a good pretence of being happy with her? The builder, she thought, a subtle reminder of what he really wanted out of their association. 'If you're depending on me to help you there,' the hot words were out before she could stop them, 'the answer is still "no" so it's no use your trying to get around me!'

The next moment she thought with horror, Why did I throw the words at him like that? But she had to tell him, didn't she? The silence seemed to last for ever.

'I get it!' His tone was steel. 'You've made up your mind about me and there's no way I can talk some sense into you.'

'No, there isn't!' If only her voice didn't have that betraying wobble.

'Why not have at shot a believing in me for a change?' The curt words flicked her raw nerves like a whip. 'You might be surprised! No?' He clasped her roughly to him and for a tense moment she imagined he was about to shake her, for his hands were holding her like steel bands. 'Seeing you're so determined—' he said harshly, and rammed home the words with a hard, punishing kiss. Then abruptly he released her and before she could catch her breath he had swung around on his heel and was striding away.

Liz watched him go, her eyes blinded with unshed tears. Stupid! Stupid! Now she had spoiled everything! Why was she trembling like this? Just because she had sent him away? She put a hand to her bruised lips. She'd had to let him know that she wasn't to be so easily taken in, hadn't she? Was it Adam or yourself that you were trying to impress? the small voice deep in her mind queried and she thrust it aside. A cold feeling of desolation was spreading through her, and scarcely knowing she was moving, she went on leaden feet to the carved wooden door and let herself inside the villa.

That night she lay wakeful, tossing from side to side in her bed through the hot hours, thinking...remembering. She had been so happy with Adam today, so terribly happy that it had been all too easy to lose sight of the real purpose behind his easy friendliness. Maybe, though, he did like her just a little, for herself? Could that be the explanation for his bitter anger at the resentful words she had flung at him? The reason for his punishing kiss? For when you came right down to it, he no longer had any urgent need to employ his tactics of makebelieve lovemaking where she was concerned. He would know only too well that faced as she now was with slender resources and no way of making a living here, soon she would be forced to call it a day, to sell up her beloved Cretan inheritance and return to New Zealand. Why hadn't she realised this before? He had only to wait, or so he would imagine, until she was forced to surrender. To him! After all her fine speeches to the contrary, her misplaced confidence in the future. Never!

CHAPTER EIGHT

SOMEHOW LIZ managed to get through the following few days. Outside the sky was the same piercing blue, the seawater as warm and caressing as ever, but the radiant sparkle of her Crete holiday had lost a little of its lustre. Blame Adam, she told herself, and added the next moment, myself rather for being so stupidly vulnerable to the sheer male attraction of the man!

In an effort to dispel her heavy thoughts she went from room to room in the villa, sweeping and dusting and cleaning—but really, she decided, it was all a waste of effort. For whatever Katina's failings, her jealousy and resentment and swift emotional outbursts, there was no doubt that in line with the reputation of all Greek women, she had kept her dwelling in immaculate condition.

Today as she wandered listlessly over the sand, warm to the touch of her bare feet, Liz's gaze moved instinctively to the deserted taverna. *Her* taverna, she reminded herself, even if it was not in operation—yet. But it would be some time in the future. 'With your state of finances?' a small voice jeered in her mind. 'You're fooling yourself!' It was the truth, she admitted on a sigh. Last night she had spent a long time with ballpoint pen and paper, working out her living costs and allowing for expenses such as souvenirs she must buy for friends at home as well as tours she might want to take to places of interest. For somehow, she tried to rally herself, she must make herself forget Adam, rouse herself to take an interest in this island so rich in mythology. It all added up to the inescapable conclusion that all the money she had in the world consisted of the amount of her return fare to New Zealand plus a small sum that with luck would cover living costs for a month or so longer. A feeling of bravado made her decide to live on her capital, such as it was, for as long as her funds would let her. After that—well, she would worry about that when the time came. One thing was for sure, and that was that never would she surrender her precious inheritance to Adam. After all her fine speeches, her misplaced confidence in the future? Not this girl! She set her soft lips firmly. She wasn't beaten yet, not by a long way. She still had some time left, and by the end of summer...

Opening the door of the taverna, she stood looking around the big room facing the sea. Strangely she felt no sense of emptiness, but rather gained the odd impression that the room was waiting for her to put her plans into action. Her plans...Across the screen of her mind flickered pictures where groups of laughing, happy tourists strolled over the sand to swim in the azure sea, sunbathing on the sand before making their way up to the taverna with its tables and blue and white sun-umbrellas, for welcome refreshments.

The worrying thoughts crowded back to mind. She could no longer hope for any financial help from Kostas, she had already written off that possibility. What *could* she do to solve her problem? Even the Delphic Oracle couldn't answer that one, she thought wryly. But there was no sense in negative thinking. She must take herself in hand, forget Adam and his compelling attraction for her, and concentrate on something constructive. The sooner she started doing something about it the better!

Back in the villa she decided that a swim in the bay was the best way she knew of taking her mind from problems, so she threw off her clothes and pulled on her bikini, still damp from the previous day's dip in the sparkling sea.

She found sunglasses, sun-lotion and a towel and stuffed them into her embroidered Greek bag. Then idly she picked

up a paperback that she had brought with her to read on the
plane trip from New Zealand. Somehow she hadn't yet got
around to reading the romance written by a popular author. She leafed through the pages, then threw the book
aside. Today romantic interludes were the last thing she
wanted to read about—especially, the thought came unbidden, when the cover picture depicted a hero who looked a lot
like Adam, though not half so devastatingly attractive. She
brought her traitorous thoughts up with a jerk. Attractive—and untrustworthy, she reminded herself. Don't forget that, my girl, or you're really in for trouble! She tossed
down the paperback and went into the kitchen, and soon she
was placing in her bag a bottle of fruit drink, bread and
some *feta,* the crumbly goat's cheese she was beginning to
get a taste for. As she moved through the sun-splashed
courtyard she plucked a cluster of white grapes from the
trailing vines, then made her way down to the beach.

On the sun-dappled waters two young men, recent arrivals in Greece she thought, judging by their pallid skins,
sailed by on windsurfers, their attention, thank goodness,
fully taken up with navigating their craft over the tossing
waves. A middle-aged couple, obviously from the nearby
tourist hotel, approached through the screen of oleander
blossoms, and a girl with long blonde hair and a young man
in a T-shirt and jeans, arms entwined, wandered along the
water's edge, oblivious of everything except each other. Liz
was thankful that the bay as usual was almost empty of
holidaymakers, for a pretty girl on her own seemed to invite company. Just to be sure of privacy she decided she
would explore the rocks at the far end of the bay, find a spot
where she could sunbathe and laze away the hours. *And
think of Adam.* She thrust the thought away.

For a long time she wandered along the shoreline,
splashing through wavelets until at last she stumbled on a
strip of sand that ran up between high rocks. In the sheltered spot water lapped around the rocks, leaving sunlit
pools where sea-creatures scuttled about their business. Far

out at sea she glimpsed the glistening curves of dolphins that were lost the next minute amongst the waves. It was very still, the only sound the crying of gulls wheeling high in the translucent blue above and the endless murmur of turning breakers.

Lazily she let the hours slip by. Again and again she climbed over the rocks and made her way down to the tossing sea, swimming and floating on her back, to splash back through the waves, enjoying the touch of salt water on her sunwarmed skin. Then at last she threw herself down on the sand, letting the sun have its way with her as it sparked lights in her drying hair and soothed away the sense of heartache and letdown. At some time during the afternoon she must have fallen into a doze, because when she awoke the sun was low on the horizon, the bays along the coast lost in a shadowy sea-haze. A fishing boat, sponges festooned over deck and rigging, cut across the golden pathway of the setting sun—no doubt, she thought, heading for the port of Heraklion after a day's sponge fishing. Heavens!—dazedly she stared down at the wrist-watch she had fished from her bag—she must have been asleep for hours!

Shaking the sand from her towel, she gathered up her bag and made her way back over the rocks. Soon she was strolling along the beach, splashing along at the edge of the waves while the fresh wind tossed her hair back behind her ears.

As she neared the taverna, the familiar thoughts surfaced. If only she could just get herself started! She paused on the shadowed sand. She remembered having closed the door opening in to the living quarters of the building, yet here it was swinging open!

Cautiously she pushed the door further open and stepped inside. Nothing wrong here. Overcoming a feeling of trepidation, she moved into the kitchen with its wide opening and counter. The next minute she stood still, rooted to the spot in amazement. It couldn't possibly be true—but it was! For fitted neatly into place at one end of the room was a spacious deep-freeze cabinet. At the end of the counter stood a cabinet filled with glass compartments, just waiting to be filled with delectable foods for serving with toasted rolls. At the other end of the counter stood an electric toasting unit. Liz blinked. There was even a big new jar of Nescafé and at its side a capacious glass container filled with orange and lemon juice. Oh, this was quite unbelievable! Swiftly she glanced around the room in search of a docket, but she could find no paper of any sort.

Kostas, she mused. It must be Kostas who was responsible for all this. Only he knew of the dimensions of the stock she required to start up her venture. No doubt, she reflected, the lawyer had decided that helping her out of her financial difficulties would be a small price to pay when it came to forfeiting his own good reputation. No doubt he was feeling apprehensive that Adam, the owner-manager of surely the most impressive tourist hotel in the island, would not keep secret the matter of Kostas having taken advantage of an unprotected woman from another country, and had endeavoured to force his unwelcome attentions on her. She shuddered at the narrow escape she had had from Kostas's advances—something, she admitted to herself, for which she had to be grateful to Adam. It was lucky for her that he had chanced to be here at the moment when she most needed him. 'Lucky?' jeered a voice deep in her mind. 'He knew you were in danger from that amorous lawyer, he tried to warn you about Kostas, but you refused to listen! Adam was protecting you, that's what! Adam...Her soft lips drooped wistfully. If only he didn't hold this overpowering attraction for her! With an effort she jerked her thoughts aside.

But all this meant—the chill thought came unbidden— that she would find herself in Kostas's debt, and suppose he came here to see her once again? This time she could expect no help from Adam. She let out a sigh of relief. But Kostas wouldn't dare, not a second time! Anyway, there would be time enough to worry about the loan when she received his letter in the mail detailing the terms of the agreement, as no doubt she would within a few days. Although she wanted no favours from his hands, she could scarcely send the goods back, since she had no idea where they had come from. All at once her spirits lifted on a wave of excitement. Wouldn't Adam be amazed when she let him know that despite his dire warnings on the subject, she now had a chance of making her own way and following her beloved project through to success after all. She couldn't *wait* to tell him that she was no longer in a position of being forced to surrender her property to him—well, she conceded reluctantly, it's half mine. Definitely, she told herself jubilantly, things were looking up!

She pressed a switch on the deep-freeze cabinet and a tiny red light flashed on. How fortunate she was that electricity was already wired to both villa and taverna—thanks to Adam and the luxury hotel he had had erected on the lonely coast.

She was looking forward already to her moment of triumph when she could tell him that his chances of acquiring the beach properties were now slimmer than ever. Not that he would seek her out again, or she him, but there might be a chance meeting. They lived not far apart, so who knew, they might run into each other. If not, she could always invent an excuse to see him—she would think of something. The prospect was exhilarating. She promised herself that tomorrow she would take a bus trip to the nearest village and visit the market there in search of fresh vegetables, eggs and fish for roll fillings.

Next day she was up early. When she had showered she dressed in the briefest of undergarments and pulled on a crisp sea-green cotton shirtwaister. Seated in front of the mirror she experimented with her hair, drawing it severely back from her forehead and catching it in a burnished knot at the back of her head. There! She looked as businesslike as she could, but it was difficult with unruly curly hair that insisted on flying out in tendrils around her face, not to mention a short, cheeky little nose.

At that moment a sound from the ornately carved door knocker brought her to the entrance, and she opened the door to face a brigand-looking Greek with a villainous moustache, wide trousers and black knee-boots. At his side stood a Greek woman wearing black garments, a dark coif shading the lower part of her sun-dried brown face. But the eyes Liz thought were shrewd and kindly.

'Kalispéra!' Liz uttered one of the few Greek words she knew. 'Come in.'

Smiling broadly, the couple stepped inside and immediately they broke into a spate of Greek, accompanied by excited gesticulations. Bewilderedly, Liz caught two names, Xenia and Nikos. As the flow of words went on, suddenly her uncle's name registered on her mind. 'Wait!'—She hurried from the room and returned with her uncle's photograph. The reaction was immediate. Beaming smiles and excited nods made Liz realise that at least these two people had known her uncle. All at once something clicked in her mind. Were they the married couple who had once lived here and worked with Katina in the taverna?

'Taverna?' she said enquiringly, and the strangers beamed with delight. 'You used to work in the taverna here?'

It was clear to Liz, however, that only the familiar word had registered with them. If only she had taken the trouble to learn something of the Greek language! She threw up her hands, palm uppermost, and the gesture of helplessness had the effect of making the strangers talk volubly in their own language. The next minute they turned and hurried out of the door, and Liz, watching from the window, saw them approach a decrepit-looking car that stood in the driveway. After a short conversation with the driver, the three came hurrying back to the villa. And pray heaven Liz thought, that the driver can speak some English.

It seemed that he did. The driver's name was Spiro, that much she understood. A Greek youth with lively dark eyes and excitable manner, he got through to Liz with the aid of much gesticulating that the middle-aged couple had heard of Liz having taken over the property and had come in the hope that they could return to the living quarters of the taverna and help with the work when the place was once again open to the public. Liz's uncle, it seemed, had promised them the use of the rooms indefinitely and only an unexpected visit to a sick relative at a village on the other side of the island had kept them away so long.

With the help of the interpreter, Liz managed to let them know that they were welcome to the use of the rooms. That she would be glad of their help in the taverna as she would soon be starting up again in business. The only thing was, she would not be serving Greek food.

The last statement brought unbelieving looks and endless explanations, but at last Liz got through to them what she meant. All at once a thought struck her. Katina? The Greek girl did, after all, have some say in arrangements, although Liz hated to admit it. She appealed to the Greek youth. 'Ask them if Katina will agree to their staying here again.'

A vigorous nodding of dark heads and a flood of excited talk make Liz realise that clearly with Katina, there was no problem at all.

'Tell them,' Liz appealed to the youth, 'that they must bring in their bags. That they are very welcome to stay for as long as they like in the taverna, just as when my uncle was here.'

The message, when passed on, brought satisfied smiles and nods, then a wild spate of Greek. It took some time for Liz to understand the import of what the strangers were saying but at last she gathered that they had asked their friend Spiro to take them in his car to the village where they could buy fresh food at the market for the taverna. Could Liz come with them and choose the freshest lettuces and peppers? It was best to be early.

'Fine!' Now it was Liz's turn to show surprise and pleasure.

'Will you tell them,' she appealed to Spiro, 'that I'm ready to go right now.' She picked up the woven baskets she had been about to take with her on her bus trip and went with the others towards the ramshackle, dust-coated car standing in the shade of the oleander bushes.

It was wonderful out in the crystalline, early-morning air, Liz thought. Xenia, a smile on her sun-weathered brown face, was offering her a blue flower plucked from the roadside. As Liz bent her head to sniff the delicate blossom she wondered if the flower had been offered as a guard against car-sickness. A little later, as Spiro sent the car rocketing up a steep incline, she reflected that had she been a bad traveller, she would certainly be in need of the curative properties of a native herb. For the road twisted and turned and the driver travelled at alarming speed, hurtling past a man riding a donkey, and taking a hairpin bend at such speed that they narrowly averted colliding with an approaching tour bus. Clutching the door handle, Liz was relieved when at length they drew up in a small settlement with its cluster of white stone cottages.

She slid out of the car, conscious of an appetising aroma of freshly baked bread that wafted from a stone bakery in the narrow, winding street. Further down the cobbled lane she noticed a small dark store with grocery lines in the window. It seemed, however, that her new friends were headed resolutely in the direction of the open market ahead and soon Liz was swept into the colourful confusion and noisy exuberance of the open-air stalls. Greek sailors were carrying in boxes of freshly-caught fish, red mullet and barbounia, heaping the fish on tables, and there were great woven baskets heaped with the golden Cretan oranges that Liz was certain were like no other oranges in the world. Straight away she purchased some. The next moment she realised that Xenia was frowning and shaking her head disapprovingly. Clearly, Liz thought, she had paid too high a price for the luscious fruit. So from then on she contented herself with indicating to Xenia the crisp lettuces, aubergines, huge tomatoes, peppers and onions, thereby saving herself a lot of drachmas. As a treat she purchased a portion of *kalamarakia,* pieces of young squid cooked in a tasty sauce that she had enjoyed at restaurant meals.

Much later, laden with baskets that overflowed with flour and cooking oil, fruit and vegetables, they took the road back to the villa. When they reached their destination Xenia and Nikos returned to the car to carry in a varied assortment of bags and bundles holding their personal possessions and the young Greek driver, with an impudent grin, threw a kiss to Liz before driving away.

That afternoon she lost no time before beginning her preparations for the opening of the taverna. In the kitchen she prepared rolls that later appeared, fluffy and appetising, from the oven. Now that they had lost the services of the Greek interpreter she imagined there might be some difficulty in explaining to Xenia the tasks she wanted done. It transpired, however, that the Greek woman, although obviously puzzled by the departure from her own traditional dishes, appeared to understand what Liz was trying to get through to her. Before long Xenia was busily slicing hard-boiled eggs and peppers and tomatoes into separate containers.

Outside, seated at one of the tables he had set out in the shade of the canopy, Nikos was fingering his worry beads and occasionally playing his lyre, his rich baritone voice raised in accompaniment to his lively native melodies.

By the end of the day the glass compartments in the cabinet were filled with fresh attractively prepared foods, and crisp freshly baked rolls were cooling on wire racks. Tomorrow, Liz mused, she would put out a notice on the taverna, OPEN, and beside it, FRESH TOASTED ROLLS. With any luck the odd hotel guest would wander in and pass on the word about the café catering for overseas tourists. Just as soon as her venture was firmly established she would let Adam in on her good fortune—and that, she promised herself, would be a moment worth waiting for! Adam...for a moment she stood motionless, dreaming. His kiss, his lips so clean-cut and firm, yet they could curve with humour or tenderness. Strength and tenderness, that was Adam. Aghast, she realised the direction in which her thoughts were moving and amended hurriedly, 'At least, that's what he *seems* like to anyone who doesn't really know him!'

My goodness, she marvelled the following morning, but news travels fast around here! For already guests from the nearby hotel were strolling over the hill and moving through the screen of pink oleander blossoms on their way to the bay below. Soon groups of holiday-clad people were heading for the small room at the end of the taverna that Liz had labelled Changing Room or dropping down on chairs beneath the sun-umbrellas that Nikos had set out on the sand. Before long the new arrivals were swimming and disporting themselves in the sun-sparkled waters of the bay—and everyone knew, Liz told herself gleefully, how fresh air and salt water sharpened the appetite! All at once she realised that groups of laughing, chatting people were approaching the open counter of the taverna and presently she found herself frantically coping with a rush of customers, while all around echoed a variety of accents, Canadian, American, English, even the Australian 'twang'.

As the busy day wore on Liz had time for no more than a quick smile of welcome for her customers as frenziedly she flipped rolls on the rack for toasting and mixed Nescafé in pottery mugs. Indeed, it seemed to her that no sooner had a party carried their trays to one of the tables spilling out on the sand than a fresh group took their place at the crowded counter.

Flushed with the temperature of the room and the heat of the day, Liz's shirt clung damply to her back and perspiration beaded her forehead as she worked on. All at once she became aware of a friendly feminine voice. 'We were so happy,' a charming Canadian woman was saying, 'when our bus courier told us he was taking us to a truly superb swimming beach and a taverna where we could get homecooking. My, but these rolls are just delicious!'

Liz flashed her a smile. 'I'm glad you like them!' Her spirits were soaring. Hadn't Adam told her that in the days when her uncle lived here, tour buses had made regular stops at the taverna that was the only refreshment centre for many miles along the lonely coast? But how, she wondered, could word have got around so swiftly of the re-opening of the taverna on the beach? The next moment she forgot the query in a rush of filling the emptied food compartments in the cabinet.

The following days flew by for Liz in a frenzied effort to keep up with the work. She had little time to think of anything else but the tasks in hand, with time only for a brief dip in the sea after the last customer had left and the doors had been finally closed for the night.

Awakening earlier than usual the next morning, she reflected that this was only the start of the summer and, if customers continued to patronise the taverna at this rate, she would be able to repay the loan Kostas had given her with no trouble at all. Wonderful to think that Adam wouldn't get his way with the property deal, not this time! It was, of course, the patronage of the tour buses that made all the difference to her takings. Something niggled at the back of her mind. How had it happened that the bus driver had known the exact date on which to resume his stop for refreshments? There seemed no answer to the mystery. Put it down to local gossip, or just plain coincidence. One thing, her thoughts ran on, she must recompense Xenia and Nikos for their help at the taverna. Xenia was a wonderful asset, she couldn't manage without her assistance, and Nikos—well, what if he did spend a lot of his time clicking his worry beads and chatting with his friends from the next bay as they sat at a table drinking endless tiny cups of Greek coffee? The fish he brought back after some hours spent in a caique with friends fishing in the bay were a welcome addition to the larder. And the liveliness and verve of his na-

tive songs that he sang in the evenings, to the
accompaniment of his lyre, were enjoyed as much by herself as by customers. Besides, there was something about his
joy of living and unfailing Greek gallantry that she found
hard to resist. The problem was, she mused, that not knowing the Greek language she hadn't a clue as to the amount
of wages she should pay the couple. Katina, of course, could
help her there—but nothing, she vowed, would induce her
to ask help of the other girl.

Adam could advise you about all that, the sneaky thought
came unbidden. He could tell you all you want to know. He
was furious with her, there was no doubt of that, but all the
same he could scarcely refuse to answer a simple question in
the matter of wages for the Greek couple. Besides, hadn't
she promised herself a visit to Adam to let him know of her
fantastic change of fortune? The prospect of scoring a victory over him was intoxicating and she intended to exploit
her opportunity to the full. Tonight she would no longer be
just a girl from down under without family or friends or influence determined to go it alone. A girl whose dreams had
faded, leaving her a temporary citizen on her own property,
in danger of being forced to surrender her inheritance to the
most untrustworthy, arrogant, devastatingly attractive man
she had ever met! A wealthy, self-centred landowner who
could, she wouldn't wonder, afford to buy up any other
property he wanted. Just as he could probably have any
woman he wanted—except her!

She wouldn't take up much of his time, her thoughts ran
on, just a brief visit. He wouldn't get the idea, would he,
that she had come to say she was sorry for the hot accusing
words she had flung at him? It wasn't as if she would be
humbling herself, giving him a mistaken impression that she
wanted to get back to the carefree companionship of their
day together at Knossos. Just a brief business call, she reasoned with herself—that wouldn't hurt, would it?

'Business my foot!' the voice deep in her mind challenged her. 'You know you long for him every day and

night. Any old excuse will serve so long as you can be with him again, even if only for a few minutes!'

Rubbish! she argued with herself. She had to find an answer to her wages problem, didn't she? And there was no reason why she shouldn't go tonight. Any tourists who came strolling down the winding goat track between the olive trees in the blue Cretan twilight would be amply catered for by Xenia, she knew. So why not?

The decision lent impetus to her tasks throughout the long tiring day. At last, as the dinner hour of the tourist hotel approached, the crowd at the taverna began to drift away and Liz pushed back the damp tendrils of hair from her flushed forehead and cleared away plates and coffee mugs and glasses. Later, when she had finished her chores, she approached the Greek woman, and pointed up the darkening slope. 'Hotel,' she said. 'Adam.'

Xenia's sun-wrinkled nut brown face broke into an understanding smile. Vigorously, she nodded her coiffed head in a reassuring gesture. *'Kali nikta!'*

'Goodnight!' Liz smiled in farewell. She knew she need have no qualms about leaving Xenia in charge of the taverna for a short while.

That evening she took her time over preparations for her visit, taking a leisurely shower and letting the water play over her sand-dusted hair. Afterwards she sprinkled fragrant talc liberally over her body. Then, clad in bra and panties, she rifled through her scanty wardrobe. Whatever happened, she mustn't look all dressed up tonight. She'd die, she'd just die, if Adam got the impression that she had prettied herself up especially for his approval, if he took the view that despite their stormy parting she was—well, interested in him.

'Aren't you?' jeered the small voice deep in her mind.

She thrust it aside and endeavoured to concentrate on what she would wear tonight. In the end she settled for a simple navy-blue T-shirt and white slacks. There, she told herself when she was dressed, that shouldn't give him any mistaken notions about the reason I've come to see him. Especially if I leave my face free of make-up and tie my hair back from my face with a ribbon for coolness.

Idly, as she slipped her feet into white thonged sandals, she mused that as a rule when a girl got herself ready for an important date she took endless pains to look her best—for him. But not this girl! All she wanted of the meeting was to have her moment of triumph, see the shock and disbelief in Adam's eyes when she let him in on her incredible news.

And yet—she paused at the mirror for a final glance—it was odd that tonight, for all her lack of feminine enhancements, she looked different from usual, her face lit with an inner excitement, lips soft and tremulous, cheeks faintly flushed—*like a girl in love.* The thought came from nowhere. What was she thinking? she derided herself, and moved to the bureau to pick up the golden pendant that Adam had given her. The bee with a sting, she reflected wryly. The tiny stylised bee held for her a fascination she couldn't explain. Tonight the jewelled eyes at the end of their fine gold wires seemed to wink at her under the light. Why not? they seemed to beam a message. What harm could it do?

Still she hesitated. The fine gold chain with its glowing ornament would complement perfectly the dark navy-blue top she was wearing, but because she was wearing his gift would he think—? What did she care what Adam thought? Swiftly she drew the chain around her throat, pushing aside the long fall of dark hair in order to fasten the clasp. She comforted herself with the thought that if Adam should have any ideas that sentiment for him had impelled her to wear his gift, the news she had to tell him tonight would soon disillusion him on that score. She closed the door behind her and went out into the star-ridden night.

Outside in the shadowed courtyard cicadas piped their summer song, taking her back to her own country. But on the other side of the world the cicadas would long have gone, chased away by the chill of winter. This was Crete, land of savage splendour and ancient pagan gods. Where high in the velvety night sky alien stars blazed in place of the familiar golden kite of the Southern Cross hanging over the Pacific Ocean. And all that mattered to her was Adam. She scarcely realised she was hurrying until her sandals felt rough to her bare feet and she paused on the goat track to shake away any sandy soil. Why was she hurrying? she asked herself. Only because she couldn't *wait* to see Adam's face when she told him her news.

All at once she was struck by a dismaying thought. Suppose he should chance to be away from home tonight? She thrust the unwelcome possibility aside. She had been so lucky, surely nothing could go wrong now! Even if he has heard rumours of the taverna being open again I still want to see him, to tell him about it myself, she thought.

As she came over the top of the rise she could see the windows of the high building below ablaze with light, and soon she was hurrying across the wide concrete surround of the hotel and into the foyer, hoping all the time that tonight Katina would not be on duty there. Once again, however, luck was with her, because a Greek girl who was seated at the reception desk, answered Liz's enquiry with a smile.

'Yes, he is in, I know,' she said in perfect English. 'Come with me and wait in the lounge while I tell him you are here.' Liz went with the Greek girl into the vast lounge room with its deep luxurious seating and great floor-to-ceiling windows looking out on a dark turbulent sea. As she went on, heads turned to watch the progress of the girl whose wide excited eyes and softly parted lips radiated an air of youth and vitality.

Liz realised that groups of guests were scattered around the immense room. Dark-eyed, elegantly gowned Greek women and foreign tourists enjoying a brief stay at the luxurious hotel on their tour of the Greek islands, expensively gowned women and men wearing light-coloured linen suits.

Liz, seating herself in one of the deep upholstered chairs in a corner of the room, tried not to show her awareness of the admiring glances beamed in her direction by middle-aged men standing at the bar and a young Greek waiter who was carrying drinks on a tray. Even a group of Greek businessmen seated at a nearby table had paused in the clicking of their worry beads to eye her appreciatively. For heaven's sake, was she the only young girl in the entire room? A swift glance around her told her that she was right in her assumption. But of course, she mused, the tour buses taking guests on sightseeing expeditions over the island would be patronised by older folk with time on their hands. This lavishly appointed hotel with its marble entrance hall and spacious grounds would be way beyond the price range of young people with packs on their backs making their own way through the Greek Islands.

The next moment she forgot everything else in the room, for Adam was striding towards her, an impressive masculine figure. Tonight, seeing him wearing a formal suit, it struck her that he looked every inch the owner of his luxurious domain. Authoritative, assured, a man who was accustomed to giving orders—except where she was concerned, of course!

'Liz!' At the warmth in his voice her heart gave a great leap, then settled again. The way he was smiling towards her, the deep soft look in his eyes, anyone would think that he was more than delighted to see her. Anyone who didn't really know him, that was, she reminded herself in the next moment.

He dropped down in a chair facing her. 'Great to see you!' The expression in his eyes underlined the commonplace words.

Just in time the thought came to her that there might be good reason for the warmth of his welcome. Could it be that he was expecting her to say 'Sorry, Adam' for the accusing words she had flung at him at their last meeting? Or more likely he was of the opinion she had come here to let him know that the property deal could go through after all.

'I didn't expect to see *you* tonight.' He spoke lightly, but his eyes met hers gravely.

Liz shifted uneasily, for the unspoken words 'after the way we parted' hung between them. She ignored the unspoken implication of his remark and rushed into speech. 'I thought you'd be surprised!' She smiled up at him and thought how easy it was to smile tonight. The difficult thing was to keep the triumph from showing in her eyes. 'I had to see you,' she grinned, 'on business! Would you believe?'

Instantly he was alert, the grey eyes that seemed to see so much more than she wanted them to fixed on her face.

'I just wanted to tell you,' the dancing light in her eyes intensified and she couldn't keep the note of elation from her voice, 'that I won't be needing those worry beads you bought me in Knossos after all!'

'No?' His voice was careless as though he were scarcely interested in her affairs, but there was a deep attentive look in his eyes. 'Come into a fortune, from another uncle, is that it?'

She laughed merrily. 'As good as! You'd never believe what's happened!'

'Try me.' At the softness and warmth of his glance, almost she could believe he was really interested in her news, regardless of how it might affect his own interests.

'You know all those electrical goods I needed for starting up the taverna again? Well,' she announced breathless, 'I've got them all now—the lot!'

She nodded excitedly. 'I've got the OPEN sign on the taverna already! It was after our trip to Knossos—' hastily she glossed over the day of such happiness that it now seemed unreal, a day that had ended on such a bitter note. 'I was down on the beach all day and when I got back just before dark there were tyre marks all around the taverna, and when I went inside—wait for it—there was a deep-freeze and a frozen food cabinet and the toasting machine I needed, all installed and ready to go. And exactly,' she cried in triumph, 'the measurements I'd written out. So of course I knew who'd sent it all.'

At his interrogative lift of dark brows she said promptly, 'Kostas, of course. He must have had the whole load sent out from the store at Heraklion. It's as clear as can be. There's just no one else it could be! Know something, Adam?' Without waiting for his comments she ran on. 'He must have had second thoughts about letting me have his personal loan to buy the things I needed to start up in business. I guess,' she added slowly, 'I have you to thank for it all really.'

'How so?'

She said thoughtfully, 'I've been thinking over all you told me about Greek men not thinking kindly about a countryman of theirs who takes advantage of a woman on her own. Kostas must have been furious at being caught out doing just that. And then for you to knock him down must have hurt his dignity more than his chin! I bet when he got back to his office he got to thinking things over and decided the best way out of the situation was to let me have the loan I wanted. A lot better for him than your letting on to his business friends in Heraklion—' She broke off. 'You haven't, have you?'

He shook his head. 'Not me.'

'Well, he won't know that. For all he knows he might be losing a lot of his clients. I figured it out that the only way he could try to make things right would be to get on the phone, put the order for me through, and have the stuff delivered. I looked all over the place for a receipt with his name on it, but I couldn't find even a delivery slip. Not that I'm worrying about that, he must have paid for it all or the firm wouldn't have delivered it to me. I expect he'll post me the papers to sign before long. I shouldn't imagine,' she flashed a smile, 'that he'll be calling on me at the villa this time! Aren't I lucky!'

'Congratulations!' There was an enigmatic note in his tone.

'That's just the start of the good news,' she ran on. 'You should have seen the crowd that came over the hill to swim in the bay and order refreshments of filled toasted rolls at the taverna! There were ever so many, I think they came from your hotel here. And then, later in the afternoon,' her blue-grey eyes glowed with excitement, 'a tour bus arrived and it seems that's going to be on a regular basis, three times a week!' She clapped her hands together. 'It's fantastic! And if that wasn't enough for one day, who do you think turned up on my doorstep? Nikos and Xenia!' Her laughter rang out. 'Nikos looked like a brigand—that ferocious-looking moustache of his and knee-boots and the beaded black veil thing on his forehead that all the older Crete men seem to wear. We finally got things sorted out with the help of a young Greek boy who'd driven them to the villa in his car. I remembered your telling me about the couple who used to help my uncle and—' she hesitated over the name, 'Katina, in the taverna. Nikos and Xenia must have kept an ear to the ground to know just the time when they might be needed again. Now we're getting along fine. Xenia's catching on fast about preparing different sorts of food from what she's used to and Nikos has promised to catch lots of fish for the table. Me, I'm learning a lot about how to hand customers their change in drachmas.'

'Good for you!' Once again she surprised an unreadable look in his eyes. 'So you're in business?'

She nodded happily. 'As from now! Things have just fallen into my lap! I really can't believe my good luck! Those Greek gods must really be on my side!'

'Looks like it.' His tone was flat, almost uninterested. Indeed, Liz mused, if she hadn't known how absurd was the thought, she could imagine that his interest was centred on her rapt young face rather than in what she was telling him. Unable to sustain his brilliant gaze any longer, she dropped her eyes and tried to pick up the threads of her story.

'This calls for a drink,' he was saying, and beckoned to a young Greek waiter on the other side of the room. 'What would you like?'

'Not retsina.' Liz wrinkled her nose at him. 'I just can't get used to the pine flavour. Oh, I know there's a Cretan saying that it takes six glasses before you know if you like it, but one was enough for me!'

Adam grinned. 'There's a native wine they make from *rosaki* grapes grown around here. I think you'll like it.'

'I'll try it. Well, that's the good news!' A flush of excitement burned high on her delicate cheekbones and she drew a deep breath. Now for that long-awaited moment of triumph! 'And now for the bad!' She ran on in a rush of words, 'I won't be selling out to you after all!'

'No?' He appeared entirely unperturbed, she thought bewilderedly. His air of polite indifference was maddening, sparking her to defiance. The impulsive words fell from her lips before she could stop them. 'You don't seem very disappointed about all this?'

His lean dark face was impassive. 'Should I be?' he enquired blandly.

Liz looked at him suspiciously. He was being deliberately obtuse, of course. Oh, she might have known he would give nothing away. Conscious of a sense of letdown, she eyed him uncertainly. The speeches she had carefully rehearsed fled from her mind and she murmured, 'But what about you?' The way in which he was leaning back in his chair, regarding her with cool detachment, was making her thoughts churn in confusion.

'I'll get by.' At the cool amusement in his tone she realised how utterly naïve she had been ever to have imagined that Adam would give her the satisfaction of betraying the slightest sign of emotion at her news. Stupid, stupid of her not to have realised that this arrogant, oh-so-attractive male would never admit to her having scored a victory over him.

With a sense of relief she turned to find the waiter setting down wine glasses on a low table between them. When the young Greek had left them, Adam raised his glass. 'Let's drink to the success of your taverna, shall we?'

She gathered herself together and managed a bright smile. 'In the Cretan way?'

'What else?'

The crystal goblets rang like a bell as they curved their hands around glasses in the traditional gesture and clinked them together, at the same time murmuring the customary *'Hyrr, hyrr,'* rolling the 'Rs' in sibilant accents echoing the vibrations of wine-filled goblets. It was a sound that had the effect of sending them both into laughter.

Could it be the sweet and relaxing wine, Liz found herself wondering a little later, or was it the heady sensation of finding herself free to put her plans into action, that was going to her head, making her say to Adam, 'I just can't believe it! You don't seem to be one little bit sorry about my staying on in Crete.'

His eyes, compelling and enigmatic, held hers. 'Why should I be disappointed about that?'

All at once she was flustered. 'I—I—' She tried to gather her thoughts together. 'That wasn't the only reason I came to see you tonight.'

'No?' Deep in his eyes tiny flames flickered and something in his gaze made her forget all about Nikos and Xenia and the matter of their wages. Dropping her eyes, she studied the white wine in her glass. 'It's funny,' the words seemed to fall from her lips without her volition, 'but I got the idea you were anxious to have those properties in the bay.'

'That's right.' His tone was laconic. 'I still am, actually.'

'But you don't seem to mind a scrap about my not selling out?'

He set down his wine glass. 'Why should I worry?' There was a mocking intonation in his tone. 'Sooner or later I'll have it. Just a matter of waiting.'

'W-waiting?' She stared at him, nonplussed. 'What on earth for?'

His glance held hers until she felt she was drowning in those brilliant depths. 'For you to say "yes", of course.'

She looked at him in bewilderment. 'You'll be wasting your time, then! You'll never persuade me to let them go, so you might just as well give up and call it a day right now.'

'Oh, I wouldn't say that,' he returned with deceptive mildness, 'I've got a lot of faith in my success with plan number two.' His bright gaze challenged her. 'I'll be getting it off the ground any minute now.'

Startled, she regarded him in amazement. 'You're having me on! But if this brilliant project of yours has anything to do with me—'

'Sure has!' His mocking grin sparked her to say with spirit, 'Then you haven't a hope!'

'Want to bet?' He studied her flushed face. 'I'll tell you something, young Liz, I usually get what I want.'

'Not this time,' flared Liz. Some devil inside her made her add, 'If it's anything like that last plan of yours—' She must have imagined the look of hurt in his eyes, she told herself. He couldn't really care about the barb she had hurled at him, not Adam. The silence seemed to last forever and she thought with an odd pang of regret, why did I say that? But he deserved it, didn't he? She regarded him from under her eyelashes and said lightly, 'Anyway, what is this big project of yours?'

Unexpectedly he grinned. She *must* have imagined that fleeting glimpse of pain in his eyes. 'Perfectly simple, really, but it's got great potential—if I can pull it off.'

Liz said, pouting, 'You might explain it to me, seeing it's such a master plan. Or don't you think,' she enquired laughingly, 'that I know enough about Greek hotel management to understand what you're aiming for?'

There was a veiled expression in his eyes. 'Oh, you'll understand this one all right.'

'Well, then—?'

'Later, later,' he waved the matter away with a lift of a sun-bronzed hand. 'Don't rush me!'

His soft laugh was infuriating. 'Let's just wait and see. Meantime,' he got to his feet and the touch of his hand on her bare arm sent a tremor running through her, 'let's dance, shall we?'

Liz was only too glad to put an end to the conversation, for she sensed in Adam a power and determination that undermined all her defences. And what if she should betray to him how vulnerable she was?

As they moved together to the rhythm of a popular dance number Liz's thoughts were in a tumult. Oh, it was heavenly to be with Adam tonight with no complications to come between them. From now on, she thought with elation, whenever he looks at me with the special glance he seems to keep just for me, it *will* be for myself. The unfamiliar feeling was intoxicating, and all at once nothing else in the world mattered but just being here, with him.

It was several dances later when she turned to him with a smile. 'I only meant to stop for a few minutes. I'd better be getting along. I'm a working girl now, remember?'

'If you wish.' A little to her disappointment Adam made no attempt to detain her. But he would see her back along the winding track through the olive trees, she consoled herself. Her senses were whirling and an irrational happiness surged through her. When he kisses me good-night in the courtyard I'll let him know, in the subtle ways that every woman knows, that from now on everything will be different between us, she thought. No more conflicts over property, that would be all in the past, for who could give serious thought to that ridiculous idea of Adam's that he called his 'plan number two'? No more subterfuges, she promised herself. Adam, his arms closing around her in the shadows of the deserted courtyard. Her senses quickened at the thought.

They were moving over the expanse of carpeted floor and had reached the foyer when an imperious feminine voice halted them. 'Adam!'

Liz's gaze went to the marble staircase where a woman leaned over the balustrade, looking down on them. Liz had a swift impression of a tall woman, slim as a wand, a dark-haired beauty wearing a low-cut black dress shot with rippling silver.

'Don't be long, will you?' It was, Liz thought with a stab of the heart, a possessive, *intimate*-sounding voice. 'Don't forget the tiz that Bill and Lena got into the last time we kept them waiting.'

Adam glanced up towards the glittering figure above, then gave a brief nod. 'It's okay.' He turned to lay a hand on Liz's arm, guiding her out through the imposing entrance and out into the soft darkness of the night.

Liz felt cold shivers creep through her body. All at once it came to her with painful clarity what a fool she had been to burst in on Adam as she had done, without warning. To have imagined in her blind trusting way that merely because tonight he had seemed warm and friendly, ignoring the circumstances of their previous stormy parting, that he really wanted to be with her, that he was even glad that she was staying on Crete, no matter the effect on his property plans. Oh, she might have known, she mused bitterly, the formal suit he was wearing, his familiar attitude towards the exquisitely dressed sophisticated-looking woman who radiated an air of self-confidence—and something else, a close relationship with Adam. She must have been crazy—the bleak thoughts rushed through her mind—to have imagined he cared for her a lot, even when there was no likelihood of her selling him her stake in this Greek island. Damn, damn, damn! she thought, hating herself for her impulsive gesture in coming here to see him tonight.

As they reached the edge of the lighted area she wrenched herself around to face him. 'Don't trouble to see me back to the villa!' Even to her own ears her laugh held a forced note. 'It's not as if I don't know the way!'

'No trouble.' He linked his hand in hers, and vibrations ran along her nerves. Determinedly she fought off the weakness. She was vulnerable to his touch, it was something that was beyond her control, and she had a sneaking suspicion that he was well aware of the effect he had on her.

The crashing disappointment she had suffered hardened her resolve and she snatched her hand from his grip. ''Night!' She was off, running up the narrow dusty track, not daring to glance back over her shoulder for fear he was following her. The next minute the query was answered for her as she tripped over a loose stone and fell to the ground, crushing the wildflowers in her headlong fall. Even before she had time to get to her feet, he had caught her up in his arms. He held her at arm's length, his tone anxious. 'You're all right, Liz?'

'Of course I am,' she mumbled, and put up a hand to wipe away the dust from her cheek.

'Sure?' His tone was warm and solicitous. But pity, she told herself, was something she couldn't take, not from him. 'You don't need to waste your time!' she flared, and struggled to free herself. He merely held her closer to him and once again she fought the excitement of his nearness, the delicious lassitude that threatened to take over. Think of his girlfriend, she told herself wildly, the scintillating figure in black and silver, the one he can't wait to get back to. It worked, giving her sufficient strength of mind to drag herself back to sanity. 'I don't need you!' she flung at him.

'Stop arguing, Liz, I'm coming with you!' There was no breaking the pressure of his fingers on her own. When they reached the courtyard he still held her hand in his. 'There's not much wrong with you, Liz, not when you bound along that goat track like a mountain goat. What was all the rush to get here?'

She said stiffly, 'I know you're in a hurry to get back tonight—'

'Me?' For a moment he sounded puzzled. Then, 'Oh, Karen, you mean?' His tone was careless. 'She'll keep.'

He was impossible! she thought angrily. Clearly a man who was so attractive to women he could have any one he wanted. He had the nerve to keep a glamorous-looking girl waiting, and to think nothing of it. He used women for his own advantage, it seemed in the same way that he had used her.

When they reached the shadows of the courtyard she wrenched her fingers from his grasp. 'Thanks for seeing me home,' she muttered and slipped away.

'Liz!' The disarming softness of his tone caught her unawares and she turned to face him. 'Haven't you forgotten something?' and before she could make an answer, 'This.' The next moment his lips sought hers in a kiss that sent fire running through her veins. Over the tumult of emotion surging through her she willed herself to passivity, while all the time her traitorous body urged her to respond to his ardent caress. At last she pulled herself free. 'I've got to go,' she murmured in a low voice, and sped towards the dark doorway.

'Wait! Come back! There's something—'

But now she was determined not to allow herself to surrender to Adam's beguiling tone or to the emotions he so easily aroused in her. Her hands were shaking, so she had difficulty in fitting the key into the lock, but at last she let herself in to the darkened house and slammed the heavy door shut behind her. Not that she need have troubled herself over him making an attempt to follow her, she realised the next minute. By now he would be taking the twisting track over the hill.

Tears trickled down her dust-smeared cheeks and she brushed them away with the back of her hand. To Adam she was no more than a stubborn girl who stood in the way of his money-making schemes, someone who had held him up tonight and caused him to be late for his dinner date with the glamorous-looking woman who had hailed him from the stairway of the hotel. Her heavy thoughts ran on. As a putdown to Adam her meeting with him tonight had been a miserable failure. He hadn't cared, he just hadn't cared about her or the property sale—not any more. All he was interested in was the eye-catching woman who spoke to him with a *belonging* note in her voice.

Liz turned away, sick at heart. She might have known that Adam would have women as friends, companions—lovers? He was a type of man to whom women would be attracted—look who's talking, she told herself bitterly. The lean dark intelligent face and male magnetism that you could almost *feel* when you were with him was a combination hard to resist, didn't she know it? So why did she feel this sickness in her midriff as if she had suffered a dreadful blow? Slowly she went to her room. Funny, she now had what she had so desperately desired, a chance to stay on in Crete to make her own way and be financially independent. Somehow, though, the matter no longer seemed of great importance. Only Adam mattered, and she knew now that he wasn't worth the anguish and heartache she had let herself in for. Somehow, she told herself on a sob, she would just have to forget him—if she could!

CHAPTER NINE

Now Liz was thankful for the long hours she had to spend working in the taverna. In the rare periods when no customers waited at the counter to be attended to, there was always cleaning to be seen to. And the baking of rolls . . . and more rolls. When the last customer had gone Liz ran down to the dark sea for a quick dip, then, too exhausted for anything else, she fell into bed. One thing, she told herself bleakly, the hard daily grind kept her from dwelling endlessly on thoughts of Adam—or did it actually work out that way? Not really, for when she was asleep she couldn't help herself, dreaming that Adam was with her once again, standing looking down at her from his lean height, his gaze warm with tenderness and *real* feeling for her.

At odd moments during the day she gave a passing thought to the letter she was expecting daily from Kostas, but so far she had received no notification from him regarding his loan. Maybe next month?

One day she was horrified to realise that she had been so absorbed in hard physical toil and her own emotional problems, she hadn't yet kept her promise to her friend and neighbour at home, to deliver the gifts and messages from Angeliké to the family in their mountain village. Swiftly she scribbled a note to Angeliké's mother, telling her she would be coming to visit her very soon and then she slipped the letter in the post. Maybe, she thought, Xenia would tell her how to get to the village. When later in the day she enquired of the Greek woman, Xenia broke into a spate of Greek, all the time gesticulating wildly. Liz was lucky, though, because a customer, a middle-aged man who happened to be standing at the counter, had taken in Liz's perplexed expression.

'Could I be of help? I happen to know the language.'

Liz turned towards him thankfully. 'Oh, please!'

'Your friend is trying to tell you that the bus for the village you mentioned leaves from the hotel stop around the point every Tuesday around two o'clock.'

'Tuesday? That's tomorrow—super!' As Liz poured coffee for her customer her thoughts were busy. 'I wonder,' she smiled across at the English tourist standing at the counter, 'would you mind explaining to Xenia, she's my helper, that I'll be going to the village tomorrow and leaving her in charge here?'

He smiled in assent. Indeed, Liz thought a few moments later, there were smiles all around.

In the morning she stowed in her travel pack the gifts that Angeliké had entrusted to her for the Cretan family. She arrived very early at the bus stop and chances were she mused, that she would have a long wait. She might even have an accidental meeting with Adam. The thought came without her volition and she thrust it away. As it happened, however, while waiting in the shade of the hotel balcony, she saw neither Adam nor Katina but only a crowd of tourists who alighted from a coach.

The local bus, when it pulled up beside her, was crowded with peasants, the women laden with an assortment of bundles. Liz pushed her way past bearded Greek Orthodox priests in their dark robes and tall black hats and found a seat at the side of a coiffed swarthy-faced woman whose bright smile revealed blackened teeth. In the noisy exuberance of the passengers, speech was impossible even had she known the language, so she nodded and smiled to a peasant woman seated opposite her who was holding towards her a flower plucked from a bunch of red and white lilies that had no doubt been gathered from her own garden this morning. Liz was becoming accustomed to this national characteristic of the Greek peasants to enjoy giving pleasure to strangers. Nor did their goodness of heart extend only to strangers, she reflected, eyeing the peasant women with their labelled bundles, each of which was no doubt a gift for a friend or neighbour. A bunch of grapes maybe, or a pot of home-made jam or a jar of olives.

As they moved up the sun-dried slopes Liz was only vaguely aware of the scarlet poppies and golden daisies that flourished alongside the roadside or the sails of turning windmills, white against the blue of distant hills. As always when she had time to dream, her mind wandered to Adam. Once, she had thought of him in the same way as the early Cretans had regarded their pagan god Zeus, someone to be looked up to, to trust, to love. *Don't think of him.*

They had been travelling for a long time under a scorching sun when she realised they were approaching a small village. Presently, together with the rest of the voluble, chattering passengers, Liz got out of the vehicle and moved into the dim interior of an ornately decorated church with its time-worn altar, richly coloured icons and flickering candles. Something of the silence and peacefulness of the age-old place of worship eased a little her sense of heartache.

It was later, when they had left the main highway and turned into a rough metal road, that Liz realised there was another vehicle on the lonely road. Idly watching, she saw that the red car had passed them to speed ahead, then pull up at the side of the road. For some reason, the driver was honking his horn, evidently as a signal for the bus to stop. Liz couldn't see any more, for as the bus ground to a halt, excited passengers left their seats and crowded around the driver, talking and gesticulating wildly. Lost in her own heavy thoughts, Liz wasn't terribly interested in what was happening, then all at once her heart gave a great leap, then settled again. Adam! She would know his deep vibrant tones anywhere! All at once she became aware that all heads were turned in her direction and everyone was talking at once.

Swiftly she got up from her seat and the excited, chattering passengers gave way to her as she made her way forward. She was conscious of Adam's tall figure, his searching glance moving in her direction, then before she knew what was happening, he had clasped her hand in a no-nonsense grip and was drawing her down the bus step and out on to the rough road.

From the vehicle she could hear shouts and laughter and loud calls in Greek. 'What on earth—?'

He was practically dragging her across the road and towards his car. 'In with you!'

But Liz refused to be manhandled in this autocratic way. She had had enough already of Adam's high-handed treatment. 'I don't know that I want to come with you,' she shook herself free of his detaining arm. 'What's all this about anyway?'

'You're coming to the village with me,' his tone was curt, 'it will be much more comfortable for you than that crowded bus.'

Still she hung back. 'I don't mind the bus. I rather like it.'

'Well, make up your mind.' His mouth was set and stern. 'Are you coming with me or not?' The staccato tone, so different from the soft accents she had known, sparked her to snap back.

'I haven't much option, have I?' For at that moment the bus lumbered past, the passengers hanging out of windows to wave and shout and call out in a flood of Greek.

'Not unless you want to walk the rest of the way,' Adam agreed. 'It's quite a step back to the villa too,' he added offhandedly.

'Oh, all right, then!' She made to hurry into the car, but he was before her, flinging open the passenger door and when she had seated herself, tucking her white pleated skirt out of the way.

They moved along the road through a cloud of dust raised by the vehicle ahead and Liz, stealing a glance towards the strong masculine profile at her side, decided that he didn't

deserve being spoken to! First of all he had let her down in
that sneaky underhanded way, then he had told her nothing about his girlfriend (don't forget that, her heart reminded her). Now he had abducted her from a public
vehicle—well, she thought crossly, you could call it an ab-
duction. He made her so *mad!* she fumed silently. On top of
all that, she thought rebelliously, he was ignoring her, staring at the road ahead without even a polite word, let alone
giving her an explanation for his extraordinary conduct.
Anger mounted in her. But she would soon change all that,
she vowed, and heard her own voice saying too breathlessly, too quickly, 'Dragging me off the bus in that high-
handed way—' The laugh she had intended to be mocking,
a trifle sarcastic, sounded even to her own ears, affected and
stupid. 'Heaven only knows,' she flung at him accusingly,
'what the Greek passengers thought of it all!' She glanced
up at him and her traitorous heart turned over. His strong
profile looked as though it was carved in bronze. With an
effort she brought her mind back to his cool tones. 'They
wouldn't have missed that little episode for worlds! They
were enjoying every moment of it!'

'What!' she gasped. 'But you—you—' she sputtered indignantly, 'for all they knew you might have been a complete stranger to me!' She warmed to her theme. 'The way
it looked you could have been intending to hold me to ran-
som or—or anything! You could see they were excited about
it!'

'Oh, they were excited all right! All that hullabaloo and
waving to us out of the bus window.' He threw her a sardonic glance. 'All the same, they didn't look all that worried about you, would you say?'

'I guess not,' she admitted reluctantly. Now that she came
to consider the matter the Greek peasants had had more the
air of a wildly excited audience witnessing an exciting drama
than people who were horrified at the unexpected happening and fearful of her welfare at the hands of a stranger.
Curiosity got the better of her and she couldn't stop the

words that had risen to her lips. 'Well then, you know the language, what did they imagine was happening?'

'They weren't too surprised. This sort of thing happens every now and again with the mountain folk of Crete. They still stick to their ancient ways. They're a bit out of touch with modern living and the primitive customs still hold good. It was a new twist to an old story, though, for them to see it all happen on a bus!' Adam's voice was deadpan, his gaze fixed on the rough metal road ahead as he swung the car around a hairpin bend.

Liz was so astonished at his words that she forgot her anger. She looked up at him with puzzled eyes. 'What on earth do you mean?'

'Oh, they just thought I was abducting you!'

'Well,' exclaimed Liz on an outraged breath, 'of all the—'

'It's quite a custom,' Adam cut in smoothly, 'when you get far enough away from the cities. You'd be surprised how many Cretan marriages start off with the bride being carried off by force by her suitor. It does settle the question, though it can cause a feud between families that can go on for generations!'

'I don't wonder!' Liz cried indignantly. The next moment, becoming aware of the twist of amusement in Adam's well-shaped lips, she hastened to change the subject. 'How far,' she asked breathlessly, 'do we have to go before we reach the village?'

He shrugged. 'Your guess is as good as mine, but I'd give it another thirty minutes. It's hard to say for sure—people living up here go along on Cretan time, say the time it takes to smoke a cigarette or for the sky to darken.'

Liz was scarcely listening, relieved out of all proportion to the cause by his change of subject. Her cheeks burned hotly at the thought of his explanation of the Cretan peasant's view of the affair. And to think she had begged him to tell her!

A little later she voiced the question that tugged at her mind. 'What I can't understand is how you knew that I was making this trip today.'

'That's an easy one to answer. I just happened to take a phone call from your friend up in the mountains. Seems she didn't get your letter saying you were planning a visit to them until today and she was hoping to be able to stop you from making the trip today. They wanted to arrange for someone to meet you at the village and take you on to their house, but I told her it was too late as you'd already have taken off in the bus that I could see disappearing in the distance. So then I accepted their warm invitation to come along too. Friendly people, the Cretans. They wouldn't understand anyone turning down their hospitality, so what could I do?'

Liz felt her cheeks flame with the humiliating realisation that he had put himself out for her, and once again she found herself in his debt. The thought made her say crossly, 'You needn't have troubled—'

A shrug of broad shoulders. 'No trouble. I happened to have a free day and I've always promised myself a run in the car to take a look at one of those mountain villages. Up till now I've never made it.'

She looked at him suspiciously, but his expression told her nothing. If that really was the reason for his chasing after her, she didn't feel so bad about his making the long trip on her behalf. But there was something about his blandly innocent stare that said, 'You'd better believe me.' She said very low, 'So long as that was the only reason—'

His sideways glance was disconcerting. 'What else?'

Stupidly, she tried for the last word. 'I'd have been quite all right, you know. I'm used to getting around by myself.'

'In the Cretan mountains?' There was a satirical note in his voice.

All at once she felt a pang of contrition. She supposed she did owe him some gratitude for his action today. She murmured reluctantly, 'Well, thanks anyway.'

'My pleasure.' The edge to his tone gave the lie to the words. Oh well—Liz stared resentfully at the hills with their silvery green foliage of olive tress—she had tried to thank him. Why couldn't he come right out with it and tell her the truth, that being forced into spending the entire day with her was the last thing in the world he would have chosen to do, and only a sense of politeness had impelled him to make the journey?

He seemed to tune in on her thoughts. 'Interesting country up this way. Like I said, it's all new to me.'

She flung him a swift upward glance, but his gaze was fixed on the curve of road ahead. 'Who knows,' he added in a careless tone, 'you might be glad of an interpreter around when you get amongst all those relations of your neighbour at home.'

Swiftly she dismissed the offer.

'Oh, I don't think there'll be any problem about that,' she said airily. 'Angeliké told me that her brother has lived for years in America and he'll be able to pass on all the messages I've brought for the family.'

Adam's mouth tightened. 'I get it.'

There was a cool politeness about his tone that told her he was still angry with her. Why then, she wondered confusedly, had he gone out of his way to see her to her destination today? It was just another thing about him she would never understand. Just because he insisted on accompanying her to the mountain village, she told herself hotly, that wasn't to say that they could get back to their old footing, and if he was expecting her to feel differently towards him, he would soon find out his error. To drive home her point she maintained a chilly silence.

They had been driving inland for some miles. Now there was nothing to be seen but the mountain crags, the only sound the faraway tinkle of sheep bells. Once, a great golden eagle swooped from a high crag, dark against the sun. It was a remote, unreal world, Liz mused. The next moment she was wrenched from her thoughts by Adam's voice. 'Not far from here, down a ravine, is the cave where, according to the myths, Zeus was born. Interested in Cretan mythology?'

Liz forgot all about maintaining a dignified silence. 'Oh, I am! I am! Who could help being interested?' She gazed out at the mountainous country around them. 'In places like this it would be easy to believe in those pagan gods and goddesses and nymphs. I'll never forget the frescoes at Knossos with pictures of the priest-king and the bull-leaping—'

'And the pendant of the honey-bee,' drawled Adam, his gaze fixed on the white dusty road. 'You liked the original when you saw it in the museum at Heraklion?'

'Oh yes, *yes!*' He had taken her by surprise. 'It's an exquisite thing, and the funny part of it is that it could easily have been made by a present-day goldsmith.'

'But you don't wear the replica,' his cold voice probed. 'Why not?'

'No.'

Her thoughts raced in confusion. She could scarcely confess to this hard-eyed man that it was the giver of the pendant to whom she had come to feel differently.

He appeared, however, to have lost interest in the matter. If only she still had faith in him!

Suddenly they swept around a bend to come in sight of a church, a cluster of white stone cottages and a tree-shaded square in the centre of a village. 'This is the last stop for bus passengers,' Adam told her. Liz couldn't help the thought that the journey would have been hot and tiring in the overcrowded vehicle compared with the cool comfort of Adam's red car. Not that she would give him the satisfaction of knowing her thoughts in the matter.

He was guiding the car down the main street, and presently he drew up in the shade of a leafy tree, where a Cretan youth stood waiting with two donkeys.

All at once Liz realised the significance of the mounts. She swung around to face Adam. 'You've arranged for donkeys to take us the rest of the way? Golly!' She burst into laughter. 'Now I know why the Greek driver on the bus got so worked up about my walking the distance, whatever it is. I suppose it's way up some mountain track?'

'So I gather.' Unfolding his long length from the driving seat, he went around the car to open the passenger door.

'This is fun!' Liz stepped out on to the dusty road. For a moment she forgot her companion, her attention centred on the strong mountain animals with their wooden saddles that were thickly padded with scarlet blankets.

She waited while Adam spoke in the Greek language with the swarthy youth, who was waving his arms and gesticulating wildly. A short time ago she would have suspected some dreadful danger lay on the route ahead, but she was becoming accustomed to the Cretans' excitable speech and lightning changes of mood.

'Up you go!' said Adam. Their glances met and something leaped in his eyes. The next minute he was hoisting her up into the cumbrous slatted saddle, holding her closer than he need, so that through the confusion of her senses she felt the warmth of his chest through his cotton shirt. How could she make herself hate him when she was a prisoner to the leaping of her senses every time he touched her?

'Thanks,' she whispered, and averted her gaze, fearful of what he might read there.

Presently the Cretan youth, whose name was Giorgios, was leading the strong animals. Like all Greeks he was loquacious and volatile, and Liz, watching his rapid gestures and flashing eyes and listening to his spate of Greek, could only guess at the conversation between the agile dark-haired youth and Adam.

Presently they were taking a track winding down a rocky gorge leading to a river bed below. It was a scene, Liz thought, of wild splendour, where pewter clouds heavy with moisture hung over the crags high above them, a silent world broken only by the clip-clop of donkeys' hooves on the rocky surface. And she was here in this magic spot, *with Adam!* Somehow today she was finding it very hard to hate Adam. Their mounts were walking abreast and it seemed silly and childish to hide herself away in a resentful silence. Especially, she mused wryly, when there were so many questions she wanted to put to him about their journey. So long as she didn't lose sight of his real reason for cultivating her acquaintance she told herself, and didn't forget about the woman he *really* loved . . .

The party followed the river bed for a long time, the donkeys picking their way amongst boulders as they followed the gorge leading ever deeper into the mountains. Never, she thought, had she been in so lonely a place, the only sign of civilization a shepherd's hut. It was as they paused for a short rest that she caught the far-away tinkle of bells. 'Would they be sheep?' she enquired of Adam.

'The *kria kia,*' he told her, 'the mountain goats. There'll be a herd of them somewhere on a patch of grassland out of sight. They don't have so much of the good life these days, not like in pagan times when they were worshipped as gods.' All at once there drifted towards them the thin, haunting notes of a shepherd's flute. 'The sheep will be somewhere down in the valleys.'

As they moved on Liz glanced up at the forbidding crags above. 'I suppose we will get to the village some time today?'

He grinned. 'Giorgios tells me we're almost there. One more climb and we'll be in the village street.' His voice softened. 'How are you feeling? Tired?'

'Oh *no!*' Her voice was alive with enthusiasm. 'I'm loving every single minute of it!' It's odd, she thought the next minute, but it's the truth. Who wouldn't enjoy the ride, she told herself, in these exciting, unfamiliar surroundings, with Adam? She thrust aside the disturbing question and tried to concentrate on clinging to her mount as he picked his way around the rocks on a steep rise. Then they reached the summit to find themselves in a small village that was ringed with mountains.

'Looks like the welcome committee's bang on time,' observed Adam, for hurrying towards them was a swashbuckling-looking Cretan of middle age with a fierce moustache. He wore dark-blue baggy trousers and jackboots and an embroidered blue waistcoat, and as he came leaping down the cobbled lane, his arms waving wildly in gestures of welcome, it seemed to Liz that even his heavy black moustache was quivering with excitement. It's Petros, she thought as he came nearer. She recognised Angeliké's father from the photographs his daughter had shown her on the other side of the world in far away New Zealand.

'*Kalimera!*'

From her seat on the donkey, Liz greeted the stranger with a smile. 'Elizabeth, Angeliké, New Zealand.' She turned towards Adam. 'Adam . . . friend.'

Petros's dark eyes flashed and Liz listened bewilderedly as a flood of Greek words poured around her. Raising her hands in a gesture of helplessness, she sent a mute appeal to Adam.

He responded with a grin. 'He's trying to tell you that you're more than welcome and that his home is at the end of the village. He'll show you the way, he says.'

'That's super!'

The donkeys' hooves made a clip-clop sound on the cobbles as the little party made their way down the narrow street. The only sign of life appeared to be a taverna, where a group of swarthy Cretans glanced up from their seats at tables in the smoke-filled room, to watch with interest the calvacade that was passing.

Petros paused at last at an entrance to a white stone cottage, and leaving Giogios to attend to the donkeys, Petros led them inside. Liz gained a swift impression of white walls hung with icons and flickering oil lamps, a loom beside an open fireplace. The next moment a black-robed woman came through an archway in the room to greet her. 'Elizabet—' In the ensuing spate of Greek Liz could distinguish only one word, 'Angeliké'. Then Maroula was kissing her on both cheeks. Tears of emotion ran down the sun-lined brown face, and the thought ran through Liz's mind that

Angeliké's mother might be garbed in sombre black, her face shaded by her coif, but there was warmth and kindness in her expression and a lively welcome for her daughter's friend in her brown eyes. The next minute she became aware of a young couple and two small dark-eyed boys, Angeliké's married brother and his family no doubt, she thought. Liz caught a jumble of names, but she couldn't distinguish between them. Not that it mattered, she thought, for suddenly she was surrounded by people, all obviously relatives and friends of Maroula and Petros, gathered here today to welcome the girl who brought news of Angeliké, whom they hadn't seen for many long years.

Once again Liz found herself regretting not having taken the trouble to learn something of the Greek language before coming to this country. If only she had she wouldn't feel at such a disadvantage when clearly Maroula and Petros were longing desperately for news of their daughter. 'English? Does anyone speak English?' she appealed to the crowd thronging around her, but she encountered only blank puzzled stares. Oh dear, now she would have to depend on Adam. She hadn't wanted to ask favours of him, especially seeing she had refused his offer to interpret for her, but it seemed she had no option. She turned towards him. 'Adam—' He was regarding her with his bright perceptive glance and she could swear there was a mocking light in his eyes. 'You wouldn't believe it,' she told him, 'but not one of them here can speak English. And there's so much they want to know about my friend in New Zealand.'

'Really?' He raised thick dark brows in a quizzical gesture and for a long moment she feared he was about to refuse. The next moment his dark face split into a triumphant grin. 'I thought you'd never ask!'

He broke into Greek, and although everyone was talking at once, Liz thought bewilderedly, evidently whatever it was that Adam was saying made sense, for Maroula was taking her by the arm and pointing up a stairway.

Adam's voice intruded on her thoughts. 'Maroula says she's sorry about her son being away. Seems he's gone back to America, he'll be so sorry about having missed your visit.' So that was why he wasn't here to act as interpreter, Liz reflected. She brought her mind back to Adam's tones. 'She says would you like to go to the bathroom and freshen up. I don't mind telling you I had to give her the idea for that one, but she caught on in the end.'

'Would I ever!' Liz threw him a thankful smile, then turned away to go up the twisting stairs with the Greek woman. When they reached the small room Maroula indicated the tap over a basin, and it was clear she was proud of the running water. She watched, smiling, while Liz washed her face and hands, then went to fetch a towel.

When Liz returned to the big room downstairs, all around her echoed talk and laughter. Petros, clapping his hands, at last managed to make himself heard, his strong tones rising above the clamour.

Liz flung Adam an enquiring glance. 'What now?'

'He's saying that everyone is to come to the table for wine and food. It seems it's a meal first, then present time. Let's hope,' he added in a low tone, 'you've brought lots of goodies with you. It looks like there are swags of relations, Angeliké's family seem to be a fruitful lot!'

She threw him an indignant glance. 'Of course I have!'

Everyone was moving, including Petros and Maroula's two younger children, an engaging-looking boy and girl who had just come in from school. As Liz, too, moved towards the table she realised that Maroula at her side was gesticulating towards the blue embroidered cloth. The next moment Liz saw with pleasure that the word 'welcome' was formed along the length of the cloth, the letters made from the bright yellow daisies that blossomed along the roadside. Liz smiled towards the Greek woman in an attempt to show her appreciation. Could it have been Angeliké who had told her mother the English word?

The volatile, laughing group crowded around the table and those who couldn't find a seat stood behind the chairs. Liz found herself seated opposite Giorgios, their guide. Despite her efforts to avoid him, Petros, with much gesticulating and a flood of Greek, was obviously insisting that Adam must sit at the side of the guest of honour. Did her hosts have the mistaken idea, she wondered, that she and Adam were a man and a woman who were in love with each other? But of course, she mused the next minute, hadn't she heard that in remote districts of Crete, the old traditions lived on and a Greek girl was never allowed to be alone with a man until the arrangement of the betrothal. Adam and herself! If only they knew, she thought wryly, and felt a knife-thrust of pain.

The crowd surged around them and she was pressed close, so close to Adam. The nearness of him, the muscular bronzed arm touching her own, was sending vibrations running through her, and flinging to the winds all her resolutions that she wouldn't let herself be so tinglingly aware of him. With an effort she brought her thoughts back to her surroundings. The chatter and laughter of the volatile peasants had risen to an uproar, and plainly, she thought, this was a big day for Angeliké's parents.

As new arrivals continued to enter the room Liz wondered apprehensively if they were friends and neighbours or close relatives. For although her rucksack bulged with parcels, there was a limit to the gifts she could hand out.

A worried frown creased her forehead and she glanced up to meet Adam's sardonic glance. It was an expression he seemed to keep just for her today, she mused crossly. Well, she hadn't asked him to make the trip, he had taken it on himself to come with her, she thought resentfully.

His forceful tones cut across her musing.

'Not worrying about the number of goodies you've brought with you, are you?' He had this uncanny knack of tuning in on her thoughts, damn him!

'I am a bit,' she admitted. 'There are so many—people, I mean.'

'Don't worry,' he said easily, 'most of these will be friends and neighbours of Petros and Maroula. The Cretans are a friendly lot, you might have noticed, and if they have anything to celebrate they want everyone they know to join in and share the fun. Today the whole of the village will be here. Your friend back in New Zealand will know the score and she'll have tossed in gifts for everyone, you'll see.'

Liz let out a breath of relief. 'Thank heaven for that!'

'You'd better learn the Greek word for "thank you",' he told her dryly. 'I've got a feeling you're going to need it before we leave. Can you remember *"Epharisto"*?'

'Epharisto,' she repeated carefully. 'Got it!'

'I'd better warn you, Cretans can be very inquisitive about folk, and devastatingly frank.'

She laughed. 'I'll leave you to cope with that! You're the language expert!'

She realised, as plate after plate was placed on the table, the long hours of preparation that must have gone to make up the varied array of Greek foods. She gazed at the great pottery bowls of salads, impressive affairs of huge tomatoes, peppers and onion, sprinkled with olives. Pilafs made of shrimps and prawns, *avgolemono,* a clear lemon-flavoured soup, boiled meat balls with rice, moussaka. There were sweets too, including honey-puffs, delicate fancies made of honey that looked to Liz like golden candy-floss, and great bowls of fresh grapes and oranges. 'Try the *tyropitta,* small cheese pies to you,' she became aware of Adam's voice, 'they're a speciality of the island.'

The food was delicious, Liz decided, and never again would she profess a dislike of Greek food. The hours in the sunlit air had sharpened her appetite and as the meal went on something of the mood of gaiety and excitement seemed to rub off on her.

'You should try the *raki.*' Adam managed to make himself heard in a lull in the tumult of voices echoing around them.

She eyed her glass. 'Dare I? I'm sure it tastes of turpentine, but on the other hand I couldn't go back to New Zealand and confess that I hadn't really sampled the fiery spirit of Crete.'

His low forceful tone reached her through the din. '*Are* you going back, Liz?'

Enjoyment of the moment had lulled her into a state of relaxed content. 'Maybe... one of these days.' She held out her glass and he poured from the carafe a portion of the native wine. As the fiery spirit went down her throat she caught her breath. 'Wow! I can understand now what they say about it, that after a few glasses of *raki* you're not really with it.'

'Try this, then,' she became aware of Adam's voice, 'it's just a local wine.'

The next minute she realised that glasses were raised and heads had turned to smile in her direction. Clearly a toast was being proposed to her. She heard her own name and laughingly acknowledged the good wishes. In the ensuing clamour of voices she appealed once again to Adam. 'What's Petros saying about me?'

She was becoming accustomed to his cool mocking glance. 'Just one of their native sayings, "Be happy always".'

'Oh!' Suddenly the heartache she had all but succeeded in smothering during the last half hour surfaced, and she was swept by anguish. If only everything could be different between her and Adam, and there was nothing to part them. If only she hadn't ever discovered his real reason for liking her—correction, making a pretence of liking her. If only... Her eyes clouded and her soft lips drooped wistfully.

'Smile, Liz!' At Adam's low urgent summons she blinked and came back to the present with a start, realising that everyone was looking at her, their glasses raised.

So she flashed her brightest smile and tried to submerge herself in the happiness and goodwill that was flowing warmly around her from these kind-hearted strangers.

The wine, sweet and flavoured with almonds, relaxed her tense nerves. It was so hard, she thought on a sigh, to remember all the time how hateful and despicable Adam was, how little she really meant in his scheme of things. His kisses that had shaken her world had been no more to him than a passing interlude.

When at last the meal came to an end Liz opened her travel pack, aware of the eager faces that pressed around her. Adam had gone to join a group of Greek men at the other side of the crowded room, she could glimpse his dark head above the others, and once again she asked herself why he had really come here with her today. The next minute she pulled herself up sharply. Why was she thinking of him all the time anyway?

Wrenching her mind back to the present, she passed around the photos of Angeliké and her family and then took an attractively wrapped parcel from her pack. 'For you, Maroula.'

Friends and relatives who were grouped around Maroula watched with breathless interest as the Greek woman shook out the folds of the fine linen tablecloth exquisitely embroidered in coloured yarns, on which her far-away daughter had spent so many hours of needlework. At that moment Liz knew that she had no need of language, for Maroula's emotion-torn nut-brown face and wet eyes said it all. Liz guessed that the cloth from New Zealand would be far too precious a belonging to be used for anything but an occasion of great importance such as a family wedding.

Other gifts from Angeliké followed—jams and preserves made from the produce of her adopted country, passion-fruit honey, chutney, rich and spicy, flavoured with dark crimson tamarillos, jars of kiwi fruit, the silvery green slices preserved in a sweet syrup.

Maroula had slipped her feet into sheepskin moccasins she had taken from a parcel and was gazing with pride at the huge fluffy slippers. 'You mustn't wear them in this heat,' Liz told her, then broke off in dismay. Oh dear, she thought, she can't understand a single word I say, and she glanced desperately around for Adam to come to her rescue. She was relieved to find, however, that he had returned to her side and had overheard the words. 'Tell her they're not to be worn in summer,' she appealed to him, 'or the poor woman will die of heatstroke! That they're only for wear when the snow is on the mountains.'

He grinned and interpreted the message, which for some reason Liz failed to understand, had the effect of sending Maroula into gales of laughter. Adam, catching Liz's puzzled glance, sent her a conspiratorial wink. 'She says she's not as silly as all that!'

As she took the presents one by one from her nylon pack, Liz realised how much care Angeliké had taken in choosing gifts for her loved ones in the Cretan village. There was a pipe fashioned from New Zealand timber for Petros, a bottle of kiwi fruit wine for the brother absent in America. The two younger children of the family smiled shyly as Liz fastened to the little girl's frock a gleaming paua shell brooch fashioned in the shape of a leaping dolphin, then flung a sheepskin lined jacket around the boy's small shoulders.

'Hey,' she caught Adam's prompting voice, 'sure you haven't forgotten Angeliké's sister and her husband?'

'Coming up!' Swiftly Liz dived into her pack and drew out a ring set with greenstone, the New Zealand jade. The expression of awed delight in Helene's dark eyes as she drew the ring on her finger was something she would have difficulty in describing by letter to Angeliké, Liz thought.

For Manoli there was a leather belt carved in the scrolls of a Maori design which he immediately put on, fastening the belt around his slim waist with the silver buckle.

All at once Liz became aware of wistful-eyed children who were standing at the back of the crowd. How thankful she was that her friend had included with her family presents an assortment of gifts for children and adults. 'The neighbours will be there to see you too,' Angeliké had told Liz, 'my parents will want everyone to join in the celebrations and share their happiness. No one must be left out, just hand things around to everyone. There are sweets and chocolates and cigarettes and pocket knives for the boys and bracelets for the girls.'

When all the gifts had been duly distributed, Liz had time to glance around her. Presents were being passed from hand to hand, and everyone exclaimed over the beauty or uniqueness of the wonderful nature of the gift. At least, that was how Liz interpreted the rapid gestures and excited talk of the dark-eyed women, a non-stop stream of words that appeared to be interrupted only by making the sign of the cross followed by a sigh that seemed to be a feature of this village life.

CHAPTER TEN

ALL AT once the noise around them died away and through a cloud of smoke Liz saw that Giorgios, their guide, had risen to his feet. Soon, his fingers sweeping the strings of a lyre, he sang a native song, and Liz found herself struggling against the haunting sensuous melody that was taking her back to a time when she had been so wildly, foolishly happy with Adam. But of course, she reminded herself as she forced her thoughts back to reality, it hadn't been the real Adam but merely a man she had dreamed up. An oh-so-wonderful male companion who was incredibly attractive, heaven to be with. A dream figure with whom for a short period she had found herself in danger of falling in love. Fortunately though, she congratulated herself, she had come to her senses in time!

Lost in her imaginings, she had scarcely realised that the song had come to an end and Petros was moving to a cleared space on the floor. Silently the crowd watched as with Cretan verve and exuberance his feet performed the intricate steps of the lively native dance. 'You mustn't applaud at the end,' Adam whispered to her, 'he's dancing for his own satisfaction, not for anyone else.'

Soon everyone was dancing, arms linked to form an open circle. As always, Adam's touch as he threw his arm around her shoulders electrified her. As she moved to the wildly accelerated rhythm she was caught up in the exhilaration around her, and everything slipped away from mind but the excitement of the moment and the sensuous beat of the singing lyre and bouzouki.

It must be the wine, she told herself in a pause in the
rhythmic beat, that was making her forget everything else
but the pleasure of the evening. Blame the music too, she
told herself, the atmosphere, the feeling of being in a far-
away world remote from everyday living. In this state of relaxation she couldn't continue to be unpleasant to anyone,
not even to Adam. Somehow tonight she was finding it very
difficult to hate Adam.

As the night wore on the music became louder, the room
thick with pipe and cigarette smoke. Dark aquiline faces
streamed with sweat as the music went faster and faster until the floorboards creaked with the stamping feet of Crete
dancers. During pauses in the dancing there was wine, the
clinking of glasses, the murmured sound of *'hyrrs'*. Liz lost
count of time until she chanced to glance down at the watch
on Adam's tanned wrist. Tonight he never seemed to be far
from her side. Maybe, she mused, he was taking his position as interpreter seriously. Aloud she said in surprise,
'Heavens, I had no idea it was so late. The night's almost
over. Why didn't you tell me?'

He raised thick dark brows. 'And ruin everyone's pleasure?'

A little later, however, as guests began to move towards
Petros and Maroula, Liz had no need of language to realise
that the party was coming to an end. As neighbours and
friends made their warm and affectionate farewells, she
gathered together the gifts that these generous people had
given to her—a hand-loomed wall hanging woven in a traditional design, freshly gathered black cherries fashioned
into a bouquet, a jar of honey and a bunch of red roses already wilting in the heat of the crowded room. When she
had placed the gifts in her pack she realised that she and
Adam were the centre of a laughing group. Swarthy faces
were pressing around them, their voices raised in words that
were repeated over and over again. Clearly, Liz thought,
whatever the meaning of the phrase it was a matter that de-

manded an answer, and something that concerned both her and Adam. She threw him a curious glance.

'I don't know what they're on about. Do you?'

Through the tumult of voices she caught his low murmur. 'Sure I know.'

'You might let me in on it,' she taunted.

'Sure you want to know?' There was a curl at the corners of his well-shaped lips. 'I warn you, Liz, you mightn't like it.'

She laughed. 'Try me!'

'Right! You've asked for it! It seems,' he said softly, 'that they're mighty curious about the date we've set for the wedding.'

'W-wedding?' she gasped. The next moment she tried to cover her confusion by saying quickly, 'Whatever could have given them that idea—no, don't tell me!' For all at once there had flashed back to her mind a recollection of Adam explaining to her the significance of a visit of a Cretan girl, accompanied by a man friend, to friends and relatives. To these mountain peasants such a visit could have but one meaning—a betrothal.

The wine, the heat of the crowded room, was making her feel slightly muzzy and far, far too relaxed. All she could come up with was: 'That must have been a hard one to answer!'

'Not really, I told them the truth.' His low vibrant tones were threaded with a note she couldn't fathom. 'That it all depends on you.'

She raised blue-grey eyes clouded with bewilderment to his face and then it happened. The wild excitement pulsing through her, the surge of happiness, drawing her to him in spite of herself. A feeling of delicious lassitude making her sway slightly towards him. Adam . . . his dark hair in disorder from the dancing, eyes alight with a message that was unmistakable: 'I love you.' The next minute she jerked herself back to sanity. 'It's the wine, the fiery Cretan *raki,* that's making him look at me like that, causing me to feel this way about him.' Through the confusion flooding through her she gathered together her rioting senses. She even managed to infuse a careless note into her voice. 'So that was why they were all looking at me?'

She turned away and the next minute Angeliké's family were crowding close, taking her hands in their warm grasp and planting affectionate kisses on both cheeks.

The group accompanied her and Adam out into the clear night air where Giorgios was waiting with the donkeys, dark shapes outlined against a silvered scene. The moon was a polished silver disc in the clear night sky, and as she looked at the mountain crags rising above, Liz was thankful she wasn't making the journey alone, for a guide wouldn't be anyone to talk to. But with Adam riding beside her—there she went once more, she chided herself, thinking of Adam, halfway to liking him all over again despite all she knew of him.

Their new friends left them where the village lane changed into a goat track winding down dark slopes, and Liz threw kisses back over her shoulder as they moved away on a gale of laughter and good wishes.

Presently, as they took a track winding down to a rocky gorge, she asked herself, 'Is this really happening?' The clip-clop of the donkeys' hooves on the stony surface sounded loud in the stillness of the Cretan night, the crags high above black against the moon, had the eerie look of a dream scene, the Cretan youth talking in a language she didn't understand, and Adam...

Oddly, the journey that had seemed so long earlier in the day now seemed to Liz to be all too short a trip, and they rode into the silent village before she realised they were so close to civilization. Adam's red car was the only vehicle in sight and when they reached it she slipped down from her mount to the cobbles of the street. Something warned her that it would be better for her peace of mind not to risk Adam's help when dismounting from her wooden saddle, not when it meant the dangerous rapture of being held close in his arms.

She waited while Adam paid the Cretan youth, then Giorgios waved them farewell and led the donkeys away. Adam flung open the car door for Liz and she slipped into the passenger seat.

As they took the dark road winding down a slope, her thoughts were busy. On this journey through the night alone together, maybe he would take the opportunity of trying to heal the breach between them? He might imagine that the attraction he held for her—why not admit it?—had been strong enough tonight to make her forget all about her sense of betrayal and her determination to resist any efforts on his part to get around her for purposes of his own. She steeled herself in readiness for any such attempts on his part, somehow she'd got to make herself strong and determined enough to resist his masculine charisma. But she need not have bothered, she told herself a little later as they sped on, because Adam made little attempt at conversation. He was seemingly intent on driving at speed as they hurtled up dark slopes and swung around hairpin bends.

Liz clutched at the dashboard as they swung around a sharp bend in the mountain road. Trying to make her voice ultra-calm, she commented, 'You're in a big hurry tonight,' and couldn't resist adding, 'Anyone would think you couldn't wait to get rid of me!'

'Not scared, are you?' He threw her a sideways glance, and she found herself wishing she could see the expression of his eyes.

'Not with you,' she said, and could have bitten out her tongue at the admission that had slipped from her lips.

For despite the speed at which they were moving, she felt entirely confident with Adam. There was something about him. You had the feeling that if he cared for a girl—she brought her thoughts up with a jolt. There she went again, romancing, dreaming, and about Adam of all men. Adam who had betrayed her trust once and would probably do it again if he got the chance. But he wouldn't, not now that she was forewarned.

She should be glad, she told herself on a sigh, that he was no longer interested in her. Clearly she had at last got through to him that she was a girl who knew her own mind, and when she said 'no sale' she stuck to her decision. But what a waste, on a night like this! If only Adam was as she had at first imagined him, he would be the one man in the world for her. Now where, she asked herself the next moment, had that absurd thought come from?

Her thoughts wandered and she wondered bleakly if he, too, were regretting the waste of this journey on a black and silver night, wishing he was with his woman friend, Karen, who was sophisticated and mature and whom he loved, really loved.

And yet somehow she gained the impression that he was angry, that the speed at which they were hurtling through the night was his way of letting off steam. Because of his inner frustrations concerning herself? She thrust the supposition aside as ridiculous. He couldn't really care about her, it had been only pretence—enough to take her in, but it had been acting just the same. Well, she stared ahead at the headlamps playing over the dusty road, if he wanted to play it that way it suited her fine. She didn't attempt to make conversation and they went the rest of the way in a heavy silence.

When at length they drew up outside the hotel, Adam turned to her, unsmiling. 'I'll see you to the villa.'

She knew it was useless to argue the matter, so she hurried along, trying to keep up with his long strides, as they took the narrow goat track together. In the moonshine she stumbled over a tree root embedded in the path and swiftly he took her hand. As always his touch sent the blood racing through her veins.

'It's all right,' she snatched her hand from his grasp. Don't touch me, please, Adam, she implored silently. She was all too well aware of the heady magic of his touch and tonight, she told herself over her whirling senses, she must keep her wits about her and concentrate on the really important things like his using her to further his business affairs and his lovemaking being just a trick. A trick that for her could have serious consequences if she didn't watch herself.

When they reached the courtyard they paused and her heart was beating fast. Adam together with the moon-silvered scene made a combination hard to resist, and she knew this was the moment when she should leave him quickly, a no-fuse moment, yet still she lingered.

'Goodnight, Liz.' She caught the tense note in his voice.

She looked up at him. 'Thanks...for everything. I couldn't have got there today but for you.'

All at once his tone was soft and deep, the tone that did things to her heart. 'Why don't you thank me properly?'

Caught in a spell, she made no move to avoid him and the next moment she was in his arms, enfolded close to him. He said huskily, 'Shall I be seeing you again, Liz?'

'No, no—I don't know,' she whispered in confusion.

'I could help you to make up your mind.' His low voice started the trembling in her. 'Why are you trembling, Liz?' Then his seeking lips found hers and she was carried away to a world of ecstasy by the heady rapture of his kiss. At last he released her and she caught his deep exultant chuckle. 'I knew I could persuade you—*my way!*'

Slowly, slowly, through a daze of happiness, Liz came back to reality. There was something she should remember. Then memories came rushing back and she wrenched herself free, pushing the dark hair back from her forehead in a nervous gesture. 'You'll never persuade me to change my mind.' She was breathing hard. 'That really would solve your problem, wouldn't it?' she flung at him. The moment the words were out she longed to call them back. But he had asked for them, hadn't he?

'So long as we understand each other!' The angry words flicked her raw nerves like a whip. The next moment he had left her.

And it was all her own fault! The sickening thought was like cold steel passing through her. But she had to fling those bitter words at him, she'd had to, for tonight his smooth technique to 'soften up Liz' had worked all too successfully. She put her hands to her burning cheeks, struck with the humiliating remembrance of how eagerly she had responded to his caress.

Blindly she stumbled towards the door and let herself into the house. Moving to the window, she glimpsed in the first flush of dawn, a masculine figure striding up the slope, then she couldn't see him for the tears that blinded her eyes. She should be pleased, she told herself bleakly, that she had kept her resolve not to be taken in all over again by his touch that could send her world spinning out of orbit. But she felt only this ache of longing. Adam had gone away, she swallowed over the lump in her throat, and this time it was forever.

A little later she decided that in this restless state it would be impossible for her to sleep. She might just as well work in the taverna, where physical toil might help to deaden this anguish and the heavy sense of loss.

Fortunately, she found as she took her place behind the counter of the seaside café, it was one of the days when the tour buses pulled in and everyone was kept frantically busy coping with the good-tempered holiday crowd. Even Nikos was helping, often pausing in his task of collecting coffee mugs from tables to burst into one of his lively native songs, to the delight of the customers. They were so helpful, Xenia and Nikos, and if business continued in this manner soon she would have no financial worries. She should be so happy, it was what she'd wanted, wasn't it? And yet...

Doggedly she went on with her tasks, even, in a brief pause in counter work, deciding to clean out a high cupboard that she hadn't yet opened. She was standing on a stool, tossing out old newspapers, when a piece of paper that was fluttering through the air caught her attention. She jumped down to the tiled floor, her gaze scanning the delivery note that the carriers who had delivered the equipment must have thrust into the high cupboard for safe keeping. But something was wrong. She felt emotion engulfing her, making her feel confused and lightheaded. For this document was made out by a firm in Heraklion for goods to be delivered to the taverna on the beach and charged to Adam's account.

Adam! A trembling seized her and as from a distance she became aware of Xenia's face, the dark eyes concerned as she tried by means of pantomime to persuade Liz to sit down.

It's just not possible! It doesn't make any sense! The conflicting thoughts tumbled wildly through her distraught mind. Not Adam! Because why would he do such a thing? But he had and that must mean that the action was to his advantage, though she couldn't imagine in what way. Dazedly she took the mug of hot coffee Xenia was handing to her. The Greek woman must be wondering why Liz, who was usually bursting with energy, was now acting so strangely. But no doubt, she reflected, Xenia would put her odd behaviour down to the all-night party in the mountain village—and the fiery *raki!*

Throughout the remainder of the day Liz moved like a girl in a dream. She supposed her hands must have performed their conventional tasks and her lips must have smiled a welcome to customers just as usual, because no one appeared to notice anything untoward in her behaviour. Except Xenia, who continued to regard Liz with friendly concern. If only she could explain to the friendly Greek woman that there was nothing wrong with her health!

In her mind she went over and over the reason for Adam having purchased the goods on her behalf, his strange secrecy in the matter. A wave of humiliation washed over her. How he must have grinned to himself at the glib explanation she had confided to him, her naïve assumption of Kostas's change of heart due to his fear of scandal. She couldn't *wait* until the end of the day when she could go to the hotel and face Adam, let him know in no uncertain terms that she knew all about his sneaky action and she wanted an explanation from him.

It was the longest day that she had ever known, but at last she said goodbye to Nikos and Xenia and hurried up to the villa.

'One thing's for sure,' she mused wryly as she glanced towards her mirror in the bedroom, 'Adam won't think I've come to see him to make things up between us, to tell him I didn't mean all those horrible things I said to him last night. Not with this ghastly white face and those awful blue shadows under my eyes.' But he wouldn't care one bit what she looked like. Unconsciously she sighed. She wasn't the woman he was interested in, so what did it matter?

Caught up as she was in her own problems and the questions to which there seemed no answers, it wasn't until she neared the imposing entrance of the high white building that it occurred to her that Adam might not be available tonight. 'He'd better be in,' she thought grimly, 'I can't bear this suspense for much longer,' and found herself looking directly into his face as he stepped from his car.

'Liz!' Something leaped in his eyes, twin shafts of pure pleasure. Surely she must have been mistaken, she told herself the next moment. No man could admire a girl who looked the way she did at this moment, especially not Adam, who didn't *really* care. Aloud she said breathlessly, 'I had to see you! It's something important! Something I just can't understand!'

'You look all in.' His eyes were dark with compassion. 'Come along inside and I'll get you a stiff whisky—'

She shook her head. 'No, no—'

'Let me take you for a drive, then,' he offered gently.

'If you like.' Dazedly she let him see her into the passenger seat of the red car.

For a moment he hesitated, his hand resting on the starting key. 'What's the trouble, Liz? You can tell me.'

'You!' She felt a wild urge towards hysteria.

He made no comment but started the engine, and soon they were taking a white dusty road winding up a steep slope. 'It's a bit more private than the Hermes, the spot I'm taking you to, and the view from the top of the cliff is out of this world.'

All at once she was feeling unutterably weary. 'Anywhere will do, it doesn't matter to me.' Leaning back in her seat, she closed her eyes, and when she opened them again he was braking to a stop on a high point overlooking a sea that was flooded with the shimmering golden pathway of the setting sun.

He turned to face her. 'Come on, Liz, tell me, what's all this about? What's the problem?'

It's strange, the thought shot through her mind, but he seems determined to overlook last night and the bitter words I threw at him. Aloud she said accusingly, 'It's you!'

He grinned. 'That's all right, then, we can sort it out between us.'

'Can we?' She raised clear grey-blue eyes to his steadfast gaze. 'Why didn't you tell me,' she said very low, 'that it was you who paid for all the goods I needed for the taverna and had all the stuff delivered there? It was you all the time! I only found out about it today when I happened to come across a printed docket from the firm who sold the goods, with your name on it. It was hidden away in a high cupboard that I've never used.

'Someone must have slipped up there, by the sound of it,' he said easily, 'but I guess you were bound to find out about it sooner or later.'

'But what I can't understand,' she pursued, 'is why you didn't let on to me about it at the time?'

'Why?' An enigmatic smile played around his lips. 'Come on, Liz, be honest with me. Would you have taken it from me, do you think?'

'No, I wouldn't!' she acknowledged quickly, and added on a sigh, 'but I guess that was because I couldn't ever trust you. I still can't believe you would go to all that trouble and expense just for me.' She raised her heavy gaze to his face. 'Why did you?'

'Just,' lifting her hand in his, he pressed her fingers to his lips, 'that you seemed to be in need of a helping hand to get that project of yours off the ground.'

'But—but—' Her heart was thudding wildly and she tried to pin down the thoughts that were rushing through her mind. 'It wouldn't do you any good. That way you'd never get the property you want so much.'

He said gravely, his eyes never leaving hers, 'I wasn't thinking of business deals, Liz, I was thinking of you.' Once again he pressed her fingers to his lips. 'I'm always thinking of you, I can't seem to get you out of my mind.' His voice was low with emotion, 'I love you, it's as simple as that.'

The unexpectedness of his words stunned her. Was this, too, part of the makebelieve? All at once it seemed very important that she be sure. Forcing down the wild excitement that threatened to engulf her, she murmured, 'Karen—'

'*Karen!*' He bent on her his incredulous stare. 'You're not telling me that you thought—good grief, she's my sister! If that's what you were thinking all this time—'

Suddenly fire was pulsing through her senses. She wasn't tired any more but gloriously, wonderfully happy!

'Why waste time in thinking anyway?' With infinite tenderness he ran his hands down her pale cheeks. 'Tell me you love me.' She barely caught the low tone, ragged with emotion.

'I've always loved you, right from the start!' The truth burst on her mind with a wild sense of elation. 'Only I wouldn't let myself believe—' The words were lost as he gathered her close and his seeking lips found hers. Without her volition her arms crept up to link themselves around his neck and her fingers curled around the soft dark hair she had always longed to touch. Then the world slipped out of focus and there was only ecstasy and a deep sense of belonging.

Adam released her at last to gaze down into her flushed, tremulous face. 'My darling,' his voice was unsteady, 'no more problems—'

Her eyes were glinting with a teasing light. 'Only one! I've just remembered about Katina and her dowry.'

'Oh, that's all taken care of now,' the words were punctuated with kisses, 'comes under the heading of project number two—remember?'

'Oh yes,' she nestled close in his arms, 'the scheme that was guaranteed to get you what you wanted? I can't imagine what you had in mind?'

'Can't you?' he whispered against her lips. 'It's a man-and-woman thing. I want you to be my wife. My darling,' his low tones were husky with emotion, 'say you will!' Her warm response to the urgency of his lips left no doubt as to her answer.

THE AUTHOR

Gloria Bevan, though born in Australia, was raised in New Zealand where she now lives with her building-inspector husband. They have three grown daughters. She has been writing stories for as long as she can remember and feels "there's a certain magic about writing even when the characters refuse to act the way I want them to." When not writing, she explores the many and varied exotic locations within reach of her suburban Auckland home.

Yours...
Faithfully
Claudia Jameson

Cindy Hetherington had a problem . . .
His name was Zac Stone, and he was the
dynamic new head of the advertising agency
where she worked.

When Zac began by giving her a stress
interview for a job she thought she already
had, Cindy stayed on to work for him for all
the wrong reasons. Mostly stubborn pride.

The false impressions each had of the other
didn't help, either. Around the office Cindy
had been nicknamed Miss Cool. But, oh,
how things changed when she fell in love!

CHAPTER ONE

'GONE? FIRED? What do you mean, he's been *fired*? What on earth's been happening around here?' Cindy Hetherington lowered herself gracefully into her chair, bewildered by what she was hearing, by what she was seeing.

She was sitting in her own office, but she barely recognised the place. To say it had been given a face-lift while she'd been away on holiday would be putting it mildly. Not only did she find herself sitting at a new desk, on which there was a sleek new typewriter, she also found herself in a room in which two of the walls had been painted pillarbox red—a colour she would never have chosen in a million years! The new carpet was a mottled brown and beige. That, at least, was inoffensive, but the only things which were completely familiar in the room were Cindy's array of potted plants. Those and her young assistant, Alison.

'Alison?' Cindy's dark brown eyes looked questioningly at the younger girl but it was Sheila who answered. It was Sheila who had met Cindy at the entrance to the advertising agency's offices some five minutes earlier, and Sheila who had done all the talking so far.

'I've just told you! Your boss has been ousted! Sacked. Fired without ceremony. Paid off. Got rid of. I can't put it more plainly than that, can I?' Sheila hitched herself on to Cindy's desk, her long and spindly legs looking thinner than ever in a skirt which finished four inches above her knees. On a woman who looked more than her thirty-five years, that was pushing it a bit. And she'd had her hair cut again, Cindy noticed. Why did some women insist on following

fashion in a sheep-like manner and never stop to consider
what actually suited them? On Sheila's pale, too-thin face
her black hair cropped severely short looked ghastly.

Cindy half turned in her chair so she was no longer face
to face with the offending pillarbox red on the wall. She
sighed inwardly, wishing it had been someone other than
Sheila who had greeted her with the news that the agency
had been taken over. There was so much cynicism in Sheila
that it was difficult to get a straight answer from her at the
best of times.

Though they worked under the same roof, the two women
saw little of one another. Sheila was a copy-writer. She kept
her own hours, coming and going as she pleased, and
worked well away from Cindy in the creative department on
the far side of the building. In the course of her work, Cindy
saw most of the advertising copy written by Sheila. She
could write ads in so many different ways, from the persuasive to the humorous to the technical—depending on the
product being sold—and it never ceased to amaze Cindy that
anything other than satire could be produced by Sheila's
pen.

Cindy didn't dislike her. Sheila was one of those people
it was difficult to dislike. But she didn't exactly like her, either. There had to be a reason she was here, sitting in Cindy's office. There had to be a reason for her taking the
trouble to come in early in order to collar Cindy before she'd
even got through the main entrance to the offices. Or was it
simply that she wanted to be the one who broke the news
about the takeover?

'No, you can't put it more plainly.' Cindy shook her head,
her blonde curls moving gently against the tanned skin of
her shoulders. 'But how can my boss be fired? John was the
Managing Director, for heaven's sake!'

'So what?' Sheila lit a cigarette, departing from her usual
drollness into something bordering on excitement. She was
grinning from ear to ear. 'John Doe might have been the
Managing Director, but he had only one share in this

agency. One share. Mr Bryant ran this place, not your boss. John Doe had about as much management ability as a juvenile flatfish.'

From behind her desk in the corner of the office, Alison giggled. She had been with Bryant's only two months, not long enough to have become used to Sheila's brand of wit and to the nicknames she gave everybody. She still found Sheila amusing, still found it hilarious when the M.D., the *ex* M.D., was referred to as 'John Doe'.

Cindy looked heavenward, her loyalty to John preventing her from making any comment, though there was a good deal of truth in Sheila's remark.

That the ownership of the agency had changed hands didn't really surprise Cindy. The chairman, Mr Bryant, who had been the founder and backbone of the agency, was way past retirement age. His tiredness and increasing lack of interest in the business had been reflected in the staff, in the lethargy which had been creeping through the agency during the past couple of years.

In the past, Bryant's had been one of the best advertising agencies in London, but these days it was surviving on its old reputation. That and a diminishing amount of business. In the four years that Cindy had been there they had lost three accounts, old-established clients. And they had won no new ones. The agency was rapidly going downhill, and whoever had bought the place would have a difficult task in reversing that process. A very difficult task.

Of course John had been at fault, as much if not more than the ageing Mr Bryant. It was undeniably true that Cindy's boss had not been much of a Managing Director. Working as his secretary had taxed Cindy to less than half her potential. Oh, there had always been something to do, but the job had never been a challenge to Cindy. She'd never had the chance to use her brains, or all her qualifications. Nevertheless, she had liked her boss enormously, and it seemed incredibly cruel that he had been ousted so sharply by the new owners of Bryant's. She said as much to Sheila.

'Knickers!' Sheila gave her a withering look. 'The ad world is tough and ruthless. There's no room for senti-ment—you should know that by now. You're too soft, Goldilocks, I've told you that before. I can't imagine why you ever came into this business in the first place.'

That was none of Sheila's business. Cindy had had good reasons for choosing the advertising world for her career, just as she'd had good reasons for leaving her home in Cheshire and wanting to live in the capital.

'Sheila, why don't you keep your questions and your opinions to yourself and just tell me, as objectively as you can manage, what happened here after I'd left for my holi-days?' she said.

Sheila groaned in frustration, her eyes sparking with amusement. 'Heavens, *when* are you going to ask me who's bought this dump of a place?'

When Cindy didn't answer, Sheila threw up her hands in despair. 'Okay, Miss Cool, I'll tell you from the top.' She wiped the smirk from her face, wriggled herself into a more comfortable if unladylike position on Cindy's desk, and spoke to the younger woman as if she were hard of hearing. 'You left on the Friday, right? On the following Thursday a staff meeting was called. Are you with me so far? We all gathered in the Board Room and our decrepit Chairman announced that he'd sold all his shares. It was done! Fait accompli! As from last Monday, we were all working for someone else.' Sheila leaned forward slightly, her eyes nar-rowing. 'Those of us who've been allowed to stay on, that is.'

'What do you mean? Who else has been fired?' Cindy blinked in surprise, still bewildered by all this.

There followed a list of seven names. Seven members of the agency's staff who had been sacked. Paid in lieu of no-tice.

'Good grief!' Cindy leaned back in her chair, flabber-gasted. 'But you can't do that! Not these days. You can't just—'

'In this business, darling, anything can happen.' Sheila's laugh was scornful. 'And when you know who the new boss is, you'll understand.'

'But—but...' Cindy didn't know what to say. In one fell swoop some of the agency's key people had been removed. Just like that! 'I've never heard of anything like it! Not on this scale. I mean—'

'I have.' Sheila sounded almost triumphant. 'I've seen it happen before. About ten years ago, when I was working for—'

Alison was looking from one woman to the next, fascinated but unable to get a word in.

'Politics,' Cindy said the word with distaste. 'It's the old internal politics game, isn't it?'

Sheila shrugged. 'Partly. Strictly speaking, those seven weren't all fired. Five of them were. Everyone else was given the opportunity of staying on, but the two account executives walked out on the spot—as soon as they were told who the new boss was... Come on!' she urged. 'I'll give you three guesses who's taking over Bryant's.'

'I'm in no mood for guessing games. Why don't you just tell me before you burst?' Cindy let out a long, slow breath, unable to decide how she felt about all this. But the idea that she was now working for someone else rather appealed to her. Working for someone who would keep her busy, be more demanding than John, might help to lift her depression. She had been depressed before she left for her holidays, thanks to James, and after spending two weeks in her father's company she was even more depressed. She shook herself mentally, refusing to dwell on thoughts of her relationship with James.

Yes, a new boss might be just what she needed. Come to think of it, she hoped he would tax her to her fullest. It would be good to be busy again, as she used to be when she first started at Bryant's. She decided there and then that she would stay on. After all, with a new Chairman, a new Managing Director and several new members of staff,

Bryant's was bound to undergo a drastic change—one way or another. It would be a new job for Cindy, without the necessity of looking elsewhere.

'And what about the other two Directors, Sheila? I mean, there was John and—'

Sheila waved a dismissive arm. 'They suffered the same fate as John—ousted. After all, they had so few shares between them, they had little choice but to sell. Mr Bryant owned eighty per cent of the shares, bear in mind.'

Cindy smiled to herself. She couldn't delay the question much longer. Having decided to stay on, she was now as curious to find out about the new owner as Sheila was anxious to tell her. 'All right, Sheila, let's have it. Who is our new Chairman?'

'Are you ready for this?'

'I'm ready.'

Sheila held out her hands with a flourish. 'Zac Stone! How about that?'

The announcement fell flat. Cindy didn't respond. For the moment, the name meant nothing to her. It was ringing a bell, but that was all.

Sheila let out an exaggerated moan. 'Good God, what's the matter with you? I think your holiday's given you moths in the brain! I've just told you that this place has been taken over by *Zachariah Stone,* and you sit there as if you're fast asleep with your eyes open!'

Two pairs of eyes were watching Cindy closely. Alison, able finally to get a word in, ventured, 'He's very nice, Cindy. I'm sure you'll like him.'

'Don't be silly, Alison!' Sheila turned round and snapped at the youngster. 'Nice is not a word that can be used when talking about Zac Stone. Not in any context. He's—er—let me see ... he's *professional.*'

Cindy nodded slowly. She'd placed the name, all right. It had only taken her about five seconds. There was only one Mr Stone in the advertising world, but... 'But Zac Stone retired about two years ago, didn't he? I mean, when he sold his original agency, didn't he make some sort of agreement not to set up business elsewhere?'

'Well done!' Sheila's voice was sarcastic, but Cindy paid no attention. Sheila's sarcasm had never affected her. There was nothing personal in it. One just had to understand the woman. She was like that with everyone.

Cindy smiled tolerantly. 'Okay, we all know that if we want to find out anything about people on the advertising scene, we've only to ask you. So why don't you fill me in on the details of Zac Stone?'

Sheila pouted as if she'd been offended—something which was virtually impossible to do. 'You make me sound like a gossip and a scandalmonger!'

'No,' Cindy couldn't help laughing, 'I didn't mean to imply that. But you are a mine of information. You pick up *everything* that runs along the grapevine.'

'Just one of my virtues. Well, Zac Stone was the majority owner of Stone, Mason and Gibbons. That much you know. It was, and still is, the top agency in London. We all know the turnover of that agency, so you can imagine the price he got for it! Anyway, in the contract of sale, Zac agreed to keep off the advertising scene completely for at least one year—obviously the buyers didn't want him setting up business elsewhere and taking all his clients with him! After all, it was his name they were paying for. Anyhow, the story goes that Zac was retiring from working life altogether. At thirty-five, if you don't mind!'

At that, Alison spoke up. 'But if he sold his agency and retired, why has he come back two years later and bought this place?'

'Shut up, Alison, you may not ask questions I don't know the answer to!'

They laughed, all of them, as Sheila continued with what she did know about Zac Stone. 'I know nothing about him personally, except that he's Welsh. They say he started out working in an agency as a mailboy! Imagine it! He's come up the hard way. What he doesn't know about the ad world, and I mean every aspect of it, isn't worth knowing. He's the tops. He'll put this agency on its feet again. He's such—'

Sheila stopped in mid-sentence as the door opened and John Crosdale walked in. John worked in the accounts department. He was a sweet man, nicely spoken with impeccable manners, and Cindy liked him very much.

He stopped in his tracks when he saw Sheila sitting there. 'Oh!' He looked from Sheila to his watch, and frowned. 'I didn't expect—'

Cindy laughed. 'Sheila's broken a record, John. She wanted to be the first to tell me the news, I suppose.'

'And have you been told? I mean, have you been told who your new boss is?'

As John looked from one woman to the next, Sheila shrugged dramatically. ''Course I've told her! But you know Miss Cool isn't easily ruffled. She didn't even react!'

John smiled, though he didn't look at all happy. Not at all. 'You've probably never met Zac Stone, have you, Cindy?'

'No. But I know of him. I know his reputation. Who doesn't?'

'He's a bastard!' John said suddenly, vehemently. 'A bastard, first class.'

This was so out of character that Cindy's eyebrows shot up in astonishment. If John hadn't been so obviously upset, she might have laughed.

'Oh, I don't know about that,' Sheila said drily. 'Where did you hear that his parents never got married?'

'Spare me,' John said stiffly. 'Spare me the puns today, Sheila. Just let me get used to the idea that starting this week I'm going to have to work within Zac Stone's orbit!'

Cindy was a little puzzled. A little puzzled and very interested. 'You know Mr Stone, I take it?'

'Yes, quite well.'

'I've met him a few times,' Sheila began.

'It's not quite the same thing,' John cut in. 'You've never *worked* for him before. But you're working for him now, so you'll find out what he's really like. Give it time.'

'And you have?' Cindy probed. 'Worked for him, I mean?'

'Yes.' John smiled at her. But then he always had a smile ready for Cindy. Always. 'I worked at Stone, Mason and Gibbons—for a total of six months.'

'And you're staying on here?'

'I haven't much choice, have I, dear? I've got a mother and an aunt who depend on me. I'll see how it goes. If I can't stand it, I'll look for another job—but I'll do it at my leisure. When it suits me.'

There was a sudden silence. Alison looked round the room as if she were sorry the show was over. 'Well, I thought Mr Stone was very nice when he had a talk with me last week,' she proffered. 'Good-looking, too. And he's a bachelor?'

Everyone turned to look at Alison, but nothing was said. Not a word. Everyone was thinking their own thoughts. Alison, young for her eighteen years and basically very shy, blushed to the roots of her hair.

Cindy felt a rush of sympathy for her and distracted the other two as quickly as she could. 'Did you want something, John? Or had you come in to tell me the news?'

'The latter. I thought you should be warned.'

Cindy looked at her watch as John closed the door behind him. 'Alison, have we got any work to do? I mean, was there anything outstanding before John—'

Sheila clicked her tongue. 'You're not very subtle, Cindy if you want me to go now, just say so.'

'I want you to go now.'

'Oh, that's charming! And I came in early especially to do you a favour. You haven't heard the rest of it yet.'

'You mean there's more?' Cindy looked at her in mock disdain. It was true that she wasn't easily ruffled. Cindy Hetherington was well spoken, well bred, well educated and

quietly confident. Whatever was ahead of her in her working life, she would cope with it. She had no doubts about her
abilities. If she could only manage her personal life as well
as she managed her working life, she'd be okay.

She looked up at Sheila coolly, her soft brown eyes smiling from a face that was exceptionally lovely, although she
personally could find a dozen faults with it. 'Go on, then.
What's the rest of it?'

'Zac's the new Chairman *and* Managing Director.'

'I see.' The note of disappointment in Cindy's voice was
plain. 'And Mr. Bryant's secretary has been given the job,
is that it? Well, I suppose that's fair enough. Miss Druce has
been here nearly twenty years, after all. Compared to my
four.'

At last everything fell into place. So this was the real reason for Sheila's presence. 'What you're really telling me is
that I have no choice about staying on. I'm out of a job, is
that it?' Cindy's mind raced ahead. It wasn't the end of the
world. She didn't need to work at all. She was in the fortunate position of having a very substantial private income. A
few weeks spent looking around for another job would
make not the slightest difference to her. Except that she'd be
bored—bored stiff. She didn't work for the money. In fact,
she spent more than she took home from Bryant's on the
rent of her luxury flat. Considerably more.

But Sheila was shaking her head and was so busy shriek-
ing with laughter she could hardly speak. 'Twin-Set and
Pearls? *Her?* You've got to be joking! Can you just see her
and Zac Stone working together? Oh, my God!'

'Will you calm down, please. If this man's coming out of
retirement, he isn't going to bring a secretary in with him.
And if Twin-Set—if Miss Druce hasn't got the job, then I've
got it. Right? Come on, Sheila, put me out of my misery!'

Sheila's laughter began to fade. 'Are you telling me you
fancy the idea of working for Zac Stone?'

'I don't know what you mean,' Cindy answered truth-
fully. 'Why shouldn't I fancy it?'

'After what John's just told you?'

'I make up my own mind about people—you should know that by now. I put up with you from time to time, don't I?'

'Thanks! Listen, seriously—'

'For heaven's sake, am I keeping my job or am I not?'

'Yes, yes. The job's yours...' Sheila let out an unpleasant snort '...subject to your having a little chat with the man himself.'

'So? That presents no problem. I'm over-qualified for this job as it is.'

'Cocky, aren't you?' Coming from Sheila, that was rather like the pot calling the kettle black. 'Qualifications have little to do with it. Zac will want to know all there is to know about you...'

'I've got nothing to hide.'

'...including where your birthmarks are and what size bra cup you take.'

Cindy put on her most bored expression, which was very disconcerting to most people. 'Don't be silly.' In truth she was stifling her mirth. Sheila really was funny at times, and Alison had collapsed with laughter. 'Unless you're trying to tell me the man's some kind of lecher?'

'Hardly!' After lighting what must have been her fifth cigarette in the space of an hour, Sheila slithered off the desk, the short skirt riding up her thighs making Cindy flinch inwardly. 'Right, Miss Cool, maybe you'll pass the test. But I'll tell you this for nothing—you won't last two minutes working for Zac Stone.'

It was the first time ever that Sheila had managed actually to needle Cindy. She probably hadn't done it deliberately. It was hard to tell. There was no real malice in the woman. Still, that didn't alter the effect of her words. 'Meaning what?'

Sheila started walking towards the door. 'Meaning you're too soft for this business. Meaning that you're not made of the right stuff. Meaning that Zac Stone will wipe the floor

with a girl like you. You're too...nice.' Somehow she
managed to make it sound like an insult. Then she added,
redeeming herself, 'Honestly, Cindy. And what I really
wanted to tell you is that there's a secretarial job coming up
shortly at Cookson Associates. I heard it on the grapevine.
The secretary to the Creative Director is pregnant, the job'll
be up for grabs soon.'

Cindy bowed her head gracefully as Sheila left the room.
Then she let out a long, exasperated sigh. 'Won't last two
minutes, indeed! Well, we'll see about that!'

Alison looked at her uncertainly. 'She's very blunt, isn't
she?'

'Yes,' Cindy agreed. 'Still, at least one knows where one
stands with Sheila.'

The two of them looked at one another and giggled. Alison was fresh from secretarial college and had been working as Cindy's assistant for two months. They got on
extremely well together. In Alison, Cindy could see herself.
When she was nineteen she, too, had been an assistant secretary, though she'd never been as shy as Alison. Still, given
a little longer in this business, that would soon be knocked
out of her.

Alison was a couple of stones overweight, and very self-
conscious about it, which probably accounted for much of
her shyness. She was an intelligent, pretty girl with a mop of
dark, tightly curled hair, and she thought Cindy was the
most super person she'd ever met—next to her aged grandmother. Cindy had rocked with laughter when Alison had
gone so far as to tell her that. But she'd been pleased, naturally.

'Listen,' Cindy looked around the office, at the two stark
white walls and the two ghastly red ones, 'are you responsible for this? I mean, did you choose this red?'

'No!' Alison looked horrified. 'Actually, I like it, but I
knew you'd hate it. I know you like pastel colours. I wasn't
even consulted. Mr Stone told the decorators what to do in

here and in his own office. I suppose he would have asked you what you wanted, but you weren't here to consult.'

'Mmm. Well, thanks for looking after my plants, anyway. I can see at a glance you've done a good job.' Cindy got to her feet and inspected her potted plants, all nine of them, one by one. She adored plants and was very successful with them. Her only regret was that she didn't have a garden to look after these days. But there were no gardens at all surrounding the block where she lived—so she couldn't even sit in one unless she walked to the nearest park. But the flat had its compensations. It was extremely comfortable, probably as safe as one could hope to be in central London, and it was just about within walking distance from Bryant's.

'Aren't you curious to see what Mr Stone's office looks like?'

Cindy's eyes trailed towards the intercommunicating door. 'Very,' she laughed. 'If it's anything like this one, it'll be—' She stopped short as the thought struck her. 'Alison, what time is he coming in? I mean, it's almost ten-thirty.'

'Oh, sorry, I haven't had a chance to tell you. He told me to let you know he won't be in till tomorrow. He said he'd talk to you first thing. He talked to everyone else last week.'

Zac Stone's office could only be described as efficient. Gone was the mahogany desk and the hefty furniture which John had used, which had at least given the room some character. The new desk was white, set in a tubular steel frame. In fact the overall impression of the office was of stainless steel and lightness. The walls were off-white, the three paintings on them steel-framed and wishy-washy. There was a row of filing cabinets in light grey, several spotlights and a couple of glass-topped coffee tables. Around the coffee tables there were four swivel chairs and sitting under the window was a four-seater settee.

'It's—er—functional, I suppose.' Cindy opened the big cupboards which were built into a recess. The top half of them still housed books and magazines, newspaper clippings and so on. But the bottom half—well, the few bottles of sherry and wine which John had kept there had been added to, and then some. There was every sort of spirit you could think of, various mixers, a crate of vintage wine, an ice bucket and assorted glasses.

'Look at this lot, Alison. Obviously Mr Stone believes in keeping the clients well entertained!' She turned from the cupboard to find her assistant looking at her rather wistfully.

'That's a gorgeous dress, Cindy. I wish I could wear those strappy little numbers. I wish I had a figure like yours! I just don't seem to be losing any weight at all.'

'Don't worry about it,' Cindy soothed, knowing only too well how the younger girl felt. 'I've told you, from the age of ten to the age of sixteen, I was overweight. Very. It's only puppy fat. It'll go in its own good time.'

'But I'm so much shorter than you,' Alison groaned. 'It's very hard to believe you were ever overweight. Are you sure you're not just saying that to make me feel better?'

'Honestly,' Cindy assured her, 'I was. I'll dig out an old photograph and show you. Are you keeping up with that diet I gave you before I went away? The health foods?'

Alison pulled a face. 'Yes. Well, I don't care much for health foods. I—I have slipped once or twice.'

'That,' Cindy said firmly, 'is entirely up to you. Nobody can do it for you.'

Cindy did some of her own shopping at the health food shop. While she was not obsessive about food, she was particular about what she ate. She believed in the old adage that you are what you eat, and if her skin was anything to go by then a varied and well-balanced diet really did pay dividends. Her skin was as flawless as her figure.

She had become body-conscious at an early age, while she was attending the exclusive boarding school her parents had picked out for her at birth. The mocking cruelty of her contemporaries had left their mark and from the age of sixteen onwards, when the excess weight finally started to melt away, Cindy had kept a very careful watch on her figure.

Never again did she want to have clothes specially made for her because she was an odd shape.

These days, she had to admit to being very indulgent as far as clothes were concerned. She loved them, and thanks to the money her grandmother had left her, she could afford to buy what she wanted. Cindy was not a follower of fashion, nor did she like clothes which she regarded as fussy. She wore what suited her and had often been complimented on her clothes sense. Especially by James.

Damn him.

At noon Cindy escaped from Bryant's and spent a quiet half hour sitting on a bench on the tiny green patch in Hanover Square. All morning she had been accosted by one member or another of the agency's staff. Gossip was rife. The grapevine was working overtime. The atmosphere at work was one of awe mingled with excitement and, in some quarters, apprehension.

When she spotted Miss Druce walking towards her, Cindy felt trapped. She couldn't just get up and walk away, because Twin-Set and Pearls—as Sheila called her—was waving vigorously.

'Good morning, Cindy.' Miss Druce lowered herself on to the bench rather tiredly. She was a middle-aged woman who had worked for Mr Bryant for almost twenty years, and if anyone was ill-suited to the world of advertising, it was she. At least, she was these days. Like the retired Chairman, Miss Druce had never kept up with the times. In fact Sheila's label of 'Twin-Set and Pearls' described Miss Druce in a nutshell. Sheila's nicknames were always spot-on.

'Did you have a nice holiday?'

'Quite pleasant, thank you,' said Cindy, somewhat evasively.

Miss Druce eyed the bare skin of Cindy's shoulders and the skimpy sun-dress with a hint of disapproval in her eyes. 'We've been very lucky with the weather lately, haven't we? You got a nice suntan, I must say.'

'Thank you.' Feeling slightly ill at ease, Cindy smiled politely. She could see what was coming. 'I spent most of my time in the garden.'

'You were visiting your parents in Cheshire, of course. How is Sir Robert?'

'He's fine, thank you.' Miss Druce spoke of Cindy's father as if she knew him, which she didn't.

'And your mother?'

'Very well. Everybody was fine, thanks.'

And then it came, but there was no hint of the sour grapes Cindy had anticipated. 'So, starting tomorrow you'll be working as secretary to Mr Stone?' There was a liveliness about Miss Druce's eyes Cindy had never seen before.

'Yes, so it seems.' She looked at the older woman curiously. 'And you're staying on at Bryant's, too.'

'Yes, of course.' Miss Druce gave a satisfied nod. 'I discussed the matter very thoroughly with Mr Stone, naturally. Cindy, let me tell you, he's a charming man! Absolutely charming! You and he will get on splendidly, I know it.'

By now, Cindy had heard such varying reports about Zac Stone that she took nothing as real. She was determined to remain neutral, unaffected by any sort of gossip. 'One hopes so.'

'Of course, I could have taken the job myself,' Miss Druce went on. 'But after discussing things with Mr Stone, I thought no, he really wants someone a little more... dynamic.' She gave a little laugh.

Cindy laughed too. 'That's hardly a word I'd use to describe myself, Miss Druce.'

'Perhaps, perhaps. However, as you know, I've had things rather easy lately, working for Mr Bryant. I mean, I've been virtually a part-timer and rather spoiled. In fact, Mr Stone asked me whether I'd rather stay on and just work part time officially. But I said no. Firstly, frankly, I need full-time money and secondly—well, we'd all rather be busy, wouldn't we? It's so bad for the character, not having enough to do with one's time. Anyway, Mr Stone suggested I might like to supervise the typing pool. There are six girls there, as you know, and I thought it a very good idea.'

As Cindy opened her mouth to make a tactful comment, Miss Druce rushed on, 'Mr Stone said that my experience and expertise could be passed on to the younger girls. He's quite a perfectionist, I believe, as I am, of course. So I agreed to take the task on, and I must say that from what I've seen so far, those girls certainly need supervising . . .'

Miss Druce went on and on. And on. The latter half of Cindy's lunch-hour was far from restful.

When she walked into the sanctuary of her flat that evening, Cindy felt exhausted. Yet she'd done nothing all day. There had been no work to do. The ear-bashing she'd taken from Miss Druce and umpteen other people had tired her out. Of course it was all a nine-day wonder. Within a couple of weeks everything and everyone at Bryant's would settle down into a routine, albeit a different one.

She was soaking in the bath when the telephone rang. All thoughts of Bryant's and everyone connected with the place had vanished. She was mulling over the two weeks she had spent with her family. It had been nice being in the country again, spending time in the gardens, doing some riding. But it had been very much a duty visit, a once-yearly duty visit. She'd done it, as she always did, for her mother's sake. And only for her mother's sake.

It was James on the telephone.

Good manners, and nothing else, prevented her from putting the receiver down. 'What do you want, James?'

'Aw, Cindy, don't be like that! Please!' The voice was half-jocular, coaxing.

'This is pointless. Look, what we had together is over. Finished. Everything our relationship stood for was negated, dissolved—by you, James. Goodbye.'

'Cindy! I *must* talk to you. You don't understand!'

'There's no point,' Cindy said tiredly, 'you're a hypocrite. You'd better face that fact.' She wasn't angry with

James. She never had been angry with him. Just disappointed. *Disappointed.* But she shouldn't have been. She should have known better than to put her trust in someone. After all, how many people were faithful these days?

'Please hear me out.' James's voice was serious now. 'I've been in agony this past couple of weeks, waiting for you to get back from Cheshire. May I come over and talk to you?'

'Absolutely not.'

There was a pause. 'Are you telling me it's over?'

'I told you that before I went away, and again two minutes ago.' Cindy promptly replaced the receiver. There was no point in continuing the conversation.

Pulling her bath towel closer around her, she went into the lounge, taking solace and pleasure from the order and décor of the room. She had her flat just as she wanted it and it was good, so good to be in the quiet and privacy of her own place.

Financially, she was a very lucky girl. She appreciated that. On the face of things, Cindy was a girl who had everything. But that was far from the truth. She lived with the feeling that life was passing her by. Deep inside her there was a discontentment which sometimes kept her awake at nights. If she could only put a name to it, she might be able to do something about it.

She sat on the settee and put her feet up, eyes closing. Life was so...so bland. It was neither boring nor exciting. It was just an unfolding of days. She wished she'd gone abroad for a couple of weeks instead of visiting her family. Perhaps a complete change would have lifted this mild depression she couldn't seem to shake off. Of course, the James thing hadn't helped. She was coming to the conclusion that she was no good with people. Perhaps she should stick to plants. They seemed to be the only thing in life she really succeeded—

The sound of a high-powered drill brought her eyes open. She groaned loudly. Since getting back from Cheshire on Saturday she had been subjected to the intermittent drilling and banging from next door. The adjoining flat had stood empty for the past five weeks, but it was clearly being altered or prepared for a new tenant. Fine. But did they have to work during the evening as well as during the weekend?

She closed her eyes again and tried to blot out the grating noise. It was impossible. Sighing, Cindy glanced towards the clock. It wasn't even eight yet, and the long summer evening stretched ahead of her. But it would be too much effort to get dressed and go for a walk in the park.

There seemed little else to do but take an early night.

CHAPTER TWO

'GOOD MORNING, Cindy.' Alison lowered her voice and jerked a thumb towards the adjoining door. 'He's in! He buzzed through about ten minutes ago and—'

Cindy started laughing. 'Speak up, Alison! He can't hear you through a closed door, can he?'

Unconvinced, Alison continued in a whisper. 'He buzzed through about ten minutes ago and said you should go in to see him when you arrived.'

'Fine. I'll just pop to the loo first.' Cindy dropped her lightweight jacket over the back of her chair. She was sorry she'd worn it, even if it did match her dress, because she hadn't needed it. It was a glorious morning, warm already, and the walk to the office had lifted her spirits.

'Don't be nervous. I've told you, Mr Stone's a very nice man.'

With a new bout of laughter tinkling on the air, Cindy did her own bit of reassuring in return. 'I'm not nervous, silly. I just want to comb my hair!'

The dress looked good with the suntan. It was white, close-fitting in the bodice, with two thin shoulder-straps, and straight in the skirt. Cindy smoothed it down and ran a comb through her shoulder-length hair, a little impatient with the curls which no amount of blow-drying would straighten out completely. It was naturally blonde, and her recent spell in the sun had added to its highlights.

She didn't bother with eye-shadow during the day, just a touch of mascara, which was all her dark eyes needed really, and lipstick. After freshening her lipstick she stood back and gave a satisfied nod at her full-length reflection. She was presentable.

After a second's hesitation at the door of her office, Cindy smiled to herself and walked on. She would enter Mr Stone's office via the door which led to the corridor. Alison would think she'd been waylaid by someone when she didn't return, and that would stop her worrying over Cindy being nervous while meeting her new boss!

'Come!'

The voice responded to the knock and Cindy responded to the voice.

Zac Stone was bent over a pad on his desk, scribbling away. It was seconds before the head of jet black hair was raised and deep blue eyes, very deep blue eyes, met Cindy's gaze.

She stood, with the sun streaming in from the windows now almost directly behind her, erect and elegant, with her head tilted just slightly to one side. It was something she always did, unconsciously, when she was either listening intently or intrigued by what she saw.

She was intrigued by what she saw.

He was wearing a crisp, pale blue shirt of the finest cotton. Through it Cindy could see the shadow of dark hair covering his chest. The top button of the shirt was open and his tie, still knotted, had been loosened, dragged carelessly to one side. His shirt sleeves were rolled up, and the depth of the tan on his forearms made Cindy look pale by comparison. On his wrist there was a gold watch; it was neat, not ostentatious, just wildly expensive.

Zac Stone's eyes seemed to be looking deep inside her. He was unsmiling but not uninterested and Cindy felt, Cindy knew, that he had taken in the details of her appearance as thoroughly as she had absorbed the details of his.

Seeing him had come as a shock to her and she mentally told herself off for it, for the brief flutter of ... *was* it nervousness? ... that was making her stomach contract slightly.

His face was—would handsome be the right word? It was
certainly an attractive face, with strong, clear-cut features,
a straight nose and... Suddenly, Cindy could hear her
grandmother's voice as clearly as if the old lady were standing next to her... 'Dimple on chin, devil within.'

Without realising it she smiled.

Zac Stone's eyebrows rose almost imperceptibly. The few
seconds' surveillance was over, shattered with the silence
when he spoke. 'Good morning. I don't believe we've met.
I'm Zac Stone, and you are...?'

There was nothing in his voice, no accent to indicate that
he was Welsh. He had an attractive voice in that it was deep,
with an unusual timbre. It was almost... almost gravelly.

He had got to his feet as he spoke, but he didn't proffer
his hand. He was a big man, lean but broad, and despite the
added stature given to Cindy by her high-heeled sandals his
height was superior by a good six inches.

'Miss Hetherington, Cindy Hetherington.' She made no
attempt to sit down. It was polite to wait until you were
asked, wasn't it?

Mr Stone's eyes left hers and flitted briefly towards the
intercommunicating door, a slight frown appearing between his brows, and when the eyes came back to Cindy's,
his frown deepened. 'You are Cindy Hetherington?'

The emphasis on the first word made Cindy wonder
whether he was disappointed—or what. Maybe he'd been
expecting someone older, someone more like Miss Druce?
Or was it simply that he hadn't expected her to come in
through the other door?

'Well. Sit down, Cindy, sit down.' The frown cleared as
he waved her towards the chair facing his desk.

As Cindy moved forward he watched her, blatantly, his
eyes moving slowly from the top of her head, over the details of her face and down the length of her slender figure.
But the deep blue eyes were unreadable and the set of his
mouth, still unsmiling, left her guessing as to what was in his
thoughts. She knew only that she didn't feel quite as confi-

dent in herself as she had when she'd entered this room. But Zac Stone couldn't know that. Nor would he. Sheila hadn't labelled her Miss Cool for nothing.

'It's nice to meet you, Mr Stone.' Cindy spoke up first, meeting his eyes levelly. Her soft, well modulated voice was clear and steady, revealing nothing but a polite neutrality. 'As you're no doubt aware, I was away on holiday for the past two weeks, so I learned the news of Bryant's takeover only yesterday.'

There was a slight hesitation before he responded. 'And how did you feel about it?'

She too, hesitated before she replied. She had to think about that one. 'Interested.'

'You want to stay on, I take it?'

'Yes.'

'How long have you worked in advertising?'

'Four years.' She suspected from the wording of his question that he wanted to discover whether his name was known to her. It was that, rather than an enquiry as to her experience, which would come later.

Mr Stone's next question proved her right. 'So you're aware that I sold my original agency two years ago, that I've been off the advertising scene since then and living abroad?'

'Of course.'

'Of course.' He smiled slightly.

'Well, the transaction was reported in *Campaign* and even so, the inter-agency grapevine is very efficient, as I'm sure you're well aware.' Cindy shrugged her slender shoulders, crossing one leg over another as she spoke. 'I want the job as your secretary, Mr Stone, and if you're asking whether I'm aware of your reputation, the answer is yes. It precedes you wherever you go.'

'I wasn't.' The answer came quickly, and the blue eyes flashed at her. There was a hard edge to his voice, letting her know she'd spoken out of turn. 'And I'm well aware of that, too.'

Cindy was unperturbed. In her opinion there was nothing wrong with what she'd said.

Zac Stone looked down at an empty space on his desk, resting his big frame against his chair in the momentary silence. It was as if he were clearing his mind of something. When next he spoke the edge had gone from his voice. 'How long did you work for John Daws, Cindy?'

'Two years. This is the only agency I've worked in. I started here when I was nineteen as an assistant secretary to the Creative Director. I was in that job for six months, then I worked as secretary to the Financial Director for a year. After that I spent six months with an Account Director and then, because I'd had all-round experience, the M.D. asked me to work for him. I was with him until he—left—two weeks ago.'

Mr Stone nodded briefly. 'Good. So, tell me something about yourself.'

The question came as a surprise and she looked at him quickly, not quite understanding. 'I thought I just did.'

'I meant tell me something about yourself, not about your career.'

'Oh! Well, I'm—er—I come from Cheshire, which is where I was born. I'm unmarried, almost twenty-four, interested in gardening, philosophy, yoga, psychology...' Her voice trailed off; he looked positively bored. 'Perhaps you'd like to be more specific, Mr Stone?'

Deliberately, insolently, Zac Stone's eyes moved down the length of her body, coming to rest on her bare, beautifully tanned legs. 'What do you do with your evenings?'

She was thrown completely now, and the first hint of annoyance gripped her. 'I'm sorry,' she said quietly, and as nonchalantly as she could manage, 'but I don't see the relevance of that question.'

'The relevance to what?'

'To my working as your secretary.'

'Don't you?' The edge was back in the deep voice. 'I suggest you answer it just the same. I suggest also that you try being a little more co-operative—if you're sure you want this job.'

If she's sure she wants the job? Cindy shifted slightly in her seat. She did want the job. She'd also taken it for granted she had already got the job, but Zac Stone obviously hadn't! Things were not turning out as she had expected. This was no informal chat by way of introducing themselves, this was an interview!

A flash of indignation rushed through her. Good grief, she could *eat* this job—and before this interview was over she'd make certain Zac Stone realised that!

She didn't care for the way his eyes had raked over her. And she still didn't see the relevance of his question, but she hadn't meant to appear uncooperative. 'I go to the theatre once or twice a week. When evening classes are in session, I go there. Of course there aren't any during the summer. I dine out quite often. I sometimes take my car and go for a drive. Fridays, I sometimes pop down to the coast and spend the weekend by the sea. You know, the usual sort of things.'

'Those are "the usual" sort of things, are they?' The sarcasm in his voice was unmistakable.

Their eyes met and held for a long moment. There seemed to be a total lack of communication between them. They seemed to be at cross purposes.

As if he were making an effort to be patient with her, Mr Stone asked, 'How much do we pay you?'

When Cindy answered that one, he nodded, as if he'd known the answer all along. 'It's not exactly a fortune, is it?'

Cindy smiled, her elegant hands making a sweeping gesture in the air. 'The so-called glamorous jobs are often poorly paid.'

'And where do you live? Do you have far to commute?'

'No. I'm lucky enough to live in walking distance, actually—well, just about. I live off Belgrave Square.'

'A very expensive place to live.' Zac Stone nodded curtly. He drew in a long, slow breath, watching her carefully as he spoke. 'So, you live in one of the most costly areas of Lon-

don, your spare time entertainment is...shall we say extravagant?...and from the look of things, you buy your
shoes and handbags in Bond Street. Am I to assume from
all this that you've got yourself a sugar-daddy?'

Cindy almost lost her composure. His remark, his assumption, his *audacity* was so unexpected that she started
in surprise. Without pausing to think, she put him right
swiftly, her voice tremulous with indignation. 'No, Mr
Stone! You're to assume no such thing!'

'A rich boy-friend, then?'

Now it wasn't his words which infuriated her so much as
the laughter which flitted across the watchful, deep blue
eyes. The nerve of the man! Was he goading her deliberately? 'Wrong again. I haven't got a boy-friend at all!'

Cindy's hands tightened on the handbag which was resting on her lap. She let her eyes drift towards the window, let
the awkward silence hang between herself and the wretched
man who was interviewing her. She didn't have to take this!
She could get up, right now, and just walk out of this place.

But the penny suddenly dropped and Cindy's indignation dissipated as she realised how odd her answers must
have sounded to someone who didn't know anything about
her. And Zac Stone didn't know anything about her, anything at all! How could he, why should he? To all intents
and purposes Cindy was an ordinary working girl who was
being interviewed for a secretarial job. What she took for
granted, her private income, her life-style—well, perhaps she
couldn't really blame him for jumping to all sorts of conclusions.

Or could she? Why did he assume she had a sugar-daddy
in tow? She knew full well that there was nothing about her
which might give a person the impression she was the sort
of girl who would... Damn Zac Stone! He'd goaded her
deliberately. She had no evidence of it; she just knew it!
What the devil was he up to?

But when Cindy turned to look at him again, she ended
up giving him the benefit of the doubt. He was looking at

her expectantly, almost innocently. She just couldn't weigh him up. But then, surely, that was the problem between them. He'd been unable to weigh her up.

'Mr Stone, I have a private income, but it obviously never occurred to me that I should start this interview by telling you that.'

'That's perfectly reasonable,' he shrugged. 'Any more than I would have started the interview by asking you if your salary were supplemented in some way.'

'Perhaps we'd better start again?'

'I think so.' He smiled at her. It was a genuine smile, and a very attractive one at that. Cindy relaxed again . . . and yet—and yet in the corner of her mind there was a doubt. About him. She'd been put on her guard; she didn't trust him. But damn it all, she was more than intrigued by him!

Mr Stone flicked a switch on the intercom on his desk. It was a moment before Alison answered. 'Yes, Mr Stone?'

'Alison, would you make two cups of coffee, please. Cindy's in here with me.'

'Oh! I thought—er—yes, right away, Mr Stone.'

Cindy suppressed a smile. At Alison's surprise—and at the near reverence in her voice.

After switching off the intercom he then picked up the internal telephone and punched out two numbers. 'Is that Bill—no, it's John, isn't it? Would you bring me the personnel file on Cindy Hetherington? Right away, please, John.'

Well, Mr Stone seemed to talk to his staff nicely enough. John Crosdale would be bringing the file. John, who'd presumed Zac Stone to have been born out of wedlock! The personnel files were kept in John's department, accounts, because Bryant's didn't have a personnel department as such.

As far as Cindy was concerned the interview was taking a turn for the better. Mr Stone would see for himself, when he looked at her personnel file, just how well qualified she was. She settled back comfortably in her seat, her confidence and

composure now fully restored. It would be a challenge,
working for a man like Zac Stone. And that, a job she could
really get her teeth into, was just what she needed to fill her
life.

'Right. While we're waiting for the file let me fill you in
on one or two things.' Mr Stone's voice was crisp and businesslike. 'Since you didn't see the relevance of my earlier
question, I will explain it to you. Had I learned that you
were on the verge of marriage, pregnancy or some similar
commitment, there'd have been no point in our continuing
this interview. The same applies if you are committed to
someone, or something, which necessitates your leaving the
office on the dot of five each evening. I take it you are not?'

'No. I'm quite free.'

'If you work for me, you'll work longer hours than those
you worked for John Daws, and that does not automatically entitle you to a raise in salary.' In a tone that seemed
slightly disparaging, he added, 'In the circumstances, that
clearly won't bother you too much.'

Cindy said nothing, she was too busy trying to decide
whether he was putting her down in some way. Was it just
her imagination, or did he seem to resent her independence?

'I start work at eight-thirty,' he went on. 'And I finish
when I've finished for the day. Where I go, my secretary
goes. When I'm on these premises, she'll be in the next
room. When I'm out seeing clients, she'll be by my side.
Understood?'

'Understood.'

'Have you got a current passport?'

'Of course.'

'But of course.' There it was again, that hint of sarcasm.
'You'd have to be prepared for all contingencies. To work
over the weekend, if I deem it necessary. Or to work halfway through the night.'

Cindy was beginning to see what John Crosdale had
meant. 'Professional', Sheila had said. My, my, what a mild

word, coming from Sheila! Cindy smiled inwardly at her own thoughts. She was almost enjoying herself now. With his sarcasm and his threats that she might have to work all the hours God sends, Zac Stone was trying to put her off the job.

'Do you still want to work for me?'

'But of course.' She said it sweetly, knowing full well that her smile would not take the sting from her choice of words. Two could play at that game.

It surprised her that his only reaction was a slight pull at the corners of his lips. Her eyes lingered there, on the firmness of his mouth. At first glance she would have described him as thin-lipped, but there was a curve, a sensuality about the lower lip which spoke of...'I'm sorry, what did you say?' Shocked at herself, at the way her mind had wandered, Cindy looked at him blankly, wide-eyed. She hadn't heard a word.

'I said, what the hell is it with you, Cindy? What's a girl like you doing in a place like this? You are, are you not, the daughter of Sir Robert Hetherington?'

Before she had a chance to reply, there was a knock on the door and John Crosdale walked in with Cindy's personnel file under his arm. He bade her good morning, but she didn't even hear him. She was looking at Zac Stone in astonishment. So he knew who her father was. Well, it wasn't all that surprising. Her father's name had been in the newspapers more than once, although not very recently. But Zac Stone had put two and two together and made four. More to the point, *when* had he realised who her father was?

John walked around the desk and placed the file in front of the new M.D. and, glancing meaningfully at the file and then at Cindy, he shrugged exaggeratedly, pulling a face as he did so. It was designed to let Cindy know that this was unusual, that in last week's 'chats' with the rest of the staff, Zac Stone hadn't bothered to go through anyone else's personnel file.

Cindy met John's eyes and nodded.

'Thank you, John.' Ostensibly, it was a dismissal, but Zac said it in such a way that both Cindy and John were left with the feeling that he must have eyes in the back of his head. He'd caught the message John had intended for Cindy. He didn't miss a thing!

'Zac.' With his eyes rolling upwards, John left the room.

'I am Robert Hetherington's daughter, yes. Have you... have you met my father?' The chances of that were slim, but it was the only solution Cindy could think of.

Zac didn't answer. He flipped open the file, took a cursory glance at the first page, an even quicker glance at the second page and then unclipped Cindy's curriculum vitae from the rest of the papers.

Cindy had submitted the CV with her application for a job at Bryant's four years ago. It comprised three sheets of paper and gave a brief outline of her life; her education, qualifications, and so on. Zac Stone eyed each sheet briefly, then let it fall to the desk.

'No,' he turned his attention back to Cindy, 'I haven't met your father. I read a comprehensive article about him in the newspaper when he retired as a Queen's Counsel.'

Cindy frowned. 'That was eighteen months ago.'

Zac smiled. 'I have a photographic memory.'

More sarcasm.

She still couldn't make head nor tail of the man. 'How did you make the connection? It couldn't have been just the name...'

'It was that and the fact that you come from Cheshire. There can't be many extremely wealthy families in Cheshire with the name of Hetherington.'

'But...' Cindy was growing quite confused. If he'd made the connection, and he knew of her family's wealth, why had he said what he'd said about a sugar daddy?

He watched her, waiting until she'd formed the question in her mind, then pre-empted her. 'I couldn't be sure it was Daddy who was keeping you in the lap of luxury, could I?'

She didn't put him right. It wasn't her father's money but a bequest from her grandmother that Cindy lived on. The thought of her accepting a penny from her father was laughable. Nor did she contradict him about living in the lap of luxury, even though it was a gross exaggeration. Cindy held her tongue because she was in danger of spoiling things. If she told Zac Stone her impressions of him, she'd talk herself right out of a job. And it was rapidly becoming a matter of principle to her that she landed this job.

Inwardly, however, she was fuming. And she got even more cross when he repeated what he had asked her just before John interrupted them. 'So what is it with you, Cynthia? Why are you bothering to work at all?'

Her given name grated on her ears, especially the way he'd used it. 'Everybody calls me Cindy, if you don't mind. I much prefer it.'

'I can understand that,' he said drily. He tapped the papers on his desk. 'There's a year unaccounted for here. What were you doing between the ages of eighteen and nineteen?'

'Nothing. I—'

'Nothing? Then why work now? Judging from the status of your family, your history, you've had everything handed to you on a silver platter. What makes you think you could hold down a job with me? What makes you think you've got what it takes? How the hell did you get into this world in the first place? Is Sam Bryant your uncle or something?'

The sound of Cindy's breath catching in her throat was made inaudible by the knock on the adjoining door. Alison walked in with a tray of coffee and placed it carefully on the desk. Cindy could feel the heat of her anger rising to her cheeks. She was so cross she couldn't have spoken if she'd wanted to. Who the hell did Zac Stone think he was? How dared he speak to her like that? He was putting her down because she just happened to be born into a wealthy family! And no one had done that before, not even Sheila.

As Cindy's eyes flitted towards Alison she saw that the
youngster's eyes had widened in alarm. Alison was busying
herself with the coffee, adding milk and just a few grains of
brown sugar for Cindy. She'd seen the file on the boss's desk
and, no doubt, the two pink patches that had appeared in
Cindy's cheeks. Cindy wasn't coping!

Cindy had the dreadful feeling she was letting Alison
down. It wouldn't have occurred to Alison that Cindy might
not get this job. It hadn't occurred to Cindy that she
mightn't get the job! Well, she'd be damned if she didn't!
What had Sheila said? Something about passing a test ...
Was this a test, and if so, had everyone had to endure it?

But of course they had! She must be getting paranoid,
thinking Mr Stone was picking only on her. A man like him,
he would want to know what motivated his staff, what made
them tick. 'He'll want to know all there is to know about
you ...'

She looked at Zac Stone through new eyes then. He was
rich, he was successful, he was powerful. Those who
couldn't stand his pace had been fired or had left of their
own accord. And Sheila had warned her that she wouldn't
last two minutes. She would prove Sheila wrong. She would
prove Zac Stone wrong in whatever he was assuming her to
be. And quite apart from that, she would prove to herself
that she could get this job, and hold it down.

And she would do it with dignity.

Fortunately, Alison was relating to Mr Stone a message
she had just taken over the phone. It gave Cindy precious
minutes in which to think. He had no good reason for refusing her the job—provided she could show him that she
had what it took. Provided she could pass his test. He'd
been trying to frighten her off. He'd been goading her, and
she'd risen to the bait. But that was all finished now. She
wouldn't rise to it again—ever!

When Alison left, with a frantic glance in her direction,
Cindy settled back comfortably in her chair and picked up
her coffee cup. She laughed softly, 'No, Mr Bryant isn't my

uncle. I was employed here entirely on my own merits. Anyway, to answer your questions—I'm working because I have a lively mind which enjoys being stimulated. And I'd be bored stiff sitting at home twiddling my thumbs all day. I don't *think* I've got what it takes to work for you, I know I have. I'll be perfectly happy to work long hours, if that's what you want, and I'll hold the job down because apart from being well qualified as a secretary I'm also well versed in all aspects of agency work, and I've got a good deal of common sense.'

Cindy was talking coolly, clearly, and she didn't pause to let him get a word in. 'I chose advertising because the psychology behind it fascinates me. I'm interested in what motivates people to buy things. I'm interested in what motivates people to do all sorts of things. I don't think of this as a glamorous job; I think I'm in a tough, competitive world where only the strong and the shrewd survive.'

She looked at him levelly, and waited. When Zac Stone remained silent, she, too, said nothing more. But her eyes were watching his over the rim of her cup. She would have given a lot to know what was going through his mind, but Zac's face remained impassive. This was make or break, she was aware of that. She was also a little nervous of all the claims she'd made, hoping that she would indeed be able to live up to them—if she were given the chance.

He grunted. He was assessing, considering, weighing. Then he picked up his cup and said nothing till he'd finished his coffee. 'Tell me, did you once consider modelling as a career? I see you took a modelling course when you were younger.'

Cindy was taken aback. He'd glanced at the papers on her file so quickly she didn't think he'd had a chance to register everything. 'No, never. I took that course because it polishes one off as far as poise and deportment are concerned. Mummy wasn't quite satisfied with the way they'd turned me out of finishing school, and the course also taught things like make-up, hair care, manicure and so on.'

Inwardly, Cindy was smiling because at the time she had taken the course she was still a little overweight. She had been totally lacking in dress sense and without the first clue as to what she wanted to do with her life. She had been floating, and she suspected her mother had sent her on the course mainly to give her something to do. But it had, in fact, done a great deal for Cindy. 'Of course,' she added, thinking aloud, 'Mummy would never have dreamt of steering me towards modelling as a career!'

When Zac threw her a filthy look, she had no idea what she'd said wrong. If he'd known her when she was seventeen he'd have seen the point in her remark! 'Is there anything else I can tell you about myself?' she asked lightly.

'Yes.' He sounded positively annoyed. 'I see you concentrated on languages during the latter part of your education, then you spent a year with friends of your family in the South of France. Just how good is your French?'

Cindy's eyes widened. He hadn't been joking about his memory. He recalled every word on the papers he'd glanced at. 'Almost as good as my English.'

'And your German?'

'Not so good. Enough to get by, though.'

'You'd use your shorthand very little with me. I prefer to talk to a machine.'

'That's fine. I'm quite at home with a dictaphone.' He had no good reason for refusing her the job, and he knew it.

He shrugged, opened the top drawer of his desk and flung a cassette in Cindy's direction. 'Start with this,' he said curtly. 'Alison will tell you how I like letters set out. She did a letter for me last week—three times. I trust you'll do better.' He picked up the personnel file, shoved the papers back into it and handed it to her. 'Take that back to John Crosdale. Then pick up some petty cash and go out and buy a decent coffee set—something modern. Throw this flowery stuff away. Buzz Sheila and tell her I want her in my office, together with everyone else who works on the Simpson account, at eleven-thirty on the dot. Then phone Simpson's and arrange a meeting with them at their offices one day next week—any time that Mr Simpson himself can be present. Then type a memo to the departmental heads and say there's to be a meeting in the conference room at three on Thursday afternoon . . . Well, what are you waiting for?'

Cindy's sense of victory was mild, very mild. There was— it was unmistakable now—a nervousness clutching at her stomach. But there was no way she would let it show. To him, or to anyone else. Calmly she gathered up the coffee cups, put the file on the tray and the cassette on the file. 'Yes, Mr Stone.'

As she moved towards the adjoining door, she could feel Zac Stone's eyes boring into her. 'And Cindy,' he said crisply, almost reluctantly, 'you'd better make it Zac from now on.'

She turned and smiled. 'Well, thank you—Zac.'

'Don't thank me yet,' he warned. 'You're on trial. We'll give it a month, then talk again. That is, if you're still here by then.'

Cindy said nothing. She'd be there, all right. She'd show him! Immediately the door was closed behind her she put down the tray, held up a silencing hand at Alison and wrote down Zac's instructions. If Alison distracted her she'd be sure to forget at least one of them.

'So you're staying?' Alison whispered as soon as Cindy's hand went down.

'Of course I'm staying. I told you I would.'

'Yes, but— Oh, I'm so glad, Cindy! I'd hate it if I wasn't working with you. Well, what did you think of him?' Alison was jerking her thumb towards the door again. 'Sexy, isn't he? Don't you think he's just gorgeous?'

Cindy couldn't suppress her smile. 'Gorgeous?' she mused. After what she'd just been through? She felt as though she'd been shoved through a wringing machine. 'He struck me as being a little—er—stern.'

'Oh, I don't mean that. You know I didn't mean that!' Alison almost gave it full voice. 'I mean his looks. Don't you think he'd just gorgeous looking? Come on, Cindy!'

'He's...well, I suppose he's attractive. Sort of.' That was as much as she was prepared to admit. She picked up the internal telephone.

'I wonder what he thought of you?' Alison queried.

But Cindy didn't want to think about the answer to that one.

CHAPTER THREE

CINDY WAS really thrown in at the deep end. Somehow, she coped. She did that because she was determined. Still, before the day was over she made her first mistake. It wasn't serious, it just infuriated her.

There were nine letters on the tape Zac had given her and she had put them on his desk, beautifully typed, by four o'clock. He emerged from his office at a little before seven and handed her the letter-folder. 'Get these off tonight, would you?'

Cindy took the folder from him and flipped it open, keeping her voice light and casual as she asked him whether they were calling it a day. He was wearing his jacket and had switched off the light in his office.

'I'm calling it a day,' he said gruffly, 'but you're not.'

'You haven't signed these...'

'You haven't set them out properly.' The satisfaction in his voice sickened her. 'I like everything set against the margin, no punctuation in the address—it saves time. Retype them and sign them on my behalf.'

'Sorry.' It was all Cindy could manage to say. She was fuming. With herself, mostly, but at his attitude, too.

'Good night,' he drawled then. 'Give the cleaners my regards.'

She glared after him. The office cleaners came in at six in the morning, as he was no doubt well aware. In her anxiety to get through everything he'd given her to do that day, she'd clean forgotten to ask Alison about the setting out of his letters. She retyped them, though it took her far longer

than it should have; she was so cross with herself that her
typing went awry. It was very late when she got home.

The next day, she saw two different facets of her boss's
personality. She saw him being flippant and she saw him
being charming.

'Now there's interesting for you!' He spoke to her in a
sing-song accent which was exaggeratedly Welsh when he
called her into his office during the middle of the morning.

When Cindy looked nonplussed he dropped the accent
and explained, still obviously delighted about something,
'I've just had a call from the Ad Manager at Barrats. He
invited himself to lunch.'

'Barrats?' Cindy stood, looking cool and crisp in a pink
shirtwaister. 'But they're not one of our clients. They do
business with Cookson Associates . . .' She caught the twin-
kle in his eyes. 'I see. So business is coming to you, is it?'

'We'll have to see. We'll be leaving at one.'

'We?'

'Of course, we.' As she nodded, he added, 'Just be sweet
to him, don't drink too much wine, and listen to everything
he says.'

Cindy did exactly as he'd told her during the two and a
half hour luncheon—and Zac said later she'd made a good
'table decoration'. There was no charm for Cindy. Not ever.
It was reserved only for the clients.

On Thursday Zac addressed the heads of department and
told them about certain changes which would take place in
the agency. Towards the end of the meeting he brought up
the subject of time-keeping. 'I'm not a clock-watcher. I want
a relaxed atmosphere at Bryant's. You can come and go as
you please—within reason.' He added that with a look in
Sheila's direction. 'All I'm interested in is that the work gets
done. When you do it is entirely up to yourselves.'

That did not, of course, apply to Cindy. She got to work
at eight-thirty on the dot and didn't leave the office until her
boss left the office. Nor was the bit about a relaxed atmosphere applicable to her—Zac saw to that. He taxed her to

her limits. He answered her questions, but he gave her not the slightest word of encouragement, or praise. Nor did he speak to her the way he spoke to everyone else. His sarcasm punctuated the day at regular intervals.

But he didn't get a rise out of her. She would not give him best. She never answered him back and she never let him guess what was going through her mind. But there were compensations for her. The job itself had already removed her depression. She was engrossed and fascinated by it even before the week was out.

She was also fascinated by Zac Stone, in spite of disliking the man. He drove himself hard, and Cindy wondered why. Why had he come out of retirement? What was the real man like? Not the Managing Director of Bryant's, not the man who was determined to make her life hell—but the real Zac Stone?

BY THE end of Cindy's second week she was really beginning to feel the strain. She was working hard, but it wasn't the strain of hard work so much as the strain between herself and Zac. He hadn't been joking when he'd said she'd be on trial.

On the Friday night, when she finally got through the front door of her flat, Cindy sank into the nearest chair and kicked off her shoes, letting her toes curl into the thick pile of the living room carpet. She didn't know which she wanted most, a cup of tea or a hot bath. She amended that to a cool bath; the weather was so sultry at the moment that even the walk home had exhausted her. Her feet were throbbing.

They had finished work around nine tonight, but at least there was no question of going into the office over the weekend. Boy, did she intend to make the most of the weekend! She would lie in tomorrow. She would stay in bed until she woke up naturally, until she'd had as much sleep as she needed! Even the thought of it was luxurious.

It was an effort to go and brew up. She leaned against the kitchen wall as she waited for the kettle to boil, her hand automatically reaching out to pluck two dying flowers from the geranium on her kitchen windowsill. Pulling a face, she ran a finger over one of the slats of the Venetian blinds as she closed them. They needed washing, but it was just too bad. They'd have to wait until she could face the task. On Sunday, perhaps. Maybe by then she would have enough energy to catch up with her household chores.

The voice of the newscaster on the television almost lulled her to sleep with her cup of tea resting on her lap. She was waiting up for a while in order to see the advertisements during the commercial breaks. It was part of her job, or at least she'd now made it part of her job, to keep up to date with the latest ads, to see what sort of stuff the competition were turning out.

Things would level off, she supposed, as far as work was concerned. Things couldn't possibly stay as hectic as they'd been over the past couple of weeks. There were several jobs she'd had to do during the past fortnight which wouldn't be in the normal run of things... like arranging the party, for instance.

There had been a meeting of the new Board. Zac and his Directors, who were hand-picked and the cream of the London advertising scene, had decided that a party would be given at Bryant's during the last week of July, no expense spared. All the clients, big and small, were to be invited, together with a number of potential clients, certain members of the press, various contacts of Zac's and anyone else whose name ought to be included. The guest list amounted to more than a hundred names and it was Cindy's task to organise the entire affair. Of course, everyone who mattered already knew that Bryant's had been taken over by Zac Stone. The party was by way of an official announcement.

Cindy didn't wake up of her own accord. At a little after eight on the Saturday morning she was wrenched from her sleep by a great, rumbling boom of thunder immediately overhead. Perspiration broke out on her forehead. She'd always been terrified of storms. She stuck her head under her pillow as white flashes of lightning illuminated her bedroom, making everything appear iridescent.

It was illogical to be afraid, she was aware of that; this was just the price to be paid for the unusually long spell of hot weather lately. But logic didn't help in this instance. The storm raged for over an hour, and as much as she was longing for a cup of coffee, Cindy stayed right where she was.

By lunchtime the storm had long since passed, but it was still pouring with rain. Any hopes of her spending a leisurely day out of doors were shot. But at least the storm had cooled things down a little. After chatting for an hour with her mother on the phone, she slipped into denims and a teeshirt, and caught up with the housework. She was ironing when the porter buzzed her in the middle of the afternoon.

She picked up the internal telephone in the hall, hoping she wasn't about to have unexpected company. 'Yes, Bill?'

There was a smile in the porter's voice. 'There's a delivery boy from the florist's here, Miss Hetherington. May I send him up?'

Flowers? It wasn't her birthday. 'Er—yes, please do.'

The flowers were from James and they were roses. Twelve of them. Twelve glorious red roses. Cindy had to say one thing for him: he didn't give up easily. Earlier in the week, he'd tried to contact her at the office, but Alison had taken the call. Now he was sending flowers. Her first thought was to drop the entire bouquet down the rubbish chute, but there was no way she could bring herself actually to do it. Her love of all things natural wouldn't allow her to do that. Besides, the roses were innocent, and very beautiful. She placed them carefully into a vase of water and found just the right spot for them in the lounge.

'Forgive me,' the card said, 'James'. Cindy tore it to shreds and went back to the ironing board.

By Sunday afternoon there was no let-up in the weather. It was still raining cats and dogs, but Cindy took herself off to the cinema regardless. She liked her own company well

enough, but spending two consecutive days alone indoors
was not her idea of a nice weekend. On the way home from
the cinema she picked up half a dozen magazines and spent
a couple of hours after dinner reading all the ads.

She was getting into bed when the doorbell rang and not
only was she naked, she was puzzled. It was almost eleven
o'clock and she certainly wasn't expecting company at this
hour. It had to be one of her neighbours, unlikely though
that was. In all the time Cindy had lived in Priory Court,
nobody had said more than good morning or good evening
to her. City life was like that.

The security in the building was good. The tenants' privacy was protected. No one got into the building unless
they'd been seen and cleared by the porter in the reception
area. But when Cindy peered through the tiny spy-hole in
her front door, she realised that the security system was by
no means infallible. It wasn't one of her neighbours. It was
Zac Stone.

'Zac?' she called to him through the closed door. 'Give
me a moment, will you? I'm—I'm...I was just in the
bathroom.' Dashing quickly to her bedroom, she pulled on
the nearest garment she could lay her hands on. It was a full-
length housecoat in pale blue and perfectly respectable, if
not quite the sort of garment she'd choose to wear in her
boss's company.

Cindy tied a firm knot in the belt at the waist before
opening the door. 'Zac... Well, I must say you were the last
person I was expecting—not that I was expecting anyone!'
She forced a smile, chattering on a little nervously. It was
strange, seeing him like this, seeing him out of context, sort
of thing. She'd only ever seen him wearing a suit until now.

He looked almost menacing tonight. In a black shirt and
black slacks, the depth of his tan was accentuated. His hair
was as black as night; it was neither straight nor curly, there
was just plenty of it and it was brushed back carelessly from
his face. Yes, he did look menacing. Dark and menacing.

He also looked very attractive; Cindy admitted it to herself almost reluctantly.

Zac Stone had the sort of face which became more interesting the more one got to know it. The cleft in the chin was very slight, the line of his jaw clearly defined. It was a lean face, a strong face, and the depth of colour in his eyes was quite unlike anything Cindy had seen before. They were so positively blue—deep blue. She could spend a long time looking at that face, enjoying it—if it belonged to someone other than Zac Stone.

'How—how did you get past the doorman?'

Zac walked ahead of her into the living room, not waiting to be invited. 'I nodded and bade him good evening. You don't mind if I sit down, do you?'

'Of course not.' What else could she say? For an instant she wondered how he'd known her exact address, then she remembered his amazing memory and the personnel file. 'What—what can I do for you?' She switched on a couple of lamps as he sat down.

'Two things. No, three.' His eyes moved round the room as he spoke, taking in all its details from the beige carpet to the plants hanging from the ceiling, the cane coffee tables and the sandy-coloured three-piece suite. They lingered momentarily on the roses. His scrutiny was swift, but Cindy knew he'd have missed nothing. 'Were you in bed just now?'

'On my way.' She was unsure whether to remain standing or whether to sit. What did he want with her at this time of night? 'Would you...perhaps you'd like a cup of coffee?'

'I'd like a jar of coffee, if you've got one to spare.'

'I'm sorry?' She looked at him blankly.

'It's the traditional thing, isn't it?' He smiled then, looking her over from head to foot as he did so. 'New neighbours usually knock and beg a cup of sugar or a packet of tea from the person next door, don't they?'

'New— *You've* moved in next door?'

'About five minutes ago. I've been living in a hotel while the place was being made ready for me. My furniture was delivered yesterday, but I've been out of town for the week-end. I've just got back now.'

He was enjoying the shock on her face, she could see it in his eyes. She'd seen the furniture van the day before, she'd even felt sorry for the men whose task it had been to un-load it in the rain. But she hadn't dreamt that her new neighbour would turn out to be her boss!

'You needn't look unhappy about it, Cindy. From my point of view it could be very convenient having my secretary living next door.'

And very inconvenient from Cindy's point of view. Didn't she put in enough hours of work as it was? 'I'm not un-happy about it.' She lied because she felt it was necessary. Well, it was a half lie. She didn't exactly feel unhappy about him living next door, she just wasn't thrilled by the idea.

The spark of laughter faded from his eyes. 'Liar,' he challenged, 'why don't you say what's going through your mind?'

'I was just . . . I was just wondering why you never men-tioned you were moving into Priory Court.'

'What? And spoil the surprise?' He did it again, just as he had a moment ago. He looked her over from head to foot, but this time he did it slowly, insolently.

It was guaranteed to put Cindy's back up because she knew he was doing it deliberately. She was well aware that on a personal level her boss disapproved of her. Why else would he do it to her? It wasn't as if he were looking at her because she was a woman, it was as if he were thinking—well, she didn't want to speculate on that.

Lifting her head proudly, she took his scrutiny with dig-nity. She wouldn't give him the satisfaction of a reaction. She took it because she wanted to get on with her job, which was the only reason she made such an effort to get on with Zac Stone.

'You offered me a cup of coffee a moment ago,' he said quietly, sardonically. 'Or do you intend to pose like that all evening, with the lamplight shining through your gown?'

Dumbstruck, Cindy marched from the room and headed for the kitchen. She was blushing to the roots of her hair. She had been standing in front of the light, but she hadn't thought about it for one minute! She glared angrily in the direction of the living room as the sound of Zac's low, rumbling laughter reached her. The nerve of the man! He'd accused her of *posing!* God, he was smart, putting the onus on her when it was his fault she'd stood defiantly rooted to the spot.

She couldn't even remember what she'd come into the kitchen for, she was too busy looking down at her housecoat. It wasn't all that thin; it probably wasn't transparent at all. Was it? But if she slipped into her bedroom and put her underclothes on, it would only amuse Zac Stone all the more. Damn him!

'On second thoughts,' he called, the amusement still there in his voice, 'make it a Scotch, will you? Neat. With ice.'

Fuming, Cindy looked in cupboards for the bottle of whisky she knew she had somewhere. She never touched the stuff herself. With an effort she composed herself before she took him his drink. 'I haven't got a spare jar of coffee. I opened a new one yesterday. I've put some in a small tin for you.'

'Fine.'

She handed him the Scotch. During the past two weeks she'd come to the conclusion that 'thank you' was not in his vocabulary. At least, not when he was speaking to her.

'Aren't you joining me, Cindy?' he asked.

'I don't drink.'

'You do drink.'

'I only drink wine.' It was all she could do to look at him, she was so angry. She sat well away from him, arranging her housecoat so that not even her ankles were showing. 'What else did you want, Zac? You said there were three things.'

His eyebrows rose slightly, but he said nothing more for several seconds. Then he nodded towards the roses. 'Secret admirer?'

'Why secret?' she said stiffly.

'There's no card, your birthday's not till the twelfth of September and you told me quite categorically that you haven't got a boy-friend. At the interview, remember?'

'I remember.' Did she ever!

'Well?'

'I bought them myself.' She was damned if she'd tell him where the roses came from.

'How interesting,' he said drily. 'You went out yesterday in the pouring rain to buy yourself a dozen red roses.'

Cindy looked down at the carpet. It was very obvious the roses were no more than a day old. She put on her bored look and hoped for the best. She wished he would go. The strain between them was almost tangible tonight.

He was just looking at her, and though his face was impassive Cindy could feel his annoyance. 'I was wondering who does your cleaning for you. That was the second thing I wanted. If your cleaning lady isn't occupied elsewhere perhaps you'd ask her to come and do my place when she's finished in here. I want someone to come in every day. Weekdays, that is.'

'I do my own housework. But if you ask the porter he'll make the necessary arrangements for you.'

'I'm surprised you know how,' Zac smiled slightly but it didn't lessen the sarcasm in his voice. He looked around the room. 'But you evidently do.'

His remark stung, but Cindy was determined not to give him any feedback. Did he think she'd been wrapped up in cotton wool all her life? 'And the third thing you wanted?'

The muscles of his face tightened almost imperceptibly. 'You know, we've spent many hours together, but we've never had a conversation.'

'There's no time for conversation at work.'

He corrected her. 'What you mean is that you have no time for conversation. There's a difference.'

'I ... didn't say that.'

'Well? We're not at work now. So why don't you say what's really going through your mind?'

Cindy was growing more anxious, and angry, by the minute. She was suspicious of him, of what he wanted. Had he come here hoping to catch her off guard? Was he spoiling for a fight? She wouldn't be surprised. 'It—I don't think that would be a good idea. Why don't we just leave things as they are? You're my boss, Zac. We get the job done. That's all we need to be concerned about really.'

'But we're neighbours, too. Remember? And I want to know more about my new neighbour...'

He was goading her again. And the more he did it, the more angry she became. He was lounging on her sofa, his legs stretched out before him and his arms spread out across the backrest. His presence seemed to fill the room, but it had little to do with the sheer size of him. Cindy felt threatened, dominated, even claustrophobic.

'...Let's take this room, for instance. This is an unusual sort of room, Cindy. It tells me quite a lot about you.'

Cindy's control was starting to slip. 'Does it? I should have thought you knew enough about me already.'

'Oh, no.' He said it quietly, too quietly. 'Not yet.' He smiled, the darkness of his skin making his teeth seem even whiter. But the smile didn't touch his eyes. 'I can't really say I like the room. Obviously it's too feminine for my liking, but it's pretty much as I expected it to be. It shows taste, it's expensively furnished and it's...cool.'

If there was a compliment somewhere in his last sentence, his tone had turned it into a backhanded one. Cindy got to her feet quickly. 'I'll get your coffee.'

She walked out briskly. What did he know about taste? After the way he'd had their offices decorated, she dreaded to think what he'd had done to the flat next door. She snatched up the coffee—only to walk smack into him as she was leaving the kitchen. Obviously his curiosity was such that he wanted to see what the rest of her flat looked like.

Zac's arms came out to steady her on her feet and Cindy took an involuntary step backwards. His touch came as a shock to her, and it was more than she could manage to hide the fact. The small tin of coffee dropped from her fingers and scattered over the kitchen floor. Neither of them noticed it. Alarmed at her reaction to the physical contact, at the way her pulses leapt in response, she felt her shoulders tense as her eyes met with his. Zac's eyes looked deeply into hers, moving downwards over her face as though he'd never seen it before. His strong fingers were burning against the flesh of her arms through the soft material of her housecoat. It seemed as if minutes passed before he let go of her but in reality it was only seconds. Seconds. Just a few seconds in which he was holding her so close that she could feel the warmth of his breath on her cheek.

But they were seconds that Cindy regretted.

Zac Stone was undeniably attractive. There was an innate strength, an animal magnetism about the man that had struck her from the moment she'd set eyes on him. He was very much the physical type, a man whom no woman would pass by without turning to take a second look.

But there was nothing else attractive about him. He was ruthless through and through. He was hard, insensitive and the very epitome of everything Cindy disliked in a man. She stepped away from him smartly, her hands going up to her arms where his fingers had touched her flesh. She regretted he'd had reason to touch her. She regretted the physical effect it had had on her. But she didn't realise how much that regret showed on her face, didn't realise how her soft mouth had grown taut, how her head had tilted upwards as if she would defy her own response.

'You bitch!' Suddenly, all hell broke loose as the deep voice hissed at her. 'You haughty, supercilious little bitch!' he grabbed hold of her so roughly that she cried out in pain. In one swift, continuous movement his lips came down on her open mouth as his fingers bit hard into her arms.

Cindy's lips parted further as pain shot through her, but her cry was smothered, drowned by the punishment of his kiss. It was more than she could endure, but she was not afraid of him. She absolutely was not afraid of him! It took everything she had to wrench her body sideways in an effort to break the contact of his lips. 'You bastard! How dare you—'

'How *dare* I?' Zac's eyes glinted dangerously. 'So you're too snooty to be touched, are you? Too haughty to be kissed! You've pushed me too far tonight, with your bored expression and your filthy looks!'

'What the hell are you talking about? You listen—oh!' Cindy gasped in frustration at the ease with which he yanked her closer towards him. She was crushed against the hardness of his chest as he claimed her mouth once more, her arms and her back immobilised by his vice-like grip. The force of his mouth on hers made her lips part involuntarily. He kissed her mercilessly, bruisingly, until her mind was screaming in indignation, humiliation. But somewhere deep inside her there was a response, in spite of everything. In spite of the way he was hurting her, in spite of the hatred she was feeling for him.

'I'm going to change this attitude of yours, madam, if it's the last thing I do.' When at last he raised his head Cindy was gasping for breath and still struggling frantically to free herself. 'Stop struggling, damn you! You'll get more of what you've just had unless you keep still and listen to me!'

The volume of his voice made her flinch then, but she glared at him defiantly; her brown eyes wide and darkened with anger. 'What's the matter with you? You're crazy! Let me *go!*' She twisted violently, freeing her right arm. Her hand flew upwards towards Zac's face, but it was caught by the wrist in mid-air. Her efforts were wasted. She'd known that all along, but her pride and her fury would not allow her to succumb.

Zac swore and lifted her bodily, moving her further back until she was pinned against the sink. His eyes were sparking with rage as he pushed both her arms behind her, holding them in the small of her back with one hand. 'If you try anything like that again, you'll find yourself on the receiving end. Now keep still and listen to me!'

She had no choice. His feet were set apart as he towered over her, his body only inches from her own. The steel of the sink was pressing against her lower back as he held her in place with the grip on her wrists. 'All right, all right! But let go of me, *please!*'

'I thought I told you to shut up...' He bent his head and Cindy drew her breath in sharply as she saw what was coming.

'No! Please! All right. Zac, for God's sake!'

He straightened, looking down at her with anger which was barely contained. 'This has been brewing for the past two weeks, Cindy. You know that as well as I do. I intend to clear the air once and for all. I'm sick of the atmosphere between us, I'm sick of your patronising little smiles, your disdainful looks, your entire attitude.'

'*My* attitude? You've got a nerve! You can't speak to me without drenching your words with sarcasm—'

'Not sarcasm. Bluntness. I believe in calling a spade a spade.'

'That isn't true!' she countered. 'If that were true, if you were honest, you'd say it directly. You'd tell me to my face that you resent my independence, you resent my background!'

She saw his brows pull together in a frown. 'Don't talk such rubbish!' he said angrily. 'What the hell has that got to do with anything?'

'You didn't want to give me the job in the first place... Zac, my back's hurting! Please let me go. If you really want to talk... I can't think straight like this. Let's—let's sit down.'

'You'll stay right where you are. This suits me just fine.' He released her at once, but he made sure she didn't move by stepping a little closer to her. Just inches. But they were inches that closed the space between their bodies so that the tips of her breasts were brushing against him. And then he kissed her again before she could even guess his intention. Cindy's mind spun in confusion. She couldn't begin to understand him, his behaviour... But his kiss was quite different now. It didn't last and it didn't punish.

'What... what was that for? I—I didn't—' She was tongue-tied, confused and very, very disturbed by the feelings he aroused in her, by the warmth which suffused her body, by the utterly ridiculous urge she had to reach out and pull him towards her so that his mouth would once again claim hers. This, while at the same time her intellect was telling her to strike out at him for all she was worth. But she didn't move a muscle.

Zac was smiling, but there was no humour in it. 'That was for being a good girl. For telling me, finally, what's been bugging you, what's been going through your mind. I've invited you to do that umpteen times before tonight, Cindy, but all I've had is a stony silence, that hauteur, that special brand of disdain you're so practised at giving.'

The smile faded, to be replaced by straightforward irritation. But at least, thank heavens, it wasn't anger. 'Now let's make this quite clear: It's all I've just described which irritates the hell out of me. As for your accusation—your history, your independence or whatever you called it doesn't enter into things as far as I'm concerned. I'm neither resentful of it nor impressed by it. But you yourself allow those things to spoil you. You're snooty, stuck-up, cold and unnatural. I like straight talk, Cindy. There's a dishonesty in your attitude—in your *withholding*—that I'm not prepared to tolerate. Do you understand?'

She did and she didn't. It had come as a shock to her to hear herself described by Zac as he saw her. Yet she began to understand, now, how she'd managed to give him that impression... such a *wrong* impression. If only he knew her, really! She'd been working on a false assumption about his resentment. He *had* resented her, but not for the reasons . . . oh, if only she had more time to think, to sort it all out in her mind. But it was too late, by the look of it. Disappointment overtook her then, and it showed. 'So—so you're telling me I've just talked myself out of a job. You've finally found—'

Zac sighed, long and hard. 'Are we having a semantic problem now or are you being deliberately obtuse?'

'Zac, I don't understand—you said . . . Oh, I don't understand *you!*'

'Evidently. Which is precisely the problem between us. I'm not firing you, for heaven's sake! Am I likely to fire you for speaking your mind, for doing exactly what I want you to do? Besides, I never let go of people who are potentially useful to me. Potentially, mark you. You've a lot to learn about your job yet, but I'm satisfied with your progress so far. You were on trial for one month, and that's how it stays. But from now on you'll loosen up a little. You're part of a team, my team, and I don't like strained atmospheres in the office.'

Cindy looked up at him in silence. Zac Stone was really a . . .

'Say it!' Zac turned his hands palms upwards shrugging. 'Just say it.'

'I—I was thinking you—you really are an extraordinary man. But my God, I dislike you!'

The blue eyes warmed with laughter and his smile parted his lips. 'Now there's a very good girl!'

Without warning, he took her in his arms and kissed her passionately. He kissed her with a passion she had known all along he was capable of. And it frightened the life out of her. Instinctively she'd inched away from him, the free part of her body swaying backwards, but Zac's arms came round her back and pulled her easily but firmly against his chest.

This time, Cindy's lips were parted by the insistence of the kiss. He kissed her slowly but hungrily, probing, exploring until her senses reeled and everything that had happened, everything that had previously passed between them faded into nothingness. She was aware only of this moment, of the hard pressure of his body against hers. In response to her unspoken longing, his hands came round to cup her breasts, his fingers moving in a slow, exquisitely sensuous rhythm.

There was no resistance in her. Cindy couldn't have stopped him if she'd wanted to. She was frightened by that knowledge and she was ashamed at her own reaction, at the way she had responded so readily, even hungrily. All too soon, it was over and Zac stepped away from her, smiling at the way her cheeks suffused with colour as he looked into her eyes. It was a smile of satisfaction.

Cindy simply didn't know what to do, what to say. She couldn't know how she looked, with her lips moist and parted, her dark eyes telling him far, far more than she wanted him to know. Unlike Zac, she wasn't smiling. Unlike him, she was bewildered. Never, *never* had she reacted physically to a man the way she had reacted to him.

She'd felt Zac's response as plainly as she'd felt her own. She watched, now, as his breathing slowed back to normal. But he was fully in control. Oh, so coolly, completely in control. Just as he had been all along, since setting foot inside her flat, since the moment they'd met.

He'd won. And she hated him for it. She was glad the air had been cleared, she was glad she was now free to be herself... But Zac Stone had a different hold over her now. A different power. A power she wasn't able to resist.

And he knew it.

She tore her eyes from his. 'I...Zac...the coffee. I'll get you some more.'

'Forget it. I can live through one breakfast without coffee. Goodnight, Cindy. I'll see you tomorrow.' He turned, but she called his name.

'I—was this what you came for tonight? To clear the air, I mean. Was it all premeditated?'

'Actually, no.' He shrugged slightly, and she believed him. 'You asked for it tonight. But it was on the agenda, I can't deny that.'

'But the third thing. Was it ... this?' She pulled her gown more closely around her, looking away.

Zac's laugh was short. 'No, it wasn't that. That wasn't premeditated, either. I wanted to mention that I've got a list of nine more names to add to those of the people we've invited to the party. Remind me to give it to you tomorrow.'

She nodded, still avoiding his eyes. 'All right.'

'Now there's a good girl!'

Like one conditioned, Cindy responded to those words with alarm written all over her lovely face.

'Relax!' Zac threw back his head and laughed. 'We'll deal with one thing at a time, Cindy. One thing at a time.'

With that, he left, and Cindy stood rooted to the spot, staring after him. He'd surprised her over and over again tonight, and she still had a lot to sort out in her mind. But Zac Stone's last remark was a cryptic one. Quite what he'd meant by it she couldn't be sure.

But she certainly had her suspicions.

CHAPTER FOUR

AS CINDY walked to work on the morning of the day of the party she reflected on the way her life—at least her working life—had changed dramatically in such a short space of time. It was the last Friday of July—and the last day of her one-month trial period.

The new Bryant's was so different from the old. She was surrounded by interesting people, in an interesting job. Working for someone other than Zac couldn't possibly have been the same. In her job she had found what she'd been looking for.

Things were going well. Life was so much easier now she was able to be herself with Zac. As far as everyone else was concerned she and Zac were part of a team, all of whom had a basic respect for one another. When in the presence of other members of staff, Cindy treated Zac in precisely that manner.

But from time to time, in their private moments, the old animosity would raise its head. Or perhaps it was simply a clash of personalities. Whatever, at least she was free to speak her mind now, when that happened. So there was no strain between them. The only strain that Cindy was currently experiencing was that which was a natural by-product of working hard and long hours. But she didn't mind that, and if her social life was non-existent, she didn't even notice.

And yet, while one difficulty with Zac had been resolved, another one had taken its place. But that was only as far as Cindy was concerned, and it was a far more controllable problem. She was acutely aware of Zac as a man. And she didn't want to be. She wanted only to think of him as her boss, and prior to the showdown with him it had been easy to do that. Now, however, it was difficult indeed to think of him only in those terms.

As a slow drizzle started to fall, Cindy edged closer to the wall as she walked. So much for the weather forecast! She didn't even have her umbrella with her. It wasn't that she disliked getting wet, it was that she hated the way her hair went very curly in the rain—and there'd be no chance whatever of having it blow-dried before the party. Today was going to be hectic, to say the least.

Quite apart from checking that everything was in order for the party that evening, she had a pile of day-to-day work waiting for her. Bryant's was buzzing at the moment because a new campaign was being planned—thanks to the new boss.

Come to think of it, she did respect Zac Stone—in a purely professional sense, that is. Zac doubled as the Creative Director. He did that because he was an advertising man down to his fingertips, and working mainly as an administrator would not have given him the pleasure he so obviously derived from being in on the action. The instigator of the action.

He had done a superb job on the Simpson account. Simpson's were manufacturers of furniture and they had warehouses in every major city from which they sold direct to the public. They advertised through television, radio and the press, and they spent vast sums of money. It was big business, Bryant's biggest account. And Bryant's had been in danger of losing them.

Simpson's factory and head office were in Middlesex, and it had been there that the meeting had taken place during which Zac Stone had not only prevented the loss of this account but sold them on the idea of an entirely new advertising campaign on a nationwide scale. Greg Halliday and Cindy had watched him do it.

Greg Halliday was one of the new men Zac had brought in. He had been appointed Senior Account Director and had done a great deal of talking at the meeting with Simpson's, whose account he would be in charge of. But it was Zac's reputation as the best TV advertising man in the business that had pulled it off.

Whereas old Mr Bryant had been very much a newspaper man, behind the times as far as TV advertising was concerned, it was in the latter that Zac Stone's real expertise lay. Greg had told Cindy this, and coming from him it was undoubtedly high praise. Greg was cast very much in the same mould as Zac; he knew the ad business inside out, though physically and personality-wise the two men could not have been more different.

Cindy's reappraisal of the past four weeks was interrupted when Zac's car slowed down beside her. He opened the passenger door and called to her, 'Hop in.'

But the damage was already done as far as Cindy's hair was concerned. She moved towards the car, but declined the offer of a lift. Zac had offered her a lift only once before, and she had explained to him that she preferred to walk to the office. On two evenings after work she had actually asked for a lift, simply because she had been too tired to walk. And after all, he did live next door to her.

Apart from those two instances, though, Zac might just as well have lived on the other side of London. As a neighbour she never saw him. He seemed to disappear during the weekends and he had never impinged on her private time except for the evening when he had asked for the coffee.

'No, thanks. I don't mind getting wet. You know I like my morning constitutional—it's the only peaceful time of the day.' Not for the first time, Cindy was thinking how very fitting it was that her boss drove a black Jaguar. She could think of no other car that would suit him better than a Jaguar. It was black, it was sleek and sophisticated...and it could be lethal if badly handled.

'I don't mind if you get wet, either,' he came back at her. 'You can get soaked to the skin for all I care. I'm concerned about your getting to work on time. You're running late and we've got a hell of a lot to do today—so get in this car, and fast! I don't want to pick up a reputation as a pavement crawler.'

She got in.

'Food, Cindy. You never told me what you'd arranged with the caterers for the party. Of course, it's a bit late to make changes now.' Zac pulled away smoothly and swiftly. How he coped with the morning rush hour in the West End, Cindy couldn't imagine. It was more than she'd like to tackle every day. Still, at least he had a parking spot in town.

'Now why should I bother a busy man like yourself with a detail such as that? The invitations were sent out by me, the drinks, the bar, the food, everything was left up to me, remember? You said spare no expense, and get on with it. So I did.'

'Point taken, point taken,' he laughed. 'And no doubt your taste in food is as impeccable as your taste in clothes.'

Cindy looked at him sideways. That sounded very much like a compliment.

'Don't you ever give that car of yours a run? That is your car, isn't it, the white Spitfire that never moves off the forecourt?'

'Yes. I'm afraid it's been neglected of late.' Cindy was attempting to smooth down her hair. She could feel the feathery little curls framing her face already. If only she'd picked up her umbrella . . .

'But you told me at the interview you sometimes "pop down to the coast and spend the weekend by the sea".'

She looked at him sideways again. Not only had he quoted her verbatim, he had also used the same inflection she had used. 'So I did. And I did pop down to the coast quite often. But frankly it's taken me some time to adjust to my new pace of work. I've been sleeping during the weekends—recharging my batteries, so to speak. Mind you, I really must make an effort. I do like to get out of London at weekends.'

'Same here,' he nodded. 'I'm house-hunting at the moment. I'm looking for a place in the country—somewhere I can make an escape to at the weekends.'

'You surprise me, actually. You seem so much a City man. I didn't think you'd have the urge to get away from it.'

Zac shrugged, manoeuvring the big car into the small, tightly-packed parking lot with enviable ease. 'I never used to have that urge. One changes, Cindy. Besides, I think when one's country-born, at some point in one's life the attractions of the countryside always come back and beckon.'

She was about to say that she hadn't realised he was country-born. She knew he was Welsh, of course, but that was the sum total of Cindy's knowledge of Zac Stone— outside the advertising world.

But Zac was already getting out of the car. He came round and opened the passenger door for her—and immediately succeeded in spoiling her good mood by telling her the rain had made her hair curl. 'I'm well aware of it,' she said shortly. 'And you're about to tell me I look like Goldilocks, right?'

Zac made an expansive gesture with his arms. 'Now would I say something like that when it would obviously upset you?'

'Yes.'

'Besides, it's Sheila who's labelled you Goldilocks... Well, that's one of your nicknames, anyway.'

'I know, I know.' They were walking quickly towards the office in an effort to escape the rain, which was now getting heavier by the minute. Cindy was well aware of her other nickname—Miss Cool. She smiled inwardly, wondering if Zac was aware of the name he'd been allocated by Sheila. Zac Stone was not Sheila's favourite person.

Zac's strides were impossible to keep up with. He was several yards ahead of Cindy when next he spoke.

'I didn't hear a word of that,' she said breathlessly. 'Would you mind slowing down if you want to make small talk?'

He turned and grinned, waiting for her to catch up witl him. 'I said I'll bet you're glad I gave you a lift now, considering the weather. Come to think of it, if I gave you a lift every morning, you'd have more energy for the job. It's silly to waste your energy on walking.'

'Thanks.'

Zac's blue eyes were laughing as he and Cindy entered the foyer of the building. He punched the lift button. 'If it comes to that, it's even sillier that we're both paying an extortionate rent when two can live as cheaply as one. Why don't you move in next door?'

'Thanks, but no thanks. I'd rather live with a rattlesnake.'

At which Zac Stone threw back his head and roared with laughter. 'Why, Cynthia, how very Freudian!'

She glared at him all the way up to the second floor.

BY FOUR in the afternoon Cindy had a pounding headache. The guests were due to arrive any time after five-thirty. She had yet to go home and change, and she was in the Boardroom, checking on the caterers' movements, when Zac came looking for her.

'Cindy, where the hell have you put that stuff you fished out of the library for me?'

'The old Eleanor ads?'

'Of course the old Eleanor ads! What else did you fish out of the library today?'

Cindy looked up from the list of foodstuffs she was checking off. 'They're on your desk, Zac.'

He grunted. 'How many times have I told you not to tidy up my office?'

'Twice.'

'And you persist—'

'Only when I walk in there and trip over things.'

Zac walked away without another word and Cindy turned back to her list. He had this weird system of running his office. There were charts and files and a hundred other such items of reference strewn all over the place—mainly on the floor. But he knew exactly where everything was...unless some well-meaning idiot moved something. Cindy shrugged it off. There was too much to do without thinking about things like that.

When she told Zac she wanted to go home and change, he went up in the air. 'You must be joking! Forget it. There's no time for that. Besides, you know it isn't that sort of party. No one's going to be dressed up—they're all coming from their offices.'

Cindy put her foot down. 'Zac, I insist. I'll be very quick, I promise. I feel so—so crumpled. I must at least pick up a fresh blouse. I'll take a taxi—'

Zac looked heavenwards, fished in his pocket and threw his car keys at her. 'Take my car—and be quick about it. You've got twenty minutes to get there and back. I want you here when people start to arrive.'

It took Cindy forty-five minutes to get there and back. It would have been quicker to walk than to plough her way nervously through the traffic in an unfamiliar car. A car which didn't belong to her, at that. She bolted up to her second floor flat and grabbed a black blouse which was sleeveless and very sheer. She'd worn a white blouse and a black pencil skirt to the office that day—so the skirt would do.

With the blouse on a hanger she raced downstairs again and got back to the office in what she considered record time.

'It took you long enough.' Zac emerged from his office as Cindy hung up her blouse on the stationery cupboard.

She cast him an apologetic look and turned to Alison, who was just preparing to leave. 'Alison, would you do me a favour before you go? Would you get me a couple of Paracetamol from the first aid box? I've got a dreadful head-ache.'

'Of course! I'm sorry you've got a headache, Cindy.' Alison's shyness had been diminishing by the day. She was no longer tongue-tied and flustered in Zac's presence, though she still looked at him as if he were wonderful.

Zac took the car keys Cindy was holding out to him. 'Alison, aren't you staying for the party?'

'No, Mr Stone. Very few of the junior staff are. I mean, it is Friday night—'

'And they have better things to do, I suppose. Quite right.' Zac smiled at her.

'Actually, I've got a date tonight.' For Alison, this was really quite something, and Cindy looked up in surprise, smiling.

'I'm not surprised,' Zac said smoothly. 'You look very nice today, Alison. That's a new dress, isn't it? And you've lost some more weight this week.'

Alison beamed at him. 'Another four pounds. It's slow but it's sure.'

'And it's paying dividends, eh? Anyone I know, this date of yours?'

'Oh, I don't think so, Mr Stone. It isn't someone who works here.'

'All right,' Zac shrugged. 'Be mysterious, then.'

Alison laughed and went off to fetch the Paracetamol.

'Oh, no!' Cindy turned to Zac, a look of horror on her face. 'Zac, give me back the keys. I've forgotten something!'

'What?'

'I've got to nip home again. Give me your car keys.'

'You've had that!' he said firmly. 'What have you forgotten? It's bound to be something trivial!'

'My—' Cindy tutted impatiently. Bother the man. 'My bra. I forgot to pick up another bra. I can't wear a white one with a black blouse!'

Zac started to walk away from her. 'So go braless.'

'Zac!'

He turned and grinned, looking from her distraught face to the white blouse she had on to the sheer black silk blouse hanging on the cupboard. 'I see what you mean.' He laughed, shrugged, and went into his office.

'No problem,' he called to her. 'Give me a minute.'

Cindy couldn't imagine what he meant. She sank wearily on to her chair and started massaging her temples. She looked up to see Zac standing there dangling two bras on one of his fingers. 'Flesh-coloured or black?' he mused, asking himself more than he was asking Cindy.

She couldn't help laughing. 'Are those the new Eleanor samples? The ones that came for the photographic session?'

'Yes. They sent a whole boxful of goodies... all sizes, shapes and colours. Here.' He handed Cindy the black bra and she stood up to take it from him.

Zac immediately caught hold of her by the waist, holding her tightly against him. His face was dangerously close to hers, and Cindy felt her heartbeat quicken. 'Unless appearances deceive...' he said slowly, an insolent smile pulling at the corners of his mouth, '...or should I say, unless I'm losing my touch, this will fit you perfectly.'

Cindy flushed with embarrassment at the memory he invoked. She wriggled to try and free herself, but it only made Zac's smile broaden. 'Mmm, that's nice. How very provocative of you, Cindy!'

She put both hands flat on his chest and tried to push him away. 'Zac, let go of me! I have to get changed!'

But Zac kept hold of her, his hands sliding down to her hips. 'Is there anything else you've forgotten?' he asked, his deep blue eyes dancing with laughter. 'I've got all sorts of things in my sample box.'

'Zac! Oh, really, you...you're...absolutely incorrigible!'

He let go of her then. He slipped his forefinger under her chin and tilted her face upwards, looking directly into her eyes. 'Not incorrigible, Cindy, encouragable. Encouragable.'

She opened her mouth to protest, but the office door opened and Alison walked in with the bottle of Paracetamol.

Cindy took them from her, draped her blouse over her arm and stuffed the bra into her handbag. She headed for the ladies' room quickly, still disturbed by the effect Zac's closeness had had on her. Encouragable? Never! Encouraging a man like Zac Stone was the last thing she wanted to do!

The bra fitted perfectly.

By six o'clock the place was thronged with people. It seemed that for every man present there was also a secretary, a wife or a mistress. The continuous chinking of glasses, the tinkle of laughter and the buzz of conversations did nothing whatever to help Cindy's headache.

But she was very much on duty, and no one would have guessed how she was feeling. She was smiling, greeting, chatting, introducing, and generally circulating. She had been briefed by her boss as to whom she should make a fuss of and she'd been told also not to stray too far from him.

She was standing with her back to Zac, among a group of people who included the Chairman of Simpson's, when she heard her boss greet someone very, very warmly.

'Well, well. I'm so glad you could make it. I'm delighted to see you, darling, delighted.' It didn't sound at all like Zac.

Cindy automatically tuned in on the conversation as she heard the tinkle of a woman's laughter. The ability to keep her mind on two things at the same time was something she'd had to learn while working for Zac. She could manage easily to chat to Mr Simpson and listen to what was happening around her.

'Not half as delighted as I am, Zac. But I'm suspicious. Why the invitation?'

'Tracy! I'm deeply offended.'

Cindy turned slightly so she could get a look at the person Zac was talking to. The woman looked somewhere in the region of thirty; she was wearing a red trouser suit which showed off her figure to perfection. It was expensive and beautifully cut, and it suited her colouring. Her straight hair reached almost to her waist and was almost as dark as Zac's. Furthermore, her face was familiar to Cindy—and it was very beautiful. Her bone structure was classical, her make-up doing it the utmost justice, accentuating very cleverly the green, almond-shaped eyes.

But Cindy couldn't remember where she'd seen that face before.

'There's so much I'd like to ask you,' the woman went on. 'I know why you retired, but I don't know why you came out of retirement. I don't know why you didn't contact me as soon as you came back to England. I don't know why you invited me here tonight…you're not thinking of picking up where we left off, are you, Zac?'

Cindy didn't hear the answer to that. Greg Halliday, the Senior Account Director, slipped a hand under her elbow and whisked her away, excusing himself and Cindy from the group she'd been chatting to.

'There's someone I want you to meet,' Greg whispered. 'Potential business, I think. Besides, Zac wouldn't want you chatting to Mr Simpson for too long. He'd see no point in it when we've already got Simpson's business!'

The next time she had a chance to look in Zac's direction she saw he was with a short, bald-headed man who was waving his arms about. The two men were standing by themselves, in a corner of the room, and there was a familiar, set look about Zac's face. He was listening and mentally recording every word the other man said. Cindy recognised the look. As far as business was concerned she'd learned to read her boss very well. She had no choice in the matter; she was supposed to be one step ahead of his requirements every minute of the day. But she didn't always succeed.

The sound of Sheila's voice in Cindy's ear some time later was preceded by a soft chuckle. 'Look at her!' Sheila nodded in the direction of the woman Zac had been talking to earlier. 'She can't take her eyes off Granite Face!'

Cindy followed the direction of Sheila's eyes and saw that the woman called Tracy was indeed watching Zac from her seat on the other side of the room. By now, Zac was ensconced in conversation with several other females and a couple of elderly men.

'You know, her face is so familiar,' Cindy said. 'Is she a model?'

'Yes. Well, she was. It's Tracy Lynn, as she called herself professionally. She's just told me she retired recently. Over the hill, I suppose.' Sheila laughed again. 'I hope I look like that when I'm over the hill!'

'Don't be silly, Sheila. She's beautiful.'

'Not enough for the close-up photographic work she used to do. Take a closer look at her if you can.'

Cindy had placed Tracy now. Her face had appeared in countless photographs in women's magazines, modelling for a popular brand of cosmetics. It had been a well-known face a few years ago, but Cindy had seen nothing of it for quite a time.

She was curious to hear more about the woman, but she didn't dare to encourage Sheila. Zac Stone was all for people picking up useful information however and wherever possible but he was dead against general gossip. And in this instance, Cindy had the feeling there might well be room for gossip. The way Tracy and Zac had looked at one another had been ... well, friendly was putting it mildly.

But Sheila didn't need encouragement. 'Yes, I think Tracy's about Zac's age, actually. I knew her quite well about twelve years ago, when I worked for my first agency. She did some modelling for us—shoes, clothes, that sort of thing. Then she did all that cosmetics work for Zac's old agency. In fact, he really made her career. They're just old friends, I suppose ... in case you were wondering.'

'I wasn't.' Cindy was lying in her teeth, and Sheila knew it.

'She's well preserved,' Sheila went on. 'You wouldn't think she was a day over thirty, would you?'

But Sheila wasn't being bitchy. She astonished Cindy by adding. 'And she's a really nice person. There's no edge to her, if you know what I mean. Her success and her looks never went to her head. She's really nice.'

Coming from Sheila that was high praise indeed. It wasn't often she didn't pinpoint a fault in a person.

By eight-thirty Cindy's headache had taken a really firm hold, in spite of a second dose of tablets. She escaped into the privacy of her own office and sat down with her head held slightly forward and her eyes closed. If she could just have ten minutes' relative quiet she might calm herself out of this and feel fit to face more of the hubbub.

'What are you doing, Cindy? Why are you holding your hands like that? Are you trying to invoke more rain or something?'

Cindy opened her eyes slowly at the sound of Zac's voice. He'd obviously seen her make her escape, but he wasn't cross with her. He was laughing.

'It's a yoga exercise.'

'Of course it is,' he said drily. 'I shouldn't ask stupid questions. Come on, let's get out of here.'

She thought he meant they should rejoin the party, but Zac shook his head rather tiredly. 'No. Let's go and have a quiet drink somewhere, eh? I've had quite enough for one day.'

'It sounds good.' Cindy didn't need asking twice. She picked up her bag and they left.

When they were seated in Zac's car, she looked at him closely. 'You're looking very pleased with yourself, Zac. The party seemed to go down well, didn't it?'

'It was money well spent,' he said quietly. 'Very useful indeed.'

His choice of words made Cindy look at him curiously. 'You've learned something of interest, haven't you? It was something that little man said to you.'

Zac took his eyes from the road. 'Now how did you know that?'

'I don't know. I just did.'

'So you've been watching me all evening, have you? Couldn't take your eyes off me, mmm?'

'You conceited devil! You told me to keep an eye on you—and not to stray too far.' Cindy laughed in spite of herself.

'How's the head?' he asked.

'Chronic.'

'Did you eat at the party?'

'Not a thing.'

'Did you have lunch?'

She gave him a filthy look. 'You know I didn't. You said there was no time for lunch!'

Zac groaned as if he were appalled. 'What a dreadful employer you've got! I'll buy you dinner, right now. No wonder you've got a headache.'

'No, but thanks anyway.' Cindy touched his arm as he indicated to make a left hand turn which would take them away from home. 'Really, Zac, it's nice of you, but I couldn't face it. I want to be somewhere quiet.'

'Then we'll go somewhere quiet. My place.' He turned left regardless. 'And we'll pick up something on the way.'

'Chinese takeaway? I know a good place—'

'So do I. The same one, no doubt.'

Cindy smiled. Zac was in a particularly good mood to-night and she couldn't help wondering about it. 'Who was he?' she asked.

'Now what are you talking about?'

'You know full well. That little man at the party.'

'Someone who wasn't on the guest list. Someone who had invited himself...thank heavens. He's the head of a per-fume manufacturing company and he was very disgruntled because his current advertising agency has told him they no longer want his business. They're pitching for business with another, much bigger manufacturer of perfumes and toiletries. The little man is small fry, so they've dropped him.'

This wasn't unusual. Cindy was well aware that the rules of advertising were such that one agency may not handle two accounts which are in direct competition with one another. Nor may they pitch for other business in the same line unless they drop their current customer. If they end up failing to get the new business after all . . . well, that's a chance which agencies had to take. 'So he wants you to handle his advertising in future?'

'Yes, he does.' Zac nodded slowly, his eyes narrowing. 'And I turned him down flat.'

Cindy's lips parted in astonishment. The downhill path Bryant's had been taking prior to Zac Stone stepping in had been arrested when Zac salvaged the Simpson account. Indeed, some new business had come to Zac without him even trying for it. But they were by no means in the position yet of being able to refuse new clients!

'Why on earth did you do that?'

In a tone of voice which Cindy had never heard him use before he said. 'Now then, my lovely, why don't we just forget about business for the rest of this evening?'

Cindy turned to look out of the window, feeling suddenly nervous and a little too warm.

CHAPTER FIVE

As CINDY emerged from Zac's kitchen, having put the rapidly-cooling Chinese food on to plates, she found him in the middle of a telephone conversation.

'...I see. Me? Yes, yes, I'm fine, thanks.' He motioned Cindy to put the plates on the coffee table. 'And you and the family?...Yes, yes, I suppose they are. Time flies, doesn't it? Anyway, when can I be sure of catching your husband at home? All right, I'll ring then... And thank you very much.'

He hung up and sat perfectly still, thoughtful.

'Zac?'

It was seconds before he turned to her. 'I'm sorry, Cindy. What did you say?'

Her head was tilted slightly to one side. 'I hadn't said anything...' She was wondering where he'd gone to in his thoughts. 'That was something to do with business, that call, wasn't it? I thought you said you were going to forget about business for the rest of the evening.'

He smiled at her warmly, a little apologetically. 'So I did, so I did. But I'm trying to fix up a meeting with someone and it isn't going to be easy. My only chance is to catch him at home. But he's away for a few days.'

Cindy was intrigued—by Zac, and whatever it was he was up to. 'Are you going to tell your secretary about it?' Softly, though she was in little doubt about the answer, she added, 'You do trust me, don't you?'

It was the last Friday of the month, and Cindy had been given her pay cheque that morning. She had been given a substantial raise, but she was more pleased about the implications than the raise in salary. It meant she was no longer on trial.

Zac looked at her steadily, his voice very serious. 'Yes, Cindy. I trust you implicitly.' He got to his feet and shrugged off his jacket, loosening his tie, just as he wore it in the office when there were no clients around. But there was something different about him tonight. Seeing him in his home was probably the reason for that. In fact Zac's flat had in itself been quite a revelation to her.

He went over to the bar and picked up a couple of glasses and a bottle of red wine. 'But I don't want to tempt providence by talking about my plans. As it is, they're likely to go up in smoke at any moment.'

Cindy nodded, understanding what he meant. He'd tell her when he was ready to tell her. She picked up her plate and started eating. 'The food's almost cold.'

'Yes, I'm sorry about that. Here, this'll help it down.'

After she had taken a sip of wine, Cindy's eyes went straight to the label on the bottle. It was expensive, delicious and far too good to accompany what they were eating. She said as much, but Zac just laughed and said hang the expense.

They ate in silence. Cindy was particular about what she ate, but she finished every last bit of it simply because she was ravenous. It was only when she cleared the plates away that she mentioned her surprise at the way the flat was decorated. 'You've had a completely new kitchen put in! So that's what all the banging was about. It's super.'

'I'm afraid it's wasted on me, really.'

'You know, I thought your home would resemble something like the inside of a spaceship.'

Zac had stretched out on the four-seater chesterfield settee. It was covered in brown leather, with two matching chairs. The bar in the corner of the room was made from mahogany, as were the coffee tables. The walls were the colour of eggshells, relieved by several paintings which were classics and rich in colour. The light from the lamps was

subdued, as was the colour of the carpet—a rich, dark shade
of rust. But it was just right; it added colour to a room
which would otherwise have been too dark.

Zac didn't seem to understand her. 'Why did you think
that?'

'The way you had our offices decorated—that appalling
red on my walls. Of course, I know what's behind that. Red
is a stimulating colour. You probably thought you'd get
more work out of me if I sat facing a red wall. It infuriated
me even before I met you.'

Zac's smile told her she had been precisely right about the
red walls in her office. As an advertising man he knew all
about the effect that colour had on people at a subconscious level.

'But the agency has an image to maintain, I suppose.'
Cindy was beginning to understand fully only as she spoke.
'Everything there has to be efficient, with-it, even ahead of
it! I like your flat. Mind you,' she smiled mischievously,
'this room is a little too masculine for my taste.'

'Naturally. Wait till you see my bedroom.'

'I have no intention of seeing your bedroom... Why, is
it more feminine?'

'No, you idiot. It's got a red ceiling.' He was so panfaced
she took him seriously for a moment. He sat up and looked
at her, curled comfortably in the big armchair with her feet
tucked under her. Her shoes had been discarded and she
looked very lovely with her unruly hair curling softly around
her face, the blondeness of it making a stark contrast where
it touched the black blouse at her shoulders.

Zac's eyes moved over her slowly, but this time there was
something different about his scrutiny. This time he was
looking at her as if she were a woman *because* she was a
woman. 'So you had me labelled and filed before you met
me?'

'I didn't say that. Don't put words in my mouth.'

'And what would have happened to us if I'd never looked
further than my first impression?'

'Just what was your first impression, exactly?'

'Your—now hang on a minute,' he grinned, 'I won't tell you the very first thing that went through my mind, not in as many words, anyway! It might offend your genteel—'

'Zac!' Cindy's tone held a note of warning. 'There it is again—your reference to my background. You do resent it, don't you?'

He let out a short, impatient breath. 'Will you get that out of your head? Look, did you resent me because I'm the son of a mid-Wales coalminer?'

'Of course not!' It was a moment before the penny dropped. 'Wait a minute, wait a minute. How could I resent that when I didn't even know about it?'

'Well, you know now. No, it was your attitude—'

'We've been through all that.' She shifted uncomfortably, recalling only too well the way Zac had changed all that.

'At the interview, Cindy. Your insolence infuriated me. You'd taken it for granted you'd got the job. You had the nerve to tell me my reputation had gone ahead of me, and gave me the impression you were merely deigning to stay on.'

'And you didn't think I'd be serious about my work.'

'That was something I had to find out. Everyone responds to a stimulus, Cindy. You don't need to work for financial reasons. Yet you were working. That in itself told me there's something lacking in your life. No, I'll amend that. Having seen how hard you work tells me there's something lacking in your life. Everyone can be provoked into action, as I say. It's a question of finding the right button. In your case it was your pride. I put you through your paces and you hated me for it. In the middle of the interview you switched from wanting the job for the right reasons to wanting it for the wrong reason—because you were too proud to be turned down.'

There was a silence.

It didn't last long and it wasn't an awkward silence. Zac Stone was full of surprises. Cindy was realising that with

every passing day. He was absolutely right, of course. In
everything he'd said.

'So why did you give me the job?'

'I decided it was worth giving you a try when you gave me
your little speech, when I saw you had some spirit. But that
spirit needed channelling, shaping to my way of things.'

'You make me sound like a wild horse!' Cindy laughed
shortly, but Zac wasn't laughing.

'No—absolutely not. Wild horses have their spirits broken, and that's something I'd never want to do to a person.
I know only too well what it's like when someone tries to do
that to you. No, your spirit just needed harnessing, redirec-
tion so that something positive could be gained with it.'

Cindy thought carefully about that, too. And how well
Zac Stone had handled her, brought about the change in her.
'Zac...thanks for the rise.'

'You earned it.' He stretched out on the settee again and
closed his eyes.

'Do you—do you want me to go?' she asked. 'You seem
tired tonight. Or distracted or something.'

For just a moment she saw the deep blue of his eyes as he
opened and closed them. 'No, don't go. Believe it or not, I
haven't had such an interesting evening in a long time.'

Neither had Cindy. She was longing to ask him about
himself, but she was afraid she might spoil things between
them. As it was, the atmosphere was good, better than it had
ever been. In another sense she was quite happy just to share
the silence. She let her eyes trail over him, enjoying his face,
the broad expanse of his shoulders, the muscular tautness
of his stomach, his hips, his legs. She wanted Zac. There was
no point in denying it to herself any longer when the very
sight of him was enough to stir an aching response in her,
the like of which she had never before experienced in her
twenty-three years.

But nothing would come of it. Of that she would make
absolutely certain. She had to. It was a question of self-
preservation. With a man such as he it would mean—

'Cindy,' he said slowly, 'do you know what the single biggest troublemaker in the world is?'

'Yes, as a matter of fact I do.' She smiled inwardly. Zac had not read her mind. Not when his eyes had been closed, at any rate. He couldn't know her reasons for saying what she was about to say. And she certainly had plenty of them. 'The biggest troublemaker in the world is sex.'

Zac's eyes opened and he smiled wryly. 'No. But that certainly runs a very close second...a very close second. Money is the biggest troublemaker in the world. Lovely, filthy, lucre.' He punched out the last three words with equal slowness and stress, and she wondered once again where he'd been to in his thoughts.

'Zac, can we talk...about you?'

'My favourite subject.' It was a quip, and it almost put her off. But not quite.

'You said earlier about my working hard when I don't need to. You work harder than I do. You push yourself as I've never seen anyone else do it. Why? You don't need the money. You're in it for the challenge. Aren't you?'

When he didn't answer, Cindy regretted having spoken.

After what seemed like a long, long time, he said, 'You're absolutely right—I do it for the challenge. It hasn't got a damn thing to do with money. Except that money's inevitable at the end of it. Come over here, Cindy, I want to kiss you.'

'Zac, please, I'm trying to understand you. You retired over two years ago. You sold Stone, Mason and Gibbons after building it from nothing into the top advertising agency in London. And you'd made yourself a fortune. You did—well, I don't know what, for two years—'

'I did nothing. Absolutely nothing...I've been wanting to kiss you all evening.'

'It was reported in *Campaign* that you made an agreement in the contract of sale that you'd keep out of advertising completely for one year, so you couldn't set up an agency elsewhere and take the clients with you. But you stayed away for two years. You had no intention of coming back into the rat-race.'

'None whatever,' he said shortly.

'But you did—because there's something missing in your life, too.'

He shifted his large frame lazily, stretched, and then re-filled their wineglasses, emptying the bottle. 'Well done! I like a woman who thinks logically.'

He went to the bar and picked up another bottle of wine, opened it and placed it between their glasses. But he didn't sit down again. He moved over to the open windows and looked up at the clear summer sky which had turned into midnight blue. 'I've always been ambitious, Cindy. And I never could resist a challenge. But I regret...'

He pushed his hands into his trouser pockets. Cindy said nothing. She just waited, seeing the tension in the muscles of his shoulders.

'...I was born in a small Welsh village. I had three sisters older than myself. My mother worked hard in the home and my father worked down the mines, like his father and his father before him.

'I was a brilliant student, with the advantage of an ei-detic memory. I won a scholarship to university, and my parents were as proud as punch. They wanted me to go to university as much as I wanted it myself. It was unheard of—a boy in that village in the middle of nowhere who would not be following in his father's footsteps. But I'd never had any intention of doing that; I was born ambi-tious, and that's something that's stayed with me no matter what I achieved. I wanted to get to the top.

'My parents were religious, and I was brought up ac-cordingly. There were a lot of subjects which were taboo in our house and I was as green as the grass, about many things. Most especially that second biggest troublemaker in the world.'

Zac turned to face her briefly, but he didn't look at her. He was looking beyond her. 'Maybe you're right. Maybe that's the biggest . . . I went through the usual adolescent yearnings and curiosity like anyone else. I did my sexual experimenting with a girl who lived in the next street. She was a pretty girl, cute as anything, and I assumed she was as virginal as I. I was seventeen when we—'

Cindy cringed at the expression he used then, but she made no comment.

'Elisabeth was a year older. Of course she told me she loved me, that that was why she was "allowing" me—'

'She probably did,' Cindy said softly. 'Why do you say it so cynically? She was young, and she—'

'And I was even younger. We only made love once. Just once. And the next thing I knew, she was pregnant. Just that one time, and my entire life—'

'Once is all it takes, Zac.'

'Who are you telling?' he said curtly, bitterly. 'Oh, hell, I'm talking about something that happened twenty years ago; I'm talking about a different era, people—a way of life totally alien to you, Cindy.'

He had his back to her again. His voice quietened so that she had to strain to hear him. 'Life was so cut and dried in those days, in that community. You worked, you worshipped, you lived by the rules. I married Elisabeth—I had no choice. My parents had a fit and so did hers. Her father practically marched me to the altar with the proverbial shotgun. It's a classic, I know, and it happens time and again all over the world.

'So I was married at seventeen and *bang* went my chance at university, my chance of getting out, making money, doing what I wanted to do with my life.'

Cindy looked at him in the ensuing silence, at the expensively furnished flat, at the successful, sophisticated man who stood before her. 'Obviously something went right for you. What happened? What happened—about the baby?'

'She miscarried. We were living with her parents, simply because there was more room in her house. She was an only child. I was working for a pittance in a local mill, handing over my wage packet to her mother, meeting my responsibilities as best I could. I'd grown up pretty damn quick. But my ambition was burning more strongly than ever.'

'So when Elisabeth miscarried, you walked out?'

Zac turned and looked at her hard and long. 'You really don't think much of me, do you?'

'Zac, I'm not judging. I don't think anything. That wasn't a statement, or an accusation, it was a question. Did you leave?'

'I left. We *both* left. The reason for my marriage no longer existed, but I thought we could make it work. I wanted to make it work. You see, in my own young, naive way, I loved her a little.

'But it had to be on my terms from then on. Elisabeth knew I was ambitious; the entire village knew I'd planned on going to university. There was no way I'd have remained poor the rest of my life—with or without the baby's presence. Once the responsibility of fatherhood had gone, though, I was obviously able to move quickly.

'I talked to Elisabeth at length. I was eighteen by then; she was nineteen. She was against the idea of leaving Wales, her family, her familiar, safe world. But she came to London with me.'

'She loved you, Zac. She'd loved you all along.'

'That's what I thought, too. You sound as naïve as I was in those days. I was a meal ticket to her. *That's* what I'd been all along. Firstly, she'd needed me to marry her. Then she discovered life was easier having a husband. It meant she didn't need to work. She refused to get a job in London, and you can imagine how broke we were. I was working in an agency as a mail boy and messenger. But Elisabeth had been brought up to think that a woman should be kept—and she never changed those ideas, regardless of how much we needed more money.

'I was fascinated by the big city, mesmerised by the advertising world. I listened, I learned, I picked brains. I was going to make it to the top. I worked long hours and I studied in the evening. I educated myself...and all the time, Elisabeth nagged me. To return to Wales, to stop working so hard, to take my head out of my books.

'After eighteen months, the inevitable happened. There was an almighty row—a very, very nasty row. In the midst of it, in her hysteria, she told me the baby she'd been carrying wasn't even mine. Before me, she'd been well and truly initiated by some kid who lived on a farm. He'd enlisted and joined the army before she realised she was pregnant. How I didn't kill Elisabeth that night, I'll never know to this day... *Then* I walked out.'

The sudden silence seemed to ring in Cindy's ears. She didn't know what to say, so she said nothing at all.

Zac lifted his glass and smiled at her. 'Admittedly, I envy you your education, Cindy, your opportunities. But I don't resent your background, for the very reason that my own background was against me. When I was working my way through the ranks, I had to compete with university graduates. But I made it regardless.

'So a person's roots, history or whatever we want to call it, never enters into the scheme of things when I hire or fire. I hire if I think they can do the job, I fire if I find I've made a mistake. If they don't like my pace, the way I run things— well, you know the old adage about the heat and the kitchen.'

Cindy nodded, watching him over the rim of her glass. By the time the second bottle of wine was finished it was well into the night. She was drowsy, and it was obvious Zac was tired. But they just went on talking.

Cindy told him something about her own family, but she didn't tell him much about herself. Talking about her innermost thoughts and hopes was something she would find difficult to do with anyone. The dawn chorus had started by the time their conversation went full circle, several cups of coffee and some rather stale sandwiches later.

'So you reached the zenith and then you retired. Why?'

'There was nothing else to do. What was left? I got tired, too. I decided I wanted to use money, that money wasn't going to use me. I bought a house in the Bahamas, just outside Nassau. It's still there; I let friends use it from time to time. I've got friends, contacts all over the world.

'I got bored, Cindy. B-o-r-e-d. You can only do so much jet-setting, attend so many parties, have more affairs than you can remember. And it palls, does it not, eventually?'

'I—suppose so.' She was hardly qualified to comment on those remarks. 'Zac . . . what happened to—to your wife?'

Draining the last of his coffee he looked at her sharply. '*Ex*-wife, if you don't mind. As far as I know she's alive and well and living in Swansea with four kids and a husband. My mother used to give me bulletins from time to time, irrespective of my not wishing to know. She used to hear gossip.'

'Used to?'

A shadow crossed his face then. 'Yes—my mother died three years ago, I'm afraid. My father went about two weeks later. I always knew it would happen like that, when one went the other wouldn't last long. They were devoted to one another.'

Cindy got to her feet and stepped into her shoes, wanting to get away from the subject of his parents. She had obviously touched on a tender spot. 'So you came back again to start from scratch. You don't need the money, but you do need the challenge. That's why you took over Bryant's.'

'Precisely so.' Zac's arms came around her from behind and she turned slowly to face him, found herself lifting her head to receive his kiss because it seemed like the natural, the only thing to do. Her arms closed around the broadness of his back as if by a will of their own.

His kiss was an exploration, a discovery, and was so sweet in its eroticism that she felt the room shift behind the blackness of her closed eyes. She pulled away from him, her breath catching on words he would not allow her to speak. Again he kissed her, and again it was different.

This time, it was a demand.

It seemed to Cindy that she had no strength at all, that it was Zac's strength, his caresses over her hips, her back, her breasts, that prevented her legs from giving way beneath her. She was pressed tightly against the hardness of his body, her response as immediate as his own, a response she was powerless to withhold. But she must, she *must*. Hadn't he just told her he'd had more affairs than he could remember? Meaningless affairs . . .

She stepped away from him, wishing she could as easily cut herself off from this impossible, impelling attraction she felt for him. 'Zac, I—I don't want things to be like this between us. You're my boss, and that's all I want you to be to me.'

Gently, he tilted her face in his hand. He looked deeply into the darkness of her eyes as if he would read her most private, innermost thoughts. 'Cindy, I know women. Quite apart from all I've told you, it's my business to know women, to know what motivates them, what they want, what they don't want, what they really hope for when they say one thing and mean something else . . .'

She closed her eyes against his words, words spoken very quietly. Dear Lord, he had no right. No right to read her so easily.

'. . . I know when a woman wants me. When the time is right, Cindy, I shall make love to you. And you will welcome it. Now go home, proud beauty, and sleep well.'

CHAPTER SIX

'CINDY, HAVE you dropped off to sleep or something?' Zac's voice boomed at her from the adjoining office. He rarely used the intercom on his desk; it was hardly worth it when his door was always open and he found it easier to shout. 'I asked you to get three phone calls twenty minutes ago—and I'm still waiting! Get on with it. I haven't got all day.'

They didn't have all day. It was almost noon on the Wednesday morning and at lunchtime she and Zac were driving down to Croydon to see a client. 'They're engaged, Zac.'

'What? All of them?'

'Yes.' Cindy refused to get flustered. The pressure was on more than ever because the presentation of the new campaign for Simpson's was due to be held on the following Monday. Everyone was working flat out.

She closed her eyes briefly as Zac shouted at her to keep trying the calls. As if she wouldn't! She wondered what on earth was upsetting him; he wasn't usually this bad. He'd been all right until about half an hour ago...

'And get Sheila in here in the meantime,' he went on. 'Like now!'

Cindy buzzed Sheila and passed on the message. But when she switched to an outside line in order to try the calls again, Twin-Set and Pearls came bursting into the office. She was obviously upset, even close to tears.

Cindy looked at her in amazement. She'd never seen Miss Druce like this before. 'What is it, Miss Druce? What's happened?' She put down the phone at once.

'I'd like to see Mr Stone.' There was a stubborn look on Miss Druce's face.

'Miss Druce, can't you tell me?' Cindy lowered her voice, 'Zac's awfully busy. I don't want to disturb him.' It wasn't only that, actually. The mood Zac was in was not a good one, and he wouldn't want to be bothered with—

'Neither do I.' Miss Druce stood erect, immovable. 'But this is very important!' Her voice rose. 'I must see Mr Stone. Now!'

Zac appeared in the doorway, frowning. 'Miss Druce, come in. Come in, my dear.'

He ushered Twin-Set and Pearls into his office and closed the door behind them. Alison and Cindy exchanged questioning looks, but there was no time to speculate as to what ailed Miss Druce. Alison didn't even stop typing. She was working as hard as Cindy these days, though at least she finished on time.

'What does he want now?' Sheila came in looking positively hung-over. She was wearing red and black striped jeans and a yellow tee-shirt and she looked like nothing on earth.

'Got a hangover, Sheila?' Alison had obviously had the same thought as Cindy.

'Less of the lip—this is overwork.' She turned to Cindy. 'I'll go in, then. Granite Face has summoned, and I must come running.'

'Hold it!' Cindy leapt from her chair and put a restraining hand on Sheila's arm. Sheila was cross with Zac because he'd rejected two lots of copy she'd written of late. 'Miss Druce is in there. Just wait a couple of minutes, would you?'

Sheila waited five minutes. She flopped into a chair and stuck her feet on the radiator. There wasn't a sound coming from Zac's office and Sheila looked at her watch every sixty seconds. 'Right! I'm off! Buzz me again when those two have finished—'

Sheila broke off as the adjoining door opened and Miss Druce came sailing out of Zac's office with a satisfied look on her face. As the door closed behind her, Sheila got to her feet just as Zac yelled to Cindy. 'So where the hell is Sheila?''

'Here, Zac, here!'

Sheila flounced in cockily, not bothering to close the door behind her. 'You sent for me?' she said sweetly, her voice dripping with sarcasm.

'Sit down, Sheila.' Zac's voice was curt, impatient.

'I would if your chairs weren't covered with a pile of junk.'

Alison and Cindy exchanged looks again. There had been a storm brewing between Zac and Sheila for over a week— it seemed it was about to break.

'Stand, then!' Zac shouted. 'For heaven's sake, what are you wearing? You look bloody awful. Don't stand on those papers, you idiot!'

There was a moment's silence, then a rustle of papers.

'Sheila, how long have you worked at Bryant's?'

'Ten years.'

'And how long have you been writing copy for the Eleanor account?'

'Five years,' Sheila's voice was both sullen and defiant. 'Since they first came to us.'

'I've just read your latest attempt on the copy that's supposed to go with the new photographs—you are aware that we've got a deadline on this?'

'Oh, for God's sake! Don't tell me you're still not satisfied?' Sheila was shouting now, and Zac shouted back at her with equal force.

'Satisfied? It's tripe! Just like your previous attempts. It's stale, clichéd and boring. *You're* stale, Sheila. You've dried up!'

'The hell I've dried up! How many ways are there to describe women's underwear?'

'An infinite number!' Zac boomed. 'Look at this. Read it! You've merely described that bra, right down to its last piece of lace. We've got the photographs to do that for us! Wait a minute, wait a minute...'

There was the sound of Zac striding angrily around his office, the rustle of tissue paper and then the command, 'Catch! Now get yourself into the ladies' room and pour yourself into that.'

At that point, Alison cracked up with laughter and Cindy shot her a warning look. True, Sheila would never be able to 'pour' herself into anything. She was as thin as a rake and she never even wore a bra.

The row flared. It was like a ping-pong match, Sheila giving as good as she got and Zac beating her down. 'We're not aiming at middle-aged ladies, we're aiming at the very young with this lot!' Zac went on. 'You haven't read the market research, have you?'

'Of course I've read the research! Of course I'm aware of the market!'

'Well, it doesn't show, lady. It doesn't show. Take these, too. And this. Go and put them on and *feel* what the garments are like next to your skin. *Feel* how comfortable they are, how natural. They're delicious, Sheila. Delicious! That's what I want you to write about. Let your imagination run away with you! Tell the readers why it's worth spending extra money on Eleanor underwear instead of buying stuff from a chain store. Tell them what it's going to do to their husbands or boy-friends when they wear these silky, seductive things. Tell them how good their figures are going to look, how this stuff is going to flatter the line of their clothes. *That's* what women are interested in. You're not writing about Simpson's furniture here, you know, you're writing about *seduction!* If you can't come up with something original next time, I'm taking you off the account!'

Sheila, tight-faced, white-faced, slammed out of Zac's office with a pair of French knickers in her hand and two bras slung over her shoulder. She was cursing generally and Zac in particular as she slammed the door to Cindy's office, too.

Alison, who had been almost prostrate throughout all this, made an effort to calm herself when she saw that Cindy wasn't in the least amused. 'I wonder why he talks to Sheila like that? You don't think he'll fire her, do you?'

'No.' Cindy sighed and started dialling again. 'He's just pressing the right button.'

'What?'

'Oh, it doesn't matter, Alison. I was just thinking aloud. He won't fire Sheila, don't worry.'

'It's strange, really, because he's always so nice to me.'

'Yes.' Cindy smiled, put the call through to Zac, and nipped out for a sandwich while she had the chance.

It was turned nine o'clock when they left Croydon that evening. Zac had invited his client to dinner when the meeting finally broke up at a little after six, and the three of them had gone on talking shop through the meal.

After she'd been in Zac's car for a few minutes, Cindy's eyes closed. She was tired, but she wasn't in danger of actually falling asleep. She was thinking about the man beside her.

She had seen Zac Stone when he was with clients, at his most charming. She had watched him relating to his staff, his team, motivating them to produce their best work and knowing precisely how to do that, according to their personalities. And in his home last week she had learned what motivated Zac. Had she seen, then, a glimpse of the real man?

But one couldn't really separate Zac's personality into compartments. The different facets of him were inextricably intertwined. One could only look at the whole, because sometimes he behaved in the most unpredictable way. Like this afternoon, for example, when at one point he'd been downright rude to his client. But he had done it in such a way that the man had taken it; had been unable to argue with the point Zac had made. Then there had been that other unpredictable moment during the morning, when he had taken time out of his busy schedule to placate Miss Druce over whatever it was that ailed her.

As much as Cindy had learned about him, Zac was still very much a mystery to her. On a person-to-person basis she trusted him, instinctively, even though she was well aware that he was a manipulator of people. Conversely, on a man-woman basis, she didn't trust him an inch! All she could really be certain of, absolutely certain, was that Zac Stone was a winner, a man who got what he wanted.

'Penny for your thoughts?'

Cindy didn't open her eyes. The very nearness of him, the fact that they were alone in his car, affected her. She didn't want to open her eyes and complicate her thoughts even further by looking at him. 'They're not worth it,' she said casually. 'They're illogical, jumbled.'

'That doesn't sound like you.' Cindy sensed, rather than saw, the look he gave her. He said nothing else. He turned the car radio on very low and they drove in silence.

He was right, too. It wasn't like Cindy. It wasn't like her to tie herself up in knots, to be so indecisive over what she felt for someone. Man or woman, she was usually quick to make up her mind about people. But most especially about men.

She had stopped disliking Zac, but what exactly did she feel for him—now? Fascination? Admiration? Respect?

She did look at him then. She opened her eyes slightly and watched him from beneath lowered lashes. The lights from the oncoming traffic were flickering across his strong, dark features, making him look more mysterious than ever.

Desire. Yes, there was that, too. And because of that she felt an element of resentment towards him. She desired Zac Stone, and she resented him because he knew how she felt.

And Zac had made it plain what his intentions were as far as that was concerned. Very plain indeed.

Cindy fell asleep then, but before doing so she managed to reach at least one conclusion: there was no way Zac Stone was going to make love to her. For him, it would be sex and nothing else. He had already admitted to having more affairs than he could remember. Well, that was not for Cindy. She wasn't going to number among his conquests!

But it was there, again, as soon as the car engine and the radio were switched off. Cindy opened her eyes to find Zac looking at her, the message in his eyes unmistakable. She had to face it, it was there all the time, crackling between them like electricity. No matter where they were or what they were doing, it was there.

'You know,' he said quietly, 'it can be quite a distraction to a man, having a brown-eyed blonde for a secretary. A beautiful, slender girl who looks like an angel when she's asleep. I don't make a habit of making love to my secretaries, you know. I don't usually go in for office romances.'

Cindy was half-drugged from sleep, but she tried to make her voice as crisp as possible. 'Then I suggest you don't try to break your habit now. And please note—I *never* go in for office romances.'

He laughed at her as she flung open the car door. 'I'll see you in the morning, Goldilocks.'

'Aren't you coming in?'

''Fraid not. I've still got a few things to do in the office... Unless that was an invitation?'

'It was not an invitation, and you know it. Good night, Zac.'

'WELL?' SHEILA looked at Zac and Cindy looked at Sheila, and held her breath. It was Friday night. It was dark outside. And tempers were raw because everyone was tired.

Zac looked up from the papers Sheila had handed to him and a delighted smile broke out on his face. 'Sheila, you're beautiful! Well, let me not get carried away—your work's beautiful.'

'Satisfied?' She ignored his remark.

'More than.'

'Right,' Sheila nodded. 'Then I'm off. I'm in desperate need of a drink.'

Zac smiled his most charming smile and Sheila looked at him warily. 'Cindy and I are joining Greg and several others in the wine bar. Come with us.'

'Are you buying?'

'I'm buying.'

'Give me two minutes.' Sheila headed for the door. 'You can buy me supper, too.'

Cindy sat back, relieved that things were on an even keel again. She picked up her notebook and stuffed it into her handbag. If several of them were transferring to the wine bar it meant that work wasn't over for the night. They'd all, inevitably, continue to talk shop. Inevitably, because the presentation for Simpson's was due to take place first thing Monday morning. And poor Sheila had had that to cope with as well as the desperately-needed Eleanor copy.

'Supper?' Zac shook his head despairingly. 'You really push your luck, don't you?'

'Always,' Sheila quipped. With an exaggerated toss of her head, she flounced out, to the sound of Zac's laughter.

Cindy stood up and stretched languorously. 'Zac, do you need me? In the wine bar?'

'I need you.' He slapped his hand against the papers he was holding. 'She's good, you know. Damn good... Why, are you eager to get off, Cindy? Have you got a late date or something?'

She didn't even bother to answer that one. She'd forgotten what a date was. She hadn't really expected to escape the next hour or so. Oh, but she was tired!

'I warned you,' Zac shrugged, 'what it would be like when the pressure's on. Working half the night, over the weekends. I hope you didn't have other plans for this weekend?'

'No. And yes, you warned me, Zac. I don't mind working this weekend, or working half the night. I know it has to be done. It's just that I'd like to have time to go shopping, to have my hair done... Maybe I can have a day off after the presentation? What about Tuesday?'

'No chance. We're going to Paris on Tuesday.' He picked up his jacket and ushered her out of the door.

'Paris?'

'Yes. I've finally succeeded in reaching that chap I wanted a meeting with. We're flying to Paris at lunchtime on Tuesday. We'll be wining and dining him in the evening, and the meeting with his Board will take place on Wednesday morning. So brush up your French.'

Just like that! No warning, no explanation!

'Zac, you haven't told me what this is all about yet! Who are we going to see? And why? And how long will we be there? And what about air tickets and accommodation?'

'I've arranged our rooms and our flights.' He switched off the lights in his office and hooked his jacket over his shoulder. 'We'll be there two nights, maybe three. As for your other questions, I'll brief you some time before we leave.'

Cindy glanced at him curiously as they met up with Sheila. She asked no more questions, but she could tell from the light in Zac's eyes that their trip to Paris was very, very important to him.

To all intents and purposes, Saturday was just another day at work. It was typically hectic and fraught. Most of the creative people were working over the weekend, two other secretaries were in, half the art department and, of course, Greg Halliday, who was actually in charge of the Simpson account. Greg and Zac worked incredibly well together. As Creative Director, Zac had spent a great deal of time with Greg deciding on their plans in the early stages of the proposed campaign and between the two men interestingly enough, there was never a raised voice, never an angry word.

It was exciting to see it all coming together. Cindy's mind went back to the day when the idea had been sold to Simp-

son's, then forward to the day when she'd see the advertisements on the television. It was an exciting process, an
exciting world.

But in spite of that she was still waiting for things to level
off a little. The pressure was catching up with her, and there
were moments when she did ask herself quite why it was that
she pushed herself so hard these days.

Maybe Zac saw her exhaustion. Or maybe he, too, was
feeling it. Whatever, he came into Cindy's office in the latter half of Sunday afternoon and told her to go home.

'Are you calling it a day, Zac?'

'I can't.' He leaned against the door jamb and looked at
his watch, 'I've got a couple of other matters to talk over
with Greg. But you don't need to be there, Cindy. Go home
and take a nap. I'm taking you out to dinner this evening,
okay?'

'Okay.' Cindy smiled at him. This was Zac's way of re-
warding her hard work.

'Wear something sensational,' he called to her as she was
leaving the room. 'I'll pick you up at eight.'

CHAPTER SEVEN

'Zac, however did you find this place? I've driven past it several times and I didn't even realise it was a restaurant. I mean, there's no sign outside. There's just a small brass plate and a rather discreet front door!' Cindy laughed. 'I really like it. It's got such...such atmosphere.'

They were sipping pre-dinner drinks, their second pre-dinner drinks. They had spent half an hour chatting over a drink in Cindy's flat after Zac had called for her. After a two-hour nap and a leisurely bath, Cindy was feeling refreshed and relaxed. She was looking her best, with her hair swept up on the crown of her head, a few wispy curls left loose to add softness to the style.

Her dress was classic, simple, made from a soft, clingy material the colour of ivory. Around the low neckline and back there was a single twist of gold thread running through the material. She would hardly call it sensational, but she knew she looked good in it.

Zac seemed pleased by her remark. 'I was one of their first customers when they opened about seven years ago. The chap who showed us to the table is new, but the owner's an old friend of mine. He runs the kitchen himself and he's an artist. Wait till you taste the food and you'll see what I mean.'

Zac had ordered for her. He seemed to know just what she liked, and the food lived up to his recommendations. They drank too much wine, which didn't matter because they hadn't brought the car with them, and Cindy grew more mellow and relaxed as the evening went on.

'Tell me, how ambitious are you, Cindy? Have you set your sights on a Directorship at Bryant's? Or are you planning to give it all up in a couple of years and settle down to marriage and a dozen children?'

'Neither!' She giggled at the two extremes of his questions. 'I wouldn't want a Directorship. I'm not that ambitious! All I wanted really was to succeed at something. If I'm doing that as secretary to the most demanding man in advertising, then I'm satisfied.'

'You are.' Zac smiled at the way she'd referred to him, his deep blue eyes intense and very beautiful in the muted lighting. 'I love it when you laugh like that,' he added quietly, 'and may I say you're looking incredibly beautiful this evening . . . But let me not digress! Why was it so important to you to succeed at something?'

Cindy didn't need to think about that. 'I suppose my family's partly the reason for that. In my teens and as a child there were so many things I wasn't allowed to do because I was the daughter of Sir Robert Hetherington, Q.C., a man who was very much in the public eye in those days.' She broke off, hearing the cynicism in her own voice. 'It . . . was the same for all of us, of course. I have two sisters older than myself. And I was never any good at anything. Oh, I was bright enough in school, but that was only because I was sent to the best places and they taught me well. I was a very unattractive little girl . . .'

'I find that hard to believe.'

Cindy bowed her head graciously. 'It's true. I was grossly overweight in my early teens, which in turn made me shy and lacking in confidence, and I had a chip on my shoulder about it. I came to London when I was nineteen, after a year doing virtually nothing at home. I wanted to live by myself, get away from the family's clutches, sort of thing. I wanted an identity of my own.'

Zac laughed quietly. 'And you wanted to have some fun. You still had that to get out of your system. You were young and beautiful by then, I take it.'

'I don't know about that.' Cindy was giggling again. One part of her mind was telling her she'd drunk too much wine, that she was talking too much, and at the same time she didn't really care. She didn't mind telling Zac about herself now. And he was so easy to talk to... 'I was young, yes. And I was slim!'

'So you tried your wings.'

'I started work at Bryant's when I was nineteen. But my evenings in those days were very different from my current evenings! I lived in Hampstead then, with a couple of other girls. We all had fun—dinners, dates, dancing, seeing the clubs and so on. We all went our separate ways within a couple of years. When I was twenty-one I inherited the money my grandmother left me—please note, my *grandmother*. My father does not keep me in the lap of luxury, as you once called it. I took the flat in Priory Court and, frankly, I like living alone. The idea of living it up these days doesn't appeal to me in the least.'

'That makes sense,' Zac shrugged. 'You got it out of your system.'

'It palled, Zac. Just as you were saying, about your retirement. I got b-o-r-e-d with it. I concentrated fully on my job from then on, working for the M.D. and all that. But it's only now that I'm getting real satisfaction from my work. I've got this *dreadful* boss, you see...'

'Out of order!' Zac summoned the waiter and looked at Cindy in mock disdain. 'You were making so much sense till you came out with that remark! Come on, I think you need a little fresh air.'

'But Zac,' she said innocently, 'if the wine's loosened my tongue a little—well, alcohol brings out the truth, doesn't it?'

They were delayed from leaving when a tall, thin man— made ever taller by the chef's hat he wore—emerged from the kitchen and made a beeline for their table.

'Zac! It's wonderful to see you. When I saw your name in the bookings for this evening—well, I was amazed. I thought we'd lost you for ever to the Bahamas.' He bowed graciously as Zac introduced him to Cindy.

'Paul Denning, Cindy Hetherington. Congratulations on the dinner, Paul. You haven't lost your touch.'

'It was superb,' Cindy added.

Paul took hold of her hand and kissed the back of it, his eyes sweeping over her appreciatively. 'You and Zac will be regulars from now on. Zac always used to be, you know. When did you get back to England, Zac?'

'Several weeks ago.'

The owner of the restaurant looked mortally wounded. 'Several weeks—and I see nothing of you till tonight?'

'I've been busy,' Zac laughed. 'I've taken over Bryant's.'

'Indeed? I hadn't heard... And why? I thought you were sick of the advertising world?'

Zac waved a dismissive arm. 'Some other time, Paul. That's another story.'

Before moving off to the next table, Paul invited them to join him and some other friends at a private dinner party he was giving one night the following week, when the restaurant was closed.

'Sorry.' Zac shrugged apologetically. 'We'd have loved to, but we're going to Paris on Tuesday.'

Paul smiled rather wistfully, his eyes moving over Cindy once more. 'Well, give Paris my regards.'

Zac laughed shortly as Paul moved on. 'He must think we're going on some sort of pleasure trip.'

'Evidently,' Cindy said quietly. 'You might have introduced me as your secretary. I'm sure he thinks I'm your mistress or something.'

'Would that be such a bad thing?'

'A very bad thing.'

He put a hand under her arm as they left, whispering in her ear, 'I thought alcohol made people tell the truth.'

'It does.'

They walked home slowly, Cindy's arm linked through Zac's. It was a beautifully warm August evening and she was heady from the wine, the superb dinner—Zac's nearness. He was looking very attractive in a light grey suit and a crisp white shirt, and the moment they stepped out of the restaurant, he loosened his tie. Cindy smiled inwardly; she could have predicted that. Even on cool days Zac tugged impatiently at his tie the instant he no longer needed to be concerned about his appearance.

'How's your mother?'

'What?' After a lengthy silence Zac's question came as a surprise. 'My mother? She's fine. I spent an hour chatting to her on the phone this afternoon. In fact, the phone was ringing when I got in. Mummy's like that. She'd spend all day chatting to me on the phone!'

'And your father, what does he think of you working in advertising?'

'I haven't the faintest idea what my father thinks—' Cindy stopped short. Zac Stone really had the cleverest way of drawing her out. The funny thing was that she didn't mind. And that wasn't due to the wine; the fresh air was rapidly clearing her head.

Zac motioned her towards a bench on a small green patch in front of a building. 'It's always "Mummy" and "my father". Every time you speak of him there's bitterness in your voice. It worries me, Cindy. What happened between you two that's made you feel like this?'

'God, you're nosey! Don't you know enough about me yet? Even now?'

'No.'

Cindy let out a long breath. 'All right. When I was thirteen I walked in on my father when he was . . . being unfaithful to my mother.' She could hardly believe her own ears. She'd never told that to anyone.

Zac made a clicking sound with his tongue. 'That was unfortunate.'

'Unfortunate? Unfortunate! For whom?'

'For all concerned. For you, at that age. For your father, who'll never forget it. For the woman, who was embarrassed. What happened?'

Cindy looked at him quickly, wondering how he could be so damned nonchalant about it. 'I-it was with a house guest. Well, a sort of au pair, I suppose. She was Swiss, in her twenties, the daughter of a family my parents knew in Zurich. She'd been living in our house for about three weeks when ... You don't want the gory details.'

'Oh, but I do. Go on.' He wasn't smiling. At least he wasn't amused.

'I was a weekly boarder in those days. I came home every weekend. My father and I were pals. As hard as he worked, he still tried hard to be the family man. He didn't mind that I was fat. I was Daddy's little girl ... my sisters were in their early twenties when I was thirteen. They never found out about this ...

'Anyway, I was home for the summer holidays and one night there was a terrifying storm—I've always been terrified of storms. I was crying. I couldn't cope on my own and I bolted for the nearest bedroom... Anna's. And there they were. There was no lock on the door, and there they were. The so-called pillar of the community, the highly respectable Sir Robert, and his au pair. I'll never forget that moment. The shock of it. The lights were on, the bedclothes were off and I burst in on them while they were actually, actually—'

Zac finished the sentence for her and Cindy looked down at the grass. 'Zac, must you be so graphic?'

He shrugged carelessly. 'Would it be fairer to describe it as lovemaking, when there's all the difference in the world between that and lovemaking? It was just sex, wasn't it? Your parents sound happy enough together now. Or was there a string of others after Anna?'

'I—no. Not to my knowledge.' Cindy was getting irritated. Just sex? Oh, where had she heard that before?

'And your mother? Did you tell her or did your father?'

Cindy got up and started walking again. 'Firstly Anna left the following morning. Secondly, I suppose my father must have told my mother, because I refused to go downstairs the following morning. I'd cried all night, and was still crying when Mummy came to me. But she knew in any case.'

At that, Zac's eyebrows rose slightly.

Cindy shrugged. In for a penny... 'My mother had had a hysterectomy. Prior to that she'd had a lot of menopausal trouble. Unlike you, Zac, I wasn't green about these things at thirteen. I understood it all, intellectually. My mother is a lady in every sense of the word. She explained to me that she hadn't given my father any "attention" in a long time. She said I should try to understand that this wasn't serious, that my father still loved her, and I should forgive him.'

'And you never have.'

'Zac, I find the whole thing very distasteful,' Cindy snapped. 'I don't want to discuss it any further. My father and I have never really communicated since that day. There's a strain between us and—well, it'll always be there.'

'That's a shame, my beauty.' Zac looked at her curiously then. 'It was one of those things. Your father fell from grace because you found out he was human.'

He held open the door for her as they entered Priory Court, bade the doorman good evening and punched the lift button.

In a quiet, tight voice, Cindy contradicted him, 'I found out he was a hypocrite. I found out he was *unfaithful.*'

'To whom?'

She stepped into the lift, glaring at him. 'To my mother, of course.'

'But she forgave him. Why couldn't you? Your father was only unfaithful to your image of him. It's always a blow when we discover that our parents are only human, with human susceptibilities. You're a big girl now, Cindy. It's about time you stopped thinking about all this in the way you thought about it ten years ago... Put the kettle on, would you? I want to talk to you about Paris.'

She had followed Zac into his flat without even stopping to think about it. In fact, it was minutes later before she realised she'd walked into a potentially dangerous situation. For the moment she was too busy thinking about what he'd said. Never once in ten years had she stopped to think what it must have been like from her father's point of view, how he must have felt when she had walked in on him. 'Your father fell from grace because you found out he was human...' But wasn't that typical of a man, to take it lightly, to put it down as being 'just sex'?

Cindy carried the coffee into the living room in a state of agitation. What was she doing here? She'd had no intention whatever of ending the evening in Zac's flat....

'Paris,' he said crisply. 'Sorry to end this evening with business, Cindy, but we'll have no opportunity tomorrow.'

'That's all right.' She relaxed slightly and poured the coffee. It was impossible to think about three things at once, despite the training Zac had given her! She would think about her father some other time. She would keep her guard up until she left Zac's flat and try to concentrate fully on what he was saying.

'You remember the man at the party?'

'The perfume manufacturer, yes. His agency were ditching him because they were going after bigger business in the same line.'

'Germaine Perfumes,' Zac nodded. 'Very big business.'

'I wear Germaine perfumes occasionally. I shouldn't have thought they were that big. They do a small but very exclusive range of—' Cindy stopped dead. Germaine Perfumes were based in Paris.

'They're launching a new range—mass market, medium price. They've got a three-quarters-of-a-million-pound budget. All that lovely lolly to spend on their launch! And you know how much profit that will mean to the agency who gets it. The follow-up business will be big, too.' Zac rubbed his hand across the back of his neck, easing the tension from his shoulders.

Cindy laughed excitedly. 'Now I understand why you re-fused the little man's business. *We're* pitching for Ger-maine's!'

'Don't get excited. I'm superstitious. I've told you be-fore. I might count my chickens before they're hatched, but I don't like talking about it.'

'But Zac, need you worry? With your reputation and—'

He held up a silencing hand. 'There are three other agen-cies pitching for the business.'

'Mmm. Well, that's normal . . .'

'Including Cookson Associates.'

Cindy flinched. Cooksons were good. 'Ouch.'

'And there's something else.' Zac drained his coffee and stretched out on the settee. 'Our three competitors are pre-paring speculative campaigns. They were given the go-ahead eight weeks ago.'

Cindy had to make an effort not to leap up from her chair. '*Eight weeks ago?* Why, you hadn't even taken over Bryant's then! We've got no chance of preparing a cam-paign in time! Zac, what you're telling me is that we're too late. Germaine Perfumes don't even want a fourth agency to pitch for the business, do they?'

'No.'

'How come we didn't learn about this sooner? Well, I mean you weren't even around when these other agen-cies—'

Zac waved an arm at her. 'It makes no difference. The whole business has been kept under wraps because it's the launch of a new product. The chap at the party told me about it because he's disgruntled.'

Cindy was shaking her head. 'And how did you manage to get an arrangement to see the Board of Germaine's?'

'I know the Chairman. Is there any more coffee in the pot?'

'Sorry. I only made two cups. Zac, please, what did the Chairman say?'

'A lot of things. It took me almost an hour to talk him into arranging the meeting.'

'So he's doing you a favour, letting you talk to his Board. What else did he say?'

'He said I'll never talk them into it. They're not interested. He said I was crazy.' Zac closed his eyes. 'Are you making more coffee?'

'In a minute. You know what I think?'

'What?'

'I think you're crazy!' Cindy got to her feet, shaking her head. There were three competing agencies preparing speculative campaigns and they'd had eight weeks in which to make their preparations. Zac had been told by the Chairman of Germaine Perfumes that they weren't interested in letting another agency prepare a campaign. Apart from that, they were too late! Why was he bothering to waste money on plane fares?

Zac was sound asleep when she went in with the coffee. It shouldn't have surprised her, considering the way he'd been working, but it did.

Cindy put the coffee down and just stood, watching him as he slept. What a strange man he was—unshockable and shocking, predictable and unpredictable, brilliant, and crazy with it. She stood for minutes, just looking at him. How often he gave her food for thought. Tonight he'd given her a feast!

She picked up her bag and left the flat very, very quietly. Looking at Zac, she had suddenly been filled with a strange, unaccountable sadness. For one awful moment, she'd imagined she was beginning to fall in love with him.

She shook herself mentally as she closed her own front door.

She was probably just tired.

CHAPTER EIGHT

PARIS WAS shrouded in grey clouds. There was a fine, misty drizzle falling, the type of rain that is far more unpleasant than a torrent.

Cindy and her boss emerged from the airport two hours later than planned, owing to a delay in take-off at London's Heathrow.

'Not to worry.' Zac ushered her into a taxi and told the driver to take them to the Hotel George V. 'Alain is coming to the hotel at seven. We've got plenty of time.'

Cindy hardly heard him. 'The George Cinq? Oh, why didn't you tell me we were staying there?' She was excited. 'I've always wanted to!'

'You didn't ask.' Zac smiled at the look on her face. 'You mean you've never seen the place?'

'Never.' The famous hotel was old and very majestic. It had been patronised over the years by maharajahs and millionaires, by Royalty and film stars. 'I've only been to Paris once before, for three days. It was a school trip.' Cindy pulled a face at the memory. 'So you can imagine the sights we took in—the museums, art galleries, Notre Dame, the Sacré Coeur. Oh, it was interesting, but we didn't exactly get the flavour of Paris, didn't see anything romantic!'

Zac was laughing now. 'But you spent a year in France with friends of your family. Didn't they bring you to Paris?'

'Paris was hardly local to where I was staying! Besides, I wasn't old enough to see any night life. I mean, places like the Moulin Rouge and the—'

'Hold it!' Zac's eyes were lit with amusement. 'We're on a business trip, remember?' He took hold of her hand and moved a little closer to her. 'But we'll have one spare evening. I'll see what I can do...'

Cindy turned to look out of the window. In a way, she was sorry she'd spoken. What she'd said could very easily be misunderstood. She didn't worry about what the rain would do to her hair. She watched the passing scenery in a state of fascination. Some people were hurrying along, some were strolling, some were sitting under the umbrellas of pavement cafés regardless of the weather. Everything in Paris was said to start at café tables, from business deals to romance.

Cindy's eyes flitted about eagerly, from the top of the Eiffel Tower to the windows of the buildings in which the Parisians were going about their daily business. She looked longingly at the smart shops on the Champs-Elysées, wishing she had time to do more than just look. How different Paris seemed now from the way it had seemed when she was a schoolgirl. She saw it now as it really was—exciting, romantic, mysterious, cosmopolitan, utterly fascinating.

Just below the Arc de Triomphe the driver turned into the Avenue George-V. The foyer of the hotel was more like the hallway of a stately home. It was magnificent, with a beautiful, pinkish Aubusson carpet which must have cost a fortune. The receptionist, immaculately clad, stood behind what could only be described as a very discreet little desk, no more than three or four feet wide.

They were greeted and treated with the utmost courtesy and a uniformed porter appeared as if from nowhere to show them to their rooms...

Except that they weren't staying in rooms. They were staying in a suite which comprised two bedrooms, with a bathroom between, and a very elegant sitting room. The suite was beautiful, but Cindy hadn't anticipated... 'I—I had no idea we'd be staying in the same suite, Zac.' She turned to him as soon as the porter left.

'I can't talk to my secretary if she's staying on the other side of the hotel, can I?' Zac tugged at his tie and dropped his jacket over the arm of a chair. Then he looked at her, as if he'd only just caught the implications. 'Hey, relax, will you?' He smiled roguishly. 'After all, you have got your own bedroom!'

'I hope the door's got a lock on it.' Cindy did not smile back.

Zac picked up the telephone. 'Why don't you go and investigate while I order coffee?' He looked at his watch. 'Would you like something to eat?'

'No. It's too near dinner time.'

'I'll order you a sandwich. Alain's coming at seven, but knowing him we'll spend at least two hours in the bar before we go in to dinner.'

'Are we dining in the hotel?'

Zac nodded as he gave his order to room service.

Cindy retreated to her bedroom. She'd had no idea Zac spoke a little French. Before doing anything else she checked the door. It had a very ornate gold handle, a sort of lever affair. Of course it was lockable. Cindy laughed at herself. But it was a nervous little laugh. She was not thrilled at the idea of sharing rooms with Zac. It was too intimate for her liking. And the bathroom was situated between their bedrooms, no doubt lockable from both sides . . .

She didn't investigate that. She was too concerned about getting her clothes out of her case and on to hangers. It seemed to Cindy that they'd come to Paris on a hopeless mission, but she would play her role to the best of her ability—which included being suitably dressed for dinner in the hotel with the Chairman of Germaine Perfumes.

The restaurant in the George V was famous for its superb cuisine and though there were countless renowned eating places in Paris, Cindy was delighted she would have the experience of dining at one of the most famous.

She looked round her bedroom with a little smile playing on her lips. The bed was vast, probably the biggest she'd ever seen. In one corner there was a cabinet which turned out to be a fridge. It was stacked with spirits in miniature bottles, and mixers of every description. She dreaded to think what a can of cola would cost in this place, let alone dinner for three in the restaurant. Zac Stone certainly liked the best in life!

The wardrobes were not immediately apparent. They were on either side of the panelled door which led to the bathroom. They were in what had at first glance appeared to be a mirrored wall, but the wall had handles and was in fact a series of doors. A laugh escaped from Cindy at the sheer depth of the wardrobes. She had literally to walk inside in order to hang her clothes!

She heard the arrival of the coffee as she took the last item from her case and joined Zac in the sitting room, still giggling about the size of the wardrobes.

'My dresses look absolutely lost in there!' Cindy laughed as she made herself comfortable in an armchair, her eyes sweeping appreciatively round the room. 'Now *this* is the lap of luxury!'

She poured the coffee and helped herself to a few dainty, prettily presented sandwiches, grateful they had at least a little time in which they could relax.

After recovering from their journey they were faced with a decision. 'Who's having the bathroom first?' Zac took a coin from his pocket and invited Cindy to call.

'Tails—never fails.'

Poker-faced, Zac told her it had this time.

'Let me see...you rogue! I win. See you later.'

The bathroom was the size of any ordinary hotel room. Discovering its eccentricities, from the glug-glug of the old-fashioned, ornate taps to the most unusual white porcelain loo which had a blue pattern on it, was an adventure in itself. The loo was tucked away discreetly behind its own little door!

Cindy was still soaking in the bath when Zac called to her. She had taken the precaution of locking the bathroom doors—from each bedroom.

'How long are you going to be in there?'

She was putting the finishing touches to her make-up when he called again. The light was better in the bathroom, and she really hadn't taken long.

'For heaven's sake, Cindy! Time's marching on!'

She pulled her gown more closely around her as she opened the door from his side. 'Sorry, but I couldn't have been much quicker.'

Zac entered and she exited. He didn't bother to lock the door, she noticed, but she did. She slid the lock from inside her bedroom and glanced impatiently at it as the sound of Zac's laughter reached her.

Cindy dressed quickly but carefully. She laddered the first pair of tights she put on, discarded the second pair because the shade wasn't right and was astonished to find Zac sitting with a drink in his hand when she emerged. And the glass was almost empty.

'I know women are renowned—' He broke off as he took in the sight of her.

Cindy's stomach contracted just as it had when she'd first set eyes on Zac. There were split seconds of silence, appraisal, appreciation, just as there had been then. She'd never seen him in a dark velvet evening jacket before, or a dress shirt. He looked magnificent as he stood up and held a hand out to her. Tall, broad, immaculate and—yes, handsome was the right word. Strikingly handsome.

'Well, this was certainly worth waiting for.' He spoke quietly as he took her hand. Cindy turned towards a chair, but Zac held her right where she stood, his glance taking in the elegant black dress with its deep vee and the provocative swell of her breasts.

The air between them was charged; the nearness of him, the sight of him, the touch of his hand making Cindy's heart pound so quickly she was sure he would hear it.

She forced her eyes away from his, away from the desire, the hunger so plainly and openly reflected there. 'Zac, please, I don't—'

'I do.' He said it very quietly as he imprisoned her in his arms. His lips claimed hers with an electrifying sensuality, tasting, exploring, the very intimacy of his kiss setting her body aflame with longing. She pulled away from him, caught in the battle between her body and her mind.

'Zac, please! *I don't want this!* If you want the truth, you frighten me. *This* frightens me—'

'*Truth,* Cindy? How can you tell me one thing when your body tells me something else? Wouldn't it be more honest to—' he caught hold of her hips and pulled her tightly against him. With one arm he held her there, impossibly, provokingly close, his free hand entwining itself in her hair as his mouth came down on hers, drugging her senses, turning her protests into lies. Slowly, subtly, the kiss changed as Cindy responded helplessly, then recklessly, everything in her straining to get closer to him.

Zac raised his head, but he did not release her. He held her against his body, his taut thighs pressing against her own, the hardness of his chest brushing against her breasts. He looked down at her, her lovely face flushed with desire, her lips parted by a small, anguished cry.

'You would deny this?' He released her, cupping her chin with his hand so she was forced to look at him. 'Still?' he demanded. 'Would you deny it now?'

Zac's eyes had darkened with a desire that matched her own, but they were not smiling. Nor was there a look of satisfaction in them.

Nor was there any warmth.

Anger flared through her at his audacity, his bluntness, his cold-blooded attitude. What right had he to assume, just *assume,* that she was there, for the taking? But even as she thought this, she could feel his lips on her neck, his hands sliding from her waist to the curve of her hip. She felt the prickle of tears behind her eyes. Tears born of anger, frustration, self-loathing because she still couldn't fight him off. Damn it all, she didn't want to fight him off!

With a man like Zac it would be all or nothing. And to a man like him, it would be meaningless. If she didn't resist him she would end up as just another statistic in his love life—his *sex* life. He didn't care for her. He only wanted to possess her! She was a challenge to him—and he'd told her he never could resist a challenge.

She pulled away from him sharply, turning her back on him and closing her eyes against the tears that threatened to spill over. 'Zac, I can't deny the physical. It was there between us from the moment we met. I know it, you know it. This is what you once referred to when you mentioned your very first impression. Is that honest enough for you?' Her voice rose as she turned to meet his eyes. 'But with my mind I reject it! Do you understand? With my *mind* I reject the idea of having an affair with my boss! I reject the idea of spoiling our relationship when we've only just established it. I reject the idea of spoiling things as far as work's concerned. I reject above all the very thought of being physically intimate with a man I don't even care for!'

The telephone started ringing before she'd finished speaking. Zac didn't even look at it. He was looking at Cindy thoughtfully, strangely, and there was a muscle working in his jaw. Dear Lord, he didn't believe a word she'd said! How much truth there was in Cindy's last statement, she didn't really know. She knew only that words were her only defence against him. Words. 'I mean it, Zac. Every word of it... You'd better—you'd better answer the phone.'

For a long moment he didn't move. He just smiled. 'You'd better go and repair your lipstick. That'll be Alain.' He snatched up the phone as Cindy told him she needed a few minutes.

'Meet us in the bar, then,' he said quickly . 'Hello... ?'

Cindy escaped into the bathroom and sat on the edge of the bath. She was suddenly dreading the evening ahead of her. How could she cope with an important business man, a total stranger, when she was being torn to pieces inside? And later, after dinner, what would happen then...?

She had been in no immediate danger just now, but there were two, possibly three, nights to get through before they returned to England.

Trembling, she struggled to regain her composure. She ran cold water over her wrists and hands and held them to her cheeks. She repaired her lipstick, combed her hair and dabbed beneath her eyes with a tissue, grateful that she'd at least managed to keep her tears in check.

Her reflection in the mirror was pleasing, that of a cool blonde who was calm and composed and had everything under control. It belied totally how she was feeling inside.

She walked into the bar looking confident, a tall, slender girl in an expensive black crêpe dress which showed off her figure to perfection. But she was unaware of the heads that turned to look at her. She saw only the sudden interest in the eyes of the man who was sitting with Zac, the way he got swiftly to his feet as she smiled at them on her approach.

Zac rose gracefully and lazily to his feet and pulled out a chair for Cindy as he made the introductions. 'Cindy, this is Alain Gérard. Alain, my secretary, Cindy Hetherington.'

It was difficult to guess the man's age. He could have been in his late fifties, he could have been in his middle sixties. He was about Cindy's height, with thick steely grey hair and dark eyebrows. He looked very distinguished, and Cindy acknowledged that he was still a good-looking man.

His appraisal of Cindy was quite open as he lifted her hand and pressed his lips to the back of it. *'Enchanté, mademoiselle, enchanté!'*

'Monsieur.' Cindy inclined her head politely, waiting for him to release her hand. He seemed reluctant to do so and when she sat, crossing one slender leg over another, Monsieur Gérard's eyes followed the movement.

'This is indeed a pleasure. Ah, indeed!' He bowed as he sat, and Cindy had to bite her cheeks to prevent her smile turning into a grin. He was typically French; in his greet-

ing, his mannerisms, his charm. But his captivation with
Cindy was perfectly genuine. 'Zac, if I had known this
business was to be brightened by the presence of such a
beautiful lady I would never have argued with you for a
moment!'

Zac looked at Cindy, a sardonic smile playing around his
mouth. 'Alain has a predilection for English ladies. You
married one, isn't that right, Alain?'

The Frenchman shrugged as if he were not going to commit himself to an answer.

'What will you have to drink, Cindy?'

'Dry Martini.' She turned to Monsieur Gérard. 'So your
wife is English? What part of the country is she from?'

'Dorset.'

'That's nice. And no doubt she is partly responsible for
your command of English. May I congratulate you, Monsieur Gérard, on an extremely impressive accent—or should
I say lack of one?'

'Alain, please!' He was delighted with her praise. 'Such
a charming secretary you have, Zac, I envy you! Such
warmth in an Englishwoman is rare, no?'

Cindy kept her eyes on Alain as Zac's answer came drily.
To her ears, cuttingly. 'Yes. Very rare.'

As Zac had anticipated, the session in the bar was a long
one. Alain was obviously a seasoned drinker and even more
obviously in no hurry to get home to his wife. He never even
mentioned business until they were drinking coffee after
their meal.

By then Cindy had a slight headache. She hadn't drunk
much, but she'd waited a long time for her dinner. There
was also the tension between herself and Zac. She was no
longer angry with him, she was simply aware of him. The
tension was a sexual one, and she felt as if she were walking
on the edge of a precipice.

'Ten o'clock,' Alain was saying. 'I and my Board will see
you at ten, but I can offer you no encouragement, Zac. I

explained the situation on the telephone. You've missed the boat, as you English would say.'

'The Welsh say it, too.' Zac grinned. 'Well, we'll see, Alain. We'll see.'

Alain looked at Cindy, shrugging expansively, and she turned her mind on to the business in hand. She leaned forward slightly. 'Alain, I understand there are three other agencies pitching for this business...'

'Ach! My dear, everyone and his dog would like to handle this launch!'

'But of course!' Cindy waved a slender hand in the air, but it was towards the low neckline of her dress that Alain's eyes flitted before he looked at her directly. 'Any launch is exciting—and an entirely new range of Germaine products is doubly so. But you haven't mentioned when these other agencies will be presenting their speculative campaigns to you.'

'Next week. At the end of next week.'

The end of next week! It came as a shock to Cindy; she'd thought Bryant's might have three weeks or so in which to prepare a campaign. Surely Zac knew this? Surely he'd been told over the phone?

Of course he had! He was just more crazy than she thought. She didn't react with any surprise, she didn't even pause before asking her next question. 'I take it the gentlemen on your Board are aware, fully aware, of Zac's expertise in television advertising? I ask this because while I'm aware that you and Zac have known each other many years, your company does not in fact advertise their really expensive perfumes through the mass media. So I ask myself, do they know that Zac is the best in the business?'

Neither man smiled at her.

'I couldn't have put it better myself,' said Zac, in a matter-of-fact voice.

'Yes, yes. A fair question, Cindy.' Alain drained his coffee cup, watching her approvingly. 'Believe me, if this were my decision alone, I would give the business to any agency

headed by Zac. I need no persuasion. There is one member
of the Board who thinks likewise. He...' Alain broke off,
searching for a word, '...lamented that we hadn't known
of Zac's return to advertising earlier. However, it isn't this
man's decision, either. You understand, the Board have to
be unanimous on this, something so important. Alas, we are
two against four others who will not be persuaded, for
purely practical reasons. The brief was given to your competitors over eight weeks ago. As I say, Bryant's are simply
too late.'

At that, Zac smiled and suggested they adjourn to the
lounge for more coffee and brandy. When they got up from
the table he kept the conversation well away from business.
Really, there was no more to be said.

'Cindy, I was wondering if you'd like to go on somewhere else?' The question came from Alain as soon as
they'd settled in the lounge. 'In Paris, the night is young no
matter what the hour! Perhaps you would like to see a
show—perhaps a little dancing? What do you think? And
you, Zac?'

Cindy's heart plummeted. She was fit to drop, her headache had worsened. Actually, the entire evening had been
quite a strain. She glanced quickly at her boss and saw that
his face was impassive. Almost. She could read those eyes
well enough to know without doubt that he was laughing
inwardly. She knew also what he was going to say. Damn
him! He was about to say that here was her perfect opportunity to see some night life—which was just what she'd
asked for in the taxi that afternoon.

But she was quite, quite wrong. 'Not tonight, Alain,' Zac
said firmly. 'Cindy has been working extremely hard of late
and it really would be unfair of me to keep her out of bed
tonight. I'm sure she's tired.'

The ambiguity, of course, went over Alain's head. Determined not even to look at Zac, Cindy turned to the older
man. 'You know, I'd have loved to, Alain. But to be honest

I have a slight headache and I am rather tired, what with the journey and all. But thank you anyway.'

Alain clapped his hands together in mock despair. 'Maybe some other time, Cindy? Who knows, when I'm next in England maybe you will offer to show me some of the night life in London?'

It was a gentlemanly acceptance of a lady's decision, but neither Zac nor Cindy made any mistake as to what was going through Alain's mind. 'Who knows?' she said lightly. 'As you say, Alain.'

Cindy excused herself after half an hour or so, pleading a worsening headache due to her tiredness. Actually, she'd never felt more alert in her life, though she honestly did have a headache.

Zac came to the suite almost an hour later. The doors were locked, of course, and Cindy's light was off, but she waited nonetheless for him to come to her room, or to hear some sort of taunt about the lack of originality in the way she'd made her escape from him.

But she needn't have worried. Zac came nowhere near her bedroom door. Nor did he make any comment through the bathroom door. Yet he was, she just knew, aware that she was awake.

' . . . WHATEVER DECISION is reached today, gentlemen, you are going to benefit from this meeting. You're planning to spend three quarters of a million pounds sterling on advertising to get your new range off the ground. The choice as to which agency will handle that for you is a major decision. Monsieur Gérard has made it clear to me that three agencies are well on their way in preparing speculative campaigns for you.' Zac shrugged slightly, looking from one face to the next. 'And I am here, as Chairman and Managing Director of Bryant's of London—rather late in the day— to give you the benefit of my experience.'

There was a nod here, a rather uninterested twist of the lips there, a wry smile from Germaine's Sales Director and a very light strumming of fingers on the boardroom table. Cindy looked around the room without moving her head, feeling a nervous anxiety which Zac Stone had long since become incapable of feeling. Including Alain, he was addressing four members of the Board, plus the Export Sales Manager and the Advertising Manager of Germaine's. They were a mixed bunch, as were their individual reactions as Zac continued to speak.

But they were listening.

Zac had been talking for five minutes, uninterrupted. After the first couple of minutes it had become obvious that the Financial Director was having difficulty in keeping up with a foreign language, at which point Cindy's nervousness had increased as she waited for Zac's signal that she should interpret for him.

But Zac had given her barely more than a glance since they'd entered the room and he was talking, now, in fluent French with a strong Parisian accent . . . far better than she could speak the language. And she spoke it well.

Would she ever really get to know about Zac? All about Zac? Would he continue forever to surprise her, to fascinate her? She glanced at him, sharp and immaculate in an expensive lightweight suit and a white shirt, his keen eyes no doubt monitoring every reaction, every facial expression of the individuals around him.

She wished that he didn't have this . . . this hold over her. She felt that she was not fully in control of herself, and that was something Cindy disliked. Still she was unable to define what it was about Zac that held her so, quite what it was she felt for him. Whatever it was, it was outside her experience. It was certainly more than physical attraction. Unlike him, their relationship meant more to her than that.

There had been that fleeting moment when she'd thought she might be falling in love with him. But how was she to recognise it, if that were the case? It had never happened to her before. She'd dismissed the idea and she dismissed it again now. She hadn't met a man yet with whom she'd fallen in love. And she'd met her fair share of them.

'...The importance of market research. I'm talking about finding out who your customers are going to be, what they want, what they *think* they want, from a product such as yours. What motivates women to buy toiletries and perfume?'

There followed a veritable hubbub of conversation. Zac's question was met with a dozen answers. The Marketing Director scribbled something on a sheet of paper in front of him, and Alain Gérard said nothing.

Zac turned his hands palms upwards. 'Of course, gentlemen, of course. Those are the obvious answers. On the face of things, I would agree with you. But would you be more specific? What is the result of the research these agencies have undertaken for you?' Zac's eyes went directly to those of the Advertising Manager and it was obvious he was put out by the question.

'Mr Stone,' the Financial Director spoke up, 'we're making only a nominal contribution towards the expenses for the work your competitors are undertaking for us. Their incentive to spend their own money is obvious. But we haven't asked them to risk their money on intensive market research.'

'Risk?' Zac parroted. 'You're talking about spending peanuts when you're offering a budget of three quarters of a million, when the success or failure of your product is at stake? Are you telling me my competitors haven't *insisted* on doing their homework?'

'Well, Cooksons are doing a certain amount of research on the—' the Ad Manager started to defend himself.

'Packaging.' Zac finished for him. 'Yes, I'm aware of Cooksons' methods, their way of thinking. They're good, gentlemen, but by no means good enough.'

Zac went into full swing; he'd seen his competitors' weaknesses and exploited them to the fullest. He fired a dozen questions as to the anticipated sales of the entire range, which was set out in the centre of the table.

In his role as Chairman, Alain did little other than maintain a quiet order about things as the meeting hotted up. The Advertising Manager had gone rather quiet, but it was he who finally spoke up and suggested to the other men that Bryant's be given the opportunity of preparing a speculative campaign. This was instantly seconded by the Financial Director.

Cindy hid her glee behind an impassive face, but her boss's next words shocked her as much as they shocked the others.

'You misunderstand me, gentlemen. I'm *not willing* to prepare a speculative campaign for you.'

There followed total silence, then ten minutes during which Zac explained to them exactly what his position was, what his methods were. He asked questions of the various men present, pertinent to their particular role, and got the fullest co-operation from everyone except the Marketing Director. The Marketing Director refused to reveal certain information about the company's sales procedures, arguing that this was strictly confidential and that it would be given only to the agency who was finally chosen to do their advertising.

Zac looked at his watch, and Cindy surreptitiously glanced at hers. It was almost noon, but they weren't in any hurry...

'To summarise,' Zac got to his feet, and all eyes were on him, 'I am not willing to prepare a campaign based on guesswork. Let my competitors come up with a series of pretty pictures; they do not deserve your business.' He looked at the Ad Manager, 'As I'm sure you will agree, *Monsieur*. Either you decide to give me the business or you don't. I appreciate that you'll have to decide quickly, and we'll leave you now to do just that. Monsieur Gérard knows where I can be contacted. I'll be in Paris until Friday noon. If your answer is yes, you must be prepared to give me all of your secrets.' He turned, then, to the Marketing Director. 'I want to know every last detail of how your sales network functions. Be assured of one thing: my creative team, my artists, will not pick up a pen until Bryant's know exactly what type of women we are aiming at with these products—and for what reason she is likely to buy them, until we have a clear idea of anticipated sales in the North of England compared to the Midlands or the South. Television advertising is an expensive business, as you're well aware. We don't want to waste money on air time in one region when it would be better to cover the area with a different approach. And so on and so on.

'Thank you for your time, gentlemen. It was a pleasure meeting you. Now if you'll excuse us, Miss Hetherington and I have other business in Paris this afternoon.'

CHAPTER NINE

'WHAT OTHER business?' Cindy asked the question the moment they stepped out into the street. The sun was shining from a perfectly blue sky and she took the arm Zac extended to her as they strolled along in the shade of the buildings.

'Lunch, of course,' he grinned at her.

Cindy giggled, but her mind was still whirling from the meeting that had just taken place. Zac had done a superb job, but she was not optimistic about Bryant's being given the business. She told him this, and she queried the wisdom of his tactics in refusing to compete with the other agencies.

'That wasn't a tactic, Cindy.' He turned left and then cut down an alleyway of cobblestones, knowing, it seemed, exactly where they were going. 'I don't prepare campaigns for people who aren't my clients. I don't need to these days. Either they entrust their business, their money, into my hands or they don't. Do you like seafood?'

'I love it.' She looked at him curiously. 'So what do we do now?'

'We wait for the telephone to ring. In the meantime, relax and enjoy yourself. It's in the bag.'

He seemed so confident that his mission had been successful. Cindy sucked in her breath, appalled. 'Zac! That really is tempting fate. I thought you were superstitious about counting your chickens... No, I mean *talking* about it?'

'I am. But not when it's a dead cert. That Ad Manager should be fired.'

'But he was on your side!'

Zac laughed shortly. 'Only because I made him aware of his incompetence. He'll save his neck from the chopping block if he votes to give me the business, and he knows it. He knows the launch will be a success if I handle it. Now, that's enough, Cindy. No more shop talk. Except...' He smiled at her, his eyes twinkling with amusement. 'Except to say you did well last night. I meant to tell you over breakfast.'

Cindy pursed her lips and shrugged it off. 'Well, I was on duty, after all. Someone had to blow your trumpet for you. It wasn't for you to do it—though you're perfectly capable!'

He squeezed her arm. 'I wasn't referring to the plug you gave me. I was referring to the diplomatic way you handled Alain's attentions—the old goat. He fancies you like mad!'

'Don't be so unkind! He's not an old goat. He's a good-looking man.'

'Do you know how old he is?' Zac admonished.

She looked at him mischievously. 'I've always preferred older men.'

'I'm glad to hear it.' His blue eyes moved over her face and lingered fleetingly on the gentle curve of her lips. She was sorry she'd spoken.

'Cindy, Alain has always been a ladies' man. He's a well-practised charmer. When he comes to London, I warn you, don't give him the slightest encouragement. For heaven's sake, he's forty years older than you! He's old enough to be your father—your grandfather!'

'Ah!' she smiled, teasing him, unwilling to let him have the last word. 'But he's not my grandfather.'

They walked at a leisurely pace through a network of streets and alleys in a romantic city that was drenched in sunshine, throbbing with activity, fascinating in its mysteries. Lunch, for Cindy, was a new experience; they took a river cruise on the Seine and ate fresh seafood and crispy salad, washed down with superb French wine. They were killing time—but what a lovely way to do it! And Zac was the perfect companion, knowledgeable, amusing, charming.

In the late afternoon they took a taxi to Notre Dame and browsed the bookstalls and art displays on the embankment of the Seine, watching the artists at work. It was turned seven when they got back to the George V and ordered a pot of coffee to be sent to their suite.

Cindy sank wearily but contentedly into an armchair in the sitting room and kicked off her shoes. 'What will we do this evening, Zac? I don't think I have the energy for more sightseeing. Oh, but I enjoyed this afternoon! Thank you.'

He smiled at her enthusiasm, at her lovely, vivacious face. 'You don't need to walk anywhere, except into a taxi which will be waiting at the door. I'm taking you to Le Moulin Rouge. How does that grab you?'

'Oh!' Cindy squealed with delight. 'It grabs me!' She was laughing at the expression he'd used, at the way he was laughing at her laughter, when the telephone rang.

Her laughter died in her throat as she looked from the telephone to her boss. Her fingers went to the thin, gold chain at her neck and fiddled with it nervously.

It was Alain.

Cindy held her breath as Zac spoke to him. If they landed this business, it would be the making of Bryant's. She wanted so much for that to happen, for Zac, for everyone concerned. But her boss's face was unsmiling, his words sparse.

'I see...' He glanced at Cindy, but he wasn't really seeing her. He was looking through her, beyond her, his mind concentrated only on what he was hearing. '...And when did they reach their decision? Ten minutes ago, eh?'

Cindy's heart sank like a stone as Zac let out a long, slow breath. He leaned back in his chair and that giveaway muscle was moving in his jaw. Whether he was angry or just disappointed, she couldn't tell.

'...You had quite a discussion, by the sound of it. Okay, Alain, thank you for letting me know at once... Of course...yes, do that.'

Zac put down the phone. He hooked one long, powerful leg over an arm of his chair and let his eyes drift towards the window, his fingers strumming against his thigh.

'Zac, I'm so sorry...'

He didn't hear her.

Cindy felt suddenly embarrassed; she didn't know what else to say to him. She also felt crushed with disappointment.

More than a minute passed before he turned to look at her. 'I'm sorry, Cindy? What was that?'

'I—I said I'm sorry. About Germaine's. It—there was nothing else you could have done this morning. You said it all; I—it was in the lap of the gods.'

Zac nodded. 'And the gods were kind. We've got the account, Cindy.' Very quietly, he added, 'It's ours, all ours. Without any conditions or reservations. Cooksons and the other people will be informed in the morning.'

Cindy's mouth opened in astonishment. She couldn't believe her ears. She wanted to wave her arms about, to jump up and down or something. But of course that wasn't her style. And quite apart from that, Zac Stone didn't seem in the least happy with the news. He didn't seem unhappy, either. He was just—just miles away in his thoughts.

'Zac, what is it? Why are you looking like that? What are you thinking?'

'Mmm?' He looked through her again. 'Cindy, why don't you go and rest for a while? I—' He smiled then, but it was as if he were making an effort to do so. 'I have some thinking to do. Have a sleep, then put on something spectacular and we'll paint the town red. We don't have to be at Germaine's until eleven tomorrow. Okay?'

'Okay.' She smiled brightly. He wanted to be left alone. The evening he was planning was for her sake, she knew. And he wasn't going to tell her what was going through his mind.

Cindy took a leisurely bath. She felt disturbed, unhappy because Zac's reaction to the news wasn't what it should be. But she was probably worrying needlessly. No doubt his mind had simply zoomed ahead. He'd probably started plotting and planning for Germaine's as soon as he received the good news!

At a little before ten she padded into the bathroom and put on her make-up. Her robe was still in the bedroom and she was brushing her hair when Zac suddenly walked in on her.

'Oh. Sorry, but the door wasn't—'

The door wasn't locked. Sleepy from her nap, she'd forgotten to lock either of them. It was entirely her own fault.

Cindy slowly put down her hairbrush as she turned to face him. He was motionless, tall and broad and frighteningly attractive as he stood in the doorway to his bedroom. He was half-naked, barefoot, covered only by a white bathtowel which was tucked in at the waist.

And Cindy's body wasn't covered by anything.

She knew, the instant her eyes met with his, that it was too late. Too late for protests, too late for words. They were about to become lovers and there wasn't a thing in the world she could do about it.

She spoke his name quietly. Just once.

Neither of them moved.

Every nerve in Cindy's body sprang to life with a yearning she would never have believed herself capable of feeling. As Zac's eyes slowly roamed the length of her naked body, her pulses leapt as they did every time he'd touched her.

His look, his absorption with her now, was in itself a caress. She, too, was like someone mesmerised as she drank in the sight of him, the slow rise and fall of a magnificent chest darkened with hair; his skin, so tanned that it seemed polished, perfect.

Zac's face was sombre, his blue eyes darkening perceptibly as he started to speak. But no words came. His lips closed and his mouth was unsmiling as he opened his arms to Cindy as she walked into his embrace.

He didn't kiss her. He just looked at her and let his hands travel very, very lightly over her face, her throat, her shoulders, her breasts. His hands trembled slightly as they moved, infinitely slowly, over every curve and contour of her body. She saw his eyes close, as though he would store indelibly in his mind every detail of her.

'Beautiful...' Zac's voice had roughened, deepened so that it was barely recognisable. 'You are incredibly, perfectly beautiful.'

Cindy closed the distance between their bodies, pressing tightly against the length of him. Her lips went to the base of his throat as her arms closed around the broad expanse of his back. Her blood was on fire, pounding through her veins. She could hardly breathe, her heart was racing so fast.

Gently, he loosened her hold on him, his breathing accelerating slightly as he spoke to her. 'Easy, my darling. We have all the time in the world. All the time...'

She was desperate for his kiss, her entire body trembling, screaming for his touch, and at the instant when she thought she could no longer stand, Zac lifted her into his arms in one easy, effortless movement and carried her into his room.

There was a moment, just one fleeting moment, when a voice in the farthest recesses of Cindy's mind tried to make itself heard. It was a voice which sounded so much like her own, barely audible but plaintive. 'Tomorrow, I'll regret this...I'll hate myself...in the morning...'

Then Zac's mouth closed over hers and the voice was obliterated. His lips trailed over her face, her eyes, her pulsating temples, as he lowered her on to his bed. 'Darling Cindy, no.' His breath was a warm breeze against her hair. 'I know exactly how you're going to feel in the morning...'

He laughed softly as he lay beside her, naked now, kissing her, caressing, stroking.

Cindy moaned under his touch, his expert exploration of her was a torch to the fire that had been kindling from the first time they met. She would never have dreamt it possible for a man to understand a woman's body, a woman's needs, the way Zac did. It seemed that there was a merging of minds, of spirits, as they caressed each other—discovering, delighting, savouring. With every passing moment, every touch, Cindy sank deeper and deeper into a state which was at once an oblivion and an awakening.

And Zac was still very much in control, of himself, of her, as he brought her slowly, deliberately, deliciously, to an all-consuming, devastating frenzy of longing. She cried out to him, unable any longer to bear the torture that was the ache inside her. Unable to wait for the moment when he would take her.

'Zac... Oh, please! Zac!' She stilled his hands, trembling uncontrollably as she arched towards him. Zac went on kissing her, his breathing ragged as his lips closed over the sensitive tips of her breasts, taunting, nibbling, gently sucking until she gasped from the exquisite torment of it.

Zac's muscles felt rigid under the smoothness of his skin as Cindy locked her arms around him, pulling him close until his mouth closed over hers in a deep and deliciously erotic exchange.

For the merest instant, Cindy's mind blotted out as Zac groaned against her lips. He drew her even closer and held her in the crook of one arm as his fingers moved towards that most intimate part of her. His lips moved lightly over her mouth in a taunting series of kisses, and within seconds Cindy was crying out as wave after wave of pure physical ecstasy shook her body.

She lay, fighting for breath, momentarily passive in Zac's arms as he smiled into her eyes and covered her face with kisses. She was unable to take her eyes from his, was unable to believe the intensity of what she had just experienced. Zac was kissing the outermost corners of her eyes, her forehead, her cheeks, as if he would reward her for her responsiveness, her very femininity.

She gazed at him with disbelieving eyes as her passion flared again, instantly, as he continued to caress her.

'Cindy...' he laid her against the pillows, his voice, his movement telling her there was no turning back now. A wave of anxiety crept unbidden into Cindy's mind. She stiffened slightly as she looked at Zac's powerful body, wanting him as she had never wanted any other man... As she had never known any other man.

She reached for him a little fearfully, the trembling of her hands, the tremor in her voice, beyond her control. 'Zac, please... Will you... I've never—I mean, I've never...'

For as long as she lived, she would never, ever, forget the look in Zac's eyes at that moment in time.

'God in heaven...' he looked at her in disbelief, his voice less than a whisper. 'I don't believe this. I don't—Cindy, *what are you telling me?*'

'I—' Cindy's voice was locked in her throat. She couldn't say it. Her eyes closed involuntarily because her mind refused to cope with what was happening. She couldn't bear the way Zac was looking at her. She had seen the muscles of his arms go rigid, his entire body stiffen as he moved, just a few inches, away from her.

'Zac, please, it's all right. It's all right—' Blindly she reached for him, but as her hands touched his chest, she felt Zac's fingers close around her wrists.

'Cindy—' he moved away from her completely, his breathing laboured as he fought for control. 'Cindy, you don't... oh, *God!*' She opened her eyes as he swore under his breath, his fingers raking the hair from his forehead. 'Did I get it wrong,' he muttered. 'Oh, boy, did I get it wrong this time! Why the hell didn't you—'

He stopped short as he saw the tears on her face. 'Cindy, I can't believe this. I had no idea. Why the hell didn't you tell me before now? How could you take such a—'

Cindy was crying silently but uncontrollably. She turned over and buried her face in the pillow, wishing she could die. She felt humiliated. Not by Zac, for he was controlling his anger far more than she deserved. She felt ashamed of herself. She'd known what he was going to say to her, and he was right.

'Stop that!' She felt his hand brush lightly over her hair, but she couldn't look at him. 'Stop it now, Cindy. It's...' She heard him sigh from the depths of his being, felt the bed give as he stood up. 'It's all right. Darling, I—I'm going down to the bar. Come and join me when you feel ready. I— we'll eat in the hotel restaurant.'

Several minutes passed before he left the room. There was the sound of drawers opening and closing as he got dressed and then, mercifully, she was alone. Her tears stopped when he'd gone and she turned over and stared blindly at the ceiling. Never in her life had she felt so wretched, so desperately unhappy. She had to face it: she was deeply in love with Zac—and it was utterly, utterly hopeless. Pointless. A man such as he would never want a permanent relationship with a woman, one woman. He'd never settle down if he lived to be a hundred. He hadn't even been able to settle into retirement. He'd missed the challenge of his work. Work made him tick. It was the only thing that really brought him to life.

And there had been, obviously, many women in his life. There would be more. One affair after the next. As there had been in the past. When he took time off from work, that was. When he felt the need.

Cindy got to her feet, only to sink wearily back on to the bed. She sat, crouched forward, her arms wrapped tightly around her ribs as if it would ease the pain inside her. What was the point of loving someone like Zac? Someone so very different from herself? There was no sense in it; there was no sense in the fact that it had happened in the first place. She couldn't just decide to fall out of love with him. Love wasn't something that could be turned on and off, like a tap.

Oh, but why, *why,* of all the men in the world did it have to be him?

After a while, Cindy got up and went to her own room. She pulled on her robe, feeling suddenly very cold. As much as she disliked strong drinks she needed one now if she'd ever needed one.

She was sipping her way through a neat whisky when the phone rang.

'Cindy, how long do I have to wait before you put in an appearance?'

'I'm not coming down, Zac.'

'I want to talk to you,' he said tiredly. 'Come down and eat with me.'

'No.' She put the phone down. She would have to face Zac sooner or later, but she certainly couldn't face him in a restaurant full of people.

More than an hour passed before he came back to the suite. He found her sitting in her room near the open window.

'I've brought you some sandwiches.' He plonked a plate on to the table at her side.

'Have you eaten?'

'Of course I've eaten,' he snapped. 'I couldn't wait for ever.'

She looked up at him then, her eyes narrowing. 'Are you drunk?'

'Nowhere near.' He sighed, lowering himself into the chair opposite hers. 'Just slightly . . . anaesthetised.'

Cindy flushed with embarrassment. 'I—I'm sorry, Zac. I—feel very badly about that.'

'Don't worry about it.' He laughed humourlessly. 'I can always take a cold bath.'

She flinched inwardly at his bluntness; she was only too aware of what she'd done to him and she wasn't exactly proud of it.

He ran a hand tiredly through his hair. 'I take it you're not on the pill? I mean, for some other reason, perhaps?'

'Zac, *must* you?' Cindy hardly knew where to look. 'I really don't—'

'Answer me, dammit!'

'No,' she said dully, 'I'm not.'

He lost his temper then—finally. He got up and stalked about the room as Cindy closed her eyes against his all too evident anger. 'I thought as much! What the devil were you thinking about? How could you take a risk like that? After all I've told you about my past. And you were so quick to remind me that once is all it takes! How could you be so bloody irresponsible? Well, you can count yourself lucky that I never knowingly take a risk. You can count yourself lucky I've got a neurotic streak about this sort of thing. We have my scheming bitch of an ex-wife to thank for that! I don't walk twice into the same trap!'

'Trap? Trap!' She glared at him, her embarrassment forgotten. She was fighting to keep her own anger in check now. 'I understand how you feel—obviously. But I'd had no intention of making love with you—ever! Kindly remember that!' The last thing she wanted to do then was to cry. But she couldn't help it. She was angry; she was loving Zac and hating him at the same time. She was confused and she felt incredibly sad that something which had been so beautiful and spontaneous should be dissected like this. 'Get out of here, will you? Just get out and leave me alone—' She choked on a sob, her hands flying up to cover her face.

Zac apologised instantly. 'I'm sorry.' She felt his hands on her shoulders, but she couldn't look at him. 'Cindy, I'm sorry. Really. Here—' he handed her his hanky. 'Don't cry—please. I can't stand it.' She heard him let out a long, ragged breath. 'Cindy, it isn't really you I'm angry with. It's me. You see, I—I never dreamt you were... I'm mad as hell because I had it all wrong! I thought I knew you, but I didn't. I thought you were just enjoying the fun of the chase. Dear God—a virgin, yet!'

He went to the fridge and took out two miniatures of Scotch. 'Since when do you drink whisky? Never mind. Here, have another!'

If he was trying to get her to smile, he failed. 'I've never encouraged you,' she said accusingly. 'Please remember that.'

Zac looked heavenward, the air whistling past his teeth. 'Your very existence is encouragement in itself.' He sat down, shaking his head. He was quiet for a long time.

Cindy said nothing. She sipped at her drink and resigned herself to his presence. He wouldn't leave her alone until he was good and ready. He'd made a mistake in his assessment of this particular woman. Maybe his professional pride was injured?

'We have to talk,' he said at length. 'You see, the more I get to know about you, the less I know you. It's—you have an amazing ability to give people entirely the wrong impression. Do you know that? At first I thought you were a stuck-up, haughty little snob. Then I discovered your sense of humour, your sensitivity, your abilities as far as work's concerned, your sophistication . . . *apparent* sophistication. Now I find out that beneath your veneers you're just an old-fashioned girl! You never cease to surprise me, Cindy.'

'If you're trying to put me down,' she said coldly, 'it won't work. Not this time. I'm not an old-fashioned girl, I just don't—'

'Wait a minute, wait a minute!' Zac held up a hand. 'I'm not trying to put you down—I'm trying to understand you. I want to talk to you. Give me a chance. I want you to see how things have looked from my point of view. All right?'

'All right,' she shrugged carelessly.

'Now, you told me that during your first couple of years in London you had a wild time. You said you did all the things you'd wanted to do, you had fun, you went out with lots of men—'

'I did. But I wasn't involved with any one of them. It didn't include—'

'Let me finish! From my point of view, Cindy, remember? I've found you to be—responsive, to say the least. I had every intention of taking you to bed . . . last week . . . next week . . . whenever the time was right.'

He laughed, making no secret of his inability to understand her. 'And now this! I'd like to know how you've got away with it.'

'I don't know what you mean,' she said dully. It had never been a question of Cindy 'getting away with' anything. But she could hardly tell Zac that he was the first man who'd ever really turned her on. Any more than she could tell him she was in love with him.

He looked at her in exasperation. 'There must have been someone, some time . . . What about the man who sent you those roses? What happened there?'

'James?'

'Whoever. How long had you been seeing him? Why did it finish?'

'He lied to me. He lied when he didn't need to.'

'How long?'

'I'd been seeing him for about four months.' Cindy shrugged. She didn't really see the point in this, but she was perfectly willing to tell Zac about James. 'I really liked him. We had a—sort of intellectual relationship, I suppose.'

'A *what?*' Zac turned and looked at her as if she were unreal. 'What was wrong with him? How could a man have an intellectual relationship with you? Didn't he try to get you into bed?'

'Yes—in the beginning. And when I made it clear I wasn't interested, he accepted it. We were friends. He was a lecturer at the technical college—I used to go to evening classes there. He lectured in philosophy and we had some really interesting discussions.'

'I've heard everything now,' Zac said drily. 'So what happened?'

'He was seeing someone else at the same time. Sleeping with someone. No, don't look at me like that. Because I didn't care. That's the irony of it—I didn't care about that. I'm not some sort of prude, Zac. But James and I were supposed to have an honest relationship. We were free to do as we wished. It would have made no difference to me if he'd been seeing six other women. But he lied to me, and he didn't need to. That's what upset me. You see, I'd trusted him, and I don't trust easily. Any more than I can...give of myself easily.

'One day, I got a phone call from an hysterical female telling me to leave James alone! Can you imagine how I felt? I tried telling her it was strictly platonic between James and me, and I won't repeat what she said to that. Then she told me she'd been seeing James for almost a year. She was in love with him, she said, and she was sick of his unfaithfulness.'

Zac was leaning against the windowsill, his hands shoved into the pockets of his slacks. He was listening carefully, but he said nothing.

'I confronted James with it, and he apologised over and over again. He said he wanted to go on seeing me. He even went as far as saying he was in love with me. Ha! He said it was just sex with the other girl. It was the same old story, Zac—just sex. Anyway—' She waved a dismissive arm. 'That was the end of James. As far as I'm concerned he was a liar and a hypocrite. Within the context of our relationship, he was unfaithful to me, too. Fortunately, unlike this other girl, I was not in love with him.'

Zac shook his head slowly. 'You've got a thing about unfaithfulness, Cindy. The frequency with which you use the word...it probably started with your father, that incident you told me about, when you were thirteen. Your father was unfaithful to you then—and you've been on your guard ever since, as far as men are concerned. You don't trust, you don't give, you make no allowances for human nature. And you don't forgive, either.'

'Spare me,' she snapped. 'Spare me the armchair psychology. I've told you, my father was unfaithful to *my*

mother. And if you think I'm an old-fashioned girl for
finding that distasteful, then go ahead!'

'And I've told you,' he said quietly, 'your father was unfaithful to your image of him. So was James.'

'For heaven's sake!' Cindy was getting more irritated by
the minute. 'Just leave me alone, will you? We're funda-
mentally different you and I. Our attitudes are different.
Let's leave it at that, shall we? I am as I am, and that's all
there is to it. And if you find my...my past...amusing in
some way, that's entirely up to you!'

'Oh, I'm not amused,' he said quietly. 'Not in the least, I
don't have an aversion to virgins, you know. But it's been a
long time since I found myself in bed with one, and as far as
you're concerned... Well, let's say I had a rude awakening.'

Cindy gave him an oblique look, still uncertain whether
he was laughing at her, and wondering what this conversation was leading to.

Zac lowered himself into a chair and stuck his feet on the
windowsill, watching her all the time he spoke, unaware of
the pain his words were causing her. 'You'll never find him,
you know—this man you're looking for. This paragon—
your ideal man who can give you a guarantee never to let
you down. This man you've been saving yourself for.'

Cindy wanted to laugh and cry at the same time. 'You're
not the first person to tell me I expect too much of people,
Zac. But it's ludicrous to say I've been saving myself for
someone! Because it sure as hell wasn't you! Yet I was willing to spend tonight in your bed—regardless.'

'Ah! But you'd have hated yourself in the morning. I
didn't believe it when you told me, but I believe it now. I
never had your acquiescence, Cindy. You wanted me with
your body but not with your mind. You'd told me that, too,
more than once.'

Cindy picked up her drink and swallowed it in one go. She
didn't know how to answer that one. She was so afraid of
giving her feelings away. If he suspected how she really felt

about him, it would certainly give him cause for amusement. 'Zac, if you're trying to tie me up in knots, you're succeeding. What do you want of me?' She threw up her hands in exasperation. 'Where is this leading?'

'I'm trying to solve your problem.'

'I don't have a problem.'

'Don't you?' he smiled sardonically. 'You're mine for the taking, Cindy—any time, anywhere. I know it, and you know it. You have no more shocks in store for me. I've discovered, finally, the real Cindy Hetherington.'

With that, he got to his feet. Cindy couldn't move a muscle. She was trembling, at a loss to understand him.

Zac put a hand under her chin, tilting her face up to his as he looked steadily into her eyes. 'I'll leave you now, Cindy. I've got some thinking to do. A little...reassessment.'

She brazened it out, meeting his gaze squarely. 'Indeed? You see, Zac, you didn't know me at all, did you?'

He kissed her lightly on the mouth. 'I wasn't referring to you, actually. I had something quite different on my mind before I walked into that bathroom tonight. But that's strictly my problem. As for yourself, may I suggest that you spend the next hour or so coming to terms with your own problem? How are you going to reconcile yourself to having an affair with a man you don't even care for? I quote yesterday's words, Cindy.' He pulled her to her feet roughly, and even as she hated him for taunting her, his nearness was affecting her more than ever before.

She snatched her hands from his grasp. 'You're a ruthless, cold-blooded bastard—'

'And you want me. What an interesting situation this is!' He walked towards the door, smiling as he turned. 'We have to be at Germaine's at eleven tomorrow. I'll have breakfast brought to the sitting room at nine. You'll be working hard tomorrow. We have to record everything there is to know about that company and their products. So don't battle with yourself for too long. Get some sleep. You've learned something tonight, after all—you're just as susceptible to the power of sex as anyone else is. Goodnight, my beauty.'

CHAPTER TEN

THE DAYS that followed were probably the strangest days of Cindy's life. She was in anguish, an agony of indecision.

In the office things were relatively slack. The Simpson campaign had been given the go-ahead and there was nothing Bryant's could do on the Germaine account until the results of the market research were to hand. It would be the beginning of September before things started to get hectic on Germaine's behalf.

Cindy had time to think. And rethink. Her evenings were free, and she went for a drive or a walk on every one of them. Zac let her leave the office at five each evening, though he stayed on himself, talking to Greg Halliday about Germaine's.

Over the weekend that followed she saw nothing of Zac. No doubt he was still hunting for a house in the country in which he would make his escape from the city on future weekends. When work permitted.

Cindy was functioning normally as far as work was concerned. Nobody could have suspected the inner turmoil she was going through. After dinner on the Sunday evening she sat down with a cup of coffee and tried to reach a positive decision.

She should leave Bryant's. If she were to hang on to her sanity, she should leave. But she couldn't. It had nothing to do with pride and nothing to do with interest in her work. In fact, she could no longer claim that. She was not, after all, so dedicated that she could work at a breakneck pace for the sake of work. Unlike Zac, she no longer found that the challenge was enough. Unlike Zac, she had found what was missing in her life. And that was something totally unattainable—Zac Stone, the man she had not been looking for. The man she had not been saving herself for.

James had once told her that she didn't know herself, and she'd denied it vehemently. But she didn't know herself now. It seemed that her life, her future, was crumbling around her. Since meeting Zac an insidious change had been taking place within her.

It was strange, really. In Paris, Zac had told her that the more he knew about her, the less he knew her. She felt exactly the same about him. She knew him better than she had before, yet she understood him less than ever.

But she loved him.

Whatever he was or was not—and he certainly was not the paragon he'd accused her of wanting—she loved him.

Nobody had told her what it was like to be in love. Nobody had told her it could be so painful. Nobody had told her how love could make a person behave illogically. She couldn't leave Bryant's, because she couldn't leave Zac.

There was neither rhyme nor reason in it, but there it was.

Nor could she enter into an affair with him. It would be the destruction of her. It would run its course, as all his previous affairs had, and leave Cindy—where? What? Empty. Desolate. As things stood, she could cope. But if Zac were to become her lover...well, the glory of that would be overshadowed by the inevitability of its outcome.

On the other hand, thinking in terms of inevitability, surely she was swimming against the tide? Oh, Zac hadn't made a move in that direction. But he would. He was playing cat and mouse with her. Maybe he was waiting, right now, for her to knock on his door and walk into his arms. Maybe he'd knock on her door first.

For more than a week, since the unforgettable evening in Paris, nothing had been said on a personal level. They had worked with one another, snapped at one another, laughed together. And beyond all that, it was still there. A burning desire, unsatisfied. With all its inherent complications, promises and mysteries. Beyond the most casual word, the most casual touch, it was there, crackling in the air. Just as if it had a presence all of its own.

Like Pandora's box.

It was on the Monday morning, ten days after they had left Paris, that Cindy finally made a decision. She walked into Zac's office with a well-rehearsed speech about why she was handing her notice in.

As soon as she got through the door Zac looked up from the chart he was working on and shoved a piece of paper in Cindy's direction. 'I've just had Miss Druce in here.' He said it without preamble. 'She's handed her notice in—finally.'

'I—You were expecting it?'

He shrugged. 'Of course I was expecting it. She's complained twice about the girls in the typing pool. You saw the state she was in the last time she came in here.'

'Yes.' Cindy remembered only too clearly. 'But she wouldn't tell me what was wrong. In what way was she complaining? What about the girls in the typing pool?'

'It's their natural—youthful effervescence,' he grinned. 'Miss Druce can't cope with it. Her ears and her sensibilities are being offended daily.' He looked heavenward. 'God bless her cotton socks.'

Cindy shoved a stack of files out of the way and sat down. 'Zac, you knew she wouldn't last, didn't you? But you had nowhere else to place her except the typing pool, did you?'

'Nope.' He picked up his pen and went back to his chart.

'So why didn't you fire her when you took over?'

'Because she'd been here twenty years. Because she'd never have understood. Because it might just have worked out in the typing pool.' He looked at Cindy then, his deep blue eyes unsmiling. 'Because I must be getting soft in my old age, okay?'

'Old age, Zac?' She smiled at him, loving him, wanting him.

'A lot older than you.' He grinned, but there was still no laughter in his eyes. 'Find a replacement, will you? Someone a little less—you know.'

'Shockable?' Cindy laughed and picked up the formally typed letter of resignation. 'So you're not so ruthless after all, eh?'

'I blame you,' he retorted. 'You have a knack of making me behave strangely.'

'You hadn't met me when you made your decision about Miss Druce.'

At that, the smile reached his eyes. 'What did you come in here for, Goldilocks? Were you about to invite me to dinner at your place tonight?'

'No.' And then she lied. 'I just came in to say good morning.'

Cindy went back to her own office. She delegated the job of ringing the employment agency to Alison, then slipped out to make a phone call from a public box. She wanted to make an appointment with her doctor for the following evening, and she didn't want to be overheard.

On the Wednesday morning, Tracy Lynn arrived. It was noon, and she was expected. Cindy went to greet her in the reception area. 'Miss Lynn—I'm Cindy Hetherington, Zac's secretary.' She held out her hand. 'We haven't actually been introduced. Zac's expecting you. And you're bang on time, he'll like that!'

'Tracy, please.' Tracy shook Cindy's hand, her green almond-shaped eyes smiling warmly from a face that was still extremely beautiful—even for close-up photographic work. 'I saw you at the party, Cindy, but I didn't have a chance to talk to you.'

She followed Cindy through reception, towards the offices. 'So what does he want?'

'I'm sorry?'

'Zac. I know him of old. Come on, tell me what he's up to, so I can be forewarned. He's got to have an ulterior motive for inviting me to lunch!'

'I wouldn't know, Tracy.' Cindy was lying in her teeth. 'I was told to book a table at Mario's for twelve-thirty, and that was all I was told.'

'Are you joining us?' Tracy's eyes were lit with amusement and, as Cindy shook her head, she laughed outrageously. 'Then he's definitely up to something if he wants me alone! Do I look okay?'

Cindy couldn't help smiling. She couldn't help liking Tracy Lynn, either. She was vivacious, outgoing—and she wasn't just fishing for a compliment. She stopped in her tracks, looking at Cindy with genuine uncertainty.

The older woman looked no less than stunning in a lemon, low-cut summer dress which was just the sort of thing Cindy would wear. It was simple, beautifully cut, and it suited her. 'Yes,' Cindy smiled. 'More than all right.' In spite of herself, she couldn't prevent the twinge of jealousy that rushed through her at the knowledge that Tracy Lynn might be around for the next few weeks—if Zac had his way.

She handed the model over to Zac, closed the door to his office, and no sooner had she sat down than Alison started questioning her.

'Who was that? Wow!'

'Tracy Lynn,' Cindy said quietly. 'A model—well, ex-model, actually. It seems she retired about six months ago.'

'She's gorgeous! Why did she retire? And why is she seeing Mr Stone? Is it something to do with Germaine Perfumes?'

Cindy shrugged noncommittally. 'It's your turn for an early lunch, Alison. Why don't you go now, while you have the chance?'

Alison switched off her typewriter. 'I'll bet it is.'

It was. Zac wanted to use Tracy Lynn in the television commercial he was planning for Germaine's. The market research was now to hand, and Zac was planning on featuring three different women of different ages and images in the ad. He thought Tracy Lynn would be perfect. So did Greg Halliday. So did Cindy.

It was turned three when Zac came back to the office. Cindy followed him into his room and asked what had happened.

He shook his head. 'She's happy in her retirement. She's absolutely, categorically not interested. She said.'

'What does that mean?' Cindy's relief was squashed by the way Zac had tagged on the last two words.

'It means,' he smiled. 'That I'm taking her to dinner on Friday night, and then maybe she'll say maybe.'

Cindy leaned casually against a filing cabinet. It was against every instinct in her to ask the question, but she just couldn't help herself. 'You and Tracy go back a long way, Zac. Were you lovers, in the past?'

Zac's eyes locked on to hers and held them. 'What's that got to do with anything?'

'Not a thing.' Cindy hated herself for giving in to her curiosity. But it was important to her. Very.

'Yes.' Zac continued to hold her gaze. 'During the last few months at Stone, Mason and Gibbons, we had an affair, though we'd been working together for a couple of years. I used Tracy exclusively on the cosmetics account. Our affair finished when I left the country. Why are you blushing, Cindy? You should have known I wouldn't lie to you. Would you feel better if I had?'

'I'm not blushing.'

ON FRIDAY evening, Cindy forced herself to go out. She took herself off to see a play, but she hardly heard a word of it. Jealousy was eating away inside her. And she hated herself for it. It was another new experience for her, and it was negative. But she'd never had reason to feel jealousy before. She'd never loved a man before. Over and over she reminded herself that Zac's date with Tracy was for business reasons.

Over and over again she wondered what they were saying to one another. Were they reminiscing? They were two extremely attractive people—and they'd been lovers.

She walked home from the theatre feeling sick. But she would have felt worse if she'd stayed at home with nothing at all to distract her. As she turned into Priory Court she saw a small BMW parked next to Zac's Jaguar. It didn't belong to one of the residents. There was nothing whatever about the vehicle which could have told Cindy it belonged to Tracy. She just knew that it did. She looked up at the closed curtains of Zac's window and saw a light come on in the living room. They'd just got back from dinner.

What now?

She had known nothing about Zac's arrangements for this evening and even as she hated herself for doing it, she walked towards the cars and touched the bonnet of each of them. They'd used Tracy's car. Zac's engine was cold. Which meant that Tracy had picked him up, or called for him at the agency.

Cindy undressed, but she didn't go to bed. She couldn't. She moved around restlessly in her bedroom. It was eleven-fifteen and she found herself looking at her watch every five minutes. Every fifteen minutes she went and looked out of her window. From the darkness of her living room, she knew, she wouldn't been seen.

At a little after midnight, Tracy's car was gone.

So nothing had happened.

She hoped against hope that Tracy had stood her ground and had not given in to Zac's persuasiveness as far as the Germaine ads were concerned. If Zac told her on Monday morning that Tracy had said yes, or even maybe, she would have to leave Bryant's. She'd have no choice. Nobody knew better than she how persuasive Zac could be. Maybe would mean yes ... and possibly a great deal more. She couldn't cope with that, with this sick jealousy eating away inside her.

It was the worst weekend of her life. On the Saturday she went to the coast and drove for miles. But she didn't even notice her surroundings. She felt as if she were coming apart at the seams. If she'd known, then, that the decision about her immediate future was to be taken out of her hands, she might have managed to eat something. She might have managed to stop hating herself.

But she didn't know, and things got worse. Late on Sunday evening, Cindy pulled into her parking spot outside the flats. Tracy's car was there. And it was still there at midnight.

At a little after two in the morning, Cindy took a last look from her living room window, and went to bed. The car was still there.

She cried half the night. She took the pills from her dressing table drawer and threw them in the rubbish bin, filled with self-loathing and humiliation. The only thing that prevented her from going insane was the fact that Zac didn't know how close she'd come to having an affair with him.

At a little after eight on the Monday morning, she was jostled from a restless sleep by the jarring of the telephone. She reached for it hurriedly, blindly, unable to bear the noise of it. Part of her mind registered that she'd overslept as she saw the hands of her clock. Then a voice in her head laughed at her for reacting. Her days at Bryant's were numbered. What did it matter if she were late? She would give notice. She would do that because her pride would not allow her to do otherwise. Zac must never know how she felt. Somehow she would work her way through the next two weeks with the dignity and composure inherent in her nature. She would tell Zac that she'd simply made a mistake, that the pace of work was proving to be more than she could cope with. That she wanted to get out before things became impossibly demanding on the Germaine account. It would, after all, be partly true.

'Cindy?'

'Mmm...? Mummy! What on earth are you ringing at this hour for? I can't chat now, darling, I'm late—'

Cindy's breath was punched from her body by her mother's next words. Her mind blanked out momentarily as tears started to trickle down her cheeks. She could never have guessed that she would take this news so badly.

'When? . . . And where is he now? . . . And what are his chances?'

She barely gave her mother a chance to answer. She was already out of bed. 'Of course I'm coming Mummy, how could you think— Let me go. I'll be home as quickly as I can possibly make it!'

She put down the phone and stood, not knowing what to do first. Her father had had a heart attack in the early hours of the morning and was lying in the intensive care unit of a hospital on the outskirts of Manchester.

And Cindy had never forgiven him.

She broke down, sobbing as she had never sobbed before. But she was on the move even as she did so. With trembling hands she stuffed clothes into two suitcases. Then she washed and dressed.

Only then did she remember Zac.

She flew to the window, wondering whether he'd left for the office. Tracy's car was there, but Zac's wasn't. She snatched up the phone and dialled Bryant's number, her hands clenching and unclenching as she waited to be put through to her boss. 'Zac, listen. I have to go home at once—my father's had a heart attack. It's bad, Zac. I have—'

She heard the sharp intake of breath at the other end of the line. 'Of course, of course,' he said hurriedly. 'God, Cindy, I'm so sorry... Ring me when you can. Let me know how he's doing.'

Cindy got out of Priory Court as quickly as she could, hampered by her suitcases. She'd just flung them in the boot of her car when someone tapped her on the shoulder. She turned to see Tracy Lynn, looking a little nonplussed at seeing Cindy, but smiling, as friendly as ever.

'Cindy? I thought it was you! Are you looking for Zac? He left about half an hour ago.' She laughed girlishly. 'I'm afraid we overslept this morning! But he'll be at the office by now, if you—'

'I wasn't looking for Zac.' How Cindy didn't bite her head off, she'd never know. But the feeling of nausea churning inside her seemed to have robbed her of the necessary energy. 'I live here, too, as a matter of fact. Excuse me, Tracy, I'm in a hurry.'

The two women got into their cars and Cindy pulled out first, her eyes swimming with tears. Only then did she question her decision to drive to the north. But it would be the fastest way. If she took a train, she'd have to get to Euston first . . . She took hold of herself mentally, acknowledging that the situation would not be helped by her own hysteria.

The rush hour traffic was chronic, even on the motorway. It was only when she left the M1 to join the M6 that Cindy was able to put her foot down. She drove fast, but carefully, her reactions automatic. In a corner of her mind she could hear her mother's voice, asking whether Cindy would come home at once. Asking. How incredibly, desperately sad it was that her mother had needed to ask. What an appalling thing that was! But she couldn't blame her mother, she could blame only herself. The strain between Cindy and her father had been tangible for the past ten years, and a constant source of sadness to her mother.

Cindy blinked against a fresh bout of tears. Dear Lord, she prayed, let him live! Let him live to be a hundred. Let him live to enjoy his retirement. Let him live that I may put things right between us.

At the dictate of common sense she pulled into a service area and forced herself to drink a cup of coffee. Not that she wanted it; it was just in an effort to halt, once and for all, the tears which were blinding her vision.

At a little after noon, she drew to a halt in the hospital car park. She saw the grey Bentley, the family car, parked a few spaces away. Then she saw George Butterworth, the chauffeur-cum-head gardener, walking hurriedly towards her.

'Miss Cynthia!' George smiled warmly and something inside Cindy snapped with relief. 'It's all right, miss. Your father's holding his own. I'll take you to Lady Hetherington.'

Cindy smiled and nodded, not trusting herself to speak. She patted the arm George extended to her and let her hand rest there, grateful to him. He and his wife, who worked as housekeeper, had been around for as long as Cindy could remember.

George escorted her to the private wing of the hospital and opened the door to a waiting room which was painted stark white, closing the door quietly after him as he left Cindy alone with her mother.

Lady Hetherington was sitting erect, quietly composed, as always. Her greying fair hair was as neat as ever, swept into a French roll with not a hair out of place. She was a petite woman, much shorter than any of her three daughters, perfectly groomed and possessed of an air of dignity which sometimes obscured her warmth. In the latter respect she and Cindy were very much mother and daughter. But her face crumpled slightly as she saw Cindy.

'Mummy!' Cindy threw her arms around her and lowered herself on to the couch. It was one of two, together with two straight-backed chairs, which filled the waiting room to capacity. 'Why are you alone? Where are my sisters? How come—'

'It's all right, darling. I'm fine, just fine. Felicity was with me until about ten minutes ago. She's gone back to the house, Jonathan says there's no point in our waiting here, but I'm not going home until I hear something positive.'

'Jonathan? Thank heavens!' Cindy sagged with relief. Jonathan Trent was an old friend of the family and an eminent doctor. Her father couldn't be in better hands. 'What about Paula? Has she been told?'

Lady Hetherington shook her head. 'She flew to California last night with her husband and the boys. We shan't be able to contact her until this evening.'

'Let's hope we'll have better news by then.'

Cindy's mother was still holding on to her hand. 'Darling, thank you for coming so quickly. It's been such a shock—'

Before Cindy could reply, Jonathan Trent came in, but he was cautious with his reassurances. 'Cindy, it's good to see you. I only wish it were under different circumstances.' He turned to Cindy's mother, motioning her to sit down again. 'There's no change, Pamela. I want you to go home. There's no point whatever in your sitting here. You know I'll ring you if I've anything to report.'

'I'm not going anywhere, Jonathan.' Lady Hetherington sat down again.

'When can we see him?' Cindy was on her feet now and the doctor slipped an arm around her shoulder.

'Not today, I'm afraid.'

'Is he going to pull through, Jonathan?' She could see the lines of strain around the doctor's face, his hesitation before he answered.

'It was bad, Cindy, but I've seen worse. Now, your father's as strong as an ox, he's been in good health and apart from that he's remarkably stubborn.' He smiled thinly. 'I think he'll pull through. But we must take this as a severe warning. He'll have to take things very easily in the future. And I shall be keeping a keen eye on him.'

'You *think* he'll pull through?' She hardly heard anything else. 'Is he awake? Can I go in and see him? Please, Jonathan!'

'No. To both questions.' He smiled to soften the blow. 'I'll have some tea sent in to you.'

Cindy and her mother sat quietly for over an hour, comforting one another without words. When Jonathan returned they could both tell, instantly, that he was feeling more confident. 'He's asking for you, Pamela. He's going to be all right.'

Cindy was on her feet instantly but the doctor put a restraining hand on her shoulder. 'Just a minute, young lady. He's asking for your mother. I'm going to allow you pre-

cisely one minute with him, Pamela. On the condition that
you promise to go home afterwards.'

'All right.' Lady Hetherington managed a smile, her voice
weak with relief.

'And when can I see him?

'Tomorrow night. For five minutes, perhaps. Bring your
mother and your sister at seven o'clock, and ask for me.'

They drove back to Cheshire in convoy, Cindy with her
mother in the passenger seat and George Butterworth ahead
of them in the Bentley. They found Felicity in the drawing
room, standing by the French windows, smoking nervously.

'Hello, Cindy. Mummy—is there any change?' Felicity
walked hastily towards them and sank wearily into a chair
when she was told that her father was going to live. She had
driven up from her home in Staffordshire that morning and
would be staying for a few days, she said.

'I'm going to my room.' Lady Hetherington didn't bother
to sit. 'Tell Mrs B. I don't want to be disturbed, Flick.'

'What about having something to eat, Mummy? You had
no breakfast, no lunch—'

'I'll be down for dinner at the usual time,' her mother said
quietly.

When Lady Hetherington had left the room, Cindy got
the details of what had happened in the early hours from her
sister. Felicity was the middle one of the three daughters and
she and Cindy had never got on terribly well. And that had
nothing to do with Flick's eight years' seniority, because
Cindy got on extremely well with the eldest of them, Paula.

'What about Charles?' Cindy asked about her sister's
husband. 'Will he drive up this evening?'

'No. He's bogged down with work. Besides, he's perfectly capable of being left for a few days. I want to stay here
until I'm satisfied that Daddy's going to recover fully.'

That, at least, was something they had in common.

'You might have hung on at the hospital,' Cindy admonished. 'I found my mother sitting there by herself, looking ghastly. Why didn't you wait till I got there at least?'

Felicity stubbed out her cigarette rather crossly. 'Because I knew you'd be there soon. Because I'd vomited twice. Because I couldn't bear to sit in that horrible room, waiting. Just waiting.'

'Are you ill? Or was it the—'

'I'm pregnant,' Flick shrugged, seeming neither pleased nor displeased over her news.

'Oh, congratulations!' Cindy's pleasure was evident. Her sister had waited a long time for this. After eleven years of marriage, everyone had long since decided it wasn't going to happen.

Mrs Butterworth came in with a jug of coffee and three cups. Inasmuch as she was painfully thin, Mrs B. was not everyone's idea of a cook/housekeeper. But she was a wizard in the kitchen and she'd been running the Hetherington household more than well for many years.

'Miss Cynthia, it's nice to see you again, though I certainly didn't expect it to be so soon after your summer visit. But George has told me the news. Sir Robert's going to be all right. Thank heaven for that!' She put down the tray, chattering more than was usual in her relief. 'Where's Lady Hetherington?'

'She doesn't want coffee or anything to eat, Mrs B.' Flick held up a hand as the housekeeper started to protest. 'She will be down for dinner, though, so please don't fuss.'

Dinner was a solemn affair in spite of the doctor's reassurance. Neither Lady Hetherington nor her daughters would relax fully until they saw the patient's improvement for themselves, although the atmosphere relaxed somewhat when Jonathan telephoned at nine o'clock with a progress report and an assurance that it would not be necessary to bring Paula and her family home from her holiday in America.

Paula had been contacted, and Cindy put through a further call to relay the latest news. After that she went to her room and flopped exhaustedly on to her bed. She had slept very little the previous evening, and she was to sleep even less tonight.

Her mind, now, seemed to be split into two separate compartments, each of which was battling for her fullest attention. Every time she closed her eyes she saw a mental image of her father lying in a white hospital bed in a white room, with a white-coated doctor standing by his side.

Then, like slides on a projector, the picture would be replaced by another on which there was also a bed, a larger bed in a room she had never seen, and on it there was Zac and a dark-haired beauty making love. Zac was holding Tracy Lynn in his arms, his deep blue eyes looking smilingly, intimately into hers, just as he had looked into Cindy's eyes...

For as long as she lived she would be grateful that she had never known the fullest extent of Zac's lovemaking. For as long as she lived she would be grateful she had not numbered among his affairs. Meaningless affairs.

Perhaps, with Tracy Lynn, it wouldn't be meaningless. They were picking up where they'd left off two years ago. Maybe Zac was in love with her, maybe that was why he invited her to Bryant's party. Maybe that was why it was she he wanted for the Germaine ad when he could have taken his choice of a hundred other models—so he could pick up where he'd left off.

There again, maybe it was just sex. Maybe Zac had turned to Tracy for the fulfilment Cindy had denied him. Oh, how quickly he had done that! How it served to demonstrate the nothingness of his feelings for Cindy.

She tried to tell herself she didn't care. She didn't care that Zac felt less than nothing for her. Didn't care that he'd made love to Tracy in a flat right next door to her own, so soon after Paris... Paris... Another woman...

Cindy pulled the bedding closer around her, curling up tightly into the embryonic attitude as if the warm softness of her bed would serve as a womb to protect her from all the hurts which life could inflict, so many of which had assailed her within the space of one day. But she did care. She *cared*. She cared because she loved Zac Stone regardless of anything and everything. But she would never see him again. Not for an instant. She had made her escape from him quicker than she had expected to, and while she desperately regretted the circumstances which had brought that about, it was an enormous relief to her.

It meant it was over. Cleanly, swiftly. Now she might start to heal, to become whole again.

If only the pain would stop.

CHAPTER ELEVEN

'CINDY...I wasn't expecting... It was good of you to come. Is your mother outside?'

Cindy forced herself to smile as she approached the bed. It was an effort to force the words past the constriction in her throat. 'Yes. With Flick. They...they let me come in first.' She sat close to her father, determined not to let him see how the sight of him affected her. He looked ten years older than he had only a couple of months ago, in June—when she had found his company a strain. His bushy hair looked greyer than ever. His face, normally jovial-looking and ruddy, was tense, almost as white as the pillows he was propped up against.

And then a momentary silence hung between them as Cindy's vision blurred. She sat perfectly still, struggling for control, frightened lest she give him any kind of stress.

'You know what this means, don't you?' Sir Robert's voice reflected his attempt at lightness, but his eyes closed wearily even as he spoke. 'It means my golfing days are over.'

'Oh, Daddy!' Cindy leaned closer to him, slipping her hand into his as the tears brimmed over and spilled on to her cheeks. Her father's eyes closed again, but Cindy felt his fingers tighten around her hand. It had been a long, long time since she had called him Daddy. That, and the way he continued to hold her hand tightly, was all they needed to say to each other really. For the time being, at least.

'Not necessarily,' she whispered. 'Not necessarily.'

'It doesn't matter anyway,' he smiled. 'There's always the putting green.'

'Yes, there's always the putting green.'

'How long can you stay?'

'Five minutes.'

'No, I mean at home—in Cheshire?' He chuckled as Cindy laughed far more than was called for.

'As long as I like. I'm—in between jobs. Now, I must get out of here or else Jonathan will chase me. Mummy will be with you in a moment. And Flick's twitching to see you, naturally.'

'One at a time, eh?' Sir Robert grimaced at the thought. 'He's a real stickler, old Jonathan.'

'And he's quite right.' Cindy broke the contact of their hands reluctantly. 'I'll see you tomorrow.'

She visited alone the following day, having arranged with her mother and sister that they would go to the hospital in the evenings and she would go during the afternoon. That way her father would have two visits instead of one. Jonathan was agreeable—provided they didn't stay too long.

Having reported to her mother and sister that Sir Robert looked a little better, still white but a little less tired, Cindy went up to her room to make an attempt at sleeping. She had just got undressed when Felicity barged in without bothering to knock.

'Cindy?'

'I'm in the bathroom. I'm going to bed for a couple of hours. I told you. What do you want?' Cindy emerged from the bathroom to find her sister sitting on her bed, smoking. 'You might have brought an ashtray with you if you intended to smoke in my room. Anyway, shouldn't you give that up now you're pregnant?'

Flick tutted, walked into the bathroom and came back without the cigarette. 'Typical! If you were pregnant, you'd do everything by the book, wouldn't you?'

'Actually, yes. What do you want?'

'There was a phone call for you while you were at the hospital. I forgot to tell you just now.' She draped herself into a chair, mischief evident in her eyes. 'From a man—a man with a gorgeous voice. I can only describe it as... gravelly.'

Cindy's stomach contracted.

'Your employer, I believe.'

'And?' She kept her voice nonchalant as she got into bed, avoiding her sister's eyes.

Flick raised an eyebrow. 'Does he look as attractive as he sounds?'

'For heaven's sake—'

'Well?'

Cindy swallowed hard, hoping it didn't show. 'Yes, as a matter of fact he does.'

'Then he can park his shoes under my bed any time!' Flick laughed outrageously. 'You must introduce me to him at once!'

Cindy shot her a contemptuous look. 'In the circumstances, that's a very strange thing to say.'

'Because I'm married or because I'm pregnant?'

'Both. You and Charles are happy enough, aren't you?'

'Happy enough...' Flick repeated the words slowly. 'I wonder what that means, exactly. Let's say there's room for improvement. Still, the baby might improve things... And there again, it might not.' She tossed back her hair, much darker than Cindy's—though her eyes were very similar. Then she stood and smoothed the skirt over her slender hips. Cindy wanted to shake her even as she realised her sister wasn't keeping her waiting deliberately.

She cleared her throat. 'What did he say, Mr Stone?'

'Zac,' Flick amended, pointedly, 'was asking about our father. What's he like, Cindy? Have you got something going with him?'

'Of course not.' She was losing patience, but she didn't want to protest too much.

'Of course not!' The other girl shrugged, not doubting Cindy's word for a moment. 'I think I'll have to knit a man for you. You'd better write down your list of specifications. You've always been faddy, haven't you? I remember—'

'Flick, please, I came up here to sleep.'

'All right, all right. There's nothing else to tell. He didn't ask for you to call him back. He didn't say he'd call back. He said he was sorry to trouble me, but he was anxious to know how Sir Robert was, and that he was very glad to hear he was out of danger and making progress. Okay, madam?' As she flounced out, Cindy put her hands up to her cheeks. They were hot.

She would have to write to Zac at once—before he telephoned again. There was no way she wanted to speak to him. It would be so much easier to explain her reasons for leaving in a letter. He couldn't protest to a letter. If he wanted to protest at all, that was. She would tell him, simply, that she wouldn't be coming back to London for quite a time, that he'd better get a replacement straight away, that she could no longer cope with the pace of work, in any case.

She wrote the letter that evening, keeping it as brief and succinct as possible. And she posted it before the last collection. With luck, it would reach London the following day.

By Friday there was no doubt that the letter had reached its destination. Two days was certainly enough time. Cindy waited anxiously for a phone call she would try to avoid at all costs. She spent all morning in the grounds of the house, which were extensive, so she might be out of reach if a call came.

But there was no call.

By Monday evening she relaxed slightly. Zac wouldn't phone now. And so much for the idea that he might protest over Cindy's resignation. Of course she knew his attitude. He would shrug and remind himself, as she had heard him do, that nobody is indispensable, nobody is irreplaceable.

Except him, of course. He was indispensable to Bryant's and he was irreplaceable as far as Cindy was concerned. There would never be anyone else for her. There was no one like him. She had never loved a man before Zac, and there was no one else for her.

The following morning, she woke up with a screaming headache and a streaming nose. She spent the rest of the week in bed, unable to visit the hospital. Flick had gone back to Staffordshire, but her mother was visiting the hospital twice daily. Sir Robert was making remarkably good progress, improving daily.

Cindy was on her feet again by the time her birthday came around on the twelfth of September, and it was on that evening, over a very nice meal prepared in her honour, that her mother told her Sir Robert would be coming home within the next few days.

'Jonathan told me this evening,' Pamela Hetherington looked almost excited. 'He's been so good, you know. I really must—' She broke off suddenly, looking at her daughter as if she hadn't seen her for years. 'Darling, are you all right? Are you sure you've got rid of that 'flu?'

'It wasn't 'flu, Mummy.' Cindy perked up immediately because she didn't want her mother scrutinising too closely. 'It's wonderful news about Daddy, isn't it? He'll have to take it very, very easy.'

'I know—I've been warned. He'll have to cut his brandy consumption drastically.'

'Totally, I should have thought.'

'Ideally, yes, but do you think he will?'

'Not for a minute!' Cindy laughed, but her mother was not easily distracted.

'There's something wrong, Cindy. With you. I've been so frantic about your father that I haven't stopped to notice until now. What is it, darling? It's something more than a cold, isn't it?'

'I—it's nothing. I haven't been sleeping too well, that's all.'

She knew without doubt that her letter to Zac had not gone astray. She knew that because she had received a birthday card from Alison in which there was a letter saying how sorry Alison was that Cindy wouldn't be returning to Bryant's, and how much she would miss her. But there had been not a word from Zac. He hadn't even bothered to acknowledge the letter of resignation.

'Which means,' her mother said softly, 'that you don't want to talk about it.'

Cindy put her knife and fork down, nodding briefly. 'That was super. It was sweet of Mrs B. to make something special for me. I must thank her...' Her mind drifted. 'I'm sorry? What did you say?'

'I said Happy Birthday, darling.' Lady Hetherington handed her a small, beautifully wrapped package. 'From me and Daddy... Cindy, you know how pleased I am—about you and your father—but I'm wondering how long you intend to stay. You know I love your being here, but what about this job of yours? From what you told me over the phone, it sounds as if Mr Stone is hardly the type who—'

'I've left,' Cindy cut in. 'I'm sorry, I should have mentioned that before. I—I've left Bryant's. It was—well, you were always telling me I worked too hard. And how unnecessary it was.'

Her mother inclined her head slightly, her small hands spread before her. It was her way of saying she'd leave the subject alone. Unless and until Cindy wanted to talk about it.

Grateful, for her birthday gift as well as her mother's understanding, Cindy got up and hugged her. 'Let's go into the drawing room, shall we? How about a game of Scrabble?'

It was rather like being young again, really young. Before things had changed between herself and her father. Before she was thirteen. The huge old house had a happy atmosphere now that its master was due to come home. Nothing seemed to change, apart from the decorations. The grounds were immaculate, the gardens beautiful in all seasons. Especially now, where September roses were still flourishing in the rose garden.

Cindy loved the house, with its antiques and its family portraits and its richly coloured carpets, old and cherished. But she wouldn't want to live in something as big as this herself, any more than she would choose to decorate and furnish the way her parents had. It was too old, a little austere, a little too quiet. Soon, she knew, she would grow bored with it. As always. It was nice to come home and it was nice to go away again—back to her own flat.

But what now? She wouldn't be returning to her own flat. That was out of the question. She wouldn't even go there to collect her things, to remove her furniture. She would pay someone to do that for her. Money really did have its uses at times. In the meantime, she'd send off a cheque for the next quarter's rent and give notice to the agents that she was vacating.

Perhaps she'd buy a small house. Somewhere on the outskirts of the capital, close enough that she'd be able to commute to her new place of work. She would have a garden, then, in which to keep herself busy at weekends. And she'd take up her evening classes again. One thing was for sure—she couldn't stay in Cheshire for ever. She was well aware that she was using the place as a sanctuary, that she'd have to sort herself out sooner or later.

BY EARLY October, after a couple of weeks' bedrest, Cindy's father was taking daily strolls around the grounds, venturing farther and longer each day. Cindy went with him, just as she used to during the holidays of her childhood. Sometimes George would accompany them, or one of the other gardeners, and they would inspect together everything which grew. Sir Robert had taught Cindy everything she knew about flowers and plants, though he had rarely had time for gardening in the past.

They got caught in a sudden shower one afternoon towards the end of the month, when, needless to say, they couldn't have been farther from shelter. They were on the edge of the woods which skirted one side of the estate, picking their way through a carpet of gold and amber leaves which quickly turned soggy.

'Don't fuss, Cindy!' Sir Robert laughed at his daughter's concern. 'I won't melt if I get wet.'

She looked up at him. He was a tall man, tall and stocky. And he still appeared to be as strong as an ox. The colour was back in his face, the tension eased, and he was looking more like his sixty-one years than he had several weeks ago.

'Go on with what you were saying,' he urged. 'You were telling me how much thought goes into the packaging of a product, the effect of colour and shape.'

'That's right.' Cindy chatted on while they strolled. She did, after all, know a lot about advertising and the psychology behind it. 'Daddy,' she said at length, 'are you really interested in all this? I mean, you've never asked me before.'

'You've never given me the chance before,' he said quietly. She nodded, biting her lip. There was no answer to that.

'Besides,' he went on, 'I wouldn't have asked if I weren't interested. Anyway, when are you going home to start looking for another job? With your experience, you'll have no trouble finding a position in another agency.'

'I—I don't know when I'm leaving. I'm trying to decide what to do. I'll . . . have to do something to fill my time.'

'How about settling down and giving me a couple more grandchildren?' Sir Robert was smiling but he was half serious. 'That'd fill your time!'

Cindy kicked at the leaves and made no comment. She looked up at the naked branches of the trees, watching a solitary sparrow hopping from branch to branch as they walked together slowly, as if it were listening in on their conversation. 'I'll probably look for something which will be a complete change. I—won't go back into advertising,'

'That doesn't make much sense! Cindy, I'm not at all clear why you left Bryant's. I mean, it sounds so interesting and that boss of yours seems like a remarkable sort of chap.'

'He is.' She had spoken of Zac, inevitably. How could she not, when her father had been asking about her work? 'He's brilliant,' she added quietly. 'And very, very talented.'

Sir Robert looked at her quickly. 'Stone,' he said thoughtfully. 'Zachariah Stone. Am I likely to know his family?'

'No. Zac comes from a small village in Wales—I can't even pronounce its name. He's the last in a long line of coalminers.'

'Indeed? Then he must be remarkable. He wasn't exactly born with a silver spoon, was he?'

'Not exactly. But he's very...ambitious.'

'And you're in love with him. Ah, Cindy...' her father took hold of her arm and linked it through his own, 'I must be getting old! I've only just realised what the trouble is.'

Cindy let out a long, slow breath. 'And I'm in love with him. No, I *was* in love with him.'

'And now you've left. You had an affair, I take it?'

She met her father's eyes steadily. 'Is this the clever lawyer probing, or is it my father?'

'The man,' he said quietly. 'Just the man.'

She squeezed his arm, understanding precisely what he was saying.

'Cindy, you said you're in love with Zac. Then you immediately put it in the past tense. Did you justify your affair with him by telling yourself you loved him?'

She smiled wryly, her eyes lit with amusement and admiration. Her father was far cleverer than she, she should have known he would be one step ahead of her. 'No, I didn't. I didn't need to justify myself. I went to bed with Zac before I realised I was in love with him—at least, before I'd admitted it to myself. I did it because I wanted him physically. So at that stage it was—just sex.' Her laughter then was brittle, hollow, self-deprecating. 'Just sex. That was something, a notion, I'd always thought of and spoken of with distaste in the past. That's one of the reasons I remained a virgin for so long. That, plus the fact that there was a switch inside me which hadn't been thrown until, until . . .'

'Until you met Zac.'

'Until I met Zac. So you see, I understood the power of sex only intellectually in the past. Which is not the same as having personal experience. I thought of it only in terms of it being a troublemaker—to me, very easy to resist.'

'Only in terms of it being a troublemaker?' Sir Robert looked at her gravely. 'How very sad, that you thought only along those lines. I—I'm afraid I'm responsible for that.'

'No.' Cindy spread her hands in a gesture of helplessness. 'I'm a mature woman, Daddy. I should have changed my thinking a long time ago. I don't—I can't—sit in judgment any more.' Quietly she added, 'It's important that I actually say this to you.'

Her father stood still, meeting her eyes. 'I appreciate that—you'll never know how much. And I'm glad your thinking has changed. For your own sake, I mean. Come on, let's sit down for a while.'

The shower had stopped, and the only place to sit was on the clean-cut stump of a huge old oak tree. Cindy pulled her coat more closely around her, looking quickly at her father to make sure he wasn't getting overtired.

How good it was to be able to talk to him, of all people, at such a level. A few months ago she would never have believed it possible. Yet here she was, and finding it remarkably easy, too. 'But it all went wrong, Daddy, with me and Zac. It was in early August. We were in Paris on a business trip when we... But it all went wrong.' Almost defiantly she tossed back her head and looked at her father directly. 'I'm still a virgin, Daddy. What do you think of that? I'm twenty-four years old and I'm still a virgin.'

He chuckled. 'Are you bragging about it?'

'No. I'm appalled by it.'

He laughed loudly then. But he never did say what he thought about it. 'But how were things when you left London? Did you have a fight? I mean, what happened between Paris and your coming here?'

It was a good question. Cindy picked up a damp twig and fiddled with it absently, her mind drifting back over the weeks. Zac, and Zac alone, had been in control, all along. He could have taken her the first night he'd kissed her. He'd known that at the time. But she certainly hadn't—not then. And when he had told her of his intentions, she still didn't believe it would happen. She thought she could escape him. What a stupid idea that had been ... And then there was Paris. Two weeks later there was Tracy Lynn. But why? Why had he taken up with her when he knew full well that Cindy couldn't resist him? Perhaps he felt the challenge had been met? But it hadn't! And that was something about Zac which just didn't make sense ...

'Cindy?'

'I dithered.' She shrugged. 'Zac didn't—I vacillated between— Oh, damn! Paula must have arrived. Look!'

In the distance she could see her sister's thirteen-and fourteen-year-old sons coming towards them at a steady trot, waving energetically. In the few remaining moments of privacy she said, 'Anyway, this is when it gets a little complex, Daddy. I decided to leave Bryant's. I decided to have an affair with Zac and just enjoy it for what it would be. I decided to stay, and do nothing. I decided I couldn't leave him, because I loved him. And I decided an affair with him was the last thing I wanted. I dithered! See what I mean?'

Sir Robert grunted, shaking his head. 'Because by then you wanted much more. My poor darling! You've had an awful time, and I'm sorry. One thing's very clear, however, from all you've told me. You're still very much in love with Zac—very much. And it's high time you went back to London and sorted things out with him. Go and talk to him, Cindy. Stop using me as an excuse to stay here—and go home. Get on with your life.'

He said it gently, nicely, and before she had time to tell him there was nothing to sort out, that Zac didn't even care enough about her to acknowledge a letter, that he'd found someone else even before she'd left, her nephews were within earshot. The conversation ended abruptly as Cindy immediately took control and made sure the youngsters didn't get too boisterous.

During the next couple of days, the weekend, Cindy diverted her nephews by taking them out to the cinema and for a meal. They were good boys, and Paula certainly knew how to keep them in check, but Cindy was anxious that their youthful exuberance might prove too much for their grandfather. She was probably being obsessive, she realised, but having found her father again after so many years, she dreaded to think what another heart attack might do to him.

Jonathan Trent was keeping a watchful eye on Sir Robert, too. He had called regularly at the house and had twice personally driven his patient to the hospital in order that he might do a more thorough examination.

But her father had been right; she was using him as an excuse to stay. When October slipped into November she realised, with a shock, that she had been at home for two months. Two months. And yes, she was bored, but she was also safe.

And what incentive was there for her to leave?

She was floating, just as she'd been when she was eighteen. She was so much more experienced, so much more enlightened, yet once again she didn't know what to do with her life.

Her parents just let her be. Over the next few weeks Sir Robert said nothing more about her going back to London. Neither did her mother. They didn't press her, one way or another. They wouldn't urge her to leave any more than they would urge her to stay. And she loved them for it.

CHAPTER TWELVE

TOWARDS THE end of November, however, Cindy was feeling a lot better. She started to heal, was no longer hurting every time she thought back. Her entire perspective had changed. Looking back on her last couple of months in London was no longer painful. She felt detached, as if she were looking at the situation from a great distance, as one might see something through the wrong end of a telescope. The details were sharp, clear, but she could stand back from it now and see it for what it was—just a chapter of her life which had passed.

On the last Friday of the month, over lunch, she told her parents she was leaving. 'I've just telephoned the porter at Priory Court and he's making arrangements for a removal company to clear out my flat one day next week. I've sent him my key. Everything will be put into storage for me until I find somewhere else to live.'

Her mother and father exchanged looks. Worried looks. 'Oh, it's all right,' Cindy smiled. 'For some time now I've been thinking of buying a house on the outskirts of London. I'll be much nearer the countryside but near enough to get into town. I shall find myself a new job immediately after New Year. I'll be leaving next Friday. I'm staying another week so I can be here for your birthday, Daddy.'

Sir Robert grunted, looking down at his plate and obviously restraining himself not to say anything.

Her mother was less controlled. 'But, darling, it's December next week. What—what will you do with yourself until New Year?'

'I shall go to Bournemouth, as usual.' Cindy hadn't spent Christmas with her parents for the past five years. It was too much to cope with. *All* the family gathered at the big house—her sisters, cousins, several aunts and uncles, and it had never been her scene. She had always spent Christmas with an old school friend, a very dear friend, in Bournemouth, and she saw no reason to change her routine this year.

'Oh.' Lady Hetherington looked quite disappointed. 'I thought this year might be different. I mean, now you and Daddy—'

'Now, Pamela.' Sir Robert shot her a warning look. 'We mustn't interfere.' To his daughter he said, 'You do whatever you feel like doing, Cindy. Will you go straight to Bournemouth from here?'

'Yes. I've already phoned Emma and David. Emma was delighted—you know how she is. She said come when you like and stay as long as you like. Actually, she'll be glad of the company because her husband has to go to Japan on business in the middle of December. He won't be back until a couple of days before Christmas.'

It would be quiet at Emma's. They would go for long walks along the sea front and they would natter about old times, as they always did. At Christmas they would be joined only by David's mother. There would be no madding crowd, nothing for Cindy to do but decide where to start looking for a house and what sort of job she would take.

Mrs Butterworth came in with a steamed pudding, and lunch continued pleasantly. Nothing else was said to Cindy about her plans.

'Now, Daddy, what on earth am I going to buy you for your birthday next week? I've been thinking about it for days and I haven't been inspired. You seem to have everything.'

'As a matter of fact,' Sir Robert laughed, 'I haven't. I'll tell you exactly what I want—a new camera.'

Cindy's mother suppressed a smile as she looked at her. Her father's request was of no help at all—she and her mother had already shopped for the camera he wanted over a week ago. That was his wife's present, so Cindy would have to start thinking all over again.

'I'll see what I can do,' Cindy said noncommittally. 'Shall we go into town on Wednesday, Mummy? There's one or two other bits of shopping I'd like to do at the same time.'

'Yes, darling, that'll be nice.'

'Who else is coming to dinner on Thursday?'

'Just Jonathan Trent and his wife.' Sir Robert waved a dismissive arm. 'No one else. I don't want a room full of people making a fuss, just because I've reached the grand old age of sixty-two.'

'Surely Paula's coming?'

'No. She's got her in-laws staying this week. And Flick isn't coming, either. She's not feeling too well.'

The conversation changed then, to Flick and the baby she was expecting. Each time Cindy had seen her sister she seemed happier about her pregnancy, though she wasn't having an easy time of it.

Cindy went shopping alone on the Wednesday. It was a foul day, freezing cold and pouring with sleet. The weather put her mother right off the idea of a trip into town, but Cindy had no choice about going. She'd left it until the last minute and she had to come up with something for her father's birthday the next day.

She took her own car into town, seeing no reason to keep the chauffeur hanging around for hours while she went from shop to shop. As a reward for her efforts she called in at a hairdresser's and had her hair trimmed and blow-dried— which was a complete waste of time, because she got wet coming out of the shop and her hair was curling uncontrollably by the time she was half way home.

As she turned into the long, sweeping driveway of her parents' house in the middle of the afternoon, Cindy's foot jerked on the accelerator and her breath left her body in a short, frightened gasp. At the top of the drive, parked directly in front of the house, there was a black car. Even from a distance there was no mistaking the sleek and graceful line of it. It was a Jaguar.

She stood on her brakes, looking in front of her as if she had come up against an invisible wall she would never be able to get past. Even as her hands started trembling she was telling herself not to be so stupid. There was more than one black Jaguar in the world. There was no reason to suppose... It must belong to one of her father's friends. But whom?

Cindy's car stalled. She looked stupidly at the steering wheel, at the keys, her mind frozen so that she had no idea how to set the car in motion again. She felt utterly sick as she realised that nothing had changed, nothing at all. So much for her healing time! So much for her detachedness!

She didn't know who the black Jaguar belonged to. But she knew for certain who it *didn't* belong to. With that in mind she made an effort to start her own car and continued slowly up the drive, her windscreen wipers beating a steady rhythm as they coped with the downpour. The sleet had turned to rain, heavy rain which looked as if it wouldn't let up for a long time.

Only when she turned off the drive and on to the gravel sweeping round the front of the house was she able to read the number-plate of the Jaguar. She came to an abrupt halt, switched off her engine and just sat, unable to move. All her energy seemed to have cut off, as the power of her engine had cut off. She reached for the handle of her door, but her fingers wouldn't obey her. Her hand fell limply on to her lap.

What did he want of her? *Why had he come here?*

Frantically she looked around, at the trees, at the garages beyond the house, at the bushes. Her instinct was to run away and hide even as she knew she had no choice but to go indoors. She didn't want to see him. She didn't want to be plunged back in time, back into the torment which was her love for him.

But it was too late. Just seeing the black car had told her that. Even before she knew who the car belonged to her body had turned to pulp, a mass of raw emotion she no longer had control over. She was, then, in precisely the state she had been in on the morning she had left Priory Court. Filled with nausea at the knowledge that the man she loved had spent the night, perhaps the weekend, with another woman. Consumed by fear over what she might have to face at the end of her journey.

The journey from the car to the house was a short one, but Cindy took each step of it with dread. She prayed that she would manage, somehow, to hide her feelings. She had once been labelled as cool... Dear Lord, she prayed, let me behave that way now. Don't let him see how much I care.

Through the closed drawing-room door she heard her mother's laughter and then her voice, far more animated than usual, 'Oh, I agree with you entirely. Please—won't you call me Pamela?'

And then there was the rumble of laughter, deep, warm and oh, so familiar! 'Only if you promise not to call me Zachariah.'

Cindy started as she caught sight of herself in the hall mirror. She couldn't go in there looking as she did. Her face was white, her lips colourless, and her dark brown eyes reflected her panic. She heard her father's voice, then her mother's, then the door of the drawing room swung open and her mother stepped into the hall.

Lady Hetherington closed the door swiftly but silently as her eyes alighted on her daughter. 'Cindy, for heaven's sake...don't worry. Darling, you're as white as a sheet!'

'What does he want?' she said lifelessly.

'Well, he wants to talk to you, I suppose.' Her mother reached out to touch Cindy's cheeks as if she would bring back some colour. 'Put some lipstick on,' she said firmly. 'And get hold of yourself.' Then she smiled reassuringly. 'I know how you feel, darling... Oh, yes, I do. I'm not too old to have forgotten this sort of emotion, you know.'

Cindy lowered herself on to a chair and took her compact from her bag, not willing to make any comment.

'I find him absolutely charming!' her mother said it as if it would help matters. 'Now go in there, Cindy. I'll be back in a moment. I'm just going to tell Mrs B. there'll be one more for dinner this evening.'

'*What?*' Cindy's voice was a coarse whisper. 'You haven't asked him to dine with us? Mummy, what are you thinking about!'

Lady Hetherington looked nonplussed. 'My dear girl, when someone calls at my home after driving two hundred miles in the pouring rain, I wouldn't dream of not asking them to stay for a meal.' And with that, she vanished.

As much as Cindy was prepared for it, it was still a shock coming face to face with him. If anything, he looked more attractive than ever. He was wearing plain slacks and a polo-neck sweater in black cashmere. He stood as she entered, tall, lithe and powerful as he inclined his dark head towards her, just as if he'd seen her only yesterday.

'Hello, Cindy.' The deep blue eyes told her nothing. They were shuttered, yet she knew he was probing her face, her mind, even as his face remained impassive. Then he smiled broadly, and Cindy's heart beat even faster because it was a beautiful sight...and because she feared he might know more than she wanted him to know.

'Hello, Zac.' Even as she said it, her eyes went to those of her father. But she knew he would have said nothing to Zac; she knew that without doubt.

'Well, this is quite a surprise, isn't it, Cindy?' Sir Robert's voice was just right, not too jovial, not too casual.

'Quite a surprise.' She sat opposite Zac as he resumed his place on the settee. Her father was in an armchair adjacent to the settee. 'Are you in Cheshire on business, Zac?'

'No.' He hadn't taken his eyes from hers for a moment. 'I can't say I was just passing so I decided to drop in. I came especially to see you, Cindy.'

'Zac's staying to dinner,' her father put in. 'Your mother's gone to have a word with Mrs B.'

'Yes, I—I saw her just now. Well, I—I'm sorry to have kept you waiting. I've been shopping.'

'So your father told me. For a birthday present, I believe.' He was not in the least put out, not in the least uncomfortable. He leaned back and stretched his long legs before him, his arms spread across the back of the settee in an attitude which was, again, so familiar to her.

She could tell her father approved of him. Sir Robert was not easily impressed by people and he had a way of making it known when he disliked someone. 'Zac's been here a couple of hours, darling. He arrived just after lunch. We've been having an interesting conversation—shop talk.'

'Advertising?'

'Law.' Sir Robert grinned. 'Zac is very well read. Aren't you, young man?'

'A mine of information.' Zac shrugged. 'Though a lot of it's useless to me.'

Feeling obliged to say something, anything, Cindy told her father of Zac's extraordinary memory. 'He—has the ability to retain almost everything he reads.'

Cindy's mother came in then, just in time to hear what had been said. 'And we've been talking politics. We've put the world to rights.' She smiled, 'And the men have made several changes in legislation which should help matters.'

'I see.' Cindy managed to laugh, but it sounded as if it were someone else's laughter. She could hardly believe what was happening. Her parents were enchanted. Zac had obviously turned on the charm, and it had worked. She forced herself to sit back in her chair. Her limbs felt lifeless, her mouth as dry as parchment. 'Have I missed tea, Mummy?'

'No, darling. Mrs B. will be in in a minute or two. Did you have a successful shopping trip?'

Cindy nodded, her mind so blank that she'd forgotten what she'd done with her day; all her parcels were on the back seat of her car.

'Had you planned on driving back to London tonight, Zac?' The question came from her father.

'That—depends.' Zac looked directly at Cindy and she shifted uncomfortably, hating the way he was putting some sort of onus on her. She could see what was coming next and she cursed her father for it.

'Stay the night. It'll be late by the time we've finished dinner, and fog's forecast for tonight. The motorway will be hazardous. We've got bags of room. I mean, if business permits.'

'Business,' Zac said slowly, in a voice which told Cindy he was thinking of something quite different, 'permits. That's kind of you Sir Robert. I accept.'

Her father nodded, satisfied. He'd like that, Zac's no-nonsense acceptance. Or refusal. No dithering. And she couldn't really blame him for extending the invitation. If he hadn't, her mother would have. She looked from one to the other, wondering if either of them really had any idea how difficult this was for her? Surely, surely if they had they wouldn't extend their hospitality so readily, even if it was typical of them.

Mrs B. came in with afternoon tea and during the next hour or so Zac and her parents continued to talk as if they'd known each other for years. They were still talking politics, obviously continuing the conversation which Cindy's arrival had interrupted. Both her parents were interested in politics; Cindy was not. She wasn't even up to date on current affairs—though it was not for that reason that she hardly contributed a word.

It was as if she weren't really present. She was sitting there, her *body* was sitting there, and yet she felt as if she were standing in a corner of the room, just looking on. She watched her mother watching Zac as only her mother could—shrewdly but not in the least obviously. Behind the dignified, polite composure which was the outward stamp of her mother's personality there was a sharp, intelligent woman who was an extremely good judge of character. From Cindy she had heard quite a lot about Zac Stone in the early days of his takeover of Bryant's—little of which had been complimentary—and now she was judging for herself.

Cindy looked at her watch, knowing what was about to happen. Her parents were creatures of habit, always had been as far as domestic routine was concerned. But she hoped against hope that they would make an exception to-day. She was dreading the moment when she would find herself alone with Zac.

They didn't make an exception today, and her mother spoke first. 'Bobby darling, it's four o'clock.'

'Just a minute, Pamela.' Sir Robert held up a hand, turning to his guest. 'There's a flaw in your thinking, young man. You don't seem to have understood my last point. If you consider—'

'Hold on.' Zac suppressed a smile, shook his head lazily. 'I've followed your argument all right. But five minutes ago you asked me to accept an assumption. What you're saying makes sense, but it's based on a premise I don't agree with.'

'Bobby...' Pamela Hetherington got to her feet and put her own full stop on the argument. 'Forgive us, Zac, but we always take a rest during the afternoon. Cindy will look after you, and it'll give you a chance to talk.'

'What? Oh, yes.' His wife's last sentence prompted Sir Robert into action. He got to his feet. 'Doctor's orders. I'm supposed to rest during the afternoon.' Then, with a mixture of amusement and irritation he added, 'we'll sort this one out over dinner, Zac.'

'I'll look forward to it,' the younger man grinned.

When her parents went out the silence between Cindy and Zac swept across the room as a heavy velvet curtain might sweep across the stage in a theatre. They were like strangers; strangers who had shared so much intimacy but knew one another hardly at all. He looked different suddenly.

Perhaps it was because he was no longer engrossed in conversation, perhaps it was because Cindy had hardly dared
to look at him properly during the last hour, being too
acutely aware that he was watching her even while he kept
up the chatter with her parents. He looked a little older,
strained, and the tension which might have been present
earlier was stealing its way into his body. Almost imperceptibly, but it was there.

'Hello, Goldilocks.' The deep voice was quiet, neutral, the
two words being used as a thermometer to measure her reaction now she was without the support, or hindrance of her
parents' presence.

She had an overwhelming desire to cry, to accuse, to tell
him to leave so that she might achieve once again the inner
calm she had known only that morning, the inner calm it
had taken her three months to achieve. 'What—what do you
want?'

'You.'

Irrationally her heartbeat accelerated. She called herself
every kind of fool for momentarily misinterpreting the single word. 'You haven't found another secretary?'

'Yes.' His eyes refused her the luxury of looking away.
'And no. When I got your letter I hired someone straight
away. She lasted half a day. So I got someone else.'

'And?'

'And she lasted two minutes.'

Sheila sprang to mind. At least Cindy had lasted more
than two minutes. She laughed shortly, hollowly, to release
the tension inside her. 'It isn't everyone who can work for
you, Zac. But you know that.'

'I made two errors of judgment.'

'That doesn't sound like you.' The remark surprised her.
'Have you got someone now?'

'No. I've—managed. With Alison, with some help from
Greg's secretary.'

'How are things going?' Cindy was trying hard to be casual. They had, after all, parted on good terms. They hadn't

fought. And he had no idea how much the Tracy Lynn business had hurt her—because he had no idea how much she cared. 'How...how's the Germaine launch coming along?'

'We've finished work on that,' He said it impatiently, as if he were glad it was out of the way. 'The first ads are due to be televised this weekend.'

'Really?' Cindy couldn't help being impressed, but she shuddered to think what life had been like at Bryant's during the past three months. Maybe that was why Zac looked so strained... 'I'm—what can I say? Congratulations.' He had wanted to launch the new range before Christmas and it had been a tall order—but he had succeeded. Of course he had succeeded. She wondered whether Tracy would appear in the ad, but it was more than she could do to ask the question. The thought of the other woman made her voice come out harshly. 'Well, if you're here to ask me back to Bryant's, forget it. I've no intention of coming back. I have little interest in the ad world at all.'

An odd expression flitted across his face. It was something she couldn't interpret, a look she had never seen before. It was almost approaching...sadness. She reproached herself instantly. What a fanciful idea! Maybe he was disappointed, but that was all. Crisply she added, 'If you'd thought it might be necessary to try and coax me back you'd have answered my letter, I suppose.'

Zac got up, moved around restlessly before sitting in the window seat. He turned, looking out of the window so she was unable to see his face. 'I have little interest in the ad world, too.'

Cindy stared at him, wishing she could see his eyes so she might understand him better. Was this some sort of tactic, a way of persuading her back to work? But no, that wasn't his style. He didn't use those sort of tactics. As if to prove her right he said, 'I want you back, Cindy. I—didn't know how to answer your letter. It was so final. I made several attempts at a reply and I discarded them all.' He turned suddenly, making her jump inwardly as if he'd touched every inch of her. 'This morning I saw the porter letting himself into your flat. When I asked what the devil he was doing, he said you'd sent him your key—asked him to make arrangements to have all your stuff removed. I'd like to know your intentions, Cindy. Why aren't you coming back to London? Your father's long since recovered, and I know you well enough to realise you must be bored here.'

His eyes swept around the room, a rather dreary room with its heavy brown curtains, its tapestries and antiques. 'What are you doing here? I realise this place is home, but it just isn't you. This place is like a mausoleum! You must feel suffocated, in spite of its size.'

She smiled because she knew what he meant. It was a gross exaggeration, but she could see his point. 'I am. Coming back to London, I mean.'

If she'd doubted it before, she knew then she was in danger. In two strides Zac crossed the room, took hold of her by the elbows and pulled her roughly to her feet. 'Then why are you leaving the flat?' he demanded. 'What have I done that you can't bear to live next door to me when you get back?'

'Zac, don't—'

'What are you afraid of? This?'

She was lost, as she'd known she would be, immediately he touched her. But when he kissed her she fought him with everything in her, fought before she drowned in the all-consuming passion she felt for him. It served only to inflame him, with anger as well as arousal. He laughed scornfully as she pulled her head away, catching her flailing arms and holding them effortlessly behind her. The movement pulled her against the length of his body, and she knew he'd never stopped wanting her, as she'd never stopped wanting him. No matter how many women he had made love to since Paris, he still wanted her. She was still a challenge to him.

He kissed her savagely until her lips parted beneath his and she was kissing him back. She returned his kiss because she had no choice. She had never known how to resist him. And he would not allow her her freedom until he had demonstrated again that she was his for the taking.

'You see?' His lips moved over her face, down her neck, pausing in the hollow at the base of her throat.

'You see why you have to come back to me? You're mine, Cindy. We have unfinished business ...'

She gasped as he bit softly into her shoulder, pulling aside the fine wool of her dress. 'I hate you,' she frowned. 'I hate you for coming here. I hate you for doing this to me—'

'Do you?' his eyes mocked her. 'You know what hatred's akin to, don't you?'

She should have known words were no longer a defence, should have known she had no defences left. Zac's hands moved over her hips, into the curve of her spine, bringing her body against his own with the grace and fluidity of a wave. As his hands cupped her breasts, he cursed suddenly, moving away from her abruptly and turning his back.

Stupidly, uncomprehendingly, she blinked and then spun around as she heard the sound of someone clearing their throat. Mrs B. stood in the doorway, her embarrassment equalling Cindy's.

'I'm sorry. I—'

If she'd knocked, Cindy hadn't heard it. But Zac had.

'I'm sorry, Miss Cynthia, but there was a telephone call for your mother and of course she's—'

'Yes? What is it, Mrs B.?' Cindy spoke more sharply to her than she had ever done.

'Dr Trent's wife. She has an unexpected visitor and wondered whether she should cancel the arrangements for tomorrow night or whether she might bring her visitor with her. I—I thought you might like to ring her back, only she's going out shortly.'

'Yes. Right away.'

Mrs Butterworth backtracked at once, and Zac swore again immediately the door was closed. 'I've got an overnight case in the car, Cindy. Show me my room before you make that call. I'll get my case.'

She went out with him to the cars and collected her parcels. Walking up the sweeping staircase ahead of him, she could feel his eyes on her with every step she took. 'You—you should be comfortable in here, Zac.' She opened the door to one of the guestrooms. 'I'll make that phone call and see you in the conservatory. We—we can talk in there.'

But what else was there to say? How was she going to cope with him during the remaining hours before dinner? With trembling hands she picked up the telephone in her bedroom and dialled Mrs Trent's number.

In the middle of her conversation her bedroom door opened and Zac stepped in. Cindy almost jumped off the bed, holding the receiver with both hands for fear she might drop it. 'Yes, yes I'm qu-quite sure.' Stammering, almost deafened to what she was hearing, she saw Zac turn the key in the lock and walk slowly towards her. She closed her fingers over the mouthpiece as his hands spanned her waist and he pulled her down beside him on the bed. 'Get out of here!... Sorry? No, no trouble at all. My parents will be delighted.' She closed her eyes, swaying involuntarily against Zac as he brushed her hair aside and kissed the nape of her neck, the palms of his hands moving ever so lightly over the tips of her breasts.

With a hasty farewell she dropped the receiver into its cradle and stilled the movement of his hands. 'Zac, please—'

'That's all right,' he murmured against her ear. 'We won't have any more interruptions. The door's locked.'

'For heaven's sake, not here! Not here, in this house!' She pulled away sharply, putting distance between them.

He made no move to come after her. 'Then where? When?'

Cindy swallowed hard, looking away from him, defeated. 'I—we'll leave in the morning. We can—can book into a hotel if you like.' Though she wasn't looking at him, she was aware of his every movement. He stretched out on the bed, his broad shoulders pushing the pillows into a comfortable position, the sheer size of him making her bed, and her room, seem smaller.

'I like.' There was the sudden flash of white which was his smile. Very quietly he added, 'So I finally have your acquiescence, Cindy.'

'My—what?' She had no idea what he meant. Then she remembered their fraught conversation in Paris. 'Oh, I see.' She looked at him levelly. 'Yes, you have my acquiescence. And if you're interested, I won't hate myself in the morning.'

He was very still, watching her eyes. 'And why is that? What's changed?'

At the threat of tears, Cindy's hands curled into fists, her nails digging into her palms. If she cried, he would know. He would know how she felt. 'I've changed. I want you. It's as simple as that.'

The silence screamed at her. She was aware of her own heartbeat, aware of the soft pitter-patter of the rain on the windows, but the silence before he spoke was an agony.

'You wanted me before. You haven't answered my question. What's changed?'

'I—' She floundered before reasserting herself. 'I've had a lot of time to think—about all sorts of things. I no longer see any reason for resisting a physical attraction.' Almost defiantly, though she was unaware of it, her head came up. 'I've told you, my attitude towards that subject has changed.'

He was looking at her now with eyes which had narrowed. He was discounting every sentence she spoke. He didn't believe her. Worse than that, he knew. He knew how she felt and he was pinning her down deliberately. It was some sort of sadistic game. She felt her stomach turn sickeningly.

'So you're willing to have an affair with me?' he raised an eyebrow. 'You're telling me this in the cold light of day, quite dispassionately?'

'Yes,' she whispered, 'I am.' As her mouth closed she bit hard into her cheeks, willing herself not to cry.

'Now...' At his tone, she braced herself. He had caught his prey and he was playing with her mercilessly. '...Can you look me in the eyes and tell me you'll be *content* to have an affair with me?'

The first humiliating tears spilled on to her lashes. 'No.'

He went in for the kill very gently. Almost inaudibly he demanded, 'And why is that?'

'Because I love you.' She said it on a sigh, the tears spilling over on to her cheeks. Then her breath caught on a sob and she turned her back on him.

CHAPTER THIRTEEN

SHE HEARD no movement. But suddenly he was there, standing behind her, his arms reaching out to cradle her against him as if she were made of glass. As he turned her gently to face him, she looked into the blue, fathomless depths of his eyes. There was no laughter, no satisfaction— just a reflection of something she couldn't name because she'd never seen it before.

'Sit down, darling.' He led her to a chair, sitting facing her as she reached for a tissue and dabbed at her eyes. Unable to resist in any way she let him take it from her and wipe away her tears. 'You haven't changed, Cindy. Oh, maybe you've grown more tolerant, more understanding of other people, but you're basically the same. It's I who's changed, not you. You don't want an affair with me now any more than you ever did. And I'm glad, because I don't want an affair with you.'

Startled by his words, she looked at him in disbelief, her brown eyes dark with bewilderment.

'I love you,' he said simply. 'I don't want you to come back as my secretary, I want you to be my wife.'

'Zac—' It wasn't a game. Over and over she told herself this wasn't a game, that he meant what he'd said. But she couldn't believe what was happening, couldn't cope with the sheer joy that pervaded her being. Nor could she speak.

'Why did you leave me?' There was a note of pleading in his voice, something else which was totally alien to her—to him. 'Why did you put me through such hell for so long?'

'Tracy—' Her eyes closed against fresh tears. 'I couldn't cope with—with that.'

For a split second Zac looked blank, then confused. He took hold of her hands. 'Tracy Lynn? But what—what's she got to do with us?'

It didn't matter to Cindy any more. She wanted Zac regardless. Regardless of what he was or was not, regardless of what he'd done. So she shrugged her slender shoulders. 'You made love to her, the weekend I left London. But it doesn't matter. Not now. I understood it even as I hated it. But I couldn't blame you. Not after...after Paris.'

Zac let go of her hand, got swiftly to his feet. 'Dear God, I don't believe this!'

'It doesn't matter. Zac, it—'

'It matters.' Tiredly he ran a hand through his hair. 'To think I've—'

He stopped abruptly. A cold fear crept inside Cindy as she wished fervently that she'd never mentioned Tracy Lynn.

'You saw her?' he asked wearily. 'On the Monday morning, when you were leaving to go to the hospital?'

'Yes.'

'And you thought I'd spent the night making love to her? With you lying in your own bed on the other side of the wall?'

'Yes.'

'Dear God! No wonder you didn't come back! I didn't make love to her, Cindy. I never even thought about it!' He turned to face her, his eyes locking on to hers. 'You don't believe me.'

'It doesn't matter—'

'Have I ever lied to you? Forget everything else I've done to you and answer me that.'

'No. But she said—she said you and she had overslept that morning. What—what was I supposed to think?' Incredibly he was making her feel guilty. 'Zac, I'm sorry, but I thought you'd turned to Tracy... I mean, after Paris you never tried... After Paris—'

He nodded, a wry smile pulling at his lips as though he understood, now, everything. 'Paris...' He sat, laughing shortly, humourlessly. 'I'd better explain what happened to me in Paris. Darling Cindy, discovering your virginity wasn't the only shock I had in Paris. I discovered that I loved you—that for the first time in my life, I was in love. And I discovered that my days at Bryant's would be numbered, that the challenge I'd come out of retirement to find was an empty one—too easy, unreal. When I got the phone call from Alain, telling me we had the Germaine business, I realised in that moment that it wasn't work which was making me happy. It was you. I'd landed the Germaine account against all odds, it was possibly the biggest coup of my career... and a hollow victory.'

Cindy closed her eyes, recalling the scene, the way he had responded so strangely to the news. She nodded slowly. 'Your reputation goes before you, as I once told you. And it works for you so much that—'

'That nothing is impossibly difficult now. I don't give a hoot. I want you, Cindy. I want children. I want time to spend with my wife and my family. I'm extricating myself from Bryant's. The Germaine launch is done, and I've been scouting round for someone who'll buy into the agency. Greg Halliday would like to hold the reins, and the way I'm feeling right now, I'd make him a gift of my shares.'

She laughed at him. 'But you won't—I mean, make him a gift.'

'Of course not,' he grinned. 'I haven't changed that much. Not quite.' The laughter faded from his eyes, 'but I've changed a great deal since I met you, Cindy. You know, in the past I've never hesitated to take what I want. With you, I couldn't. I couldn't take what you were unprepared to give, to give willingly with your heart, your mind, as well as your body. After Paris I waited for you to come to me. Two weeks, Cindy. Two weeks passed and you avoided even coming for a drink with me. I thought it was hopeless. You'd denied it, but I was convinced you'd been saving yourself for someone very special, and I knew it wasn't me. You were mine for the taking...but I couldn't take that from you.

'After you left—when I got your letter—I fought with myself daily not to ring you, to come after you. I had no idea that you cared. Do you see that? I only discovered what you felt for me when you walked into the drawing room this afternoon.' Smiling, he reached for her hands. 'My cool, level-headed darling! Your composure had slipped. I knew what you were feeling, because I recognised the symptoms. I felt it, too. I've been unbearable to work with these past weeks. I've even bawled at Greg. I—when I saw them taking your furniture away, I—I can't tell you how I felt. I'd been waiting for you to come home—not to Bryant's, but home. When I learnt that you weren't coming back I got straight into the car and drove up here. The realisation that you were disappearing completely brought me to my senses. I came to ask you to marry me. Cindy, you're all that matters in the world to me.'

He broke off, turning the palms of her hands upwards and kissing them tenderly. 'I've found a house in the country. You'll love it, darling, I'm sure. It's perfect for us. It has a rose garden and an orchard, extensive grounds. I left a deposit on it some time ago, but I—I've done nothing about it since. If you like it, it's yours. Will you marry me, darling?'

Cindy reached for him, locking her arms around his neck as he pulled her on to his lap. 'Yes, I'll marry you, my love. Just as you are! Changed, unchanged—' She lifted her face for his kiss, a kiss which spoke of tenderness, caring...

'Cindy, how many men have you made love to since you left London?'

She didn't even bother to answer that one!

Zac's eyes danced with amusement. 'Precisely. And that's why I didn't make love to Tracy. She was quite willing to be...persuaded...into doing the Germaine job. But her price was too high—far too high. She's got herself a boy-friend. He's married, wealthy, and possessive enough for him not to want her to model any more.'

The broad shoulders lifted in a shrug. 'When I took her to dinner on the Friday, she said maybe. But I didn't know why she was hesitating. She'd have made a lot of money from doing the ad. We made a date for the Sunday evening and when I took her home for a nightcap, she asked me if she were staying the night. I said no.'

'I don't quite follow, Zac. I take it her boy-friend keeps her. Did she think you might be a replacement for him?'

'Something like that. And I've no doubt I would have picked up where our relationship left off . . . if I hadn't met you. We talked, she and I. You must remember we were friends in the past, as well as lovers. We talked well into the night, catching up on the past two years—though she did most of the talking. She told me what she'd been doing, about her boy-friend and how they met . . .'

'And then?'

'And then I kissed her goodnight—and all the time I was thinking about you. You can believe it or not, Cindy; I put her in the spare room. She looked at me as if she'd never seen me before. "Who is it, Zac?" she said. She teased me mercilessly. "I've told you everything and you've told me nothing! Who is it that's wheedled her way into that ruthless heart of yours?" I went into my own room in a kind of . . . shock. Kissing Tracy was absolutely meaningless.'

He let out a long, slow breath, shaking his head as if he still couldn't believe what had happened to him. 'I don't have your morals, Cindy. And I'm far less scrupulous than you—but if that night with Tracy Lynn is anything to go by I can safely say I'm yours . . . faithfully.'

'Oh, Zac, Zac! All I ask is that you love me.' She nuzzled against his neck, feeling their hearts beating in unison as he held her tightly against him. 'Just make me feel secure in your love.'

'That's easy enough,' he murmured, as he kissed her tear-filled eyes.

THE AUTHOR

Claudia Jameson lives in Berkshire, England, with her husband and family. She is an extremely popular author in both the Harlequin Presents and Harlequin Romance series. And no wonder! Her lively dialogue and ingenious plots—with the occasional dash of suspense—make her a favorite with romance readers everywhere.

Sweet Vixen

Susan Napier

Max Wilde had taken over as executive editor of New Zealand's leading fashion magazine just to create havoc, Sarah thought bitterly.

He wasn't content with changing the magazine's format, however. Now he was focusing his attention on Sarah herself, taunting and challenging, forcing her to admit that her desires as a woman hadn't died with her husband.

She hadn't felt so alive in years—and she resented it!

CHAPTER ONE

"COME ON, Sarah, get a move on! The plane was due in fifteen minutes ago." Julie Somerville gave her assistant a harried look over the top of her typewriter.

"Don't panic, it'll only take me twenty minutes to get out there. They won't even have got through Customs. You know how notorious Auckland airport is at processing jumbos," Sarah Carter replied calmly from the opposite desk.

She hated being rushed. To rush was to risk being unprepared and in her job that was tantamount to a crime. As editorial assistant on the monthly fashion magazine *Rags & Riches* she was constantly meeting new people—writers, models, advertising executives—and all expected her to know instantly what they wanted and why, and what Sarah was supposed to be doing about it. Usually she did, thanks to the overstuffed green filing cabinet squatting within arm's reach of her chair.

"Don't say 'don't panic' in that maddening way, I think I've earned a good panic!" Julie declared. "While you've been lolling about the city's beaches for three weeks I've been working at shriek pitch. Not only running this madhouse, but also trying to fend off the rumours that Wilde Publications has bought us out with the aim of rationalising their Australasian operations...by dumping *Rags*."

"Well, from today, you'll be able to let them do the fending," Sarah soothed.

"If they don't spend their whole visit stranded at the airport, yes." Julie jabbed viciously at the keys of her machine. "I had everything nicely laid on for Thursday. This is going to completely derail my timetable. I nearly had a nervous breakdown when Janey brought in that telex first thing this morning. Damn!" The dark blonde head bent as Julie back-spaced and X-ed out an error in her copy.

Sarah grinned. Julie's nerves were an in-house joke, never in danger of being bent, let alone broken. She loved it when things went awry and she was called on to extract order from chaos, completely confident of her abilities. She was a good journalist and an excellent editor; ambitious, hard-headed, yet possessed of all the elegant femininity expected of a woman who edited a fashion magazine.

"Stop grinning and start moving." Julie looked up again as she heard the rumble of a filing cabinet drawer. "What are you up to *now?*"

"Looking for the file on Wilde's. I'd better know who I'm supposed to be meeting."

"It's not there—I've got it. Anyway you haven't got time. Indulge your fetish for facts later, all you're doing is greeting them, not entering *Mastermind!* Max Wilde you *must* know, Tom Forest is a fellow director—financial expert."

"But—"

"Oh my God!" Julie sat suddenly upright in her swivel chair, china-blue eyes focussing properly on Sarah for the first time.

"What's the matter?" The crack in the clear soprano voice was unnerving.

"Grape! You had to wear the dreaded Grape, on today of all days."

Sarah looked down at her dress, a short-sleeved shirt-waister with a matching belt. It had been the first thing to hand in her wardrobe, so she had put it on.

"I had vain hopes you might have done some shopping during your holiday." Julie rolled her eyes. "What kind of impression do you think the Grape is going to make? If only I didn't have this meeting...what's the weather like outside?"

"I am not wearing a coat. Not in Auckland. In February," said Sarah firmly.

"This is the son and heir of a world-famous couturier we're trying to impress here," Julie wailed. "He'll be expecting style...panache..."

"He'll be expecting you," came the mild reply. "And we can't all look as good as you do."

Julie was in her late thirties but with her rippling shoulder-length blonde hair, glowing, peachy skin and lithe figure she could have been ten years younger.

"You don't even try, Sarah. Why don't you—"

The phone on Sarah's desk rang and she snatched it up. Once Julie started on the subject of clothes she could go on for hours.

"It's Keith." She hugged the receiver to her chest. "He wants to know if the panic's still on and whether you want to see the paste-ups now?" Keith Moore was their art director. It was the triumvirate of him, Julie, and photographer Mike Stone who were responsible for creating *Rags'* distinctive, successful, identity.

"Yes and yes. I may as well see them, I seem to be suffering from terminal writer's block here." She tore the paper out of her typewriter and screwed it up in disgust.

"What paste-ups?" asked Sarah, replacing the receiver.

"We've done a mock-up of the April issue," Julie explained. "New ideas for new publishers. We were going to get a dummy printed, but we won't have time now."

"Isn't that assuming rather a lot? Wilde's may not want to make any changes."

"We're a little on the staid side, sweetie, you must admit and Wilde Publications isn't noted for its conservatism—nor is Max Wilde. Since I don't think he's coming all this way just for his health it stands to reason he has plans. There's a memo of mine about it somewhere—Janey, don't you ever *walk* into a room?"

"Sorry." Julie's young, freckle-faced secretary looked anxiously at Sarah. "I just rang to check for you about whether the flight from London was on time. It wasn't."

"There, I told you not to panic, Julie. How late is it?"

"Not late," yelped Janey. "Half an hour early! Tailwinds or something." Her voice rose to follow the blur that was Sarah.

So much for not rushing. Fleeing for the stairs, Sarah cursed the fact that they were on the fourth floor of an old building. There were only two lifts and they always seemed to be rattling up when you wanted to go down.

She was still panting as she manoeuvred the bright orange office Chevette through the streets of the inner city. It was all the fault of the grape dress, really. If Julie hadn't started on that she might have left before the phone rang, and not learned that the plane was early, and not be chauffeuring a stomach-load of butterflies around now. It was always worse having to anticipate disaster.

She knew, however, that none of her clothes would have met with Julie's unqualified approval. The easy, comfortable blouse and skirt combinations were "boring", the suits "too severe", the dresses "wallpaper clothes". The root of the problem, according to Julie, was that Sarah lacked the prime motivation to dress fashionably: the desire to attract men.

As she swung out to pass a slow-moving container truck the tiny diamonds that studded her wedding ring caught the light and points of white fire blazed briefly, mocking her thoughts.

When she had first joined *Rags & Riches* as a nervous, inexperienced secretary Sarah had been grateful for Julie's help and advice. In fact she had spent her first few weeks' wages buying clothes, most of which, though dated, she still wore. Simon had made it clear that he resented the idea of her drawing money out of their joint account to buy clothes for a job he didn't want her to take, another petty attempt to make her feel guilty about wanting some independence.

Yet when she had gone ahead and used her own earnings it had provided him with a fresh grievance...now she was trying to make *him* feel guilty and inadequate. Most of his complaints had been similarly confused and contradictory but at the time she had been too involved to see it and had suffered agonies of self-doubt as a result.

Her husband's death had come only four months after she had started her job and the resulting gradual ingrowth hadn't been a conscious process, but an instinctive reaction to inward and outward pressures.

A plane roared low overhead as Sarah turned into the airport approach road, reminding her of her mission, and she wished again that she knew something about the people she was to meet. Perhaps she could try some logical deductions.

She knew that Sir Richard Wilde was about 70, very rich and very famous. Therefore his son must be about 40, born with a silver spoon in his mouth, attending the best schools, gaining entrée to all the best places by virtue of his name. He would be sleek and well fed, impeccably dressed, of course, and probably rather aloof, as befitted his wealth and position. His companion would be much the same, perhaps the junior of the two.

There—they couldn't be too difficult to pick out of a crowd, thought Sarah smugly, especially as most of the flights from England at this time of the year were filled by families returning from Christmas reunions. And she had made her trip in record time—fifteen minutes.

Time is relative. To Max Wilde it seemed that he had been waiting an awfully long time and he found himself becoming increasingly irritated with each passing minute. Surely they would be met as arranged, in spite of the last minute change of plan? It was common courtesy, not to mention good public relations. He would allow the tardy Mrs. Somerville another ten minutes.

Restlessly he shifted position in the cushioned chair. He felt flat, drained of energy. He shot an envious look at the

man sitting next to him. Tom looked perfectly comfortable, quietly finishing off a cigarette, not at all depressed by
the functional lifelessness of the terminal. The bulky body
was relaxed, the heavy head tilted back, thinning grey hair
fluffing out from behind large ears. He looked like a big,
amiable teddy bear, but the simile was only apt in the physical sense. Tom's refined manners were anything but bear-
ish and his brain, when it came to debits and credits and the
ins and outs of tax laws, was the equivalent of a sophisticated computer. At the moment the computer was switched
off, and Tom seemed to be very much looking forward to a
few weeks of semi-relaxation in a Southern hemisphere
summer. Max was not.

He only had himself to blame, of course. If he hadn't
been so over-confident as to risk flying in marginal weather
last April he wouldn't be facing exile now. It had been a
needless risk and one that had very nearly ended in his
death. And for what? For temporary gratification. For a
woman whose body he enjoyed no more and no less than he
had enjoyed others, and whose mind had begun to bore him
utterly.

Max's social life had figured briefly in that last, blazing
row he had had with his father before his rapid exit from
London. Their relationship, always precarious, had suffered one of its recurrent blow-ups and this time Max, usually able to ignore his father's frequent provocative moods,
hadn't even tried to avoid it.

He had arrived home from a particularly grinding session with the executives of a company that Wilde's was in
the process of buying out. A number of problems had
cropped up unexpectedly and it was nearing ten o'clock by
the time he got into his car. Ice on the road had made driving a chore and negotiating his route Max regretted the impulse that had led him to agree to the meeting at the other
company's offices. If it had been held at Wilde House he
would have been only an elevator ride from home.

By the time he reached the door of his penthouse apartment all he wanted was food, drink, sleep . . . not necessarily in that order. But he was greeted by Brandon, his butler, who apologetically informed him that his father was waiting in the study.

"Oh God, what has he come visiting for at this time of night?"

"He has been waiting some time, sir."

"Lying in wait you mean. Bring me in a large brandy, will you? Nothing for Sir Richard, we don't want him to settle in."

The study was his retreat, jealously guarded. Sir Richard had instructed that the apartment be designed as a showcase for Wilde Interiors and since Max spent so little time at home he made no demur. But he had put his foot down over the study and the quiet, understated elegance of the room contrasted with the dramatic brilliance of the living areas. Booklined walls and a long ebony desk warmed the deep-pile cream carpet and the cream velvet chesterfield. The wall behind his desk displayed a few favourites from Max's extensive art collection.

Sir Richard Wilde did not possess the kind of personality that complemented the room. Even seated at the desk, absorbed in some papers, he managed to radiate a volatile aura.

"You've been avoiding me for weeks, Max. I want to know why," he announced, taking up the conversation as though they were already in the middle of an argument.

"Hello, father." Max refrained from mentioning that he had been out of the country for most of that time. His father was well aware of the fact. Besides, it was true.

He walked over and twitched a paper out of his father's hand. "Well, what is it that's so pressing it can't wait? Other than your enduring, endearing interest in my paperwork." He flicked a sarcastic finger at the untidy pile on the desk.

His father squared off the papers with pale, neat hands while Max watched objectively. For the first time he no-

ticed the thin black cane leaning against the edge of the desk
and stifled a sigh. That meant his father was role-playing
again. The aged parent, he supposed. It would be laughable if it were not so tiresome. Max was in no mood to play
games.

"You're my son, my only child, of course I'm interested.
I'm worried about you." The quavery note was nicely balanced by an injured air.

"Well stop worrying," Max said callously. "I'm thirty-
five not fifteen. I've been running my own life quite satis-
factorily for a long time now. And if it wasn't for you I'd be
running Wilde's the same way." He turned and took the
amber glass from a silent Brandon, approving the large
measure with a dismissive nod.

He took a gulp, expecting a sour look from his father, but
instead he got a quiet smile and the younger man's eyes
narrowed. Usually a remark like that produced an explosion and usually Sir Richard, who only drank champagne,
made some pointed remark about Max's drinking.

"That's exactly why I've come to see you. I can't put it off
any longer, I wanted to tell you my decision right away." He
paused dramatically for effect. "I'm getting on—sixty-eight
at the end of the next month—too old to be taking on a lot
of unnecessary work."

"Don't tell me you've decided to give up designing?"

He received a rigid stare. "Don't be ridiculous. I'm an
artist, artists never give up their work. Millions of women
depend on me to dress them in a style to which they are unaccustomed." His father's jokes were always execrable.
"No, I'm talking about the business side of things. I've decided it's time you took over the chairmanship of the
Group." He sat back with the air of a magician who has just
pulled a rabbit out of a hat, but the response was disap-
pointing. Max refused to applaud.

"Indeed?" He walked over to the chesterfield and sat
down, nursing his drink, contemplating his father. Tall and
lean, like himself, Sir Richard was health personified. The

desk lighting was flattering, but even in broad daylight his father didn't look his age. His face was lined, but they were the strong lines of character, and his hair, though white, was still the thick leonine mane it had been in his youth. His mind was as clear as a bell and he was still a powerhouse of energy.

He had talked about retiring before, but never seriously. In fact he had fought tooth and nail to retain his control, firmly resisting any efforts to dislodge him.

"And what are the strings?" inquired Max pleasantly.

"Strings?" Innocently. "What strings? You're my son."

"I've never known you offer anything without conditions. Perhaps you want me to merge with a textile heiress."

"Don't be facetious, Max," Sir Richard snapped, then stopped. "Have you got someone in mind?"

"No, I have not."

"Well, you should think about it anyway," plunging down a sidetrack for a moment. "A chairman should have a solid home background, the shareholders like it. Wenching is fine in your youth and I've no objection to the press you've been getting, but when you get to your age people begin to wonder if there's instability. You've got to start thinking about heirs, you know."

"I don't have to do anything," Max interrupted. "I'm not marrying the first available candidate simply to provide you with grandchildren. In my considerable experience it's an overrated institution. Certainly you and mother were no blissful advertisement for the delights of matrimony."

True to form his father waved the unpalatable away with an elegant gesture. "Your mother was a very beautiful and intelligent woman but she could be very wilful."

"As wilful as you."

Sir Richard frowned. "We're digressing. We're supposed to be talking about you. The fact is..." he reached for his cane and made a play of using it to haul himself up. Here it comes, thought Max, cynically. "The fact is that my age is beginning to creep up on me. I can't be bothered with all these new angles your whizz kids are dreaming up... new companies, new directions. It's distracting and these days I need all my energy and concentration for my real work—designing. I had hopes, of course, that you would follow in my footsteps, but no matter, you've chosen other fields. Talent has many guises and I respect yours. You have a rational yet intuitive sense for business, you're demanding but fair, you have experience and all the qualities of leadership that would make you a good chairman.''

"Why do I get the feeling this is a funeral oration?"

"You have all these things," his father continued inexorably, "and yet, I hesitate. Why? Why do I now feel some doubt that you're ready for it?"

That brought Max up sharp. He set his half-empty glass down on the black coffee table beside him with a sharp click.

"What in the hell do you mean by that?"

"Just what I say. Something's not right, and I think you should tell me what it is. I should like to know, both as your father and as present chairman of Wilde's. For the past few months you've been like a cat on hot bricks, working like there's no tomorrow."

"I've always worked hard. Dammit, you wouldn't want me as a director if I didn't pull my weight." Max stood up abruptly, thrusting his hands into his pockets.

"I agree. But there is a difference between working hard and over-working. You're driving yourself close to the brink, physically and mentally."

"Which one of your tame executives has been keeping tabs on me this time?" Max enquired caustically, aware that this was a rare reversal—he was losing control while his temperamental father remained cool. The thought only angered him more.

"It's not a matter of telling tales, Max, and if you were reacting less defensively you'd see that. If your health is in jeopardy, naturally that affects the companies you control and the people you employ. And this is not just a straightforward case of overwork. It's been going on ever since that crash. I can't put my finger on it exactly but you seem to have lost your sense of proportion. What you're doing doesn't seem to satisfy you any more and that worries me. What are you trying to prove, and to whom?''

"I'm not trying to prove anything!'' Max was furious now. "I don't have to. When I fail in my job, then you can worry. But don't accuse me of doing it too well.''

"But you're not doing it well, that's the point. Not as well as you used to. If you're not happy in your work how can you expect others to be happy working with you, or for you?''

"Thank you for the honesty—it's the company that's worrying you, not my personal welfare, so you can drop the aged parent act, it cuts no ice with me.''

Unabashed, his father abandoned the cane and stood tall. "Up until now the two have been virtually indivisible, perhaps that's the problem. I built my empire out of blood, sweat and tears as well as talent, and I want you to inherit it. But more than that, I want you to want it as much as I did. I've never doubted your ambition or your determination to take over from me but if that changes, I want to be the first to know. I've seen too many good men crushed by the sheer weight of responsibility at the top to want to see it happen to any son of mine.''

"Is that what you think? That I'm cracking up? That I can't handle the responsibility any more?'' Max demanded tautly. It was the nearest his father had ever come to conceding that Max was more than the extension of his own ambitions, but there was too wide a gulf between them now to bridge with words. Ever since he had left university Max had been aware that beneath the casual affection and respect they had for each other ran uneasy currents—a competitiveness that inhibited any real closeness between them and tempered trust with wariness.

"You tell me. Can you honestly say that there is nothing troubling you?'' Sir Richard paused expectantly but Max merely compressed his lips. "All right...I didn't expect that you would tell me. Perhaps you haven't even worked it out for yourself yet. Maybe you need time to think."

"Not about the chairmanship."

"Fine. Then there's something you can do for me before you take it on."

"I knew there would be strings."

"I've already discussed this with the other board members—individually, of course—and the consensus is that I resign at the March board meeting and you are voted in to my place. Naturally I'll still retain a seat on the board, but you will be Group Chairman. There'll be shufflings on some of the subsidiary boards as well, but when you come back we can discuss that further!"

"Come back!" Max rapped out. "Come back from where?"

"New Zealand." Sir Richard avoided his son's incredulous stare. "You know that the publishing company has taken over this fashion magazine—*Rags & Riches*—there. I've been through the paperwork. It's a good little magazine, that's the general opinion, but it could do with a shot in the arm—hook it into our syndication network, inject a little more cash, that sort of thing. I see our first official issue is the April one; it will be going into preparation about now as a matter of fact, and will come out the week that we introduce the new collection in Australasia. Great possibilities there. I suggest you're the man to explore those possibilities. I want you to go down there, look at the situation, deal with it as you see fit. You've worked in this area before—you spent some time on *Elan* in Paris, as I recall, and enjoyed it, so you can't say it isn't in your line—"

"It isn't. Not now. Five years ago maybe!" Max exploded, unable to listen any longer. "If you think you're going to exile me to the back of beyond until I shape up to some nebulous ideal—"

His father over-rode him with ringing tones. "You can take your time. A month I think. You and Tom Forest."

"So I get a nursemaid now! You're the one who needs the nursemaid, you must be going senile. I can't leave London now. I've got a thousand and one things on my plate. I'm not going to walk away from delicate negotiations now, it could kill a dozen deals."

"We did without you while you were in hospital," his father pointed out drily. "You're not indispensable, Max, not yet anyway. As to your workload, that proves my point. I want the pressure off you for a while and I can't think of a better way of doing it, short of a complete holiday, and to get you to do that I'd have to commit you. You'll have one task and one task alone down there and I'll instruct head office to that effect. No long-distance conference calls. As for Tom, he damn well deserves time off. He's kept up with your pace in spite of the fact that he's more my generation than yours. I won't have you risking his health without good reason. If the thought offends your work ethic I suggest you get him to investigate the possibility of other interests Down Under."

Max had the grace to feel uncomfortable. Tom had worked closely with him ever since Max had first joined Wilde's and had remained his right-hand man through all the learning years. Originally Sir Richard's man, he was now indisputably Max's; a source of sound advice and trusted wisdom, and taken too much for granted.

"If you don't want Tom, it'll have to be one of the whizz kids," his father added cunningly and Max shook his head absently.

"Tom." His head jerked up and he glared at Sir Richard when he realised the admission. His father was looking his usual sprightly self. "What happened to creeping old age? Changed your mind about retiring?"

"My word is my bond."

"And if I don't go I suppose you'll refuse to step down. I could force you to, regardless."

"You could," his father agreed complacently. "But you won't. It would take time, you'd alienate a lot of good peo-

ple and it would damage Wilde's reputation . . . not to mention me. But the choice is yours."

"It's no choice, it's blackmail," Max snapped and Sir
Richard fell back on the age-old parental maxim:

"It's for your own good."

Looking at it from a distance Max realised that if he had
pursued his argument with his usual ruthless determination
he would have prevailed in the end. In spite of his father's
position and reputation Max wielded a great deal of power
in his own right, not only in the votes of the many boards he
was on but also in personal loyalty. He had never fully
flexed his muscles because he had never needed to, and when
it came to the point he had held back. And here he was,
wondering whether he was going to regret it.

"You did inform Mrs. Somerville it was Tuesday not
Thursday, didn't you?" he asked Tom who had stood up to
stretch his legs.

"The telex should have arrived first thing yesterday. I'll
go and call their office, they may have got the times mixed."

Max glanced at the flat silver watch on his wrist. "It
would be quicker just to find a taxi."

"I'll phone first. Give them the benefit of the doubt."
Ever the diplomat. Max watched as he disappeared in the
direction of a row of telephone booths.

Easing the tension out of his neck and shoulders he began an idle survey of the comings and goings around him,
noting the summer fashions. A woman coming through the
automatic sliding door at the main entranceway jolted him
out of his torpor.

My God, if that's our typical New Zealand reader I can
see our work cut out for us, he thought sardonically.

She hesitated and looked around. Max couldn't take his
eyes off her, spellbound by a kind of detached horror. She
looked about thirty years old but it was difficult to tell in
that awful dress. The dated style did nothing for her and the
muddy colour was further flattened by the deep tan of her

skin. Her hair, scraped back into a severe pleat, emphasised the undistinguished features. Poverty, carelessness, or sheer lack of taste, decided Max critically.

He watched her walk briskly over to the British Airways desk. Surprisingly, she moved well. His experienced eye detected that beneath that apology for a dress was a good body, tall and well-proportioned, though a trifle voluptuous for Max's taste.

He was still staring, lazily amusing himself by imagining what she would look like in some of his father's designs, when she turned impatiently from the desk attendant who was shaking his head. Their eyes met. Full face, the triangular line of her jaw and high cheekbones gave her a pointed, vulpine look and he smiled at the comparison.

He was rewarded with a cool disdainful look that held a hint of contempt. The kind of look that it was usually his prerogative to deliver. Caught on the raw he deliberately dropped his eyes in insolent appraisal of her body and when he raised them again he was gratified to see her reddening as she turned away. Her bag swung on her shoulder as she turned and he caught sight of the magazine tucked there.

Surely *she* couldn't be Julie Somerville? No fashion editor would be so unfashionable! However, it would be as well to check. He sighed.

Leaving his single case beside Tom's two bulging ones he picked up his briefcase and strolled over. He was half amused, half irritated to see her stiffen as she became aware of his presence and a slightly malicious impulse prompted him to make his first words ambiguous.

CHAPTER TWO

"ARE YOU waiting for someone?"

The voice was rich and brown, flavoured with harshness, like bitter chocolate. It made the back of Sarah's neck prickle oddly and, disliking the sensation, she turned defensively.

It was him of course. The man with the insulting stare.

She had noticed him even before she entered the terminal, framed by the glass rectangle of the door. He was isolated from the rest of seething humanity as much by his expression as by the fact that he was sitting alone. No happy traveller there, but a world-weary cynic. The thin, dark face wore a look of intense boredom almost amounting to sullenness. His body was long and slim, disposing itself with an easy elegance, but the indolent attitude didn't entirely conceal the latent strength. He was dressed with a studied casualness—off-white linen shirt, open at the neck, and dark trousers. And he was attractive, sinfully so, in a dark, gypsyish kind of way.

He had watched her walk across the arrival lounge. She knew because she could feel it, just as she had felt his approach now. It had been a critical gaze too, and, irrationally, she had resented it. She was used to being superficially judged and found wanting by male eyes, usually it didn't bother her. But he did. And when she had seen that smile, that narcissistic expectation that she would smile back, overwhelmed with gratitude that he had condescended to notice her, she was seized by the desire to prick that peacock pride. And she had. His reaction to her non-reaction had been typical. Handsome men often thought themselves irresistible.

She lifted her chin and looked past him. "Yes. If you'll excuse me." She made her voice as clear and cold as her slate-coloured eyes.

He moved at the same time she did, blocking her path, the smile tightening on his lips. At close quarters he was even more attractive. Sarah felt the impact of his masculinity as an almost physical threat and instinctively she shrank from it. A gypsy, but an aristocratic one, the slight signs of dissipation giving him an additional, dangerous, edge. The blue-black of his hair was reflected in the blue shadow on his chin and upper lip and there were shadows too under his eyes; those curious eyes that were not dark as one would expect, but light hazel, disturbingly brilliant.

"Do you mind? I said excuse me!"

"And I asked you a question."

Sarah licked her lips. His persistence was vaguely menacing. "I told you—"

"Excuse?" A pretty blonde British Airways stewardess materialised beside them and thrust a folded piece of paper at the man. "Sorry I missed you when you left. Here's my number. If I'm not there my flatmate knows my schedule." She flashed a brief, insincere smile at Sarah and dashed away again.

The man tucked away the piece of paper in his shirt pocket and raised a bland black eyebrow at Sarah.

"Now, where were we?"

"Nowhere!" snapped Sarah. She should have moved while she had the chance. Smug, egotistical devil! "If you're so desperate for company why don't you catch another flight and collect a few more numbers!" The words sounded ridiculously priggish even to her own ears, but what with being late and not being able to spot her executives, and trying to cope with God's gift to women, she was rapidly losing what was left of her cool.

"I was going to suggest a good one for *you* to call," he said evenly. "A psychiatrist. You have quite an aggression problem there."

"The one you go to no doubt," responded Sarah sweetly. "But doesn't he specialise? Egocentric males?"

There was a taut little pause.

"Are you always this rude to strangers?"

It was a farcical situation, exchanging insults in public with a perfect stranger. Already appalled by her uncharacteristic behaviour, Sarah searched for some way to defuse the conversation. Why hadn't she just ignored him, or frozen him off?

"Ah, there you are! You must be Sarah Carter. I've just been on the telephone to your editor."

Sarah gratefully took the outstretched hand, smiling tentatively at her rescuer. Broad shoulders and a rather kindly middle-aged face.

"Mr. Wilde?" she asked, questioningly.

His handshake was firm and dry and the polite smile widened appreciatively.

"I'm flattered, but no. I'm Tom Forest. Hasn't Max introduced himself yet?" He propelled her gently towards the other man. "This is Max Wilde."

In place of Sarah's brain sat a large chunk of marshmallow, pink and mushy and incapable of coherent thought. Luckily none of her body's other systems appeared to be working either—she didn't flush or stammer or burst into tears of humiliation. She just stood there and stared blankly at him.

"Pleased to meet you, Sarah Carter, at last." The very lack of expression in the low, harsh voice was a mockery in itself. He extended a hand, like a challenge, and Sarah took it, avoiding his eyes by looking down at her hand almost engulfed by his. His knuckles whitened and she winced at the fierceness of his grip and looked up involuntarily to catch the gleam of amusement in his eyes.

He had known. All along he had known—or at least suspected—who she was. He had let her make a complete fool of herself and now he was enjoying her discomfiture. She fought in vain to stop the wave of heat from climbing into her face. She hadn't blushed in years and it was infuriating that this awful man should be able to make her do it twice within a few minutes.

"I'm sorry if you've been kept waiting." Embarrassment rushed her into speech. "But yesterday was the city's Anniversary Day, a public holiday. We didn't know about your change of plan until about half an hour ago." An acceptable compression of time in the circumstances, she felt.

"It was rather short notice; and we haven't really been waiting long," the older man replied, but with a quick glance at his companion that spoke volumes to Sarah. That expression of boredom hadn't been feigned.

"If... if you'll bring your bags and follow me—the car's right outside."

She followed them over to their luggage. The two men were both the same height, but Tom Forest's large frame gave him an amble whereas Max Wilde glided with an almost feline grace.

The world outside was a vivid contrast to the controlled environment of the terminal. The warm humidity rolled into their faces with surprising suddenness and out in the direct sunlight colours everywhere seemed bright and hard.

"I think I'll go and find a cigarette machine," Tom Forest said. "I didn't buy any duty-free, I'm trying to give up. But I think I was a bit optimistic to think I could do it all at once. Now I've smoked my last one I think I need the security of an emergency pack." With a smile he inclined his head at Sarah and she watched with regret as he walked away.

There was a long silence as Max Wilde moved forward and leant his forearms across the top of the car. He looked up into the arc of cloudless blue, narrowing his eyes against the glare. The heat from the metal soaked into his body soothing away some of the stiffness. The effects of the crash still lingered in his system even if, as his father had said, he didn't want to admit them. There were scars, not all of them physical, and considering the length the company went to play down the details of the accident, it was fortunate that there were no obvious disablements to explain away. Just this damned unsettling dissatisfaction with the world in general. Even the challenge of merger and takeover had lost its edge.

The longer the silence stretched, the more nervous Sarah became. What was he thinking about, to give his face that brooding, impatient look?

Damn the man! If she was going to be working with him for the next few weeks—working *for* him—she had better make her peace now and get it over with.

She cleared her throat. "I'm sorry I spoke as I did just now, but I had no idea who you were..."

His head swivelled and for a moment she had the idea he didn't know who she was. Then the hazel eyes narrowed.

"Just a passing wolf on the prowl? Did you think I was moving in for the kill?"

"Of course not," she floundered. She had, though goodness knew why. The man carried a positive masculine charge, he would never have to make the first move. Women, like that stewardess, would naturally gravitate towards his field of attraction. *Most* women, that is.

He inspected her again, with the curiosity of a scientist studying an interesting, but odd, specimen.

"You flatter yourself. Or is there something I don't see? Does every man who looks at you follow through with a pass?"

"That isn't what I—"

"Do you treat all men as potential rapists? It must make for a very exciting life."

"Only the ones who look capable of it," she rapped back, hating him for his deliberate taunts.

To her annoyance he merely laughed. "From you that's a compliment, I'm sure. Sorry to disappoint you but public ravishment is not my style. I'm trying to remember what I read about you in the personnel files, nothing that prepared me for the unique quality of your welcome."

If anything was calculated to haul Sarah up short, that was. What was she doing? Julie would *kill* her. And dance on her grave! How was she going to get out of this one?

"I'm—" The word jammed in her throat and took some pushing to release. "I'm sorry...I—I'm not really back in the swing of things yet. I've only just come back from holiday. Everything was very much up in the air when I left. The deal must have gone through very rapidly." She was beginning to babble but at least she wasn't saying anything that could be construed as insubordinate.

"I like to work quickly. It keeps everyone on their toes."

"Are you going to be here long?" she asked, striving for normality.

"Long enough."

"Have you ever been here before?"

"No."

It was like trying to get blood out of a stone. Sarah made one last attempt. "Well, you've picked the right time of year. February weather is usually the best of the summer."

"I came here to work, not lie in the sun."

"I'm sorry," she said, dismayed by his sharpness. It seemed nothing she could do or say was right. She was always either insulting him or apologising to him. "I was just making conversation."

"Aimless chatter I can do without."

Sarah would have liked to slap his supercilious face. Instead she gave him a brief vitriolic look which completely passed him by, and subsided into rigid silence.

Shortly afterwards Tom Forest arrived back, and together the two men loaded the three bags into the boot of the car. Max Wilde then got into the back seat with his briefcase while the other man eased himself in beside Sarah.

"You're Julie Somerville's assistant, aren't you?" he asked. "Have you worked for *Rags & Riches* long?"

"Three years," said Sarah, concentrating on her driving. An accident would really round off the morning! "I started off as a secretary, the rest was sort of gradually accidental. Julie seemed to think I had the potential to do more than type letters and answer phones."

"With the idea being that you eventually graduate to editor?"

"Oh no." She had never ever thought about it. "It's a job for a journalist and I'm no writer. I prefer what I do, which is a bit of everything and everything of little bits."

"More managerial than creative."

"Yes. But management involves creativity, too."

The large head nodded thoughtfully. "I'm glad you think so. Too often organisational skills are underrated. Not everyone has the flexibility to do it well, particularly when control involves the interaction of artistic temperaments."

Sarah grinned. A very subtle way of saying the crazies who inhabit the extended world of fashion journalism.

They discussed the point in general terms for a while, then moved on to specifics—Sarah's job at *Rags* and the magazine itself. Aware she was being sounded out, she spoke honestly and intelligently, hoping the man in the back seat was listening. At least he wouldn't be able to dismiss her as brainless.

She could see him in the oblong of the rear-view mirror, head tipped back on the seat, eyes closed. The lines of tension around his mouth and eyes were quite pronounced and the rigidity of the jaw showed that even now he wasn't relaxed. She felt a moment's uncertainty. She should have made allowances for the fact that he had just spent nearly twenty-fours in the air, been effusively humble instead of being offended at his sarcasm. Then she remembered that Tom Forest had been on the same trip and *he* had managed polite civilities at the end of it. Flashing another look at the closed face behind her, Sarah shivered. For all the charm that had lit his face when he had smiled at that stewardess, there had also been a certain cool calculation. Not a man given to impulse. Not a man to make an enemy of.

If only she hadn't been so hasty. She cringed to think of his incredulity when he realised she thought he was trying to pick her up. She would have to try and put it from her mind, try to forget, too, that instinctive dislike she had felt. It could make her job over the next few weeks very difficult and could even jeopardise her future with the magazine.

When they reached the hotel Sarah double-parked and offered to check in for them, but Tom Forest declined with thanks.

"We'll sort ourselves out and give Mrs. Somerville a phone call," he said. "Thank you for meeting us, we'll see you again soon."

Back at the office Sarah resigned herself to a wasted morning. Everyone wanted to know what the advance guard had discovered about the new arrivals. With difficulty Sarah managed a fairly accurate physical description and a less accurate description, because of the deliberate omissions, of her own feelings on meeting the great man himself. One by one her colleagues trotted back to their departments in the mistaken belief that they had pumped Sarah dry of information.

It wasn't until Julie got back from her meeting at ten-thirty that she really spilled the beans. Reluctant as she was to confess her stupidity, it was better that Julie heard it from her than from the Wilde man.

Wondering how to present her case Sarah had finally decided on a bald statement. Julie's sense of humour was a bit unpredictable and trying to dress up the facts as a funny story could well backfire.

Disbelief, annoyance, mock-sobs and heavy sarcasm was the result, followed by a short, sharp homily on the merits of being polite to strangers, even importunate ones. Quite mild for Julie, really.

"Honestly, Sarah, you are the limit," she finished up. "The one person I thought I could rely on not to foul up! What happened to your celebrated soft answer...the Carter trademark?"

How to explain about the prickle on the back of her neck? The instinct. The "feeling". She could imagine the beautiful blue eyes widen at such impracticality from practical Sarah. Besides, her complaint was quite justified, Sarah's job was to smooth down feathers that other people had ruffled, not do the ruffling herself.

"He should have introduced himself first," she said unwilling to take the entire blame. "He definitely didn't look my idea of an English tycoon. More like a male model."

"What did you expect—bowler hat and umbrella? Don't let the Hollywood looks fool you, honey. Men have done that before now and gone on to commit commercial suicide. He's got a brain with a capital B—commercial degrees up to here and the midas touch as far as money's concerned. Let's just hope he lists a sense of humour amongst his other attributes. I hope you apologised."

"Of course I did!" She was not going to enlarge on *that* conversation.

Julie slammed drawers and shuffled papers noisily for a few more minutes and then to Sarah's relief she began to laugh.

"Here. You'd better take this."

She tossed over a large green envelope. It landed with a soft "phlop" on Sarah's desk, disgorging some of its contents—light cardboard sheets to which printed clippings were pasted. "It's the file on Wilde's, you'd better do some homework."

It took a while for Julie's mirth to subside. Sarah closed her eyes and ears to the distraction and settled down to read the file in front of her. It was certainly comprehensive. There were clippings from overseas newspapers and magazines, press-releases, notes and sketches from the various Wilde fashion collections as well as cross-references to letter and photographic files, which Sarah also looked through. She read through everything once, putting her speed reading to good use, sifting out the references to Max Wilde and putting them aside for further study.

From the tenor of the news reports she could deduce that his attitude to the press was ambivalent. When he wanted publicity for his ventures he appeared charmingly frank and forthcoming, welcoming questions. But equally, he could be a reporter's nightmare. "Mr. Wilde had no comment to make", "Mr. Wilde was unavailable for comment", "Mr. Wilde refused to answer further questions".

Where his private life was concerned there wasn't even a "no comment". There were plenty of photographs—smiling, stern, frowning, quizzical—action flashes grabbed on the run, of him at nightclubs and theatres, fashion shows and functions. Always there was a beautiful woman on his elbow, or the suggestion of one just outside the frame, a slender hand clutching his, a wisp of skirt, the direction of his gaze. The captions were all gossip and hearsay of the "Millionaire Max's Latest Love" type. Sometimes there were coy little comments from the women in question but discretion was obviously something he expected from his female companions. Max himself never bothered to deny or confirm anything from what she could gather—not even the stories that were patently outrageous. Perhaps he knew that nothing generated publicity power like the suggestion of secrecy. His reticence made him a gossip columnist's dream.

Most of the financial news reports that mentioned him were also favourable, admiring even, in their restrained fashion and by the time Sarah had finished her homework she was sinkingly aware she had crossed swords with a very powerful and important man. However, nothing that she had read made her like him any better. All that money, all those boardroom and bedroom successes. How could he not be arrogant? Conceited?

It was some time before she became aware of the pangs of hunger and realised that it was lunchtime and she was alone in the office. She was just thinking of going out for a bite to eat when the phone rang.

"Sarah?" It was Julie, her voice raised over a background of restaurant clatter.

"Hello. I wondered where you'd got to."

"A last minute luncheon engagement."

Hearing the suppressed note of excitement in her voice, Sarah didn't have to ask with whom.

"Having met the man in the flesh I can sympathise with your crass idiocy of this morning. Fathomless charm. It would be interesting to plumb the depths."

"Rather you than me." Sarah hadn't even received a puddle of charm from the man. "What time will you be back?"

"I don't know... I don't care," floated the answer gaily. "I probably won't be back at all. I cunningly brought an idea or two with me to run up the flagpole, so we may spend the rest of the afternoon saluting. Incidentally, he wants a full staff meeting tomorrow morning—send a memo out, will you? If anything urgent comes up, I'll be at the hotel. I'll see you this evening."

"This evening?"

"You haven't forgotten the *Sappho* launching, have you? I sent the invitation out to you. I want you to be there, Sarah, it's a major new line."

"More flag flying?"

"It's a good way of keeping up our contacts... learning what's going on in an informal way. Talking of which, I'm having an informal party on Sunday afternoon. Coming?"

Sarah hesitated. "Of course." Julie's Sunday afternoon barbecues by the poolside of her lovely home were legendary and few people passed up the chance to attend. Everything was very relaxed, you didn't even feel obliged to make conversation if you didn't want to. Just swim and eat and lie in the sun. The only type of party Sarah *did* enjoy.

"I had forgotten about tonight, thanks for reminding me. What time?"

"Seven. And Sarah?"

"Yes?"

"Wear something . . ." she sniffed, *"different."*

Sarah hung up with a sigh. *Sappho* was a new cosmetics line coming on sale in New Zealand shortly and the American-based company was holding a "happening" to introduce their product to the trade and media. They'd hired the top floor of the Intercontinental Hotel as the venue.

The trouble with me is that I'm becoming blasé about "happenings", she told herself. As a novice she had gone to promotional evenings wide-eyed, but now they were just a small part of a full, demanding job.

CHAPTER THREE

By THE time Sarah arrived at the Intercontinental Hotel everything was swinging. The noise-level was high, upbeat music competing with a voluble crowd, most of whom were watching a series of fantasy make-up demonstrations in one corner of the large restaurant. Drink was just as abundant as noise.

She greeted several people she knew and accepted a tall glass of something before being expertly cut out of the crowd by a young man from Sappho's advertising agency. Sarah glanced around the room while she listened politely, managing to look interested and impressed as she wondered whether the preponderance of unfamiliar faces meant the evening would be more of a chore than usual.

"Hello, Sarah. I wonder if I might have a word with you? Excuse us, Peter."

Sarah was whisked away to the other side of the room by a pretty girl wearing a stunning combination of black lurex "boob tube" and slinky, skin-tight gold satin pants.

"Thanks, I think he was just getting his second wind," said Sarah gratefully. Her rescuer was one of *Rags'* staff writers.

"You looked as though you might be building up to a yawn. I would have come over sooner but I didn't want to break up what might have been a promising encounter."

The two girls chatted for a few minutes about what Chris thought of the *Sappho* range, then a short speech signalled the end of the fixed agenda for the evening and the arrival of a mouthwatering array of food laid out on long, white-covered tables.

"Oh goody, I'm famished," said Chris, who could eat like a pig and never put on an ounce. She slanted Sarah a sly look. "I don't suppose you have any room?"

"What?"

"A little bird tells me that you got your foot rather firmly wedged in your mouth this morning. Still there, is it?"

Sarah pulled a face. It had been too much to hope that Julie would keep her gaffe to herself, once she had seen the humorous possibilities.

"A little bird with a big mouth. I suppose it will be joke of the month now."

"Are you kidding? Of the year! Did you really—!" She broke off to give Sarah a sharp nudge. "Speak of the devil!"

Near the door at the other end of the room was Julie, still in yellow but looking as fresh as a daisy, her arm tucked smugly through that of the tall dark man.

"Oh, Sarah," breathed the girl beside her. "How could you?"

Very easily, thought Sarah, her nerves tightening a notch. The dark head was tilted to one side as Max Wilde listened to Julie's introductions. He looked totally at ease, the supreme confidence of power and wealth unmistakable. And the men he was meeting were shaking hands with a hint of deference that showed their awareness of it. He was wearing a dark suit, blue shirt and tie, yet he looked considerably cooler than many of the more casually dressed men around him. A state of mind rather than a physical condition, thought Sarah enviously.

"Lucky Julie," drooled Chris. "It looks like a take-over in more ways than one. Steven Somerville will have to look to his laurels. Hey!" Another nudge. "He's looking at you! Give him a smile, Sarah."

She had no choice. Forcing her reluctant cheek muscles into action she achieved a polite smile and inclined her head.

To her intense embarrassment, conscious of the audible gasp beside her, he made no answering sign of recognition. He continued to look straight through her for several moments, a blank expression on his face. Then he turned away.

Sarah's whole body burned as she stared unseeingly at the back of his head, feeling as if the whole room had witnessed that snub. She knew precisely what he was doing—paying her back in kind, but most unkindly, and unfairly. In the midst of her angry embarrassment she was surprised that he would stoop to such a thing. Perhaps spite was part of his nature—look how he had enjoyed watching her squirm at the airport when she found out who he was.

"Do you think he didn't recognise you?" Chris looked from Max Wilde to Sarah's pale face. "It's a big room, maybe he's short-sighted."

In a pig's eye! thought Sarah, but she didn't say it. Stouthearted Chris was unwilling to think badly of anyone, particularly a man whom, she had cheerfully informed everyone that morning, she had lusted after for years from afar.

"He was probably miles away," Sarah said stiffly.

"Sure. But—"

"Forget it, Chris."

Sarah could see her friend was dying to ask a flood of questions, but those three final words told her she would get nowhere. Her colleagues knew that there were clearly defined lines within which it was unwise to step where Sarah was concerned. One heavily scored line involved men and her personal relationships with them, her husband included. Sarah could take good-natured ribbing with the best of them but real curiosity was an intrusion. Because they liked and respected her they obeyed the unwritten rule, knowing that Sarah reciprocated by respecting the privacy of others.

"Okay, but seeing as you're obviously not going to introduce me, I'll drift on over myself. Maybe I can pry him away from Julie long enough to try my luck!"

Luck would have nothing to do with it, Sarah decided as she elbowed her way through to the buffet. That man made his own luck! His arrival seemed to have taken her appetite away but she piled her plate with chilled oysters in the shell, crayfish mayonnaise and salad, anyway. She would eat every scrap, just to prove to herself that it made no difference what he thought or did to her. She wasn't going to let herself be intimidated by someone else's opinion. It had happened once before in different circumstances and had brought nothing but stress and strife.

She had almost finished her meal and was sitting alone at her table after sharing it with a succession of companions, sipping on a light, cold white wine, when she suffered the shock of seeing Max Wilde sit down on the vacant chair opposite.

At her sharp intake of breath some of the wine went down the wrong way and sent her into a fit of coughing and spluttering, eyes watering furiously. The man was a jinx!

"Drink some more wine."

She did as she was told and immediately felt better. Why did her common sense desert her in his presence?

"All right?"

She nodded, not trusting her voice, hating that grin.

"Good." He sat back. "Lost your tongue? Or minding your manners? How did it feel to be on the reverse end of a glacial stare?"

Struggling for composure, Sarah stole Chris's line without compunction. "You mean when you arrived?" She shrugged casually. "I assumed you must suffer from short-sightedness."

He followed her further than she meant him to: "And too vain to wear glasses?" She got a view of a hard, olive throat as he drew back his head to laugh uninhibitedly. If Sarah hadn't disliked him so much she might have found it an attractive sound. "Nicely said. Unfortunately—for you—I know you better than to believe you thought anything so innocent."

"What makes you think you know me at all?"

Lids veiled the glitter of his eyes. "I told you. I've read your file."

He made it sound like a scandal sheet, although Sarah knew it only contained unadorned facts and figures.

"And I've read yours, Mr. Wilde," she said, imitating his tone.

"Checking up on me?"

"It's part of my job to know what's going on." Perhaps the conversation could be steered on to more conventional lines. She must remember what Julie said about him, albeit in rather exaggerated terms: "He's life or death for us, sweetie. We don't need the extra aggro that antagonising him could give us. Be *nice* next time you see him." Sarah would as lief be as nice to a tiger. This one had intelligence as well as speed and strength; a wicked combination.

"Then you didn't do your job very well this morning, did you?" he replied, not diverted.

"There were circumstances . . ."

"Julie explained," he cut her off. "What conclusions did you come to then, about me, from your file?"

"None," she lied. "I prefer to make my own judgements."

"So do I. That's what I'm doing now." Just the kind of remark to set her at her ease! "Do you like your job?"

"Yes." He must know that already if he had listened to her conversation with Tom Forest.

"Ambitious?"

"In what way?" she asked carefully.

"How many ways are there?"

Sarah licked her lips. Why couldn't she treat him as she did any other person showing a casual interest in her job?

"I suppose I'm ambitious in that I want to be the best at what I do."

"That's not ambition, that's human nature. Ambition is *needing* to be the best. According to Julie you're the best

Editorial Assistant she's ever had, and that includes her stints in New York and Paris.''

His voice was slightly dry and Sarah searched his face for signs of sarcasm. There were none. Mind you, he was only repeating what Julie said, not complimenting her.

"She demands a lot and usually gets it," Sarah said, giving credit where it was due. "Julie's taught me practically everything I know."

"I doubt whether modesty was included." That touched a chord of humour in Sarah but she didn't let herself smile. "What about writing? If not being a journalist precludes you from editorship—" he *had* been listening "—do you not feel your job self-limiting?"

"No. There are other directions. I didn't want to be a writer, I still don't."

"No talent?"

"No inclination." Annoyed. Writing was like offering up a part of yourself on a platter for the world to pick over. Sarah had never even been tempted.

"Then you don't have any frustrated ambitions?"

"Why should I? Ambition isn't everything."

"It is if there's nothing else," he murmured and Sarah met his enigmatic gaze. Once again she had the feeling that for him, for the moment, she didn't exist. Had she imagined that faint bleakness?

"Well, I suppose wanting to be happy is an ambition, and in that sense everyone is ambitious," she said slowly, looking out of the window at her elbow. The view was quite spectacular, the city below settling into dusk, lights beginning to prick on in the streets which criss-crossed down to Quay Street and the bright port illuminations. Over on the North Shore, beyond the out-flung arm of the harbour bridge, comfortable suburbia was also lighting up and to her right Sarah could see the shadowy hulk of Rangitoto Island receding into the darkening sky.

Unconsciously, Sarah's voice had contained the gentle reassurance that she had so often used when Simon was suffering from bouts of inadequacy, real and imagined. It was an automatic response that would have worried and disturbed her if she had realised she was doing it. She didn't, but the man opposite did, and was struck by the irony of this odd, prickly female offering him reassurance. His curiosity was aroused, too.

"That most difficult of all ambitions to achieve," he said, prompting softly.

Yes. And the most fleetingly held. It ran like dry sand between your fingers...one moment you had it warm and soft in your hand, the next it was gone. Sarah's happiness with Simon had been like that. And now she had found a new, different kind of happiness. Contentment. But already she could hear the rustling flurries of a rising wind that threatened to disturb it. Nothing stayed the same, no matter how much you wanted it to.

"Don't you think so?"

"I—" With a shock Sarah realised that she had nearly said what she was thinking, spoken the unspoken fear out loud. The shutters dropped immediately and the eyes which had been almost sea-green became hard as pebbles.

"Perhaps."

"Perhaps?" His mouth twisted. "You don't want to agree with me but you don't like to disagree. I think I preferred it when you were spitting at me, at least you were being honest."

"There are times when honesty defers to diplomacy," said Sarah undiplomatically, still agitated by the way he got under her skin.

"Fortunately I'm not hampered by any such restriction. Tell me, do you deliberately dress like that or is it merely innate bad taste?"

Sarah's jaw nearly dropped at his incredible affrontery. New Zealanders were generally a tolerant race with a "live and let live" philosophy that usually enabled them to accept people as they were. It wasn't often that people remarked on Sarah's personal appearance, other than those who knew her well enough to essay a gentle joke or, like Julie, adopt a maternal exasperation.

"I'm sorry if the way I dress doesn't meet with your high standards, Mr. Wilde," she said stiffly. "But it really isn't any of your business."

"I think it is. You work for me, remember? Or you will in a couple of months; and you're a rather poor advertisement for a fashion magazine."

"I'm not advertising anything. We employ other people to do that. It isn't a condition of my employment that I make the Best Dressed lists. My clothes are perfectly respectable."

"Oh, they are," he agreed pleasantly. "'Respectable' is the kiss of death as far as fashion is concerned. You don't deny, I notice, only defend."

"I dress as I please," said Sarah desperately. She could feel her grip on the conversation slipping.

"Then you're too easy to please. I'm not. But this is neither the time nor the place to discuss it. I can see your editor looking anxiously over this way. Smile, or she'll think you're saying something she'll regret later."

Sarah resisted the urge to look furtively over her shoulder. He had a nasty habit of springing verbal surprises, the kind that left you hanging over a cliff wondering where the solid ground had gone.

"Julie knows me better than that."

"And knowing you, wouldn't expect you to smile, mmm?"

Sarah stared at him for a moment, then out of sheer perversity switched on a brilliant smile, the kind that she had seen Julie use on less-than-intelligent men. Except Julie also fluttered her eyelashes slightly and Sarah couldn't quite bring herself to do that. Besides, her soft, natural ones wouldn't be quite as impressive as Julie's artificial abundance.

"Why, Mr. Wilde, whatever gave you that idea?" she said coyly. If he wanted her to pander to his ego, she would comply, with a vengeance!

Being more than intelligent he immediately got the point. But his reaction wasn't what Sarah expected. She had half hoped, half feared he would be annoyed, but he wasn't. He showed a very genuine amusement, appreciative of the way she had very neatly turned the tables.

"Touché," he acknowledged. "I fear my pique was showing. I won't ask you to smile again. I'll leave it to your discretion. You're right of course, a response must be spontaneous to be honest. I believe that a person's instinctive reaction to a given situation is a far truer indication of their nature than a modified response, which is a social imposition."

Like this morning, for instance, Sarah thought. Is that what he was saying? And just now—that urge to annoy him by simpering like a feather-brained idiot? If so, Sarah didn't agree; social conventions were important, they protected, restrained, aided inter-personal relationships. Following your instincts was dangerous and often wrong. Wasn't the attraction to Simon instinctive? And also her initial reaction to his possessiveness—to be flattered, to baby him out of it instead of standing up for herself?

Deep, dark thoughts and she resented Max Wilde for making her think them. A tactical withdrawal was called for. She should have kept her mouth shut from the first. Been *nice*. *Modified* her responses. He would have been none the wiser.

Sarah looked at the dark countenance now in profile. He certainly was a handsome man. No, she corrected herself, not handsome—beautiful, yet in no way feminine. There was a fine-boned, thoughtful arch to the brow and the hard, high cheekbones and hawkish sweep of the nose gave him a touch of nobility. Those strange eyes were fringed with thick, dark lashes and the tanned skin was smooth and finely grained.

His hair was straight, trimmed just above his collar, jet-black but for the gleam of grey in the short sideboards. The etchings of strain around the features were deepened by tiredness; the cynicism she guessed was habitual. A man of culture, a man of passion... The mouth and eyes held sensual promise, a promise that from all accounts had been often made and probably just as often fulfilled.

Seated, he still retained a grace of carriage and poise that reminded her of a dancer; an alert, controlled, potentially explosive strength masked by grace.

At precisely that point in her thoughts he turned his head, quite casually, and she was caught openly staring. Sarah's throat closed in the grip of an unidentifiable fear and every muscle in her body tensed. The room receded and his image came into ultra-sharp focus, claustrophobically close, and her heart thumped hot and heavy as the moment stretched into eternity.

Simultaneously, they both looked away and Sarah discovered that she had been holding her breath...waiting. For what? She released her breath slowly, carefully, wondering what he had seen in her face. Had that panicky feeling showed? She glanced surreptitiously at him out of the corner of her eye but the classic profile was unreadable. She was being overly-sensitive, allowing a vague apprehension to run away with her. Everything would be all right tomorrow. She would be back in a familiar environment, on her home ground, when she met him next. And he would have other things to concern him, to draw his attention; Sarah could sink gratefully into the background again. Let Julie answer his questions, deal with his unpredictability!

Sarah got up, clutching the wooden back of the chair. "If you'll excuse me, Mr. Wilde, there are several people I should speak to..." He looked up again, eyes light and faintly mocking.

"Of course. I'm sure there'll be plenty of other opportunities for conversation."

It sounded like a threat, and as he rose Sarah slipped away. She didn't know whether he was watching her, but the back of her neck was prickling like mad as she skirted the couples now disco-ing on the dance-floor. Once she was screened from him by the crowd she broke for the door.

"Leaving already, it's only nine?" It was Julie, eyeing Sarah's batik skirt with disfavour.

"I think I've done my share of flag flying."

"Okay; at least you came. Did you tell everyone about tomorrow's meeting?"

Sarah nodded.

"Good. Good. Er... What did he say?"

Max Wilde must have been telling the truth about the anxious look. Sarah hesitated. "That you'd explained about this morning. I think we cleared the air." She crossed her fingers.

"Terrific!" Julie beamed. "He was very reasonable about it, you know, considering it wasn't his fault. We had a little laugh over it and everything was as smooth as apple pie."

Had a little laugh about it! Sarah repeated savagely to herself as she rode down in the lift, changing a frown to a polite smile as a clutch of Japanese businessmen boarded at the next floor. Smooth as apple pie! What did Julie know? He hadn't withered her with sarcasm, or snubbed her, or laughed at her! Julie *liked* him.

Sarah didn't. Not at all.

CHAPTER FOUR

As THE week came to a close Sarah told herself that at least she had tried. Julie couldn't fault her for that. She had attempted to be as pleasant, co-operative and efficient as usual, but the good ship *Resolution* foundered in the sea of unpredictability that was Max Wilde. Self-effacement didn't work with him, he liked to make waves, get opinions—provoke them, if necessary. He certainly seemed to take delight in provoking Sarah out of her cool composure.

The constricting self-consciousness she felt in his presence got worse. She dropped things, and forgot things, and made stupid mistakes, all of which made her even more nervous. It was a vicious circle.

Grudgingly she had to admit that as an Executive Editor he knew his stuff. He immersed himself in the job as though it was the most challenging of his career, and in doing so challenged the *Rags* team to keep up with him. He worked with aggressive speed, absorbing information like a sponge, tapping the minds around him and handling the reins' of command with easy confidence. He made himself approachable, yet had sufficient presence to instil respect. And he was a master at the art of persuasive reasoning, the subtle manipulation of argument in his own favour.

By Friday the tacit agreement was that however dynamic a brain he was, Max Wilde wasn't an easy man to work for. He was uncomfortably impatient—smiling one minute and snapping the next. Wherever he went he created a natural surface tension which Sarah found as irritating as it was stimulating.

After the first burst of hyper-activity he settled down to mere over-activity. Surely he didn't work at this sort of intensity all the time? Not even the devil himself could keep that up, thought Sarah, appalled by his sheer drive. No wonder he had been curious about her ambitions, and so sceptical when she said she hadn't any. Work to him was as natural as breathing and he regarded everything in the light of a debit or credit.

He was generous with praise where it was due, quick to appreciate a good idea. But he was also extremely caustic in his criticisms, and brusque to the point of rudeness with excuses, however justified. He did not suffer fools gladly and at times used words like weapons, striking straight to the heart of the matter regardless of personal feeling, exposing hidden weaknesses and dealing with them ruthlessly. It was unpleasantly like a trial by ordeal to be on the receiving end of his critical dissection, as Sarah found out on several occasions.

It didn't help that he continued to make derogatory remarks about Sarah's clothes or that he seemed to be amused by the references to the manner of their meeting. He may have forgiven, but he wasn't forgetting!

On Friday morning Sarah arrived at work to find that Julie and Chris, together with two more colleagues, Nora and Mike, were already settled around the big oval oak table in the interview-cum-conference room. Sarah was about to take the seat nearest the door when Marie and Keith arrived and Sarah took a playful swing at the art director with her note pad. He executed a neat side-step and to her horror she ended up hitting Max Wilde himself, who was following close behind. It was only a light tap but it hit him squarely in the chest.

"Sorry," she blushed, and hurriedly sat down, trying to avoid seeing Keith's smirk.

Max Wilde, in a grey suit and shirt but without a tie, looked slowly around the table before uncapping the nib of a silver pen. Like unsheathing a sword, Sarah thought.

"Let's get straight down to business, shall we? I'm impressed, both by your obvious commitment and by some of the ideas you have put forward for this." He indicated the artist's board beside him displaying the *Rags* mock-up. "However, I have some points to make. The emphasis I question. You're changing masthead, layout, typeface—all the things that are your signature. All right, change the cover to indicate your new affiliation, change the order of your columns and add new ones, but not the type. It's clear, it's clean, it's *Rags*. Changing it would be too much of a shock for your readers. Certainly we want to startle, to challenge, but not to shock.

"The content is a different story. You have tried to broaden the base of your appeal, but you haven't gone far enough. You've put in furniture, interior decoration—why not food and wine? They're also part of *ambience.*"

"But we're a fashion magazine, a specialist magazine," Nora interjected.

"How specialist is fashion? It's custom; not only of dress, but of manners, of tastes in everything—even thought. Think of your name. You're not only *Rags* you're *Riches* too. Money and everything that it can buy. In fact, why not have a regular financial column, money from a woman's point of view—how to get it, invest it, enjoy it?"

That interested Chris, who was knowledgeable about stocks and shares and bought jewellery as an investment. She was always telling Sarah that it was important to make your money work for you. But her advice fell on stony ground. To Sarah money was something you either banked or spent.

Having tossed his suggestions into the ring, Max Wilde now sat back and watched the dogfights that ensued. The pale eyes followed the rapid exchanges with a piercing intensity and the slim fingers played ceaselessly with the pen. Sarah found her eyes drawn to that little bar of silver as it was twisted and twirled, rolled back and forth and occasionally used to make notes. She had rarely seen him completely still, except just before he pounced on an unfortunate victim of his displeasure, like a predator pausing to judge speed and distance.

Although she wasn't taking any part in the discussion herself, Sarah listened closely. She had heard these arguments many times before but seldom with the sense of urgency they had now. This time what they said would have meaning and effect, it wasn't just letting off steam, stirring the creative juices with complaint and argument.

Sarah began doodling on her pad with her very prosaic ballpoint, sketching the man at the end of the table with reasonable proficiency. Simon had been quite helpful when she had mentioned she would like to learn to draw, but his fiercely professional criticisms of her dabblings had defeated their own purpose. The enclosed room was very warm and Sarah blinked hard as she added horns and a tail to complete the picture. For some reason she hadn't been sleeping very well lately.

"Are we boring you, Sarah?"

Her pen slid off the paper and she straightened in her chair.

"Of course not." The give-away was her voice, squeezed high by the yawning bubble that had frozen in her throat. "Just making notes." She tilted her pad sharply away from Keith who was craning for a look.

"Good," came the crisp reply. "Then you can make a few comments."

"I...really haven't been involved in the new developments. I was away—"

"I know. But you must have formed an opinion. You have some very definite opinions, and you have been making copious notes. Enlighten us, please."

The voice was redolent with sarcasm and Sarah felt even more like a recalcitrant schoolgirl caught cribbing at an exam. Some of the faces around the table grinned expectantly as the prospect of some entertainment loomed.

"I haven't had time to study the mock-up in any detail—"

"Even better. Your regular readers won't get time to study it either, before they're presented with the *fait accompli*. What are your first impressions?"

"Well..." she pretended to look down at her non-existent notes to give herself time to curb her wayward mind. "I did think the changes a bit dramatic, especially, as you said, the typeface..."

"I think I can guess that you would prefer to retain the status quo. But putting the preference aside for a moment, what about some constructive comment," came the dry response.

"That is constructive," Sarah protested. "Our circulation figures are holding steady, surely that's a vote in favour of the status quo."

"Holding steady is another way of saying remaining static. You're keeping your hard-core readers but not acquiring new ones."

"But we can only expect to hold a certain percentage of the market."

"A percentage you haven't quite reached yet. And there's the floating buyer, the one you have to grab at the magazine stand with an eye-catching cover and the promise of good, readable, varied material within. *Rags* has been on the market long enough to be secure, familiar. Now is the time to stimulate the reader by adding a little unfamiliar spice."

"Why not herbs instead of spice? They have a more subtle flavour." One part of Sarah's mind noted that he had stopped fiddling with his pen. Was that a good sign or bad?

"Specify." That singular challenge he was so fond of issuing: explain yourself, talk, convince me. Now she was started she would not retreat. She might be wary about caring for people, but she cared *about* them, about *Rags* and its readers and contributors.

"I don't like Male of the Month," she said baldly to a chorus of disapproval.

"It's a great idea," cried Chris. "It'll be tremendous fun to do."

"Don't be such a stick-in-the-mud, Sarah," said Julie. "Everybody's loosened up these days. It's really just male fashion shots with a bit of personality thrown in."

Backed into a corner Sarah came out fighting.

"It's not the idea that I don't like," she told the room at large. "It's the way it's presented. It's the worst kind of sexism."

"I might have known you were an ardent women's libber," came from the head of the table.

"If that means I have confidence in our women readers' intelligence and taste, yes I am," Sarah shot back.

"What is it precisely that a woman of intelligence and taste would object to?"

The dry cynicism infuriated Sarah. He had asked for her opinion, hadn't he?

"The whole tenor of the article. The captions are pure cheesecake. It may be fun to write, but I think it should be more than just a stereotyped joke."

"You mean . . . take it seriously?" asked Julie sceptically.

"More or less. A sophisticated version. A mood interview piece. There are plenty of attractive men around—" she ignored the laughs and whistles "—from entertainers, to politicians, to businessmen, to the stranger in the next car at the red light. Each month let's get a guest columnist to take out the man of her choice and do an impressionistic story about the evening. Team it with one big colour shot and a few black and white and you have . . ." she searched for the words as her enthusiasm for the idea outran itself.

"The ultimate female fantasy," Julie finished for her. "Sometimes, Sarah, you really surprise me. I like it! I like it very much. It could be very sexy."

"Bags I go first," laughed Chris. "The perfect excuse to ask a man for a date, and on expenses too!"

A light-hearted squabble broke out, relieving the strain of the past hour or more of vehement discussion. Even Max

Wilde relaxed, as much as he was able, chin resting on his steepled fingers, looking every inch a candidate for Male of the Month. Maybe she should suggest it, thought Sarah with an inward giggle, knowing he would detest the very idea. But what a scoop it would be! She was very, very tempted, thinking of all the times he had been provocative, but bit hard on her tongue. Giving in to impulses like that to annoy him invariably got her in over her head, he merely took it as a sign that he was succeeding in getting under her skin. Which he was, dammit! She already spent too much idle time thinking up crushing remarks with which to slam the stable door after the mocking devil had bolted.

Back at her desk after the meeting had broken up, Sarah quickly searched out some documents, intending to slip along to Tom Forest's room at the end of the corridor and inveigle him out to a conveniently early lunch. She was not fast enough, however, because when she looked up Max was standing in front of her desk. He was only half a head taller than she was but he always seemed to *loom*. Come to that he loomed even when he was sitting at his desk which had been placed for his use several paces away. It was most unnerving. Sarah was used to meeting men on her own level, often looking down on them. It was easy to be firmly offputting to a man who was shorter than you. This one was not only tall, but tenacious, with a visible aura of masculinity that offended Sarah as much as his on-again off-again charm did.

Simon had had the charm; getting his own way was easy. Until Sarah discovered that he used it the way he used everything—temper, depression, jealousy—as therapy. He worked out his moods by manoeuvring people into responding in a certain way and then attacking them for it. It gave him a sense of power when his own self-respect was at its lowest ebb. Only when Sarah had refused to play the game, had been angry at his charm, laughed at his depression, shrugged at his jealousy had the real person begun to emerge. But by then it was too late, Sarah's emotions had

been exhausted into apathy. Charm was merely one of the
trappings of personality, no guarantee of inner warmth or
depth.

To Sarah's dismay Max Wilde leaned over until his face
was only inches from hers. He spoke with a slow precision
that was more alarming than his fiery spurts of temper.

"Just once I would like to see you react to me naturally,
and smile as though you mean it, not just out of politeness,
or as a weapon. I don't like it when you're polite and silent.
It makes me curious to know what is going through that
oddly constructed brain of yours."

Sarah shied backwards, almost knocking over her chair
in the process. His words were obscurely threatening but at
least it was some consolation to know that he wasn't om-
nipotent. Her thoughts were still safely wrapped up inside
her head.

He sauntered over to his own desk and sank into the
scoop-backed chair, legs outstretched, crossed at the ankle,
acting as a pivot for the slight movement of the swivel. With
his hands still in his pockets he looked a picture of indo-
lence. Sarah, tense and wary, recognised the all-too-familiar
signs. Eyes half closed, jaw muscles relaxed, mouth deceptively bland—he was about to indulge in some Sarah-
baiting. Killing time until lunch.

"What I can't quite reconcile," he said lazily, "are those
two images, the outraged spinster of Tuesday and the rational, liberated Mrs. Carter of this morning who has sufficient worldly wisdom to recognise the subtle power of the
intellect. The appeal of the sensuous over the merely sensual...that was the gist of your argument about the Male
of the Month, wasn't it?"

She hadn't thought of it in precisely those terms, but in
essence that was exactly it. However, she had no intention
of being drawn into agreement or anything else with him.
He could tie her up in verbal knots, and who knew what she
would end up admitting.

"I really must go..." she said, gathering up the papers she had been looking for, and her handbag, but he wasn't listening. He suddenly seemed to find the gleaming black tip of his shoe interesting.

"Two images," he said softly, and his eyes narrowed even further, then closed altogether. In spite of his olive skin, the lids had an almost translucent quality and Sarah felt a strange disquiet on seeing the delicate blue tracery just under the bony ridge of the eye socket. She didn't want to think of him as flesh and bone and blood, a man. He was an adversary, someone—a person—she neither knew nor liked. She didn't ask herself why.

She was almost out the door when he spoke again, his voice no longer soft.

"One more thing, Sarah."

"Yes?" She half turned to show she wasn't coming back into the room.

"My name is Max. Use it. You're the only one who doesn't. You don't call me anything, but you know very well who I am."

"Very well—" but it still wouldn't come. She wasn't even aware of giving him a name in her thoughts. Ridiculous when she called Tom, older and more deserving of the respectful "Mr." by his first name.

He smiled unkindly. "It'll come. Practise at home, in front of the mirror." He looked at the dark green skirt and blouse she wore. "If you have one, that is."

Even a leisurely lunch with Tom, talking about the points of interest he should see during his visit, couldn't completely banish the sting of that last remark.

CHAPTER FIVE

THE FIRST few moments of consciousness, before she opened her eyes, were the most precious; her mind still adrift among the soft rags of dreams, her senses beginning to register the beckoning warmth of a new day. Summer Sunday mornings were sweet and ripe and made to be enjoyed with slow pleasure.

Tossing back the feather duvet Sarah pulled on a cotton robe. She would breakfast outside.

A few minutes later she carefully mounted the black wrought-iron staircase that spiralled from the dining area to the upper floor, a bowl of muesli and fruit in one hand, a cup of steaming black coffee in the other.

She slid open the ranchslider and settled down on the sun-warmed canvas chair on the balcony, resting her coffee cup on the low wooden divide which separated the stretch of decking next door from her own.

As she ate she surveyed her domain. The sun was well clear of the horizon but it was still quite early, the air fresh and unsullied by the racketings of the human race, except for the quiet purposefulness of the morning church-goers and the far-off meanderings of yachties out pursuing their salty pleasures in the aquamarine bowl of the harbour. A few clouds punctuated the sky but they were innocent flosses of cotton candy, weightless, seemingly unmoving, though the white sails below were plump with satisfying breezes.

"Waiting for me, my love?"

The muesli tilted dangerously as Sarah jumped, hearing echoes of another time, another place.

"Quite the contrary, Roy. Go away and leave me in peace."

Roy Merrill's face, what could be seen of it under thick curling red hair and full matching beard, creased in a grin. He rested stocky, ginger-frosted forearms on the divide and took a sip from her cup, pulling a face at the bitterness.

If one trusted apparel to proclaim the man then Roy, bare-chested and in faded, paint-encrusted cut-off jeans, was easy-going, good-natured and somewhat disreputable. But he was also intelligent and talented; meticulous even—but only on canvas. To Sarah he was the brother she had never had, the one person who seemed to understand her feelings. He was certainly the only man she felt comfortable with, for he had never shown the slightest sign of being interested in her as a woman. That, she supposed, was the strength of their relationship, their complete physical indifference to each other, and their mutual respect. That was how they could live in such close proximity, wandering into each other's home at will, with an easy intimacy uncomplicated by tension.

Considering that he had been such a friend of Simon's, the accord between them was surprising, but it had always been so. Roy, American-born and educated, had been a guest tutor during Simon's first year at art school and had been one of the few people to get really close to the young man, nurturing his talent and using his own well-known name to further his protégé's career. They had even moved into the adjoining town houses when Simon had inherited several thousand dollars and been able to match Roy's investment, an arrangement which had suited them professionally as well as privately.

From the first, Sarah had felt that Roy accepted her as a person in her own right, not just as his friend's wife, and after Simon died their affection for each other had not changed. Roy had been unstintingly kind and asked nothing in return, not even questions. She knew that he was concerned about her, especially since he had been the one to break the news about Simon that awful night, the one to whom she had sobbed out her fear and anger and grief. But he had conspicuously respected her silence since. Until a few months ago. Until now.

"I can't go away, honey," he said. "We had an appointment. Remember?"

She did. Too well.

"I haven't finished my coffee."

"I'll do that. I haven't had any breakfast." Roy was incredibly cavalier about his eating habits. He wasn't above making midnight raids on Sarah's refrigerator, which was well-stocked for just such an eventuality, when working late and smitten by a hunger that wouldn't be satisfied with beer and cold baked beans. "I'll just go and empty a packet of sugar into this while you climb over."

"I'm still in my nightie," she called desperately as he disappeared inside his own sliding door.

"You're wearing more than me then," came the answering call and Sarah sighed. He had finished the painting two weeks ago. She had to see it some time.

She finished her muesli first...she might need the blood sugar. She was just as reluctant now as she had been five months ago when Roy first asked her to pose for him. Not out of embarrassment, for having moved in artistic circles for three years she had acquired a very practical approach to life studies and she had posed many times for Simon. It was a measure of the almost schizophrenic nature of her husband's mind that although he painted nudes of her as an innocent young girl—Eve before she tasted the apple—and quite happily sold them on the open market, if a man so much as smiled at the real, fully clothed Sarah he was immediately suspicious. What did he say to you? What did you say to him? Did you like him? I don't want you to see him again. He seemed to think that because she was young she was easily led, malleable. *That* she had never been.

Embarrassment was the excuse she used on Roy, of course, but he knew her better than to believe it. His insistence and scoffing derision had at last worn her down. He had even gone as far as to reassure her that if she thought the finished portrait was too "revealing" (a grin as he said it), he would arrange for a private sale through his brother, Anthony, who ran a New York art gallery and acted as his American agent.

"We shall make sure you aren't flooded with propositions from hordes of gumbooted philistines and smutty representatives of the gutter press," Roy had boomed idiotically and won his case when Sarah had collapsed into helpless giggles. The posing had been easy, sandwiched in between various commissions Roy was working on, and now it was over the hard part had arrived. Confronting herself.

Slowly she clambered over the wall and walked diffidently into the twin of her own lounge, although this was still a working studio, strewn with canvases and paints, tins and bottles, stacks of junk and crates that doubled as furniture.

"Over here." A shaggy red head rose from the rubble, knocking back the hot coffee with the confidence of a cast-iron constitution.

"The dramatic unveiling," said Sarah nervously as she rounded on the covered easel. He hadn't even let her have a glimpse at the work in progress. "Are you pleased with it?"

"It's good." That could mean anything.

Prepared as she was, Sarah still experienced a shock of recognition, a split-second of envy eclipsed by mental rejection of the voluptuous creature in front of her. Then followed the awesome realisation that Roy was right. It was good. As good as she had feared it would be. A blending of technical skill and raw emotive power so complete that it was impossible to view the painting objectively.

The size was disconcerting to start with. Sarah felt an urge to step back to a safe distance, outside the circle of its compelling, magic spell. It was so lovely... the dramatic chiaroscuro and glowing colours creating an aura of seductiveness reminiscent of Renaissance paintings.

The woman—*not me, that's not who I see in the mirror
every morning*—was half sitting, half lying on a bed. The
background was dark and indistinct, mere glints hinting at
objects concealed in the velvet blackness surrounding the
shadowy frame of the brass bedstead. Warm golden flesh on
the rumpled sheets in the foreground was lit by the soft yellow light from an unseen lamp.

At first glance the nakedness was explicit, but it was an
illusion. The glowing light stroked the subtle contours of the
body, melting away into secret shadows in a subtle por-
trayal of the timeless allure of woman. There was allure, too,
in her expression. Though the face was not classically
beautiful it had a luminous warmth and vibrance that would
outlive mere beauty. She was sensuous, provocative, passionate, and the curve of the full mouth showed un-
ashamed awareness of the fact. But it was a natural, earthy
sensuality that was not too far removed from innocence.

The soft lines and curves evoked physical reality, the
weight of breast and thigh, the play of muscle where the
body stretched and turned, the texture of the downy skin.
The hair was touched with fire as it tumbled in a disordered
mane over sloping shoulders, falling to a rippling pool on
the sheets. Fire slumbered too, in the wide, darkened
eyes . . . inviting eyes, proud and joyfully alive.

Roy, who had been watching her face with some satisfaction, distracted her attention but not her eyes.

"Well, what do you think?"

"I don't know," she said shakily. "Who's it supposed to
be?"

"Don't you recognise her, at all?"

"You have the likeness . . ." she had assimilated that immediately. "But for the rest . . ."

"Not bland, pretty-pretty chocolate-box enough for
you?"

"From you?" That was laughable. "She's very . . ."

"Sexy?"

Exactly. Sarah wrinkled her nose.

"Warm? Loving? Giving?" he continued, arms folded across his barrel chest, a short, almost stumpy man whose flaming hair made such an impact that people usually didn't notice his lack of inches. "What did you expect?"

"I don't know," she repeated and he snorted loudly.

"What kind of artist would I be if I only painted what people wanted to see? You know the kind of work I do. I've wanted to paint you for a long time, you knew that too. Ever since I saw those of Simon's and was so sure I could do better. I had to wait until he was dead, and until you decided you were mature enough to handle what I might do with you. I'm damned if, after five years of waiting, I should have to settle for half a woman!"

Sarah looked back at the painting, surprised by his vehemence. "But *she's* only half a woman." The half that operated on instinct, on feeling, that half that couldn't be trusted, the half that betrayed the *self*.

"Why do you say that? She knows what she's doing and why. Which is a damned sight more than you do, you're just too damned afraid to admit it!"

He grabbed her unexpectedly by the shoulders and said fiercely: "Look at it, Sarah, and like it. It's the best thing I've ever done. You trusted me, enough to sit for me—put yourself in my hands—so trust me now. I wasn't inhibited by living inside your skin—I could see where you wouldn't look. Look now. Be honest. You always used to be."

He didn't wait for an answer. He strode out to the deck and vaulted over on to her side. Probably off to raid her fridge, whistling a tuneless song that told Sarah the rest was up to her. He hated explaining his art, declaring it should speak for itself to those who were willing to understand. Sarah, at last, was willing.

For too long she had been afraid, cheated on the courage and strength she had so grimly gained from living with Simon—her medals of honour, dishonoured by cowardice. She had been afraid of the woman who now looked at her with such sensual pleasure in the satisfied smile. Afraid of her power. Afraid of her vulnerability. So, like a child afraid of the dark, she had pulled the bedclothes over her head and tried to deny the existence of the temptress. "Don't be silly, there's nothing there" her nurse used to say when Sarah awoke in the dark in the grip of a nightmare. Nothing but herself. The most frightening and persistent fears were always the ones that came from within.

Since Simon's death her imagination had had a field day. Her guilt that she had failed him in some way had grown all out of proportion. But what did she owe him now? Only memory, the memory of the good times. To herself she owed life, fulfilment, the realisation of her full potential as a woman and she couldn't do that by refusing to acknowledge her basic drives. She had been frustrated, angered and hurt by the limitations that Simon had tried to impose on her personality, yet here she had been, imposing even stricter limitations on herself in an ultimately more damaging way.

Stepping closer to the mirror-image-that-wasn't, Sarah appreciated for the first time the composed, natural delicacy of the painted image. A woman welcoming her lover, or perhaps bidding a temporary farewell, quite unselfconsciously—a moment of joyous feeling suspended forever.

If only such moments, such feelings were not so rare in real life. When was the last time she felt happy? Not just content but truly happy, the kind of happiness that grabbed the throat and sharpened the perceptions. It was chilling to realise that the answer was not counted in weeks or in months, but in years. She had held herself in like a tightly clenched fist . . . clutching nothing.

Be honest, Roy had said, and she was honest enough to admit that these things did not come as a blinding revelation. She had known for some time that her life had lost its cutting edge, that she was marking time on the brink of change, waiting for the final push that would provide the impetus to finally free her from the constraints of the past. And Roy had given it to her—a gift of all the things that had been unsaid between them. A gift that, in spite of that first, nervous rejection, she had never seriously considered refusing to accept.

For was she, secretly, not curious? She had not allowed herself to be attracted by, or attractive to, men for fear of being trapped again in a suffocating relationship, but the thought of endless, empty, arid years stretching ahead was equally suffocating. Freedom was an internal, not external quality.

Sarah had experienced, and enjoyed, the physical side of love and knew that her body had needs that were no longer being fulfilled. Simon had been her first lover, and her last. But not *the* last... she had never consciously made that decision. Yet she was too intelligent and fastidious to go in for casual sex, too wary to fall in love again so soon. Perhaps the answer was merely to be *receptive,* to begin to test out those womanly instincts that had been so long ignored.

She shivered. What would it be like? she asked silently of the enigmatic painted image in front of her. To feel another man's hands upon her body? To reach out and touch, be touched? To offer herself up to the drenching sweetness of male invasion? The prospect both excited and frightened her, but she no longer feared to think it. She smiled into the dark, desirous eyes.

"Hello, Sarah," she said.

Out on the balcony she found Roy wolfing salami, cheese and olives.

"For breakfast?"

"And last night's dinner, and lunch yesterday. I was busy. I finished the McKenzie portrait, did you see it on the other easel."

"No." The word spoke volumes.

"Well, it's not as good as yours anyway." Roy grinned.

"I've decided I do like it."

"What made you change your mind?" he asked, innocently, knowingly.

"I like it. *But ...*"

"Ah." He sighed. "You're going to raise the spectre of that promise."

"Do you mind?" The private part of her still rebelled at the thought of the public speculation the portrait would cause if shown in Auckland. Roy's work inevitably attracted a lot of publicity. If it hadn't been so... *good*...

"No." He scrubbed some crumbles of cheese out of his beard. "Actually I had decided to send it over to Tony when I was still halfway through. I knew it was going to be special. My market in the States is pretty strong at the moment, it'll fetch a far more inflated price there than here."

"Mercenary beast. That's me you're blithely offering for sale."

"Tony'll make sure you go to a good home, a very expensive home." He rubbed his hands together and cackled. Sarah gave him a friendly thump.

"So my cowardice is doing you a favour."

"If you were such a coward you wouldn't have sat for me in the first place."

"The honour was too great to refuse," she said gravely, and was amused to see the worldly Roy, used to critical acclaim, flush at her sincerity.

"Your freckles are joining up," she said innocently and found herself bundled across to her own balcony.

"On your bike, brat, I've got work to do. Oh, by the way..." Sarah paused. "My hot water heater went on the blink again last night. Can I use your bath until I get it fixed?"

"Well, get it done by a registered electrician this time," said Sarah with a long-suffering sigh, "not a mate's mate. And maybe you'd better stick to showers, last time I recall being locked out of my own bathroom for hours at a time while you turned yourself into a wrinkled prune."

"But a clean prune, love, and didn't I clean the paint off the bathtub when you asked?"

"The place stank of turps for a week," said Sarah, unmollified, and they parted with grins, Sarah lazing around until two o'clock, when she left for Julie's party feeling very light and carefree.

The Somervilles' house was a low L-shaped bungalow with a lounge that opened on to a stretch of glazed quarry tiles spreading around the rectangular pool, which was screened from the neighbours' backyards by a high wooden fence.

Smoke was rising slowly into the still air from the corner barbecue as Sarah slipped in through a side gate. Most of the thirty or so people present seemed to have taken advantage of the trio of changing cubicles to strip down to bare essentials and Sarah had to pick her way over prone bodies scattered around the pool as she headed for the shade of the vine-covered pergola which jutted out from the house. Julie was there, organising drinks at the bar.

"I thought you weren't coming. Where have you been?" she demanded.

"You said any time after noon."

"Did I? Well, you're here now. Help yourself while I farm these out." She picked up a tray of drinks and carried them off, leaving Sarah with the distinct feeling that she had been very relieved about something.

Mindful of the heat and the way these parties stretched, Sarah contented herself with a fruit punch and moved over to watch the dying moments of a violently disorganised game of water polo. She could see Keith and Marie in the middle of the mêlée, slugging it out, and Keith's wife, Danielle, splashing around, helpless with laughter at their antics.

When the game broke up Sarah decided to take advantage of the lull and grabbed an empty cubicle, changing into a plain, streamlined one-piece bathing suit.

The water was deliciously cool on her hot skin and she swam languidly up and down the pool a few times. Though the heat of Auckland's summer sometimes palled, swimming never did and Sarah tried to do a few kilometres every day, at the beach or a local pool.

Just as she was contemplating getting out, she saw Steven Somerville come out of the house with Max at his side. Since he had told her to use his name, she had slipped surprisingly easily into the familiarity in her mind. The verbal barrier remained as yet insurmounted.

Although Sarah had suspected he would be here today she still felt an unpleasant little shock of surprise, and floundering, nearly choked on a mouthful of water. He was wearing only brief navy swimming togs and had a towel slung over his shoulder as he stood talking with Jack a few feet from the pool. Sarah trod water, allowing herself a critical study; there was little enough to criticise.

There wasn't an ounce of spare flesh on his body and although he didn't have a tan, neither did he look unhealthily pale. His olive skin had a natural dark cast that indicated that when he did tan he would do it easily and quickly. Although he was slim he had a hard muscularity; his chest was broad with a fine smothering of dark hair which arrowed down to the flat plane of his stomach. Sarah's eyes slid over narrow hips and strong, lean thighs and she felt an odd feathering sensation inside as he changed his position slightly. He was very nearly naked and for one traitorous instant she wondered what he would look like without that brief covering.

The dark head turned casually towards the pool and Sarah hurriedly turned and swam to the far end. She didn't want him to catch her staring. Mind you, he was probably used to it. It was that arrogant assumption of his that so got on her nerves. She hoped that her new, fragile awareness of herself as a woman wasn't going to manifest itself in mentally stripping every man she looked at. Especially a man like Max, who was overpowering enough covered neck to toe! What had she hoped to discover, anyway? Some hidden defect? A beer belly or knobbly knees? Instead he was like a fined-down version of Michelangelo's "David".

She rested her folded arms on the edge of the pool at the deep end and sought to return her thoughts to the mundane by chatting for a few minutes with Marie, who was dangling her feet in the water and munching on a thick, juicy barbecued steak. When she got up to go and refill her paper plate Sarah was left alone and reluctantly pushed off to swim back down to where she had put her towel. Halfway she came face to face with Max doing a slow, well-disciplined crawl. She returned his pleasant greeting calmly and continued on her way, but he turned to accompany her.

"I watched you from inside, you're an excellent swimmer. Do you swim a lot?"

"Quite a bit. There's a beach on my back doorstep," she replied politely as she reached the steps.

"You're lucky." He forestalled her intention to get out. "I enjoy it too, but I rarely get the chance. When I do, I like to do it in style. I take my boat out on a long cruise and spend as much time under the water as on it. Have you done any scuba diving?"

Conscious of the silver drops slithering from wet sinewy shoulders through the dark curls on his chest, Sarah struggled to keep her eyes level with his. They slowed an unnerving tendency to drift downwards.

"I've had the opportunity but it's never really appealed."

"Afraid of getting out of your depth?" The familiar mockery was a relief, sparking as it did familiar annoyance. "I suppose I shouldn't be surprised that you prefer the shallows. But you should try diving, it's quite an experience, you might even surprise yourself."

"No thanks," she replied tartly. "As you just pointed out, there are all sorts of nasties lurking in the deep."

"I'm sure a water-baby like you would have no trouble outdistancing any...er...devils from the deep," he said, amused by her little dig. "If you wanted to, that is. Or aren't you as confident in the water as you'd have me believe? Another false trail?"

Unsure of what he meant, Sarah frowned. Standing waist-deep in water, hair blue-black in the sun and wet face sponged of several years' age, he did not seem quite as intimidating as usual. Or perhaps it was Sarah who was not her usual self. She was seized with a sudden recklessness, a desire to beat him at his own game of *double entendre*.

"So confident that I don't feel the need to constantly prove myself. That's the prerogative of the male ego," she drawled sweetly.

"You have a thing about the male ego, don't you?" he replied smoothly. "How about indulging mine. A race? There and back…if it's not too much of an effort for you," he added drily.

"No. But it might be for you. Are you sure you're up to it?" That seemed to strike a nerve, for the amused eyes hardened.

"I'm up to anything you can deal out," he told her and the words were barely out of his mouth before she was off. She had no intention of giving him any advantage, fair or unfair, and thus had a fractional start. She deserved it, she told herself, for all the times he had taken unfair advantage of her, knowing she was battling to stay polite in the face of his mockery, yet still pushing, pushing until she cracked and lost her temper. He always looked triumphant when she snapped or got flustered.

She turned at the wall still ahead but he quickly moved up beside her, cutting through the water with an ease that spurred her to fresh effort. His strength was superior but Sarah was quick and light and very much in condition. She was a mere hand's touch ahead when they made the steps again and both rose up, sparkling wetly, to face each other.

There was laughter and desultory clapping from the rest of the party and a few shouts of "*Viva* women's lib" and Max waved away the catcalls with a joke.

"I think she went easy on me."

"Of course I did," Sarah taunted, elated. Victory over him gave her fierce pleasure. "I didn't want the male ego to suffer too much damage."

"And provide my psychiatrist with more work? You obviously have hidden resources, you're constantly surprising me. Congratulations," he told her flushed, triumphant face.

"For surprising you? Or for beating you?" Sarah dared.

"Both. How many more talents are you hiding? One thing at least, that's no longer hidden—you're in excellent shape."

He leaned slightly towards her, placing a forefinger on her shoulder and running it lightly down to the crook of her elbow. She could hardly believe her eyes when he put the finger to his mouth and tasted the water he had stroked from her arm. The lazy flicker of his tongue seemed an intimate suggestion and the look in his eyes confirmed her suspicion that he had made the gesture deliberately, to disconcert her. He did. She could almost feel the rough, moist warmth of his tongue on her skin; the sensation was indecently real and her reaction was to dash water against her arm, washing his touch away.

"And I've discovered that you're not invincible after all," she returned quickly, ignoring a prickle of unease at his rather smug smile.

"Did you think I was?" he asked softly. "I freely confess I'm not. But remember that I don't like to lose too often. It brings out the devil in me." She didn't think the devil *needed* bringing out! "Come on, come and dry off."

"I want to stay in a bit longer," she protested, automatically wanting the opposite to what he said.

"Really?" He looked sceptical. "All right, I'll join you."

For a moment they stood engaged in a silent tussle of wills before Sarah gave in. She had won, she could afford to be gracious...this time. She followed him out of the water and held out her hand for the towel he stooped to pick up for her. But instead of handing it over he held it against himself, just out of her reach, and stared at her body.

Sarah tensed, this wasn't an idle glance, and was fiercely glad that she had not worn a bikini. If she had looked down she would have been aghast to realise that the wet green suit revealed more to the experienced eye than even the skimpiest of bikinis. The shiny, silky fabric clung lovingly close, outlining every curve and hollow like a second skin. Although it took an almost superhuman effort she remained, hand patiently outstretched, as if she didn't give a damn that he was looking at her.

She was momentarily distracted from her agonising self-consciousness when she noticed a faint, almost imperceptible tracery of scars radiating down from underneath his left arm. They were thin and pink and quite obviously permanent. Simultaneously Sarah felt a pang of sympathy and a grim satisfaction that he was flawed, albeit in a small way.

When he moved he took her by surprise, throwing the towel around her shoulders and pulling her close.

"That suit is rather like you," he murmured close to her ear. "Misleadingly demure; until studied in detail."

He held the ends of the towel more firmly, as she wriggled, then stiffened into stillness as her damp thighs brushed his hair-roughened legs. He was so close and she was electrically aware of what seemed like acres of bare skin, his and hers.

"Don't be embarrassed," he continued smoothly, watching her blush with interest. "You have a lovely body. You should wear less more often."

She gasped and he let her go with a laugh. She went straight back to the cubicle where she peeled off the offending suit and used the towel roughly, externalising the tingling feeling. Wretched man! He hadn't seemed very put out at all by his defeat, considering the way he had reacted to her questioning his capability. He should have been annoyed, not amused. She could handle his annoyance, it even made her feel superior in fact, but that way he had of smiling as if at a private joke, a joke on her, was infuriating.

Sarah slipped on the underwear she had packed in the shoulder-bag and pulled the black-and-white sundress over her head. It was a simple uncrushable cotton sheath, elasticised at the waist with a slit to mid-thigh on one side. Simple but flattering the proportions of her body, which most of her other clothes failed to do. Today, for the first time in a long while she had felt the urge to wear something pretty. Now she wished she hadn't. *He* would think she was dressing to impress *him*.

She wrung out her suit over the little grate in the corner of the cubicle and tucked it into a plastic bag. Then, looping a couple of errant strands of wet hair into the dampness of her pleat, she re-emerged, thankful to have her sandals on again as protection from the blistering heat of the quarry tiles.

Over at the bar where she had left her drink Max was mixing something in a short glass. He was wearing white trousers and a slim-fitting body shirt, unbuttoned. He had been quick. No doubt he gets a lot of practice at rapid dressing, Sarah thought bitchily under cover of a smile.

He smiled too. "I think this is the first time I've seen you out of swamp colours. What happened, did the military appropriate your wardrobe for camouflage manoeuvres? Open sandals too. My God, it's positively obscene!"

"It's my day off," she replied, taking a firm grip on the smile.

"And mine. However there is a little matter of business we must discuss. Julie said we can use the privacy of her study." He turned towards the open french doors, pausing with an exaggerated sigh when he realised Sarah had not moved.

"Are you waiting to be proved wrong again?"

"Pardon?" Where was Julie? Why did she get the feeling she had been manipulated yet again into an unwelcome situation?

"This is the second time you've suspected me of having designs on your virtue, isn't it? Never mind, maybe it will be third time lucky!"

CHAPTER SIX

SARAH SANK into the depths of a plush leather chair and eyed Max Wilde across a large coffee table strewn with books and magazines as he did the same. He smiled, the charming smile he so rarely directed at Sarah . . . she wasn't usually worth charming.

"Well?" she asked, with wary politeness. "What business do we have to discuss?" She was almost certain she was about to be chewed out for something.

Silently, he reached for a large black folder lying on top of the magazines, swivelling it around so that it faced Sarah.

"Open it, it won't bite," he said, amused, as she looked at it suspiciously. "I'd like to know what you think. Take your time." And he settled back in his chair as she slowly did as she was bid.

It was a design folio, crammed with a collection of beautiful, bold, dashing sketches. Sarah didn't need to check the sharp, angular signature to recognise the unique style of Sir Richard Wilde.

The contents of the folder were so fascinating that for once she was able to ignore the disturbing man opposite. What a fantastic collection of clothes—feminine and elegant, practical too! As she leafed through, a pattern emerged, a co-ordination of cut, cloth and contrast which was obviously intended to extend the versatility of each basic outfit. There were suits, trousers, skirts, jackets and soft blouses to mix and match; dresses classical and timeless, dresses dramatic and different—casual yet classy, designed for living, breathing women, not just models and mannequins.

The evening clothes were rather more exotic. There was a breath of the East in the high collars, cross-over fronts and formalised lines; the teaming of short, jutting, buttonless jackets in brilliant racing-silk colours with gowns of softer hues. There were also sleek lounging suits and a more glamorous kind of mix-and-match with cobweb-fine shawls and scarves and camisole tops.

With each page were a selection of fabric samples which Sarah fingered appreciatively. They were lightweight wools and wool-blends, silks and soft, easy-fitting knits. The colours were striking and unusual combinations of muted colours with pure, clear primaries. It was not difficult to imagine the myriad ways one could combine the individual elements of the wardrobe to produce variations on a theme.

"You obviously approve," the dark chocolate voice melted into her thoughts.

"Who wouldn't?"

"You. Considering that you seem to be totally uninterested in your own clothes. Yet you must have some fashion sense to be able to do your job properly." He retrieved the folder and put it into a leather briefcase which he then locked and placed back on the floor by his chair. "I thought that anything that didn't feature sack-cloth and ashes mightn't appeal to your introverted taste."

Sarah was too curious to rise to the bait. "Is this the Pacific Collection that there have been rumours about?"

"There's no Pacific Collection as such," she was told. "That's just a convenient smokescreen. What we are releasing here, and in Australia and the West Coast of the States, is a new label—*Images*. Not only a new label, a totally new market for Wilde Fashions—not couture, not mass-market, but somewhere in between."

"What has this got to do with me?"

"Everything. I want you to model a selection of *Images* clothes for a feature in *Rags & Riches.*"

"I beg your pardon?" She must have misheard. That or he was joking in spite of his bland expression.

"Wilde's has offered Julie an exclusive on the Collection for the April issue—it'll come out the week we hold the preview. *Rags* is going to do an eight-page feature in a 'before and after' format, aiming it specifically at the type of woman for whom *Images* is designed. Consider yourself lucky to be the chosen one."

Lucky? Sarah stared blankly at the figure lounging in his chair. To exhibit herself in such a farce?

"It's a preposterous idea," she said coldly. "I've never heard anything so ridiculous in my life."

"On the contrary," he said calmly. "It has many merits, not least as a good PR exercise, both for Wilde Fashions and for your magazine. And there's a more personal reason for you to give your co-operation. When the photographic session is over the clothes you model will be yours."

Sarah opened her mouth but no sound came out. Did he seriously think that made any difference? She was familiar with the type of feature he had in mind, where a bevy of beauty experts turned an ordinary unprepossessing woman into a poised and glossy advertisement for the benefit of clothes and make-up. Done well, with style and imagination, it could be tremendously effective. Done on somebody else!

"I can think of better reasons not to," she told him flatly. "It's still a ridiculous idea—" She broke off and stared at his smug expression. "It was yours, wasn't it? I should have known. No!"

"Of course it was mine. No one else would dare suggest you do something you didn't want to," he replied drily. "But you're perfect. I've never seen a more genuine example of 'before' in my life. This feature will at least have realism on its side."

"It's got nothing else!" snapped Sarah. "You've made it very clear that you don't approve of the way I look. Isn't this a rather extreme and expensive method of pointing it out?"

"Cheap at the price," he mocked. "Since the clothes will be altered to your fitting and since Wilde's isn't in the business of selling second-hand goods, you're being offered them in lieu of payment. Although when I discussed this with Julie on Friday afternoon she did say you'd be delighted to do it for love."

Oh did she? No wonder she had left it to him to break the news. Traitoress! That his comments were logical did nothing to soothe Sarah's ruffled spirits. Why didn't he lose *his* cool for once? He was too damned sure of himself...and of her eventual capitulation! But she didn't want to be reasonable. She was a woman and women were allowed to be perverse, weren't they?

"I'm not delighted and I won't do it," she said sharply, but it had no effect. He continued to look quite unmoved. Sarah searched for something that would emphasise her distaste for the whole idea. "And if you think I'm being coy, you're wrong! Should I feel grateful that you've condescended to play the great benefactor? Does it give you some kind of kick to think of yourself as fairy godmother to poor little Cinderella employees?"

His mouth tightened and there was a flicker of movement in the jawline that made her think that she had hit very close to the mark, but when he spoke it was with a note of boredom that was far more crushing than his anger or sarcasm.

"Don't take it so personally. I was merely pointing out the beneficial side-effects accruing from a business proposition. If you think that I have anything other than a professional interest in the matter then you grossly exaggerate your own importance. And if the idea of owning a Richard Wilde wardrobe is so unthinkable, by all means refuse it. Doubtless we can come to some other arrangement."

Feeling like a child who has just thrown a tantrum in public—foolish and chastened—it was a moment before Sarah registered the implication of that last, throwaway line.

He was still assuming her agreement a foregone conclusion.

"The question of accepting the dresses is irrelevant, since I have no intention of modelling them," she said, at her stubbornest. "Find someone else."

"Don't be in such a hurry to reject an idea you know nothing about," he said patiently, reasonably... infuriatingly. "I admit I expected some opposition from you, but I was sure that at least you would approach it with an open mind. Let me tell you something about *Images*. Then you can make your own decision, and I'll abide by it." He ignored the way she was perching on the edge of her chair, ready to leave, and rolled straight over her half-articulated protest.

"Recent market research has shown that there's a growing, untapped market here for designer fashion in the middle price range. Women want three things: a name designer, a dress that's ready-to-wear but not anonymous, and thirdly and most importantly, one that's not going to break the bank. *Images* satisfies all those criteria."

He continued, outlining the motivation behind the collection with concise rapidity, sketching the progress of *Images* from idea to reality. He made it sound dramatic, appealing and assured of success. Like himself, whispered a tiny voice in Sarah's brain.

If it had been anyone other than Max Wilde describing the idea Sarah would have applauded. But she instinctively hesitated to like anything he did.

"A 'before and after' feature would strike at the heart of the market. Clothes are a confidence-builder and the aim is to show the average woman just how confidently she can wear a Wilde design. You look good, you feel good...it will show."

"So why not find an average woman to model for you?" Sarah inserted.

"I have. You. You may not really be average, but you look it," he said cryptically. "To work, this thing has to be honest as well as dramatic, and with you it couldn't be anything but. We'll do a few paragraphs about you, have a couple of shots of you in everyday wear and let *Images* do the rest."

"You're very confident that it will work."

His face took on a look of hauteur. "I am. I wouldn't help promote a line if I didn't believe in it."

"But why me?" That sounded weak, so she tagged on: "Why not Jane, or Nora?"

He drew a long breath, and Sarah wondered whether that spurious patience was at last running out. Would he give up?

"They already make the best of themselves, you don't. Nor do thousands of other women, women who read *Rags*. They would, if they could; if somebody showed them *how*. You're also quite photogenic—I've seen some of Mike's shots of you when you've been assisting at sessions. In fact you look better in photographs than you do in the flesh, which is another bonus."

"Lucky me!"

"Yes, you are lucky. You have exactly what *Images* is trying to sell—potential."

He moved his arm casually, draping it over the back of his chair so that his hand swung down, touching the folds of his open shirt. The muscles of his chest tautened and relaxed as he did so and Sarah couldn't help being acutely aware again of his body, the separate components that made up the virile whole—nerve, muscle, sinew.

He was watching her now, a faint smile on his lips, as though he guessed the effect he had on her and Sarah felt her old antagonism flare up again. She forced herself to concentrate on what he was saying, to ignore the visual stimuli.

"Most women associate high fashion with beautiful models, thin as rakes and just as human. Something that's fine to look at but never seriously considered as wearable. But basically a model's stock-in-trade is self-confidence, and the high they get from consciousness of their own attractiveness. Beauty is in the mind, not the eye—of the wearer as well as the beholder.''

"I'm still not interested," she cut in on his persuasive flow. "You'll just have to find somebody else."

"Aren't you being rather selfish?" He picked up the drink that he hadn't touched since he came into the room and took a pull, as though he needed it. "You'd be helping your readers, *ergo* your magazine, *ergo* your colleagues. Not to mention yourself. Most women would give their eye-teeth to own ten Wilde creations. You're getting them for nothing."

"I'm not most women—"

"My God, you don't have to tell me that!"

"And I'm not getting them for nothing."

"All but." He finished the drink, fast, then leaned back and pushed his hands into his trouser pockets, pulling the stretch fabric tight against powerful thighs.

"What is it you're afraid of, Sarah... besides yourself? You're not being asked to sacrifice anything. A little publicity won't turn you into public property—it'll be the clothes that are famous, not you. No one will even remember your name. And what is so embarrassingly dreadful about being made to look attractive?" Put like that the two main lines of her defence looked painfully thin.

"I just don't want to do it," she said sullenly, unable to say why she *really* didn't want to do it. It wasn't her own importance she was in danger of exaggerating, it was his! She couldn't shrug off the fatalistic feeling that this man got whatever he wanted, regardless of what obstacles were thrown in his path.

"You mean you don't want to do it... for me," he said, with uncanny perception, and his voice hardened. "Let's take that as read, shall we? Personal considerations aside— your professional good sense should tell you it's a damned good idea. If you like the collection, and you've said you do, you can't claim you have any ethical objections."

Sarah moistened her dry lips with her tongue, feeling herself weaken. He was right, she should put aside her dislike for him personally and consider it purely on merit.

Her hesitation finally exasperated him. "For God's sake, what do you want me to do? Grovel?" All that sweet reasonableness was tossed out of the window when it seemed he wasn't going to get his own way after all. Grovel? She should live to see the day! "I can't believe that even *you* are that self-centred, that humourless. Can't you even do it for a bit of fun? If you forgot about your own hangups for a moment we might get somewhere. It's not as if I'm asking you to strip off for a nude centrefold!"

The absurdity of her intransigent stand suddenly struck her and Sarah laughed, the first genuine laugh she had ever given in his presence. She laughed again when she saw the jerk of his head, the surprised expression that briefly crossed his face. What would he say if he knew she *had* stripped off? Not for a centrefold but for the artistic equivalent. That would be one in the eye for a man who thought he knew all about her just because he'd read her file!

On the heels of the comparison came another. In a way both he and Roy were offering the same thing—a chance for her to step outside herself and see how others saw her. Except Roy's assessment was based on the firm foundations of friendship, whereas the brooding man opposite, who was less of a stranger than she might wish, was dealing with superficialities. Certainly he wanted to use her for his own purposes, for his own profit, but if she accepted would she not be using him, too? A satisfying thought. And why shouldn't she? Why cut off her nose to spite her face? Deep down she really did want to wear clothes like those in the folio, spread her wings a little, explore beyond those limitations she had set herself. It was *time.* And to hell with Max Wilde and his opinion of her.

"What's so funny, all of a sudden?"

"Nothing," she said, not quite removing the grin from her face, seeing and understanding his wariness. He didn't trust her any more than she trusted him. "You're right, of course. When do we do it?"

"Do what?" he asked, very still.

"The feature. I agree. Isn't that what you wanted?"

He recovered himself. "What made you change your mind?"

She shrugged, aiming for maximum annoyance. "But I still think you would be wiser to get someone else."

"No. You're the one who gave me the idea. You're a little on the voluptuous side for photographic modelling, but that's to our advantage in this case." He looked her over again, but this time it was completely dispassionately and Sarah felt none of her former embarrassment. "You've got good skin tone, and eyes and teeth...we may have to do something with your hair—"

"Not cut it," she said quickly, touching the dark mass protectively. There were limits to what her newly restored sense of humour would take.

He shrugged. "That's up to Teresa Grey, our beauty consultant. She and a fitter will be arriving on Wednesday with the dresses. The complete collection won't be sent out until just before it's to be shown."

"Wednesday! So soon?"

"I rang the salon on Friday and gave them your measurements, plus the selection which Julie and I had chosen...they're probably being made up right now. Time is of the essence, I want to see the page proofs before I leave or it will mean sending them to me in London for approval—and frankly I'd prefer that not to happen. A leak at this stage of any of the designs could prove extremely costly."

Only his first few words were important, the rest she recognised as a red herring.

"You gave them my measurements on Friday, before you'd even asked me? That was taking things for granted, wasn't it?"

"It was a calculated risk, I'm used to taking those," he said coolly. "Naturally I was relying heavily on your practical good sense, though sometimes you show remarkably little of it."

Now that he had what he wanted he was prepared to be flippant. Sarah glared at him as he unfolded his graceful length from the chair and strolled over to the small french doors which opened out into a tiny courtyard at the side of the house, lined with tubs of flowering plants and ornamental trees. It was intended to be a little haven of peace but Sarah thought the clutter too studied. Her own tangle of half-wild shrubbery was much more satisfactory.

It really was unfair that the man had so much going for him, Sarah thought as Max braced himself with effortless elegance against the door jamb. It was distracting trying to carry on an argument in the face of such stunning good looks, and even more demoralising when you realised that he had the brains to match. A natural winner.

"We can do the 'before' shots on Tuesday, they shouldn't take very long," he was saying without turning his head. "Bring in a few clothes tomorrow and we'll choose what we want. Wednesday we'll do the fittings and let Teresa take a look at you. The actual shooting will probably take three or four days, full days."

"Well, don't expect me to shout for joy when you wave your magic wand," she said.

"Why? Don't you want to be the belle of the ball? Have the princes paying homage at your feet? Perhaps you're the type who prefers to do the kneeling, though I can't quite see you playing the role of passive submission with any great conviction."

She refused to acknowledge the sexual innuendo.

"I certainly wouldn't go down on my knees before *you*," she scorned. "I'm a little choosier."

"More than a little, from what I can gather," he said obliquely, then settled more comfortably against the door. "Anyway, I can think of far more interesting places for a woman to be than at my feet. Pliancy bores me."

"What a shame, and you must meet so much of it," Sarah said in a breathless little-girl voice, his conceited impudence raising her hackles as usual.

He laughed. "You forget when you smile so sweetly that you also show those needle-sharp teeth! Personally, I find the struggle between predator and prey far more stimulating than a submission without a fight."

She walked into the trap with charming naïvety.

"The idea of man as the predator is rather dated isn't it? Women are no longer hobbled by male prejudices." That wasn't quite true, as she had good reason to know. Several times she had been the victim of one particular male prejudice—the assumption that because she was a young widow she must be sexually frustrated, only too willing to fall into bed with a man, any man, at the mere suggestion of interest. Some of the men she had met hadn't even had the decency to wrap up their opinion in courtesy and had appeared surprised when she very firmly disabused them. She had long ago determined that peer pressure would not rule her life.

"This is the liberated half of the century," she went on hardily. "But perhaps at your age one does tend to live in the past."

"I wasn't referring to *man,* little girl," came the silky reply. "Woman has always held the ultimate power. What chance do we poor males stand against the honeyed webs that are woven around us?"

"None, if you're weak-minded."

Black brows arched. "Do you think I'm weak-minded?"

"Not at all, you're still free of the silken trap, aren't you?" she retorted, rattled that she had let herself be drawn into a discussion that had crossed the borders into the personal.

"You mean marriage? So you see it as a trap, too. Was that what your marriage was?"

Her withdrawal was instant and obvious, like a snail shrinking from a probing finger.

"Was it?"

"I don't wish to discuss it." Not when she was trying to put it all behind her. Not with him, he was far too skilful at recognising evasions.

"Why not?"

"Because it's none of your business." Unfortunately her adamant refusal to satisfy his curiosity only succeeded in arousing it further. She should have been off-hand, joked about it. He was such a dominant man that a sign of weakness was like a red rag to a bull.

"He was a painter, Julie said—your husband. I would like to see some of his work."

"Why?" Sharply.

"Because art is one of my interests, a special interest. Also it might help me peel away another of your layers."

"Why should you care?" she demanded. "I thought I wasn't your type."

He crushed a head of jasmine in his fist and inhaled the fragrance: not a gesture that a lesser man would have made. Much as she hated to admit it Sarah knew his sensitivity was innate, not a pose. He was genuinely perceptive and alive to the subtle variations of human response. That made him so much more dangerous as an opponent—he could follow the complexity of the feminine mind.

"My mind is always open."

"Always? Too busy to keep union hours; you must be a success." Something drove her on in spite of herself.

"When you get to my level, you don't have to belong to a union," he said levelly, eyes watchful. "And I balance my books, thank you."

"I bet you do, you're an expert at juggling figures."

There was an icy silence, during which he levered himself slowly upright. "Be very careful, Sarah," he warned softly. "My patience isn't infinite; you are beginning to annoy me." And then with steel unsheathed: "Is that what all this personal antagonism is about? The fact that I enjoy the company of women and they enjoy mine?"

"That has nothing to do with it!" Even as she said it she was aware that it was a lie.

"But you do disapprove of me, that much is patently obvious. And since I don't think you can quarrel with my professional abilities, it can only be my personal conduct that doesn't meet with your impeccably high standards."

Sarah stiffened angrily at the sarcasm. "Just because I don't fall over myself at your charm—"

"Oh, so you admit that I have charm, we're making progress," he sneered. "Is it me you resent, or the sex in general? Or sex in general?"

"Don't be so disgusting—"

"So you think sex is disgusting," he deftly twisted her words to his own purpose, looking at her with a cold, clinical interest. "Is that what was wrong with your marriage?"

Every time she retreated he was there, baying at her heels. Now she rounded on him, fiercely.

"I told you it was none of your business. Is a woman not a woman simply because she doesn't appreciate your overblown attractions!"

"Overblown?" His thin smile held a glitter of real annoyance. "How Victorian of you, you're the one who's out of date. Coming from a woman, and I use the term advisedly, who is so afraid of her own femininity that she deliberately de-sexes herself, I must take that as a compliment."

The remark, with its grain of unarguable truth, flicked her on the raw and her eyes flashed green sparks of temper.

"And I should be complimented by *your* interest? I suppose I'm impressed that you get as much pleasure from dressing women up as you do from undressing them!"

The instant lift of his head was like that of a hound catching the scent of his quarry and Sarah swallowed nervously as the lean body went into fluid motion, circling slowly around in front of her, coming to a stop a few feet away.

"You really go for the jugular, don't you?" he drawled with ominous restraint. Sarah knew she should apologise but pride imprisoned her tongue. He shouldn't have started asking personal questions.

"Regretting your agreement already?" His mockery was the last straw, and Sarah took from him the one weapon with which she could strike back with impunity.

"What agreement?" she said coldly and turned to pick up her bag from the chair.

Although she had been half expecting something it was a shock to feel his hand lock around her wrist and pull her back to face him.

"You're not going back on your word," he told her tightly.

"I didn't give you my word!"

"As near as dammit!" He jerked her so that she stumbled, nearly crying out from the pain in her wrist. Those elegant-looking hands had the strength of the devil. He looked as if he wanted to hit her almost as much as she wanted to hit him. "I'm warning you, Sarah, don't push me."

"Don't push you!" she exploded, her temper past flashpoint. "How can you push a juggernaut? Why don't you just go away and leave me alone!"

"I can hardly do that now, I'm in too deep," he said tautly, and then, considering her animated face and splendidly blazing eyes, uttered with studious insolence, "Fascinating, you look quite vivacious for once. Want to go one further and take a swing at me?"

She had never wanted anything as much in her life! Sarah lashed out in fury, catching him on the side of the forehead with her tightly clenched fist. His hold slackened enough for her to pull away and dart towards the door, her bag forgotten.

Before she had got three steps he was there in front of her, grabbing her forearms, pinching the flesh between rigid fingers. There was a flush on the high cheekbones and for the first time she saw him fighting for control of his temper. They glared at each other until Sarah, her anger still undiminished, began to struggle.

"Let me go, you're hurting me."

"Not half as much as I'd like to," he ground out, tightening his grip until she whitened.

"I didn't mean to hit you," she gasped. "You shouldn't have invited me to."

"I didn't know you were going to take me up on it. Not the shatterproof Mrs. Carter. Your self-control isn't what I thought it was."

"Nor is yours. *You're hurting me.*" He didn't loosen his grip and a yellow light smouldered in the hazel eyes, promising retribution.

"Well, at least you got it out of your system. You've been dying to do that since we first met!"

"It was your fault."

"Oh no, don't unload your neuroses on me. If you weren't so emotionally stunted you wouldn't have been so bloody hostile in the first place."

"There's no need to swear," she said automatically, her mind functioning on its lowest level. He had a fluent command of the language that rendered swearing obsolete and made his use of it sound doubly vicious.

"I don't suppose you ever do that, do you? You prefer foulness by implication. Very civilised of you."

"Civilised is the last thing I'd call you!"

"Then you won't be surprised if I act the savage," he snarled and shook her hard, until her head fell back and the predatory mouth swooped and fastened on her trembling one in a grinding, relentless travesty of a kiss.

The assault was bruising, insulting in its intensity; the pain in her arms and the soft inner surfaces of her mouth as they were crushed against her teeth excruciating. He meant to punish, to humiliate and subdue, and he succeeded. Although she clamped her mouth shut against the angry invasion she was agonisingly aware of being completely at his mercy. His strength was overpowering, never before had she been so conscious of her physical vulnerability as a woman and her mind sheered off in panic at the thought of what he could do if he chose to exercise the privilege of his strength.

She would have tried to cry out but she didn't dare open her mouth. She wanted to beg him to stop but she couldn't find the breath. He was holding her tight, so tight she could feel his heart pounding against her crushed breasts like a trip-hammer. She was helpless, she couldn't breathe, she was suffocating, she could taste blood on her tongue, she could feel . . . oh, God, she could feel . . .

As suddenly as he had swooped he lifted his head, the yellow light gone from his eyes to be replaced by one she couldn't identify. But she could identify the sudden uncoiling in the pit of her stomach, the smooth, heavy shift. Dazedly she shook her head in repudiation. How could she have felt anything but pain and fear?

"That has the distinction of being a first for me," he murmured huskily into her confused face. "I've never kissed a woman in anger before, at least not in genuine anger."

Her treacherous imagination wondered briefly what dangerous, exciting love games this man might play when aroused. Perhaps he sensed the thought because his hands loosened their hold and the deep, dark pupils of his eyes seemed to expand into her mind.

"I expected you to use some of that athletic ability of yours against me." He let his fingers trail over the marks his grip had left on her arms and felt her tremble. "But you didn't."

"I . . ." She hadn't even tried, she realised, just accepted his strength as superior without testing it . . . *without wanting to.* And where had her anger gone? She should be furious with him for mauling her. "You didn't give me time . . ." she began weakly as his hands slid up to her shoulders. He smiled, an enticing, sexy smile that warmed his face from within and he pulled her towards him again, slowly, gently.

"You have time now . . ." came softly, liltingly.

The change from aggressor to seducer was so swift and complete that Sarah was bewildered, and beguiled. She had wondered, hadn't she, what it would be like to be in a man's arms again?

Curiosity warred with caution. He was no longer threatening, he was almost apologetically gentle and the gentleness lulled her into a false sense of security. A kiss was only a kiss, after all. Just one couldn't hurt.

She forced herself to relax as he murmured her name coaxingly and at the first, light, restrained touch of his firm lips her relaxation became genuine. It was strange...a pleasant, cool caress, demanding nothing, nothing but acquiescence and that was easy.

She leaned lightly against him and he let go of her shoulders to move his hands delicately over the fabric at her back. His skin against hers was smooth and warm, the fresh tang of chlorine mingling with his male body smell. He nuzzled the corner of her mouth and discovered the tender spot where her lip had split against her teeth, touching it with his tongue and gently sucking away the pearly drop of blood.

"Open your mouth, darling," he whispered seductively, "let me taste you properly."

Dreamily, without volition, her mouth opened beneath his, her hands sliding up to rest on the silken shoulders under the thin shirt. It was so warm, so enjoyable, so pleasurable that she let herself drift in the backwash of contentment and when the quality of their embrace began to change she was a prisoner of her own response before the danger even registered.

The strong, slender hands touched her neck, moved up to her face, cupping it, positioning it so that he could explore her mouth more freely, deepen the warm, rapid kisses to slow, sensual ones. Her own hands slipped on the tense muscles of his chest, fingers tangling in the dark hair there, clenching as her body clenched with impossible yearnings. She could no longer think, only feel, her senses reawakened to passionate life. And as the ravishing fantasy continued it was no longer curiosity that drove her to arch against the virile hardness but something more compelling, more elemental, that strove for expression.

Without knowing it she murmured his name and as he felt her body strain against his he gave a small grunt of satisfaction, shifting his stance and allowing his hands greater licence. They roved over her body in a journey of discovery, burning through her thin dress, describing slow, erotic circles.

His mouth roamed too, nibbling her tender ear lobes, gently biting the apple-smoothness of her shoulders left bare by her cutaway sleeves, burying itself in the sensitive arch of her throat. She shuddered as his hands slid into the small of her back, pressing hard, and she moaned into his open mouth, losing the final shreds of her reserve, feeling his tongue flickering against hers as though drinking in the sound. She had never known such darkness and heat and sweet, sweet, sensation.

How long they remained like that, fused into a sensual world bounded by each other's arms, Sarah had no idea, for time was out of joint. It was a sharp, alien sound that divided them. A door slamming and nearby voices.

He still held her by the arms, she would have fallen if he had not; but only for a moment. Then he blinked, and the wide, dark pupils narrowed again like camera shutters and he stepped back, breathing with the same shallow intensity that he had after their race in the pool. The world steadied and righted itself and Sarah was appalled by the damage done. Nothing had changed, yet everything had. Herself especially. She could feel herself shaking like a stupid schoolgirl and stuttered into stupid schoolgirl speech.

"I thought you didn't have any designs on my virtue." Her voice was a thread of sound but he heard, and his mouth twisted.

"It's not your virtue that tempts me," he said softly, with wry self-mockery and Sarah felt a renewed surge of heat through her body. God, what was the matter with her? She wasn't a green girl. Had she kept herself under control for too long, ready to fall like a ripe plum into the hands of the first man who kissed her? She closed her eyes in embarrassment and backed away. Even a man whom she found personally objectionable? She looked around for her bag, desperately trying to avoid looking at Max. She couldn't bear to see amusement on his face.

"What shall I tell Julie your reaction was?" he asked as her hand connected with the door handle. For one awful moment she thought he meant the kiss and spun around to regard him with apprehensive stone-grey eyes. "To *Images,*" he added helpfully and she flushed.

"I...tell her you charmed me into it!" It was a lovely exit line but unfortunately she fumbled it. The door handle seemed to stick and he had to come to her aid. He didn't laugh though, he was quite kind, which to her oversensitised mind was worse.

CHAPTER SEVEN

IF SARAH had harboured any remaining illusions that modelling was an easy, glamorous profession, working on the *Images* feature would have completely eradicated them.

After a deflatingly brief morning posing in her own clothes for the merciless eye of the camera, Sarah was hustled unceremoniously into a world of discomfort and tedium. She was made-up and made-over, pinned and poked, pushed and pulled, primped and posed. She was stared at, talked about, teased and tested, treated like an empty-headed puppet dancing obediently for anyone who pulled the strings. And of course it was Max Wilde pulling the strings.

There were compensations. The clothes were lovely, *she* looked lovely in them, and she didn't need Julie crowing over her to tell her that...it was self-evident. And the experience itself was interesting, if exhausting.

Teresa Grey had been an unexpected bonus. Not the glamorous, intimidating sophisticate that Sarah had dreaded, but a dizzy gamine-faced blonde prone to fits of the giggles, and given to ordering Max about with an easy familiarity that was enviable. She was also a whizz at her job and Sarah watched, fascinated, as the girl rang the changes of make-up and hairstyle, searching for precisely the right look for each *Images* ensemble—and finding it.

She had been cheerfully disgusted at Sarah's lack of interest in herself.

"You should be ashamed, letting yourself go at your age," she had scolded on the first day, testing Sarah for colour and skin-type and pointing out all her weaknesses with professional frankness. "I bet you've even been lazy about using cleansers and moisturisers. Now is the time to take care of your skin, before it's too late, especially if you spend a lot of time in the sun.

"You've got fantastic hair!" Her hair had surprised them all. Not even the colleagues she had worked with for three years had known of her great abundance. "And great bone structure and you're just letting it all go to waste. Watch me and you'll get the idea...it's all a matter of colour and contour and balance."

Max had been irritated that the project was taking a little longer than he had anticipated, conscious no doubt of the limited time available to him, and being the most convenient whipping-boy at hand, Sarah often felt the sharp edge of his impatience. He seemed to take little account of the fact that she wasn't a professional model and expected her to anticipate his demands before he made them—then was angry when she didn't. It was very hot in the tiny studio with the lights on and Sarah found her own temper shortening appreciably, but she tried not to let it show. She was intelligent enough to appreciate that they were all working under pressure, the pressure of time and the more subtle one of making a success of what they did, though no one really seemed to believe that Max's idea could fail—not even Sarah.

He was a perfectionist too, which made him all that much more demanding. Sarah spent endless hours hanging around, waiting for some infinitesimal lighting fault to be corrected, or listening to an incomprehensible discussion about angles, or lenses, or shutter speeds. Max revealed a technical and artistic knowledge of photography that Mike Stone, the magazine's talented photographer, was forced to respect, even to the extent of letting the other man override his professional opinion on occasions.

Sarah being an amateur among professionals, wasn't supposed to have opinions. She was just supposed to obey orders without question. And she was frustratedly aware that it amused Max to have her in a situation where she couldn't refuse or obstruct him without seeming childish and churlish; where she had to smile when he told her to, put up with being critically discussed over the top of her head as if she wasn't there, and touched... always he was touching her, twisting and turning her, arranging her limbs or the tilt of her head. Usually it was with a remote concentration that belied the odd physical sensations that Sarah experienced at his hands, but sometimes his fingers would linger a fraction too long, or his eyes would gleam with a knowing light as she tensed at his touch, a tacit reminder that he knew she wasn't as indifferent as she affected to be.

It was annoying, after she had expended so much effort in reassuring herself about that kiss. How it didn't matter, how it made no difference. She was convinced that her explosive response to his lovemaking had been quite normal in the circumstances. She had recognised right from the start that he had sex appeal, but her intellectual acknowledgement hadn't prepared her for the potency of the physical reality. She was, after all, a relative innocent in terms of male-female relationships, whereas he was an expert. His sensual technique had been polished with practice... it wasn't surprising that she should feel overwhelmed by it.

She had been naïvely curious, but his motives for kissing her that second time had been more obscure. Pique? Reflexive masculinity? Anyway, what did it matter? To ponder his reasons implied that she wanted to know, and she didn't. Far safer to dismiss it as a flash in the pan on both sides. Max was a graduate in the volatile science of body chemistry and it would be extremely unwise for a mere beginner like Sarah to start experimenting with him. At least she knew that she still had normal female reactions, she needn't worry that she had let them wither away through lack of use. And apart from anything else she still didn't *like* the man, he was too cynical, too hard, too... unsettling!

Even when he was being pleasant to her, it was in a back-handed sort of way.

"You're a natural," he told her on the second morning of the "after" shots as she stood in the small, white-painted dressing room while Teresa made a few last-minute passes with powder and hairspray. "You don't even have to do anything. Your face isn't expressive, but it has that touch of aloofness that photographers kill for."

Sarah looked into the mirror. The jumpsuit was silver and white with quilted, slightly pointed shoulders, a wide silver cinch belt and narrow legs. Silver threads and beads had been woven into dozens of long, thin plaits which had taken Teresa and a local hairdresser hours to do but which looked spectacular. Too spectacular for Sarah. "I look like something from outer space."

"Extrovert is the word I think you're looking for," Max replied, watching her turn to see her back view. "Agreed, it's totally different from the other clothes we've chosen but a touch of fantasy will give the sequence a lift. It may not be what you would choose yourself to wear but it symbolises the *Images* message: the way you dress can alter the way that other people perceive you, and the way that you perceive yourself."

How do you perceive me now? Sarah wanted to ask, but prudently held her tongue. It was enough that the mirror gave her an odd sense of displacement, showing her a fantastic, wayward creature who didn't appear to give a damn about conventions. Who had never heard the word "safe". A dangerous perception.

"I think I like the grey best of all," she said firmly. The dove-coloured three-piece suit in fine wool was her idea of high fashion—pencil-slim skirt, tapered trousers and pert stream-lined jacket with narrow revers.

"It suits you, I'll admit," came the amused reply. "A very soothing, understated elegance ... until one receives the shock of the sexy, passionate pink blouse. Then it's diffi-cult to see anything else." He sauntered out, leaving her wondering whether she detected wider implications in the remark.

She was instructed to leave the plaits in overnight, and a most uncomfortable night it was, too. The next day Teresa unbraided them with startling results. Sarah's hair fluffed out like a woolly pelt, floating over her shoulders in a mantle of tiny waves to complement the Pre-Raphaelite look of a thin, flowing white-tiered gown with a bodice embroidered with a glowing William Morris design.

As she stood among the masses of perfumed flowers that were to provide the backdrop for the dress, Max had come close to arrange a drift of hair so that it would not conceal the beautiful embroidery across her breasts. He took some time to do it to his satisfaction and then briefly touched the tiny corkscrew tendrils at her temples.

"Ah, yes. Perfect," he murmured, regarding his work. Then he looked into her eyes and the abstraction on his face slipped—he smiled very faintly, making an intimate secret of it. His eyes dropped to her mouth, lingered, and came up again. A kiss by proxy. A delicious tingle shot through Sarah's body and for a moment it was as though she could feel those hard arms around her, the black head coming down to block out her vision, the warm spicy breath of him in her nostrils. It made her feel weak, lethargic, passive.

"Just relax this time. Don't try and project anything, in fact keep your mind completely blank. Let whoever looks at this picture project their own thoughts into you." His eyes went to her mouth again. "Open your mouth."

"W...what?"

"Not that much," he told her impatiently and she realised he was completely businesslike again. He lifted an imperious hand to her jaw and applied a controlled pressure. "Slightly. That's right. Teresa! Could we have the gloss off her cheeks, please?"

Shakily, Sarah wished she could keep up with his rapid changes of mood. Probably he'd forgotten those enticing words he had muttered against her lips that day. She hadn't, and his using the same phrase had almost panicked her. She had thought he was going to kiss her again, right then and there. She had *wanted* him to. She really had to pull herself together!

Fortunately for her nerves, Friday was a free day. Max and Tom flew down to Wellington to attend a national fashion award luncheon and the shots of the last outfit, a red evening dress, were scheduled for the following Monday. The fact that the day seemed rather flat Sarah put down to the anticlimax of nearly having finished her part in the feature. Rattling around in the office she even found herself looking forward to the harbour cruise that Julie had organised for Saturday. Nothing to do with the fact that Max would be among the twenty or so guests!

As it was she didn't see him for the first forty minutes of the cruise, he was too busy charming all Julie's valuable business contacts. Sarah, meanwhile, had a pleasant, undemanding conversation with Tom at the stern rail of the blue-and-white motor yacht.

"It's a beautiful location for a city," he told her as they watched the busy marina recede, framed in the background by the grey arch of the harbour bridge. "So unspoilt compared with many I've seen."

As they creamed around the southern end of Rangitoto Island past the armada of small craft, crewed it seemed by clowns in brightly coloured life-jackets and sunhats, their faces smeared with the ubiquitous white zinc protective cream, Sarah listened to Tom talk about some of the exotic places he had visited.

"Have you ever considered working abroad?"

Sarah swung around at the interjection. Max had obviously overheard her conversation with Tom about faraway places. He was dressed in a red-and-black striped T-shirt and white trousers, with mirrored sunglasses masking his eyes. He casually moved up beside them and repeated his question about working overseas.

"Does the prospect appeal?" he pressed.

"No." Up until now she had been too securely wrapped up in her comfortable life.

"It should. You have a good head for the publishing business, sound managerial skills. The opportunities in a country like New Zealand must be very limited; you might consider the challenges and opportunities that exist elsewhere."

"But..." She raised her eyebrows at him and he looked amused.

"But what?"

"You don't usually pay me a compliment unless it has a sting in its tail."

"I'm not paying you a compliment. I'm voicing a simple truth...of which you are already aware. If I was paying you a compliment I would tell you how delicious you look in that green thing."

She glared at him, recognising the teasing inflexion. It probably stood out like a sore thumb that the stretch towelling playsuit was new. Stung into action at last by seeing the inescapable contrasts from the early proofs of the photo shots, Sarah had splurged out, buying more clothes in a week than she had in the past two years.

"I think I prefer the one about managerial skills," she said severely, trying to ignore the fact that he had moved closer, and the long muscled forearm braced against the rail was nearly touching hers. She shifted her weight on to her other foot so that she could lean away slightly. It seemed important that he shouldn't touch her.

"Why? Because the other's too personal? We've worked quite well together this past week, I thought you might have changed your mind about not liking me. Most people like me, why not you?"

"Such arrogance," Sarah sniped, knowing what he said was fact, not fiction...he wasn't given to boasting. "I suspect you mean most *women*, and that you're talking about loving, not liking."

Her sarcasm rebounded as he grinned rakishly. "I don't think love has much to do with it either."

"That doesn't altogether surprise me."

"Because I don't debase the currency? People use the word too freely and rarely mean it in the truest sense. If I said I was in love with every woman I went to bed with I'd be fickle, or a liar. If I don't say it, I'm a satyr. Either way I can be accused of something, but personally I prefer honesty. If ever I fall in love I'll be able to use the word in all its pristine purity."

"You might never use it at all at that rate," Sarah felt constrained to point out, though his words echoed an answer in her heart. She too believed that love was too precious a word to be bestowed willy-nilly on everything from ice-cream to the deepest of human emotions. At least a woman, if she got involved with Max Wilde, would always know where she stood. There would be games, but no pretence, and freedom on both sides.

"Perhaps not," Max drawled. "But I'm having a hell of a time discovering what love *isn't.*"

As if to demonstrate, the rather lovely daughter of a wool yarn manufacturer gravitated over and so obviously hovered that Sarah was bound to introduce her. Hazel eyes glinted briefly into grey as Max switched on the charm. As she withdrew, Sarah suffered twin impulses—one was to push Max overboard, the other to give the lovely young thing a ducking! Instead she decided to take one herself and clear her head which was fizzing with notions of what love *wasn't* for that long-limbed devil. The *Pacific Lady* had reached its destination, a private island, owned by Julie's friends, just south of Cape Rodney. Sarah could hear the rattle of the anchor chain, and with any luck she would be able to experience the matchless feeling of stepping on a shore unmarked by footprints, human or animal.

She changed into her bikini in one of the guest cabins and tipped the skipper a wave as she quietly swung herself over the side and into the water. It was quite cold at first, but invigorating, and she struck out strongly for the beach several hundred metres away.

The small, deepwater crescent was the island's only bay, sheltered from the Gulf winds by rocky promontories at either end which formed a small natural harbour free of hazardous currents. The narrow band of white sand rose steeply to a ridge of boulders, beyond which was sandy tussock grass and the first close stands of trees. A pole house nestled in among the trees somewhere, a "bach" the owners called it, a palatial spread was Sarah's term.

As soon as she made land, Sarah clambered over the rocky ridge to settle out of sight of the boat on the soft upward slope of grass. She lay on her back with a gusty sigh, her head in the shade of the contorted pohutukawas, letting the heat of the early afternoon roll over her. She felt her skin tighten as the sea-water evaporated, leaving tiny encrustations of salt caught in her silky-fine body hair. Wrapped in a cocoon of peace she drifted in and out of a light, refreshing doze. So warm and peaceful . . .

She awoke to a shiver of water drops and at first thought it had begun to rain, but when she opened her eyes she was dazzled. The shade of the trees had shortened and she was lying in the sun's full heat.

More droplets and she shaded her eyes and squinted at the wet figure which dropped on to the grass beside her. A brief dizziness which could have been the effects of the sun overtook her—her companion was Max.

He lay on his side and propped his head on one hand and Sarah let her own head drop back. She closed her eyes again, forcing herself to lie unmoving on her back for a few minutes more. In her imagination her already brief green bikini was shrinking further under his interested stare. At last she allowed herself to turn over casually and bury her hot face in her folded arms.

Long, long moments passed and when he laid a flat palm on her back she felt scorching shock.

"Don't."

"You're sandy," he said quietly, and began dusting her back. She lay rigid until his hand moved to the backs of her thighs.

"That's enough!"

His hand was removed immediately, but if anything she was even more conscious of his presence.

"You are quite the most nervous female I know. And lately you're even more tense. Did you expect me to apologise for kissing you?"

"No, of course not," came the muffled reply. Perhaps if she buried her head in the sand...

"No. Not when you showed such unmistakable signs that you enjoyed it as much as I did." And when she stayed silent, "Didn't you?"

She shouldn't have come. She should have stayed with the crowd on board the boat. Safe. Why hadn't she? *Because you wanted him to come after you,* niggled her illogical brain. *Because you knew he would.* Not through any reasoned process, but by instinct.

"Didn't you?" he demanded with rough impatience. "Damn you, Sarah, look at me!"

He was quite capable of forcing her to, if impatience turned to anger. Sarah rolled on to her side, putting plenty of grass between them; she couldn't meet his eyes though, and looked instead at the scarred chest.

"I meant my face, not my body," he mocked and she flushed and stammered.

"I—I was just wondering about the scars."

"I was in an accident," his hand came up to stroke them lightly and the voice changed subtly, insinuatingly. "I was in a great deal of pain for some considerable time."

She looked at him suspiciously. The hazel eyes were wide and innocent. He was exaggerating in the hope of softening her up. The scars didn't look that bad.

"I suppose a champagne bottle exploded over you, or the lady got over-excited."

He showed his teeth in appreciation. "Vixen. Do *you* scratch when you get over-excited?"

Again things were moving too fast for her and she closed up. "No. I slap faces," she said distantly and half sat up to look over the rocks. No sign of anyone else taking to the water and the rubber outboard dinghy still rocked emptily where it had been lowered beside the yacht.

"Did he hurt you very much?"

"Who?" She tensed. Max gentle was Max devious.

"Your husband."

She caught her breath and speared him with dark accusing eyes. "Why are you always asking questions?"

"I'm interested. If I'm curious I ask questions. It's normal. So is answering them."

Quite. And she would have to get over her almost pathological reluctance to talk about Simon some time. But now? With Max? It could lead to all kinds of complications. However she knew from experience that evasions only whetted Max's appetite for information.

"I just don't happen to think it matters any more," she said with almost complete truth.

"But it does if it affects your attitude to me, to men in general. What was he like?"

"If he had lived he would have been a great painter," she stated non-committally.

"I meant as a man," he said, adding to her ruffled profile. "I'm not your enemy, Sarah."

No, nor friend neither.

"He was very—" she hesitated, how to put it into words that said not too much, but not too little? "He was very...possessive." It was a relief to say it, to relinquish another stubbornly held piece of the past. Easy, too, once said.

"Did you resent that?"

"Not at first. I was very young when we married, but it became very wearing. And painful, for both of us," she told the rocks, the sea, the sky...the world.

"Jealousy is often indivisible from love, I believe," came the remark, challenging in its very neutrality.

"He wasn't just jealous," she turned on him fiercely, "he was obsessive. He expected me to live through him, for him—"

"Aaah," his sigh filled the silence as she broke off and he lay back, his hands under his head, with a ripple of glistening muscle across his chest. Sarah looked at his closed eyes, the slight smile on the sensual mouth.

"Why do you say it in that tone of voice?" she asked.

"Because it explains a lot," he said without opening his eyes.

"What?" Sarah demanded, goaded by his reticence, for once able to appreciate how irritating he had found her reserve in the past.

"Why you're so scared of involvement. Why you're so wary of men. Why you back off at the slightest sign of interest."

"I didn't back off at Julie's party," she said, feeling defensive without knowing why.

"Only because you were curious," he said lazily. "Did you think I didn't know that? I'd hurt you and you wondered what it would be like to be kissed better." One eye opened, catching her out in a flush. "I hope I managed to satisfy your curiosity."

"Adequately," retorted Sarah curtly and he grinned.

"You must practise these put-downs in private." He could read her like a book, it seemed. Both eyes now fixed brightly on her as she plucked a blade of grass and studied it.

"How was he killed?"

She was used to the abruptness by now, and had discovered that an abrupt reply was the best answer.

"A plane crash." There was an instant's stillness, then he sat up again.

"I'm sorry."

"You didn't know him."

"No. But I know you."

For some reason his gentleness upset her.

"Well, I wasn't sorry. At least not for us. For him. For me. But not for us."

If she had hoped to shock him she was disappointed. He just, very softly, lifted one hand to her chin and tilted it up towards him.

"And now? What now? Are you still sorry for yourself? Still afraid?"

She pulled her chin away, eyes sparkling greenly.

"No. And I don't need your particular brand of therapy, thank you."

"And what brand is that?"

"Sex!" she blurted out. It was a mistake, an admission of a kind, and physical awareness snaked out to encircle them both.

"You should wait until you're asked," he murmured mockingly, "but would that be so awful? Sex has nothing to do with possession, not in the psychic sense—it's a sharing, giving and taking in equal measure. I have no intention of hurting you, Sarah."

"Then leave me alone." That smooth, creamy, coaxing voice slid insidiously along her sensitive nerves.

"Your lips say one thing, your eyes another," he said, reaching out for her.

"You arrogant, conceited—" she gasped as an arm fastened around her waist, curving her close to him on the soft cushion of grass. His other hand came up behind the damp coronet of her hair and his mouth neared hers, lips curving, parting. Fearful...wanting...she closed her eyes and waited for the soft touch of his mouth and when it didn't come she opened her eyes again to find him grinning at her.

"See?"

Her teeth snapped shut and she wrenched herself away and scrambled to her feet. So he thought she was going to succumb easily to that practised charm! She almost made it away from him, but he was too fast for her, grabbing her ankle as she stepped out, and the result was an ignominious tumble down the slope almost to the foot of the rocks.

She was still lying, breathless, in a little sandy hollow when he reached her, placing his hands on her bare waist, holding her down, laughing openly as she hit out wildly. It was all a great game to him, he didn't care whether he was hurting her or not.

Her blows had no effect. He merely held her until at last she stopped and lay panting, glaring at him, hot and flustered by the sun and the struggle and the pressure of his hands against her ribcage. She was terribly conscious of their lack of clothing, only her two scraps of fabric and his thin blue swimming briefs between convention and nakedness. She moved restlessly, feeling the delicious languor of desire begin to weight her limbs.

Suddenly, disappointingly, he let her go and sat back on his heels. Sarah, bewildered by a sense of loss, lay staring at the thin, serious face. No trace of his former mockery remained, only a kind of tender restraint that made Sarah's heart lurch oddly.

"That was unfair of me," he said, amazingly. "I don't want to make you do anything that you will regret. All I want to do is kiss you...or rather, for you to kiss me."

Sarah's eyes widened. Max humble? Max *asking*? She must be hallucinating! In her experience men didn't usually ask, they took first and asked later!

"I..." What could she say? Yes, I want to kiss you but I don't want to want to? Remembering what had happened the last time she shivered, she had gone in over her head.

Max met her uncertain gaze quite openly as she too got up on to her knees, wanting to brush the sand from herself but afraid to draw his attention to her betraying body, which still felt warm and tingly.

"Look, no hands," he said softly, and spread his arms, palm up, out from his sides.

Was this another part of his game? Sarah, distrustful, was yet bewitched by that uncharacteristic supplication of his.

Her eyes were drawn to that firm, flirtatious mouth, and she imagined renewing her acquaintance with its pleasures.

"Promise?" she murmured absently.

"Cross my heart," was the grave reply.

Her eyes fell from his mouth to his chest, where the dark hair curled damp, now matted with sand and a few thin strands of grass. As she watched, the tenor of his breathing changed, became slower, the rise and fall of his chest acquiring a deep, hypnotic rhythm. There was a peculiar attraction in knowing that he was waiting on her, that he had placed the situation firmly in her hands. That she was in control.

Tentatively, she touched him, she couldn't help it, resting a hand just above his heart, feeling the strong, rapid beat. It was like feeling the beat of her own heart.

"Sarah?" the word was low, husky, almost strained, and she looked up. The expression on his face made her tremble inside.

Very carefully she moved closer and kissed him, very quickly and lightly on the lips and drew back. No threatening reaction, he merely knelt there, waiting. Feeling bolder, she kissed him again. Again no reaction; it was like kissing a warm statue, and just as unsatisfactory.

"What's the matter?" he asked of her frown.

"You're not helping," she told him, piqued.

"You want me to?"

She eyed him silently.

"All you have to do is say 'stop' and I'll stop," he said and Sarah found the thought immensely liberating. In this she could trust him. He was not a boy, likely to lose his head, and he was too civilised to attempt a complete seduction here on the beach where they might be interrupted at any moment—she could hear the outboard motor spluttering to life across the calm bay. She felt safe, and she leaned forward again and put her mouth against his, a streak of pleasure shooting through her as he allowed her to coax his lips apart.

She edged closer so that the tips of her breasts brushed his chest and he began to move his tongue, slowly and erotically against the sensitive lining of her mouth. They kissed slow, sensual, heat-drugged kisses and Sarah yielded herself up to the entrancement of the moment; the fragrance of the crushed grasses, the salty tang of his lips, the soft warmth of the air all combining in a heady invitation that she had no will to resist. She would never have believed that there was such pleasure to be had from a mere kiss. Her hands stayed pressed against his chest, measuring the beat of his arousal, while his stayed obediently at his sides and yet his mouth was so skilful at enticing her enjoyment that her whole body became suffused with sensation.

"Max..." she sighed as the kiss was broken at last, her eyes stormy with passion, her head thrown back as she looked up at the hard-edged face above her.

"Will you let me touch you?"

Sarah nodded automatically, aching for the stroke of his hands upon her body, still trusting.

He made a soft, murmuring sound and lowered his head to hers, moving his powerful body against her in a sensuous, sinuous movement, one hand slipping in between them to cover her breast as her arms linked around his neck. At the sudden, more aggressive thrust of his tongue in her mouth, the fine tremor that shook his body, the iron-hard pressure of his thighs, Sarah dazedly took fright, alarm bells ringing frantically.

"No, stop—" was muffled against his mouth yet he instantly pulled away, or rather pushed her away, hands gripping her shoulders tightly.

"See?" he said thickly, with a crooked little smile. "Gentle as a lamb. Putty in your hands."

"I think that's one metaphor too many," Sarah mumbled distractedly and his smile became more natural as he dropped his hands from her shoulders and flexed them by his side.

"We'll see. Have dinner with me tomorrow night?"

She wasn't that naïve. "I'm tired—it's been a busy week."

"For us all. A very quiet dinner, at a very quiet restaurant."

"At a very quiet hotel?" she asked drily.

"The thought never crossed my mind," he told her, looking innocently hurt. "Julie has recommended several fine restaurants and I would like to try one in congenial company."

"I'm sure Tom would love to go.'

"I can dine with Tom any day of the year. I want to go with you. I want to talk to you, get to know you. Haven't I just demonstrated how trustworthy I am?"

Only in the sense that he could exercise self-control when it suited him...to serve a purpose. She didn't doubt that he was using the verb "know" in the Biblical sense, he wasn't proposing to give her dinner just for the intellectual pleasure of good conversation.

On the other hand, she admitted to herself, she wanted to accept the dinner invitation. Even at his most dislikeable, Max was stimulating company and her very mistrust of his motives would protect her from the verbal seduction she was sure he would attempt. It would be a challenge, in a way, as no doubt he found her a challenge. There was no reason why she should not participate in the game, providing she obeyed her own rule: remember who he was, what he was. She would enjoy herself as an adult woman in the company of an attractive man, but she wouldn't enjoy herself *too* much. She had the rest of her life to explore relationships with men; no sense in rushing her fences simply because she had come to terms with the fact she was a woman, free to pursue her own life, her own desires, accountable to no one but herself.

"It's Sunday, there mightn't be many places open." She made a last, half-hearted salute to the boring demands of common sense.

"We'll find one." He held out a hand to help her up, which Sarah pointedly ignored.

He was sounding smug again, which she thought was one of his least attractive habits. So when he headed up towards the track which led to the concealed holiday home, Sarah turned and made her way back down to the water's edge, intending to swim back to the yacht forthwith. A demonstration, she hoped, that one Yes didn't concede submission. She hoped.

CHAPTER EIGHT

SARAH TOOK more care over her appearance on Sunday evening than she had for a long time. She needed to feel sleek and well-groomed, a nice thick coat of plaster over the cracks in her confidence. Was she ready for this?

Deciding what to wear had put her in a quandary. She had not yet got around to buying evening wear and, anyway, she didn't want Max to think she was trying too hard to impress him. On the other hand she didn't think he would appreciate being seen with a woman who didn't wear her clothes well. In the end she had fossicked out her dateless "basic black". Simple, long and figure-hugging, it was in a silk-knit jersey, slightly gathered under the breasts, with delicate shoe-string straps.

Trying to damp down her feelings as the hour approached, Sarah wished, for the first time in her life, that she had a sister, or a close female friend, someone who could give her some sound advice on how to approach the evening. With care, of course...but should she be off-hand, flippant, or should she try a serious appeal to Max's better nature—if he had one! Tell him that he was going too fast for her, that she was not prepared to indulge in anything more than a light flirtation? To her fevered brain even her reflection in the bedroom looked slightly sceptical. Just what *are* you prepared for, Sarah? she asked herself, and shrugged. What the hell, she would take things as they came, one at a time. For tonight she would have no past, no future, just a present. That would have been Roy's advice, if he had been here to give it.

Sarah turned off the upstairs lights and made her way
carefully down the spiral staircase. The last time she had
seen Roy was the previous morning, when he had bounded
in as she was getting ready to leave for the marina, wanting
a shower and staying on for a bacon and egg breakfast.

"I'm taking off up north for a few days, tomorrow," he
had told her, wolfing his food. "Do a bit of sketching, look
up a few friends, so I shan't be monopolising the bathroom
any longer. I have a guy coming in to fix the hot water cylinder on Tuesday evening, could you let him in for me?"

Sarah nodded. Each possessed a key to the other's front
door for just such back-scratching eventualities.

"I'm dropping you in for framing on the way," he had
added. "Carerra has some sort of exhibition opening at the
gallery tomorrow so it'll be a cast-iron excuse to barge in and
see if there's a free feed." He had grinned at her brief frown.
"Don't worry, I'll make sure he knows the rules."

Finally, as she had dashed out the door, he had called out
slyly: "I see life is imitating art. You'll be beating them off
with a stick in no time, darlin'." A not-so-subtle reference
to her smartened appearance she guessed, and he had no
reason to think otherwise. She had only mentioned Max to
him on the vaguest of terms, in an attempt to prove to herself that, outside work, Max didn't matter. And she hadn't
mentioned modelling for *Images* at all. She too had a sense
of the dramatic. She would casually toss him a copy of the
April issue when it came out and enjoy the expression on his
face. Life imitating art, indeed! She grinned; of the two men
who loomed largest in her life at this moment, each considered her transformation all their own work.

The doorbell. It sliced through her thoughts, setting her
nerves ajitter and she brushed her trembling hands against
her dress, making herself move slowly as she walked down
the hall. Be cool, she told herself, keep your head...it should
be easy as long as he doesn't touch you. Her quick tongue
could defend herself against words but her body, she had
discovered, was less easy to control.

It was dusk, the summer air warm and heavy and slightly salty. He stood in the deep indigo shadows of the large puriri tree which grew up against the house, spreading its crooked branches and glossy, evergreen crinkled leaves out over the doorstep, and Sarah's first sensation on seeing him was a faint prickle of unease. The feeling gained strength when he moved and the light from the hallway fell on to the narrow, unsmiling face. A beautiful face with a hint of ruthlessness, made even more intimidating by the impeccable formality of the black jacket and stark white shirt, the jagged edges of the black tie. The light made his eyes glow like a cat's and she had the absurd impression that he was crouched, cat-like, ready to spring.

For a moment they stared at each other and in spite of her determination to keep her head, Sarah felt a slow, disruptive charge of excitement, mingled with apprehension, shock through her. Then he smiled and the illusion of menace was dispelled.

"Something else new?" he mocked softly at the dress.

"Years old," she told him with obvious satisfaction.

A husky laugh swirled around her. "Unrelieved black, very dramatic. Or is it supposed to indicate mourning?"

Only Max could ask such a question. "Ask me that in a few hours time," Sarah fenced and he laughed again and extended a flat hand, revealing a flash of silver at his cuff.

To avoid having to touch him Sarah turned and made a business of shutting the door and checking the lock, transferring her clutch-bag to the hand nearest him. When she faced him again his arm was back at his side and he merely stood back for her to precede him to the car, an ironic twist to his mouth.

He settled her in the passenger's seat, then slid behind the wheel and started the engine, backing out with swift economy of movement and accelerating smoothly away from the curb. He seemed preoccupied by more than just his driving and apart from a few remarks about the car, a hired BMW, and a request for directions, was silent on the drive. At least it was not a stiff, awkward silence, Sarah consoled herself.

She was not surprised when they drew up outside one of Auckland's most prestigious, and expensive, restaurants... only the best for Max, always. *So what are you doing here, Sarah?* Why did he give her this inferiority complex?

The two-storeyed wooden building had originally been a family home, on the grand old Edwardian style and the atmosphere of a gracious upper-class residence had been retained in the conversion. They were shown, by a deferential *maitre d'hôtel,* to a table outside on the verandah, screened from public view by a trellis of vines which grew from balustrade to eaves along its length. Enclosed lanterns at each table provided the soft lighting.

It wasn't until they were seated, waiting for the wine steward to return with pre-dinner drinks, that Max looked at her fully again, with an odd intensity.

"I don't think we said hello, did we?" She was the focus of a magnetically attractive smile. "Hello, Sarah."

"Hello..." She was annoyed at the breathlessness of her reply.

"Still stumbling over my name? Do you realise that the only time you use it easily is when you're in my arms." He paused, musingly. "I suppose I shouldn't object if you choose to make my name an endearment."

She avoided his teasing eyes. This was another man again, a relaxed, almost whimsical one without that careful control that had seemed such an intrinsic part of his personality. Consequently, he looked younger, less jaded, more dangerously attractive than ever.

"Black suits you," he continued, appraising her further. "A pity there wasn't something black for *Images.*" He leaned back slightly to allow the wine steward to place their drinks on the table. "Although what we have is quite sufficient—more than sufficient. It's shaping so well that the feature may be syndicated to other Wilde publications."

Sarah wasn't sure she liked that idea and her doubt must have shown for he said, with mild exasperation: "Don't tell me you haven't considered the possibility, it was always on the cards. You're not going to turn coy now, it won't wash, in view of—"

"In view of what?" she asked, when he stopped and took a pull at his Martini.

"The fact that you've enjoyed yourself on this assignment," he continued smoothly after the tiniest of hesitations. "Barring minor...er...differences of opinion, that is. What do you think of the proofs?"

Sarah shrugged. "They're excellent." But he didn't need her to tell him that.

He made a derisive sound. "No self-congratulations? Don't you possess any vanity at all?"

"As much as anyone, I suppose."

"No, you don't." The hazel eyes gave her a curiously baffled look. "You frequently walk past a mirror without even a glance...even when you're wearing my father's best efforts. You never touch your hair, or make any of the subconscious gestures a woman makes to check her appearance. I can't believe that you're so genuinely unaware of the effect you're creating."

"What effect is that?"

"It's not necessarily a strength you know," he said, ignoring her question. "A small dose of vanity or envy would round off some of those edges that other people bark their shins upon."

"Is that what you prescribe. A teaspoon of the seven deadly sins?" said Sarah lightly.

"Perhaps not all seven...but I think I've made myself clear on that subject before."

"Crystal. You have a winning way with an insult," Sarah told him, a trifle tartly.

"Learned at my mother's knee."

Sarah's over-sensitised ears detected a hint of underlying bitterness in the smooth reply. Was he speaking the literal truth? Was this another tiny splinter of vulnerability threatening to work its way under her skin? She resisted it, remembering how skilled he was at manipulating people.

"You're lucky," she replied. "The only things I learned at my mother's knee were already thousands of years old. I decided not to embark on a course of continuing education, whereas *you . . .*"

"Now, now," he admonished, with a gleam of appreciation, "no fighting tonight. Shall we declare a truce?"

Sarah took a cautious taste of her sherry. She had better be careful, she didn't have much of a head for alcohol.

"Sometimes I can't help it," she confessed.

"I know what you mean," he murmured. Thick, dark lashes lay briefly against his skin as he looked down, idly stirring his Martini with the olive on a toothpick. Then the lashes swept back revealing the large dark pupils ringed by a halo of hazel. "Why do you never wear any jewellery?"

"I . . . I don't own much."

"Except your wedding ring."

Sarah looked down at her left hand. "That's an heirloom. It belonged to Simon's grandmother."

"No engagement ring?"

She was past resenting his inquisitiveness. Besides, by answering some of his questions yesterday she had given him tacit approval to ask more. "We didn't have a formal engagement. And anyway, Simon didn't believe in over-adornment, or in acquiring possessions for the sake of it."

"Except you."

Sarah's fingers curled into her palms at the quiet irony. "That's not quite fair," she protested, equally quietly. "There was more between Simon and me than . . . perhaps I shouldn't have said what I did yesterday."

"Why not? Who was it who said that one owes respect to the living; to the dead one owes only the truth?"

"Voltaire," replied Sarah automatically, having come across the quotation in her extensive reading after Simon's death, when she was trying to come to grips with her feelings about grief and guilt and the resulting emotional mess.

The man across from her smiled. He was too clever by half. Sarah gave him her haughty look.

"You should wear jewellery—gold perhaps, something warm and yellow, or rich and red, like rubies," he said, to punish her, his eyes drifting over her bare ears and throat, to the beat of the pulse above her collarbone. "But perhaps you're right," he continued provocatively, "bareness makes its own statement . . . and it's often a more interesting one!" His eyes dropped lower and glinted with satisfaction as she hastily brought her arms up on to the table in front of her, resting her chin on her hands, shielding the warm swell of her breasts from his gaze.

Sarah felt herself flush with a mixture of embarrassment and annoyance. Damn him for a disturbing devil! She had worn the dress braless before and not felt self-conscious, yet he made her feel a brazen hussy. In fact she had tried a strapless bra under the dress this afternoon, but the lace had been bulkily obvious under the thin silk and she had stuffed it back into her drawer, feeling a coward for having tried it on at all.

"Calm down, Sarah," he said mockingly. "I'm not going to leap on you in the middle of the restaurant. Credit me with a little finesse."

"Oh, I credit you with more than a little," she managed sarcastically, "and it's not exactly a calming thought."

"I'm glad you find it exciting," he said, wilfully misunderstanding her and then disconcerted her by changing the subject. "I meant what I said about your working overseas. Why don't you consider it? London perhaps? Wilde's has several publishing concerns there. I could make some enquiries if you like."

"I already work for Wilde's," she said, not sure whether he was serious or whether it was just part of his line.

"You're being obtuse," was all he said.

"Still intent on playing the fairy godmother?" she taunted, deciding to take him lightly, fearing to do anything else.

His mouth turned down at the corners. "I admit that at the time you accused me of being condescending my attitude may have been rather patronising, but I've since been cured of that. I suspect that Cinderella possesses more than enough of her own brand of magic."

And with that enigmatic utterance he turned his attention to the listings in the leather folder beside his plate, and suggested that she choose from the menu for them both.

"Tom told me that cooking is one of your hobbies." Sarah had a momentary frisson at that, remembering the other things she had told Tom during their numerous conversations. "Well, wine is one of mine, so let's collaborate." And, drily: "Your surprise is most unflattering. I know I open car doors for women but that doesn't mean I'm the complete chauvinist pig. Have I ever given you reason to think I was?"

In truth, he hadn't. He was quite prepared to meet a woman on her own intellectual level, whatever it was, and certainly showed no signs of treating them as second-class citizens. And, Sarah realised with a flash of wisdom, he was confident enough of his own masculinity not to have to reinforce it by acting the macho male.

Together they decided on champagne to accompany the first course of smoked roe pâté and vichyssoise soup and with the main course of chateaubriand a distinguished French red. Both agreed that dessert would be superfluous.

As the conversation flowed easily back and forth, Sarah relaxed enough to enjoy herself. She was seeing yet another facet of this most complex of men, a fascinating one. Max was cultured, witty without effort, mining a rich vein of humour which abhorred posturing and pretentiousness. They discussed books and music, people and current events, exploring mutual ground and areas of irreconcilable difference alike, sometimes earnestly, sometimes humorously. Yet

Sarah was ever aware of the undercurrents to the conversation and whenever she seemed in danger of forgetting the fact that they were man and woman, Max would re-introduce that note of seductive intimacy to which she was increasingly vulnerable.

"I'm glad Teresa gave you a fringe," he said suddenly, in the middle of a discussion about New Zealand wines. "It means you can't hide your hair away any more, even when you scrape it back as you have done tonight. Is that piece of not-so-subtle body language directed at me?"

"I always wear it up," Sarah said, put off her stride.

"Not always, surely," he murmured.

"I sometimes wear it loose at home."

"In bed?"

"Yes, I mean, no," stammered Sarah. It was amazing how evocative a couple of words in those chocolate-flavoured tones could be. It raised all sorts of images between them. "I usually plait it at night, otherwise it gets very tangled."

"I imagine it would, but it would be a pleasure to untangle," he said softly over the narrow rim of his champagne glass. "Does confining it so strictly during the day enhance the nightly private pleasure of letting it loose?"

Sarah's mouth went dry. "You make it sound almost wicked," she said faintly.

"It is wicked, a wicked waste." He finished his creamy, chilled leek and potato soup and rested his chin on linked fingers, as he often did when thinking. Sarah concentrated on her pâté, her face a serene mask while her heart skipped erratically, waiting...waiting...

Yet again he indulged in a verbal retreat, leaving her poised on the edge of frustration. When was he going to put into words what was in both their minds, so that she could get her little rehearsed refusal over and done with? This time he was talking about Sir Richard, describing his working habits with a mixture of respect and unfilial sarcasm.

"He sounds rather formidable," Sarah commented. "I should be in a constant state of terror if I had to work for him."

He looked amused. "People call me formidable, but you're not scared of me...quite the reverse."

"Perhaps they mean *formidable*," said Sarah, giving the word its French pronunciation.

"Is that a compliment?" he pounced.

"From me? Never!" Sarah hid her smile in her second glass of champagne. The heady brew was so fine and light and dry that it almost crackled in her mouth. She felt she could drink it all night and not be affected.

"Never say never, Sarah, that's tempting fate. I'll get a good word from you yet."

"I think you have a surfeit of those already."

"Not from you. But I can wait."

"Somehow I get the impression that you're not very good at that."

"I'm learning," he said, with wry self-mockery. "You like getting your own way almost as much as I do. You'd have made a good schoolmarm...or mother. Were you and your husband planning children?"

Sarah shook her head abruptly.

"Don't you want to have children?" He sounded vaguely shocked.

"Your chauvinism is showing," she told him with a trace of the schoolmarm. "But yes, I do; some time."

"Then it was your husband who didn't."

Recognising the relentless look on his face Sarah gave in gracefully. It no longer had the power to hurt her, anyway. "Simon was the child in our marriage," she said candidly. "Or rather, his talent was."

"My God, it seems to me that you got precious little out of that marriage," he said, with what she thought was unnecessary harshness.

"I got myself. I grew up. I learned about art, and beauty and truth, and about love," she smiled wistfully.

"And where have you put all this education to use?" he asked brutally. "How many men have you been out with, like this, since Simon died?"

"A few." To relieve the intensity of their conversation Sarah made a bright joke about some of her matchmaking editor's pushier candidates, but it fell flat and Max muttered something under his breath. "What did you say?"

"I said—clumsy idiots."

"My clumsiness as much as anything," Sarah admitted. "I went out with them for all the wrong reasons. At that stage I wasn't ready to make any kind of concession to any man."

"But now you're ready to experiment a little," he said, deceptively casual.

Her reply was too quick, too emphatic. "No. No. Not at all."

"Liar," he challenged and she stilled, like an animal cornered. Max's steady eyes were almost straw-coloured in the lamplight—the colour of the champagne in her glass. Champagne eyes and champagne, they both beckoned her to recklessness.

In a moment she was lost, her own honesty defeating her, at last giving in to the strength of the attraction he held for her. She had tried to avoid it, been careful to nurture dislike, explaining away the tension that she felt in his presence as antagonism. But it wasn't. It was more complex than that, and more simple. It was sexual tension, and she felt it enveloping her now, prickling across her body like a rash. She lowered her lids, flustered, and lifted them again. He was still watching her, with a virile certainty that was intoxicating; he was way ahead of her, on all counts. He knew she wanted him, he wanted her—the desire in his eyes no longer veiled, but burning a steady flame. Sarah didn't want to fight him, or herself, any more. There was a sense of inevitability about it, as though every encounter, since their first meeting, had been leading up to this. Deep within her the battle had been fought and lost some time before; only her timidity, her fear of the unknown depths of her own passion, had prevented her from admitting it.

The searing moment of mutual recognition was interrupted by the waiter, who took their silence as a cue to offer a few pleasantries, cleared the table and re-laid for the main course. The red wine was delivered, opened, tasted and poured, and the chateaubriand, a tender, succulent fillet of beef, crusty brown on the outside and meltingly pink at the centre, arrived on a silver salver surrounded by an array of crisp-tender vegetables.

Max calmly began to eat while Sarah wondered where her appetite had gone, and tried to ignore the pangs of a more urgent hunger.

"Eat. It's good," she was told, and Max smiled approvingly as she obediently picked at her food.

"What a good child you are when you're not arguing."

"I'm not a child."

"You are in some things," he said, supremely confident. "You don't know very much about men. About the way they think and act, about how they feel in relationship to you. Don't you know that coolness and disinterest is a challenge to any man's masculinity?"

"Is that all I am to you, a challenge?"

His smile glittered at the note of chagrin. "Mere challenge I can resist; mystery is something else. The question is, what am I to you?"

That was a question Sarah didn't even want to consider.

"A challenge, perhaps," she murmured, trying for archness and achieving mockery.

His eyes narrowed. "Perhaps you do know. Perhaps this nervous apprehension is just a pose."

She didn't pretend to misunderstand. "I loved Simon. I never looked at another man while he was alive, and afterwards I never wanted to." Then she felt embarrassed at the blatancy of her statement, but Max simply nodded and began to draw an intricate pattern with his fork on the white linen table-cloth. A lock of straight black hair fell forward over his brow and he was frowning slightly with concentration. Sarah longed to lean over and make contact, sooth out those furrows, make him look at her again with that warm, sensuous gaze.

"What about friends? People you knew before and during your marriage...other artists?"

"I more or less lost touch with them all," she said meekly. "Quite a few of Simon's so-called friends were just hitching a ride on his reputation. After he had gone we had no common interest any more."

The pattern became even more intricate. "All of them. You have no contacts in the art world now?"

"Acquaintances. Except—" she paused, fascinated by the convoluted wanderings of the fork, and the fork paused also.

"Except?"

"I have one friend, a painter...I owe him a lot."

"You have a close relationship?"

"Not the kind you're implying."

"No romance?" He seemed to tire of this game, throwing down the implement and stretching his shoulders back against his chair. He sounded vaguely triumphant, Sarah thought, annoyed. It was a bit late now, asking whether she was involved elsewhere, when he had already made his dishonourable intentions clear.

"No romance," she repeated neutrally.

"What about before Simon came on the scene?"

"Do you want the story of my life?" she asked, exasperated, and sighed when he nodded. "No, there was no one before Simon."

"Just establishing precedence," he mocked. "So there's only been one man in your life, and he put you to sleep. It's about time you were woken up."

"Have we swopped fairy-tales now?" Oddly enough she did feel as if she had woken from a long sleep—dazed and heavy, and filled with languid longings. She used her cutlery slowly, deliberately, aware of the eyes on her mouth as she ate, making of it a sensuous act. The rich white *béarnaise* sauce was redolent of tarragon and chives, which she would forever after associate with this meal...this man. She sipped her wine, and the ruby liquid left her mouth warm and red.

"I think we're going to create a tale all of our own," he replied. He seemed on the verge of saying more, but restrained himself. At times this evening he had seemed almost hesitant, as if pondering the consequences of what he was doing, and at others he had given her potent reminders that he was not a man to give up easily, if at all, once his mind was made up.

Sarah waited until their plates had been removed before bursting out with: "This is absurd, I hardly know you!"

"That's the way it takes you, sometimes." He declined coffee with a brief gesture of his head while a steaming cup was set in front of Sarah. "But if you want to know anything, ask—I can't guarantee that you will like the answers you get, but they'll be honest answers."

Sarah opened her mouth and shut it again, and laughed ruefully. "I can't think of a question now, not when you're looking at me like that."

"Is this better?" He dutifully averted his eyes, chin on hand, to study the ornate silver salt-cellar on their table. It was; relieved of the searching intensity of his gaze Sarah found her tongue, and asked, her interest stimulated by their earlier conversation:

"Are you and your father very close?"

The slender fingers stilled on the scrolled silverwork and his lowered lashes flickered. She knew he had been expecting a question about past love affairs, or whether his rakish reputation was earned, but strangely neither really mattered to Sarah any more. She was with him now, and that was enough. But she *was* interested in what made him tick as a person—what motivated his singular drive. "You can look at me now," she told him blandly.

"You make a career of being unexpected, don't you?" he told her and linked his hands as he applied himself to satisfying her curiosity. "No, my father and I are not close. We're too alike in some ways to get on well, in others we're too different."

"How different?" she prodded, pleased to be the examiner for once.

"He believes talent and temperament are inseparable. I don't. I believe that self-discipline enhances and concentrates a talent, in whatever field. My father does everything to excess, except parenting. He had a distinct lack of talent in that area, as did my mother."

"So you don't live together?"

"God no!" He looked appalled at the very thought. "We deal very well together at a distance. In spite of his failings as a father, or perhaps because of them, he seems to be developing a compulsive need to meddle in my life—both personal and business—and refuses to concede that I am more than capable of dealing with my own problems."

"A fairly common complaint among sons, I would imagine," said Sarah, amused by the aggrieved note in his voice, and wondering what specific remembrance had induced it.

"Perhaps," he allowed. "But I have achieved my present position with very little help from him—" He saw her scepticism. "It's true, intentionally or unintentionally he made things very difficult for me during my formative years with the company. Perhaps he feared that one day I would push him out."

"And would you?"

A faint smile. "No. I think that has been proved beyond doubt."

"What do you mean?" she asked curiously.

He seemed to give himself a mental shake. "I mean I recently discovered that I have no wish to crush the old man, even if it's in my power to do so. He may infuriate me, but he is my father, and a designer of undisputed genius."

"Is that why you didn't become a designer? Because you didn't want to compete with him on his own ground?" asked Sarah with sudden insight.

"No, I—" He stopped, and a brief expression of confusion passed over his face. "At least I don't think so, I've never been interested in designing—"

"That doesn't answer the question."

"No, it doesn't, does it?" She saw him smile and erect the "no entry" sign. "I think this conversation is getting a little... involved."

"You didn't say that when I was the one under the microscope," Sarah accused, not wanting to let him off the hook so easily.

"You're a more interesting specimen than I," he told her, with adroit insincerity and she had to laugh.

"How clever you are at evasion."

"Almost as clever as you," he agreed smoothly, and Sarah felt a small spurt of rebelliousness.

"Are you secretly insecure?" she taunted. "Is that why you never let your women get too close to you?"

Black brows rose. "We haven't established yet whether you are one of 'my women'."

Sarah glared at him and his mouth twitched temptingly.

"It is commonly known that you like to flirt. That your attitude to your... to female companionship is easy come, easy go," she said, and felt ridiculous as he clicked his tongue.

"Sarah, Sarah," he said, with mock-disappointment. "You've been reading the newspapers again. Who are you going to believe, them or your own instincts?"

"Both, they both tell me the same thing!"

The hazel eyes gleamed with pleasure and laughter as he leaned forward in a confiding manner and Sarah instinctively leaned forward also.

"Do you know what the dictionary definition of 'flirt' is?" His face was disconcertingly close and as she watched the words form on his lips she was swamped by a sudden surge of desire. She wanted to pull his head even closer, run her fingers through that silky black hair, feel the movements of that mobile mouth against hers. The feeling was so intense that she had difficulty controlling it, and grasped her hands tightly in her lap to prevent them betraying her by reaching out for him.

"'To pretend to make love,'" he quoted softly, insinuatingly. "I don't qualify, Sarah. I don't *pretend*."

"You told me you didn't use the word 'love'," said Sarah, her voice husky, eyes fixed on his face, inextricably caught in a web partly of her own making.

"I'm not talking about emotion. As the description of a physical act the word is very apt. When I go to bed with a woman we don't just 'have sex', we engage in a mutual ravishment of the senses. Purely physical gratification doesn't require a partner—but to make love..."

Sarah felt her skin bloom with colour and struggled to overcome what seemed to be an acute lack of oxygen. Her breasts rose and fell quickly as she began to breathe rapidly to make up the deficiency. She could not have felt more flustered if he had suited his actions to his words.

"Does that frighten you?" He seemed to be flattered by the idea, so that she would have liked to deny it, but she didn't.

"Yes." It was like being on a high board, wanting to feel the exhilaration of the dive, and aware that fear played a part in that exhilaration.

"But it excites you, too," he read her perfectly. "As you excite me." He moved in for the kill, catching the hand that came up as though to fend him off. "But it's more than purely physical, Sarah. I like your mind, I admire your independence ... I understand it, we're two of a kind in that respect."

In the midst of the toils of desire, Sarah denied that. "I want to be free because I know what it's like to be a prisoner. You want me to be free because it absolves you from any kind of responsibility, because an independent woman won't clutter you up with emotional demands."

"Isn't that the pot calling the kettle black?" Max said drily, the banked fires still visible in his guarded eyes. She was aware that he was stepping delicately and she couldn't blame him. It had been a stupid thing to say, because she was going into this thing with eyes wide open, as selfishly as he was. She too was scared of emotional clutter. Desire without responsibility, that was what she wanted.

"Don't you want us to meet as equals?" he asked, and suddenly she found her answer, looking at her hand enveloped in his.

"No." His face altered, though he masked his uncertainty well, and Sarah smiled, putting all the feeling she could into the lazy invitation in her darkening eyes. "I don't want to be an equal partner—" she paused, deliberately heightening the tension between them—"I want to be seduced, I've never been seduced before. What's it like?"

There was an incredulous silence. Then he laughed abruptly, with as much frustration as humour. "Just when I think I'm beginning to work you out—! My God, that's another first...I've never been asked to seduce a woman before, at least not in words. I begin to wonder who is seducing whom." He gave her a long, slow look—her eyes, her mouth, her bare shoulders, the golden promise of her breasts. "But I accept the invitation, of course, how could I refuse without ruining my reputation?" Now both of his hands held her submissive one. "You're so elusive that even the colour of your eyes shifts. They're dark, almost purple at the moment. What colour will they be when you're aroused, I wonder? Or are you aroused already?" The last word slurred to almost a whisper and one hand slid to her wrist. Her pulse beat hard and fast against his thumb and she could feel a slight ridge of hardened flesh on his palm. Another scar? Soon she would feel it on the soft skin of her body and she went weak with imagining it.

With slow deliberation he brought her hand up to his mouth, palm upwards and bit gently, voluptuously into the soft base of her thumb. It was a statement of sexual power and Sarah's eyes half closed as she felt a deep, molten flowering inside her, her body softening in a way that made the man across from her catch his breath.

She was hardly aware of leaving the restaurant, or of the journey home. Only of Max beside her, controlling the powerful car with ease, glancing sideways every now and then with barely concealed impatience.

He followed her up the darkened stairwell to the studio where she had left a single, soft orange lamp burning. She kicked off her shoes and floated over the polished wood floor towards the light, like a moth drawn inexorably towards the flame.

CHAPTER NINE

THE DARK volume of the night pressed against the wide expanse of uncurtained window; cloud hung like smoke across the thin, pale face of the moon. There was no wind, not a sound but the chorus of crickets outside in the darkness, no witness but the large, soft moths beating their wings against the glass, drawn like Sarah to the spell of the light.

She was trembling. Here in familiar surroundings what had seemed so inevitable now seemed less certain.

She heard a soft footfall, felt hands descend lightly on to her shoulders.

"Have you changed your mind?" There was a thread of amusement in the voice that caressed her ear. He knew so much about women, he must know what she was feeling. "If you have, tell me, this is supposed to be seduction, not rape."

He turned her slowly around and she stared hard at the black tie, sensing rather than seeing his mouth curve.

"Shy, mistress? You wanted me to take the first step and I have. All you have to do is say yes." His hand tipped her chin up and held it until her eyes lifted to meet his. What she saw there made her tremble anew. "Say yes, Sarah," he urged softly. "Say yes. I won't hurt you. I promise."

Without really being aware of it she allowed her body to sway, drawn by the magnet of his. Her voice held a question as well as an answer.

"Max?...I..."

It was enough. One lean, dark hand slid around to the back of her head, gripping her firmly, pulling her forward.

He bent and brushed his open mouth tantalisingly across hers, drawing back as she stirred and tensed like a warm, wild animal in his arms.

"Relax. Don't be frightened," he soothed.

"I'm not, it's just..." Sarah gasped as he nuzzled her neck, finding with his tongue the throbbing pulse at the base of her throat. "I don't remember—ever—feeling like this." The words slowed and slurred as she threw back her head to allow his mouth access to the sensitive skin just under the curve of her jawline.

"You never have," he muttered against her with sensuous satisfaction. "Nor have I. We're a unique combination and the way we feel and fit together will be unique too. I want to pleasure you and show you ways to pleasure me...we have all the time in the world...we can take it slowly, gently..."

He was keeping a tight rein on his passion and Sarah rebelled. She was a woman and wanted to be treated like one. She didn't want restraint, she wanted Max as she sensed he could be—fierce, passionate, volcanic—excitingly male. The driving need inside her would be content with nothing less.

She freed her hands, crushed between her body and his and held his head, stilling it. The hard shape of his skull in her hands was strangely affecting. Such fire and strength and intelligence inhabited that delicate structure. Such a man. Her eyes widened, showing him dilated pupils almost swallowing the violet-shadowed irises.

"Not too gentle, I hope." Her bewitching dismay died under the ravishment of his lips. She made a soft, contented sound and his mouth hardened, deepening its erotic penetration. The darkness grew in around them, the orange pool of light like a glowing bubble of sexual tension enveloping them, isolating them.

Sarah stretched her arms and wound them around his neck, leaning into him on tip-toes, closing her eyes and drinking him like an intoxicating draught. She felt his hands move on her head, then the weight of her hair began to shift and she realised what he had done. Her head jerked back and he let her go, watching as she moved out of his arms and raised shaking hands to struggle with the unanchored pins.

"Let it down," he ordered thickly. "I want to see it down around you, I want to hold it in my hands."

Impatiently she shook her head to release the knot and the heavy, luminous mass fell down. She heard a sharp hiss of indrawn breath as Max stared, following with his eyes the rich, rippling glow as it veiled the curves of her body. He had seen her with her hair down before, in the studio, but now he was looking at her as if he had never seen her before, the expression on his face fascinated, absorbed. For the first time in her life Sarah felt a true sense of feminine power.

As the seconds ticked by the tableau remained, Sarah as fascinated by Max as he was by her. He stood as if transfixed, feet slightly astride, hands hanging loosely at his sides, breathing slowly and deeply, eyes half-closed, face drawn tight, nostrils flared. He looked magnificent, savage, stripped of all that elegant charm that masked the elemental man. And in Sarah the elemental woman was fired in response.

Provocatively she turned her back on him, finding the last of the pins and drawing them out of her hair, placing them on the table beside the lamp. Then she began running her fingers through the tresses, pretending she had forgotten the man behind her.

He moved at last, with sudden violence, pulling her back against him so that she felt the hard muscularity, sliding his hands around her waist, splaying long fingers over her stomach as he buried his face in the scented curtain at her nape.

"I've run you to earth at last, little vixen," he growled. "There's no escaping me now; no laying of false trails or doubling back. Just you, and me, and this." He moved his body deliberately against her so that its heat penetrated to her very bones, turned them soft with exquisite anticipation. She tried to twist around in his arms, but he wouldn't let her, hands tightening over her hip bones, tangling in the fine ends of her hair.

"Don't be so impatient," he tantalised, a warm, exultant note of laughter in his voice. "You must earn your satisfaction. I promise you, my wanton innocent, the pleasure will be all the more intense for it. Relax. Enjoy what I'm going to do to you."

There was nothing she could do but obey, arching towards his hands with a sigh as they slid up to cup the aching fullness of her breasts, his thumbs brushing teasingly over the hardening tips. Her head fell back on to his shoulder, her safe, ordinary world exploding into a rapturous excitement of the senses beyond anything she had ever known. A stinging desire that streaked along her skin and nerves until her whole body was afire with it. At last, when she thought she could bear the slow, tormenting caresses no longer he turned her closely in his arms, the hardened contours of his body evidence of his own arousal.

He kissed her eyes and nose and mouth, and her hair where it waved thickly over her ears, and lifted his head to look at her dreamy face, touching her dark tresses.

"I know now why you keep it hidden. Like this it's too much of a temptation. Glorious, beautiful, infinitely sexy..." he said the words slowly, tasting them on his tongue, taking fistfuls of the softness and winding it loosely around his hands, drawing her mouth back to his. Her arms went around his waist under the jacket, locking him closer.

His hands stroked her hair and it clung, crackling, to him like a live thing. Sarah's mind blurred and tumbled weightlessly, the song of the crickets outside merging to vibrate with the high, unending song of longing that Max was creating with his hands and mouth. Like a virtuoso with a beloved instrument, he handled her with consummate skill, touching the chords of forgotten notes, discovering new ones.

At some point her dress slithered into an insubstantial heap at their feet and Sarah shivered at the friction of his clothes on her heated skin.

"Still no compliments for me, darling vixen?" Max taunted softly, forcing her back over his arm so that the weight of her hair pulled her head back, but she could only moan helplessly, eyelids fluttering closed not wanting him to stop. Not wanting him to ever stop...

"It seems I shall have to use force..." and he took the bare sacrifice of her throat, trailing fire with his lips and tongue to the taut offering of her breasts. Tiny cries escaped her as he kissed the captured peaks, his mouth opening, moist, knowing, as he explored her arousal with a sensual expertise that had her twisting in voluptuous agony.

"Give in?" as his mouth returned to hers for the final onslaught.

"Yes...yes...yes to everything...please..." Sarah felt disorientated and clutched wildly at him as she felt herself whirling, falling, but he was only pushing her down to the soft white sheepskin rug beneath their feet.

It seemed an age that he stood staring at her as she lay, satin body framed in auburn silk, a strip of delicate black lace her only covering. Then slowly, deliberately, Max stripped off his jacket and tie and threw them down, tugging open his shirt, scattering cufflinks with a soft patter across the floor, and then threw the discarded shirt down, too.

The smooth olive skin gleamed bronze in the lamplight, silvered with dampness and rippling as he moved to kneel beside her. He plunged his hands into the broad swathes of her hair and lifted them, letting the strands run through his fingers like water to splash over her body.

"How could I ever have thought you anything but what you are—lovely, desirable..." His voice roughened into harshness and his hands clenched her waist. "My God, I want you—"

Breathless with impatience Sarah reached up to pull him down, flesh against flesh, stroking her hands over his chest and shoulders, feeling him shudder like a man with a fever at her eager touch. He shifted his weight over her and her fingers flexed, nails sinking into his back as she felt the powerful thrust of his body.

"Don't hurt me, sweet vixen, I'm at your mercy now," he groaned as her nails raked downwards but she was beyond controlling herself, her body arched like a bow to his, her head rolling helplessly from side to side in an erotic transport of delight, all consciousness lost to the foaming excitement as the waves of sweet, piercing pleasure built up to tidal force. There were a thousand exquisite pulse-beats in her body; resounding desire in every cell and nerve ending.

The frantic movements of her body beneath his took the final shreds of his own control. There were no concessions now to her doubts, but she welcomed him, mind and body longing for the release that he had been so skilfully denying them both, hands seeking the belt buckle that dug into the soft flesh of her belly.

The interruption, when it came, came with brutal suddenness. A splash, a curse, a muffled thud and an explosion of bright white light from the direction of the half-closed bedroom door.

Max was on his feet even before Sarah's sluggish brain registered what had happened. She lay for a moment, dazed, shaking, gulping great breaths of air, then jackknifed up to grab the flimsy dress that lay an arm's length away. She stared blearily at the door with an awful premonition of disaster.

"Is that you, love? It's only me. I know I said I'd be away for a day or two—" Roy broke off, aghast, as he appeared in the doorway and saw the two frozen figures.

"Roy!" Sarah despaired and the unexplainable guilt she felt must have shown on her face for Max looked from the other man to her with dawning suspicion. Roy was wrapped only in a towel and dripped damply on to the floorboards.

We're all undressed, thought Sarah with hysterical irrelevancy...with Max, of course, wearing the most of all!

He stooped now, to shrug into his shirt, and to pick up his jacket and tie, which he thrust into the pocket.

"My mistake," he said with bleak and deadly quietness and Sarah recoiled at the brief look of icy hostility he gave her as he passed by. Her throat was so jammed full of anger and explanation that she choked helplessly, unable to utter a word.

Max hesitated at the top of the stairwell, half-turned towards Roy and, unbelievingly, Sarah heard her friend repeat with contemptuous precision:

"Your mistake."

Sarah squeezed her eyes shut on the nightmare, but the distant, distinct click of the front door confirmed the sick reality.

"Wait here," she heard Roy say as he ducked back into the bathroom. Where did he think she would go? Dashing out half naked into the street after Max? The thought prompted her to scramble up and pull on her dress, doing up the zip with clumsy fingers. Her whole body was racked with agonising cramps, she felt as though part of her had been torn away, leaving a great, gaping wound.

"What was he doing here?" Roy came back into the room wearing denim jeans and carrying a white T-shirt screwed into a ball. She could hear bathwater gurgling down the pipes.

"What do you think he was doing?" She found her voice, small and tight. "I would have thought it was pretty obvious. What were *you* doing? You aren't even supposed to be in Auckland!"

Roy shrugged, unembarrassed. "My car broke down on the motorway, so I called the trip off until it's fixed. I didn't get back until late and I was filthy, I needed a bath."

"At—" Sarah looked at her watch and gasped. "At midnight!" She and Max had been here for nearly an hour. The pain and frustration intensified.

Roy ran his hand through his wet hair. "Is it that late? I came over about ten—you weren't here so I let myself in...I thought I'd just have a quick dip. I must have fallen asleep. Where were you?"

"Dinner. We went to dinner. You shouldn't have come in, Roy," her voice rose sharply.

"All right, I'm sorry, there's no need to shout," he said. "You've never come back with anyone before, how did I know tonight was going to be different? I've used your bath before at night, and I didn't fall asleep on purpose, just to break up your cute little scene with the boss."

Furiously angry, Sarah lashed out with her tongue. She had never until now regretted the closeness of their friendship and in the short, heated exchange that followed said hurtful things that were unfair and untrue, and was stung in turn by Roy's retaliations.

"And who the hell are you to make sarcastic remarks about cute scenes! You're the one who told me I was only half a woman," Sarah finished desperately.

"I didn't mean you to jump into bed with the first man who asked you. I thought you had more self-respect."

Sarah stiffened. "You make it sound cheap and sordid—"

"Instead of romantic? Come off it, Sarah, you're not the type for one-night stands with strangers."

"He is not a stranger and it wasn't a one-night stand," said Sarah icily. Instinctively she knew that the passion she and Max had shared was more than just a brief, animal urge easily satiated.

"If you were capable of going to bed with a man without any kind of emotional involvement you would have done so by now, taken the easy solace it offered," Roy continued implacably. "I may be an advocate of free love, but not free sex. There has to be a relationship first!"

"But there was!" Why did he find that so hard to accept? "You don't understand—" and to her shame and horror Sarah burst into a flood of tears.

Instantly she found herself enfolded in a great bear hug, her head pressed against Roy's damp chest.

"Don't cry, honey," he rocked her. "You never cry. I'm sorry, I don't know what came over me. I was just shocked, I guess, I let rip without thinking. You must be feeling ghastly. I'm sorry." The words rumbled reassuringly in the ear that was pressed against his chest. Roy was Roy again, and not that accusing stranger.

She let herself be led over to the two-seater settee against the wall and felt herself pushed into the squashy cushions. She sat, sniffing, feeling drained and deathly tired.

"I'm the one who should be saying sorry," she said at last, wiping her face on the offered T-shirt and handing it back to the hunched figure beside her. "I yelled first. I didn't mean what I said. I don't know what came over *me.*"

"I do."

She coloured. "Oh God, what must he be thinking!"

"Nothing complimentary," he replied in an odd, flat voice.

"I should have said something...but I couldn't. I couldn't believe it was happening." She turned. "But you said something. Why did you say that? It implied—"

Roy pulled moodily at his beard, avoiding her eyes. "What should I have said—'we're just good friends'?"

"You could have said—"

"Look, Sarah, he was in no mood to listen to anything—reasonable or unreasonable."

She remembered the glacial look and winced. No. Max had drawn his own conclusions. He thought he had been made a fool of, used as a stop-gap while her live-in lover was away. But, remembering also what they had shared, she did not think that he would believe that for long. Once he had had time to consider he would realise that there must be another explanation. They would probably even be able to share a rueful laugh over the incident. Should she ring him? No, better wait until tomorrow and speak to him face to face. He would probably hang up on her in his present mood. And she had better ponder on the best approach to take.

When Roy saw some of the tension leaving her face, he chanced a gentle probe.

"What sparked this sudden mutual interest then?"

"Not sudden," Sarah yawned, the late hour catching up with her.

"Regular date, huh?" he jeered lightly.

"Regular from now on," she grinned.

Roy slumped back on the settee, frowning. "I never thought you would be attracted to a man like that," he muttered. "I thought you had more taste."

Fleetingly, Sarah wondered at his tone. Could he be jealous? Then she dismissed the thought as ridiculous. Roy might love her, but only in a brotherly way.

"A man like what?" she asked.

"A cunning, cold-blooded, worthless bastard," Roy said in a grim, alien voice.

"Roy!" Sarah sat up, utterly confounded. "How can you say that? You don't even know the man."

"I know enough. Next time I see that lecherous swine I'll punch his head in!"

"Roy!" There was no doubting his sincerity. "He didn't rape me! He was here because I wanted him to be. Are you going to do this every time I bring home a man you don't approve of?"

He gave a twisted grin. "You sound as if you're planning to bring them home by the dozen. No. Just this one. He's special."

"That's why he was here," Sarah told him. "Actually, when he first asked me to have dinner with him, yesterday on the island, I wasn't sure either. But—"

"Yesterday?" Roy's flaming head snapped round.

"Yes. During the cruise."

"He asked you out? Yesterday?" It was unlike Roy to be so slow on the uptake.

"Not until after we'd kissed," said Sarah impishly, but Roy didn't smile, he looked quite white and taking pity on him Sarah told him all about her meeting with Max and their subsequent roller-coaster relationship. If anything, Roy began to look sicker, so she threw in the story about *Images*.

"Why the hell didn't you tell me all this?" he demanded hoarsely. "You hardly ever mentioned him. I had no idea you had such close contacts with the guy!"

"I didn't want to talk about him," said Sarah, aware of how lame that sounded. "I didn't even think I *liked* him."

"Oh God!" Roy buried his face in his hands.

"What's the matter?"

"You're not going to like this." He lifted his head apologetically.

"Is it something you've heard about him? I probably know it already," said Sarah confidently.

"Why do you think he immediately assumed that we were lovers, not just living together—or brother and sister, or cousins or something?"

"I told him I had no family here...and that I lived alone." One way and another she had told him quite a bit about herself in the course of the evening.

"He and I have met before, Sarah."

"You never told me," she said, surprised.

"You never told me about you and him," Roy pointed out. "Anyway we only met this morning. At Carerra's gallery. He was opening the exhibition."

A starburst exploded in Sarah's brain. Max's strange mood, his intense curiosity, the way he had looked at her and talked—the look on his face when she had let down her hair.

"You showed him the painting," she breathed, appalled. "You let him see it!" Her voice peaked on a squeak.

"No...at least—" Roy spread spatulate hands helplessly. "It was Carerra. When I said it was for sale overseas he dashed off and came back with Wilde in tow."

Sarah groaned.

"I didn't know who he was," protested Roy. "Carerra was fluttering around like a mother hen, and when he got around to introducing us it was too late. I had no idea there was anything between you and Wilde—especially since I could have sworn he didn't recognise you. Why should he? The resemblance is quite slight to the casual eye."

"His eye is never casual," stressed Sarah.

"Well, he didn't say anything...although he did ask later who the model was."

"Oh God—"

"But only in a casual way when we were discussing some technical points. I said you were a friend."

"A friend," echoed Sarah stupidly. No wonder Max had jumped to the wrong conclusion. That beautiful, damning painting. It gave her a strange, curling sensation in her stomach to think of him standing there before that canvas, studying her naked image. Somehow it seemed more indecent than when he had done so in the flesh.

"He didn't comment. Perhaps he didn't know it was you," said Roy without hope.

"He knew all right." Her skin tingled when she remembered the fire in Max's eyes when he saw her hair swirl down around her hips. "But why didn't he say anything at dinner?"

"He would have to be insensitive not to realise why the painting wasn't being offered for public sale here. He was probably waiting for you to tell him."

"It never even occurred to me," said Sarah absently. He *had* given her several openings, she realised now, but she had ignored them. Such mundane matters had been far from her mind! "What did he say about it?" she asked, stricken with curiosity.

"'Exceptionally fine'," Roy gave a creditable imitation of Max's drawl and grinned. "Among other things. I rather liked him. Knows his art, has a shrewd intelligence, and wasn't the least impressed by Carerra's outrageous flattery.''

"So how come you were uptight about me coming back here with such an admirable character?"

He winced at her sarcasm. "Brainstorm, darlin'; still half asleep, etc. As good at jumping to conclusions as he is. I thought I'd read him all wrong, that he was one of those slimy creeps whose interest in art is covertly prurient. I thought he was getting his kicks from possessing the original of a work of art, so to speak.''

"You thought an awful lot in a very short time."

"Didn't I just. And way off beam, too."

"Were you?" She *wanted* to think so, but wanting didn't make something so.

Roy seemed to understand what was in her mind. "*I* think so. If he was as corrupt as all that he would have left with a wave and a philosophical shrug. Instead he looked like a man who had just received a massive kick in the guts—"

"As poetical as ever," said Sarah to hide her relief. Roy could be trusted to read facial expressions, he had made his fame and fortune from them.

"Anyway, his interest in you obviously started way back. He spotted your potential and had the means and desire to exploit it. I'm not surprised that his desires took a more personal turn, they often do between model and artist— witness you and Simon, and me and—" he ticked a few names off his fingers and Sarah laughed. "I won't say that seeing the painting mightn't have spiced the dish for him; it's not a clinical study after all, but the main ingredient is you. On brief analysis, I'd say he was too cultured to equate art with pornography and too virile to need the stimulation that pornography provides, hmmm?" Green eyes crinkled as Sarah began to fiddle intently with her hair, twisting it into a long tail, and he continued musingly, "In fact, he would make a good subject. I'd like to resolve some of those complexities on canvas."

"Perhaps you could do a nude," Sarah needled.

"Sorry," he gathered himself. "Just thinking aloud. Though he certainly has the body for it."

"Goodnight, Roy." The sly dig shot Sarah to her feet.

"Okay, okay, I'm going, I can take a hint. Will you be all right?"

"I'm not about to commit suicide," Sarah said in revenge. "Not over a cold-blooded, worthless—"

"Don't repeat that, will you? It was quite an excusable error."

"In quite a comedy of errors." Sarah walked over to the balcony door and slid it open.

"Never mind, all's well that ends well," Roy punned. "If you need a written statement to convince your once and future lover of our platonic friendship, just ask." Sarah pushed him out the door, but he poked his head back in to add:

"I hope you don't singe your wings with this one, love. He's a high-flyer."

Sarah sighed as she shut the door after him. She was touched by his concern but he was worrying unnecessarily. She wasn't going to make the mistake of taking Max's attentions seriously. They were worlds apart. But who knew better than she that vows of permanency held no guarantees of permanent happiness? A temporary adult relationship, brief, satisfying, compromising no one, suited them both.

She turned off the light and padded across the floor to the bedroom, wincing as she trod on something hard. She felt around in the darkness and picked up the forgotten cufflinks. Here was a ready-made excuse to speak to Max tomorrow. There would be a few nasty minutes to brave but it would be worth it. He was worldly, sophisticated, had a well-developed sense of humour—he had displayed some of it tonight. He would understand, once she explained. She fell into bed, warmed by the certainty and slept, deep and dreamless.

CHAPTER TEN

SWATHED IN protective towels, Sarah stared at her reflection in the large mirror rimmed with lights.

Teresa had surpassed herself this time. Her swan-song, she called it, for later this afternoon she was flying on to another assignment in Australia. Sarah's hair had been swept up into a soft, romantic knot secured by red enamel combs and trailing short, feathered wisps at the sides and nape of her neck. Her face had been subtly rounded out with blusher and highlighter and a dramatic blend of silver-grey, blue and violet on her eyelids and a provocative deep red gloss on her lips drew attention away from the pointed jawline to the central features.

It was a sophisticated, elaborate mask and the white walls in the background and white towels around her neck gave her head a floating, disembodied look.

Sarah shivered, not at the macabre thought but on recalling her brief encounter with Max that morning. She had arrived at work full of determination, relieved to find Max alone in the office, poring over a series of marketing surveys. It encouraged her to see that he looked so normal, no clouds of thunder lowered upon his head.

"Can I see you?" she had asked, after greeting him, standing tentatively in front of his desk.

"You see me now." He read on. Not so encouraging. Still, who would expect him to be effusive after the night's fiasco?

"I..." she fumbled in her bag. "I want to return these..." she placed the cufflinks on the desk and stared hard at the dark crown of his head, willing it to lift.

"Thank you." He wrote something in the margin on one of the sheets, and added a footnote.

"And...I want to explain; about last night," she said mesmerised by the pen flowing smoothly over the paper.

"I wasn't aware that the situation required clarification," came the tinder-dry comment.

"But it does." *Look at me, damn you,* she longed to say, as he had said to her. But of course she didn't. She kept her voice quiet and steady.

"I know it must have looked...well, odd. But—Roy is the friend I mentioned. We don't live together; he lives next door—"

"How convenient," he said pleasantly. His pen paused and he looked at her for the first time since she had entered the room. The hazel eyes had a strange, opaque quality, quite empty of expression.

Ignoring her sinking heart Sarah rushed untidily into her story, about Roy and the trip, and the hot water cylinder, and his habit of falling asleep in the bath. Shorn of background and atmosphere it sounded painfully thin, even to Sarah. The more she became aware of it the more tangled her explanation became. He listened with an impassive, unblinking, lack of interest for a few minutes before cutting in as she faltered for a third time:

"What are you so uptight about? Forget it, Sarah, it doesn't matter." He smiled, a thin unpleasant smile that went no further than a faint movement of the lips. "Post-mortems bore me."

He bent his head again, adding, a few seconds later when he became aware that she was still standing there, stunned:

"Teresa's waiting for you in the studio. Let's get this over and done with, shall we?"

Nobody, but nobody, ignored Max when he spoke in that clipped, impatient fashion, not even Sarah at her bravest, and at that moment her bravery was at its lowest ebb. His studied indifference had a devastating effect on her self-confidence. Did he really care so little? Or was it all a front? With Max it was difficult to tell.

Sarah stretched out a hand to touch the dress which hung alongside the mirror. Perhaps he wouldn't be so indifferent when he saw her in that. He had been mildly complimentary at the fitting and mild approval from Max was equivalent of rave reviews from anyone else. Perhaps he needed something to jolt him into remembrance of what they had shared, of the husky words of promise he had murmured to her last night. This dress could do it, if anything could. It was beautiful.

The long, pure silk dress was the same toffee-apple-red colour as her lips, the broad straps supporting a low, square-cut bodice, the narrow waist stitched in a V-shape at the front, giving the dress a slightly medieval look, with the skirt falling in soft folds to the floor. Over the bodice fitted a high-necked, long-sleeved silk chiffon camisole, embroidered with dark red sequins, fluttering to a scarfed hem at waist-level.

"Sorry to be so long," Teresa bounced through the door carrying a pair of strappy red high-heeled shoes which she stood neatly under the hanging dress. "I must learn to organise myself more... Now, where was I? A dab of freshener to set you, I think. Are they ready yet, do you know?"

"Mike's still setting up." Sarah closed her eyes as the other girl dabbed on some cold, fragrant lotion with a cotton wool ball. Then with a flick of her wrist she whipped off Sarah's cloak of towels, eyeing the two wisps of lace which were all she wore underneath.

"I know you complain about skinniness being the fashion, but I wouldn't mind a few of your curves. It's almost a pity to put on the dress. If you walked around like that you wouldn't have to worry about make-up. No one would look at you above the neck!"

"This is supposed to be an Autumn Collection," Sarah grinned, used to Teresa's frankness by now.

"That's better. You looked a bit down in the mouth—" she broke off as the door swung open behind them. Sarah's whole body tensed as she saw the reflection of their visitor.

"You could have knocked," Teresa said, in her mildly bossy tone.

"Sarah's not shy. Are you, Sarah?" Her heartbeat accelerated as she briefly met sardonic eyes in the mirror. Was he going to say something in front of Teresa? She looked hastily around for her towels, but they had already been stuffed into the laundry bag in the far corner of the room and not for anything was Sarah going to stand up and expose herself to that subjective appraisal.

"That's not the point," said Teresa, unaware of the undercurrents. "It can be most off-putting to have people barging in on you unexpectedly."

Fortunately, Max wasn't required to make a reply for at that moment Julie poked her head around the half-open door.

"Excuse me, Max. I know you're not set up yet, can I borrow Teresa for a few minutes? I need some advice and I might not get the chance to ask her later on."

"Ten minutes," said Max, not taking his eyes off Sarah.

"Thanks." She disappeared and Teresa took off her thin protective wrap and hung it on the hook on the back of the door.

"Don't do anything I wouldn't do," she said cheekily, as she scampered out after Julie.

The skin prickled all the way down Sarah's bare spine but she controlled the impulse to squirm. He had taken off the light jacket he had worn in the office, she noted as her eyes avoided his, to reveal a cool white shirt, tailored in some rough linen weave, tucked into oatmeal trousers with a snakeskin belt. He had rolled up his sleeves for work in the hot studio and undone two shirt buttons, and the black mist of body hair on his forearms and rising from his chest brought back memories that made Sarah swallow nervously. She cleared her throat. By now she should be used to the way that Max used silence as an intimidating weapon.

"Would you mind passing me that wrap behind you?"

"A bit late to worry about covering yourself up, isn't it?" he said laconically.

"It's quite cool in here," Sarah said with incredible casualness.

"Odd. Such a small room. And no air-conditioning."

There wasn't either, Sarah suddenly noticed, and flushed furiously, glaring at him. He was using that sarcastic, supercilious voice she so detested. The more so because she suspected it was assumed. He wasn't looking in the least bored.

"And I don't like being stared at," she said rashly.

"You surprise me." Icicles dripped from every syllable.

"I thought that was what interested you . . . my unexpectedness," she mocked softly and for a moment the bored mask slipped and hazel eyes blazed yellowly at her, to be veiled immediately. But Sarah felt a surge of triumph. She had penetrated that blank façade, now she must cut off his retreat. Get his anger out in the open where she could fight it. She twisted round in the chair to look at him properly. He was a long way up. "Do you think that I'm an exhibitionist simply because I have my picture painted?" She caught the thought which hardened his face. "All right, it was in the nude but Roy is a fine artist, a serious and dedicated man. I wouldn't have posed otherwise."

His eyes had flickered at the mention of Roy. "Oh, I agree he's good. It's a superb piece of work. So good that one can forgive it its sheer dishonesty."

"Dishonesty!" She felt a prick of anger on Roy's behalf. "That's unfair. Roy has great integrity, he's the most decent and honest man I know!"

"Then I pity him!" Sarah shrank from the full force of his contempt, shocked by its intensity, beginning to appreciate the magnitude of the task she had set herself. He turned and she thought, with a mixture of fear and relief, that he was going to walk out. But, ominously, he merely closed the door, then leaned his long length against it while his narrowed eyes crawled slowly over her half-naked body. "Does he still see you as the innocent temptress? I doubt it, after last night. No one's that gullible."

"Will you pass me the wrap, please?" Sarah asked, waveringly.

"You're not showing me anything I haven't already seen." Carelessly he unhooked the wrap and tossed it across, watching cynically as she put it on and stood up to tighten the belt, facing him proudly. "Less, thanks to your...shall we say, enthusiasm? And your...*friend's* artistic skill. Next time, though, he should paint you as you are. A temptress indeed, but with all the innocence of a whore!"

"I thought postmortems bored you," Sarah said, stunned by his crudity but still grimly holding on to her composure.

"I thought that would hit home," he told her, betraying pleasure. "Incredible, isn't it, that any man could resist your injured innocent act?"

"I hope you enjoyed your petty revenge," Sarah threw at him fiercely. "So much for your much-vaunted sense of justice! You won't listen to the facts because you don't want to hear anything that will challenge your infallible assumptions!"

"The operative word being facts, not your brand of pretty fiction," he said with a bitter clarity. "There's nothing wrong with a whore, as long as she's an honest whore."

"You have a twisted sense of morality," Sarah choked in wrathful indignation. "No wonder you confuse fact and fiction. You were taking me to bed last night, not to church, and it's only your pride and vanity that got hurt. You're not going to save face by indulging in cheap name-calling—"

Max elbowed himself off the door with a suddenness that had Sarah clutching the chair between them.

"Cheap?" he snarled. "Why not? You were mine for the price of a meal!"

"And you were mine for nothing," Sarah flung back. "What does that make you?"

His nostrils thinned. "At least I offer exclusivity."

Sarah laughed; a shrill, brittle sound. "Of what? Club membership? Mistresses and ex-mistresses of Max Wilde? I thought *that* was open to the public."

"Jealous?" he thrust, harshly mocking, and something inside Sarah writhed briefly and died.

"Of you? Don't be ridiculous!" she spat, tempted to throw the chair full in his sneering face. "I was just pointing out that you're the last one to preach morals to me. Maybe you're too corrupt to be able to understand that a man and woman can have a platonic relationship like Roy and I. Well, I don't give a damn what you think anymore. Roy and I have known each other for seven years. He was a good friend of Simon's, and of mine—"

"I'll bet he was," Max inserted silkily. "And with whom was he the more intimate—your husband... or you?"

"You... vile... hypocritical *swine,*" Sarah gasped out, flushed and trembling so hard she had to grip the back of the chair. Leaning into it frantically, eyes glittering brilliantly, she was unaware of how excited and exciting she looked in the grip of raging temper. "How dare you make such foul, such *rotten* accusations. You know *nothing.* You're a bigot and a coward—you're *afraid* to listen, to admit any weakness or wrong, because that would mean you'd have to come down off your self-created Olympus and let the rest of us see how fallible, how *human* you are! You're not a god, Max—I don't think you know what you are!"

The narrow face darkened and Max made an indistinct sound in his throat, hands curling slowly into fists at his sides, balls of bone and muscle. He took a step towards her, as if he couldn't help himself and Sarah recoiled, letting the chair fall with a sharp clatter. He wouldn't resort to physical violence would he?

"It won't work, Sarah, not this time," he told her through his teeth. "I know you now for what you are: a treacherous, amoral little slut!" His mouth twisted in contempt, his voice filled with loathing. "You're clever, I'll give you that—a woman has to be to fool me. But I never make the same mistake twice." He took on a cruel mimicry: "*I don't remember ever feeling like this.* You must have a singularly short memory!"

Each word was a drop of acid etching itself into her fiery brain. Sarah tugged the thin wrap tighter, as if it could protect her from the merciless onslaught. The whole situation had exploded in her face and she was too hurt now to retract anything, or even want to. Perhaps she had provoked him, but only because she refused to be ground into the dirt as a result of his intransigence.

As she hugged herself, drawing the slippery material taut over her breasts, she saw the smouldering eyes drop by the merest flicker of a lash and fix themselves again on her face with a strained intensity. And suddenly it hit her *why* he was so bitterly contemptuous and how she could exact bitter payment for all his insults.

She rubbed her crossed hands up and down her arms, feigning weariness, watching Max's reaction through lowered lashes, noting the way his eyes unwillingly followed the slow, massaging movements. *Yes.* She let one hand drop and moved the other casually up to slide inside the neckline of the wrap. A muscle jumped in the lean jaw as she shifted the material slightly so that he had a brief glimpse of golden bare skin to her waist, the more enticing because it was now supposedly concealed.

"What's the matter, Max?" she asked huskily. "Does my body bother you?" His eyes jerked back to her face, shocked, and she gave him a slow smile. "Not bored, Max. Never bored. My body fascinates you, doesn't it...my body, my hair. Did you dream about it last night? What you missed, what you wanted..."

Dark blood ran up under the taut skin of his face and Sarah felt a hot, hard thump of victory in her chest. "Poor Max," she simpered. "I turned you on and you don't know how to turn yourself off..."

He cracked wide open then, in a way that appalled her even as it sent adrenalin racing through her veins. The hard, arrogant lines of his face blurred with rage, the eye insensate and she panicked immediately, realising that in driving him over the edge she too had lost what little control she had.

He came towards her, off the balls of his feet, and she held up a feeble hand to ward him off.

"No, Max—I didn't mean—"

"Oh yes, you did, you—" he struck her hand away, backing her up to one smooth, blank white wall. "Haven't you got the guts to finish what you started?"

"No—" she whispered, terrified at the demon she had released; at her own swirling, reckless excitement.

"Are you a masochist as well as a nymphomaniac? On the lookout for new sensations. By God, I'll give you one!"

He reached for her, and reacting instinctively Sarah clawed at him with elegant blood-red nails, but he shackled her wrists with steely fingers, holding her at bay. "Hit me, Sarah, and I'll hit you back. The only reason I didn't last time was because I thought you were a lady. But the lady's a tramp." A thin razor-sharp smile sliced into her. "You're the hypocrite, not me. I never pretended to be inexperienced, and at least I'm capable of being faithful to one woman at a time. My lovers don't have to worry about queues in the bathroom."

"I didn't know he was there," she moaned, stupidly, hardly aware of what she was saying. He was just talking to feed the inferno inside him, building up to an explosive climax. His face, so close to hers, looked gaunt, scraped to the bone.

"No? Maybe threesomes turn you on. Was I supposed to ask him to join us?"

"You're disgusting." She turned her burning cheek aside, but he was relentless, remorseless.

"He looked fairly shattered, though. Did he kick you out after I left? But no doubt you've kept other options open ... was I going to be one of them?"

"Bastard," she gritted, closing her eyes against the withering scorn, feeling the hot salty pressure against her lids.

"A whore and a bastard. Perhaps we're made for each other. Shall we find out?"

Slowly, inexorably, he pulled her wrists up and out until her arms were spreadeagled along the wall. She fought him

every inch of the way, silently, with all her strength, but her
futile struggles seemed to compound his enjoyment.

"You're getting excited, darling," he drawled savagely
into her hectic face. "Does it excite you to be handled
roughly? Is that all part of the game?"

He moved on to her, anchoring the center of her body to
the wall with his hips, his every deliberate action exuding
sexual menace that was frightening and repelling. Yet dark,
furious, threatening, he was still attractive and Sarah moved
frantically, trying to twist away, horribly aware of something inside her that was responding to the physical stimulus. He laughed and laid the full length of his body against
hers, rock-hard muscle from shoulder to knee and she was
shaken by a compulsive betraying shiver.

"No, please ... not like this," she cried weakly and the
answer came, raw and insolent:

"Hell, isn't it, Sarah, when you want something you
know you shouldn't? Beg if you must, but try and make it
a little more convincing!"

He lowered his mouth to hers, taking his time, indicating
he would use all his considerable skill to get what he
wanted—complete submission. When she kept her mouth
obstinately closed he moved sharply, crushing her against
the wall until the pain in her shoulder-blades made her give
a muffled sob. Immediately the enemy invaded the vulnerable territory, thrusting a coaxing, questing tongue into the
deep moistness, tasting victory. Whichever way she moved
her head he followed easily and soon she stopped, feeling
hot and helpless and giddy, accepting him. He began to
grind his hips against hers in a slow, sensual rhythm that
mimicked the act of possession, rousing a sweet, familiar
ache that made a mockery of Sarah's protest. But acquiescence wasn't enough for him and he kept up the forcible
arousal until stark, awful reality faded and Sarah was swept
back into a world of pure sensation, of touch and taste and
feel. An involuntary groan broke from her lips as the blood
began to throb at her pulse points, sing along her veins.

The sound was absorbed into his mouth as he loosened his hold on her wrists, keeping her pinned with his body while he untied the belt at her waist.

She freed her mouth long enough to plead:

"No, Max—someone might come . . ."

"Let them."

He kissed her again, and again, overcoming her brief resistance, roughly stripping the wrap from her shoulders, baring her body to his touch. His mouth was warm on her neck and she felt his practised hands run knowingly over her tingling skin, her body lifting and tautening to meet them. Desire raced along sensitive nerve endings and she moaned softly as his fingers stroked down the silken curve of her breasts, slipping inside her flimsy bra to find and caress the burgeoning nipple.

Her trembling increased. She was made for this, this blissful pleasure; and he to reveal it to her. It felt good. It felt right.

She whispered his name, hands coming up to settle on the soft dark hair at his nape, cupping the shape of his head.

It seemed to trigger a nerve and suddenly she felt him shudder and tense, swearing thickly against her throat, a vicious sound of self-disgust that tore the lovely fabric of her dream. He thrust himself violently away from her and she swayed, mind blunted by sensation, skin incandescent with heat, damp palms pressing back against the cool of the wall behind her.

With an effort Sarah lifted heavy lids, bewildered at the swiftness of his withdrawal. Max had his back to her, bending stiffly to pick up the fallen chair and straighten it meticulously. His shirt was clinging damply to his skin and she saw the muscles beneath clench briefly before he turned around.

"Well, that's one thing you don't have to lie about. You certainly seem to get job satisfaction." He wiped the redness from his mouth with the back of his hand as though the taste of her revolted him.

Sarah steadied herself against the wall, the only stable thing in a shifting universe. She sought his face for some indication of passion, of softness, but there was none. Savage lines of satisfaction grained the skin around his mouth and his eyes were like knives, cold and merciless, dissecting her.

Her stomach lurched violently. She felt bruised, violated. What had happened to her self-respect? He had treated her with the same contempt that a rapist must feel for his victim; with anger and disgust. And she had enjoyed it! Invited it even, for she had provoked him to breaking point. God, what was the matter with her? She was acting as if every vile thing he said about her was true!

She watched, hypnotised as he tore a tissue out of the large box on the make-up table and wiped his mouth and hand. Then he began to sort through the lipsticks until he matched one with the smear on the tissue.

"No!" Her skin crawled as she realised what he intended to do.

He smiled cruelly. "Lost your taste for being touched? If you prefer, you can wait for Teresa...explain to her how you smudged her good works."

Sarah submitted frozenly as he tilted her chin to the light and skilfully re-coloured her bloodless lips. She could see the faint beading of sweat on his upper lip, but his hand performed its task without a tremor. He was inhuman. How could he do it...while she stood there beaten, humiliated...she remembered her wrap and scrabbled blindly for the gaping edges.

"Thanks for letting me test the merchandise." He threw the lipstick back on to the table. "But I think you've overestimated its value. You ought to consider the strategic advantages of withholding your assets."

Sarah didn't have the strength to fight back, she leaned her head tiredly against the wall and stayed unmoving until she heard him leave.

She collapsed at last on to the chair, blinking fiercely. It would take ages to repair the damage if she cried, and *he* would know the reason for the delay. She would not give him such a complete triumph.

She hated him. He was arrogant and crude and so *wrong*. She wasn't promiscuous...she didn't think...at least, only with him. But why? Was it only because he had been the first to tap the deep well of her suppressed sexuality? She could see, from the bleak vantage point of a new physical maturity, that Simon had never done more than skim the surface of her passions. He had been too selfishly concerned with his own needs to be able to fully satisfy hers. Max, on the other hand, confident of his prowess, had been willing to wait on her, taking as much pleasure in discovering what pleased her as in fulfilling his own desires...in fact they had seemed inseparable.

Sarah buried her face in her hands and groaned. Her hands felt icy, her body numb. That was twice in two days Max had brought her to the pitch of desire then abandoned her, though this second time was by far the worst. She shouldn't have tried to fight him, he could always annihilate her physically and verbally. She couldn't even feel angry at him, though she had every reason to be...just this terrible numbness.

It was pride alone that saw her through the nightmare session that followed. Pride made her smile, and sparkle and *project* by order of the shadowy figure beyond the half-circle of bright lights, when inside she felt shrivelled and old.

Afterwards, in the semblance of normality, she allowed herself to be bullied into going to lunch with Tom, though the thought of food was nauseating. They went to a tiny coffee bar not far from the office, one they had been to several times before, situated below street level, down a narrow flight of stairs.

Playing with her salad Sarah let Tom's ramblings about the new contract with *Rags'* printer, the busy London schedule he would be returning to at the end of the week, and other inconsequentials flow soothingly around her. Suddenly, out of the blue, he said something that riveted her attention.

"Max came under duress? What kind of duress?" It was no use telling herself she wasn't interested.

"He only agreed to come out to New Zealand in exchange for certain...ah...concessions in the board-room," Tom explained, seemingly absorbed in the disposition of tea-leaves in the bottom of his cup. "Sir Richard insisted that he take a break from his rigorous routine, but Max would have none of that, so *Rags & Riches* was compromise on both sides." Tom paused maddeningly. He was being uncharacteristically indiscreet and Sarah prayed he wasn't going to realise it now and clam up. If she had been thinking more clearly she might have wondered about his sudden desire to impart gratuitous information on a hitherto avoided subject.

"Max resigned himself, if only because he knew it was basically his own fault. When he came out of hospital after his accident he was ordered to convalesce for at least a month. Instead he put himself under psychological pressure to perform, and at a level which exceeded even his pre-accident optimum."

He lost interest in reading tea-leaves and watched Sarah as she grappled with the one fact that she had plucked out of his statement. *He* had told her—but she hadn't believed—those scars hadn't looked so awful...

"Accident?" came out shrill and cracked.

Blue, blue eyes, calm and unfathomable as the sea, looked into hers. "It was played down at the time: these things can and do upset the balance of the market. Last April Max crashed his plane on a flight from Paris to London. Nearly killed himself—"

Somebody was operating a drill in her head. The bright red-flocked wallpaper of the coffee bar sprang at her, sharp, vivid, threatening suffocation, and the warm, spicy coffee-laden air grew strong and bitter in her nostrils, a sour bitterness that also flooded the back of her throat.

"I'm sorry, love, but at least it was quick. They said he would have been killed on impact..." Roy's caring voice floated through her chaotic mind. Killed? Had Max been killed? Her whole body was one silent, suffering, scream.

No. *Nearly.* That's what Tom had said. Nearly. A year ago she hadn't even been aware of Max's existence, let alone... The world began to revolve slowly around her, then faster, and cold sweat broke out on her forehead as she groped for meaning. She laid her head in her arms on the table, waiting for the turbulence to subside, hoping she wasn't going to disgrace herself by being sick. If he had died, she would never have met him. Never have fought those exhilarating battles; and won, and lost, and hated, and loved. *And loved.*

The numbness of the past hour dissolved as a wave of terrible futility washed over her, flooding her with exquisite pain. She loved him! That was why she lit up like a torch whenever he touched her, that was why his indifference, his rejection had been so utterly devastating. She loved him. In spite of herself, in spite of him... the man who never used the word *love,* except in the physical sense. God, it was almost funny!

"Sarah, are you all right?" A voice penetrated the fog.

She lifted her head. "Yes. Yes. I just felt a bit odd there for a moment." An odd kind of love, indeed.

"Sure? You're very pale?"

She nodded, though it hurt. Everything hurt.

"I'm sorry, I didn't mean to upset you." The round face was gentle, understanding. Appallingly so.

"I... that's how my husband died, you see. In a plane crash. It was a shock," she improvised, a transparent half-truth.

"I know, Julie told me," he said, unembarrassed, and she was aware that she hadn't fooled him one bit. Was he offering his shoulder to cry on? What had prompted him to draw his bow at the venture? "A shock for Max, too. People tend to think of Max as being invulnerable—I think he had even come to believe it himself. He lost something in that crash, an ability to *enjoy.* I think he might have found it again, here."

Sarah looked at him, pain in her heart—for herself and for Max. Perhaps that explained his savagery. She had taunted with weakness and that barb must have sunk far deeper than those he had hooked into her flesh, for she knew their falsity. She shook her head wearily, not really knowing why. If Tom was implying that Max had found it with her... but there was no reason for him to think that. Max must flirt with hundreds of women. The pain intensified—she was one of hundreds. No, not even that now!

Tom appeared quite concerned about her lack of colour and Sarah found herself meekly allowing him to shoo her on home. Overwork, he said; the strain of doing two jobs at once. He would square it with Julie.

At home she roamed restlessly around the house, wishing it was possible to go to bed and pull the covers up over her head and summon up those calm, uncomplicated days so recent, yet so far behind her.

She dragged herself into the bathroom and was horrified when she looked in the mirror. A wraith! Dark, burning eyes in a white face. No wonder Tom guessed. Her hot eyes felt dry and sore, her mouth parched, her body feverish, as if pain had absorbed all the moisture from her system.

Maybe it wasn't love, she thought desperately. Maybe it was infatuation, hormonal imbalance—something you could take pills for. All she had to do was hold out until the end of the week, until Max left. Plod on, endure, hide the pain—she was good at doing that. Could she trust Tom? Yes. He understood, he was sorry for her. Curious he might be, but not cruel, not like Max would be if he ever found out. He would laugh, his triumph complete; he would delight in making her suffer. And she would suffer enough without his help. The two things she wanted most in the world right now were the two things he would never give her. His love, and his trust.

CHAPTER ELEVEN

"I DON'T believe this!"

In a luxury suite at the Intercontinental Hotel Sarah confronted a tall, lean, hazel-eyed man over the remains of a luncheon trolley. She was gripped by an uncanny sense of *déjà vu;* this had happened to her before, a little over a month ago. Was the nightmare going to begin all over again?

"You can't—" She stopped, a hand lifting to her heavy head, mesmerised by that familiar expression of hauteur, by the quizzical lift of the brow.

"Can't?" Slowly. Exploring the new word. "Are there laws in this country of which I am unaware? Are you not a free agent?"

"Of course—I—" Sarah put a hand over her heart. It was beating at an alarming rate. "But you can't possibly ask me to work for you on the basis of four days' acquaintance! It's not—"

"My dear child," Sir Richard Wilde looked deeply pained, one thin hand lifting languidly from the arm of his chair, "if you're going to work for me you must learn to stop thinking in clichéd terms. Originality is my trademark. One must not allow oneself to be hidebound by convention, it stifles creative thinking. It is because I have acted on intuitive decisions that I am where I am today. Would you have me abandon my formula for success now, on your behalf?"

"No...no, of course not," said Sarah hurriedly, still finding the conversation difficult to believe. She had received a casual job offer once before, from a member of the same family—one which, not surprisingly, had never been renewed. She doubted that Sir Richard would deliberately mislead her, but over the past few days she had learned something of his penchant for whimsicality. "But there is a question of suitability—"

"Ahh." Shoulders moved expressively under the dark velvet jacket. "I would never have brought the subject up if I did not think you were suitable," he said, dismissing the point with his own unique brand of logic. "And you wear my clothes so well; I knew as soon as I saw your photographs that if we ever met we would be...sympathetic."

He had said as much on his first visit to the *Rags* offices. Sarah, though having had plenty of time to prepare herself, had still been winded by his likeness to Max, and flustered by having her hand kissed instead of shaken.

"You do not have to introduce her," he had told Julie, who had brought him in from the airport. "I recognised her at once. But that is not mine," frowning at Sarah's apricot voile dress, "and you have lost weight."

"I'm dieting," Sarah had lied. She couldn't very well have said, "I'm pining for your son."

"It does not suit you," she was informed, with an exquisite disregard for tact. "You have height, you need the proportions to match. If you lose any more weight my clothes, which make you look so chic, will be useless to you. An ill-fitting garment is an abomination, do you not think?"

It was skilfully phrased so that in agreeing to the last Sarah was agreeing to the whole. Sir Richard Wilde, she had since discovered, was adept at getting people to agree with him. Not that it made any difference, for if they did not, he ignored them.

"Looking good in your designs is unavoidable," Sarah pulled herself back to the present, sitting earnestly forward in her chair. "And it's scarcely a recommendation for a personal assistant."

"For me it is. You will be constantly at my side; of necessity you must be a discreet advertisement for my talent."

"But, I have no experience—"

"I should soon give you that. Tell me," he changed tack with disarming smoothness, "are these . . . trivialities an attempt to hide from me the real reason for your refusal?"

"What?" Sarah only just prevented herself from leaping to her feet in shock.

"Do you have a personal dislike of me?" came the bland reply. "I had the impression that you had enjoyed the last few days, in spite of your reluctance to oblige me. Was I wrong?"

His observance disconcerted her. She had been greatly reluctant, too aware of the poignancy of the situation. Every now and then an intonation, a turn of the head, a phrase would strike a responsive chord and she would be shaken by helpless, hopeless longing. However, she had been given little choice. When Julie had heard that Sir Richard's private secretary had suffered an attack of food poisoning the evening they arrived in Auckland she had immediately offered Jane's services.

"No, no." Sir Richard had dismissed the possibility with an imperious wave. "I cannot work with a stranger. Sarah will do—we are already acquainted by proxy. Do you take shorthand?" And when she nodded slowly, "Good. That is settled."

A complete autocrat, but a charmer. He had a grasshopper mind and an uneven temper which he made valiant efforts to control for Sarah's benefit. She was surprised by his thoughtfulness, the small considerations he gave her, and disarmed by his elegant manners. Max had called him a despot, but he was a benevolent despot and not half as formidable as his son had suggested. But then, she thought bitterly, Max's judgements about people had not proved infallible.

Sir Richard was a formidable showman, though. He had been delighted at the stir he had created by deciding to come to New Zealand for the *Images* preview and it had taken little persuasion from Julie to get him to say a few light and witty words at the christening party for the new *Rags & Riches,* held the following day.

Sarah had obediently trailed everywhere after him, jotting down his constant flow of ideas and memos to himself and to his staff, and watched in awe as he effortlessly extracted every ounce of publicity from his brief visit. Controversial comment and bons mots were scattered in a manner carefully calculated to reach a maximum audience. Sir Richard seemed to positively encourage the pursuit of journalists and photographers.

"Fame, wealth, success—these things I have sought all my life," he told Sarah confidently. "In my younger days I struggled against poverty and anonymity in a fiercely competitive field. It took more than just talent to achieve my aims. Why should I now seek to hide from fortune?—that is the action of the weak, the insecure. Privacy—bah! Only what is inside the head and the heart is private, the rest is window-dressing—meant to be seen."

He spoke, gesturing with passionate intensity—the same intensity with which he approached life. Everything was related to the senses, to feeling, to instinct, to perception. Like now.

"No, you weren't wrong. I like working for you very much...you've been very kind." A faint smile of amusement lit hazel eyes. "But what about Kevin Matlock?" She had only glimpsed the untidy, bespectacled young man briefly, confined as he was to his hotel bed, but he had looked nice. She would hate to think she was doing him out of his job.

"What about him? You do not imagine that I could function without additional assistance? I have several secretaries, although admittedly I shall be shedding most of them when Max takes over the chairmanship of Wilde's at the end of the month. He will inherit them, or rather disinherit them if I know my son's mania for efficiency."

Sarah tensed inwardly. Would she never get used to the mention of that name? Thankfully Sir Richard didn't mention him often. She watched warily as the aristocratic figure leaned forward to pour himself another glass of champagne from the chilled bottle on the trolley.

"You seem surprised. Did he not mention his imminent elevation while he was here?" he continued casually.

"No. Tom did, Tom Forest...indirectly," said Sarah, remembering that momentous conversation in the coffee bar.

"Ah yes, Tom. He gave me a report. He was very impressed with you... as I am. I have been thinking along the lines of a personal assistant for some time—it is fate that brings us together, perhaps."

Lately Sarah had regarded fate with a jaundiced eye.

"What would I be doing, in this job?"

"More or less what you have been doing for the past few days."

"Oh." Dare she mention her misgivings? She had no need to, for they were shrewdly analysed.

"Of course, I am limited here. My real work, my only work from now on, is designing, but on a scale which you may yet find difficult to appreciate. I travel the world in search of inspiration, I attend showings, receive clients, visit the factories that make my exclusive fabrics, entertain the rich and famous, all in the cause of fashion. I think you will find your job sufficiently challenging and certainly it will be educational. Why, in ten years' time you may be utilising the valuable experience you have acquired with me in the running of your own fashion empire."

"As long as I don't aim for yours?" murmured Sarah, half laughingly, then quailed at his expression, fearing she had presumed too much.

"I believe Max has ambitions in that direction." He smiled, with a brief gleam of maliciousness. "Though you are quite welcome to fight it out, postmortem. You might even beat him. Tom told me that you were quite capable of standing up for yourself."

"But how can you know that I will—" Sarah began, returning to her best defence.

"Know? What is this obsession with knowing?" Sir Richard demanded, white-maned head tilting impatiently. "I do not know that the designs of my hand will sell, but I have confidence in my talent. I have confidence in you."

"But—"

"Please," he begged, setting down his crystal champagne glass with a frown. "Do not begin all your sentences with the word 'but', it begins to grate."

"I'm sorry, b—I mean, you must know many women capable of filling the position."

"Capable, yes, but acceptable? There is a difference. I receive many requests it is true, but usually those who seek my employ have an ulterior motive. They wish to get into modelling, or design, or my bed." He paused, on that startling note, giving Sarah a moment to realise that he was still, though elderly, an attractive man. "Such motives inevitably lead to conflicts and I do not need the distraction. I do not want temperament—I have more than enough of that myself." It was a relief to discover he had a sense of humour, that was the first time she had heard him being remotely humorous about himself. "I want calmness and common sense, and intelligence, of course. Most important, I must have a woman who is not going to burst into tears every time I shout."

"And you think I wouldn't?"

Hazel eyes narrowed. "You have courage, and you are no sycophant." He pursed his lip. "Were you afraid of my son?"

Sarah swallowed. "Sometimes."

"Hmm. He has a devil of a temper when roused."

"That's what he said about you."

He acknowledged it. "But mine blows over as quickly as it occurs. Max is less flexible. He tries to be logical and life is not logical. I am logical only by accident."

"Do...? Would...?" the burning question was difficult to phrase, but it had to be asked, even though she intended to turn down Sir Richard's offer. "Does your son have much to do with the Salon?"

"Nothing at all." Sir Richard clasped his hands over the ruffled white front of his shirt and smiled with self-satisfaction. "I do not permit it. In fact we meet but rarely, and never socially. Max always was a solitary, secretive boy—" He pulled himself up. "But we digress. I can see you wish to do some thinking—no!" when she would have protested, "I insist. You may have until tomorrow to consider your answer. Now, pass me my cane and I will see you to the door."

Sarah handed over the thin, ivory cane which rested against the trolley, noticing as she did so that Sir Richard seemed to be having some difficulty in rising. Walking across the room with him she could see that the cane wasn't the purely fashionable accessory she had first thought it to be.

"Are you all right, Sir Richard?" she couldn't help asking.

Sir Richard sighed and reached out a hand for hers. Looking down at it she saw he was wearing two rings she had not seen before, gold with some dark stones. They were so heavy that they made the thin white fingers look quite frail.

"Age, I'm afraid, Sarah. I'm no longer a young man. I cannot expect to enjoy the constant good health of my youth. Yet my work drives me on. I cannot afford to show weakness, it is not good press." He closed his eyes briefly and Sarah was struck by the pallor of his skin. Sir Richard seemed to be so vital, yet even his energy could not be limitless. She remembered the times in the past few days when he had faltered until, conscious of being watched, he had drawn himself up and gone on. Such an active, mentally agile man must fear the encroachments of age, the strictures that it was gradually placing upon him. She felt the stirrings of compassion.

He opened his eyes and smiled, a faintly wistful smile. "Think well on it, Sarah, and think not only of yourself, but of me too. I need you."

Stranded in an emotional wilderness, Sarah was tempted. In the past month she had come to the disquieting realisation that she no longer filled her old, comfortable niche at

Rags & Riches. She had out-grown it and hungered for something more demanding to fill the gaps that had opened in her life. She knew that if it had not been for Max she would have accepted Sir Richard's offer without a single question. But Max was inescapable. What would he say if she turned up under his nose, working for his father? He would think she was chasing him, grovelling for his attention, might even guess the truth. He would have nothing but contempt for her. But so what? He could not despise her any more than he did already and she could not let thoughts of Max rule her life forever, no matter how much she loved him.

How naïve she had been to think that once Max's disturbing physical presence left her shores the tide of her emotions would begin to recede. It was quite the reverse, rolling in like a great wave, gathering strength and momentum, washing away all her feeble attempts to rationalise her love into something less dramatic, less shatteringly painful.

What she had felt like after Simon's death paled by comparison. She had never ached like this... the phantom ache of a lost limb; unable to eat properly or sleep, consumed by the effort of keeping his haunting image at bay, so that she might at least *appear* normal. She dreaded the dark, lonely nights, lying awake for hours with her thoughts, but she dreaded even more closing her eyes and falling into that void where her subconscious released all the raw agony and despair that she wouldn't allow herself the luxury of feeling during the day.

Anything would be better than the limbo she was in now, she thought that night as she tossed and turned in the large bed. Even the daily prospect of running into Max, and enduring the kind of cold, empty courtesy he had accorded her during his last week in New Zealand. The scene in the dressing room had obviously been a catharsis for him, so perhaps she was flattering herself to think he would care what she did. Given the relationship between Max and his father, his new responsibilities as Chairman, and the fact that London was a city of millions, the chances of their meeting were really rather slight.

Sarah groaned, burying her face in her pillow, torn by conflicting feelings—wanting to see him again, but afraid of what it would do to her. Max had taught her a harsh lesson about herself. It was true that there was a deep-seated sensuality in her nature, but it was inextricably tied to an equally deep-seated desire for love and commitment. In the final analysis her intellectual need for independence had proved secondary to the feminine desire to seek a mate—yet for Sarah that mate must be one she could respect for being as strong, or stronger than she was.

Simon had tried to dominate her in his fashion, but because he had been basically weak he had not succeeded, and his failure had driven him to intolerable extremes. Max, if he wanted to, could do it effortlessly. He was the kind of man she had thought, in the pseudo-sophistication of her teens, that Simon was. Max had bullied her back into life, into love, and she should be grateful to him for that alone, regardless of the painful consequences. In a few short weeks he had shown her emotional heights and depths she had not been aware existed.

Towards dawn she came to a decision. Love might change—grow or die—but regret was forever. If she didn't take this chance now she would regret it all her life. It was an opportunity to escape the humdrum, to make something of herself, and at the same time perhaps, just perhaps, she might be able to go some way towards healing the breach between Max and herself—regain his respect if not his friendship. Maybe. Perhaps; the stuff dreams are made of.

SARAH STARED out the car window at pedestrians quickened by the prospect of another cool April shower, umbrellas unfurling, eyes beginning to turn streetwards, in cynical anticipation of the magical disappearance of every taxi at the first spit of rain. I'm glad I've got mine, she thought, three weeks in London having taught her that a certain amount of selfishness was a necessity if one was to survive in the big city.

Selfishness was also necessary to survive the rigours of her employment. Sarah had found that if she didn't strive to have her needs and opinions acknowledged they were often completely overlooked according to the unwritten law that Sir Richard knew best. Frequently though, he did—as witness the ease with which he detached her from her old life, just as he said he would. In no time at all Sarah found her resignation accepted, notice waived, passage booked with all the red tape in tatters behind her. She was duly farewelled with envious enthusiasm...and a whisper in her ear from Julie that if she should ever come across the makings of a good exclusive...

When it came to the crunch Sarah had left her job, her home, her country with surprisingly few regrets. Only Roy was a wrench and he was his usual disgustingly cheerful self as she wept over him at the airport.

"Hell, don't ruin my only good T-shirt," he told her. "Now go on, cut the apron strings. Be good. Be happy. And if you can't be both at the same time, forget the good!"

"Here you are then, miss." Sarah realised with a start that the taxi had stopped. She looked out at the multi-storey building shooting up into the darkening sky from a slick, rain-swept pavement.

"Oh, thank you." She fumbled for change and opened the door, drawing her cream woollen coat tightly around her for the dash to the double-glass doors.

Crossing to the reception desk she glanced around the warm, brightly-lit foyer with interest. This was the first time she had been to Wilde House. Since he had relinquished his chairmanship, Sir Richard no longer had offices here and he actively discouraged his staff making contacts with the wider organisation, in the interests of security. Sarah was more inclined to believe the reasons more personal—Sir Richard, having narrowed down his activities, was jealousy guarding the autonomy of his private kingdom. It was true that gossip flowed in torrents through the Wilde Salon, but respect for their monarch's talent and an even healthier respect for his pyrotechnic displays of temper engendered an almost fanatical loyalty amongst Sir Richard's staff—not a whisper escaped their lips outside the Salon walls.

Living-in at Rawlings, Sir Richard's Berkshire home, was one of the conditions of Sarah's employment and she couldn't help but enjoy her sudden ascent into luxury. Work and leisure time tended to become intermingled but at first Sarah was too busy finding her feet and coping with the realisation that her new employer enjoyed better health and a worse temper than he had led her to believe, to find the insularity restrictive. Now, however, she was eager to try her wings.

For three weeks she had done little more than shuttle between Rawlings, where a design team worked under Sir Richard's personal direction, and the Salon in Oxford Street, where the main business was carried out. In either place she was directed to researching records—"learning the ropes". There would be no trips or social engagements until she was adequately prepared, she was sternly informed, and when she dared to question the value of heavy tomes on the origins of the fashion industry, or etiquette...

"There is a purpose in everything I do." Sir Richard was at his most pompous. "You are no longer a classless New Zealander, you are part of my entourage and as such I cannot have you embarrassing me with exhibitions of ignorance or ill-breeding. You still have much to learn...besides, your new wardrobe has not arrived yet. Those clothes you're wearing—*they are not mine.*" The ultimate condemnation.

Fortunately her custom-made clothes had now arrived, and at last she had been let off the leash. That morning she had been resigned to yet another day "swotting" in the office at Rawlings while Sir Richard and Kevin Matlock attended an exclusive showing for a very famous client. A phone call after lunch had provided the diversion.

"Sarah, I need you."

At last. "Yes, Sir Richard," she replied meekly.

"Kevin very carelessly omitted to bring some papers that I must study before my evening engagement. You will find them on his desk, in a yellow envelope. Can you bring them to me?"

"Of course. Are you at the Salon?"

"No, I'm at the Duchess' residence in Mayfair, but I don't wish to be interrupted here. I shall be going to the penthouse to change at six, you had best meet me there."

"The penthouse?" Sarah faltered, clutching the receiver with suddenly slippery fingers.

"Max's place, at Wilde House," came the impatient reply. "I often use it when he is away—"

"Away?" A rush of cowardly relief washed over her.

"New York, I understand. For several days. When I was chairman I made a point of being in London for at least one week in four; Max makes no such concession . . . I must discuss it with him when he returns." A pause as he rearranged his thoughts. "Yes, meet me at six; and wear something formal, the red velvet I think. You may come with me this evening. It is only a small celebration for a minor member of European royalty, but it will be an experience for you—a chance for you to practise the despised etiquette, hmmm?"

Riding up in the small private lift, Sarah watched the lights flick on and off—sixteen, seventeen, eighteen. Her stomach tightened with every floor. Ridiculous to feel scared of an empty apartment, or even of an occupied one. Max was the real reason she was here after all, in spite of all that cleverly contrived mumbo-jumbo about the job being the thing. She hadn't even come close to seeing him, let alone exchanging unpleasantries since she had arrived, but the hopeful fantasies continued to tantalise her. Therein lay the root of her fear—wasn't it better to travel in hope . . .

The lift doors rolled back and she was facing a single, heavy black-padded door across a width of white carpet. She stepped up and took a deep breath and pushed the lacquered button beside the door. She waited in the thick silence, feeling like a spy. This was Max's home, his lair, and she was here without his knowledge. She felt as guilty as if she was contemplating stealing something.

The door opened with quiet suddenness to reveal a short, middle-aged man in a dark suit. He regarded Sarah with a brief expression of consternation before habitual deference reasserted itself.

"Mrs. Carter?" he asked, as if he really wasn't sure, but Sarah had distinctly heard the security guard down below ring the penthouse to check that she was expected.

"Yes. Sir Richard's assistant," she added unnecessarily, disturbed by the odd vibrations she was receiving.

"Please come in," he invited, with now impassive politeness. "My name is Brandon. I'm Mr. Wilde's butler." He took her damp coat as she juggled her handbag and the large envelope of papers. "If you will come this way."

Sarah followed the upright figure over the white ceramic tiles of the entry hall, past masses of sub-tropical greenery and into the deep luxurious pile of an electric-blue carpet which covered the floor of the split-level lounge.

On the upper level was a large formal dining area. Steps led down to the lounge proper, acres of it, bounded on one side by floor-to-ceiling windows which looked out over a roof garden with a kidney-shaped pool, calm waters reflecting the dull grey sky.

At first glance Sarah was dazzled by the magnificence of it all. White and a myriad of blues from eggshell to turquoise, rough-textured fabrics contrasted with smooth velvets, glass and steel, ceramics and laminated woods. All the lights were recessed, including the ceiling spots which were directed on to paintings and prints lining the walls. Sculptures from small to life-size were scattered around the room. It was beautiful, but sterile. There were no personal touches, no warmth, no soul.

She turned and caught the butler's black button eyes on her face and wondered whether her ambivalent opinion showed. Certainly the unspoken question did.

"Wilde Interiors were given a free hand, madam."

"Oh." She walked slowly down the steps. If she had Max's money she wouldn't leave the decoration of her home to someone else, she'd have the fun of doing it herself. If she had *Max* she wouldn't care if she lived in a hovel! She pulled herself up sharply. "Where are the gilded cherubs?" she enquired facetiously, not expecting to be understood.

"Madam has been to Rawlings?"

Sarah looked at the close-cropped head suspiciously. *Madam has.* The butler at Rawlings used the third person too, but never with the hint of dryness she detected in this bland-faced man. And he was actually condescending to engage her in conversation...not etiquette at all, and she should know!

"I'm living there at present," she explained, and with a faint smile. "I don't think baroque is quite my style." At least this had an open, uncluttered look, whereas Sir Richard's taste for flourishes had been indulged to the full at Rawlings, with almost claustrophobic results, Sarah thought.

"Indeed, madam." The black eyes gleamed. "My tastes are also rather more modern. Would you like a drink while you are waiting for Sir Richard?"

Sarah glanced at her watch. Five-thirty. Sir Richard's timekeeping was at best erratic, prone as he was to distraction, he might arrive in five minutes, or not for another hour.

"That would be nice. A brandy and ginger ale, please."

She put her bag and envelope down and sat on one of the long white couches that formed an open-ended square by the windows, sinking into the well-padded velvet cushions as Brandon opened a white louvred door in the wall to reveal an extensive array of bottles and glasses. After handing her the amber glass tinkling with ice, he pressed a button concealed in the wall and the raw silk curtains, one shade lighter than the carpet, whispered across the windows. At the same time the ceiling lights dimmed and a collection of small glass spheres heaped on various tables throughout the room began to glow softly.

"How beautiful!" slipped from her involuntarily. "But I don't see any cords, how do they work?"

"They are operated by microwave. It was Mr. Wilde's personal recommendation."

Here was a chance to ask the question she had been dying to ask, and with as much casualness as she could muster said, "When is Mr. Wilde due back?"

"Due back?" The neutral repetition stopped Sarah's heart in mid-beat.

"Sir Richard told me he was in New York, for several days," she said quickly, staring at him with wide, dark eyes.

Brandon cleared his throat. "Ah yes, New York," he agreed, to Sarah's unutterable relief. His face moved stiffly and she realised that he was actually attempting a smile— butlers would spin in their graves! "Mr. Wilde flies Concorde. It renders the distance so negligible one scarcely considers the United States to be 'abroad'. I dare say it would take you longer to come down from Berkshire in the rush-hour."

And with that pleasantry he withdrew, with the request that she call him if she required anything further.

Sarah admonished herself for panicking, it was becoming too much of a habit. She must be cool and composed at all times—how often had Sir Richard drummed that into her? It used to be second nature until Max gatecrashed her life and reduced her to a mass of sensitive nerve-endings. Now she needed it more than ever, now her hopeful travelling was drawing to a close. Damn, her hands were shaking.

Sarah finished her brandy and thought about another, to help calm her nerves. Why not? Max owed her something. A couple of brandies was a bargain price for a broken heart. She got up and found the intercom switch that Brandon had indicated and rang. Brandon delivered without comment and she drank. Better. She was only shaking inside now. Why did she have this awful feeling . . . ? Perhaps the apartment was haunted, guarded by Max's unquiet spirit.

She got up and wandered, inspecting herself in the distorted surface of an aluminium sculpture. Lovely dress; pity that the colour held such unfortunate memories. Even though her image was made lopsided by the curving surface of the sculpture, she could see that the deeply-slashed neckline and long, figure-smoothing line of the red velvet suited her. What an angel Sir Richard was! He had designed her hair too—a long braid encircled the back of her head with the rest of her hair cascading in waves from its centre. Regally sexy, he had decreed.

"Regally sexy," she repeated out loud, feeling less intimidated by the elegant luxury around her. These were the kind of surroundings in which Sir Richard was training her to feel at home. So feel at home she would. She took off her shoes. She put her feet up on the couch, a warm, vibrant splash of colour in the cool room. She didn't even move when she heard the apartment door open and, simultaneously, the phone ring. There was a faint murmur of a voice as Brandon answered the telephone, and the sound of footsteps across the ceramic tiles. Sarah smiled serenely, alcohol warming her veins, waiting for Sir Richard to appear.

CHAPTER TWELVE

"WHAT IN the hell are you doing here?"

Sarah blinked at the hostile, brandy-induced apparition at the top of the carpeted stairs.

"Sarah!" The voice was harsh and demandingly savage. In a charcoal-grey suit and tie and white shirt, Max looked formal and remote, every inch a Chairman of the Board. His face was sharper than she remembered, more angles and less flesh; paler too, and the grey strands threading the black sideboards seemed more numerous. But he was still Max, still the man who held her bruised heart in the hollow of his uncaring hand.

Paralysed by the shock of his sudden appearance Sarah could only stare and wait as he set down his briefcase and came slowly, frowningly down the steps and across the room towards her.

"Sarah?" The husky question came as Max narrowed his eyes and half raised a hand from his side as if to touch her, as if he doubted the evidence of his senses.

"Max...?" was all her poor vocal chords could manage, but it was enough. His hand dropped and he took an audible breath.

"You seem as surprised as I am," he said, after a moment. "Yet why should you be? You must have come here to see me."

He undid the buttons of his jacket, not taking his eyes off the sudden flush on Sarah's face. He shrugged it off and sat down on the couch opposite, stretching out his long legs, hands splayed tautly over his muscled thighs. He looked her over and the ghost of a smile touched the hard mouth.

"You look very much at home."

The faint sarcasm thawed Sarah's frozen limbs. She hurriedly swung her legs off the couch, sitting up to search for her red shoes with her feet.

"Did I say I objected?"

"I..." Sarah stopped, confused by the hint of humour. He had been unmistakably angry when he had walked in and seen her there. Why was he now looking as though...as though... "I thought you were in New York."

"I was; until this morning. Now I'm here. And you're here too. And you still haven't told me why." He was mocking her, but gently, and it completely shattered her composure—it was so unexpected...so *impossible*. That he should smile, like that, at her, after all that had passed between them.

"I—I've brought some papers," she said vaguely, eyes going hungrily over the lounging body, storing up the memory of his nearness.

"You came all this way just to bring me some papers? How kind of you, Sarah. But couldn't you have posted them?"

He didn't even ask to see them, didn't even really seem interested, he just stared at her with that disturbing smile.

"They're not for you."

"Not for me?"

"Your—Sir Richard asked me to—"

"My father!" It was as though she had slapped him, the smile vanished in an instant, his face hardening with suspicion as he stood up. Sarah stood up too and was dismayed to find that without her shoes she only came up to his shoulder. "What has my father to do with it?" Suddenly something else registered with him. "And where did you get that dress, it's from the Wilde Spring Collection? What's going on?"

"You don't know?" breathed Sarah, one hand coming up to cover her horrified mouth. "I thought you knew. I spoke to Tom on the phone last week. He knew. I thought you knew, too." She had been unsure what to think, whether to be relieved that Max had made no effort to jeopardise her new job or depressed that he obviously didn't give a damn. But if he hadn't known...

"Knew what?" articulated Max dangerously, and Sarah shivered wordlessly. "So help me, Sarah, if you don't stop stalling and tell me, I swear I'll—" He had actually slipped rigid hands around her slender neck when they were interrupted.

"Excuse me, sir." Brandon showed no surprise at finding his master on the verge of strangling a female visitor. Perhaps he was used to such strange scenes, thought Sarah a trifle hysterically, before she realised she was being addressed.

"That was Sir Richard on the telephone, Mrs. Carter. He apologises for the delay. He has been held up at the Salon, but he still wants you to wait. He had a message for you, too, sir," he addressed the ominously quiet Max. "He asked me to convey his best wishes. He said you would understand."

"What?" The uncomfortable grip on Sarah's throat dropped away as hazel eyes glared at the bland-faced butler. Seconds ticked away before Max said softly, through his teeth, "Get out."

"Will you be wanting—?"

"Get out!" Max bawled and with remarkable calm Brandon bowed to Sarah and withdrew, managing to exude dignity through every retreating pore.

"Now..." Eyes that held a brilliant glitter were turned back on Sarah. She drew on the remains of her Dutch courage.

"I work for him."

"Work for whom?" said Max blankly. Obviously never in his worst dreams had it occurred to him...

"Sir Richard," she whispered. "I'm his personal assistant."

He looked incredulous, furious. "When? How?" he shot at her.

"He offered me the job when he came out to New Zealand," said Sarah, endeavouring to conquer a sudden queasiness. "I've been working for him virtually ever since."

"You're living here?"

"A—at Rawlings."

A red flush covered Max's cheekbones and he gave her a look of baffled anger. "My father doesn't need another personal assistant, and you damned well know it!"

Sarah's chin lifted proudly. "He says he does."

"I'll bet he does, and I bet you weren't hard to convince." Max drew his lips back from his teeth, but it was more a snarl than a smile. "You must have been glad you lost your chance with me. My father is much richer and not likely to be as *demanding* as a younger man."

It was clear what he meant and the insult rendered Sarah icily sober. "You're insane—can you hear yourself?" she said in a cold little voice. "If you have no respect for me, you should at least have some for your father. He—"

"Oh, for God's sake shut up!" Max ground out rudely and went over to the bar. "I don't need your lectures." He didn't come back with his drink but prowled about beyond the square of the couches. Sarah found her shoes and put them on, feeling shattered. This was it. The end of the journey. And nothing had changed. She watched his restless pacing helplessly. He moved fluidly, like the big cats at the zoo, back and forth, a resentful captive. Eventually he stopped and glared at her sullenly.

"And you can stop looking at me like that, damn you. You know I didn't mean it." He thrust an impatient hand through thick black hair. He sounded for all the world like a sulky boy who knows he has done wrong but doesn't want to admit it. In spite of the sheer awfulness of the situation Sarah felt a dull flicker of amusement.

"I'm glad I amuse you!" The growl wiped the smile off her face and she snapped back:

"Well, it's laughable. He's old enough to be my grandfather and most of the time he treats me like a recalcitrant child. We're only going out tonight because he's finally de-cided he can trust me not to eat peas off my knife.'' For an instant she thought Max was going to smile but he was still simmering.

"All right, I get the message. I've already apologised. Should I go down on my knees?''

A glorious surge of righteous indignation freed Sarah from the last bonds of nervousness. To hell with the surly brute! Had she actually imagined that she loved the moody devil?

"Only if it'll improve your temper! You were right about you and your father being alike in some ways. You both sulk if you don't get things exactly your own way. I should be used to it by now."

Max hunched his shoulders and stared at her with thinly veiled dislike. Some of the drink slopped out of his glass as he moved. He swore softly and rubbed at the mark with a careless shoe then refilled his glass before coming over to sprawl opposite her again, asking with a restrained belligerence:

"Why do you work for him then? I seem to recall you once shuddered at the very idea."

"I didn't say I don't like working for him. Actually he's been very kind." Since Max made no move to reply, unpleasantly or otherwise, Sarah plugged on, making polite conversation to a stranger. When she mentioned, in passing, that this was her first expedition on her own Max roused himself to interruption.

"That doesn't sound like you. I thought you didn't like to be caged in any sense."

Sarah shrugged. She was not about to confess to the slightest tinge of frustration. "Sir Richard said my rough edges needed polishing. And they did. I feel much more confident now, quite equal to anything he might throw at me."

"Knowing my father, that could be termed literally. I take it then, that he requested you work for him and not vice versa."

"I couldn't believe it at first." She explained briefly about Kevin Matlock's illness and the circumstances surrounding Sir Richard's surprising offer, warily eyeing the now expressionless face opposite. Max seemed to have calmed down but his stillness could conceal anything.

"So here you are—polished and perfumed to perfection," he murmured at last. "Tell me, why did you think I was still in New York?"

"Your father said you were," Sarah replied, thankful that they were at last communicating normally. "And Brandon—" Black eyebrows flew up as Sarah endeavoured to remember just what his butler had said. "Well, he didn't actually *say* you were still there, but he . . ."

"Implied it. How well I know Brandon's implications," drily and then, almost under his breath. "Damn him for his interference! My father can resist everything but the temptation to organise the world to his own dramatic satisfaction."

"He really does need an assistant," Sarah insisted loyally. "He told me himself that his health—"

A short amused laugh greeted this bit of naïvety and Max gulped half his drink without enjoyment before saying, savagely: "I don't like being manipulated."

"*You* do it all the time," Sarah pointed out, beginning to think that all this moody, broody behaviour had nothing to do with her at all. His anger seemed more directed at his father than at her, and she was just the convenient whipping boy. "Anyway, now that you're chairman I don't see how your father can manipulate you."

"Don't you? My God, you're a dumb little cow sometimes."

Sarah stiffened at the casually uttered insult.

"Intelligent enough to be damned good at my job."

"Intelligent, but dumb," agreed Max infuriatingly.

"I don't know what you're talking about."

"That's what I mean." Her irritation seemed to have restored his good humour. "If I thought you *did,* you'd have been on the doorstep by now. And you didn't land the job, the job landed you...well and truly." He laid his head back against the cushions and studied her through thick, dark lashes. "You look thinner."

"So do you," countered Sarah nervously. He had always been unpredictable, but never this much—blowing hot and cold with one breath. "You look tired, too." The blue shadows were back around his eyes, the bones of his temples more pronounced, giving him a lean and hungry look.

"I am." The admission surprised her. The Max she knew would have denied it. "Have you been homesick?"

"I haven't had time. In any case, there wasn't a lot to feel homesick for." *Only you, only you.*

"What about lover-boy?"

"If you mean Roy Merrill," said Sarah, in a carefully neutral voice, "he was very pleased for me. And he was never my lover."

They measured glances for a few seconds, and Max was the first to look away. "Well, it doesn't matter now." The flat voice hammered a shaft of steel through her heart.

"No."

Suddenly the effort of sitting there, trying to appear unmoved, was too much. She got up and walked restlessly, as the man had done before her, revealing her agitation more with each passing minute. She wished she had never come. She wished she was sophisticated enough to smile and mean it. She wished the polish was diamond-hard and not just skin deep. She forced herself to display an interest in the various works of art, though in reality she saw nothing, too acutely aware of the dark man watching her every move. She had never known such silence, like the end of the world, and the longer it grew the more impossible it was to break. She almost jumped out of her skin when, on consulting her watch for the tenth time in as many minutes a velvety voice floated in from the edges of eternity.

"You may as well relax, Sarah, you're in for a very long wait."

"What?" She gave him a hunted glance.

"We may as well make ourselves comfortable...find a pleasant way to pass the time. Come over here."

Sarah's skin prickled as she registered that certain lilt. "What for?"

He smiled lazily and her eyes widened. Surely he wouldn't have the gall to...

"Come here and see." *He would.*

"No," she said, violently, staying where she was, a safe distance of several metres. Even so she took a hasty step back as Max rose slowly to his feet, yawning and stretching until the long body shuddered, every muscle seeming to settle back into complete relaxation. He no longer looked tired, but somehow refreshed, his smile widening as if her increasing nervousness amused him, pleased him.

"You always were nervy around me," he observed. "Some things don't change, do they, Sarah?"

Sarah licked her lips and his eyes dropped to her mouth. "Like that. You always do it when you're scared; and I always find it erotic." He paused and the blood thundered in Sarah's ears. She was convinced that either she was drunk, or he was, or they both were. "Are you scared of me now, Sarah?"

"Should I be?" She meant it to be discouraging but it came out a squeak.

"Yes. Oh, yes." He came towards her on catlike tread and she backed away.

"Max, stop it!"

"Stop what?" he asked innocently, still coming.

"This stupid game, whatever it is."

"No game, Sarah," he said, grinning wolfishly as she backed up against a large white stone sculpture, hemmed in by the back of the couch on one side and a table topped with the glowing globes on the other. "I've had enough of games. This time it's for real."

Sarah's nerves were as taut as wire as she watched him stop an arm's-length away, resting a lean hip against the back of the couch, casually unbuttoning and removing his waistcoat, and undoing several of his shirt buttons. Butterflies began a frantic dance in Sarah's stomach. She craved his touch, his soft words, but not like this. He thought she was an easy lay, a body with which to relieve the frustrations of a tiring day.

"Your father will be here any minute," she said desperately, but Max was ignoring her flutterings, his mouth twitching as he looked at her.

"How clever of you to wear red, it's so...evocative. I remember the last time you wore a red dress. All I could think of was what was underneath it—the honey-flavoured skin, those little shreds of lace...kissing you up against that wall, arousing you until all you could do was moan for me. Remember?" His voice had dropped to a husky murmur, his eyes almost clouded as he watched the rapid rise and fall of her breasts. Sarah almost moaned then. She remembered. Every inch of her body tingled with the memory.

"I see you do," he said dreamily and she, struggling weakly in the silken web of sensuality, only gave him token resistance when he pounced, pulling her towards him until their bodies bumped together.

"That's better. Little fool, stop fighting me. This is what you're here for."

With one arm around her he thrust his other hand into her hair and tilted her head back kissing her roughly. It was as though he had never stopped.

Still holding her he let himself fall over the low back of the couch, carrying her with him so that she lay on his chest, hair falling in a silky curtain around their faces. His mouth moved against hers hot and hungry, parting her lips with an eager tongue. It happened so suddenly, that much-desired, long dreamed-of embrace, that Sarah was instantly excited—pride, scruples melting like sugar in the mouth. He was rough, but it was a roughness born of passion, not anger, and Sarah welcomed it, welcomed also the change of that first devouring assault to a mutual exploration.

She closed her eyes, sighing as his mouth moved over her delicate ear, moving her own mouth against the warm muskiness of his neck, loving the feel of domination it gave her to lie on top of him, to feel his body tremble beneath hers.

His hands moved through the warm softness of her hair and he used it to pull her sideways and roll with her so that now he was lying half on top of her, his thighs heavy on hers, hands moving over her as he kissed her face, her throat and the upper curve of her breasts above the dress. She twisted, pressing herself feverishly closer to him, hair spilling in a cascading wave over the side of the couch to the floor.

She felt the warmth of his hand on her leg, sliding up the heavy velvet of her dress, stroking her thigh with soft, circular movements and felt his slurred murmur against her throat.

"How I've waited for this...moan for me, sweet vixen, like you did before..."

His hand moved up under her dress, sliding across her satiny stomach as he brushed his mouth back and forth across her skin just above the deep curve of her bodice. The fabric suddenly felt tight and constrictive, heavily encasing her, inhibiting her enjoyment. The blood rushed dizzily to her head as it drooped over the side of the couch. A physical sensation that was close to swooning, a voluptuous sighing, straining sensation took hold of her. She was gasping for air in his arms, dying of sweetness and love...

Next moment she was being shaken out of her daze, the caressing hands had become a vice about her waist.

"What did you just say?

"Hmmm?" She didn't care, she tried to pull his head back down but he wouldn't let her. He dragged her so that they were both sitting up.

"What did you say?"

"I don't know...I don't remember," she said, frightened. She didn't want to think, or talk, she wanted to make love. She no longer cared how little he thought of her, she wanted one beautiful, intimate memory to take away with her. To sustain her against the bitter truth she had faced tonight.

"Something about loving me."

"No." Not even in the incandescent heat of the moment could she have betrayed herself so utterly. "No, I said— make love to me."

"You lying bitch, you said you loved me!" He shook her brutally hard and she choked back a sob. Was he angry because he thought she had said it as a form of blackmail to try and worm her way back into his good books?

"You must have misheard me—"

"The hell I did!" He put a hand on the side of her face and forced it back as she would have looked away from him. " 'I love you,' you said—and you meant it. That's why you took that job with my father, because you wanted to get close to *me:* because you were desperate enough to settle for whatever you could get—isn't it? *Isn't it?*" His eyes burned yellowly into hers and she knew by his look, his grip, that he was intent on forcing an answer. God, how he must hate her, to do this to her!

"Perhaps I did say it," she said wildly, giving him the lesser victory, "but you already know how responsive I am to you physically. You can make me say anything, do anything, when I'm in your arms—"

"And have done so...but not tonight. I wasn't asking anything of you tonight. I wasn't taking advantage of your sexual thrall," he gave a peculiar, excited laugh. "What you said you said of your own free will. And you'll say it again."

"No!" With an anguished cry she tore herself out of his hands and fled, plunging through the nearest door, down a short hallway into the dimness beyond. A dead end; she turned at bay.

"You're always trying to get away from me, darling," came the silky drawl from the dark silhouette in the doorway. "Haven't you learned yet how hopeless it is?" He couldn't know how true that was. "This time you've made a truly Freudian slip.

The room leaped into life as he touched a switch by his side and Sarah realised with dismay that she was in a bedroom—his bedroom. It had to be. All white and black and silver, the tubular chrome curves of the bedstead rising flatly from the wide, wide, black fur-covered bed.

Sarah could feel herself beginning to shake, beginning to weaken. What did pride matter? He was right, she would settle for whatever she could get...

"Max...your father..." she panted, a last fatalistic attempt to put him off the scent.

"My father, my sweet little innocent, won't be coming to the party."

"What?" Distractedly she stared at him.

"Didn't I say you were dumb?" He didn't move from the doorway, just looking, savouring her nervous fear. "He set you up, and me. We may as well go along with it. Did you know it was my birthday today?"

Sarah stared at the madman. Did he want her to sing "Happy Birthday"?

"He likes his presents to be unique, extravagant...and superbly wrapped..." She didn't need his eyes wandering over her to tell her what he meant.

"You're mad," she breathed.

"Insane," he agreed. "You told me that before. And my father told me, when I spoke to him on the telephone this morning that when I got back from New York, he had a present for me that he would deliver tonight." His eyelids drooped. "And that it was something I wanted... very...much."

"He wouldn't," Sarah whispered, feeling used, confused.

"He did. It's the kind of devious game he likes to play." Max smiled, too kindly. "I imagine you're feeling now like I felt when I found out you worked for him. You'll get used to it, and him."

"But how, why should he?" Sarah's fear had receded on impact of this new bombshell, as she slowly fathomed the implications.

"No doubt he was concerned about my mental health. My convalescence in New Zealand didn't seem to have had the effect he was hoping for—so he obviously did some detective work. And if Tom knew you were here, I can guess where he got his best information from."

Oh, God—Tom! What sort of information had he provided Sir Richard with? His suspicion that she loved Max? No wonder Sir Richard had been so smug when she accepted his job, and all the time he had been planning this—coolly working it all to a precise timetable. And all because...her eyes stopped looking inward and refocussed on the man who had moved into the room without her realising it and now stood an arm's-length away, watching the expressions chase across her face. Watching her reach the unbelievable conclusion.

"Why should he think you wanted me?" she asked, hardly daring to voice the question out loud.

"Perhaps he came here snooping." His steady gaze went past her. "And saw that."

Numb as her brain was, she knew what she would see before she turned. Knew, feared, hoped. And there it was. On the wall, by the bed, displayed by the soft lighting. The picture, Roy's picture—that alluring, inviting Sarah—safe in some rich American's private collection, so she'd thought. She closed her eyes, and opened them. It was still there, telling her something, and she was terrified of misunderstanding the message.

She turned back, skin milk-white, eyes huge and dark.

"Why?"

"You know why."

But she didn't. She couldn't make the step, the leap from fantasy to fantastic reality.

"Tell me."

He moved to touch her and stopped, warned by her expression. "Did you mean it when you said you loved me?"

She knew what he wanted. He wanted her to make it easy for him. But he had hurt her too much. Let him risk rejection, know the pain of uncertainty.

"Tell me."

He began stiffly, guardedly. "I knew it was going to be sold in America so I had my dealer put up a standing bid for any new works of Merrill's that came on the market. I got it two weeks ago." His voice became rough, and he wouldn't look at her, staring instead at his fingers playing lightly over the chrome of the bed end. "I didn't have you, so I had to have the next best thing, no matter what it cost me. And it cost me quite a lot." The smile was a mere twitch. "I flew it out first-class Concorde on a seat all of its own, with an escort."

"You wanted it that much?"

He looked at her, dark lashes flickering, sweat breaking out on his forehead as though this was a labour of physical strength. "I wanted *you* that much. It didn't start out that way. In the beginning I just wanted to go to bed with you, to draw out the fire that I sensed inside you, for my own pleasure. Yet the more I got to know you the more I wanted to know. You tried to be so dull... but with me you were sharp and fierce and passionate, and you had an inner strength and intelligence that I liked. And then, and then—" he broke off and swallowed, and his voice became thick with effort as he forced himself to continue.

"That night at your place the whole world crashed in on me. I felt humiliated, betrayed, as if I had some moral claim on you when in fact I had none. I felt angry, jealous, things I've never felt before about a woman. I didn't know what was happening to me and I hated feeling so... so helpless before you."

The bewilderment was there on his face and in his voice, as he had felt it then. He was carrying on an internal struggle, grimly intent on stripping away a lifetime's defences— on holding up each imperfection to the light for her inspection.

"The next day, when you told me about your relationship with Merrill I wanted to believe you so badly that it scared me. I wouldn't let myself listen. For the first time I was in an emotional situation I couldn't control. It was important that you be a cheat and a liar and a promiscuous tart, because that gave me the perfect excuse to reject you, to regain control. But it didn't work like that. I still wanted you, and I hated myself for it so I—I—*God!*" He closed his eyes briefly, clinging tightly to the cold chrome and sucking in a painful breath. "When I think what I did, what I said...I thought you must know and be laughing at me for my weakness."

He jerked his head sideways, but not before Sarah had seen the strange glitter in his eyes and was awed. Tears...for her...and bitter self-condemnation. Suddenly she didn't want to hear any more of this forced confession. She didn't want to hurt as she had been hurt, she wanted to protect him, to enfold him in her love, never to demand but to give and give without counting cost.

She reached out and put her arms around him tightly, resisting his attempt to detach her. She laid her head against the slightly damp skin of his chest, feeling the soft body-hair tickling her cheek, hearing the erratic beat of his heart.

"No more," she begged softly. "You don't have to explain anything to me, Max...I understand."

He pulled her head up, cupping her face with gentle hands. "I hurt you. I owe you this. I can only hope you will forgive me. I came raging back here like a wounded tiger; no wonder my father and Tom decided that drastic measures were called for. I realised, you see, as soon as I left, that I had bungled my chance of real happiness. That like a blind fool I had run away from the very thing I'd been seeking all my life, and given up hope of ever finding."

He groaned and Sarah was amazed that he couldn't see what was in her face. She knew now what he meant about Roy not mattering, the past only mattered in the sense that it had brought them here, together, in the present. Couldn't he see that she no longer wanted, or needed to receive his complete submission?

"I love you," she said softly. Then with force and passion: "I love you and I'll say it, in your arms and out, for as long as you want me to. I'm yours for as long as you want me."

He looked white, shaken, so that she smiled and said:
"You knew." And he smiled too, rather crookedly.

"Wishing made it so." His voice took on a tone of wonder that caressed Sarah with warmth. "I never thought I'd fall in love. Take a wife, have children eventually, yes—if only to placate my father. But love? It's a strange country, I don't know it, I don't know the language—"

Sarah laid a small soft hand over his mouth, feeling joyous, generous—

"I'll teach you. But as long as you feel it you don't have to say it."

She felt his warm breath against her palm.

"Oh, but I want to. I want to be very explicit." The smile faded and his voice took on a deep, new strength. "I love you, Sarah. You're the only woman I've ever said that to. First love, last love, my love." He kissed her to punctuate the phrases, and the kisses grew, slower, longer, as they swayed together, locked in each other's arms, affirming the vow.

"No more objections to being set up?" Sarah enquired huskily at length, as Max nuzzled the long, lovely curve of her throat.

He lifted his head and grinned. It took light years off the charcoal-suited chairman. "You know why I was so furious? I had my own plans and I saw them go up in smoke before my eyes. Come and see."

He led her over to the bedside table and sat her, very properly on the edge of the bed while he drew out a small, rectangular case. He placed it in her hands and sat beside her to watch her open it.

Sarah found the hidden catch and gasped at the sight of an exquisitely wrought brooch, a golden fox with flashing, ruby eyes and lolling tongue, surrounded by an intertwining of chased gold vines. There were two tiny earrings to match, each a copy of the fox's head.

"For me?" she breathed and Max smiled tenderly at her disbelief.

"I have airline tickets too. I intended to come out and prostrate myself. To woo you properly," he said softly with wry self-mockery. "I had them specially made to my own design. I made myself wait until they were finished, hoping that the breathing space would give you time to stop hating me for the things I did to you."

"They're beautiful." Sarah touched the delicate jewellery with a shaking hand. "Nobody's ever given me anything so beautiful."

"And unique, like you," Max said, immensely satisfied by her words. "And this, too..."

No box this time. A ring—aflame with rubies, afire with diamonds.

"Put it on. No, this hand," taking it from her nerveless fingers. "To celebrate what I hope will be the shortest engagement in history."

"Engagement?" Sarah thought she was going to faint, the jewellery forgotten. "You want to *marry* me?"

"Of course I want to marry you," he said violently. "What do you think I've been saying? That I love you and want you to be my mistress." Her face gave her away. "You must have a very low opinion of me! I suppose I can't blame you for that."

"No." Sarah laid her hand on his arm, felt the rigidity of his muscles and hastened to reassure him. "I only meant that I never thought...I mean..." she floundered, knowing it would hurt him if she told the truth, that she hadn't thought his love sufficiently strong for him to give up his celebrated freedom for it.

"God, is it marriage that's the problem?" he said suddenly, a raw note of uncertainty in his voice. "Has your experience with Simon put you off?" The emotional struggle showed on his face as he said, slowly, "I don't want a so-called 'open marriage', but if you'd feel trapped with anything more conventional—" he broke off, wounded by her laughter at this most serious of moments. "What are you laughing about?"

"You. So abject." Sarah could hardly speak for giggles, he was so far *wrong*. "I'm enjoying it while I can, once we're married I suppose you'll be your usual arrogant self again."

His eyes gleamed with a return of masculine confidence. "You can't refuse me now, darling, my father would never forgive you."

Sarah sobered. "But he didn't know you wanted to marry me. Will he ... approve, do you think?"

It was Max's turn to laugh. He slid an arm around her velvet waist and hugged her against his hard body. "Approve. Darling, you've been signed, sealed and delivered by his own fair hands. You've domesticated the tiger, of course he approves."

"Hmm, I always was good with wild animals," Sarah murmured, tremors beginning to build up in her body as the strong, sensitive hands began to wander.

"Don't distract me," came the order. "I'm unwrapping my birthday present."

Before she realised what had happened Sarah was flat on her back on the bed, being ruthlessly kissed. With practised economy of movement Max neatly extracted her from her dress, so obviously eager that her mischievous streak was awakened. Secure in his love, she pushed him away, wide-eyed when he slid his hands over her lacy red bra.

"No, Max, not until we're married, it wouldn't be right."

He looked stunned. "You want to wait? It'll be at least three days before—" he choked to a stop as Sarah's eyes began to dance.

"Vixen," he growled, threateningly. "For that bit of heresy I shall make love to you until you beg for mercy."

"Try and make me," she teased provocatively, enticing him with her lace-clad body, and trying half-heartedly to escape as he lunged for her.

They wrestled playfully until it was no longer play, until desire caught up with them, overtook them, and the rhythms of love established themselves in soft, sighing sounds.

Sarah gave herself with delight, with love and uninhibited joy and was rewarded with unimaginable pleasure when he finally took her, with infinite skill and a kind of gentle savagery that carried her with him to the far peaks, breathing as one the thin, rarified air of ecstasy, sharing a passion that was pure and white and blindingly fierce.

And afterwards when he held her trembling body against his, and licked the sweet salt tears from her cheeks, she knew at last the peace of utter contentment. That this love she had found was not a trap, but a door to a new, exciting and enriching life.

THE AUTHOR

Susan Napier was born on Valentine's Day, so perhaps it is only fitting that she became a romance writer. She started out as a reporter for New Zealand's largest evening newspaper before resigning to marry the paper's chief reporter. After the birth of their two children she did some free-lancing for a film-production company and then settled down to write her first romance. "Now," she says, "I am in the enviable position of being able to build my career around my home and family."